Zindedi has attacked Koblan, and Deccia is a prisoner of the insane leader, General Greisn.

In order to defeat the Zindedis and rescue her twin sister, Methusal and her community must ally with her mortal foe, Mentàll Solboshn, Chief of Dehre. He has been put in command of the Kaavl team, but can they trust him?

KAAVL CHRONICLES
(Book Two of Quadrilogy)

KAAVL
QUEST

Jennette Green

DIAMOND PRESS

Kaavl Quest

A Diamond Press book / published in arrangement with the author

ISBN: 978-1-62964-013-6

Library of Congress Control Number: 2016910090
Library of Congress Subject Headings:
Man-woman relationships—Fiction
Paranormal—Fiction
Paranormal romance—Fiction
Courage—Fiction
Individuality—Fiction
Fantasy fiction

Diamond Press
3400 Pegasus Drive
P.O. Box 80043
Bakersfield CA 93380-0043
www.diamondpresspublishing.com

Published in the United States of America.

So many

to appreciate…

Know I sincerely appreciate

you--every

encouraging word.

Koblan

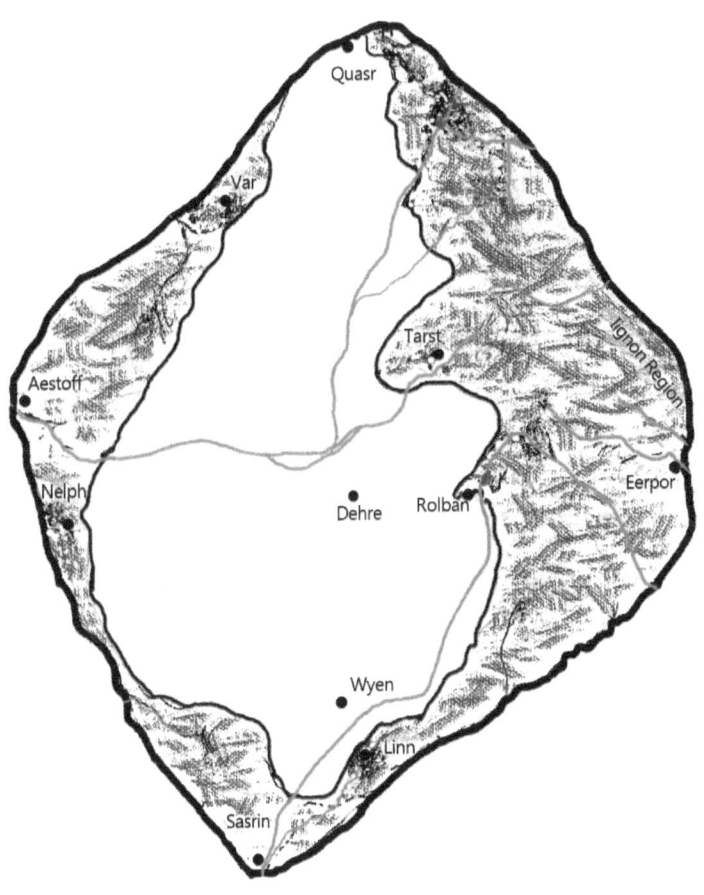

Quasr

Var

Tarst

Aestoff

Tignon Region

Nelph

Dehre

Rolban

Eerpor

Wyen

Linn

Sasrin

Pronunciation Guide

Kaavl (Kah' vl)

Kaavl levels (from highest to lowest):
Ultimate level (only Mahre ever achieved)
Primary level
Bi-level
Tri-level
Quatr-level (Kwah' tra level)
Quint-level (Kint level)

Places

Aestoff (Ay' stoff)
Carachki (Ka ra' chki) capitol of Zindedi
Dehre (Deh' ree)
Dehrien (Deh' ree un)
Eerpor (Ear poor')
Eerporian (Ear por' ee un)
Koblan (Koe' blun)
Koblani (Koe blane' ee)
Rolban (Role bane')
Rolbani (Role bane' ee)
Quasr (Kay' zer)
Quasrian (Kay zar' ee un)
Tarst (Tarst)
Wyen (Why en')
Zindedi (Zin deh' dee)

Characters

Rolban

Aalicaa (A lee shaw') (Aali (A' lee)) Deccia's sister/cousin, Methusal's cousin, Quatr-level
Barak Mehl (Bare' uk Mel) Kitran's brother
Behran Amil (Bee' hrhun/Beh' rhun Uh meel') Tri-level
Ben Amil, Behran's father
Deccia (Day' shuh) Methusal's twin sister
Erl (Earl) Methusal's father
Goric (Gor' ik) Tri-level
Hanuh (Han' nah) Methusal's mother
Kitran Mehl (Kih' trun Mel) Barak's brother, Primary level
Mahre (Mah' ree) The Old Kaavl Master
Methusal Maahr (Meth u' zul Mare) Tri-level
Petr (Pet' r) Deccia and Aali's father, Bi-Level
Pogul (Poe' gull)
Poli Amil (Pol' ee Uh meel') Behran's mother
Sims Nalg (Sims Nalg) Supply room supervisor
Timaeus (Tim' ay us)

Dehre

Hendra (Hen' druh) Quatr-level
Jascr (Jas' kr) Bi-level
Mentàll Solboshn (Mn tall' Sole' bah shn) Chief of Dehre, Primary level
Efron (Eff' ron), Bi-level, Mentàll's first-in-command
Tabor (Tay' bor), Bi-level, Mentàll's second-in-command
Wortn (Wor' tn) Dehrien, Tri-level

Tarst

Aenill (Uh neel') Pan's wife
Dastn (Das' tn), runner for Tarst
Pan Patn (Pan Pat' tn) Tarst Chief, Primary level

Zindedi

General Greisn Rohasch (Gree' shun Ro' hash) (brother of Zindedi Presidente)
Presidente of Zindedi

PROLOGUE

CARACHKI
CAPITOL OF THE ZINDEDI CONTINENT

THE PRESIDENTE OF ZINDEDI inhaled deeply from his cigar, and allowed a smile to curl his lips. He puffed a smoke ring up toward the ceiling. Watched it billow out and dissipate into nothingness. Just like Koblan's defenses would vaporize to mist. By his calculations, his brother had arrived in Quasr, Koblan's northernmost village, two days ago. Was he too greedy to hope the entire continent had fallen already?

Perhaps. The Presidente inhaled another lungful of smoke.

But he knew his brother. By now, the people of Quasr were already suffering from the terror of being under the General's boot. Soon, all of Koblan would suffer.

He chuckled to himself. He almost felt sorry for the Koblani people. Defenseless, unsuspecting. Truly, they were uncivilized. They championed independent tribal towns, and had no central government. No Presidente. No national defense.

His lids drifted closed, imaging with pleasure the horror plaguing the far continent. They had no hope of winning against him. How quickly they would realize that. For two and a half years, he had assembled and prepared an undefeatable army and navy. Koblan would fall in a matter of days. And then all of Rolban's ore would belong to him.

△ △ △ △ △

QUASR
KOBLAN CONTINENT

THE STONE FLOOR HURT her shoulder, and her entire body ached. She opened her eyes to blackness.

The sound of metal grating against metal assaulted her ears. A door creaked open, allowing a thin stream of light inside. A short, hunched man, clad in a rough brown tunic scuffled inside and lifted a taper high to illuminate her cell.

He cackled. "Your presence is required...again."

Terror exploded in her mind.

"No," she screamed, but he yanked her to her feet. She collapsed back, forcing him to drag her. Another guard arrived and threw her over his shoulder. She gasped, and struggled with all of her strength.

"No!" Her scream reverberated down the hall as he carried her to a place she did not want to go.

△ △ △ △ △

ROLBAN
KOBLAN CONTINENT

"No... No! DECCIA!" With a gasp, Methusal Maahr sat upright on the cold stone floor. Her heart raced.

Her clothes clung to her damp skin, and she trembled as a chill invaded her soul. *Deccia.* The nightmare was about her twin. But it hadn't felt like a dream at all. It had felt so real...

CHAPTER ONE

HARD GUSTS SWIRLED around the Tarst Range peaks and swept south, across the southern plain, and crashed into the Rolban Mountains. The strengthening winds meant winter would arrive within days.

Methusal sat cross-legged on Rolban's cropland plateau, her knees inches from the cliff's edge. Icy northeast wind lifted her hair and brushed its chilly fingers across her scalp. A high, strange note keened through the gale, and far away dark clouds obscured the Tarst Peaks.

Methusal felt it. Something awful would happen. And her mother confirmed it.

Last night's nightmare replayed through her mind. It couldn't be true.

Then why had she slept-walked last night? She had woken up sprawled in the middle of her living room compartment. Methusal could count on one hand the number of times she'd slept-walked in her life. All had been preceded by nightmares. All of which had come true.

Strike that. Her last nightmare, two and a half years ago, had only partially come true. Their fiercest enemy had attacked Rolban. But the great war she'd foreseen—that had not yet come.

Was her sister all right?

Shivering, Methusal rose and lifted the trapdoor. She climbed down the rough-hewn steps into one of the passageways inside the mountain. Lunch had finished hours ago. She'd be lucky to get a few scraps, but the dream had upset her so much that after working nonstop in the supply room this morning, she'd needed time alone to think.

As Methusal slipped into the dining hall, a tremendous shout erupted from downstairs in the Great Hall.

"*Halt.* Halt, I say!"

Methusal's father and uncle rushed down the Grand Staircase and into the Great Hall. Two guards closed ranks behind them, preventing others from following.

She slipped back into the main passageway to see what was happening. The shouts quieted. Murmuring voices touched her ears. The guards moved, and her father and Petr Storst climbed back up the Grand Staircase. Guards followed them, blocking the view of the man behind them.

Methusal craned her neck. When the guards turned the corner a man with white-blond hair and broad, powerful shoulders strode into view.

A horrified gasp choked her lungs. Fear cut through her, as swift as a blade.

Mentàll Solboshn. Chief of Dehre—the man who had tried to take over Rolban two and a half years ago. The man who had threatened to kill her. And the man who had been warned over pain of death never to return.

What was he *doing* here?

Shock trembled through her. He'd pass right by her. She wouldn't let him see her fear. She would betray no sign of weakness to her mortal enemy. To Rolban's mortal enemy.

Erl Maahr, Petr, and the two guards approached and passed. Only one length separated her from the giant, blond-haired Dehrien Chief. She slipped into kaavl and in a heartbeat took in everything about her enemy.

He was probably just over thirty now. A bleached leather tunic and breeches outlined his sleek, powerful frame. He strode sure and silently down the hall, like a wild beast scouting its prey. She forced herself to scan his face. Still the same high, wide cheekbones, the same short, white-blond hair...and the shock of the coldest, palest blue eyes she'd ever seen.

Those wintry eyes impaled her, like spears of ice through her soul.

Fear accelerated her pulse. The Dehrien Chief said nothing, but his hard face and freezing gaze, directed only at her, clearly stated, *I have not forgotten. You will pay.*

And then they were gone, down the hall and filing into the Chief's office—her father's office.

Methusal crossed her arms and heaved an unsteady breath. The Dehrien still hated her. He certainly hadn't mellowed over the last two and a half years. The rapid beats of her heart unnerved her, and she willed it to slow down. He couldn't hurt her. For whatever reason the guards had allowed him in, they'd escort him back out. She was safe.

Why had her father allowed him back into Rolban?

For ethical reasons, Methusal usually didn't use her extraordinary kaavl abilities to eavesdrop, but right now she needed to understand what was going on. The man was a huge threat to everyone in Rolban.

She slipped down the hall and stood outside the Chief's door. Although she didn't need to be this close to hear, she *needed* to be close, for a reason she could not name. She wanted to analyze every nuance of the conversation, too. Focusing completely into kaavl, she listened.

"Tell us why you're here, Mentàll. You have five minutes."

"I just returned from Quasr." The Dehrien's low, harsh voice triggered too familiar memories...and nightmares. Fear prickled, and the hairs stood up on Methusal's arms.

"The northern coastal town," Erl agreed. "Go on."

"I had planned to speak with Chief M'ntoyan. But when I arrived, half the town was burned to the ground. Foreign ships filled the harbor. The Chief is dead. An invader General from across the sea sat in his chair, and enemy soldiers filled the mansion."

"An *invader?*" Erl said sharply. "From the continent across the sea?"

Methusal drew a quick breath. She pressed her hand to her mouth. *Deccia.* Two weeks ago her twin had traveled to Quasr to learn the latest teaching techniques. Last night's nightmare returned in a rush and she felt sick. It *couldn't* be true. And yet, if Deccia was captured by a sadistic brute, she didn't believe for one minute it was one from across the sea.

Her impulsive nature, which she had so successfully controlled over the last two and a half years, abruptly overcame her better sense. She burst into the room and glared at the Dehrien Chief.

"What about Deccia?" she demanded. "What's happened to her?"

"Methusal!" Erl frowned.

Mentàll ignored her outburst. "I barely escaped with my life. Invader soldiers have taken over the entire town. Many people are dead, and the others are under house arrest."

Methusal didn't believe one word the Dehrien said. If anyone had taken over Quasr, it was Mentàll. Just like he had tried to take over Rolban.

She trembled with emotion. It all suddenly became quite clear. Mentàll had taken over Quasr, and now he was planning to trick and attack Rolban. Again.

Petr Storst, Deccia's adoptive father, said in a strangled voice, "Deccia is in Quasr. Did you see her?"

"Captives were taken, and your daughter was one of them."

Horror choked Methusal. So. He admitted it. Her dream was true. Even worse, Mentàll had captured Deccia and was abusing her!

With an inarticulate gurgle, she leaped forward and grabbed the Dehrien Chief by the tunic. She jerked at the leather cloth, but his powerful body did not move.

"What have you *done* to her?" she said in a low scream. His hard hands easily caught her wrists, painfully immobilizing her, but she struggled furiously against him. "How dare you throw her in jail? How dare you hurt her! Did you hurt her because you hate *me?* Answer me, you dirt eating *whip!*" She could barely see through her tears.

"Methusal," Erl said. "That is enough. Methusal!" He grabbed her arms and dragged her away from the Dehrien. "Sit down. Calm yourself!"

Methusal refused to sit. She hugged herself and glared at Mentàll through her tears. She'd never wanted to hurt anyone in her life like she did now. The horrible man! What had he done to her twin?

"I don't believe anything you've said," she spat. "You're a lying whip. The past proves it!"

Rage flared, warming those icy eyes to frostbite blue, and searing his cheekbones a furious red. However, he made no move to retaliate.

Belatedly, caution warned her to take care.

After a long, uncomfortably prickling moment, he gritted, "I do not lie. *Ever.*"

"Your Alliance was a lie!"

"The Alliance was a tool. Petr approved the second treaty, which gave me power in Rolban."

Her uncle's face darkened in color and mottled into shades of purple. He'd been stripped of office because he'd conspired with the Dehrien Chief. Petr's letter of agreement had also convinced Chief Patn of Tarst to sign the Dehrien's second treaty, which had provided the flimsy legal grounds for Mentàll's attempted takeover of Rolban.

"You meant to capture Rolban all along," Methusal said. "By force, if necessary."

Mentàll returned his attention to Erl. The cold mask had returned. "The fact remains—I did not lie then, and I do not lie now." He flicked a condescending glance at Methusal. "What would be the point?"

"You said Deccia is in jail, Methusal. How do you know?" Petr's color had paled to a sickly puce.

"I didn't know for sure. Not until now. But I had a nightmare last night. It seemed so *real,* but I didn't think it could be." Tears again filled Methusal's eyes, and she turned to Erl. "She's hurt, Papa. We have to save her. We have to *do* something!"

"That is why I am here," the Dehrien Chief asserted. "We need to assemble an army. We need to defeat the invaders in Quasr before they spread south and threaten our towns."

"Methusal has a point," Erl said. "How do we know you're telling the truth? Sending our best soldiers would leave Rolban defenseless. Then you could attack us again."

The Dehrien's jaw clenched. "I speak the truth."

Silent moments passed. Mentàll turned his wintry gaze upon Methusal. His hatred for her seemed to have intensified, if that was possible.

She couldn't care less. All that concerned her right now was rescuing her twin sister. "Arrest him, Papa," she urged her father. "Until we learn what has happened to Deccia."

"You will *not* throw me in jail," snarled the Dehrien. "I have told you the truth."

"Of course I will not put you in jail," Erl soothed, possibly sensing that the situation was about to spiral out of control. "I appreciate the information. However, surely you understand that I'll need to verify the facts. One of my messengers should report back from Quasr soon."

"Timaeus left to visit Deccia five days ago," Methusal said. Timaeus Rolnnt was a messenger for Rolban, and also her sister's fiancé. Their wedding was set for next month.

"He should return tonight," Erl said. In addition to the title of Chief, he coordinated all of the Rolbani runners who relayed messages between the different communities on the Koblan continent.

Methusal shot a dark look at the Dehrien Chief. "Unless he was captured, too."

"I did not see Timaeus," the Dehrien claimed.

A knock rapped on the wooden door.

"Come in," Erl called out.

When the door opened Timaeus stood there, panting. Sweat dripped down his tanned face. Behind him stood another young man who was almost as tall as Timaeus. He had dark hair too, but he was a bit more sturdily built. Methusal recognized him as Dastn, one of Tarst's runners, and also Timaeus' good friend.

"I have news," Timaeus gasped.

"Come. Sit," Erl ordered. "Methusal, pour some water."

She quickly complied, and the two young men sank onto the offered chairs.

Timaeus didn't touch his water. "Invaders have captured Quasr. Deccia...I couldn't find her. I don't know where she is."

"Mentàll said she was captured," Erl said.

Instead of looking relieved to discover that his fiancée was alive, Timaeus' face crumpled. "That General is a beast. He's *insane*. Oh, Deccia!" He began to weep.

Horror gripped Methusal. She looked from Dastn to Timaeus. "You mean it's true? Invaders took over Quasr?"

"Invaders from Zindedi." The chamber fell silent.

Zindedi.

Verdnt had been from Zindedi. Timaeus had killed that murderous traitor two and a half years ago. At that time Verdnt's personal papers had mentioned an accomplice in Tarst. That man had never been found, although Kilum, a Tarst runner, had disappeared soon after.

Now the Zindedis had come to Koblan again. An army of them, apparently. Was this the time of trouble the Prophet had predicted? Was it the trouble she'd seen in her first nightmare two and a half years ago? A sick feeling oozed through her.

Erl rubbed a hand across his pale, drawn face. "Zindedi. I never dreamed... Timaeus, how many?"

"Hundreds. And they have death-sticks. They can blow a hole right through a man."

Everyone fell silent at this horrific announcement. Methusal had never before heard of such a killing device.

"And more invaders are coming," Dastn put in. "We overheard a man say more ships will attack Aestoff on the west coast. And more will arrive in Quasr, too. They plan to march south to capture us—specifically Rolban—and then head farther south."

"*What?*" Petr roared. "They want to take over the entire continent?"

"Yes."

Methusal didn't want to believe it. But Timaeus would not lie. That meant Mentàll...she looked at the Dehrien Chief. His condescending gaze cut her to the quick. Difficult as it might be, she owed him an apology. She said, "I accused you unfairly. I'm sorry." But her hard look told him she didn't trust him. And never would.

Seeming to ignore her apology, he turned to Erl. "We must form an army and attack the invaders."

"We need to warn Aestoff. And the other communities, too," Petr said.

"I'll send runners to warn them all," Erl agreed. "If Pan agrees, I think our three communities—Rolban, Tarst, and Dehre—should form our own army and march out immediately for Quasr. I'll send my fastest runner to Tarst."

Dastn spoke up. "Tarst already knows. Another runner came with me, and I sent him to tell Pan the news."

"I sent a runner to Tarst as well, asking Pan to meet us here as soon as possible," Mentàll said.

"Good," Erl said. "As soon as Pan gets here, we'll form a battle plan. I'll send out the runners to the other communities immediately. I'll also call a community meeting. Petr, will you set it up?"

"Right away." Petr moved his bulky frame toward the door. Erl followed. Evidently, the meeting was over.

"What about him, Papa?" Methusal shot a glance at Mentàll. "You won't let him stay in Rolban, will you? Pan may not get here until tomorrow."

"Mentàll is welcome to stay for the meeting with Pan. His four travelers outside the gates may not, however. I'm sorry, Mentàll. Security reasons."

The Dehrien Chief inclined his head. "I will send them home to begin preparations."

"Good. Methusal will show you to the guest quarters. Make yourself comfortable. You're welcome to stay the night."

"Papa... *Papa!*" But Erl had disappeared down the hall. Only the exhausted runners remained in the room with her and the Dehrien Chief. Where had all of the guards gone?

"Frightened, Methusal?" the Dehrien asked with a curled lip.

She gritted her teeth, but did not reply. Even though her behavior so far hadn't proven it, she had matured quite a lot from the hotheaded girl she'd been two and a half years ago. She could certainly treat the Dehrien with the courtesy required of her. "I'll show you to the guest compartment. Then you can speak to your minions."

Timaeus gave a muffled snort.

Apparently Mentàll did not like her comments or her orders, for his condescending smile disappeared. If looks could kill, she would be dead now. Fear bit into her. What was she thinking? She'd be stupid to tour the dim hallways alone with him. She wondered where Behran was at the moment. Even though he was still occasionally a thorn in her side, she'd welcome his presence right now.

Methusal left Petr's office first, which forced the Dehrien to follow in her footsteps. She headed toward the junction of the Grand Staircase and the main hall. The Dehrien Chief, however, quickly strode ahead of her, his long strides eating up the distance. Did he know where the new guest quarters were located? Methusal increased her pace to keep up. At the Grand Staircase the Dehrien turned left and headed down.

She scowled after him. "Where are you going?"

The Chief of Dehre didn't acknowledge her question until he'd reached the bottom of the staircase.

"I will speak to my men. You have one minute to find an escort—if you fear you need one." His contempt was evident.

Methusal bit her lip. Of course he wouldn't let a mere girl order him around. As far as an escort was concerned, it galled her to admit that she did want one. She didn't want to be alone with the Dehrien.

She found Behran in the dining room dumping his dishes into the dirty utensils tub. He was tall, lean, and good looking, with sharp features and dark blond hair. In her opinion, he was the best looking young man she'd ever seen. Two years ago they had been rivals in the kaavl games. Actually they still were, except now they competed at the Bi-level instead of the Tri-level. But after the Dehrien Chief's failed takeover of Rolban, their tenuous friendship had slowly developed into something more.

"I could use your help," she told him.

A straw colored brow rose and deep blue eyes smiled at her. "Anything for you." His mocking tone was half serious, half in fun. Even though they'd been seeing each other for a year now, he still liked to get under her skin. In truth, she liked it too, but right now she needed him to be serious. Together they walked to the main hallway.

"Mentàll is here."

"I heard."

"Papa asked me to bring him to the guest quarters. But I don't want to be alone with him."

"Methusal, afraid?" he teased.

The Dehrien Chief appeared on the stairway with his pack on his back.

"Behran," she whispered.

"Don't worry." Behran's warm, strong hand closed over hers. "I'm here."

The Dehrien reached them. He took in their clasped hands with a derisive lip twist. "The happy couple. Eager to make your wedding vows?"

Methusal ignored the question and headed down the hall, anxious to complete the distasteful task.

Behran, however, spoke up. "We're in no hurry."

"Why pay for what is given for free?" the Dehrien agreed.

Methusal gasped, outraged by the insinuation. "Behran is not...we are not... Behran is a gentleman, unlike you!"

"I offered to marry you. Or don't you remember?" He gave her a nasty smile.

"Marriage or *death*. I couldn't decide which would be worse."

Behran's hand tightened around hers. "Here we are. Guest quarters." He pushed open the door.

"Thank you Behran. Methusal, we will meet again." That promise was a threat. The look he gave her could have frozen the sun.

Taking deep breaths to calm herself, Methusal headed back to the dining hall.

"You haven't told me what is going on."

She stopped abruptly. "Invaders took over Quasr."

"What? You mean invaders like Verdnt?"

"Yes." She quickly explained. "Deccia is captured. And I know she's hurt. We have to do something to help her, Behran. Anything!"

Without a word, he pulled her into his arms. Finally, she let herself cry. "We'll save her," he said softly. "Don't worry, Thusa."

△ △ △ △

Several hours later, Methusal sat in the packed out dining hall waiting for the meeting to start. Her mother sat at the table, and so did Old Sims—Methusal's supply room supervisor and also adopted grandfather. Behran and his parents sat with them as well. Her young cousin, Aalicaa, slid in next to her. The young girl had turned fifteen several months ago, and was now a highly skilled Quatr-level contender. Kitran had recently told Aali that she would soon advance to the Tri-level.

"What's going on?" Aali hissed. "And why is that whip beast here?" Her blue eyes narrowed and shot daggers at Mentàll, who stood on the platform with Erl, Petr, and Pan Patn, who had just arrived from Tarst. Tarst's Chief had left home at first light—apparently the minute he'd heard the news from the Tarst runner.

"He told us about the invaders," Methusal whispered.

"Invaders! Where?"

Aali had been in class this morning. Evidently she hadn't heard yet. Methusal gave her wide-eyed cousin a worried look, and said softly, "Quasr."

"Quasr! But Deccia..." The young girl heaved a sharp breath. "Deccia!"

Deccia was not only Methusal's twin, but Aali's adopted sister, too. Almost twenty-one years ago, Hanuh Maahr had given birth to twin girls—a double blessing in Rolbani culture—and she had decided to give one of the girls to her childless sister, Juni, and her husband Petr. Five and a half years later, Aali had been born to Juni. Not long after, Juni had died of an illness. The dark-haired twins and the fair-haired Aali were like three sisters.

"She's alive, Aali." Methusal comforted her cousin with a gentle squeeze around the shoulders. "She's captured."

Tears wobbled on Aali's lashes.

"It'll be okay." Methusal wished she believed her own words. Fear, like an empty ache, cramped in the pit of her stomach. "We'll rescue her." Or she'd die trying.

Erl blew the slug monster shell. The low, mournful note quieted the excited chatter in the room.

"We have bad news about Quasr." He scanned the crowd. "Invaders from across the sea have taken over Quasr. Many are dead. Many are captured. The situation is grim."

Cries of outrage burst out. Beside Methusal, Aali tensed.

Erl motioned for quiet. "Worse, the Zindedis intend to take over all of Koblan. I've spoken with Pan Patn of Tarst, and Mentàll Solboshn of Dehre. We have all agreed to join forces to fight the Zindedis in Quasr.

"Most of you don't trust Mentàll. And for good reason. But he came here first with the news, and we owe him a debt of gratitude for that. Now we can strike back quickly and expel the invaders from our continent."

"I'm ready! What can I do?" a man shouted.

"Kill them," roared another.

Chief Patn stepped forward. "We will fight. Rolban, Tarst, and Dehre have agreed to join forces. But we'll also need to leave men at home to defend our communities, should that become necessary. Also, Rolban and Tarst have agreed to provide shelter for Dehrien women and children if the invaders penetrate this far south."

"We can't trust them!" shouted Goric. He was a medium height, slight young man with a sly eye and a proven ability to cheat.

The crowd muttered agreement.

Erl waved for silence. "True. But we'll only take women and children under twelve."

A disjointed murmur swelled. On the surface, the decision seemed humane. But Methusal wondered if it was wise. The Dehrien Chief could be charismatic when he chose to be, and he was a proven genius at manipulation. Had he already asserted his mind warping influence over her father and Pan? With narrowed eyes, she watched her enemy on the stage. Her father was smart. Surely he wouldn't make any decisions that would hurt Rolban.

Erl cleared his throat. "We will leave for Quasr the day after tomorrow. In the meantime, we'll form our army. Anyone who wants to fight for Koblan, please meet with the four men stationed at the two tables in the front. They'll determine if you can fight, and in what regiment. Recruits will be responsible for packing their own supplies. We'll post lists of necessities that you'll need to bring. Swords, knives, and bows and arrows will be distributed this afternoon, and weapons practice will begin immediately. Training will continue every evening of our three day journey to Quasr."

Rolban and Tarst had begun making weapons again after the war with Dehre two and a half years ago. The short war had marked the end of the two hundred year old Great War Peace Plan. Dehre had already broken the peace agreement, and the other communities wanted to be ready in case of another war. The possible threat Zindedi posed had played a factor, as well.

But they had no Zindedi death-sticks; whatever they might be. So they'd have to fight with old style weapons. Hopefully they would be adequate.

"What about Aestoff and the other communities?" asked Ben Amil, Behran's father.

Pan spoke up this time. "Runners have been sent to every community on Koblan. Aestoff is in immediate danger. Nearby communities will aid them. We hope that Eerpor and Wyen will help us in Quasr."

Erl spoke again. "This evening I'll give another update on the situation. That is all."

He descended from the stage, and Pan and Mentàll followed him. Erl motioned to Kitran and his brother Barak to follow, and he nodded at Petr, Ben, and Behran to do the same. Other high ranking council members followed.

Methusal quickly figured out that a meeting was about to take place, and she decided just as speedily to join it. She stood up.

"Methusal." Her mother's gentle hand touched her sleeve. "Your father didn't call for you."

"I need to be there."

"Me, too." Aali stood eagerly.

"No," Hanuh firmly told her young niece.

Methusal said, "I'm sorry, Mama. I have to go. I have to be there for Deccia." And she also suspected that she'd need to attend the meeting in order to fight for her right to join the war team. In the past, all women had been forbidden from fighting in wars.

A frown pinched Hanuh's brows, but she nodded to Methusal, giving her blessing.

CHAPTER TWO

METHUSAL SLIPPED INTO her father's office. Every chair was occupied, so she leaned against a rocky wall near the door.

"Methusal." Warning sounded in her father's low tone. All eyes in the room turned to her.

"My sister is in danger. I want to be a part of the war movement." She slid a glance at the Dehrien Chief. His pale eyes burned hatred into her. She stared back, fighting to keep her features expressionless, although fear knotted her stomach. She distrusted that man completely. "I'll do everything in my power to protect both Rolban and Koblan."

The Dehrien's only reaction was a slight tensing of his shoulders. Methusal returned her attention to her father. "You won't know I'm here."

Behran coughed behind his hand. It sounded suspiciously like, "Right!"

Her father swiped a hand over his balding head and briefly closed his eyes. Besides Methusal, he was the only one standing in the room. They were the same height—he, stocky and medium height for a man, and she, tall for a woman, and slender. "Very well, you may stay," he sighed. "Let's begin."

"I have a plan," stated the harsh, grating voice of the Dehrien.

Methusal muttered under her breath, "When don't you?"

Erl sent her a sharp glance, but Mentàll ignored her. "We'll need three war parties. Two to fight with weapons, and one to fight with kaavl."

Pan nodded. "Not a bad idea."

"Rubbish!" Petr Storst clenched his fists. "We can't trust that Dehrien. We should keep his ideas out of the discussion. I don't trust anything he says."

"Because I humiliated you?" Mentàll inquired.

Behind his white beard, Petr's face turned red and darkened to purple. "You are an abomination!" he shouted. Apparently this was one insult too many for him to stomach today. "If it was up to me, I'd throw you out!"

"Petr."

Mentàll said, "No. It is time for the truth. You hate me, Petr, but you hate yourself more. It is true I took advantage of your lust for power. But your greed laid the foundation. You made it possible for me to take over Rolban."

Petr leaped to his feet. "Throw that Dehrien out!" he roared.

The Dehrien's muscles tensed. "Because I speak the truth?"

Petr's stocky form trembled with rage. "Your army killed our citizens!"

"Five," Mentàll agreed. "I regret that."

"You regret nothing! You'd take over Rolban right now if you could. Speak that truth!"

Mentàll remained silent.

Petr raised his arm. "See?" he questioned everyone in the room. "The Dehrien slug has lost the right to speak in this assembly!"

Mentàll relaxed back in his chair. It almost seemed like a taunt. He said, "Koblan needs Dehriens to fight the invaders. If you want my men, you will accept my leadership."

"Leadership? Ha!" Petr spat, and sat again.

"Petr," Erl said. "Let me do the talking." He turned his attention to the Dehrien Chief. "It's true we don't trust you, Mentàll. What assurance will you us give that you'll deal honorably with us? That you won't turn your forces against us after the war ends?"

"My word." The pale eyes glittered. "I will not break my word. Ever."

Erl stared at him for a full minute. Finally, he said, "Very well. I accept your word. You say we should have three teams? I agree. If Pan also agrees, I think he and I should each lead a war party." He looked at his friend, the Tarst Chief.

Pan nodded. "We both have strengths in strategy. A wise decision."

Kitran spoke up next. He was Methusal's kaavl instructor, and at the Primary kaavl level. "I volunteer to lead the kaavl team. I grew up in Quasr, and I know it well."

"I will lead the kaavl team," the Dehrien Chief stated. "I am Kaavl Master."

Kitran's thick black brows beetled together, and he clenched his fists, which surprised Methusal. Normally her level-headed instructor was impossible to read. But then again, Mentàll had tricked Kitran two years ago, just as he had tricked Petr. Except that deceit had probably hurt more, because Kitran had idolized the Dehrien for his kaavl abilities. And he'd trusted Mentàll. He had thought they were friends.

"You forfeited the honor of Kaavl Master when you attacked Rolban," Kitran gritted.

"On the contrary. I remain the best in kaavl. You know this. And I'm a proven leader." The Dehrien spoke with cold logic. "The kaavl team requires both qualities in a Kaavl Commander, and that is me."

Kitran's jaw muscle clenched, and for the first time ever Methusal sensed the deep rage bubbling in him. He spat, "I will not follow a manipulating whip!"

"Then you may choose to serve on a different team," the Dehrien countered.

Kitran heaved a deep breath, clearly trying to calm himself. He turned to Erl. "I will follow Erl and Pan's leadership. I will abide by their decision, not yours, Dehrien."

All eyes turned to the Rolbani and Tarst Chiefs. Erl looked uneasy, and a frown pinched Pan's normally jolly features. They conferred quietly.

"We've made a decision," Erl said a few moments later. The Dehrien Chief still looked calm, and Kitran had relaxed a little in his chair. "Mentàll is Kaavl Master. And he is the Chief of Dehre. He will be the Kaavl Commander for our kaavl war team. Kitran, if you don't want to be on his team, I will accept you on mine. However, Koblan needs your kaavl talent. You would serve our continent best on Mentàll's team."

Kitran's frown blackened like a thundercloud. His brother Barak, who shared Kitran's dark features, but possessed a bulkier build and a volatile temper, scowled as well.

"It is decided," Erl said. "All the best kaavl players will unite under Mentàll's command."

A sick feeling clawed at Methusal's gut. She wanted to join the war effort, and kaavl was her only skill. But she couldn't submit to Mentàll's leadership. Kitran may hate Mentàll for tricking him, but Methusal loathed him for a deeper, far more personal reason. And she distrusted him. She didn't care that he'd been given her father's trust. He hadn't earned hers.

"Papa." Methusal suspected the opposition to her next statement would be strong, so she straightened her shoulders. "Papa, I want to fight, too. I want to help rescue Deccia."

Her father didn't look surprised—or happy—to hear her request. "Methusal, women have no place in war." He spoke gently. "It's brutal. And I know you have a soft heart. Look at all of the animals you help heal. Could you kill a man?"

"I don't know," she admitted. "But I need to go. Please assign me a place."

Although he shook his head, he appeared to be thinking it over. Finally, he said, "I don't like this. But you're almost twenty-one. You have the right to decide."

"Thank you, Papa," she said softly. "Will I be on your team?"

"You will be on mine." The Dehrien Chief's harsh voice startled her.

True, with her skills, it was where she belonged. But she could never be on his team. Fear rippled through her, but she stiffened her muscles so he wouldn't sense it. "Never!" she said. "You threatened to kill me two years ago. And violate me, too. I'll never be on your team. *Never!*"

"I did not kill you," the Dehrien said softly. "And I did not violate you."

"You would have, if I hadn't escaped."

"No." The denial came, sharp and fast.

"You *liar!*" she cried out. "You told me to take my clothes off and...and climb in your bed."

Erl stared. This was the first he'd heard of it. "Is this true, Mentàll?"

Fury lurked in the Dehrien Chief's gaze. "It is true I threatened Methusal. She endangered my entire plan."

"You were going to *rape* my daughter?"

"No. I came to my senses. That would have been wrong. When I returned to tell her, she was gone. Hendra had taken her place."

Erl watched him, his face hard. The Dehrien Chief matched his gaze.

Erl said, "You know I have no way to verify your story."

"Then judge my actions. I did not harm Methusal." The freezing gaze flew her way. In that flash, she saw the deepest truth. He still burned to hurt her; somehow, some way—even now.

"I can't be on his team, Papa!" She instantly regretted blurting that out, because now she'd just revealed fear to her enemy.

Erl's gaze remained on the Dehrien Chief. "Your word seems to mean a great deal to you, Mentàll. Is that true?"

"It is," he returned. "I will not lie. Liars are weak." Pride glittered in the pale eyes.

"Then give me your word, and I will accept it." Erl folded his arms across his chest.

The Dehrien Chief narrowed his eyes. "Name it."

"Promise you will not harm my daughter during the war."

Mentàll glanced from Methusal to Erl, and then back again. Although his face remained expressionless, his eyes told the truth. She saw the battle waging within him. His desire to extract revenge for the pivotal role she had played in his humiliating defeat two and a half years ago fought his desire to lead the kaavl team as he saw fit.

"I will not," he said at last, harshly. "She will be safe during the war."

"Methusal?" her father asked. "Do you accept his word?"

Mentàll clearly still hated her. And although she didn't trust him, she did believe he hated liars—she'd learned that fact the hard way. "I will accept it." Unease, however, swelled.

"Very well," Erl said, "you will be on Mentàll's team. He needs the best, and that is you, Methusal."

"Thank you, Papa." She glanced at her enemy in order to gauge his reaction. Hatred simmered in that cold gaze...and a cruel warning. Her time on his team would be no picnic. Maybe he wouldn't physically harm her, but he could torture her in other ways. And he was brilliant enough to think of many.

"Welcome to my team, Methusal. I will expect only your best."

"And of you, I will expect nothing." She averted her gaze and crossed her arms.

Erl frowned at her, but directed the meeting on to other matters. Methusal took a deep breath and tried to calm the fear shivering through her soul. Mentàll would not lay a hand on her. She would be fine. She would do her job, and she'd help rescue Deccia. And when the invaders were defeated—hopefully in short order—they'd go home, and she'd never see him again.

She could do it. She could do anything to save her sister.

Δ Δ Δ Δ Δ

Aali tip-toed down the hall to her Uncle Erl's office. She knew the top secret meeting was taking place right now. It wasn't fair she couldn't participate, just because she was only fifteen. She was Deccia's sister.

But she could spy. And, by flying aptes, she'd learn every secret they whispered in there.

She relaxed back against the wall next to the Chief's closed door, and kicked up a nonchalant foot on the black rock wall behind her. She strained her ears and heard a low murmur of voices. Methusal's indignant tones rang clear.

If only she could hear better! Aali pressed her ear to the door. A few sentences filtered through.

"Spying?"

Aali gasped in a startled breath and glanced into the amused brown eyes of the Tarst runner, Dastn. She had noticed him before. Mostly because he was cute. He was tall—she barely topped his shoulder—and sturdily built, but in a lean sort of a way. She especially liked his spiky brown hair at his temple that tipped just so to the left. It made him look wicked and exciting. She guessed he was about twenty years old.

Aali quickly gathered her thoughts. She tried to sound lofty. "I need to speak to my father."

"Petr?"

She smiled her brightest smile. "Why, yes! I don't believe we've met. I'm Aali." She stuck out her hand. After a pause his hand closed around hers, warm and strong.

"I'm Dastn."

"Pleased to meet you, Dastn."

He folded his arms across his broad chest. "Do you enjoy spying?"

"Spying!" Aali said indignantly. Really, the nerve of him. "You know nothing about me."

"Timaeus has told me plenty."

Timaeus, the traitor!

Aali frowned. "So? I'm spying. What's that to you?"

"Not much." But the corner of his mouth curled up, as if he found her amusing.

"You are disagreeable," she told him.

"Nice to meet you, too." The office door opened and he straightened.

With a final glower, Aali darted down the hall. Her father would be mad if he caught her spying. Hopefully that troublesome Dastn wouldn't tell him. But at least she'd learned a tiny bit—enough to set her plan into motion.

△ △ △ △ △

After the meeting finished, it was time for the evening meal. Methusal's stomach rumbled as she waited her turn in line, and then she scooped up meat and mashed tubers from the buffet line sculpted out of black rock. A lot had been decided during the meeting—and she had tried to pay attention to the details. But what she cared about most was going on the mission and rescuing her sister. And, of course, defeating the invaders. More meetings would take place tomorrow, but she would not attend. She had accomplished her goal. Now she would get ready for the trip.

As she navigated through the dining hall toward her family's table, she thought about what she should pack.

A movement and a frisson of danger alerted her to the Dehrien Chief's presence. He had appeared out of nowhere, and now silently stalked beside her.

Fear flared, but she struggled to suppress it. "Step off," she told him, turning aside to her table.

"I want to speak to you, Methusal. Give me your attention."

She set her plate down and faced him. She wanted to cross her arms, but didn't want to appear defensive. "Speak, then."

"We will work closely together during the next few weeks."

"Oh, goodie." Teeth gritted, she stared into Mentàll's cold eyes.

"You will treat me with respect." His voice was low with threat. "I am your commanding officer."

"You have not earned my respect. But I will follow your orders—on the field, only. Out of respect for my father."

"Then we understand each other."

"I understand that you hate me."

Amusement tinged that icy gaze. "Enjoy your reprieve."

He was clearly warning her of his intention to retaliate after the war. After all agreements had ended.

"Will you be able to control yourself that long?"

The Dehrien's features tightened, and red tinged his cheekbones. "Test me, and you will suffer," he promised.

"You already plan to break your word?"

"I will not need to break my word. I think you understand that."

"Whip!" she muttered.

The Dehrien Chief stepped closer. His sheer size intimidated her, but she refused to back up. "Choose your words wisely, Methusal." That low hiss shivered through her soul.

"Threaten me," she returned, "and I'll make sure you lose your job as Kaavl Commander. Kitran would make a much better leader."

Mentàll smiled, clearly unmoved by her threats. "I look forward to many days together, Methusal. But I will leave you with one word of warning: Choose insubordination at your peril. You will not enjoy the consequence." His threatening smile told her that he would.

Methusal stilled a quiver of fear. "Harass me, and *you* will know the consequence."

"Is he bothering you, Thusa?" Behran's voice spoke behind her.

The Dehrien flicked a condescending glance at Behran. "I will leave you to your prickly thorn, Behran. A woman so prideful and arrogant cannot possibly make a comfortable companion. Perhaps that is why you will not sample her nectar."

Methusal's mouth opened in shocked outrage. She crossed her arms tightly against herself to suppress her desire to punch the Dehrien hard in the gut. "You *horrible* man," she spat. "*You* are the prideful one. You're the arrogant beast! The whole world isn't big enough to fit your ego. Step off!"

Mentàll only smiled. A grim, curiously triumphant light sparked in his eyes. "Enjoy the cut of her tongue, Behran. Unless you tame her, she will destroy you." He turned on his heel and left.

"I hate him!" she snapped. "I *hate* that horrible man."

"Don't let him get under your skin." Behran pulled her into his arms.

Methusal heaved an agitated breath. "I'm not like that, am I, Behran? Prickly? Prideful, arrogant?"

She felt his faint chuckle. "You can be prickly. And you come across as confident, but inside..." he pulled back, so he could look at her. His deep blue eyes were warm. "Inside, you're like a soft pastry. Sweet and tender." He kissed her, and she kissed him back.

"Thank you, Behran," she whispered.

He hugged her tight. "And remember, I'll be with you on the kaavl team. You'll never be alone with Mentàll."

She relaxed a little more. "Thank you. You always make me feel better."

"I love you, Thusa. Don't you know that?" His gaze looked tender, but hesitant. It was the first time he had ever said those words to her.

Wonder filled her, and she smiled. "I love you, too, Behran." She kissed him again.

CHAPTER THREE

METHUSAL LOOKED AT THE ITEMS strewn on the pallet in her room. She needed to pack clothing, of course. A water skin. Soap and a hairbrush. And she also needed to visit Old Sims and collect her rations from the supply room. But what was she forgetting?

Kaavl strips and her kaavl stick.

She added a handful of the thin leather strips, banded in blue, along with the half-length long, stout kaavl stick to the growing pile. She also added a shorter, quarter length kaavl stick for good measure. Although kaavl sticks weren't used in the annual Kaavl Games, they were a remnant from wartime, and all kaavl contenders still learned how to use them. Her skill level with the short stick was mediocre. But she'd used the longer stick several times in the past to defend herself from whip beast attacks.

"Methusal." Her mother's soft voice spoke from behind the leather door hanging. "May I come in?"

"Of course, Mama." When Hanuh entered, Methusal said, "What else should I bring? What am I missing?"

Her mother's gray hair, once as dark as Methusal's, was gathered back with a scrap of leather. Tendrils wisped around her gentle face and framed her bright blue eyes.

Hanuh surveyed the mishmash of items piled on Methusal's bed. "An extra coverlet, in case you need to keep your pack strapped up?" she suggested. The pack, when unfolded, also served as a blanket. "And what about a hooded cloak?"

"Yes." Methusal hurried to fetch those items. Then she saw her medical pouch. She always carried coltac leaves and tacky leaves wherever she went, in case she found a wounded animal. Surely she'd need those during the war. She added the pouch to the pile.

Hanuh drew a breath. "I think you'll need this, too." She extended her hand. A dagger with a red bone handle rested on her palm.

Methusal felt repulsed. "Mama! No. I won't need that. I don't even know how to use one."

Her mother pressed the cool bone object into her palm. "You're going to war. You'll need to defend your life."

She shot a quick glance at her mother. Just as she had feared, a far off, distant look clouded Hanuh's gaze. "You see something, don't you? What's going to happen to me...and to Deccia?"

Her mother refocused. "I don't know. But I do know you'll need to defend yourself. Learn how to use it." Her lips tightened. "I wish you wouldn't go."

"I have to. For Deccia."

"You're on the Bi-level now. Your kaavl will help find Deccia."

"You know that?"

"I sense it. Beyond that, I don't know." Pensive lines worried her brow. "Methusal," she said hesitantly, "I feel like I need to warn you about something."

She felt more dread. "What?"

"Thusa...if you go, your life will never be the same again."

"What do you mean?"

"I can tell you no more."

Methusal tried to read her mother's troubled expression. Either Hanuh didn't know more, or she wouldn't tell her. Sometimes Hanuh felt deep warnings in her heart that she should not share certain premonitions.

"Be careful, Thusa. Choose wisely." Tears brightened her eyes, and Methusal hugged her.

"I love you, Mama. I'd stay if I could, but even if Deccia wasn't captured, I'd have to go. Do you understand?"

She patted Methusal's cheek. "Of course. You're Mahre's descendent. Your kaavl is a gift. You feel responsible to help defend Koblan."

"Yes. Isn't that the true reason for kaavl? Not for kaavl games, but to save and protect us all."

"I'm proud of you." Her mother smiled. "So is your father."

Methusal smiled, too. "Maybe the war will end soon. Maybe we'll rescue Deccia in time for her wedding next month."

Hanuh's gaze shadowed again. "Perhaps."

Methusal wanted to make her mother smile again. She offered, "And maybe soon after that Behran and I will marry, too."

Hanuh did smile then, and the sadness in her eyes turned to hope. "I'd like nothing more. You know I love Behran. He's a fine boy." Another frown pinched her brow. She opened her mouth, hesitated, and then said in a rush, "Be careful, Methusal." And then she looked distraught.

"Why?"

Tears sparkled in Hanuh's eyes. "I'm sorry. Nothing is clear. I can't tell you much more. But take care with your choices. Your entire future rests upon them."

"I will. Don't worry."

"You're a good girl. I trust you to do what is right." With those oblique words, Hanuh left her.

With a frown, Methusal wondered what her mother meant.

Thinking of premonitions, another memory returned to mind—of meeting the Prophet two and a half years ago. And his warning that a time of trouble would come. Could this Zindedi invasion be the trouble he had envisioned? Probably. She couldn't help but remember the disturbing nightmare she'd had then, too. In it Mentàll had hunted her, and she'd run for her life. The One had warned her to listen...to follow him. Were all of these things about to come true now?

△ △ △ △ △

DEHRE
DAY 2 continued...

Hendra rapped on the wooden board knocker beside the tent's door.

"Come in," Mentàll said brusquely.

Hendra stepped inside and watched as her cousin—still Dehre's Chief after a rough two and a half years—packed his bag for the upcoming war. Thankfully, a war he had not started this time. A war she was determined to join. Last time she had failed everyone. Now she was determined to make up for it.

"I'm coming, too," She'd decided to present it as a fact—not as a request. After all, she was twenty-three years old now.

"You are not." He continued to pack. Three knives and two swords lay on the table, and so did several bleached leather tunics and breeches.

In the past, a confrontation of any kind would have sent Hendra into a fearful panic. She still preferred to avoid conflict, but the last war had taught her courage. That didn't mean she wasn't scared. Right now her heart pounded in hard, sickening beats. "I'm an adult. You can't stop me."

He stopped packing. His cold, pale gaze made her shiver. "You choose to live in my tents, and under my protection and authority. You will obey me. I am responsible for your safety."

Hendra had already anticipated that reply. "I'm at the Tri-level. I can scout in the war. I don't need to fight. I don't want to fight, either."

He returned to his packing. "Fighting will be inevitable."

"I won't stay here." Alone. But she didn't say it. She didn't need to.

"Jascr will be on the kaavl team." Her cousin's words cut like a sharp knife.

If he thought that bit of news would scare her off, he was wrong. "I want to come," she said stubbornly. "I want to help Dehre. I want to help Koblan. It is my right."

Her cousin could be fair when he chose to be. He had always protected her to the best of his ability, too. She understood little else about him, even after all of these years. She suspected he had a soft spot for her—that was the only explanation she could find for why he hadn't thrown her out of his tents two and a half years ago. That was when she had betrayed him and warned Rolban that he planned to take over their community. But even her betrayal hadn't helped Rolban, because she'd warned them too late. Innocent people had died. So she had failed Rolban, and she'd betrayed her cousin, too. Hendra hated herself on both counts. When she'd arrived home after the battle in Rolban, she had packed up all of her things and waited for Mentàll to order her to leave Dehre. He never had.

Mentàll had spent months, however, not speaking to her. Of course, he'd been preoccupied, trying to provide food for the starving Dehriens. Eventually the seed grain they'd bought from Tarst, in combination with the newly diverted Tarst River, had helped solve the famine. And he'd met challenge after kaavl challenge to keep his position as Dehrien Chief.

"You want to see Behran," he said.

Hendra's face warmed. "No. I want my life to mean something. I want to make a difference. I don't want to sit in my tent and twiddle my fingers! Mentàll, I feel useless. Purposeless. Like my life has no meaning. Even if I die, it would be better than sitting here, doing nothing. Don't you see?"

"You help the orphaned children."

"For a few hours each day. I won't be missed. I've already asked Gelda to take my place while I'm gone. I need to help Koblan."

"Do you still give half of your food to the children? Because there is no need."

"Yes. How did you know?" She had begun sharing her food rations during the famine.

"I know everything that happens in my tents."

She finally realized that he'd neatly changed the subject. "I want to do something that will help everyone, Mentàll—not just the children."

Hendra encountered the cold blue of her cousin's stare.

"You're still angry that I betrayed you." How she guessed this now, she didn't know. They'd never spoken of it before. Fear curled up inside her, and she waited for the lash of his anger. Just like her father and brothers had always delighted in hurting her in the past.

"You disappointed me," he bit back. "But you are my responsibility. I will not cast you out."

Hendra felt a cautious bit of relief. He had not attacked her. "I didn't want you to kill innocent Rolbanis."

"Innocent Dehriens died instead. Including the children you care for."

Hendra looked down. "I didn't want anyone to die."

"The responsibility does not lie with you. Methusal is to blame."

Puzzled, she looked up. "How?"

He gave the laces of his pack a vicious jerk. "I do not want to speak of it."

"So you'll let me come?" she persisted. "I want to prove my worth to Dehre, to you, and most of all to myself."

Her cousin remained silent for so long that she wondered if it was his way of dismissing her. She waited with patient stubbornness.

"Very well. You may come."

She gasped with delight.

"But you will follow my orders to the letter," he warned. "You will be on my kaavl team. But if I decide to move you somewhere safer, you will go."

"I understand. Thank you."

"Then pack. Here is a list. We leave tomorrow at first light."

Hendra clutched the list and ran to her tent. Maybe she was crazy to want to join a war. Fighting, and men in particular, scared her to death, but she had to do this. She didn't want to live in fear any longer.

△ △ △ △ △

ROLBAN
DAY 2 continued...

Methusal heard the clash of weapons down in the Great Hall as she headed for the supply room. Men were practicing for the battles ahead. Certainly an activity in which she had no desire to take part. Although Hanuh had given her a knife, she only wanted to use it for self-defense.

Now she needed to see Old Sims and gather up food supplies. She also wanted to say goodbye to the man she considered her grandfather. Sims had been a wanderer for many years, but he had settled in Rolban over thirty years ago. He had no family of his own. When Methusal had begun working as his supply room assistant, she had developed a deep affection for the elderly man. So had her parents, and they'd unofficially adopted him into their family. He often ate meals with them now, and he participated in their family celebrations.

Surely she would see him again when she returned, but she just couldn't be sure. He was almost old enough to be her great-grandfather, although he was still spry and sharp.

"Sims?" She poked her head in the supply room's doorway.

The tall, stooped man with thinning white hair stood in the corner. A gnarled finger counted sacks of grain discs. He turned at the sound of her voice, and a smile creased his leathery features. "Methusal, my girl. Come in. You've come for your supplies."

"Yes." She hesitated. "I'm sorry I won't be here to help you if the Dehriens come."

"No need, my girl." He smiled. "I'll find help. The Dehriens can do their share of the work, too. That's the least they can do to enjoy the safety of Rolban's walls."

"Will you watch out for my mother while we're gone? She'll be alone."

"Hanuh is a strong woman. Just like her daughters," Sims's faded blue eyes twinkled.

"Will you, Sims?" she pressed.

"That I will, my girl. What an old man can do, I will do. Remember, Hanuh and Poli's garment room is right next door. I'll watch over them. And if the Dehriens come to Rolban, I'll keep a sharp ear tuned for any talk of mutiny, too."

"Thank you. I know only women and children will come, but I don't trust any of them."

Sims nodded. "I'll keep in close contact with Petr and Ben. Don't worry, Methusal." Petr and Ben Amil would be acting as Co-Chiefs during the war.

"Thanks, Sims." She gave him a tight hug. "I'll miss you."

The gnarled hands gripped her shoulders. "Be careful. You'll face more Dehrien tricks than I will." He peered intently at her. "I understand that you'll be on Mentàll's kaavl team."

"Yes."

"He's not a man to trifle with." Concern quavered in the old voice. "Be careful with him, Methusal. Make your decisions with care."

Sims' words echoed her mother's. She searched his eyes. "What do you mean?"

Sims gave her shoulder a final pat. "I'm saying there's far more to the Dehrien than meets the eye. Be careful. When you get as old as I am, you learn to read people. And that young man..." he hesitated. "That man is either heading for triumph or ruin. Only time will tell. But *you* be careful, my girl. You know the danger."

"I do. Thank you, Sims."

"Now," Sims turned to the sacks of food stacked on a shelf, "you'll need to carry your own rations. Two sacks of meat and a sack of grain discs. And tagma berries."

"Those will get heavy fast."

"War won't be easy. Carrying your food will be the least of your hardships."

Sims' words weren't comforting. Methusal hoped she would be able to overcome all of the challenges she was about to face. Was she naïve to think the war would go smoothly, and that they'd be able to rescue Deccia right away?

Sims patted her back. "You look troubled. I have full confidence in you. If anyone can make a difference in the war effort, it's you, my girl. The Old Kaavl Master's blood runs thick through yours. With it, you can help save us all."

"I'll do the best I can. Will I see you at dinner tonight?"

"That you will."

Tonight she'd say most of her goodbyes, which she did not look forward to. Part of her couldn't wait until tomorrow, when they would finally start hiking north to rescue Deccia. Maybe then the uneasiness in her soul would settle.

CHAPTER FOUR

AALI HURRIED ALONG, cap pulled low, and with her long blond hair piled up high beneath it. They'd left at first light that morning, and had marched without stopping all day. It was terribly boring and tiring, but necessary, of course. In a few days they'd attack and defeat the invaders. And rescue Deccia.

Troops of Rolbani soldiers trotted ahead of her. Almost a hundred, Aali guessed. She followed close behind them, but not too close. She didn't want anyone to recognize her. Not until they were at least two days away from Rolban. She didn't want to be found out and sent home. She would be a part of this mission, whether they liked it or not. And she'd be a great help, too. Didn't she know kaavl? Maybe they'd put her on the kaavl team with Methusal and Behran.

But then she'd have to take orders from that whip beast, Mentàll.

A soldier looked behind him, and she ducked down her head, pretending to adjust her pack. She peeked back up.

Good. Free and clear.

The afternoon was almost gone. Soon it would be time to set up camp. Good, because her feet hurt.

Might as well practice kaavl, so she'd be ready for battle, she reasoned. And it would help to pass the time. She sharpened her listening skills and tracked systems of movement. She also practiced pinpointing their location. The soldiers ahead were loud and hard to filter out. What about behind her?

A soft scuff of footsteps were almost upon her.

With a gasp, she glanced over her shoulder. Dastn! That troublesome runner. What was he doing here?

"You're falling behind, soldier." Dastn strode by, wearing a large pack secure on his shoulders. She stuck out her tongue at his broad back. That's all she needed—to be found out now.

Suddenly, the runner turned back and snagged her arm, pulling her to a halt. His fingers quickly flipped off her cap, and her long blond hair cascaded to her shoulders.

"I thought so," he said grimly.

Aali snatched back her hat. "What's it to you?" She piled up her hair again and tugged the cap back on.

"I have to report you."

"Step off," she scorned.

He gripped her arm, and none too gently. "You'll step with me. Now come on."

Aali struggled, but quickly realized it was useless. Although she was wiry, he was much bigger than her in every way.

"I'm not going home! Bother you."

He smiled in a thin sort of way. "Didn't plan to be caught yet?"

"Not until tomorrow." Then she snapped her mouth shut.

He hustled her along, making her seethe.

"Hands off!" she spat. "I'm not a child."

"You're acting like one. Not exactly mature to sneak after the war campaign. Your father doesn't know, does he?"

"How is that your business? Let me go!"

"I can't have you following so far behind. It's dangerous. You'll walk in the middle of the pack while I talk to Erl."

"Dangerous? How? I've been walking by myself all day."

He did not reply, which infuriated her still more—almost as much as knowing she'd soon have to face the music with Uncle Erl.

Dastn pulled her through the crowd, searching for her uncle. Aali saw him the same instant the runner did. She lifted her chin. "Let me go," she said coolly. "I won't run off."

Dastn gave her a sharp look, but did as she bid. Head held high, she marched up to Erl.

"Uncle Erl."

His steps faltered. "Aalicaa! What are you doing here?"

"Thank you." With a faint blush, Hendra touched the ends of her long, straight, white-blond hair, which was almost exactly the same shade as Mentàll's. Only her eyes were a warm dark brown, and instead of coldness, she projected a cautious warmth. Not for the first time, she reminded Methusal of a fragile, hurt animal.

"Welcome to the girls club!" Aali said. "I haven't seen any others, besides us."

Hendra said, "Maybe we're the foolish ones, to want to come to war."

"We get to live the excitement, you mean," Aali interjected.

"I'm sorry about your sister," Hendra offered quietly.

"We'll rescue her, just wait and see. Right, Thusa?"

"Hendra." Methusal turned quickly at the sound of Behran's voice. He grinned, obviously pleased to see the Dehrien girl, and the old insecurity twisted through Methusal's heart.

Hendra's face lit up when she saw her former Dehrien teammate. They had trained in kaavl together before Behran's family moved to Rolban.

Behran reached out to give her a hug, but stopped when Hendra flinched. Red suffused her face. "I'm sorry, Behran. It's wonderful to see you." Briefly, she clasped his hand. "I'll be on Mentàll's kaavl team, too. I reached the Tri-level last spring."

"Congratulations," Behran's warm smile lingered.

Trying to ignore the discomfort she felt, Methusal looked away and discovered that the Tarst had just maneuvered a log over the narrowest part of the river. "Look! We can cross."

They waited in the long line to cross.

"Behran. Methusal..." She bit her lip, and her faint frown looked distressed. "I...I well... You're long overdue an apology from me."

"For what?" Methusal said with surprise.

"For the war two years ago. I should have warned you sooner about Mentàll."

"Don't worry. I suspected he was up to something the whole time. Don't feel bad." Then, because she was curious, she said, "Did you know any facts for sure?"

"No. But I did have suspicions. I didn't want to believe them. And I didn't want to betray Mentàll. He's been so good to me."

"Really?" Methusal found this difficult to believe. Then again, she'd only seen the cold, power hungry side of the man. It was hard to imagine that a human side could exist.

Softly, Hendra said, "Even after I betrayed him, he wouldn't cast me out of his tents."

"I don't blame you for anything," Methusal told her. "Mentàll is responsible. And you saved me from him. If it hadn't been for you..." The old terror made a lump form in her throat.

Anguish darkened Hendra's eyes.

The Dehrien's outrageous claims in Rolban flew to mind, and Methusal clenched her teeth. "Two days ago, he actually had the gall to say he wasn't going to violate me in Tarst. That he'd changed his mind!" She heaved a choked, furious breath. "The lying whip."

"I'm sorry." Hendra bit her lip again. "I know he frightened you. But you should know...that night, when he came back in the cabin, still thinking I was you, he ordered me to get dressed."

Methusal listened to this with disbelief. Apparently the Dehrien girl still blindly clung to her misguided hero-worship of her cousin. "Well, if he did change his mind, it was because he'd decided to kill me, instead."

Hendra flinched. "I'm sorry. I'm so glad he didn't do any of those things to you."

Methusal looked down the long line of people to the Dehrien Chief, who was waiting to cross the Tarst River. She was glad, too. But what tortures did he plan for her now? She wasn't naïve enough to think his plans for revenge would remain on ice until the end of the war.

△ △ △ △ △

The sun had set, and dusk slid across the plains and low lying hills when it was finally Methusal's turn to cross the Tarst River. Behran went first, then Hendra, Aali, and finally it was her turn. The log looked skinny, and it bowed in the middle as her friends carefully shuffled to the other side, which was four lengths away.

Methusal cautiously edged sideways onto it. Her moccasined feet curled over the rounded edges. Step by step, she sidled toward the far bank, trying to forget how far she still had to go, and trying to ignore the furious rush of the white water below her.

"Scared, Methusal?" The taunt came from her left. Her gaze slid to Goric, who had followed her onto the log. The slight, wiry young man was the one she'd managed to get expelled from the kaavl program two years ago for cheating. He still hated her for that humiliation.

His dark blond hair spiked down his forehead, punctuating his murky gray eyes.

"Cautious doesn't mean scared, Goric."

"Really?" He bounced on the heels of his feet. The log shifted.

Methusal's arms flailed, but she caught her balance just in time.

"Goric!" Barak roared from the bank. "You'll answer to me if you do that again."

Goric smirked, and edged closer to Methusal. She increased her pace. He said, "Kitran reinstated me in kaavl. I'm back at the Tri-level."

"Good for you. I hope you can compete now without breaking every branch on the plain." Maybe that wasn't nice, but it was true. He was a noisy kaavl player. That's how she'd easily defeated him at the Tri-level.

"I'll be on the kaavl war team," Goric said. "With you."

Finally, she'd made it across. Methusal jumped to safety and turned to Goric. "Great. Try not to get yourself killed."

He drew in a sharp breath of fury.

It really was too bad Kitran had reinstated Goric into kaavl. He must have been desperate to build up the war team.

"Methusal, look!" Aali called. "Pan brought an extra tent for us girls!"

For the first time Methusal noticed the huge, slow moving beasts of burden which were tethered to boulders on the far edges of camp. Urchets. The large, four-footed animals had high, pointed ears, long necks, and broad backs. Urchets liked to live in the hills and the Tarst tended herds of them. They were useful for their milk, and for their ability to carry loads of supplies through treacherous terrain. Perfect for their mission now.

Methusal and the other girls soon discovered that a Tarst young woman would share the tent with them. Her name was Oona, and she seemed nice, but reserved. Moments later Aenill, Pan's wife, appeared out of nowhere. With a cry, she hugged Methusal and Hendra. The plump older woman turned to Aali. "And who would you be?"

"I'm Aali, Thusa's cousin. Petr Storst's daughter."

Aenill nodded. "I see you've met Oona, my niece. She'll help me cook on the trip, and at base camp. Will you girls help, too?"

Aali sighed. "We know all about kitchen duty."

"Don't worry. Tonight we're having dried rations. And I brought spices, Methusal." Her eyes twinkled, obviously remembering Methusal's mission to spice up Rolban's dull diet two years ago. "We will eat well, never fear."

The last bit of daylight disappeared as the girls settled into their tent. When Methusal came out, she was happy to see the large fires burning in a protective half circle around the camp. The Tarst River protected them on the south side. Both fire and water were deterrents to the huge, fanged wild beasts that emerged from their caves at night. They could tear a man limb from limb in a few horrifying seconds. Daylight blinded their sensitive eyes, so they scoured the plains only at night to search for fresh meat.

She spotted Aenill near the largest bonfire. A metal contraption had been set over it, which was made up of two sets of metal legs and a cross bar at the top. Pots hung from this. Methusal hurried over. "Can I help?"

"I'm boiling water for tea. One pot is ready. Help me get it down."

Methusal helped wrestle the heavy pot to the ground, and then they hung another in its place.

Aenill put two fingers in her mouth and whistled. "Hot water! Form a line." She pushed a ladle into Methusal's hand. "Here. Dip it up. Oona will help me lift the pots. She's a bit stronger than you."

The men lined up, and soon Aali stood with a ladle beside another pot, and Hendra helped when either of them tired. Dastn and Timaeus appeared, and with a frown, Aali served

Dastn. Methusal offered the tense-looking Timaeus a smile. "We'll rescue her soon."

"I'm trying hard to believe that."

"Will you be running messages between our war teams?"

"Yes. And coordinating with teams from other communities. And as we travel north Pogul and I will scout ahead for invaders who might be heading toward us."

Methusal glanced at the flickering bonfires surrounding their camp. They were meant to scare off the wild beasts, but what if they lured a wild beast of another kind? "Is someone scouting for invaders now?"

"No. At first light we'll go out again. I'll head west and Pogul will go north, following the range, like the war party will."

"I didn't know Pogul was a runner." In fact, Methusal didn't know of any praise-worthy things about Pogul. She knew he often slept while on guard duty back home. The fact that he was rude and lewd didn't help her opinion of him, either.

"He's not." Timaeus' lips thinned. "But we take what we can get." He moved on.

Methusal greeted several men from Rolban, and then continued dipping up hot water for strangers. Most people smiled, but others looked grim and unfriendly. Dehriens, she guessed. Two years ago she'd noticed that the Tarst generally seemed cheerful, while the Dehriens looked unhappy.

"Hendra!" A brawny man with curly black hair pushed forward. The Dehrien girl instantly shrank back. His crooked teeth flashed. For a split second they reminded Methusal of fangs. "Glad you'll be on the kaavl team too, sister."

Hendra's lips barely moved. "Jascr." Her hands jerked as she poured water into his cup.

The man's black gaze turned to Methusal. "Who is this vision of beauty?" His finger swept down her cheek. "Nice."

She did not flinch. "Step off."

"I like fiery women."

"Then find another."

He laughed and gestured toward camp. "But where?"

"Next," Methusal said pointedly.

By now Hendra had retreated another full step.

Jascr laughed again. He leaned forward and tugged hard at Hendra's hair. "Sister," he smiled, and vanished into the night.

Hendra dropped the ladle and pressed her trembling hands together. "I'm sorry for my brother."

"He's your brother?"

"Yes. My oldest one. He's at the Bi-level."

"He threw you out of the house after your father died," Methusal remembered.

"Yes. And I'm glad."

What an awful family. It must be, if Mentàll was the best of the bunch. Poor Hendra. No wonder she looked frightened so often.

△ △ △ △ △

Methusal sat beside Behran near one of the bonfires. She'd eaten her rations, and the warmth of the fire made her feel sleepy. She didn't think she'd fall asleep, though, because half of the men were sword fighting. Grunts, clashes, and shouts peppered the still night air.

The thought of actually killing someone made her feel sick. She shivered.

"Cold?" Behran slid an arm around her shoulders, and drew her close to his warm body.

With a smile, she leaned into him. "Actually, I was thinking about the war. I hope we don't have to fight." Blades flickered in the firelight.

"Are you ready? Have you practiced with the knife Hanuh gave you?"

"No. But I can use a kaavl stick."

"We won't be able to bring kaavl sticks on our spying missions. They're too big to hide. Unless you brought a short one."

Behran had a point. "I did, but I'm not as skilled with that one. Still, I don't want to practice. I don't want to kill anyone."

"You may have to, in order to save your life."

Methusal said nothing.

"You need to learn how to use the knife so you can defend yourself."

Methusal pulled away. "Kitran told me the same thing."

"Listen to us. It's for your own safety. I'll teach you." He scrambled to his feet and held out a hand to help her up.

"Behran..."

"Come on."

Reluctantly, she gained her feet.

"Are you turning in?" Hendra's hesitant voice made Behran pause.

Methusal felt grateful for the small reprieve.

"I'm going to teach Thusa how to use a knife. What about you? Do you need to practice?"

Hendra glanced between the two of them. "I have some skill. I don't want to interrupt..."

"Come on." Behran reached for Hendra's elbow, but the girl flinched. His hand dropped. In a gentle tone, he said, "Help me convince Thusa that she needs to practice."

With a small smile, she glanced quickly at Methusal. "Well..."

"The more the merrier," Methusal agreed, shoving aside her ridiculous twinge of insecurity. It was selfish to want to spend time alone with Behran, too. She offered the other girl a grin. "Come on."

A smile lit Hendra's features. "All right."

The next half hour was fun. Behran made it so. Methusal learned three ways to unsheathe her weapon without detection. Behran also showed both girls how to hold the knife, and various methods of attack. Methusal made sure she stood far from her friends while she practiced. Still, the deadly arc of the blade frightened her, even though she controlled the weapon. The damage it could inflict deeply disturbed her. She'd spent so much of her life healing hurt animals that the thought of hurting another living being on purpose made her feel sick. She prayed that she would never have to use the knife to defend herself.

Hendra had difficulty mastering one knife hold, so Behran spent a long while with her, correcting her finger position. Hendra laughed with him, and Methusal felt uncomfortably like an outsider. She watched them quietly talk to each other. Unable to help herself, she intensified her kaavl hearing to eavesdrop. Although she felt guilty about it, she had to know...

Behran said in a low voice. "Will you be able to fight? I know how you feel about violence."

"I'm hoping kaavl will help me avoid fighting."

"That's unlikely."

"It doesn't matter. I want to be useful. I don't want to hide behind my fear anymore, Behran."

"I can see that. I'm proud of you."

Feeling more disturbed than ever, Methusal stopped listening. The proof of their close connection was what she deserved for eavesdropping.

Clearly, the friendship from their childhood was still as strong as ever. She wondered if Behran had ever developed romantic feelings for Hendra. And what did Hendra feel about him? The soft smile she gave him now seemed to border on hero worship. And why *wouldn't* she like him? He was a wonderful man. Certainly none of the Dehrien men she'd met so far were as nice as Behran.

Behran chuckled, and the two headed her way. Methusal slid the knife back into its holder.

"I have to go," Hendra said. The faint frown she sent Methusal appeared troubled. As if she'd sensed what Methusal was feeling. "Thank you, Behran. Good night, Methusal."

"Night."

Behran's arm slid around Methusal's shoulders. "That was sudden," he observed, watching Hendra go.

"It's getting late."

"Walk with me for a minute."

"Okay." Happier again, Methusal snuggled against him, with an arm around his waist, and they walked to a large boulder just outside the fire ring. Behran helped her up.

Weapons practice had quieted. Out here, away from the fires, the cold night air nipped through her tunic. The air smelled sweet; perhaps from the plants dotting the nearby hillside. The plain lay quiet and still, bathed in the green light of Ryon, which had just crested the peaked, snow-capped mountains. The moon looked especially large tonight. A bright halo surrounded it, and wispy clouds drifted across its face. Methusal had never seen Ryon look so bright or so close before. Or so large. It seemed portentous, as if the moon knew it was about to give light to a battle for a continent.

Methusal shivered. "The calm before the storm?"

"Probably. The day after tomorrow we'll reach base camp. Then we'll face the invaders."

"If we don't meet them sooner."

"Behran?"

"What?"

"Are you scared?"

"Sure. Who wouldn't be?"

"It's strange, but I feel like an innocent. That the peace we feel right now...that *that's* the illusion. I'm scared of what's coming."

"Thusa." His arm tightened around her.

"Deccia's living in a nightmare," she whispered. "I think we're going to step into it. My mother said if I go on this mission my life will change forever. I'm afraid she's right. I'm scared."

"Look at me." His blue eyes looked very dark. "We have each other. I won't leave you. Nothing will change. It'll be all right. And we'll find Deccia."

"I hope you're right."

△ △ △ △ △

Voices woke Methusal soon after she'd curled up on the hard ground with her leather coverlet pulled up to her chin. Of course she'd checked it first to make sure no nasty rochers had crawled into her pallet. The black, shiny bugs lived only on the plains. Their bites burned for days.

She shivered from cold now, and a rock dug into her hip. At first she thought the pain had awoken her, but after she moved the pebble and relaxed back toward slumber, voices tickled her ears again.

Mentàll's voice was one. She stiffened. Two and a half years ago his voice had woken her several times. Both times from clear across camp. Nothing like that had happened since then.

Her kaavl abilities were extraordinary hearing, coupled with carrying—mentally transplanting herself to the origin of the sound, and then fanning out her hearing from that spot—it was as if she stood in that very place and heard what a normal person would hear while standing there. But those carries were conscious and deliberate. Hearing Mentàll's voice had been an unconscious event. Methusal believed she'd figured out why she'd heard his voice during those unconscious carries. He was a threat. Maybe her subconscious mind listened for trouble while she slept.

The Dehrien Chief spoke again. "We can make the war work to our advantage."

"How?" Methusal didn't recognize the other voice. It sounded thin and reedy.

"Leave that to me, Efron. But rest assured, Dehre will win the prize long denied to us."

"The Rolbanis must not learn about it." The new Dehrien voice was deeper than Efron's.

Mentàll said, "They are ignorant about what matters most. Spoils belong to the victor. If they do not know there is a quest, how can they win?"

A soft chuckle. "You are clever, Chief."

"This war will fortify our position. Now we only need to win it. The quest will accomplish our other goal. When we arrive in Quasr, give the Chief's descendant that note."

"Yes, sir." A soft sound of a tent flap dropping reached her ears, and two sets of footsteps whispered over the earth. Then silence.

Methusal sat up on one elbow. What was that Dehrien plotting now? And how would winning the war help him fortify his position? What position? And what did he mean about spoils and a prize?

CHAPTER FIVE

THE NEXT MORNING the war party packed up at first light and marched north. Methusal and the others munched on dried rations while the sun slowly warmed the earth.

As she ate, she told Behran what she had overheard last night. He still was the only one who knew about her extraordinary hearing ability.

"We can't trust him," Behran agreed. "We'll need to watch him. And you should probably tell your father what you heard."

"I will." But right now Erl was walking with Mentàll and Pan, so it probably wasn't the best time to speak to him.

Aali ran up then, and so the subject ended.

Methusal spared a brief glance for the blond-haired Chief. So far, he'd made no effort to harass her during the trip. Either he took his word to Erl seriously, or he was avoiding her for reasons of his own. Either way, as long as it lasted, Methusal would gladly take it.

After a while, a Tarst boy who looked a little younger than Aali joined them as the morning heated up. His round baby face beamed when he introduced himself as "Taltn at the Tri-level." He told them he would be on the kaavl team, too.

"Are you Methusal?" A bit of awe warmed his green eyes as he looked up at her. He was short and a little plump. "You're Mahre's great great, great, etc., great-granddaughter, right?"

"Yes." Methusal smiled at his wonderment. As if she was any different from anyone else!

"Fight with me." He brandished his kaavl stick. "Show me how it's done. I want to learn from the best."

Methusal grinned at his enthusiasm. "The kaavl stick isn't my best event."

"Come on," he encouraged, prancing ahead of her.

Aali sighed audibly.

"Okay. For a minute." Their little group moved to the east so the others could march by. Methusal first demonstrated how to spin the kaavl stick, and then how to strike with lightning precision. The Tarst boy enthusiastically copied her, and soon they battled against each other. Methusal easily disarmed him, but when he eagerly picked up his stick again she decided to go easy on him, in the hope of boosting his confidence. He was actually pretty good.

As their sticks clacked, a low howl moaned from the rocky jumble at the base of the mountain behind them. An animal. In pain. Its misery called to her heart. Methusal flicked her kaavl stick a few more times and called a truce. "Good job."

The boy panted and grinned, clearly pleased with his prowess.

Aali rolled her eyes. "Please! Thusa, move aside. It's my turn to battle the boy."

Taltn flushed, and his happy smile faded. Grimness tightened the soft lines of his mouth. "Bring it."

"Happily." Eyebrow arched, Aali proceeded to attack him with vigor.

"Ow!" he howled.

The injured beast keened again.

"Ow!" poor Taltn snapped.

"Careful." A red-haired man with a close-cropped beard approached. "I don't want to fix up injuries before the war starts."

Behran extended his hand. "I'm Behran."

"Doc. From Tarst. Dastn's cousin." The wiry, medium height doctor shook Behran's hand, and Methusal smiled a greeting, but slipped away from the little group when the beast howled again. Maybe she could help it, but she'd need to hurry. She didn't want to be left too far behind the war party.

"Thusa, where are you going?"

"Be back in a minute. Don't worry." She sprinted toward the sound of the animal's whimpers. At the base of the bluff she silently climbed over and around the rocks, and slowly edged forward when she neared the injured beast. A wolmite, she guessed, by the low timbre of the howls. Wolmites walked on four paws. Her moccasins slipped on a pebble, and the beast's moans stopped.

Methusal cautiously eased around the last corner. Just as she'd thought. A silver-furred wolmite lay on the rocky ground. Its pointed ears twitched. One paw was caught in a trap.

Who would lay a trap out here, more than a day's run from any community? Maybe it had been a runner, wanting to catch his supper. He must have laid the trap a while ago.

The beast's yellow eyes watched her. Its lips curled back to reveal sharp fangs, and its silver fur ruffled out in a thick mane about its neck. Methusal stopped moving. "It's okay, boy," she murmured.

The beast continued to watch her. It did not growl, which she took to be a good sign. She'd rarely been bitten by the beasts she helped. Most trusted her. This one was helpless and knew it—that could either be a good or bad thing. Some animals were too frightened to accept help. They would rather attack a helping hand than allow someone close enough to help them. She'd encountered a wolmite like that in the past. She'd had to let it go. It had died soon after.

Methusal knelt and extended her fist. The wolmite nosed forward the tiniest fraction. Another good sign. "I'll help you, boy," she murmured. "Will you let me?"

She slowly extended her kaavl stick and the beast sniffed it, too. Next, she angled it between the jaws of the trap. The beast yelped when the trap snapped open. He shook his paw free and pranced to his feet. He stood on three legs, and his deep yellow eyes stared at her.

"I'll help you," she said again in a low, soothing tone. "Come here." She extended her fist in a gesture of peace. With the other hand she pulled coltac and tacky leaves from her pouch. Also a kaavl strip from her pocket. She moved closer. The beast did not move away. She looked him straight in the eyes. "Come here," she whispered.

The beast crept forward. She let him sniff her fingers.

"Let me help you."

The beast sat on its haunches, but watched her warily.

"Let me see that paw." Moving slowly, and then with a firm touch, she took the beast's mangled front paw and held it above the injury. She felt it carefully. It didn't feel broken, but it was a bloody mess. One toe was torn off; probably from trying to free itself.

Quickly, she squirted on thick coltac juice. It would prevent infection. Then she wrapped on tacky leaves and swiftly tied up the whole package with a thin leather kaavl strip. There. Now the leaves would stay on long enough to do some good. Without the kaavl strip the beast would chew off the leaves within minutes.

She released the beast. The wolmite stared at her for a long moment, and then turned and limped away on three legs. It stopped and looked at her again, and then moved on. When Methusal heard a movement behind her, the beast disappeared among the rocks.

"Good job." It was the Tarst doctor. "Thought I'd see if you needed help. Obviously, you don't." His direct gaze made Methusal feel instantly at ease with him.

She packed up the remainder of her supplies. "It's not the first beast I've helped."

"You have a gift." They walked together to catch up with the war team. "Do you have medical training?"

"Not really." The idea of receiving medical training had never even crossed her mind. Kaavl had been her only focus for over seven years. "Just the basics. I got into a few scrapes when I was young. I paid attention when the doctor took care of me. Then I found myself helping hurt animals."

A small smile lifted his lips. "Never humans?"

Methusal laughed. "I don't think a human would trust me. I don't exactly have a good bedside manner. I'm more of a doer than a nurturer."

"Doesn't matter. I could use your help. I'm the only doctor. We'll have a lot of injuries."

Rolban's doctor, D'Wit, had been too elderly to make the trip to Quasr, and she'd heard that Dehre's doctor was in Wyen, getting training when the invaders arrived. It was unlikely he'd travel north to help with the war effort. She didn't envy Doc. It was a lot of responsibility for one man.

She didn't like thinking about war injuries. "I'll be on the kaavl team."

"Even better. Each team needs medical help." His direct gaze caught hers again. "Are you up for it?"

Methusal felt honored that this man, whom she barely knew, already believed that she would do a good job. "Yes. I'd be glad to help in any way I can."

"Good." He smiled. "You'll probably live to regret that offer."

△ △ △ △ △

Pogul reported back to the war team after they'd stopped for lunch. He'd seen no signs of invaders to the north. Methusal knew she should feel relieved, but strangely, did not. The trip seemed too quiet. Too easy.

"We'll travel to the Cormak River, cross it, and camp for the night," Erl said.

Timaeus, who had reported that all was clear to the west, joined Methusal, Aali, and Behran for the march north that afternoon. He was unusually quiet. Methusal knew he was worried about Deccia. So was she. Something Timaeus had said back in Rolban had bothered her for a while. Now was her chance to ask him about it.

She moved up to walk beside him. "Are you all right?"

His face looked drawn and grim. "I hope I'm wrong."

"About what?"

"The General. I keep thinking..." He said through gritted teeth, "He'd better not hurt her."

Methusal's nightmare again seared her mind; as it had done repeatedly over the last several days. But she wouldn't tell Timaeus about it. It would only worry him more. "What is he like?"

His jaw tightened. "I've only heard stories, but they're bad enough."

"From the Quasrians who escaped?"

"Yes. The stories they told.... He ordered children cut down in cold blood. One family wouldn't leave their house, so he set it on fire and barricaded the doors and windows. They screamed while they burned alive."

Horror choked Methusal. "And he has Deccia," she whispered.

"If he hasn't killed her yet." A tear ran down his cheek, but he swiped it away, hard, with the heel of his hand. "But if she isn't dead, he could be doing horrible things to her."

Tears filled Methusal's eyes, and she looked away so Timaeus wouldn't see. She *knew* what the General was doing to her. Nausea churned in her stomach.

"We'll rescue her. Soon," she said fiercely, but tears finally escaped. A silent, agonized wail worked its way through her soul. Her sister. Her *sister* was suffering horribly right now. And she couldn't stop it.

Timaeus put an arm around her shoulders and hugged her tight. "Deccia's strong. She'll make it. That's the only thing that keeps me going."

"She has to know we're on our way." Deccia sensed things; sometimes even before they happened. "She *has* to know we'd never abandon her."

"She knows." The grim, tough note in Timaeus' voice didn't match the fear in his eyes. He loved Deccia with his whole heart.

"She's lucky to have you," Methusal said softly. "She'll need you, after..." And they *would* rescue her. At the first opportunity. She couldn't think anything different.

"She'll need you, too." His silent look said he knew Deccia would be fragile and broken. She would need all of their love and support to recover from the horror she was living through now. If only they could rescue her before the General tired of her and killed her.

△ △ △ △ △

In the late afternoon they reached the lush, bushy banks of the western flowing Cormak River. It was wider than the Tarst River, but shallower, according to Timaeus. They'd been hugging the soaring mountains all day, and the place where they'd cross was nestled in a small green valley. The rolling hills on the northern side of the river looked quiet and peaceful, and were dotted with bushes and a few small trees. The tall, eastern mountains intersected the hills about twenty lengths to their right, and erupted fairly quickly into tall, rocky jumbles and towering cliffs of whitish gray rock. Some rocks were small, and some boulders were as tall as a man. Scraps of vegetation clung to the inhospitable earth. It was strange to see such barrenness soaring above the lush green of the river valley.

The first men of the war teams sloshed across the river. The water came to their knees, and then thighs, but no higher.

Methusal waited her turn in line. She felt bone weary from marching for two days. While part of her knew she needed to rest, the other half wanted to run to Quasr and immediately rescue her sister. But even when they arrived in Quasr that plan would not be practical, of course. They'd need to scout and plan their attack first. But she chaffed at the delay, and the delays sure to come.

Protect Deccia, The One, please. Methusal wanted to believe The One was real, and that he heard her plea now. Her meeting with the Prophet two and a half years ago had made her think more about The One than she ever had before in her life.

Methusal splashed through the icy river and climbed the bank on the other side. She was glad the warm sun was still beating down, so her breeches would dry before dark. She dropped her pack near a rock at the base of the rocky mountain. Aali scampered up the closest, stony hill to the east. She stopped and peered down at something. "Thusa," she called. "Come look!"

Although tired, Methusal scrambled up after her cousin.

"Look. It's like a perfect bowl."

At their feet the gray, pebbled hillside dropped into an oval, rocky crater several lengths deep. Maybe when the river ran higher, a pool or lake formed there. The earth beneath Methusal's moccasins felt gritty, like chalk mixed with sand.

"Neat," Aali commented. She scampered back down into camp. "I'm hungry. Are you going to eat, Thusa?"

"In a minute." She should actually help set up the tents, but she wanted to explore for a minute. This land looked so different from Rolban's fertile mountains. She headed north, following the lip of the gorge. Gray rocks jumbled in piles on the hillside up ahead. In some places, the mountains sheared high into cliffs, and in other areas jagged, rocky paths curved between stones and soaring cliffs, providing ways to climb even higher.

Methusal glanced over her shoulder. Camp had disappeared from view. Maybe she should head back. Instead of heading back south, though, she headed west and climbed down over the rocks. Now she saw the green hills ahead, and the squat trees. A shadow moved beneath one.

Instinctively, she crouched down behind a boulder. It was too early for the wild beasts to be out, and too big for an apte or whip beast. Another wolmite?

Movement flickered behind another bush. Her heart beat faster, and she glanced north for more signs of movement. Nothing. She intensified her hearing and placed it where the first shadow lurked. She heard quiet, even breaths. Then a rushing scuffle came from the north, and a series of metallic clicks.

Danger. Her instincts screamed it, and she darted toward camp. The scuffling sounds grew louder. At last she reached the edge of their quiet river valley.

"Invaders!" she screamed. "*Invaders!*"

The men looked up, surprised. But the first person to reach for his weapon was Mentàll Solboshn. His thin sword, encased in a long, narrow pocket in the thigh of his breeches, flashed to hand. Other men took their cue from him and lunged for their packs.

Barely in time. A yelling horde of black and red clad men hurtled down the hillside. In horror, Methusal watched two peel off and head straight for her.

CHAPTER SIX

THE ZINDEDIS LOOKED like men from her worst nightmare with their wild, long dark hair, grinning yellow teeth—and their black sticks. Methusal ducked behind a boulder. Beside her something exploded, and rock fragments spattered her tunic. *What was that?*

She scrambled up the hillside and slid behind another boulder. Another explosion. A whine pinged by her ear, and a small section of the cliff exploded into a spray of dust.

Death-sticks. Timaeus had warned that the invaders carried them. They must shoot a hard projectile out the end. Maybe a rock? Clearly the invaders could kill people while still a long distance away from their prey—a much further range than bows and arrows. Methusal didn't have those, either, since only runners or hunters were skilled in that art. She'd have to use her knife. But hand combat would be impossible unless she tricked the enemy into coming close.

The thought of killing a man in cold blood made her feel sick.

Methusal tore on, and the grunting invaders followed her. Was she a coward to run like this? Or maybe it was a smart move. She was luring two invaders away from camp. That meant fewer men for the Koblanis to fight.

They were gaining on her.

Methusal intensified into kaavl and became sharply aware of each foot placement. She was careful not to let pebbles roll. She sprinted up the mountain and ducked left and then right, leading them on a confusing chase.

Methusal realized she'd unwittingly circled south now, and was heading toward camp again. Probably not the best idea. She turned north again, but now she heard three more systems of movement. They were a two minute run west. To the south, death-sticks blasted and men grunted, apparently fighting in hand-to-hand combat.

Her pursuers increased their pace. Methusal heard another system of movement now, startling in its closeness. It was swift, and virtually silent. It had to be a kaavl contender. A good one, too. No one else could be so silent on these pebbled hills. The three men running from the west chased him.

What if it was Behran?

She trained her hearing on the unknown ally. Three additional systems of movement sprang up out of nowhere near the Koblani she was tracking. The kaavl player grunted when they attacked. Then came the ring of a sword. An explosion. Then the sound of fleet steps.

Her fellow Koblani had escaped, but four men still followed him. He was heading straight for her.

She didn't want her two pursuers to join forces with his four. Then again, maybe she and her kaavl ally could work better together as a team against the Zindedis.

Methusal didn't have time to decide, for as much as her path zigzagged, the kaavl contender continued to head right for her. As if on purpose. But how could that be? Unless his hearing was as sharp as hers—or he possessed a skill she knew nothing about.

She had to lose the ones following her.

She sprinted up and to the right, around a huge boulder, and then through a strange, natural archway and into a small area protected by a rocky overhang. She slammed back against the curved wall. Her heart pumped hard. She'd have to make her stand here.

Trying to quiet her panting breaths, she listened. Her two pursuers had stopped fifty lengths southwest. Another man had joined them—one of the four pursuing the other Koblani.

The Zindedis muttered to each other, and she wondered if they had lost her trail. But her kaavl ally was approaching fast, and three Zindedis still pursued him.

Heart pounding, Methusal waited. Her ally knew where she was; of this, she felt certain. Again, she wondered how.

Unless he possessed an extraordinary sixth sense...one of the rare ones, barely described in the *First Book of Kaavl*.

She waited, knife gripped tightly in her fist, and then her compatriot slid backwards into her hiding spot. A gasp caught in her throat.

The Dehrien Chief glanced at her and froze. His pale eyes turned to daggers. Needles of fear prickled into her heart as his palpable hatred seared through her. Wonderful. Could things get any worse?

No time to think. Two Zindedis snuck up on her enemy's side, and one on hers. She automatically held of up two fingers and pointed, and then crouched at the ready. She noticed a big stone nearby and grabbed it with her free hand. Her palm felt slick with sweat on the red bone handle of her mother's knife. Her hand trembled.

The Zindedis rounded the corner on the Dehrien's side. Mentàll killed the first man with cold, brutal efficiency.

And then a Zindedi charged around the corner nearest Methusal. His long, black death-stick was pointed straight at her. Terrified, she threw the rock with all of her strength. The death-stick jerked and exploded. For a second, she wondered if she'd been hit. But she felt nothing. She briefly wondered if he'd shoot at her again. But no. The invader charged at her. She flung up her knife wielding hand in self-defense. He swung his death-stick at her and she blocked it with her other arm. A blade flashed in the Zindedi's hand and arced toward her. She stumbled backward.

He charged for her again, and she staggered back. An unholy glee lit his black eyes, and he swung the stick again. It connected with the side of her head. Pain exploded. He dropped his death-stick and lunged at her. Now Methusal wished she'd practiced more with her knife. Without thinking, she flung it at his neck. It missed. Horror stabbed her. She'd lost all sense of kaavl. She lurched backward and tripped on a rock.

The invader didn't give her time to regain her feet, but she saw him coming and rolled away. Too late, she saw a sight that horrified her even more. She lay less than a length from the edge of a cliff.

The invader landed on top of her. She struggled, twisting and rolling, struggling to keep his knife away from her throat. The invader had clearly spotted the cliff, because a slow, vicious smile revealed broken yellow teeth. He forced her to roll with him. When they stopped, she lay on her back, her legs dangling off the ledge. The Zindedi lay beside her.

He smiled at her. "Now you will die."

He swiftly sat up and raised his knife to plunge into her neck. That was his mistake. He sat on the edge, too. A little too close. A little too confident.

Methusal bucked up her legs and hit him square in the chest. Surprise circled his eyes, and he tilted backward. He screamed, and grabbed her leg as he toppled off the edge. His weight jerked Methusal and she sped for the edge. Desperately, she clawed at the ground, but pebbles and dust ran through her fingers. She couldn't stop.

She screamed.

△ △ △ △ △

The attack of the invaders came as a shock to Hendra. Their shrieking whoops and deafening death-stick blasts terrified her. Pandemonium stampeded through the Koblani camp. Urchets brayed in panic and tore free of their tethers.

Hendra yanked out her knife, panting with horrified panic.

A Tarst soldier—one she'd seen drinking in the stream at lunch—staggered backward and fell two lengths away. A round wound bubbled blood out of his chest. He twitched, and was still.

She gulped in horror. How could Koblanis win against death-sticks?

A hard hand gripped her shoulder and she spun. Mentàll said, "Go to the valley Aali found. Follow Doc. Stay and help him." And then he was gone

Hendra spotted the red-haired Tarst doctor climbing a hill, carrying a wounded soldier over his wiry shoulder. His cousin Dastn followed close behind, carrying another man.

Hendra ran toward them, and on the way she saw Aali, Methusal's young cousin. The girl's round blue eyes looked stunned and she stood very still, as if frozen. Hendra grabbed her arm. "Come on. Follow me."

They both climbed down into a small valley. Doc lay his patient on the rocky ground and ripped his bloody shirt off. Hendra had never spoken to Doc before, and normally would shy away from speaking to strange men, but adrenaline eased her fear.

"We're here to help. What can we do?"

The Tarst doctor didn't look up. "Bring my bag."

Hendra quickly went to work handing him supplies, pressing on wounds to stop the blood flow, and then moving on to the next patient as the doctor directed. Time sped by. So far, no invaders had crested their hill. Maybe the Koblani team was successfully defending their camp. Part of Hendra felt guilty that she wasn't fighting, but the other half knew she was doing important work here, too.

Aali collected water from a nearby stream and cleaned the wounds as best she could before Doc treated them. Dastn and several others carried in the wounded as fast as they could carry them

Men moaned around her, which made Hendra's heart twist in anguish. She was glad she was here, because she wanted to help them. Heal them. Normally she'd avoid touching anyone because physical contact frightened and repulsed her. But these men were defenseless, and she discovered she could touch them without fear.

The sounds of the battle quieted. Maybe it was moving into the hills. She wondered how many invaders there were, and if they could defeat them.

The thought that they could lose this first battle was unthinkable.

A quiet lull came. Dastn and the others had been gone for a while. Hendra watched Doc's quick, deft fingers sew up a wound. She knew a little about healing, and could tell he was a gifted doctor. She cast a quick glance at his down-turned face, and for the first time wondered what he looked like. She had paid little attention to him until now. He looked to be about thirty. Her glance took in his short, dark red hair, and the closely trimmed beard that hugged his lower jaw. His shoulders looked muscled, and his hands were lean and well-shaped.

Feeling strangely flustered, Hendra returned her attention to the coltac leaf she held at the ready. When Doc reached for it, his fingers brushed hers. A charge snapped through her at the contact and Hendra jerked back, her heart pumping in a wild terror.

"Bandage," he said, paying no attention to her ridiculous reaction.

"Bandage," she said, quickly handing him a tacky leaf. He pressed the sap sticky leaf over the wound.

"Good work." He finally looked up. Smoky blue eyes met hers, and he stared for a long, inexplicable moment. "I don't believe we've met. Everyone calls me Doc."

"I'm Hendra," she said, her heart still pumping ridiculously fast.

"Mentàll's cousin."

She nodded.

Another patient appeared. They continued to work silently and easily together. Hendra steeled herself not to wrench away at every accidental brush of his fingers. He wasn't the enemy. He would not harm her. But something inside her feared him—and not because he was a dangerous man. But because he might be a good one.

Oona and Aenill arrived and quickly set to work.

Long minutes...perhaps hours later, Dastn appeared, smudged with blood and dirt. "The Zindedis are retreating."

Hendra sat back on her heels. "Thank heavens."

"We have more wounded on the battlefield. Can you come?"

Doc climbed to his feet. "Hendra, come with me. Aenill, will you finish bandaging this man, and keep the rest comfortable?"

"Of course."

Hendra followed Doc to the top of the hill, and the devastation below made her steps falter. Scores of men lay dead; many fallen at grotesque angles. Half were Koblanis. A few moaned. One screamed in agony.

Hendra's heart palpitated with the horror of it all. Too much death; too much blood. It was too much. Something inside of her turned off. The familiar, icy sensation was welcome for once. The cold space inside Hendra billowed and engulfed her heart in ice. It was a defense she had learned while living in her fist punching, bone breaking childhood home. It had been the only way she could survive the horror.

She stumbled after Doc, and bandaged patients while he scouted among the fallen for those who could still be saved. On closer inspection, more Zindedis than Koblanis lay dead.

That was a poor comfort. Minutes turned into hours. Blood crusted Hendra's hands.

They managed to save a dozen more men. All were Koblanis. No Zindedis had survived. Hendra helped Doc administer precious pain powder to the ones suffering the worst agony. All received blood builder, which was made from mashed taric roots.

The coldness in her heart felt like an unmeltable ice block. Even as it protected her now, Hendra hated it. She felt inhuman, incapable of feeling or caring about the agony surrounding her. Even so, feeling compassion wasn't necessary to complete her tasks. She'd learned that long ago. As long as she did all she could to help others—somehow that made up for the deficiency that lived inside her.

It would go away. Eventually.

With a cold sort of detachment, Hendra scanned the valley for Mentàll and her friends. She saw no one she recognized.

△ △ △ △

Desperately, Methusal clawed at the dry, pebbled soil as she shot over the cliff's edge. Her fingers scrabbled, clutching for anything as she fell. A scraggly bush slid through her fingers and she grabbed for it and caught one slender branch. It stopped her fall with a yank, snapping, but still holding her. The jerk made the Zindedi lose his grip on her leg. He shrieked and Methusal heard a dull, sickening thud when he landed far below.

She hung by that one slender, broken twig, her heart racing. A desperate glance proved the cliff top was at least seven handbreadths overhead. In her right hand the bush's roots shuddered, releasing a shower of dust. It wouldn't hold much longer. Quickly, she scanned her surroundings. The cliff was sheer. No hand holds or footholds—except for one tiny rock ledge, just to the left of the bush. She swung her hand overhead, scrabbling for it. But it was just out of reach.

The root shivered, and tiny snaps indicated the roots were breaking. Time was running out. She hauled herself up on the root and clawed again for the rock ledge. Her fingers gripped the stone outcropping just as the twig gave way. Methusal hung on, swinging, by her fingertips. Her heart pounded in terror. She barely had a grip on the tiny ledge.

Was this how it would end?

She couldn't hold on for long. Another glance confirmed that the sheer rock offered no other holds for her right hand or her feet. And if she moved even the tiniest bit, her left fingertips would slip free.

A shadow fell over her, blocking the sun. Zindedi, or...

Mentàll Solboshn. Her mortal enemy stood above her. Anger, hatred, and other, unknown emotions battled across that cold face.

Despair closed like a fist around her heart. She would die. Tears burned.

She wouldn't beg for her life. Methusal closed her eyes. Her fingers slipped a fraction. She hung only by her nails now.

Against her will, her mouth quivered. One more second, and she would plummet to her death.

She opened her eyes, but couldn't stop them from filling with tears.

She wouldn't cry. She *wouldn't*.

Eyes wide and watery, she hopelessly jerked up her chin, expecting Mentàll to be gone, or to see triumph on his face. But she saw neither, as her fingers slipped for the last time.

Instead, she saw a hand swoop through the air.

He caught her by the wrist and pulled her up bodily, one-handed. The Dehrien clamped his other hand under her armpit and jerked her up to safety. She staggered into him, but instinctively put out her hands to stop herself. His bleached leather tunic felt warm, and his body beneath, hard and alive with muscle.

Shaking, she stepped back a fraction from the giant Dehrien, trying to regain her equilibrium without stepping off the cliff. Defensive, automatic kaavl noted that she barely topped his shoulder. Never before had she been this close to her enemy.

Words clogged in her throat. Her chest felt tight.

"Thank you," she forced out when Mentàll turned away. He did not respond.

And then she saw the blood on his back. His tunic was soaked red, and rivulets trickled down his breeches. An invader sword had slashed him from shoulder to waist. The wound was on his right side, which explained why he'd pulled her up one-handed.

"You're injured!"

"I am fine."

Maybe he was. He moved normally. Maybe the wound wasn't deep. But blood ran down his leg. Soon it would drip onto the ground and provide a trail for the invaders to follow. She retrieved her knife and listened. The remaining invaders were thirty lengths south, but rapidly hiking closer.

Methusal followed him ten more paces, and then he stumbled over the rocky ground. He halted and put a hand on a tall boulder. The sounds of the three approaching Zindedis grew louder in her ears.

"Why are you stopping?" Then Methusal drew in a sharp breath. His face was white.

The danger of the situation screamed through her mind. The invaders...the blood about to drip to the ground, the Dehrien Chief losing strength to walk, and being out in the open, ripe for the kill. And she couldn't leave him alone to die when he'd just saved her life. Even if he hadn't, she'd never let a whip beast suffer in such a way, let alone a fellow human being. ...Even though he acted more like the former than the latter.

"Come on." She grabbed his arm, draped it over her shoulders and gripped him around the torso, over the wound. He didn't make a sound as blood squished out, soaking her arm and tunic sleeve with warm wetness. She pulled him to the left.

Methusal intensified her kaavl concentration, pinpointed the location of the three remaining invaders, and charted the best course to evade them. If only the blood didn't fall to the ground... If only Mentàll could keep walking. She'd never be able to drag him anywhere. He was too big and heavy.

It must be sheer determination that kept him moving. Blood soaked her arm now.

Rocks scattered nearby. The invaders were close. Methusal pulled the Dehrien around a large boulder. Here the ground sloped downhill. She had no choice. The easiest way was down. Then left, around that next corner. If they could just stay quiet enough, the invaders wouldn't spot them.

"Quiet," she breathed. "Quick."

They moved as fast as possible. Mentàll's gait was a soft shuffle, and his weight on her shoulders grew heavier. He wouldn't make it much further. He was losing a lot of blood, although it thankfully still soaked into his clothes, instead of dripping a trail onto the ground. Where could they hide? Methusal swallowed back her rising panic. One thing at a time. Down the slope, around the corner, around another corner...what was that, up the hill a bit? A dark shadow. A cave? Possibly.

"Twenty more paces," she panted. "Then we're safe."

His steps lagged with each number she whispered. By number ten, most of his full weight bore down on her, and she was partially dragging him. Sheer panic leant her the strength to carry on.

"Five," she grunted softly. Had he passed out? No. He still managed to move his legs, albeit late, at each step. And it was a cave. A low one.

Staggering under her enemy's weight, they reached the entrance.

"Here?" came his thread of a whisper.

"Yes." Methusal thought quickly. "I'll need to drag you in on your stomach. Down you go."

He collapsed onto his knees, and only his arm, still slung over her shoulders, prevented his face from smashing into the pile of boulders strewn at the entrance.

Methusal still heard the invaders around the corner, and up the hill. She had to move fast. No question of *if* she could move him. She had to. Lowering his upper body, she gripped under his arms and, gritting her teeth, backed into the cave, bent double. Handbreadth by slow handbreadth, she pulled him. Her back ached, her shoulders felt like they were being pulled out of their sockets, and her muscles burned, but finally he lay in the long, low space.

Methusal darted outside. Blood probably marked their location. Sure enough, red smeared the rocks closest to the cave.

The sound of rolling stones indicated the invaders drew closer.

Her heart pounded as she scattered white dust over the rocks, hiding the blood. She had easily spotted the cave. Would the invaders, too? She had to be prepared.

She slipped back into the cave, slid Mentàll's razor sharp sword from its sheath, and hid behind the lip of the cave opening. She'd completed only three visual carries in her life. Two during the war with the Dehrien Chief, and one later, but only after intense concentration and practice. She had to do one now. Their lives might depend upon it.

Relaxing, she focused deeply into kaavl and peeked out of the cave entrance. The invaders' footsteps placed them downhill now, around the next corner. She mentally placed her hearing in that spot and fanned it out, hearing all sounds as if she stood in that exact location. And suddenly she stood there, too, and saw the cluster of invaders.

"Four of them," she breathed. Where had the other one come from? How could she take on four Zindedis at once? Two men pointed in her direction, and the other two turned away. She could maybe take on two, but if she did, the others would come looking for them. No. It would be better to stay undetected.

Mentàll lay silently. Had he passed out? Hopefully. If so, he'd stay quiet.

Heart pounding, she retreated fully into the cave when the two invaders rounded the corner. Silence was her only weapon. She listened as they climbed the hill. She gripped the needle sharp sword tighter, palms perspiring, ready to kill if necessary.

"That big one should be dead by now. He could never make it this far."

"What about the girl?"

"Brinc went off the cliff with her. I saw it from higher up."

"We need to go after the others," the first complained.

"The General wants the big one dead."

"You stabbed him. He's as good as."

"Come on, then." The apparent leader hiked up the cliff, away from Methusal and the Dehrien.

Slowly, her heart rate returned to normal as the invaders hiked further north. Safe. For the moment. Now for her patient. Mentàll would bleed to death if she didn't do something now.

In the dim light of the cave, she pulled the Dehrien's tunic away from the injury, and then gulped back nausea when she saw the wound more clearly. A deep cut sliced down two thirds of his back. It started a handbreadth left of his right arm pit, and slashed straight down to his waist. Peeling back his tunic hadn't been the best of ideas. Areas had started to clot, but now they began to bleed again.

Quickly, she used her knife to cut off a thick strip of leather from the bottom portion of his tunic and pressed it, one hand above another, onto the wound. She pressed firmly, applying pressure to staunch the flow. Blood dripped down his side and onto her hands, and panic filled her. What if it didn't stop? What if he died right here, right now, under her inexpert care? She wished she knew what to do.

"The One, help," she whispered. "Please stop the bleeding. Help me know what to do!"

"Fnn," the Dehrien Chief slurred.

"You're awake?" Methusal felt incredulous. With the pain and blood loss he should be unconscious. Not talking.

No response. Apparently he drifted on the brink of consciousness.

The blood flow stopped. "Thank you," she breathed. After a few minutes she slowly, increment by increment, lifted her hands from the wound. He needed Doc. The wound needed cleaning and stitches. More pain lay ahead for the Dehrien, and although she hated him, she felt sorry for him. But at least he was alive.

Shallow breaths made his back rise and fall.

She no longer heard the invaders. "I'm going for the doctor," she whispered. "Stay here. I'll be back soon."

No response.

She ran back to camp, afraid of what she might find, and skirted around a few skirmishes along the way. The river valley was quiet, but littered with bodies. The sight made her feel sick.

She saw the doctor's red head not far away, and Hendra knelt beside him. He applied a dressing to Taltn's injured leg. Thankfully the wound didn't look too serious.

"Doc." She sprinted up. "Mentàll's injured. A knife wound this long." She measured with her hands. "He's lost a lot of blood."

"I'm there."

Doc spoke to Hendra, gathered up his supplies, and followed Methusal up the rocky hillside.

"What happened?"

Methusal described the attack. With reluctance, she added, "He saved my life. I was about to fall off a cliff."

"Really." Surprise lurked in the word. Doc probably knew that no love lived between her and the Dehrien Chief. Word traveled fast, and Dastn was Doc's cousin.

"I don't understand it, either."

"Be thankful. Maybe it's a step of peace."

Methusal doubted that. She'd be a fool to trust the Dehrien a fingerbreadth.

The Dehrien was still unconscious when they arrived. "Probably better this way," Doc said grimly, after taking a look at the deep, deadly gash. He set to work cleaning the wound, and Methusal helped as he directed.

Doc had packed in healing coltac juice and had begun to sew up the wound when Mentàll stirred. The needle pierced his skin again, and he groaned. He tensed a shoulder, as if ready to spring up.

"Steady," Doc said. "You're injured. I'm sewing you up."

The Dehrien gritted his teeth and averted his face. Doc continued to sew, and Mentàll lay very still. Probably in agony, but he was unwilling to show it.

Doc's needle pierced in and out of the Dehrien's skin. Methusal felt vaguely sick, and had to look away. It didn't matter that he was whip beast. She hated to see any living thing suffer.

Finally, Doc finished. "Mentàll?"

Nothing for a very long moment. Then a faint, "What?"

"I'm leaving blood builder and water with Methusal. Drink it when you're able. I'll be back soon with some men to help you back to camp."

She followed Doc out of the cave. "You want me to stay here?"

"Already regretting your vow to help me, Methusal?" Doc handed her a water skin and a small bag of powder. "Put a half-handful in the water. I'll be back as soon as I can." He jogged down the hill.

"But..."

He glanced back. "You can handle it, can't you?"

"Yes. Of course."

"See you soon."

With a sinking feeling, she watched him go. It wasn't forever, she reminded herself. Doc would be back soon.

Feeling apprehensive, she edged back into the cave. Her patient had somehow maneuvered into a sitting position, but his face looked as white as death. His breaths sounded shallow and quick.

"Doc left me blood builder," he said harshly. "Give it to me."

The arrogant man. Turning her back on him, she mixed the brew like Doc had instructed. The Dehrien ripped it from her hand the instant she offered it. He gulped it all down and then cast the water skin to the floor.

With a curled lip, she said, "What pretty manners you have."

He bared his teeth in a snarl, and sank down onto his elbow. His skin looked like chalk.

"Lie down, you prideful man," she told him. "Whether you like it or not, I'm supposed to watch over you."

He sank back onto his stomach, but only because he clearly had no strength to do anything else. How he must hate being the weak one! For the first time in their long, unsavory acquaintance, Methusal held all the power. She smiled faintly at that happy thought. If she was a mean person, she might try to take advantage of it.

Instead, she sat in the cave entrance with her back to him. She wanted to ignore him. Really, she wished she could run away. But she wasn't a coward, and Doc needed her to stay at her post. She noted the length of the shadows. How much longer until he returned?

Long, silent moments passed.

Methusal heard a scrape behind her. In a thin thread of his normal voice, the Dehrien said, "How did you do it?"

"Do what?" Why was he speaking to her?

"See the invaders around that corner."

Alarm fizzled. No one knew she had the ability to carry visually. Not even Behran; mostly because she'd done it so infrequently that she didn't consider it a true skill. "What do you mean?"

"You said there were four of them. I know where they were. You could not have seen them."

"You were in and out of consciousness."

"Tell me," he demanded, his voice weak.

She glared over her shoulder, but his eyes were shut in obvious pain. "I have nothing to say. Have you forgotten we're enemies?"

Mentàll made to go up on one arm, and then sank back down again. "I saved your life," he gritted. "You owe me the rest of it."

Methusal laughed at his audacity. "You believe that old myth? And, by the way, I saved yours. But I free you of that obligation."

The pale eyes were open now, and Methusal shivered at the look he gave her. He said, "You will never be free of me."

Methusal quivered again, and drew further away from him. "You're a horrible, nasty man."

"I deliver on all promises, and collect on all obligations."

"So you will fulfill your promise to my father."

"Until the end of the war."

"Why didn't you let me die then, on the cliff? Two years ago you vowed you'd make me pay for humiliating you. Wouldn't death be your ultimate penalty for me?"

He gave a harsh laugh, and then groaned. "You do not know what will satisfy me."

"Maybe I should have let you die." Methusal couldn't believe the words left her lips.

"Compassion may be your weakness."

"A fault only to a man with no scruples."

He gave her a nasty smile. "I look forward to many more days together, Methusal Maahr."

Disturbed, she fell silent. Hopefully Doc would return soon. She couldn't wait to escape from this miserable man.

△ △ △ △ △

The battle was finally over and the last patient bandaged. Doc had said Aali could take a break, so she gladly staggered away. She needed to be alone. How could Hendra and Aenill and Oona keep working? They looked so calm and tireless. She didn't feel that way. Not at all.

Knees trembling, she climbed the slope and slipped down the other side into a quiet hollow. Her stomach heaved, and she vomited. She gulped and began to cry, and then vomited again.

Shaking, she pulled leaves off a nearby bush and wiped her mouth. She stumbled back up the hill to a boulder so she wouldn't have to see the mess.

All of the killing. All of the suffering.

She buried her face in her knees and sobbed. She'd thought war would be exciting and dangerous. Not miserable and heart breaking. She wept because her stupid, blind trust that the world was good was gone. Bad things could happen. Bad things did happen. People were suffering now, and they would continue to suffer. Some would die. Even Doc couldn't stop it.

Aali cried until her face ached and she felt raw inside. Then she sat there for a long time, looking out over the quiet, rocky valley. Soon she'd have to return to camp and continue her duties. But not yet. Not yet.

Minutes...maybe an hour passed, and then she heard footsteps. Pebbles scattered down the hill. Her solitude had ended.

Dastn appeared in her side vision. "Doc sent me. He needs you back at camp."

Aali looked away. Not Dastn. Probably he'd come to point out how foolish she was, and how she'd never belonged here in the first place. "I'm coming."

"You're hurt."

She looked down at her arm, only now vaguely noticing that it throbbed. Blood had congealed over a long slash on her forearm. "It's not bad," she said dully. Not compared to what she had seen today.

"It needs to be bandaged." Dastn pulled coltac leaves from his pocket and hunkered down next to her. His large hands felt gentle on her arm.

Aali quietly watched him work.

Dastn said, "Kind of overwhelming, wasn't it?"

"Don't say I told you so."

"Have I?" He smoothed on the tacky leaves and released her arm.

"You're thinking this pesky girl got her eyes opened. That I shouldn't have come."

"You did well, Aali. I'm proud of you."

"You are?" She was surprised. And his words actually made her feel a little better.

"I judged without knowing you. I was wrong."

"Not entirely. Be honest."

One corner of his mouth curled up, looking quietly amused. "You're unpredictable, I'll say that. But I'd rather you be on my team than against it."

"Thank you." Aali smiled. He really was cute, with that half smile and with his right eyebrow tilted up at that same wicked angle as his spiky hair. "I'm going to be a big help for the war party," she promised. "Just wait and see."

"I believe you will. As long as you stay out of trouble."

"Oh, pooh. I never get in trouble," she said, following him back up the hill.

"Uh huh."

△ △ △ △ △

Doc appeared at Hendra's side while she spooned mashed tubers into an injured man's mouth.

"You're doing a great job."

Surprised, she glanced up. His smile unexpectedly warmed a bit of the ice still encasing her heart. She lowered her eyes for a confused second. "Thank you." He was still smiling when she glanced back up, which flustered her still more. She noticed then that he carried two packs on his shoulders—her cousin's and Methusal's.

She sat back on her heels. "Where are you going?"

Behran appeared. "What's wrong?"

"Mentàll is injured, and Methusal is looking after him."

"Where?"

"Up in the hills."

"Is she okay?" Behran asked. "Mentàll hasn't hurt her?"

"He saved her life. I need to go, but I'll be back soon."

The Tarst doctor strode off. Already the sun was setting. It wouldn't be long before the wild beasts came out—as if they needed *more* things to worry about tonight.

"You okay?" Behran's deep blue eyes looked concerned. Hendra noticed a small gash on his cheek.

"Looks like you're the one who's hurt."

"It's nothing." He glanced at the men lying in the gorge. Nine of them still lived. "Erl plans to march to base camp in the Quasr Mountains tomorrow."

"What will happen to these men?"

"Timaeus ran to Var. It's not far. They'll send men and carry the injured ones to their community."

"Will Var help in Quasr?"

"No, I've heard they're going to stand with Aestoff. They should be here by midmorning. We'll march after that."

Hendra was glad that her patients would be well cared for.

Behran turned around as Dastn and a few other men descended into the gorge. "We've lit fires in the valley to scare off the wild beasts. We need to move these men over there now."

More pain for the poor men—but that was better than being eaten alive by the beasts. And what about her cousin? How bad were his injuries?

Frankly Hendra was shocked that Mentàll had saved Methusal's life. She hoped it meant he'd changed his mind about her. In her heart, though, she suspected that was not the case. His hatred ran too deep. If Mentàll had saved Methusal, it was for purposes of his own.

Hendra prayed for their protection. And for Mentàll to see beyond the hatred simmering in his soul for Methusal...and, she suspected, for all things Rolbani.

△ △ △ △ △

Doc arrived at the cave alone. He carried Methusal's pack and Mentàll's, too, which caused unease to slide through her. "Where is everyone? I thought you said you'd get men to carry him to camp."

"I talked to Erl and Pan, and both agree with me. Mentàll can't make the trip tomorrow. He'll be safer here."

"I can make it," the Dehrien grated from the floor.

Doc knelt beside his patient. "The blood builder will take twenty-four hours to take effect. You've lost a lot of blood. You can't even sit up, Chief, let alone walk all day to base camp."

"Erl doesn't know where base camp must be. I do." Pride leant strength to his voice.

"So do your men."

Mentàll fell silent and closed his eyes.

Methusal knew the Dehriens had recently scouted in the mountains around Quasr. What she didn't know was why. Part of the plot she'd overheard?

Doc glanced up at her. "I'll need you to stay with him. His bandages need to be changed tomorrow morning and tomorrow night. If he's doing better, he can try to walk the next day."

"I need to stay?" she said in dismay. "With *him?*" Her voice rose.

"You know what to do."

"Surely you could train one of his Dehriens! How hard can it be to change a bandage?"

"I can do it myself," muttered the man on the floor.

Doc ignored him, and his gaze held Methusal's. "I need you to stay here. You have the basic training, and I need to show you what to do in case he goes into shock. You can build a fire to keep away the beasts, too. And you know kaavl."

Methusal bit her lip. She understood his reasoning. Unfortunately, the idea of staying with him made her want to run screaming from the cave. With a small smile, she reluctantly dismissed that idea.

"He'll probably sleep most of the time," Doc said, urging Mentàll to drink from a water skin. "I'm giving him pain powder. It's a sedative, too. Give it to him again in the morning and tomorrow night, along with the blood builder. He'll need sleep to regain his strength." The doctor turned his attention to Mentàll. "Follow my instructions, if you want to reach base camp any time soon."

The Dehrien muttered something unintelligible.

Doc explained the dosages of the different powders and other safety instructions, and then he stood. "You're on your own. I trust you to take good care of my patient."

"I will." It was hard to say those words, although she did mean them. She followed him out of the cave. "What about my father, and Behran and Aali? Are they all right? And Hendra?"

"Yes. Aali and Hendra have been helping me. Your father got a slash on his arm, but he'll be fine. Behran is fine, too."

Methusal was relieved to hear that, at least. With a sinking feeling she watched the doctor disappear down the hill. Now she was alone with her mortal enemy. Two nights and one day to endure in this tiny cave! Not to mention the hike to base camp. Her spirits sank to her moccasins.

She glanced at the Dehrien. It looked like he'd already fallen asleep. Fast working powder. One thing to be thankful for, at least. For the sake of peace, she'd better feed it to him on a regular schedule.

Outside, the dusk sky was a dark blue, tinged with pink. Night was falling. She'd better hurry up and gather wood for the fire. The idea of being eaten by wild beasts appealed only a little less than spending time alone with the Dehrien.

The long night slowly passed. Methusal slept at the mouth of the tiny cave, as far from the Dehrien Chief as she could possibly be. She woke in fits and starts when odd noises outside awoke her. The fire crackled and popped outside the cave entrance, and every time she awoke, she put more wood on the fire. Thankfully, no wild beasts or invaders attacked. When dawn lightened the sky, she finally drifted into a deep sleep.

CHAPTER SEVEN

DAY 5

SHUFFLING MOVEMENTS awoke Methusal at midmorning, and she sat up fast.

Wild beasts!

But the sounds came from behind her. A glance told her it was a different sort of wild beast.

The Dehrien was sitting up. Somehow, he'd stripped off his tunic. Tanned skin stretched over sleek, powerful looking muscles. A silver medallion on a chain hung from around his neck. Twin peaks were etched into it. What significance did that hold? ...Not that she would ask.

He twisted now, trying to look behind him. His hand worked at the wound on his back. His lips contorted in a grimace. Methusal was tempted to let his foolhardy behavior make a mess of it and rip his stitches out. Then she realized she'd be stuck with him for even longer.

"I'm supposed to do that."

The Dehrien ignored her. He'd already ripped off the leaves. Now he appeared to be trying to rub coltac juice into the wound.

Let him try. If he could take care of his wounds, maybe she could leave him here alone. Surely he could make the trip to base camp on his own.

Unfortunately, she didn't know the location of base camp. And much as she wanted to escape, it would be wrong to leave him here alone in this condition.

The Dehrien seemed to be having trouble reaching his lower shoulder blade region. Methusal didn't offer to help again. He obviously wouldn't accept it. She just folded her arms and watched the flickers of pain that contorted his mouth.

Now he reached for the bandages. His fingers looked bloody. Not a good sign. This fiasco had gone on long enough. If she let him bandage up an incomplete job, he'd get an infection.

"Let me look at it," she ordered.

He continued to ignore her. Irritation heated her temper. The rude man. ...Not that she'd been exhibiting any better behavior qualities, she had to admit.

"You'll get an infection if you mess up the job."

An angry muscle flexed in his jaw, but still he ignored her. He lifted a clean leaf to press onto the wound. If the wound wasn't clean, the leaf would become soiled and useless. And she had no intention of scouting these desolate, rocky hills for more. Methusal lunged for it and snatched it from his hand.

The next minute, she found herself flat on her back on the floor, his hard hand pressed against her throat. Cold eyes stabbed through her like an icy sword. Fear bled out.

"Do not *touch* me," he hissed.

Methusal refused to reveal the raw panic pulsing through her. She glared. "Doc said to follow instructions."

"I need no help. And no medications."

"Let me go!"

"Then you will follow my instructions. Go tend the fire."

She clenched her fists. "Be a fool, then."

"You are in a precarious position, Methusal. Do not anger me."

"Kill me, then." She couldn't believe the words left her lips.

He stared at her, as if considering it. Her mouth went dry. Stubbornly, though, she refused to take back the words or beg for her life.

"You like danger, Methusal?"

"I don't run from it." But her heart pounded like a herd of wild beasts.

To her surprise, he removed his hand from her windpipe. She bolted upright and scooted away from him.

Those chilly eyes watched her, but a faint smile curled his mouth. "You pretend courage. But you fear me."

"Wild beasts can't be trusted."

"You know nothing." He pulled the tacky leaf from her hand and attempted to adhere it to his back.

Frustration churned. "You're going to waste those leaves!"

He halted, and gave her a cold stare.

"If you haven't properly cleaned the wound, or put on enough coltac juice, then the wound will get infected. And the leaves you put on will seal in the infection."

He looked at the blood-smeared leaf in his hand.

"You could die. It's your choice."

With a disgusted motion, the Dehrien Chief crumpled the soiled leaf. "Do it. Clean my wound."

Now she felt like a servant, expected to respond to his imperial command. She bit her lip, struggling to control her temper. At least he had decided to comply. That meant they might make it to base camp tomorrow.

"Lie on your stomach," she ordered.

With stiff movements, he obeyed. Blood trickled from the wound. Doc had done a good job of stitching the skin together, but areas already looked red and angry.

She broke open a coltac leaf and dribbled it down the wound. It took five of them to cover the area. She did not want to touch him, but needed to smooth the thick gel over the wound. Lightly and tentatively, she accomplished the task. The skin felt puckered under her fingers. It must be terribly painful. Not that she cared, she told herself.

She affixed the bandages. "I'm done. Now for the powder."

He sat up and rested his good shoulder against the cave wall. "I will take the blood builder. Nothing else."

"Fine." Why should she care if he suffered? She measured the correct amount and placed it on a leaf. "Drink this with water." In silence he did so, and they both ate a sparse breakfast of dried rations.

Then Methusal gathered up their water skins and left without a word. It was rude, she knew, to leave him there alone with no idea of where she was going, or how long she would be gone. Frankly, she didn't intend to return for a good long while. He brought out the worst in her. She wasn't proud of herself, but that was the truth.

△ △ △ △ △

Methusal filled the water skins and rinsed off her face, hands, and as much of Mentàll's blood from her tunic as she could. She felt filthy from traveling for three days with no bath, but could do little to remedy the situation right now.

Then she took her time browsing the hills, searching for firewood. It was quiet. Only the sounds of small animals scampering over the rocks reached her ears.

A shower of pebbles scattered down the hill behind her. She froze. A human—or a large animal—had made that sound. She ducked behind a huge boulder and peered around the side.

A stooped, wizened man appeared with a staff in his hand. His skin was the color of bark, and his hair was snow white, like the far peaks. He stood very still and stared at the boulder. She had the uncomfortable feeling he could see right through it.

The Prophet.

"Come out, Methusal." There was no mistaking that deep rumble.

She rose from her hiding place, but left her assortment of sticks and water skins behind. "Prophet." She experienced a strange desire to bow her head. "I was hoping to see you."

He chuckled. "As you know, The One sends me to all true seekers."

"I haven't done much seeking since the war," she admitted.

"It is during conflict that we realize we need The One. We understand how puny we are."

"Will we win this war?"

The Prophet eyed her. "Take care, Methusal."

Unease slid through her. "Everyone keeps telling me that. Why?"

"You have many choices to make. Each will affect your future. I've been sent to challenge you to follow The One's higher path. It is time for you to listen."

Methusal remembered that she hadn't listened very well the last time the Prophet had spoken to her. He'd told her to pray for her enemies, and she had—but only once, and half-heartedly, at that. Her old nightmare from two and a half years ago flashed to mind. In it, The One had told her to listen. The Prophet had said that instruction was for a later time. Now?

Methusal still felt uncertain. "You mean he's seeking me out?"

"He always seeks us. We need only search for him with our whole heart and we will find him."

"Then what do I need to do?" The Prophet was right. It was time for her to listen. While she hoped she was more mature than the headstrong, hot-headed girl she'd been two years ago, she also knew there was definite room for improvement. As an afterthought, she added, "Will it help me rescue Deccia?"

"It is the way for you to live."

Why did she have the feeling she wouldn't like what he'd say next?

"Are you ready to listen?"

"I think so."

He smiled. "Your choices will make all the difference."

"That's what Sims and my mother said. What does that mean?"

The Prophet raised his staff. "Choose the way of peace with The One, and with man."

"In a *war?*"

"You tend to your enemy now?"

"Yes." Her unease deepened.

"It is a test to be repeated many times, until you understand."

"Understand what? And I don't want any tests. I want to rescue my sister and win this war. That's it."

"Life consists of tests. Heed, Methusal. Repay no one evil for evil."

"But..."

"Love one another. Love your enemies."

"But that's impossible," she blurted. "I hate Mentàll. And if I turn my back on him, he'll kill me!"

"You need not like him or trust him. Or approve of his actions. Or of those of your other enemies. Act with kindness. It is the higher way."

"That's impossible. I can't."

A frown creased the Prophet's brow. "You will not?"

She gasped, unable to believe what he was asking of her. "I wouldn't know where to begin."

"You are kind to animals. Be kind to humans, too. It is the higher path. Choose it well."

"Will being kind help me make the right choices?"

"Choose well, Methusal, and you will not go astray."

"How can I possibly be kind to my enemies?" She crossed her arms. Her soul recoiled at the thought of treating any of her enemies—the Dehrien especially—with kindness. The Prophet asked the impossible of her.

And yet she hadn't listened last time. Would things have turned out differently if she'd followed his advice? Could the bloodshed in Rolban have been prevented? Although she'd never know, now she had another chance. Wasn't it time for her to stop being stubborn and listen?

And then a few of the Prophet's words registered. "Oh! You mean I should be kind when I tend to his wounds—to heal him?"

The deep brown eyes gazed at the far off, white-capped Tarst Peaks. He nodded once. "When you heal him."

Methusal relaxed. Yes. She could treat the Dehrien like an injured wild beast. It would be difficult, but not beyond her abilities.

"I will leave one last word for you. Take it to your enemy."

She waited obediently, although she'd prefer not to speak to the Dehrien at all. An unrealistic desire, of course. They would spend at least twenty-four more hours together. Conversation—if crossing verbal swords could be called that—was inevitable.

"Tell Mentàll this: What he seeks draws nigh. He needs only to see to believe." He chuckled to himself, as if at a good joke.

"Is that a riddle?"

"He must choose the right path. It is up to him to find the prize he seeks."

Methusal found it difficult to believe the Prophet would help the Dehrien achieve any prize he sought. "He's dangerous. Why are you helping him?"

"Everyone has choices. It is only too late when death calls."

She muttered, "You mean he's not already assigned to the pit of hell?"

The Prophet frowned. "Choose well, Methusal. I leave you." He turned and slowly hiked back the way he had come.

Feeling unsettled, Methusal watched him go. She was supposed to show love to her enemies and treat them kindly. When they were injured? Or all the time? This last idea made her feel uncomfortable, because it unfortunately rang too true.

She made a mental inventory of her enemies. Mentàll, of course. And Goric, and possibly Jascr. Pogul. How was she supposed to show kindness to them? In actions only, she quickly assured herself. But still. The Prophet, with The One speaking through him, asked the impossible of her.

She lifted her eyes to the blue heavens. "How?"

It seemed completely impossible, even if she *did* want to obey. Truthfully, she did not. She wished she was a better person, like Deccia. *Deccia*. She closed her eyes. She had to rescue her sister. Would following the Prophet's advice help? She didn't see how. With a frustrated noise, she went to search for more firewood.

△ △ △ △ △

No Zindedis had attacked last night. Aali hoped they had retreated to Quasr. She'd overheard Uncle Erl and Pan talking last night. Meaning she'd spied on them while they talked in Pan's tent. They believed the Zindedi attack force had been about forty men strong. At least their Koblani warriors had beaten them. This first victory was important, Uncle Erl said. It sent a message to the Zindedi leaders that Koblanis were a force to be feared. Aali agreed. Her hope of rescuing her sister had recovered that morning.

At midmorning the people from Var carted away the critically injured men, and runners rounded up the skittish urchets. Only two animals had been killed.

Then Aali helped strike camp. Finally! She was impatient with the delays. Wasn't the goal to rescue Deccia? Well, of course to win the war, too. It bothered her that she hadn't heard any strategies to rip Koblan from the foul Zindedis' hands yet. It didn't matter. She'd already cooked up a plan of her own that might help.

On the hike to base camp, she decided to put it into action. She skirted around the group of injured men who marched in the middle of the warrior pack, and searched for her kaavl instructor. There were too many people.

Maybe if she climbed a hill she'd spot him faster.

Pleased with the idea, Aali scampered up the nearest rocky hill and scanned the war party. They turned a corner and marched out of view. Hurrying, she dodged around massive boulders. If she could make it around that next bend she'd have a clear view.

She darted around a knee high rock, around a stunted bush, and tripped over a pair of legs lying in the dirt.

Aali screamed.

"Shut it!" Pogul sat up. His eyes looked bleary from sleep.

"What are you doing here?" she gasped. "Aren't you supposed to be scouting?"

He must have hiked out here a good while ago, to be so deep in a nap. The *slug,* escaping the chores of tearing down camp!

"A little girl like you doesn't know what's what."

How dare he speak down to her? He was the one lying in the dirt! Suspicion struck. "It's your fault!"

Rocks tumbled down behind her. "Aali! What are you doing here?" Kitran. "I heard you scream."

"I tripped over Pogul. He was taking a nap."

The stocky, blond-haired young man scowled. "I slipped and fell."

"Right." She rolled her eyes.

"Why aren't you scouting, Pogul?" Kitran asked tersely.

"I told you. I slipped and knocked my head." He glared at Aali.

"Is that what happened yesterday, too?" she demanded. "Is that how you missed all those invaders sneaking up to attack us?"

Kitran's black brows lowered.

"I looked!" Pogul's eyes shifted. "I didn't see them."

"Get back into position," Kitran ordered. "If this happens again, I'll report you to Erl."

Muttering to himself, Pogul staggered down the hill, dislodging pebbles and showers of soil with every step. If the invaders were close by, they'd definitely hear him.

"Why are you here, Aali?"

"I was looking for you!" She bestowed her most charming smile upon Kitran.

His brow raised, and he headed down toward the warrior party. "Why?"

"Uncle Erl agrees that I can stay on the war party."

"Aali."

"Okay, I know I pushed my way onto the team. But that's why I'll be such a good help to everyone."

"Erl doesn't want you here."

"But I am, and that works out best for you, too." She hurried on before Kitran could dampen her spirits with any more gloom. "I know kaavl. You know I'm good, Kitran. I could be a vital member of the kaavl team. I'm small and skinny, and can get in places men can't. I'd make the perfect spy!" She felt excited by the logic of her plan. Kitran *had* to say yes. "What do you say?" she urged. "Will you work it with Mentàll so I can be on the kaavl team?"

Kitran's jaw clenched. "If I had my way, that whip wouldn't be Kaavl Commander. But will I help you? No. It's too dangerous, and you're too young."

"I am not! I want to help rescue Deccia. You have to let me on the team!"

"Even if I was the leader, which I'm not—*yet*," he bit out, "I wouldn't put you on the team."

Aali wilted a little. Kitran had never spoken so harshly to her before. "Then what will I *do?*"

"Work at base camp. Help Aenill with the food. Be safe."

"That's not fair!"

Kitran sent her a black glare and her steps faltered. He said, "What *is* fair? Following the orders of a whip? Deccia kidnapped? *None* of it is fair."

"We can make things better if we try."

"I *will* try. You can be sure of that."

Disappointed, Aali slowed her steps. Kitran would try? Well, so would she. Even if it temporarily meant being banished to base camp.

Somehow, she'd find a way to rescue Deccia. And when her perfect opportunity came, no herd of wild beasts, and certainly Kitran Mehl would not stop her.

∆ ∆ ∆ ∆ ∆

The sun swiftly sank toward the tops of the white, rocky hills when Methusal gathered up the water skins, clumps of kindling, and a bunch of slow burning branches and headed back to the cave to spend the final night with her enemy.

She found him sitting outside the cave, tending the fire in the deepening dusk. Somehow he'd dragged a few branches near the cave entrance. Fresh blood dripped down his back.

She frowned. "What are you doing?"

He slowly turned his head. His face was gray, and eyes hostile. "You did not return. I believed you had left."

She dumped the wood at his side. "I don't break my word. It's time to change your bandages."

Ignoring this, he wrenched his water skin from her hand and took long, deep gulps.

Then she realized what she had done. "I'm so sorry! I forgot you had no water."

He ignored her.

"I mean it. I'm sorry I left you without water. I didn't think..."

The dismissive set of his jaw made her feel even worse. Clearly, he had expected no better from her.

Treat him right, she told herself. Do the right thing now. Deep regret for her thoughtless actions made it easier to adopt a gentler tone with him. It was one that usually soothed wild animals. "I need to tend your wound."

He made no effort to move. "Do it, then."

Methusal supposed she could tend it just as well when he was sitting up. Although fresh blood dripped, the wound looked less red and inflamed than it had this morning. However, it was hard to see it clearly in the dim light. Again, she didn't like the thought of touching him, but she did so quickly and efficiently. She kept her touch light and soothing, as she did with the injured animals. Then she applied the dressing.

"There. Now it's time for the blood builder. And you should take the pain medication so you can sleep."

He drank the blood builder, but when she offered the pain powder on a leaf, he crushed it into the dirt.

Her temper kindled. Unfortunately, the Prophet's instructions to be kind returned to mind and she frowned. Fine. She would try one more time.

Methusal measured more pain powder and again offered the leaf. "If you want to build your strength, you'll need to sleep."

His teeth bared in a feral snarl. "I will stay alert."

"Why? The invaders are gone. I've seen no one, except for the Prophet."

"The Prophet."

"He sent a message for you."

Mentàll frowned, clearly suspicious of any words she might speak to him.

"He says the prize you seek draws near. You need only to see to believe. And choose the right path."

The Dehrien blinked and looked away. Clearly the words meant something to him.

"Now take the pain medication."

He looked at her, and the pale blue ice froze into her soul. "I do not want to waste pain powder. Put it away."

A war waged between their clashed gazes, but the threat and intimidation in his caused fear to shiver through her heart. "Fine," she said at last, dropping her trembling hand. "Suffer, then."

Methusal left him to tend the fire, and entered the cave to gobble up a few rations. She was famished because she hadn't had lunch. As she sat alone, however, anger festered. The One was asking too much of her. It felt wrong and uncomfortably dangerous to be kind to Mentàll. Hopefully the Prophet's words would soon leave her mind, because she could not stomach doing another kind act for that miserable man.

Twilight deepened into night, and the Dehrien entered the small cave. Methusal squashed to the far right side of the cave entrance so he would not accidentally touch her. She sat with her knees drawn to her chin. He dropped down on the other side of the entrance.

She scowled at him. "I plan to sleep soon. Move to the back of the cave." Belatedly, she added, "Please."

"I will sleep here tonight." To give proof of his intention, the Dehrien Chief stretched out. Alarmingly, his legs slid her way.

"Stop," she snapped. "This is my spot. Go to the back of the cave!"

His eyes glittered in the pale green moonlight. "I am your commanding officer. You will obey me, Methusal."

"You are injured. It's my job to care for you. I will tend the fire."

"No. You will not."

How dare that man tell her what she would and would not do? Methusal refused to move from her position at the entrance, which forced him to stretch his long legs out behind her. She dropped another branch onto the fire. She sensed him staring at her, but ignored him.

"You want to sleep at the cave entrance, Methusal?"

Was he surrendering? Victory leaped. "Yes."

"Very well. Lie beside me."

Methusal froze. "You *whip!*" she hissed. "How dare you?"

He smiled, a nasty one. "You can have your way."

Why did he always win these battles? "You are a wild beast, you mean!"

"Choose your preference, Methusal."

Fury dripped through her heart, but without another word she crawled over his legs, loathing every point she accidentally touched him, and scrunched into the far, back corner of the cave.

"Fine," she said. "Stay up all night. Suffer. Tomorrow I'm leaving, whether you're able to go or not."

"I will be ready, Methusal," said the hated harsh voice. "I will be well enough to bring you safely to base camp."

Methusal shut her eyes and willfully closed her ears. She hated him. Hated his condescending, sneering, manipulative power games. She couldn't wait to reach base camp. At least there she could finally escape from him.

CHAPTER EIGHT

METHUSAL AWOKE TO SILENCE. Bright sunshine announced the new day. Outside, all that remained of the fire were blackened embers. Mentàll was nowhere to be seen, and a quick scan proved his pack was gone. Had he already left?

Alarm kicked through her. That would be just like him. Especially since she didn't know how to get to base camp. By forcing her to track him, Mentàll would satisfy his unending desire to torture and humiliate her.

Springing to her knees, she tucked a meat strip between her teeth and strapped up her pack with shaking hands. The fresher the trail, the easier it would be to track. Trembling now with fury, she burst out of the cave and into the bright morning sunshine. She was momentarily blinded.

"Sleep well, Methusal?" That grating voice made her spin. Her enemy sat on a nearby rock, tying up his pack.

Methusal took deep breaths, trying to calm the adrenaline rushing through her. "I thought you had left," she said without thinking.

"You felt frightened that I would leave you alone?"

"No!" The brief relief she'd felt at seeing him dissolved into anger. "I expect only the worst from you. Why didn't you run off?"

Those cold eyes cut like daggers into her. "I keep my promises. But I will wait no longer." He stood and strode up the rocky hillside. He moved easily. Only the stiffness of his right shoulder indicated he suffered from an injury of any kind.

Methusal gritted her teeth and followed. She should check his wound, but the last thing she wanted to do right now was touch him.

Morning passed to noon in complete silence. Methusal followed several paces behind him. There was no sense walking beside him or talking to him. He'd only be condescending, anyway.

At lunch time the Dehrien stopped by a tiny stream which meandered through a rocky gorge. A few tufts of hardy grass sprang up from the hard, stony ground near the stream. No trees lived in these hills. Little vegetation, either—although with the water running through, it seemed like there should be more. Maybe the ground was too hard to allow plants to grow roots. Or maybe it didn't contain enough nutrients to nurture tender plants.

The barrenness of the area seemed like a fitting analogy for the man who sat on a boulder beside the stream with his back to her. He drank deeply from his water skin.

Methusal knew she had neglected her duty for too long today. She had a job to do. Doc trusted her to take care of the Dehrien's wound, and her own sense of decency demanded it, too.

She lowered her pack to the dusty earth, which was littered with tiny white and gray pebbles. Reluctantly, she approached the Dehrien Chief with her medical supplies in hand.

"It's time to change your bandages."

He did not spare her a glance, and instead took another swallow. "You are derelict in your duty, Maahr."

Her spine stiffened, but she refused to be baited. "Take off your tunic."

He grasped the back of his tunic with his left hand and pulled it over his head. The wound dripped blood. It looked wicked, red, and ugly. Methusal also realized this was the first time she'd seen it in the full light of day. It looked awful.

The knife wound looked raw and inflamed. No protective leaves remained, and she felt guilty for neglecting it for so long. The Prophet's admonition to be kind to her enemies also lashed at her conscience. His wound could be infected now, and it would all be her fault. She felt sick about it.

She quickly set to work, unable to look away from the inflamed, puckered skin. More remorse twisted through her soul. She cleaned it as well as possible. Luckily, Doc's stitches still held, which was one good thing, at least. She broke open all of her remaining coltac leaves—seven in all—and smeared them over the long gash. She hoped the thick, juicy gel would kill any infection that might be starting.

The wound looked considerably better after she had cleaned it and applied the gel, so she felt a little better, too. It still looked inflamed, but hopefully it wasn't too late to prevent an infection.

She smoothed on the first tacky leaf bandage where the knife cut ended at his waist. For the first time she noticed the fine white lines crisscrossing his back. They began just above his breeches and extended up his back, across his wide shoulders; a hundred, or perhaps more. Scars. Deep ones, by the look of most of them.

She couldn't stop a soft gasp. "What happened to you?"

Mentàll stiffened and lunged to his feet. Fists clenched, he drew in two harsh breaths and faced her. "Tend my wound," he snarled. "That's all that is required of you."

The threat in his voice chilled her. Refusing to reveal her fear, she stared up at him, unblinking. "Sit, then."

After a moment he did so, his shoulders stiff. When she pressed on the remaining tacky leaves, his muscles felt like ore beneath her fingers. She couldn't prevent her gaze from returning to his scars, though. So many. And old, too—they looked faint and smooth. In fact, she probably never would have noticed them if it wasn't for the bright sunshine and unfortunately, being so close to him.

The healer in her wanted to touch the old lines...to guess how deep they had gone, and how quickly they had healed. It was the part of her that cared for all injured, suffering animals, whatever type they might be.

Clearly, the Dehrien had suffered at some point in his life. But when?

As she adhered the last leaf, Methusal remembered a conversation two years ago at the Tarst games, when Hendra had revealed a glimpse into her family life. She had said her father had beaten all of the children. And that he'd hated Mentàll most of all.

Had those terrible lashings been delivered to Mentàll when he was a *child*? She felt horrified. Images flew to her mind of a thin, white-haired boy beaten by his large uncle. Beaten into the merciless, hate-filled man he'd become today? It certainly didn't excuse the actions he'd chosen as an adult. But maybe it partly explained why it had begun.

△ △ △ △

Hendra awoke early in the morning. The war team had arrived at base camp at dusk last night, and after a quick meal everyone had tumbled into bed.

Today they'd begin to set up camp. Hendra wanted to help, but she wasn't sure what to do, besides setting up the women's tent.

She rolled up her pallet and scanned the barren area that was to be their temporary home. It was located in a small valley. A stream and waterfall rushed down the northern slope. Gray dirt, strewn with pebbles, comprised the valley floor, and matched the color of the mountains towering around it. A few scrubby bushes with dull, gray-green leaves clustered on the slope near the stream, and the urchets grazed on the stubbly vegetation.

The whole place felt like a forgotten wasteland. Hendra certainly knew from the walk yesterday that it was far enough into the mountains that the Zindedis would have a hard time finding it.

After a quick breakfast, Hendra helped Aenill set up the women's tent, and then she stashed her pack inside and exited. She wondered what to do next.

"Hendra!" Not far away, Behran and Doc struggled with a massive leather tent. "Will you help us?"

"Of course." She hurried over. The next hour passed quickly, although sometimes Hendra wondered what she'd gotten herself into. Setting up the tent required being in close proximity to both men. Although she trusted both of them, and she'd had little trouble working with Doc during the battle, her ingrained fear of men had apparently returned in full force since then. She hated it. She hated that she had to fight against recoiling each time one of them accidentally touched her. She struggled to focus on the job and ignore her insane reactions. She wished she was a normal girl and not this timid, fearful apte.

"Last pole," Doc said with a triumphant grin. At the moment she was working with him inside the tent. He struggled harder to push the last support beam into place. "There. Grab it. I need to tie it down."

Hendra gripped the thick pole a safe distance below his hands.

"Move your hands up here for better leverage," he urged.

Tentatively, she slid her fingers up the pole.

"Here." He took her hand in one of his firm, sure ones, and directed it into place.

Stark terror surged through her. She felt dizzy, and noise roared in her ears. Every fiber in her screamed to escape. She couldn't *bear it*. She stumbled backward.

The pole shuddered and tilted sideways. Doc grabbed it and shot her a bewildered look. But when he saw her face, instant concern replaced it. "Hendra. Are you all right?"

"I...I'm fine." Tears burned her eyes. What was *wrong* with her, she wondered with despair. Why couldn't she do a simple task without freaking out?

Legs trembling, she made herself move forward. She forced herself to grip the pole above and below his hands. Doc stood very close to her because he needed to help support the pole, and she was quite aware of him. He still looked concerned.

"Are you all right? Do you need to sit down?"

"No. Please. I'm fine. Tie down the pole."

After a small hesitation, he secured the pole into place.

"Great job." Behran entered. "Now what?"

"We'll need to set up a table and pallets. Behran, why don't you work with Hendra and make up the beds?" Doc sent her a sharp, discerning glance, and retreated to put together a crude table for a desk. Hendra felt unexpectedly exposed, as if he had seen into her soul; as if he had seen a part of her that she didn't allow anyone to see.

Feeling uncomfortable, she gladly set to work with her old friend, Behran. Behran wouldn't push her. Doc, however, she wasn't so sure. Hopefully he would forget about the whole incident.

Hendra set up a pallet next to the one Behran had made.

"You okay?" he asked.

"Of course. Why wouldn't I be?"

"When I came in, you looked like you'd seen a ghost."

"It was nothing."

"Are you sure?"

"Yes." She wouldn't look at him.

"Hendra." After a reluctant moment she looked up. As always, his deep blue eyes calmed her in a way that only Behran could. "If you ever want to talk, I'm here."

"Thank you," she said softly, and ducked her head. Behran did care. He was a true friend.

He said no more, for which Hendra was grateful. She didn't think Behran knew about her home life, although for years they'd practiced kaavl together as children. She'd kept the abuse a careful secret, and still wanted to do so. She didn't want him to know how little she was worth.

Years ago, kaavl had been her only escape from real life. But more than the violence and verbal abuse of those early years had destroyed her. Hendra smoothed out a blanket for a new pallet, and closed her mind to the past. She wouldn't think about it. In fact, if it was up to her, she'd never think about it again.

The sun rose over the high, rocky hills as they worked to store supplies. After they'd finished, they invited the mildly injured men, who had still managed to make the hike to camp, to spend the night in the medical tent. All needed attention, and Hendra helped change bandages. Behran helped too, until Kitran popped in and asked him to practice with swords.

Late in the afternoon, after finishing up with the last patients, Doc said, "Thanks for your help, Hendra."

She smiled and pushed a lynnte cleaning weed into a leather bag.

"Will you help me tomorrow, too?"

She quickly glanced at him. "I..."

"I mean until the kaavl team leaves."

A soft sort of trepidation beat inside of her. Doc's direct gaze held hers. Here was a man who would not play games. He needed help.

She was sick to death of allowing fear to rule her life. "All right," she said softly.

He smiled, and his white teeth looked straight and strong. A nice smile. A warm flutter beat in her stomach.

The wounded soldiers needed her. Doc needed her. And by helping, she'd fight her debilitating fears, too.

Soon she'd spy and work with the kaavl team, which would be made up of all men, except for Methusal and herself.

If she couldn't handle working with Doc, then she'd be in deep trouble on the real battleground.

△ △ △ △

Methusal and Mentàll hiked all afternoon across the plain. They skirted the Quasr Mountain foothills the entire time. Fatigue ached through her muscles, and she wondered with increasing frequency how the Dehrien Chief was holding up regarding his wounds. She still trailed behind him, reluctant to walk in close proximity to her enemy.

Unfortunately, walking four steps behind didn't give her a clear view of her patient's expression.

She wondered if she should check on him. But wasn't he a grown man? He could stop if he was tired.

Methusal wanted to reach base camp soon. She longed to see Behran, her father, and Aali. Anyone friendly.

Her conscience nudged her again. She glanced heavenward. How could she possibly continue to be nice to her enemy? It was so *hard*. She directed a brief prayer to the heavens. *If you want me to be kind, The One, please help me. I can't do it on my own.*

She eyed the Dehrien, who still strode ahead of her. She didn't feel any different.

At least she could see if he was all right, she reasoned. It would only take a second to check. And it wouldn't require any soul draining, impossibly kind acts, either.

Methusal trotted ahead, pretending to ignore the Dehrien Chief. She felt his gaze upon her, but ignored him until that uncomfortable feeling vanished. Then she slid a quick glance sideways.

The Chief of Dehre's face was white, and his lips thinned. He was in obvious pain.

Great. Now what?

If she tried to help him, he'd probably snarl at her. So? Did that matter? Was she afraid of him?

Yes.

Strangely enough, that made her feel even more determined to do the right thing. Calmly, she said, "You should stop and rest."

"No." He strode on.

Stubborn, prideful man. Let him walk until he collapsed. Methusal frowned and bit her lip. Wrong attitude.

"Are we close?" she wanted to know.

"Another hour," came the terse reply. The Dehrien Chief slowed down and turned to climb up into the steep rocks. After a few dozen steps, he paused and placed a steadying hand on a boulder. Gray tinged his skin.

If she didn't intervene, he'd probably walk until he collapsed. Letting the Dehrien injure himself wouldn't do anyone any good. Least of all the war effort. He was the best at kaavl on Koblan—maybe on the entire planet. Unfortunately, they needed his skill to win this war—provided, of course, he could be trusted.

Ahead, the Dehrien Chief stumbled, but swiftly caught his balance.

Enough.

"I need to rest," Methusal announced. Not sure if that would be sufficient, she sat down on a nearby rock and uncorked her water skin.

The Dehrien glanced over his shoulder. A long moment elapsed, during which he clearly battled whether or not he would concede to her wishes. Finally he sat down too, but a good distance away from her.

Methusal remained seated after she recorked her water skin. She pretended to relax. From time to time, she slid a glance his way. Normal color slowly returned to his face.

Long minutes passed, and then the Dehrien Chief looked at her in the same instant she sent him another assessing glance.

Suspicion flared, and his face hardened. "Enough," he snarled. He slung his pack over his good shoulder and stalked off.

Methusal smiled to herself. At least The One would be pleased with her one kind act for today. Certainly, the Dehrien would never thank her.

The next hour passed, and the sun sank toward the horizon. They climbed steadily higher into the barren, rocky Quasr Mountains. Twin white peaks towered far to the east, but Mentàll headed north now. Clearly, the peaks weren't their destination. She hadn't seen water in hours.

They climbed still higher, and in the distance, beyond another high slope, scrubby trees dotted the mountain. Were they heading up there? It looked like another three hour walk.

Mentàll twisted left at the next high hill and then descended down, out of view. Methusal hurried to follow. Of course he'd love to leave her behind, lost and confused. She sprinted to catch up, and then caught her breath when she topped the hill. Below lay a huge, deep basin. Camp.

Tents populated the dusty gray earth. Perhaps at one time it had been a lake. Several fire pits blazed. Pots hung over each. On the east side of camp loomed five large tents. Probably three of them belonged to the Chiefs. Certainly the bleached leather one belonged to her favorite Dehrien. Maybe the other two remaining large tents were the medical tent and the dining hall. Smaller tents lay scattered to the south.

To the north, a small waterfall cascaded down the mountain and disappeared behind big clumps of bushes. From there a stream emerged and meandered down the remaining hillside and flowed west, bordering the northern side of the valley. Tiny figures climbed the rocks above the waterfall. Urchets ambled in the low hills.

Home. A bit of peace slipped into her soul. Although it looked barren, it also looked welcoming.

As Methusal jogged down into the valley behind the Dehrien leader, she spied Aenill Patn stirring a large pot. The delicious scent of stew tantalized her nostrils. To her left, Kitran and Behran practiced sword play in the open field on the west side of camp.

Behran. She smiled. It had been a long two days. She'd talk to him as soon as he finished practicing.

Mentàll strode ahead of her, obviously heading for his own tent.

Her eager gaze searched the camp for her father or Aali. She didn't see either of them, but she'd find them soon.

Doc ducked out of a smaller tent and altered his path to intersect hers. "How's our patient?"

"I'm not sure. I let the wound go untreated too long this morning." Guilt again reared its ugly head. "It looks inflamed."

"I'll check it out. Looks like he's regained his strength." Doc nodded at the Dehrien, who'd stopped to speak to one of his men.

"Mostly. He was close to passing out on the trail because he refused to stop."

"He doesn't want anyone to see his weakness."

"You're right about that."

"Why didn't you treat his wound on time?"

"I'm sorry. I have no excuse, but to be really honest he's tried my patience over the last two days. I know we need him, but I'll never trust him."

"Because he tried to take over Rolban."

"Yes. And now we have to ally with him to save Koblan. In fact, I'll be on his kaavl team. Ironic, don't you think?"

"Are you up for the challenge?"

"Yes. I'll do my duty, if that's what you're asking."

"So I'm right to trust you to take care of his wound?" Again, that sharp, assessing glance.

Methusal felt rebuked; as if he had expected a higher standard of behavior from her. And he was absolutely right. Neglecting the Dehrien's wound this morning had been wrong. It made no difference how he treated her. She had failed in her duty.

"I'm sorry. I won't let personal feelings get in the way again. I'll give him the best care I can."

"Good." Doc looked ahead. The Dehrien was about to enter the bleached leather tent. "Mentàll!" The Dehrien Chief turned his blond head. "I'd like to check your wound. Meet me in the medical tent."

The Dehrien nodded and disappeared inside his tent.

"I used my last coltac leaves today. I'll need more supplies."

"Come in and I'll get you set up." Doc pushed aside the leather tent flap to the medical tent. She glimpsed Hendra at the back of the large tent, sponging a man's brow.

"Hendra's helping you?"

Doc smiled. "She's my best nurse. I'll miss her when she leaves with the kaavl team."

Hendra looked up and an instant smile blossomed. After finishing with the man, she dropped soiled lynnte weeds in a bucket and hurried over. "Methusal!" she said. "And Mentàll? Is he all right?"

"He's fine, but needs rest. Not that he'll listen to anyone. Except maybe you, since you're his cousin."

Hendra gave a breath of a laugh, and her brown eyes danced. "Mentàll listens to no one. Least of all me."

"And here he is." Doc said. They all moved aside as the large Dehrien entered the tent.

"Mentàll!" Hendra said. "Are you well?"

"I am fine. Do not worry."

At his abrupt tone, Hendra lowered her gaze and glanced at Doc. "I'll attend my next patient. Glad to see you, Methusal. You, too, Mentàll."

The Dehrien did not respond. However, his gaze briefly followed Hendra to the back of the tent.

"Let's take a look at that wound." Doc cleared supplies off of a make-shift bench and indicated that the Dehrien Chief should sit down and take off his tunic.

Doc went down on one knee in the dirt to get a better look.

Methusal saw when Doc noticed the scars. His left hand went out, as if to touch them—which had been her first response, too—and then it dropped. His frowning glance met hers. She shook her head a tiny bit.

He nodded. "The wound looks raw, Mentàll, but it should be fine. Methusal, make sure you work the coltac juice in well. Watch." Doc squirted a dollop of gel on the puckered skin, and then used the heel of his thumb to gently knead it into the wound. "You try."

Methusal would much rather squirt on the juice and lightly dab it over the Dehrien's skin. The less contact with him the better, was her philosophy. Tentatively, she slid the ball of her thumb over the slick skin.

"Firmer, Methusal."

"Won't that hurt?"

"You care?" the Dehrien mocked.

Methusal glared, and pressed a little harder. Mentàll drew in a quick breath.

"Careful." Doc did not sound pleased. "Like this." His fingers guided hers this time, and Methusal felt bad.

"I'm sorry. I have it now."

The Dehrien Chief said, "Finish it, then."

Methusal wanted to do nothing less. "Doc is the expert on healing wounds. Maybe he should..."

"You will tend my wound every day. Prove your competence."

Doc looked at her, clearly expecting her consent. The Dehrien glanced over his shoulder. The chilly blue gaze demanded her capitulation.

"Of course," she said tightly. "Nothing would make me happier."

"Accepting your place, Methusal, is half the battle," the Dehrien murmured.

"Accepting my *place?*" She stiffened, anger pulsing through her. "What exactly do you mean by that?"

Beside her, Doc sat back on his heels.

"I am your commanding officer," Mentàll returned. "If you want to stay on my kaavl team, then you will obey me without question. At all times. Is that understood?"

"We're not on the kaavl team right now."

"I am your commanding officer. Now."

Words stuck in her tight throat. "I will obey your orders on the field. But at base camp my father is my commanding officer."

"I will happily reassign you to your father's team. Is that your wish? You need only speak it."

She counted to ten in an effort to control her temper. He knew she had to be on his team. Not only because of her kaavl skills, but more importantly, it was her only hope to rescue Deccia quickly. The other teams would attack. The kaavl team alone would gather intelligence and discover Deccia's location first. She had to be on that team, no matter the cost to herself. She had to rescue her twin as quickly as possible.

"No." With difficulty, she acknowledged, "I want to be on your team."

At least she was finished working in the coltac juice! With shaking fingers, she pressed on the tacky leaves. She could not finish fast enough. The Dehrien got under her skin much too easily. She wanted to run screaming from the medical tent. A reluctant smile twitched her lips at the thought. Certainly, that wouldn't be her finest moment. And the Dehrien would not scare her off.

She affixed the last leaf.

Doc said, "Good job. Change it twice a day for another day or two. Then once a day will do." With a narrowed glance at them both, he gathered up the extra supplies and moved on to the next patient.

Mentàll pulled on his tunic and stood. Methusal quickly stood, too. She didn't like him towering over her.

He said, "We are agreed, then."

Methusal didn't answer. Further acquiescence cost her too dearly.

"Speak, Methusal. Are you on my team or off?"

"On," she said, through thinned lips.

"So you will follow my orders."

"In everything with respect to the war, yes. If you think you can order me to fetch water for you or plump your pillows, you are sadly mistaken."

His teeth bared in a poor smile. "I use no pillows, Methusal. But you may be certain if I did, I would not want you to touch them."

"Then we are agreed."

"Do not disappoint. One infraction, and I will cut you from my team." The Dehrien strode from the tent.

Methusal abruptly crossed her arms, trying to squelch her rising anger. Thank goodness her friends would be on the kaavl team. Without them, she didn't know how she'd endure the coming war.

△ △ △ △ △

"Thusa!" Aali threw herself at Methusal the moment she entered the tarp-covered food preparation area.

"Aali." She hugged her back. "Is this your job? You're going to help Aenill?"

Her cousin grimaced. "For now."

"For now?" Suspicion registered. She knew her cousin too well. "What does that mean?"

"Nothing." She innocently widened her eyes. "Don't worry. I know my place."

Methusal didn't believe that for one second.

"Dinner will be in an hour. Want a meat strip?" Aali fished one from a tub and Methusal took the jerked meat, glad to have it. Her stomach rumbled.

"No offense, Thusa, but you stink."

"Thank you so much."

"It's not your fault. You were stuck with that stinky Dehrien for two days." Aali grinned. "But you can take a bath. Want to see where?"

"Definitely."

Aali quickly spoke to Aenill, and then scampered with Methusal to the women's tent. "Get clean clothes and come quick, before that vile Dehrien finds it."

Grabbing up a handful of clean clothes, her soap, and a drying cloth, Methusal followed her cousin to the north end of the small, dusty valley.

"This way." Aali scrambled up the rocks, following the stream, which rushed downhill over smooth stones. A faint path appeared between two clumps of bushes, which were also flanked by large boulders. A sheer cliff rose to the left, and from it cascaded the waterfall.

Following Aali, Methusal slipped between the bushes and stopped in amazement. A large, clear pool, sculpted from rock and fed by the waterfall, shimmered in the late afternoon sunlight. Its privacy was perfectly protected on all sides by high, thick bushes and by the curved cliff wall, from which the sparkling waterfall fell.

"I'll watch and make sure no one comes," Aali offered. "But be quick. Aenill needs me to rip up logne leaves."

"Thanks so much," Methusal breathed.

The thought of being clean again felt like pure heaven after four days of dirt and climbing and marching. She quickly disrobed, and then brought her old clothes and soap in with her. Might as well clean those, too. After quickly washing, she relaxed in the pool. The water eddied around her. She felt buoyant and light, and oh, so clean.

If only troubles could be washed away so easily. Thinking about her sister brought her mind back to Aali.

Something about her innocent denials a few minutes ago had set off Methusal's internal alarms. Sneaking and following the war team wasn't the first time Aali had formed her own secret plans. In addition, she knew her cousin well enough to suspect that Aali wouldn't want to stay at camp like a good girl while everyone else participated in the "adventure"—as she would see it.

"Thusa!"

"Coming!" She quickly dried off, dressed, and wrung out her wet clothes before heading back to camp in Aali's fast wake.

"Aali, please tell me the truth. You're not planning to go off and do something on your own. Right?"

Her steps faltered. "No."

Her suspicions solidified. "Aali. Promise me you won't follow the kaavl team to Quasr."

"I wouldn't." However, she did not sound convincing.

"It's too dangerous. It's not like following the war team here, or even following the kaavl team to Dehre two years ago. Please! Promise me."

"Then what am I supposed to *do?*" she cried out. "Sit here and twiddle my thumbs? Stir porridge until my arm falls off? How will that help Deccia?" Angry tears gleamed.

Methusal gently pulled her into a hug. "I know you want to help. Look for opportunities here, at base camp."

Aali's pooched out lip looked mutinous. "What opportunities?"

"I don't know," she admitted. "But promise you'll stay here."

"Thusa's right." Behran swung in to walk beside them. Methusal grinned at him, and he put his arm around her waist, drawing her close. She relaxed, and finally felt happy. When she was with Behran, everything always seemed like it would be all right. Sternly, he said, "Promise us, Aali."

"Fine!" Her cousin scowled. "I'll stay here. But when an *opportunity* comes, you know I'll follow it. Nothing will stop me from rescuing Deccia."

"That's our job."

"It's my job, too! I'm not a child anymore. I wish everyone would stop treating me like one!" Aali stormed for the cooking area.

"Do you think she'll listen?" Behran murmured.

"Yes. For now."

"I'll talk to Timaeus and Dastn. They'll help keep an eye on her while we're gone."

"And I'll talk to Papa and Aenill." The more people watching Aali, the better, Methusal thought, watching her cousin viciously rip up logne leaves. Aali was a determined girl. She smiled. A quality she understood too well.

Δ Δ Δ Δ Δ

After supper, Methusal felt peaceful as she sat beside Behran in the dusk, close to one of the blazing bonfires. Cool night air made her skin prickle up in bumps. She shivered, and Behran tightened his arm around her shoulders. He felt warm beside her, and secure. Methusal wanted to soak in the peace of this moment. It might very well be her last one.

The Chiefs had met, and Mentàll had just announced that the kaavl team would break camp and head for Quasr tomorrow afternoon. They'd find a safe place for the kaavl camp, and then infiltrate Quasr at dark to spy and discover as much information as they they could. Runners would wait at the base of the mountains, and then relay that information to the two waiting war teams. Then the battle to win back Quasr would begin.

"Are you nervous, Thusa?"

She leaned into him. "A little. Actually, a lot. We'll have the wild beasts to worry about tomorrow night, and the Zindedis, too. But finally, we'll start doing something to rescue Deccia."

Behran kissed her hair. "We'll find her."

"I know." They had to. Maybe they'd even find her tomorrow. Methusal barely dared to hope it.

A spray of pebbles hit her back as someone scuffed by.

Her gaze shot left, and she met Goric's sneer.

"Sorry. Guess your kaavl didn't see that coming," he taunted.

"You little..." Behran's arm restrained her.

Goric only laughed and dropped down next to Jascr. Now, how had those two struck up a friendship? Maybe their equally stellar characters had drawn them together.

"Let it go, Thusa."

"You and the Prophet. You're both giving me the same advice."

"You met the Prophet?"

"Yes. In the hills when I had to watch over Mentàll." Methusal explained what he had said about treating her enemies with kindness. "It feels impossible," she finished, still irritated with Goric. "If they attack me, they'll regret it."

Behran chuckled. "Fiery Thusa. One of the reasons why I love you so much."

Ruefully, she said, "And why some people hate me so much."

"Don't change." Behran kissed her. "But be careful. I think the Prophet is right. It might be best to treat our enemies like friends during the war. I'm not saying we should trust them. But we can't fight each other if we want to win against the Zindedis."

"You're right." A tall figure caught her eye. Her fiercest enemy strode between their bonfire and another one, and for a second his black silhouette looked rimmed in fire against the dark night. A deep shiver worked through her soul. A warning.

Her life would become very unpleasant if she couldn't control her tongue with him. At all costs, she must stay on the kaavl team to rescue Deccia. If following the Prophet's commands would help her accomplish that goal, then that is what she would do.

△ △ △ △ △

Methusal had a hard time falling asleep. Fires crackled around camp, although wild beasts weren't likely to roam this rocky, desolate region. They much preferred the plains, where plenty of aptes and whips burrowed. Kaavl camp would be located on the plains, though. Probably in the rocky foothills closest to Quasr.

She shivered and rolled over, thinking about the possibility of seeing wild beasts on her spying mission tomorrow night. The entire kaavl team would infiltrate the Zindedi stronghold then. Again she wondered if she would find Deccia. Worry knotted her stomach. Her sister was suffering. She knew it. If only she could help her *now*.

At last, she drifted into the shadow world of sleep.

Deccia cowered in a corner of her dark cell, shuddering each time a door clanged shut, each time footsteps shuffled in the corridor, and every time the flicker of a torch brightened the hall outside her wooden door. A barred window let in light from the corridor. Otherwise her cell would be pitch black.

Deccia knew she was underground in a Quasr dungeon. She felt buried alive. Suffocated by fear. Would she ever be rescued?

"The One, help me," she whispered.

Familiar, shuffling footsteps approached.

She shuddered and hoped they'd pass by her door. "Protect me," she whispered, and tears rolled down her cheeks.

The steps paused outside her door.

The jailor's low cackle made her skin crawl. "Take your food like a good girl," the fiend lisped between the bars. "Perhaps the General will reward you later."

Deccia pressed her fist to her mouth and hunched tighter into her corner. A key scraped in the lock.

Terror soared through her. Deccia choked back a soundless sob. If only he'd leave! She'd gladly starve to death, if it meant the General would never summon her upstairs again.

The hunched form looked like a dark lump in the door-way. The torchlight momentarily blinded her eyes.

"I see you," he chuckled. "Come get your food."

Deccia hunched tighter into her corner. Not for the first time, and with shame for her weakness, she wished she was dead.

CHAPTER NINE

METHUSAL WOKE UP at dawn, exhausted. At least she was lying on her pallet. Last night she'd woken up multiple times, cowering in a corner of the women's tent, drenched with sweat. She was thankful she hadn't wandered through camp or stepped into a bonfire.

All night long she had suffered with her twin.

Was Deccia truly in a Quasr dungeon? Was the dream real? Had Deccia suffered, terrified, all night long in a dark, dank cell? Starving, too, because the monstrous guard had taken the food away.

Tears burned her eyes as she dressed and quickly packed up the supplies she wanted to take to kaavl camp. The dreams *felt* real. As real as her prophetic nightmare had felt two and a half years ago, and that one had foretold this awful war.

She wanted to believe the dreams were only nightmares spun in the nether world of sleep, where fears and fantasies twisted together.

Aali poked her head around the tent flap. "Mentàll is ordering your presence."

Methusal closed her eyes and drew a calming breath. She'd been plagued by her sister's demons all night, and now she'd be tormented by her own.

She would find Deccia, and soon. Then both of their nightmares would end.

"I'll be there in a minute."

"You tell him. I'm not talking to that wild beast again."
Aali disappeared.

Methusal finished packing. She wasn't sure why, but
Aali's unfortunate announcement also reminded her about
Mentàll's suspicious conversation with his cohorts the other
night. She still hadn't told her father about it.

As she tied up her pack, she wondered if she should. But
she had no proof. And her father could take no action without it. So maybe she should wait find the proof she needed.
Then Erl could take appropriate measures with the Kaavl
Commander. Kitran would love to take over that role, she
reflected as she stepped out into the overcast morning.

Low clouds enveloped the Quasr peaks. Although rain
wouldn't be pleasant for the hike to Quasr, it might keep the
Zindedi soldiers inside while the kaavl team did reconnais-
sance.

With reluctance, Methusal's gaze slid toward the Dehrien's
tent. He wasn't in sight. Terrific. She'd grab breakfast first.
She hurried toward the tarp covered eating area. New,
roughly hewn tables and benches had appeared overnight.
Behran sat, chuckling, across from Hendra. Hendra's soft
smile seemed to border on hero worship.

Methusal's steps slowed, and a knot lodged in her stomach.
Once again, she wondered about Behran and Hendra's past
relationship. How deep had it been? How close were they
now?

Behran clearly liked Hendra a lot. Maybe he felt protective
of her, too. Something about Hendra projected an aura of
fragility, but Methusal suspected a slender core of ore lived
inside the other girl. Hendra had defied her cousin in order
to save Methusal's life two years ago, and now she had joined
the war effort. If she was afraid, she was trying to fight it.
Methusal admired that. It was difficult to distrust the other
girl when she liked her, too.

"Methusal." The harsh voice jerked her attention from
the two at the table. Mentàll's chilly gaze said he'd seen her
watching Behran and Hendra. Did it please him to see her
feeling a little disturbed? Probably.

"Aali delivered your message. Why did you ask for me?"

"My wound needs tending."

"Fine."

She followed three steps behind the Dehrien, but stopped when he lifted his tent flap. The nerve of the wild beast. "I won't go into your tent."

He smiled nastily. "If you are afraid, then you may tend my wound outside."

He enjoyed her discomfort. He deliberately provoked it, relishing the power he held over her. Two years ago, he'd promised to make her pay for his humiliation and defeat. A few days ago, he'd promised her father that he wouldn't harm her during the war, but this subtle intimidation and the needle skewering power plays...these, she must suffer now.

Methusal struggled to calm her simmering temper while the Dehrien shucked off his tunic and sat on a boulder outside his tent. What had the Prophet said? To treat her enemies with kindness.

She pulled the coltac leaves from the medical pouch she always carried and tended the vicious slash as quickly as possible.

"How does it look?" he wanted to know.

"Unpleasant. Just like you." She speedily moved past him to escape. His large hand curled around her wrist, stopping her.

With a quick twist, she jerked free. "Don't *touch* me. Ever!"

"Heed me, Methusal." The cold gaze held hers. "Fear builds healthy respect."

"Respect is earned. And I don't respect you."

"You will listen to my instructions."

She crossed her arms, and then realized how defensive that looked and dropped them. "Speak, if you have something to say, or I'm leaving."

"Practice with your knife. I may not be available next time to save your life."

She gasped, unable to help herself. Then she scowled. With one sentence, he made her face three unpalatable truths: she had failed, he had saved her life, and now he could order her around as he wished. She hated every reminder.

A pleased smile curled his lips. Another victory for him.

Teeth clenched, she turned away.

"Is that a 'yes,' Methusal?"

He wouldn't let it *go*. She heaved a short breath.

"You are not grateful I saved your life?"

The man too easily flayed under skin. "Why did you save me, anyway?" She felt pleased with her cool, even words. A new question flew to mind. "You sought me out, didn't you? You followed me in those hills. Why?"

The Dehrien Chief didn't answer, although his reprehensible enjoyment at her expense fled, replaced by an expressionless mask. He stood and pulled on his tunic.

"Why?" she pressed.

"I did not know it was you."

Meaning if he had known, he would not have come.

"So why did you save me, then?"

He eyed her coldly now, as if she was something foul he'd found in a trash heap. "You're worth more to me alive than dead."

"So you admit you need me on the kaavl team."

"I need a warrior who follows orders. Practice with your knife, Maahr."

Methusal said nothing.

"Yes, sir," he prompted.

Her temper abruptly snapped. "Devil take you, Mentàll! *Yes,* I will practice. But you can't order my tongue."

"On the contrary. By the time this war is over, you will understand exactly how much authority I hold over you." Arrogantly, he finished, "And you will willingly submit."

Methusal gasped in fury. "You are insane! I'll never *submit* to you. Ever. In fact, by the time this war is over, you'll wish *you* were the one who'd fallen off that cliff!"

He took one step toward her. Instant threat oozed from his formidable frame. "Test me to your peril, Methusal."

She drew a quick breath. Why couldn't she follow the Prophet's one, simple directive? "I said I'll practice. But don't ask anything else of me."

He was not pleased. And he'd make her pay for that insubordination in the future, somehow, someway—she saw that in his gaze, as clearly as Ryon lit a bright summer night. She turned and walked quickly away.

As much as she wanted to take the high road, she had failed again. And she'd antagonized her biggest threat of all. Could she be anymore foolish?

△ △ △ △ △

After breakfast Methusal found the weapons field. Taltn, the Tarst boy, ran up, eager to practice with her. They each took turns—one with the knife, and one with the long, blocking kaavl stick. The kaavl stick was made of an extremely strong, dense hardwood, and in the old days of war they had held up well in battle.

Her knife skill level equaled Taltn's, she quickly discovered.

A few minutes later Kitran arrived with Goric. He watched her spar with Taltn, and then signaled for a halt. "Practice with Goric, Methusal. I'll practice with Taltn. You're not learning much from each other."

Goric hefted the kaavl stick in his hands. "Use the knife first. Go ahead," he jeered. "Try to get past me."

She still hated the feel of the knife in her hand. Although she didn't like Goric, she didn't want to accidentally hurt him, either. She swung for his arm. Goric's kaavl stick smacked into her fingers. Pain burst in her hand and she dropped the knife.

Goric circled, smiling, and watching her through murky gray eyes. "Try again."

Fingers tingling and smarting, she retrieved the knife from the dirt. Moving quicker this time, she lunged toward Goric and then twisted left, struggling to avoid his kaavl stick. The rod hit her shoulder, her elbow, and then her leg. He swiftly struck her again and again. She barely had time to wield the knife at all. Each minute seemed like an hour. Goric beat her back and forth across the weapons field.

Frustrated fury churned within her. This wasn't practice!

"Give up?" he taunted.

Sore and angry, Methusal snapped, "My turn with the stick."

Still grinning, Goric unsheathed his knife. It was a large one with jagged edges, and too big for his slight frame. Methusal had no intention of letting Goric slice her up—*accidentally*, of course.

Lightning fast, Goric lunged forward. Thankfully she had more experience with the kaavl stick than with the knife. She spun it, deflected the blade, and at last slipped into kaavl. Goric had rattled her before, but now...now everything seemed to slow down. Every sense sharpened to acuity.

Every reflex responded with practiced precision. She easily parried his thrusts, and she began to understand his patterns, his facial expressions, and the stances he took before certain strikes. Anticipating them, her stick was there before his knife could begin the move.

She whipped her kaavl stick faster. It was effortless—and totally surprising. She'd never wielded a stick like this before. She saw rage contort Goric's features. Spit flew from his snarling mouth as he threw his weight into each lunge. He wanted to hurt her. In fact, maybe he would kill her if he could, because now she was humiliating him.

And how simple it would be... The thought came, and with a quick wrist flip, she unarmed him. His face turned dark red.

"More?" she wanted to know.

"Enough, Methusal." Kitran's voice seemed to come from a great distance, but she didn't relax until Goric picked up his knife and resheathed it.

"Shake hands," Kitran ordered.

Goric crushed Methusal's hand, squeezing her bones together. She bit her lip, but refused to cry out. Hatred burned in his eyes. And then he was gone. Gingerly, she shook out her hand.

"Good job, Methusal." Her kaavl instructor smiled, and she blinked in surprise. She'd rarely seen Kitran smile, and never a wide one, like that. "I've never seen you better with the stick. You made a breakthrough."

"It was awesome," Taltn exclaimed, his eyes shining. "Will you show me how you did it?"

"It was kaavl. I wish I could do the same with the knife."

"It will come," Kitran assured her. "You're afraid of the knife. With more practice you'll overcome it."

"Goric hates me even more, now."

"During the war we'll have to work with people we hate. But *you* be the one to take control, Methusal." His eyes darkened. "We will win the victory over our enemies."

"What do you mean?"

"Each of us will do what we must to win the war." An unreadable mask hardened his features.

Unease slid into her spirit. "What are you planning?"

Kitran didn't reply for a moment. "Nothing. Yet. But if it becomes necessary, I'll do what it takes to make sure the kaavl team is led right."

△ △ △ △ △

Rain sprinkled the dusty earth when the seventeen members of the kaavl team headed west over the mountains, toward Quasr. Nervous excitement made Methusal feel tense and a little jittery. Finally, she'd get to spy in Quasr. She wondered if she would find where Deccia was being held, and if she would be able to rescue her twin tonight.

More immediate, practical matters forced their way to the front of her mind. When they spied in Quasr tonight, would they meet Zindedi soldiers? Would they have to fight?

Methusal knew her knife skills were still poor, and that she needed to improve, even though the thought of killing someone made her feel sick. Beneath her cloak, she wore the short kaavl stick strapped to her waist. She wished she could carry the long one into Quasr. But at least the short one was a familiar measure of defense, should she get into a sticky situation.

The wild beasts would leave their dens at dusk to hunt.

"Ready, Thusa?" Behran gave her the cocky grin she knew too well. When they'd been rivals, he had used it to get under her skin. He still used it to ruffle her feathers.

Unwilling to disappoint, she said sweetly, "I'm ready to make a bet."

He grinned. "Tell me."

"I bet I'll find the most valuable piece of information tonight."

"You're on. What are the stakes?"

"If I win, you give me a backrub."

"I'll take the same prize."

"Good." She grinned. "Then we're agreed."

"What if we're on the same team?"

Kitran joined them. "No chance of that."

"Why?"

"The Kaavl Commander issued orders. You're with me, Thusa. We'll scout the east side of town, near the docks. Behran, you and Hendra will scout the west side. Your mission will be a lot safer. Crops grow out there, and not much else. At least that's the way it was when I grew up there."

She said, "Will our mission be dangerous?"

"Not if we're careful. I could walk through that town in my sleep."

Methusal grinned at Behran. "I guess you'd better accept defeat now." She tried to ignore the ridiculous feeling of discomfort that Behran would scout with Hendra. She trusted him. For that matter, she trusted Hendra, too.

It took almost three hours to reach the final, rocky foothills which ended just before the Quasr coastal plain. The sun dipped toward the western mountains and cast intermittent rays through the rain clouds, turning them a bright pink. Mentàll led them down to the flatland, and then they walked south for half an hour until the sunset deepened into a grayish purple twilight. Finally, he slowed.

Tall, jagged rocks lay jumbled against the base of the cliff in this area, and more boulders lay scattered over the plain, too, as if thrown by a cosmic hand. Mentàll led them through a narrow opening, and she discovered that the tight cluster of the gigantic boulders formed the letter "O" near the base of a particularly steep hill that erupted into a towering cliff. A winding stream trickled inside of its rocky arms.

The enclave was about eleven lengths deep and seven wide. And except for the opening near the stream, completely protected on all sides from wild beasts. A small cave, far up the hill, was too small and too steep for the wild beasts to use as a lair.

"Camp," he announced, dropping his great pack.

Methusal found a level piece of ground near a big boulder at the base of the hill, and dropped her pack there. Behran dropped his beside it. Hendra moved away, looking for a place to put hers.

"Hendra," Methusal immediately said. "Over here."

Hendra looked back, hesitation clear in her averted body language. "Are you sure?"

"Of course. We're the only two women, and we're all friends. We have to stick together."

Pleasure suffused Hendra's face, and she made her way back. "Thank you," she said with a shy smile.

Behran said, "We wouldn't want you to be anywhere else."

Sunshine beamed in Hendra's smile to Behran. Methusal smiled, too, and told herself to stop feeling so insecure. It was ridiculous. Behran loved her. It was good he was a friend to Hendra, too. Clearly, the Dehrien girl needed all the friends she could get, if her dysfunctional family was any indication of her life in Dehre.

After dropping their packs, all of the kaavl players gathered in a loose circle to listen to their leader's final instructions. The rain drizzled a little harder now, and Methusal pulled the hood of her cloak up, as did the other team members.

"We'll head out when it's dark." Mentàll wore no hood, and the short blond hair that kicked up at his temple had turned into wet spikes. His pale gaze drove into each person, demanding their full attention.

"Each team member has his assignment. Each person has a partner. Hear me now. Never spy alone. If your partner is captured, return to camp immediately so we can plan a rescue. Never try to rescue your partner alone. Is that understood?" His hard tone demanded unquestioning obedience.

A mumble of assent came.

Kitran said, "Who is your partner, Mentàll?"

"I require no partner."

"Sounds pretty arrogant. You don't think you'll be captured?"

Displeasure thinned the Dehrien's lips. "I require no assistance. And I want to be able to move about as I see fit. That way I can assist those who need help the most."

Suspicion stirred in Methusal's mind. Maybe Mentàll wanted to be freed of the inconvenience of a partner because he didn't want anyone to spy on *him*. What did he plan to do? Meet up with the Quasr Chief's successor? Put his nefarious plan into action? Maybe pursue the unknown prize he lusted after?

Kitran seemed to read her mind. "How do we know we can trust you, Dehrien?"

"I understand that you feel humiliated, Kitran. But I am the Kaavl Commander, and you are not. Your pride is wounded. But do not challenge my authority just because you cannot stand to take instruction from one who is more skilled in kaavl."

Methusal gasped, and Kitran's tanned face darkened.

"If that is all." Mentàll turned his attention to the group. "Report back at dawn."

"Be careful, Thusa." Behran scanned her face for a moment, as if memorizing something precious to him. He kissed her, and it lingered. Even though Methusal felt chilly on the outside, warmth blossomed inside.

She smiled softly. "You too, Behran. Remember, I'll be expecting my prize later."

He chuckled. "Come on, Hendra."

△ △ △ △ △

Rain sheeted down onto the grassy plain in the dark, gloomy night. From time to time Ryon's rays broke through, which helped keep them on course. Kitran led the way through the downpour.

So far, they'd seen no packs of wild beasts. Kitran moved at a pace that was easy for Methusal to match, but he was silent, and clearly lost in thoughts of his own. His dark, handsome face looked hard and unhappy.

"Don't let Mentàll get to you," she offered after a while. "He's an expert at hurting people."

"He's a ruthless *wild beast*. He'll do anything to stay in power."

"Yes."

Kitran's dark eyes searched her face. "Did he hurt you when you were trapped with him in the hills?"

Methusal sensed that Kitran wanted her to say that Mentàll had. He wanted to find more reasons to hate the Dehrien and strip him of power. "Not physically," she said carefully. Her normally calm kaavl instructor seemed on edge. Anger boiled in him, and she didn't want to stoke it. How would that help the kaavl team? "I can handle him. Don't worry."

"Good," he muttered.

"I know you're angry about what happened two years ago."

"He made me look like a *fool!*" he growled. His tone reminded her of his volatile brother Barak—not the calm kaavl instructor she'd known for half of her life. "I trusted him as a friend, and he betrayed me!"

"I know." Maybe she shouldn't have raised this topic. She didn't know what else to say. But after a while, as the lights of Quasr grew brighter through the darkness, hard words came. "I don't like him either, Kitran. You know that. But don't you think it would be best to try to work together? We all have the same goal. We want to beat the invaders."

"I can't believe you're taking his side. After everything he's done to you."

"I'm *not!*" Methusal said, aghast. "But Papa thinks he should be Kaavl Commander. I have to trust my father's judgment. I want to rescue Deccia, and I want to win the war. And Behran said something that makes a lot of sense: how can we win the war if we're fighting each other?"

"I *am* following his orders," Kitran said shortly. "But don't talk about that whip anymore."

Methusal didn't want to talk about the Dehrien, either. It had been hard to advise Kitran to pursue peace with the Dehrien Chief. But logically, Behran was right. Fighting with Mentàll would not help win this war.

A cool breeze blew in from the sea, and dark clouds scudded across Ryon by the time she and Kitran circled into Quasr from the east. Instead of the fresh, clean scent of rain, though, Methusal smelled something charred and acrid.

A wet, icy gust of wind blasted against her and she shivered, glad that her cloak was waterproof. Most of her body was dry, but mud squished inside her moccasins. Her toes felt slippery and disgusting. And her wet leather pants clung to her cold legs.

They approached a line of shacks leading to the beach. Kitran slowed down when they reached the first building, and Methusal intensified her kaavl to listen for Zindedis. Rain spattered on rooftops and on the pebbled ground. Up ahead she heard voices. But right where they were was silent. And she saw no signs of movement.

Kitran peered into the nearest shack's window and Methusal did the same. Ryon's unreliable light illuminated a dark shack filled with men lying on bunk beds or on the floor. It appeared that they were sleeping, although it wasn't very late yet. At last twenty men slept in the one hut. Methusal counted twelve shacks, just in this row. Maybe soldiers lived in all of the shacks on Quasr's perimeter. And she guessed that more Zindedis lived in the heart of town and in the Quasr Chief's compound, too.

Methusal uneasily wondered how many invaders occupied Quasr. Certainly more than the two-hundred fifty troops their own war party had managed to muster.

She and Kitran sidled forward. Noise came from the next shack and light streamed from the window. She counted eighteen men inside. Some played cards. Others arm wrestled. Shouts of laughter punctuated the night.

Good thing it was raining. Hopefully the men would stay indoors. She momentarily wondered why some men were sleeping, and others awake. The answer came quickly. they probably took shifts at soldier duty, so regiments were ready around the clock.

At the edge of the next hut Kitran paused and looked around the corner. He held up two fingers. Two soldiers. He looked again, and then silently slipped across the alley to the next shack.

Methusal's turn. Her quick glance spotted a cloaked guard hunched against the wall. His black hood was pulled low over his face. He didn't seem to be worried about an attack. But surely the Zindedis knew the Koblani war team was coming.

Kitran swiftly made his way to the beach. Strung out along the shoreline were shacks fronted by tables and chairs. Some shacks sported large, boarded up windows. Were they shops? Places to eat? Maybe Quasrians had spent their free time here before the invasion.

A beaten pathway linked the shacks, and short sets of stairs led down to the beach. A narrow dock poked into the harbor, and several small boats bobbed next to it. Out in the bay the intermittent green light of Ryon illuminated thirteen ships.

Kitran grunted, "Five are Quasrian fishing boats. The other eight are Zindedi warships. But look." He pointed. "Another one is coming."

A bright circle of light rose and dipped above the black surface of the water. It was too dark to estimate how far away it might be, but it appeared to be large, and was coming closer.

Another ship filled with Zindedi soldiers? No wonder the Zindedis didn't seem worried about the Koblani war team.

"Come on." Kitran slipped left, down an empty street leading toward the heart of town. Following swiftly, Methusal scanned the little she could in the gloom. Here the acrid smell of smoke permeated the damp air. Half of the buildings had burned to the ground. The other half were scorched.

The only untouched structure on the street was a large building with no windows visible from the street, and only one door. Four soldiers huddled in the rain outside the front door, death-sticks held at the ready.

Across the street, Methusal and Kitran crouched behind a pile of blackened, broken beams. "What do you think is in there?" she whispered. "Weapons?"

"Or food. Or supplies."

"I haven't seen any Quasrians. Where are they?"

"Probably under curfew."

Under house arrest, in other words. The Zindedis didn't want the Quasrians meeting in the middle of the night to plot an uprising.

"The invaders will probably shoot on sight," Kitran muttered. "We'll need to be careful."

Moving in a zigzag pattern around burnt buildings, he led the way through Quasr. Pairs of Zindedi invaders patrolled the streets, but they were easy to skirt around.

On the southern edge of town they encountered a large group of soldiers and a number of sprawling tents. Methusal hid in the shadow of a building and counted the number of men marching in the rain. Easily fifty. And more were probably sleeping in the tents. Here were the soldiers she'd been anticipating.

"Come on." Kitran melted into the shadows, heading back north, toward the beach, and she hurried after him. Before he'd gone far however, he ducked into a gutted shack on the west side of the street. He crouched down and peered north. Methusal followed his line of sight and gasped.

A towering white wall, three lengths high, and at least fifty lengths long, stretched down the street. A gigantic gate constructed of vertical bars bisected it, and soldiers patrolled before it. Through the gate's bars, Methusal glimpsed a paved walkway and lush plants. If they crept closer, she could see more, but a quick glance proved why Kitran had stopped here. The buildings directly across from the structure had been burned to the ground.

Kitran slipped west a block, and then headed back toward the beach.

"What was that place?" she whispered when they again crouched in the shadows of the shacks lining the beach.

"The Chief's compound. The General's compound, now."

Methusal's heart beat faster. Deccia! Her sister was inside that compound. The impressions from her dreams all pointed to Deccia being held in an underground prison beneath a large complex. A complex the General inhabited. It had to be the compound they'd just seen. Excitement overwhelmed her. She clutched Kitran's shoulder. "We have to go back!"

Kitran's black eyes gleamed in the darkness. "Our mission is to watch the beach."

"Then why have we been spying all through town?"

"I wanted to see for myself what's going on." So Kitran had decided to flaunt Mentàll's orders.

"Deccia's in that compound. We have to go back."

"How do you know?"

"I've had dreams..." She realized how silly that would sound to a logical man like Kitran. "I *know* she's in there. I'm going back."

"No, you're not."

"Why not? Why can you scout wherever you want, but I can't? This is my sister's *life* we're talking about!"

"We need more intelligence. We can't just break in."

"Right! So let's get more information."

"Another time. The ship has anchored. We need to watch it."

So near to Deccia, and yet so far. Frustrated, Methusal struggled to think of a way to change Kitran's mind.

The crunch of boots on wet pebbles took her by surprise. Soldiers. Only four lengths away. She'd slipped out of kaavl because she'd forgotten the mission and had been worrying about her sister. Constant kaavl concentration had always been a challenge for her, but it was something she must overcome if she wanted to stay alive during this war.

Chagrinned, she touched Kitran's arm in warning. They couldn't move, because the soldiers were too close. Any movement would capture their enemies' attention, and unfortunately several clouds had moved and Ryon's green light shone clear and bright right now. Even worse, one of the men carried a lantern.

Methusal hunched over, hoping her cloak would look like a sack of grain, or maybe a lumpy bush. The bright light of the lantern licked toward her feet, and she bit down hard on her lip, fighting her instinct to flee.

△ △ △ △ △

Hendra knew Mentàll had sent her to this far, western edge of Quasr in order to keep her safe. Frustration simmered as she brushed aside tall, wet stalks of lynnte weed, following fast after Behran. What Zindedi secrets would they discover in these damp farmlands? None, of course. She'd come to war to *help*. If Mentàll refused to let her scout in Quasr, why had he let her come at all?

It also disturbed her that Mentàll had sent her on this mission with Behran purely to upset Methusal. Hendra had seen the satisfaction in his small smile when Methusal had sent a backward look at Behran when they'd struck camp. Although Methusal would never say it, it bothered her a little that Hendra and Behran would scout together. Equally clear, Mentàll relished her discomfort.

Hendra negotiated clumps of soggy weeds, and scanned the terrain for wild beasts. She'd seen the way her cousin baited Methusal, and the subtle, yet purposeful ways he sought to pierce her heart and make it bleed out pain.

Hendra hated seeing that side of her cousin once more. The last time had been two and a half years ago—again, to Methusal. He hated her, plain enough. But why? Just because she had humiliated him in the past?

But it had started well before then.

Hendra slogged after Behran through the wet, dark night. Maybe she should try to talk to Mentàll. Maybe she could convince him to stop.

At the very least, she could set Methusal's mind at ease. She would never steal her boyfriend. Methusal didn't know that. After all, Hendra was a Dehrien, and Rolbanis had distrusted Dehriens for over two hundred years. Worse, she was Mentàll's cousin. And Mentàll had certainly given Methusal plenty of reasons to hate and distrust him.

Methusal didn't know that Hendra could never have a close relationship with any man—even Behran, the man she trusted more than any other. The very thought made her tremble with fear. *Never.* Never.

Hendra blinked back tears of self-disgust. Again, she despised herself for remaining a prisoner of the fear. She hated it. *Hated it!* She'd give anything to be a normal girl, and live an ordinary life.

But to become free, first she had to face her fears and conquer them.

Frustration surged, because tonight she'd neither fight nor win any victories. Not out here in these safe, desolate farmlands.

When she returned to camp, she would demand that Mentàll give her a more dangerous assignment next time.

△ △ △ △ △

Methusal froze when the light shone a finger's breadth from her foot. She barely dared to breathe as the soldiers' footsteps crunched closer. Surely the Zindedis would see them. How could they not? Even without the lantern, Ryon shone right down on them. Kitran and she were in full view.

Her panicked mind wondered what to do if they were caught. Fight? Let them drag her to prison? Maybe to the dungeon where they held Deccia.

The boot steps squelched by.

Kitran and Methusal crept to the edge of the shack so they could see the beach more clearly. The soldiers—twelve of them—stopped short of the lick of the tide. One held the lantern high and waved it. After a moment the light on the ship blinked, as if someone passed a black cloth before it. A code?

The hiss of fresh rain on sand filled Methusal's ears, but she struggled to compartmentalize it and focus only upon the soldiers.

The ship's light shone clear and steady now. A soldier on the beach passed a dark cloth over their lantern, clearly responding to the first message from the ship.

"What are they saying?" Kitran muttered in frustration.

"I don't know. Wait."

The ship's light blinked again, and then went dark.

The soldiers on the beach headed back the way they had come. Methusal and Kitran flattened themselves against the shack's wall, and then sidled around to the beach side once the soldiers had cleared that area.

Soldiers' mutters now reached her ears.

"Tomorrow morning?"

"We'll unload the powder and ammunition then. Hope this blasted rain stops."

A chuckle. "A little wet powder won't stop us. Those Koblanis haven't tasted real fear yet. I can't wait to blow up the whole continent."

"When will the other ships arrive?"

"In a few days. They'll head south. We'll take Koblan like a tidal wave." Laughter rasped. "What'll you do with your share of the ore, Commander?"

"Buy me a nice piece of land in the Carachki hills."

"Right up there with the Presidente?"

More laughter.

"You have grand plans, Commander."

"I've in mind to become a General. If the position opens up, of course."

Subdued laughter followed that statement.

"Kill that Dehrien, Mentàll, and you'll move up to Chief Commander. And get plenty of coin, too. The General wants him dead. Today he screamed that he wants to see him rot in the sun."

"Didn't Oric kill him?"

"He went back to find the body. It's gone."

Another said, "Challenge the General head to head, Commander, and you'll move up quick enough."

Laughter rumbled. "No! I want to rest at leisure the rest of my days. My woman complains of the smell of blood. She's threatened to throw me out, right along with the wash."

The men's chuckles faded into the drizzly night.

Methusal's legs felt like gelatin. They'd almost been discovered. And Mentàll...the General obviously wanted him dead. Even more interesting, his vendetta against him sounded personal.

"Mentàll has a bounty on his head," Kitran said grimly. "Wonder how he earned that."

"Well, we know he's on our side, at least."

"He's a liability. Nice he warned us the Zindedis are after him. Anyone who scouts with him will be sentenced to death, too."

"He's scouting alone."

"Doesn't matter. If anyone sees him, they'll know Koblanis are near. Mentàll had better stay out of Quasr, period. Come on," he ordered. "We found our information. Time to head back to camp."

It wasn't anywhere near dawn, which was when Mentàll had told them to return.

"What about Deccia? We still have time..."

"No." Kitran's abrupt tone put an end to the subject.

Although Methusal wasn't happy, she didn't argue. At least now she knew where Deccia was being held. The next step would be to formulate a plan to rescue her. And, in truth, she was ready to leave Quasr. She'd experienced enough close encounters with the enemy for one night.

She followed Kitran east into the black night, and they quickly left behind the lights and danger of Quasr.

A few stars shone overhead now, and the light of Ryon revealed thick clouds scudding toward the Quasr Mountains.

Although it was only lightly sprinkling at the moment, it felt colder than it had earlier—maybe because her water-soaked pants and moccasins clung to her skin. She especially hated the feel of the cold mud sliding between her toes.

Kitran increased his speed to a jog, and she matched his pace. She couldn't wait to put on dry clothes, roll up in her coverlet, and fall asleep.

Husky pants tickled her ears.

"Kitran! Run!" She catapulted into a sprint. In her relief to escape Quasr, she'd forgotten about the wild beasts. At least she hadn't completely relaxed her kaavl. But she should have heard them long before this; another reminder that she needed to work on her concentration.

Methusal sharpened her senses. A pack of wild beasts, at least eight strong, had caught their scent. Their flying paws gouged the wet earth, spraying out clods of mud. She whipped out her knife and kaavl stick and ran like the wind.

The panting beasts growled. One licked its slobbery chops.

"Kitran!" she gasped.

He veered for the rocks jumbled together at the base of the Quasr Mountains. A cave! If only they could find one, they could fight the beasts head on, without worrying about them circling behind and trapping them.

Ryon slid behind a cloud. Now she could only make out shadowed details of the foothills. Caves? Or black boulders?

Methusal flew over the rocky, muddy plain, sharply aware of each stone, each puddle, each hole beneath her feet. Overhead, Ryon shone bright and clear again. And then she saw it. A tiny opening, just beyond the next great boulder.

"Kitran, there!" she gasped, pointing.

"I see it."

To her kaavl intensified senses, the hot, putrid breaths of the wild beasts seemed to singe Methusal's neck. But two lengths still separated them from the ferocious animals.

One wild beast clicked its jaws, and the scrabbling claws flew faster. Methusal had seen wild beasts chase down a wolmite before. The wild beasts, which normally ran upright like a man, stretched to run flat out, loping with their longer back legs. Their shorter front legs enabled them to hop, which lengthened their stride. There was no time to warn Kitran. No time to do anything except gasp for each burning breath and hurtle toward the shadow.

Kitran made it around the boulder first. Methusal slammed into him. Despair choked her. No cave!

Then she spied a narrow passage one length south, between two rocks. "Come on!" She slithered between the cliff and a monstrous boulder. Hard rock squeezed into her ribs, and she hoped Kitran could make it through. The passage opened up a little after that, and a quick glance proved Kitran had forced his thick-chested body through the narrow opening.

Would the wild beast be able to wiggle in, too? Would she and Kitran be safe, or trapped in this slim crevice, fighting for their lives?

Methusal stopped where the cliff and the huge boulder met. A dead end. "We're trapped!" Overhead, a wild beast howled. More scrambled up onto the rocks. Would they jump into their narrow pit and rip them limb from limb?

"Now what?" she whispered.

"*Shh.*" Kitran retraced his steps.

A scratching, snarling beast had clawed halfway through the narrow opening. Knife clenched in his fist, Kitran lunged forward. And then the moon swam behind a cloud, trapping them in pitch blackness.

Snorts snuffled, and something screamed in pain. Breathless with horror, she whispered, "Kitran?"

Her heart pounded faster. She clenched her knife tighter. *Please, The One. Protect Kitran.*

She heard the awful sound of ripping flesh. "Kitran," she cried out.

"I'm here." Her instructor appeared at her side. She smelled blood.

"Are you hurt?"

"I killed a beast. They're feeding on it now."

"They're *eating* one of their own?"

"That's what wild beasts do. They devour the weak and the helpless."

She hugged her arms tight around herself, trying to stop her teeth from chattering. No more claws scrabbled overhead. Probably those beasts had jumped down to dine on their companion, too.

"Stay still," Kitran whispered. "They don't have good memories. Maybe they'll forget us."

Methusal didn't need further urging. She was too scared to do anything but shiver in silence. She tried to shut out the sounds of sinew ripping from bone, and the slobbering, snapping snarls as the beasts fought for the choice bits. Moisture rolled down her cheeks, and she realized she was crying. Her nose dripped, but she didn't dare sniff. She silently wiped it with her sleeve.

Kitran put a heavy arm around her shoulders and pulled her close. He'd never offered a personal, comforting gesture to her before. He'd always seemed so remote—the idolized and respected instructor. Now, during the war, she was learning that he was human, too. His hot fury at Mentàll, and comfort for her. It made her like him even more.

The sounds of the beasts faded.

"We'll stay here until dawn," Kitran muttered.

Methusal didn't argue. They sat in the narrow gorge on the gravelly earth, backs against the stone wall, with their knees bent. Methusal fell asleep with her head on Kitran's shoulder.

Chapter Ten

METHUSAL WOKE UP when Kitran moved. Pale sunlight shone overhead, but shadows still filled their protected crevice. She shivered in the cold.

"We need to go." Kitran slowly clambered to his feet.

Methusal felt just as stiff as her instructor looked. Pins and needles tingled as she stood. She squeezed through the narrow passage after him, and onto the sunlit plain. Yards from the crevice entrance lay the mangled, skeletal remains of the wild beast. Methusal shuddered, because she realized those polished bones could have been their own.

Even in the sun, the morning felt cold. The first crisp taste of winter had arrived.

Kitran set a fast pace for kaavl camp. When they arrived, Methusal spotted Timaeus and Dastn talking to the Dehrien Chief. The two men would run their information to the war teams.

"Kitran," the Dehrien Chief said, as they approached. It didn't pass Methusal's notice that he ignored her utterly. Just to her liking. If only she could always be so lucky. "We have been waiting for you."

"We were attacked by wild beasts." With clipped words, Kitran outlined the information they'd uncovered last night, including the report of more Zindedi ships sailing south, and the ammunition arriving in Quasr this morning. He made no effort to hide the fact that they'd spied all over town.

To Timaeus, Mentàll said, "Tell Pan the ammunition is ripe for the plucking. But they'll need to attack the beach fast. Surprise will be their best weapon. Also tell them that we estimate there are seven hundred Zindedis in Quasr." A few more words, and the runners sprinted up into the hills, where the war teams waited close by.

Seven hundred Zindedis! It was worse than Methusal had imagined. Quasr was the size of Tarst, which held about two hundred men. How many Quasrian men had survived the initial invasion? Even if all had survived, which was unlikely, how could their small army Koblanis and the Quasrians ever defeat so many invaders?

The Dehrien Chief finished speaking to Kitran. Out of the corner of her eye she spotted Behran washing his face in the stream. Hendra was nowhere to be seen.

Eagerly, Methusal slipped toward Behran.

"Methusal." That hated, familiar voice stopped her. "Are you forgetting your duties?"

"What du... Oh." The small smile curling his lips made her frown. Clearly, his opportunity to torture her had arrived. Time to clean his wound. She had managed to escape that pleasure last night, thanks to the rain and the mission.

"Of course," she said evenly.

The Dehrien Chief turned back to Kitran. "You have retrieved valuable information. You did a good job."

Uncertainty flickered over her kaavl instructor's face.

"However," Mentàll continued, "you did not follow instructions. You were assigned to one area in Quasr, and you left your post early. If you had remained, you would not have been attacked by the wild beasts."

"We trekked to Quasr in the dark. We could have been attacked then," Kitran stated. "Don't talk to me about wild beasts."

"You are a valuable team member, Kitran." Mentàll's gaze looked like blue ice. "I would hate to lose you."

"Is that a threat?"

"The kaavl team must work as one. In order to achieve our goals, each member must scout where I say to scout."

"Do you think you know everything?" Kitran's lip curled. "I grew up in that town. If you want to be efficient, you should ask *me* for advice."

"I know Quasr well. But you are right. I would like to confer with you on a few issues."

Disbelief flickered across Kitran's dark face. "You belittled my kaavl a few hours ago. Now you're asking for my help?"

"I cannot allow insubordination, Kitran. You, of all people, should understand that. Do not challenge my authority again." A short silence elapsed. "If you agree, I would be happy to hear your views on infiltrating Quasr."

"You mean that in your arrogance, you've finally realized you need my help. You can't do it alone."

The Dehrien's stare became glacial. "Do not make this difficult, Kitran. I am offering a flag of peace."

"You mean you won't humble yourself or admit you need my help. But you expect *me* to humble myself to you. Is that it?"

"Your answer is no?"

"I will give my opinion," Kitran gritted. "But I will be surprised if you actually listen."

"Meet me after the meal, and we will discuss strategy."

The Dehrien clearly wanted Kitran's opinion. Methusal was surprised. Was he admitting that he respected Kitran? Or did he truly need help? Somehow, she doubted the latter. She followed her kaavl instructor and murmured, "That's progress, don't you think?"

"We'll see what happens. He uses people. He'll pick my brain, and that'll be it. That wild beast will never share power."

Methusal slowed down and allowed Kitran to go on without her. She did agree that the Dehrien would never share power with Kitran. And he probably did want to use Kitran's knowledge. But still, asking Kitran for help must have cost him a little of his enormous pride. Certainly, a move she'd never seen him make before. Either he really needed help, or—he couldn't possibly regret his earlier, condescending words to Kitran, could he?

No. Mentàll certainly didn't regret any of his awful words to *her*. Regret surely couldn't live in a man like him.

"Methusal." The Chief of Dehre reclaimed her attention. "You forget your duties so quickly?"

Methusal pressed her lips together, but did not respond to the subtle dig. "I'm ready."

"Follow me." The Dehrien moved eastward, down the stream past Behran, and even past the turn in the creek where more rocky jumbles hid the temporary camp from view. Methusal felt more uneasy with each stride that took her further from camp. Her steps slowed.

"Where are you going?"

"Afraid?" he mocked. The Dehrien stopped beside a medium-sized boulder and stripped off his tunic.

Two steps still separated them, but Methusal chose not to close the distance. "Why did you drag me so far from camp?"

"You fear for your reputation?" Nastiness glinted in the pale gaze.

"Answer my *question*."

"I like privacy. Others do not need to know the severity of my injury."

"You don't want to appear weak."

"I am not weak." His gaze held hers, threatening her. Challenging her. "Am I, Methusal?" She did not answer. "Tend my wound." Again, the imperial command.

With gritted teeth, she finished the distance between them and pulled the necessary medical supplies from her pouch. A glance at his broad back proved that wilted green tacky leaves were still adhered to his skin like a bandage. That was a good sign. The wound had remained protected during the last twenty-four hours.

She did not want to touch him. Everything within her urged her to run from him right now.

The Dehrien's large hand unexpectedly whipped out and caught her wrist. He pulled her closer with a jerk. Those ice blue eyes were much too close. Fear spiraled, but she swallowed it back.

"You fear me," he hissed. "Will you admit it now, Methusal?"

Never. Because that was exactly what he wanted.

She glared. "You may be a wild beast, but I do not fear you."

"Prove it, then. Now." He released her.

Freed, Methusal trembled with reaction and delayed fury. "Don't *touch* me again. Or you'll tend the wound yourself."

His fingers curled around her wrist again, but they were deceptively loose this time. "Do you truly want to threaten me, Methusal?"

"Stop *touching* me!" With a quick kaavl move, she freed herself, but her heart pounded. Fear—she hated it—slithered through her like a whip.

"Then prove your bravery. Stop procrastinating." He sounded so cool and reasonable, and yet still he baited her. He relished making her squirm.

Abruptly, Methusal stepped behind him. She'd tend his wound all right. She ripped the first tacky leaf from his back, and then the next. His muscles flinched. Blood oozed from the wound as the red crusted leaves fluttered to the pebbled earth.

Methusal felt sickened by her actions.

His wound must burn like fire after the treatment she'd just given him. But he silently waited for her next ministrations. Expecting more hurt?

The blood trickled down his back, toward his breeches.

Would she treat an injured apte like this? Never.

Biting her lip hard, she carefully removed the remaining leaves. Then she broke open a coltac leaf and dribbled on the juice. Tears of self-condemnation stung her eyes as she rubbed in the healing gel with a firm, kneading precision, like Doc had ordered. Surely that must hurt, too.

Then she pulled out new tacky leaves and adhered them to the wound.

"Finished," she said shortly. Heaving a breath, she whirled and strode away. Tears slipped down her cheeks. She'd just behaved like Mentàll. She had inflicted pain on him. And she hated herself for it.

△ △ △ △ △

Hendra had just finished washing her face in the stream when she saw Methusal hurrying toward her, heading back toward camp. She'd seen Mentàll lure her friend back among the rocks, and guessed it was because he needed the Rolbani girl to change his bandages. At the time, Hendra had wondered if she should intervene. He had promised not to hurt her, and in her heart, Hendra couldn't believe he ever would.

The Rolbani girl came closer. "Methusal?" With alarm, she noticed the tears streaming down her friend's face. She hurried over. "What's wrong? What did Mentàll do to you?"

The Rolbani girl gave a poor smile and wiped at the tears. "Nothing, Hendra. Don't worry." She looked ahead, her gaze scanning camp, clearly searching for someone.

"Behran's at the fire," Hendra said softly.

"Thanks."

With a frown, Hendra looked in the direction where Methusal had come from, and where her cousin still remained. Much as she both dreaded and feared the confrontation to come, it was time to talk to him.

She intersected Mentàll's path when he walked back toward camp.

"Hendra." He didn't look surprised to see her. In fact, she read nothing in his expression. A normal occurrence.

"How is your wound?" Cautiously, she circled around to her subject.

"It is healing." He continued on, so she was forced to walk beside him.

"Methusal tended it?"

He did not answer.

Hendra gathered up her courage. "She was upset. What happened?"

"It is none of your concern."

"You're my cousin, and she's my friend. It hurts to know that you're treating her wrong."

Mentàll stopped. His icy gaze flayed straight through her. Hendra trembled and swallowed back a surge of fear. This man had never harmed her, and she knew—she believed—he never would.

To her shock, he snarled, "Methusal deserves everything she gets. It is her fault Dehre has suffered over these last three years. It is her fault our people died."

Hendra dared to say, "It's her fault she defended her community?"

Her cousin's freezing look scared her. Nonetheless, she said, "You've always hated Rolban, haven't you? Is that why you hate Methusal, too?"

"Methusal has earned her own fate. But yes, little cousin, if you must know, she embodies everything I despise about Rolban. She is arrogant and cares for no one but herself."

Hendra frowned. "Mentàll..."

"Do not talk to me about Methusal," he gritted. "I will *not hear it.*"

Holding tight onto her courage, she said, "Treat her right, Mentàll. You'll come to regret it you if you don't." Why did she feel so certain about this?

Silkily, he said, "She possesses the man you want. Why are you defending her?"

Hendra flushed. "I don't want Behran."

"I see things, little cousin." He let that sink in. "And do not tell me how I should behave. I know how to handle Methusal Maahr. I am accomplishing exactly the goal I desire."

Although his chilly look forbade further comments, Hendra said, "You're wrong about her. I hope you figure that out before it's too late." She decided not to argue about her scouting assignment right now. She turned away, but her cousin's voice made her pause.

Softly, he said, "I am proud of you, little cousin. You stood up to me and spoke your mind. Remember, however, that I am your leader. Your Chief, too."

"I understand." He did not want her to defy his authority in camp. But he would hear her words now, because he cared about her, in his own way. Whether he'd consider those words remained to be seen.

Hendra grabbed her pack and left her stiff-necked cousin alone. Or maybe ice-encased would be a better description. Not for the first time, she wondered about the similarities between Mentàll and herself. Did ice freeze his heart, too? Sometimes she felt like she was frozen from the inside out. Of course it was a defense mechanism that shielded her from pain.

Hendra thought about her cousin, and with intuition gently probed the coldness that always permeated him. When she combined the little she intuitively sensed with all of the facts she knew about him, she realized something new. His ice just might be the opposite of hers—thick on the outside. But did it freeze his heart, too? Or did it encase it, protecting it, so nothing and no one would ever hurt him again?

She still wanted to believe—perhaps blindly—that deep down, he was still the same sensitive boy she remembered from childhood. And also the man who had rescued her that awful afternoon, so long ago. Hendra shuddered, and shut her mind to those images. She wouldn't think of that time, ever again.

Maybe Mentàll wasn't that person any longer. Her father had permanently corrupted her brothers. Perhaps he had twisted that same lasting, cruel impression into Mentàll's soul, too.

△ △ △ △ △

Mentàll sent two Dehrien kaavl teams to spy on Quasr late that morning.

After talking to Behran and eating dried rations for breakfast, Methusal felt a little better. Her conscience still bothered her, but she didn't want to think about the Dehrien leader—a difficult thing to do when Mentàll called a meeting when one of the teams returned.

"We are fighting the Zindedis on the east side of town. Our war team is also fighting to steal the ammunition that has arrived on the beach from the new ship."

The Chief of Dehre glanced about, making sure he held everyone's attention. "The Zindedis are on full alert. From now on, every scouting mission will be dangerous. Jascr and Wortn just returned. They reported that the Quasrians may walk through town during the day if they wear brown cloaks, which identify them as Quasrians. We will do the same."

Kitran spoke. "We'll scout during the day now?"

"Yes. Then we will not need to fight the wild beasts at night."

"Won't the Zindedis see us?" young Taltn asked.

"They will think we are Quasrians."

"All except for you," Kitran countered. "They'll recognize you, won't they? Because you have a bounty on your head."

The Dehrien Chief said nothing, but his expression became glacial.

Jascr swaggered forward. "We Dehriens leave an impression." He spit on the ground. "Leave your mark, if you can, Rolbani. Then we'll listen to your bleats."

Kitran shoved forward. "Arrogant fool. You sent this preening pup to Quasr, Mentàll. What if he's caught the General's attention, too?"

A snarl contorted Jascr's mouth and he raised his fists. Wortn, a short, broad man with thinning, dirty blond hair appeared at his side. Methusal remembered his name because he'd beaten her in the Dehrien Kaavl Games two and a half years ago.

"Looks like someone is itching for a fight," Jascr sneered. He rammed a finger into Kitran's chest. "Step up, Rolbani. Prove you're a man."

Methusal wanted to roll her eyes at the male posturing. A pained expression crossed Hendra's face.

"You're proving your lack of self-discipline." Disgust curled Kitran's lips. "Tell me, Mentàll. Why are they on the team?"

"Jascr. Wortn," Mentàll said harshly. "Step back."

With a final chin jut, Jascr swaggered over to Mentàll's side. During the confrontation, all of the Dehriens had lined with Mentàll. The Rolbanis and Tarst faced them; all except for Hendra and Goric, who had switched sides. Goric sidled closer to Jascr, as if wanting to be associated with that boastful cretin.

"Tomorrow, all teams will leave camp at dawn," Mentàll said. "You will keep the same partners you had last night. I will give each team their assignment later."

"What will we do today?" Kitran said. "We're wasting time. We should be scouting around the clock. The war parties need up-to-date information. Why are we twiddling our thumbs at camp, Dehrien?"

"I need scout teams this afternoon. Are you volunteering, Kitran?"

"Of course."

"I'll go again, too," Jascr asserted.

Goric shoved his way to the front. "So will I."

Mentàll scanned the group. "Any other volunteers?"

Both Methusal and Hendra raised their hands. Mentàll's gaze rested on them, but moved on.

"I'll go," Behran volunteered.

"Good. Kitran, Behran, Jascr, and Goric. I'll give you assignments. Everyone else is dismissed."

Methusal did not like being ignored or dismissed. Even worse, she'd heard no mention of rescuing her sister.

"I don't think Mentàll will ever give me a good assignment." Beside her, Hendra sounded frustrated.

"Why not?"

"He wants to protect me. But I came here to help win the war!"

Maybe Mentàll intended to protect Hendra, but Methusal knew that wasn't why he'd passed her over for the scout teams. "Let's find out what their assignments are," she proposed.

The two waylaid Kitran, and Methusal asked, "Will you be gathering information about the General's compound?"

"No. I'll make contact with old friends."

Jascr and Goric brushed by. "What are they going to do?" Hendra asked.

"I don't know." Kitran headed for Behran.

Frustrated, Methusal called after him, "Did Mentàll mention rescuing Deccia?"

He didn't answer.

"I'm sorry, Thusa," Hendra offered softly. "Maybe tomorrow."

"Tomorrow what?" Jascr had circled back, and Goric followed close on his heels, like a pet apte. Maybe a pet whip would be more appropriate. Jascr slid an arm around Hendra's waist, who visibly blanched. "What are we talking about?"

Hendra twisted free. Face pale, she said, "Step off, Jascr."

He smiled, clearly enjoying her response. "No brotherly affection, sister mine?"

Goric sneered.

"Don't you have an assignment, Jascr?" Methusal said pointedly. "Or maybe you're reluctant to speed to your death with Goric at your side."

Red flushed Goric's face. "I'm at the Tri-level, Methusal. Don't talk down to me."

"Did you earn the Tri-level? Or did Kitran give it to you because he was desperate to find kaavl players for the war team?"

"You little..."

Seeing that he barely matched her height, Methusal suppressed a smile. "Let's see if your kaavl finally matches your boasts."

Goric clenched his fists. "You think you're better than everyone, don't you? Just wait. You'll be the one who's humiliated."

"Prove yourself, then. You know I can beat you with the kaavl stick. If you want more humiliation, I'm ready."

Jascr's black eyes narrowed. They looked like mean pebbles, and sent a splash of sense, like cold water, through her brain. Belatedly, Methusal wished she could take back her foolish, confrontational words. When would she ever learn to watch her mouth?

The Dehrien turned his attention to his sister. His knuckles scraped her jaw. Hendra went very still and closed her eyes, but didn't flinch. "Goodbye, sister mine," he said in a low voice. "I will see you later." He shot Methusal a quick, sly glance...it almost seemed like an afterthought, and yet she knew it was a calculated action. Pure evil lurked in his twisted smile. Without another word, he clapped a hand on Goric's shoulder and the two strolled away.

"I'm sorry," Methusal immediately told Hendra. "I shouldn't have baited Goric."

"I try to ignore Jascr. He gets bored if I don't react." The Dehrien girl looked pale, but remarkably calm.

"I'm sure you're right." Methusal didn't feel very happy with herself. First, she'd mistreated Mentàll's injury, and now she'd attacked Goric. "I don't know if I'll ever learn," she said with regret. "I used to mouth off all the time, and made all kinds of enemies. I thought I was past that."

"No one's perfect. And remember you're making friends, too." Hendra waved at Taltn, who offered them both a big grin.

Methusal smiled back. "Thanks, Hendra." Maybe she had taken several steps backward today. But overall, maybe she was growing in the right direction. "I'll take your advice. From now on, I'll ignore Goric."

Δ Δ Δ Δ

An hour later, Methusal wondered what she was supposed to do at camp. She wanted to be scouting the General's compound and searching for a way to rescue Deccia.

Everyone but Hendra had disappeared. Methusal had already washed out her dirty moccasins, and currently wore her other pair. She'd washed her face and hands and feet. Now she wandered around the deserted camp.

It was odd, but she had the strangest feeling that someone was watching her. But when she intensified into kaavl, she heard nothing. She tried to ignore the unsettled feeling.

A short distance away, Hendra sat against a large boulder, writing on bound parchment leaves. Maybe a diary. The remaining men had vanished into the hills, knives at the ready to slay some unwary beast.

Mentàll had disappeared, too. Where? What nefarious plots was he working on now? Maybe he was figuring out how to infiltrate Quasr or how to seize that prize he'd talked about the other night—the prize the Prophet had promised would soon come within his grasp. Methusal wondered what it could be. And she wondered again why Mentàll had been meeting with the Quasrian Chief before he was killed.

She glanced around camp. Only Hendra, deep in thought, was in sight. Mentàll's pack lay just over there, partially hidden behind that rock. What if she wandered over and accidentally kicked it open? What might she find inside?

Heart thumping faster, Methusal strolled over and perched on the boulder. She pulled off her moccasin and pretended to shake out a pebble. She glanced at Hendra. The Dehrien girl seemed lost in her own world.

Good. Methusal sharpened her hearing and listened for the returning men. Nothing. All was quiet. Overhead the sky was a bright blue, and the sun felt warm. The beautiful day felt like the perfect benediction for her underhanded plot. If she couldn't spy in Quasr, then she'd spy on her own enemy instead.

Methusal tugged at the string securing Mentàll's pack shut. He'd tied it in a tight double knot. She took careful note of what the knot looked like, because she'd need to put everything back exactly the way she'd found it. Two years ago she had searched Mentàll's tent in Dehre. At the time she had noticed that he kept everything neatly organized. He paid attention to details. He would notice if something was out of place.

She worked at the tight leather knot for a good minute, while at the same time keeping her senses tuned into kaavl. Hendra's quill continued to scratch on the parchment.

Finally, the knot loosened. One of her nails was jagged by now. Quickly, she pulled open the pack. She had to be fast, before Hendra noticed what she was doing, or before any of the men—especially Mentàll—returned to camp.

Bleached leather tunics lay on top, and breeches lay beneath them. A thick bag of rations came next, an extra water skin, and then three sharp knives. The edge of one caught on her skin and caused a thin line of blood to bubble up. The knife blade was honed to kill. She shivered and carefully searched a little faster.

Methusal found personal items, soap, and then finally, at the bottom, a small leather book and a sheaf of parchments. The book was a copy of the *First Book of Kaavl*, which was written by Mahre, her ancestor—the greatest Kaavl Master who had ever lived. Legend said he'd written a *Second Book of Kaavl*, but it had disappeared two hundred years ago during the Great War. Dehriens had stolen it from Methusal's ancestor, Jotham, while he was their captive for several weeks. Legend also said that Jotham had scratched the location of the missing book on the back of his tablet necklace.

Methusal hadn't learned this legend until the Dehrien Chief had stolen her tablet necklace from her two years ago. After examining the tablet, he and the traitor Verdnt had thought they'd figured out the location of the book—Rolban.

They had been wrong. The book was not in Rolban. And the two peaks and the barely legible scratched letters which ended in the letter "R" did not stand for Rolban. No one knew where it was hidden. That truth had died when the Dehriens had killed Jotham.

Methusal wasn't surprised that the Dehrien Kaavl Master was carrying a copy of Mahre's first book. But what about the parchments? What were they? Carefully, she lifted them out.

They were letters, she quickly discovered; letters to Quasr and Aestoff, and letters from their chiefs to Mentàll. She swiftly scanned them. They seemed cordial, and even friendly. Trading bargains were agreed to: pots of wild beast oil for a barrel of dried fish, and Dehrien baskets for coastal fruits. Benign enough documents. And yet Methusal knew Mentàll well enough to realize that far more lay behind the seemingly innocuous letters. The Dehrien was laying the foundation for friendship—as he had with Rolban two and a half years ago. He was possibly constructing the foundation for another Alliance.

Rustling tickled Methusal's ears, and she hastily shoved the parchments back where they belonged. The noises became louder. Men scuffed closer, laughing loudly. They were still some distance away, but she didn't have much time. The hunters had made a good kill, from the sound of it.

Fingers shaking now, she quickly straightened Mentàll's clothing and hastily knotted the bag again. A double knot, she remembered just in time.

Trying to look nonchalant, she rose to her feet and wandered toward Hendra, who still wrote furiously in her book. "I'm going to scout for berries," she said. "I'll be back soon."

"Okay," Hendra mumbled.

Quickly, Methusal escaped from camp. Her heart beat rapidly. Thank goodness no one had seen her. No one would ever know that she had rifled through the Chief of Dehre's bag.

The sounds of the returning men grew louder. Taltn scampered ahead of them.

"Thusa," he cried out. "They killed a wild beast. We'll have fresh meat tonight!"

"Wonderful." She stood beside Taltn as the men came into view. Four carried the great beast. Its fur looked gray and matted, and foam still dripped from its razor teeth. "Yum," she mumbled.

The men, mostly Dehriens, grinned at her as they marched by. An unusual occurrence. She smiled back, and tried to look approving and enthusiastic about their kill. They jogged down the hill to camp.

"Where are you going, Thusa?" the Tarst boy wanted to know.

"I thought I'd look for berries or logne leaves."

"Where's your bag?"

Methusal hadn't thought that far ahead. "Um. I guess I forgot."

"I have one," Taltn said. "Can I come with you?"

"Sure. Come on."

Following the stream, they hiked into the gray hills. From experience she knew berry bushes usually hugged creek banks. But they found nothing along the stream. Only thin, scraggly bushes adorned with spiked, gray-green leaves.

Methusal again got the feeling that someone was watching her.

She paused and surveyed the unpromising landscape. No one was in sight—human or beast. And she heard nothing. The hills looked like a barren moonscape. "I guess we're out of luck."

"Hendra scouted the farm lands last night. Let's ask what she saw," Taltn suggested.

Still, that vague feeling of being watched followed her as they trotted downhill to camp. She didn't feel frightened, but wondered if maybe she should.

Back at camp, Taltn asked Hendra what plants she'd found last night.

"Plants?" Her brows lifted. "Why?"

"For food."

"Or medical supplies," Methusal added.

"Of course! Why didn't I think of that? And I thought Mentàll had sent me on a pointless mission. I saw lots of lynnte weed, and some coltac leaves, too, and lots of tagma berries." She frowned a little. "Do you think we should go now? Mentàll hasn't ordered us to go to Quasr today."

"We won't be in Quasr. And we need supplies. You said it wasn't dangerous. What else do we have to do?"

Hendra still didn't look sure. "Well, I..."

"Come on!" Taltn appeared to be eager for a new adventure.

Methusal grabbed her water skin and her cloak to use as a makeshift bag, and the others did the same. Hendra led the long way across the plain to the west side of Quasr. Green and brown mottled fields stretched west of the town.

"Almost nothing has been harvested," Hendra said when they stopped and surveyed the land. No people were in sight. Just bent, wilting stalks. Further to the west loomed huge, prickly tagma bushes. Methusal wasn't sure if they were wild bushes, or planted on purpose.

The sun felt warm on her head as she set to work. She wished she had a bigger cloak. She harvested coltac leaves and lynnte weed, while Taltn scrounged up tagma berries and Hendra scouted for other edible plants. As the time passed, Methusal occasionally caught a flicker of movement through the tall weeds. But when she listened, she heard nothing but the wind.

Their tied up cloaks bulged by the time the sun dipped toward the western horizon.

"We should head back." Hendra's faint frown looked worried.

"Mentàll won't be mad," Methusal encouraged. "We found food." Of course she had no idea how Mentàll would react, but she didn't particularly care, either. They had done a good thing this afternoon. They needed food, and runners could send most of the coltac leaves and lynnte weed to Doc, which would help in the war effort.

Hoisting the heavy bags over their shoulders, they headed back. On the way they nibbled on a few of the delicate green vegetables that Hendra had found. They were pods the size of a small finger, and tasted sweet and delicious.

Once again, more strongly than before, Methusal felt like she was being watched. When they were close to camp, she stopped near a small boulder and told the others to go on. She wanted to figure out who was watching her. Perhaps foolishly, she didn't feel afraid.

Taltn and Hendra disappeared behind kaavl camp's protective rocks. Methusal scanned the horizon again. There! A brownish sliver of movement. A beast of some sort.

Methusal wasn't afraid of animals, except for wild beasts and the occasional whip. This animal was neither. Patiently, she waited.

A faint sound touched her ears. She spotted pointed ears sticking up from behind a boulder to the northwest. A surprising thought hit her. Maybe it was the wolmite whose paw she had fixed up on the way to base camp. Had he followed her all the way here?

It seemed unlikely.

The wolmite slunk around the corner of the boulder. He stopped and watched her with yellow, unblinking eyes.

Methusal smiled and extended her fist. "Come here, boy. How is your paw?" she asked gently.

The wolmite still didn't move. But he watched her carefully. Methusal lowered her hand and waited.

Finally the wolmite walked toward her, head held high, but tail down. He walked with a limp. The bandage on his mangled paw was long gone. Only a chewed leather strip stuck out to one side.

"Is your paw better, boy? Does it hurt?" Of course it still hurt. As the animal drew closer, Methusal saw the bloody stump where the lost toe had been. Dirt was imbedded in it.

It looked awful. Pus bubbled out one side, and her heart twisted. It needed to be tended or the wolmite could die of infection.

The beast stopped a half length away and sat and looked at her. She extended her fist again and he leaned forward to smell it. She whispered, "Let me fix your paw. Come here."

The wolmite moved closer, and to her complete and utter surprise, put his mangled paw on her lap. She was moved by the sweet trust of the gesture. This wild animal trusted her to take care of him. Moving slowly and carefully, she stroked his head. "It'll hurt, boy," she whispered. "Will you be brave?" The beast blinked at her.

"Okay, then." She pulled lynnte weed and coltac leaves from her bundle, and uncorked her water skin. She poured a dribble of water over the lynnte weed, and then rubbed it to make it foam. Gently, she washed the beast's paw. Dirt and rocks fell away, and the wound seeped blood. The pus area was the worst. She felt sure the wolmite would run away, but he didn't. He yipped once, but did not move. Still, he stared at her steadily, as if he was afraid if he blinked, she might disappear. Carefully, she worked at the wound until it was completely clean.

The beast did not cry again. He trusted her. As she gently worked in the disinfectant, healing coltac gel, she thought about how differently she was treating this wolmite than she had treated Mentàll this morning. The Dehrien was wild and unpredictable, just like this wolmite. But certainly no less deserving of kind, considerate care for his wound.

The Prophet's words returned to mind. "Listen, Methusal. Love your enemies. Treat them with kindness."

Guilt again assaulted her. She had behaved exactly like Mentàll had treated her. Mean and cruel. It made her feel sick. And she hadn't treated Goric any better, either.

She didn't want to be that kind of a person.

Maybe Mentàll intended to continue acting like a hateful wild beat, but she didn't have to do the same. She could choose the higher way. The right way.

And she would. From now on.

No matter how the Dehrien treated her, she would obey The One and do the right thing. Because at the end of the day she had to like herself. More than that, she wanted to be a person her parents could be proud of—and Aali, Behran, and the Prophet, too. Hadn't she been taught since childhood that each decision she made shaped her character? Well, from now on, she would choose the right path, no matter how hard it might be.

Methusal sliced off a thin strip of her cloak and tied a bandage around the wolmite's paw. She rubbed his nose. "Now," she said in a low, confidential tone, "don't tear that off. It needs to heal. Do you understand?"

The wolmite stared at her for a moment and then pulled free. After another unblinking look, he limped away. "Good-bye," she called softly, but he didn't look back.

There went one wild animal. Soon she would have to face another. But for once she felt prepared to deal with that particular man. She was ready to conquer his efforts to convince her to hurt him, just like he hurt her.

This time, she would win in the battle of their wills.

△ △ △ △ △

When Methusal returned to camp it was dusk, and growing cool. A new fire had been lit, and the wild beast roasted on a pole above it. Fires could only be lit at night. It was the only time the invaders wouldn't spot the smoke and find kaavl camp. Fortunately, the rocks around camp hid the flames from Quasr, too.

Taltn and Hendra tended the fire. Nearby, Methusal spotted men jostling and shoving one another, ransacking Hendra's sack of green vegetables. Few manners on display there.

"Thusa!" Behran strode toward her, and with a flutter, she again realized how handsome he was. He looked so tall and broad shouldered in his brown leather tunic. His dark blond hair fell carelessly across his tanned forehead.

She smiled and closed the distance between them.

"What have you got in your cloak? Another wild beast?" Behran teased. He tugged it from her shoulder, relieving her of the weight.

"Thanks." In answer to his question, she explained about the medical supplies she had harvested.

"Mentàll should be happy to hear that. Seems like we have a lot of good news this afternoon."

"What do you mean?"

Behran grinned. "The war team captured the whole boatload of ammunition the Zindedis rowed ashore."

"All of it?" Methusal exclaimed.

"The Zindedis didn't see them coming. The first strike team grabbed the supplies and ran for the hills, and the second team fought the Zindedis to cover their retreat. Timaeus was just here. He reported that teams have already transported boxes of powder and death-sticks to a valley near camp."

Methusal could hardly believe this good news. A few more successful missions like that, and the war could be over before they knew it.

"By the way," Behran said, "the Zindedis call the death-sticks 'guns.'"

"Guns." Methusal rolled the unfamiliar word on her tongue. "What will our team do with the guns?"

"Figure out how they work. Maybe practice with them, too."

"At base camp?" Methusal wasn't sure if that would be a good idea. "The Zindedis might hear the shots. It might lead them to camp."

"Pan already thought of that. They'll practice at night, far from camp."

Behran carried her cloak to their protected sleeping area near two large rocks, and there Methusal transferred the supplies into an extra tunic she'd brought. Tying the sleeves together made it into a strong sack. She'd need her cloak tomorrow to scout Quasr. "How was your scouting trip?"

"Dangerous. Zindedis stopped Kitran right after we entered town."

Horrified, she said, "Did they stop you, too?"

"No. I was following him a few steps behind him."

"What happened?"

"While the soldiers talked to him, someone started a disturbance down the street. That got their attention, and Kitran and I ran to the next road. Turns out the Quasrians who started the fight recognized Kitran. They distracted the Zindedis on purpose. A man led us to their meeting house."

"So Kitran met with the people he wanted to today?"

"A few. Not the new Chief of Quasr. He and his family are deep in hiding. The Zindedis killed the Chief's father and mother, and are looking for him now."

"How awful!"

"Chief Calbn M'ntoyan has a lot of friends. With any luck, they'll stay safe."

"So what's next?"

"Kitran set up a meeting with one of his friends for tomorrow. You'll go with him. That man has been spying on the General's compound. He knows all the latest information."

The General's compound! Finally, a step toward rescuing Deccia. Tomorrow she and Kitran would hopefully discover exactly where Deccia was located, and how to infiltrate the compound. "Finally," she breathed.

Behran's deep blue gaze held hers. "We'll rescue her, Thusa. Don't worry."

She smiled, feeling love and gratitude to have this wonderful man in her life. And he loved her! She could barely touch the wonder of it.

"If you're hungry, you might want to grab some of those vegetables. Looks like they're ready to finish them off. That wild beast will take a while to cook."

Methusal followed Behran's gaze. The horde of men clustered around Hendra's cloak had increased. The sack looked nearly empty now. A few pods lay scattered on the ground.

A movement caught her eye. Mentàll strode alone into camp. Now, where had he been this whole time?

Since Methusal knew the Zindedis wanted his head, it seemed safe to assume that Mentàll wasn't plotting with their enemies. That wasn't to say he wasn't working on some unknown plot of his own, designed to benefit only himself.

She remembered the papers she'd found in his bag, and wondered again if he wanted to set up an Alliance with the other communities. She wished she'd had time to look at the book in his pack. Maybe that had contained more information.

She glanced at Behran. "Want me to bring you some pods?"

"I've had some, but thanks."

Methusal moved to the huddle of scavenging men. She didn't really feel like wrestling between their bodies to get to the food. "Excuse me."

Jascr emerged. He smiled and kicked a pod her way. "We've left a few scraps. You can crawl at my feet to fill your belly."

Methusal frowned, but remembered Hendra's sensible words to ignore her brother. Averting her gaze, she spotted an opening between two Dehriens and plunged in. One of the Dehriens was a tall, skinny man with receding black hair, and the other was more muscular, with mud colored hair and eyes. Efron and Tabor. She'd often seen Mentàll talking to them on the march to Quasr. She guessed they were his first and second-in-command in Dehre.

A wild scrabble at the bag secured a handful of pods. She escaped and headed back to Behran.

As she did, she noticed that Mentàll had finished speaking to the men, and now moved toward his pack.

Unease slid through her. And guilt. Would he notice...?

Surreptitiously, she watched him. Mentàll bent over his pack and reached for the knotted cord. His other hand moved forward to untie it, and then stopped. He stared at the knot for a very long moment.

Alarm squeezed faster and sharper through her. It felt like a cold blade poking at her innards.

He looked sideways, at camp.

Thankfully, he didn't look directly at her. She nibbled on a pod and kept her pace steady. The Dehrien Chief's gaze roved over the rest of camp and touched on her. A blush of guilt warmed her cheeks. Hopefully the dusky twilight hid it.

He couldn't know that she had infiltrated his bag. But he surely knew someone had.

To her surprise, he stopped untying the pack and walked away.

Methusal felt increasingly uneasy, and hurried to join Behran in their protected alcove.

"Time for my backrub," she joked, reminding him of their bet yesterday.

Behran grinned. Slowly, he said, "You *did* find us a boatload of Zindedi ammunition."

Methusal had to be fair. "But you and Hendra found the fields. Now we have food and medical supplies."

"After you picked them."

Methusal grinned. "I guess I win, then."

Behran leaned close and his breath whispered across her cheek. "I guess you do." An almost kiss. A teaser.

She shivered in happiness and crossed her arms against the increasing chill in the air. The leaping fire looked more inviting by the moment. Soon she'd move closer. For now, though, she wanted to enjoy her private moment with Behran.

Behran's strong fingers worked at the knots in her shoulders. "You're tense."

Should she tell him what she'd done? She again glanced toward the fire. During the last few minutes, she'd been keenly aware of Mentàll stalking through the camp. Now he watched her.

"Now you're even more tense."

Methusal averted her gaze and tried to relax. The Dehrien Chief could pin nothing on her. And she'd stolen nothing. But she felt guilty anyway.

Because she had invaded his privacy. *For the greater good.*

It didn't ease her conscience.

Behran's fingers gradually loosened the knots in her shoulders, and she relaxed. Long, soothing moments passed.

"Better?" he murmured.

"Yes. Thank you." She smiled up at him.

He kissed her temple. "You're welcome."

Movement registered in her peripheral vision. The Dehrien Chief was striding toward them.

Tension crept back into her body. Methusal wished she didn't feel so guilty. She hoped it didn't show on her face.

The Chief of Dehre came to a halt near them. Methusal wished she could ignore him. In fact, she pretended not to see him.

Behran said, "What do you need, Mentàll?"

"I have come to congratulate Methusal."

Cautiously, she met his pale, glittering gaze. "For what?"

"For your bountiful harvest. Did you find all you were seeking?"

Did a double meaning edge his words? "I picked as much lynnte weed and coltac leaves as I could carry."

"Good. Save some for yourself. Give the remainder to Timaeus when he returns. Doc will need them at base camp."

She nodded.

"I require Methusal's assistance," the Dehrien told Behran. "Will you excuse us?"

Methusal quickly glanced at Mentàll and then back at Behran.

The Dehrien smiled. "Surely you have not forgotten your duty, Methusal."

Reluctantly she climbed to her feet. To Behran, she mumbled, "He needs me to tend his wound."

"Are you all right?"

"Of course." She forced a smile and met the Dehrien's penetrating gaze. "I'm ready."

Her brave front couldn't ease the sick jitters in her stomach. She followed him to the isolated place where she'd cleaned his wound that morning. The two bloody leaves still lay on the ground. It was a reminder of her earlier behavior, and it also reminded her of her vow to treat him gently, like an injured beast.

Now, so close to him, and about to actually touch him, it seemed utterly impossible.

Methusal stripped off his bleached tunic, revealing tanned, broad shoulders and the bloody slash down his back. Several of the tacky leaves had fallen off.

"Begin your task," he ordered.

Methusal clenched her jaw, but told herself to relax. At least he hadn't asked her about the pack. Not yet, anyway.

She stared at the wide shoulders, girding herself up for the chore she must do. *Pretend he's the wolmite,* she told herself. *What did I do for him?*

Dampen a lynnte weed.

She dampened it in the cold stream, and then touched it to the first tacky leaf. Mentàll flinched—probably because it was cold. The wolmite wouldn't have liked that, either.

If Mentàll was the wolmite, what would she do? As she gently worked off the first tacky leaf, she knew. Warm up the lynnte.

Feeling a terrible sort of revulsion for the kind act, she rubbed the lynnte weed between her palms to take the chill off. Then she applied the damp fibers to the next tacky leaf and gently peeled it off.

This was so *hard.* Methusal drew a steadying breath. It went against everything in her to treat this man with kindness. Forcing tenderness into her touch, she carefully wet the next leaf, and with gentle strokes, carefully removed it, too.

Mentàll jerked forward. He twisted to look at her. A snarl bared his teeth. "What are you *doing?*"

"Taking off the leaves."

Distrust glared back.

"I'm trying to be gentle. Like with the wild animals I help. You qualify."

"Tend my wound. And be quick about it," he snapped.

She had upset him. An unexpected bonus. Carefully, she removed the rest of the leaves. The muscles in his back twitched. She knew he was itching for the treatment to end.

Perversely, now she took pleasure in lingering over his wound, making sure the coltac juice was massaged in properly, and the new leaves perfectly adhered.

By now, Mentàll had stopped fidgeting. In fact, he sat very still. She tied her medical pouch closed. "Done."

Mentàll rose fast and pulled on his tunic. When he faced her, his menacing glare made her swallow.

"Did you enjoy yourself?"

"I'm pleased to do a good job."

An unknown emotion flickered, but ice replaced it. "Do you want to play games with me? Because I play *hard.*" Threat edged his tone. "And I play to win."

Fear fluttered, but she narrowed her eyes. "You're paranoid. I treated your wound nicely, like Doc ordered. How dare you attack me?"

"We both know your *treatment* had nothing to do with being nice. You hate me. Don't lie to me with your touch."

"If you don't like how I treat you, then ask Hendra to tend your wound. I'll happily give her the job."

A smile curled his lips. "I am sure you would."

"If that's all..."

"It will never be *all,* Methusal." A shiver slid through her at his tone. "We will have many days together. I intend to enjoy every last one."

"More threats?" She clamped her teeth together, forcibly biting back rash words. "If you're finished with me, I'll go."

The Dehrien said nothing.

What was this? Victory? With a feeling of triumph, she marched away.

"Methusal."

She paused, but did not look back.

"Dehre has strict laws about violating personal property."

She froze.

"I have your attention, do I?" he asked silkily. "Face me, Methusal."

Everything in her told her to run. She did not. Expression as chilly as she could make it, she met his gaze. "What are you accusing me of now? *Stealing* from you? Because you have nothing I want, Dehrien."

He stalked toward her. "Kaavl Commander. Sir."

Methusal remained stationary, but unease clawed inside her.

Threat oozed from his every pore. "I will not allow insubordination, Methusal. Most especially not from you."

Half a length separated them now. Never would she admit to rifling through his pack. What's more, he could never prove it. "Step off."

"Kaavl Commander. *Sir,*" he snarled.

She hated that he was larger than she was. She hated that he could physically overpower her, and easily, too. Methusal felt like an apte, toyed with by a wild beast. If she didn't do what he wanted, he'd kick her off the kaavl team.

Or would he?

He relished tormenting her. If she transferred to another team, he wouldn't be able to pursue his favorite entertainment.

"You *are* the Kaavl Commander, true. But you've earned none of my respect."

He whipped back, "You have earned a day in kaavl camp. Tomorrow you will gather firewood and prepare the meal..."

"No!" She and Kitran would discover the secrets of the General's compound tomorrow. Maybe even rescue Deccia. "No. I have..."

She stopped. It would be stupid to let him know how much she wanted to scout. Then he'd rip the opportunity away for sure.

"You have to what? Learn how to treat your leader with respect?"

The backs of her eyes burned with tears. "I *hate* you!"

"Kaavl Commander. Sir."

She averted her face and bit her lip hard. Fury seethed hot in her heart. With loathing, she muttered, "Kaavl Commander. Sir."

"Say it again, like you mean it."

"Kaavl Commander. *Sir!* Are you happy? Can I scout now?"

He watched her for a long, predatory minute. "Yes."

Shaking, she spun and stalked away.

"Remember your place, Methusal." That hateful, harsh voice followed her. "It is half your battle."

Methusal balled her hands into fists. She wanted to punch that arrogant wild beast.

The violence of her emotions scared her. Biting her lip harder, she burst into tears and ran to the tall rocks that protected camp. In the deepening dusk, she wove through them until she found a quiet spot. Then she crumpled to her knees and wept.

She'd tried to be kind—well, mostly. And look what it had brought her. More suffering.

Help me find Deccia soon, The One. Please! I can't take any more of this.

△ △ △ △ △

Late that night, after eating roast wild beast, Methusal curled up into her coverlet. Cold air bit through the thin blanket. Maybe she should pull out the extra covering she'd brought. Or maybe not. Soon winter would arrive, and it would be even colder. Maybe it would be better to let her body get used to the cold.

Behran quietly lay a length away, and Hendra lay another length beyond him.

Cold permeated her body, and seeped down into her very bones. Shivering, Methusal decided to put on her last, extra tunic. After pulling it on, she curled up into a tight ball, trying to get comfortable on the hard, pebbled ground. During the day, this spot had looked perfectly clear and level. Now she realized the ground sloped downward at her head.

She would live.

Camp was quiet now. Only a few men moved near the fire. The last of the wild beast had been chopped into hunks, and now was drying on a spit over the fire.

Methusal closed her eyes. The frustration of the day ate at her. She'd done nothing to help Deccia, and worse, the Dehrien Chief had succeeded in burrowing under her skin twice. Methusal struggled to remember the good things:

Behran's backrub, and finding the coltac leaves. And tomorrow she'd scout with Kitran. Maybe they'd even rescue Deccia. With that hopeful thought fixed in her mind, she finally relaxed into sleep.

Methusal stood in the middle of a long, shadowed hall. Torches sputtered on the walls. They were spaced out every five lengths.

Wooden doors punctuated the hallway. Each had a small, barred window.

A short, hunched man in a brown cloak approached. A circle of keys clicked in his hand. Behind him strode a stocky man. This one walked with clipped steps, and he wore a black military uniform crossed with a red, sideways sash. Stripes and gold clusters decorated his uniformed shoulder. His black and silver hair was cut short, his face jowly, and his lips looked thin beneath his mustache. Methusal couldn't see his eyes, but she didn't need to. He was a cruel man; she sensed it in her bones.

The guard twisted the key in a door lock and it swung open. The door was the fourth from the end of the hall.

"You have a visitor," the bent man cackled. "You may leave your cell today."

No sound emerged from the room.

"Move aside." The military man's quiet voice bubbled with barely restrained glee.

"Yes, General."

General! Methusal watched the invader move into the dark doorway. "Come, my sweet." His breathy chuckle made Methusal's skin crawl. "That's right. Come on."

The General stepped back and Deccia's pale face appeared in the doorway. Methusal gasped. Her dark hair looked matted and unwashed, and so did her clothes. Her shoulders were bowed, and only the small lift to her chin indicated that her sister still possessed any of her normal spirit.

The General chuckled, and when he turned, his amber eyes glowed in the torchlight. They appeared peculiarly unfocussed. Terror shivered through Methusal's soul.

"Today, my sweet, we will take a stroll." He gripped Deccia's arm. She did not resist. They headed toward Methusal.

"Deccia," she whispered, but her sister did not hear.

They passed right by. "Deccia," she cried out.

"Where are we going?" her twin mumbled.

"The garden. You remember our enjoyable time there, don't you?"

"No!" Horror vomited out in that one word. A sharp twist, and Deccia broke free and ran. The General didn't chase her. Instead, a chuckle gurgled in his throat, and he followed her at a slow, steady pace.

Deccia was trapped. She'd reached the end of the hall, and now faced a closed door. Frantically, she rattled the handle.

The General laughed.

Horrified, Methusal ran down the hall and joined her sister. Both of them yanked at the locked door. Wild-eyed, Deccia glanced over her shoulder. Frantic gasps escaped from her lips. She renewed her frenzied rattling of the door handle. The clicks sounded pathetic in the silent hall.

Suddenly the door flew open, revealing a soldier. Off balance, Deccia staggered backward and fell. Confusion twisted the soldier's features into a frown.

"Run, Deccia!" Methusal cried out. "Here's your chance. Run!"

Deccia didn't move. Instead, she cowered on the floor. The General was almost upon them.

"Deccia!" Her twin didn't respond. Helplessly, Methusal watched the General stop beside her sister.

He extended one hand and beckoned. That's when Methusal saw the bloody stump where his thumb should have been. Revulsion convulsed in her throat. "Deccia, run!" she begged. "Come with me."

An explosion made Methusal jump. "Deccia!"

Her sister did not respond.

The General said, "If you come to me now, all will go well for you."

"Deccia!" Methusal sobbed out. "Come on! Come now!"

Someone gripped Methusal's shoulders, dragging her from her twin. "No!" she cried out. "No. Deccia!" She struggled violently. She had to help her! Methusal tried harder to break free, but the arm around her would not let go.

"Trust me," he whispered.

The unknown man pulled her over rocky ground. Deccia disappeared from view. Methusal sobbed harder. He urged her to sit down, and she obeyed. Smooth leather touched her fingers.

Where was she? She resisted lying down.

"It's okay, Thusa. It's only a dream." Behran's voice.

Methusal struggled to open her eyes, and fought to free herself from the entangling threads of the nightmare. A dark face loomed above her, backlit by the starlit sky. Behran.

"You were sleepwalking," he murmured.

Her heart pounded. Half of her mind was still entangled in the throes of the nightmare. "Deccia," she choked out. "The General has her. He was...he was..." She burst into tears, and Behran pulled her into his arms.

"Shh," he whispered into her hair. "It was only a dream."

But was it? It had seemed so real. Methusal wept, and Behran held her tight. A muffled explosion ripped the night. She flinched, and Behran held her closer.

It sounded like a gun, just like in her dream. Were invaders shooting someone? Or—memory flashed—was it the war team in the mountains, practicing with the invaders' guns? More shots punctured the silence of the night.

Behran finally urged her to lie down. He pulled his coverlet closer and then lay beside her, pulling her against him. He felt warm and solid and real.

"What happened?" she whispered. "You said I was sleepwalking?"

"Through camp."

"Oh, no." Sleepwalking was a childish activity. It was a weakness, and a vulnerability. "Did anyone else see?"

A silent second elapsed. "Most people are asleep. I don't know."

Methusal bit her lip. "Thank you for bringing me back here."

"My pleasure." More quietly, he said, "I didn't know that you sleepwalk."

"I usually don't. Only when I'm really upset. I've been doing it a lot since Deccia was captured. It's like..."

"Like?" he prompted, when she hesitated.

"This will sound crazy, but in my nightmares, I'm with her. I see everything she sees. Sometimes I'm *her*, but this time I was me. I tried to help her escape, but she couldn't hear me. She didn't know I was there." More tears welled.

"I'm sorry, Thusa."

"I hope the dreams aren't true."

"We'll rescue her. Soon," he promised.

"I hope so," she whispered. She relaxed a little, glad that he was so close. What would she do without him?

"Thanks, Behran," she whispered again, and snuggled into his chest. Everything would be all right. It had to be. Tomorrow she and Kitran would learn the secrets of the General's compound. And they'd rescue Deccia, too.

We're coming, Deccia. She hoped her twin heard her heart.

Please keep her safe, The One. Protect her and deliver her from that awful man! At last she fell into an unsettled sleep.

CHAPTER ELEVEN

DAY 9

METHUSAL AWOKE BEFORE DAWN feeling stiff and exhausted. Behran had returned to his own space, which was for the best. Methusal didn't want anyone getting the wrong impression about their closeness. She'd been brought up to believe that intimacies belonged only between a married couple. Behran believed the same.

Quietly, she prepared for the day by washing in the cold stream. She longed for a full bath, but that wouldn't happen until they returned to base camp, because she didn't want to undress in a camp full of men. By the time she'd eaten dry rations for breakfast, everyone else was up.

"We'll leave in a few minutes," Kitran said. "Are you ready?"

"Almost." Behran and Hendra sat with Methusal, finishing their breakfasts, too.

"What's your scout assignment, Hendra?"

"I don't know. Here comes Mentàll. I'll ask."

Last night's humiliation flooded back. Methusal didn't want to look at the Dehrien. But what if he took her revulsion for fear? He'd relish that victory. She glanced up at the Dehrien, her expression purposefully blank. But he paid no attention to her. Good.

"Hendra and Behran. You and Taltn will gather supplies from the farms."

"But I want to scout!" Hendra sounded upset.

"No argument. It is a necessary task. Return by mid-afternoon. Timaeus will carry the medical supplies to base camp."

Hendra said no more, but she frowned. A puzzled frown pulled at Behran's brow.

"Tomorrow you will scout, Behran."

Behran nodded, clearly not liking it, but accepting it.

Hendra said, "Will you let me scout tomorrow, too?"

"We will see," he said shortly. "Methusal. Time to tend my wound."

She did not want to continue to tend his wound twice a day. Once was torture enough. "Of course," she said in a pleasant voice. "If you feel that is necessary. But Doc said that after a few days the leaves can be changed once a day."

The Dehrien stared at her for an uncomfortable moment. "Come with me now." He strode away.

With a frown, she scooped up her medical pouch. "I'll be back soon," she promised Behran. Hendra sent her a quick, sympathetic glance. Methusal followed the Dehrien to the familiar boulder near the stream.

He stood waiting for her. She didn't like his expression. As a consequence, she stopped a good distance away from him, and almost crossed her arms defensively, but thought better of it. "What?"

"Do not question me when I assign you a task, Maahr."

"Doc said..."

"I do not care what Doc said. This conversation is about you, Methusal. If you challenge my authority, you will lose. Every time. When will you realize that?"

After his foul behavior last night, and after suffering through the awful nightmares about Deccia and that horrible General, her temper snapped. She had had enough. "How insecure you must be. Every time someone challenges you, you attack. Not the best way to build respect for your leadership."

"*You* are the only one who challenges me."

"And Kitran."

"Kitran chooses his battles with purpose. You do not. I wonder if you belong on this team."

"You won't kick me off."

He moved toward her. "Won't I?" An unpleasant smile touched his lips.

"No. Who would you torture then? All your fun and games would end."

"I would keep you at camp, Methusal." The calculating smile remained. "Unfortunately, you would find it quite unpleasant. You would have no opportunity to search for your sister. No opportunity to help the war effort. Keeping camp would become your sole responsibility."

Temper flushed her cheeks hot. "I only *asked* if I could change the leaves once a day."

"You *will* respect my authority. Until you do, we will repeat this conversation."

Her anger boiled hotter, making her want to match the Dehrien's nastiness. She hated that. And yet she hated even more his manipulative power plays, which were designed to squish her beneath his moccasin, like an insect.

"Fine. Then tell me, Kaavl Commander. *Sir*. Shall I tend your wound twice a day? Or once?"

His features contorted into anger, and his hands tightened into fists. "Your insubordination has reached the limit, Maahr! Now..."

"No!" Her heart pounded. *What was wrong with her?* "I'm sorry, okay? I'll tend your wound twice."

She had to stop reacting to his attempts to provoke her. Staying in control of her temper was key, if she wanted to gain any sort of power over this situation. And if she wanted to like herself at the end of the day, too. She regretted now that she'd just regressed into the behavior of a rebellious teenager.

Hands trembling, she pulled out the coltac leaves.

"Accept your place, Methusal." The Dehrien stared at her for another long, sickening minute, and sat on the boulder.

As gently and swiftly as possible, she removed the old leaves, rubbed in the juice and adhered the new leaves.

Mentàll pulled on his tunic the instant she was done. "Good job, Maahr."

"What?" She stared at him in disbelief.

Satisfaction flickered. He had liked surprising her. She also saw it in his small, nasty smile. "Take pride in a job well done. And listen to Kitran when you scout today." He strode toward camp.

What game was he playing now?

Methusal couldn't begin to understand that man. Thankfully she wouldn't have to deal with him again until tonight. Long hours from now. Hopefully by then she and Kitran would rescue Deccia. After that, she wouldn't care if Mentàll banished her to camp, or if he kicked her off the team entirely.

△ △ △ △ △

By midmorning Hendra's back ached from picking vegetables in the field. Worse, frustration churned like a hot fire within her. She should have demanded that Mentàll give her a scouting assignment. Why hadn't she? Why was she still such an apte?

She straightened, pressing a hand to the small of her back. Off in the distance, Behran harvested coltac leaves, and Taltn, the lynnte weeds. She glanced to the east, over her shoulder. She was the one closest to town. Dark gray shacks edged the skyline. They were probably only a minute's run away.

She'd picked all of the pods where she was, so she bent double so the tall, wild grass hid her, and moved closer to town, looking for another good pod bush. She bypassed a few dead bushes. Finally she found a good pod bush, and when she peeked above the waving grass, discovered she was only a stone's throw from town.

She bent to pluck more green pods. Why wouldn't Mentàll let her scout? Didn't he think her kaavl was good enough? Was he being overprotective? She suspected the latter. But both were possible.

How could she prove herself, if he never let her try? How could she scout, if she never demanded the chance?

Anger mixed with her frustration. Vegetables now overflowed her partially tied up cloak. She glanced west, and didn't see Behran or Taltn for a minute, but then she saw their heads moving west, toward the tagma bushes. They must still have room in their cloaks. She, on the other hand, could only fit in a few more pods. And then what? Was she supposed to sit here and do nothing, when only a short distance away Zindedis held Quasrians captive? The Koblani war team needed every scrap of information they could find.

Town lured her. It was so tantalizingly close.

Surely if she quickly snuck to the edge of town she'd learn something useful.

No more pods fit into the makeshift bag. In fact, pods spilled out when she cinched it closed. She plopped down on the moist, prickly earth and wrapped her arms around her knees. An ocean of tall, swaying grasses rippled above her. She felt protected and cocooned. After a few minutes she again peeked above the grasses. Behran and Taltn looked like tiny figures on the western horizon.

Nerves danced in the pit of her stomach. They wouldn't notice if she ran into town for a few minutes.

Her heart beat faster. She'd never disobeyed Mentàll before. But wasn't this why she'd come to war? To defeat her fears, and to help Koblan win the war?

Of course. And here was her opportunity to stop behaving like an apte. Even better, if she could discover the tiniest scrap of information, it might make all the difference in the war effort.

A foreign sensation prickled through her. Excitement. Yes. She could do it. No one would know—unless, of course, she discovered important information. Then she'd have to tell Mentàll. He'd approve of her actions then, she reasoned. Even better, she would have proven herself. He'd see that she was a competent spy, just like the others.

Hendra crept to her feet. With a final, backward glance at Behran and Taltn, she sprinted for Quasr.

△ △ △ △ △

BASE CAMP

Aali was happy at base camp. Really, she was. She didn't mind fetching water, and cooking food, and cleaning dishes, and helping Doc.

Okay... Yes. She did. It was so *boring!*

She longed to do something *vital.* She daydreamed about sneaking into Quasr. In her fantasies, her cunning kaavl skills rescued Deccia every time. And yet how could she rescue her sister when she couldn't leave base camp?

Aali brooded over the fact that she'd probably never see an invader again. Although she *did* know where the warrior team had stored the invader plunder. She had spied yesterday, and seen it piled high in a valley to the northeast. She had seen boxes, bags, and guns—those deadly weapons that blew holes in men. She shivered at the memory.

She wanted to see a gun up close. And why shouldn't she?

But how?

An idea popped into her head. She could ask for scout duty. Then she could explore to her heart's content.

Uncle Erl needed lots of scouts to protect the hills around camp.

Why hadn't she thought of it before? Even better, her Quatr-level kaavl skills would qualify her for the position!

Uncle Erl and his war party were at camp, so she could ask him now.

Thrilled by her idea, Aali hurried to Erl's tent. The flap was shut, but that didn't stop her. "Uncle Erl," she called out. "Are you there?"

"Come in."

She swept aside the door and stepped inside. Erl's tent was huge, like Pan's and Mentàll's. Her uncle sat frowning over a makeshift table strewn with parchments.

Aali rushed across the room. "I want to be a scout. Can I? I'm at the Quatr-level. I'd be great at it!"

Erl's frown deepened. "I have plenty of scouts. My war party has it covered."

Disappointment stabbed her. Ignoring it, she pressed on, "But what about when you leave? I could help then."

"What are you up to, Aalicaa?"

"Up to?" She widened her eyes.

He raised a brow and waited.

She frowned. "Fine. I'm bored. I'm tired of peeling tubers. I want to do something exciting."

"Your work is important. And you're doing a good job."

"Thank you. And I'll keep doing it," she rushed to assure him. "But sometimes I'd like to scout, too." She offered her most charming, persuasive grin.

"I understand how you feel. But no." He focused on his parchments again.

"Why not?"

Erl sighed. "Because you're reckless and headstrong. Look how you forced your way onto the war party. You'll stay in base camp so Aenill and Doc can watch over you."

She scowled. "I am not a child anymore!"

Erl's gaze cooled to ore. "That is my last word on the subject. Close the door on your way out."

Aali burst outside, trembling with anger at Erl's inflexibility. He was just like her father. The injustice of it all! She had behaved in an exemplary fashion at base camp. How dare he accuse her of being willful and uncontrollable!

Frowning, Aali stalked to her tent and collapsed onto her pallet. It was wrong. Unfair. And foolish! She sat up then, thinking harder. When Erl and Pan and all the warriors left base camp, only three scouts remained. Base camp *needed* more lookouts.

Who was in charge of the scouts? Maybe she could ask *him* for a job. Then she frowned. Whoever he was, he'd ask Erl's permission first.

Thwarted again.

Her forehead hurt from frowning so hard.

Suddenly the perfect solution dawned on her. She didn't need to *be* a scout to go on an adventure! She just needed to *substitute* for a scout. The scout who watched the weapons valley. Pogul.

She smiled to herself. Pogul was lazy. She'd offer to take his shift, and then he'd get a whole afternoon to nap. He'd snap at the chance. Then she'd explore the valley all by herself, and no interfering scout would stop her.

Soon she'd get to inspect a gun up close. She'd talk to Pogul at lunch.

△ △ △ △ △

Methusal and Kitran sat on the floor of a deserted, dirty hut in Quasr. Her bottom hurt from sitting for so long. Across the room, a candle burned in a bowl which was placed inside the blackened fireplace. No furnishings decorated the stark shack, except for two shelves, which held broken pieces of pottery.

Kitran had been instructed to wait in this hut for his informant to show up. And so they had been sitting here—for hours, it seemed like. She couldn't wait for the man to arrive. Once they'd learned every detail about the General's compound, perhaps they could rescue Deccia. Maybe even today.

"Do you think something happened to him?" she whispered.

The thin-walled shack was located on the north side of town, near the sea, and dozens of Zindedis patrolled the area. Luckily their brown cloaks had disguised them as Quasrians as they'd cut through town. No one had accosted them. It had seemed almost too simple.

Outside, footsteps scuffed by.

"I don't know." Kitran stood and paced the small area.

As more time slipped by, Methusal felt increasingly uneasy. She tried to quiet her fears with logic. The hut was obviously deserted. The Zindedis wouldn't check it unless they heard a suspicious noise.

She sharpened her kaavl and listened for approaching footsteps. Boots crunched on the pebbled road. Precise, concentrated kaavl determined that five sets of boots strode closer. Five men.

"They're in that one?"

A faint chuckle. "The little one sang like a girl."

"Kitran!" she hissed, leaping to her feet. "Zindedis."

Kitran shot for the far, open window. Zindedi boot steps clumped three lengths away...two. Grabbing the top ledge, he swung his legs up and through. Methusal did the same thing just as the door crashed open.

"Koblanis!" came a guttural cry.

Methusal and Kitran took off at a dead run.

∆ ∆ ∆ ∆ ∆

Hendra crept down the eastern line of shacks. Although it was too late for her to do anything about it now, she remembered the Quasrians wore cloaks. If a Zindedi saw her, she'd be arrested.

Well then, she'd stay undetected.

So far, she'd seen no one. The farm shacks were deserted.

She came to a dirt street, and stopped. Sparse huts populated the other side of the road. Several had been burned to the ground. All appeared deserted. Through the gaps between the shacks, she saw that homes had been burned on the next street, too.

Where were all of the people?

Had the Zindedis killed them all? Sickened by the thought, Hendra sharpened her hearing and cautiously slipped across the street. In the distance footsteps crunched over gravel. Fear pulsed through her.

The footsteps faded, but still she hesitated. What should she do now?

She forced herself to cross the next road, and then voices made her tuck up flush against a tilting shack. Her heart hammered, and she didn't move. After several slow, calming breaths, she peeked around the corner. The people appeared to be Quasrians, because they wore brown cloaks.

She jerked back, heart pounding. Black and red clad invaders mixed with them.

Why was she here? What had she hoped to find?

Shouts erupted down the road. Taking a breath, she peeked out again, keeping her back pressed to the wall. Her senses felt more sharply tuned into kaavl right now than they ever had before in her life. In a flash, a man streaked by. He was short, balding, and wore no shirt.

Then why was the commotion centered down the street? Why weren't the invaders chasing the escaping man?

A long minute passed, and then suddenly the man streaked by again, exactly as she'd seen him the first time.

What was *that,* she wondered, bewildered.

Zindedis barreled by. An odd, tingling sensation slid down her back, and Hendra turned to glance at the street behind her. The man sped by, heading in the opposite direction this time.

It hadn't happened yet.

Her pulse skipped. How did she know that? And how had she seen it?

More importantly, could she help him?

Following her intuition, she darted back and slipped around the other side of the shack, which faced the next street. She tried the front door. It was jammed shut. Hendra flipped back against the side wall. Now what?

A window!

Quickly, she pushed one open, climbed inside, and closed it again. She ran for the front door. It was bolted from the inside. A quick glance confirmed that the one room shack was deserted, except for rochers scuttling into the far corner.

The bald man was almost upon her. Again, Hendra did not know how she knew that. She swiftly unbolted the door and peeked out. Here he came, running like the wind. No Zindedis were in sight. Hendra flung open the door.

"Here!"

The man stared at her, and then swerved inside. Hendra slammed home the bolt, heart pounding almost as fast as the man was breathing.

That's when she saw the lacerations on his back. A score or more, obviously made with a whip.

Horror gripped her. In that instant she saw another man—a much younger one—and her father's whip slicing deep into his skin. Her cousin had not made a sound. He never had. In that battle of the wills, he had always won, but the lashes from that particular whipping had taken months to heal. It was also the last beating her father had ever administered to Mentàll.

Following that memory, another one shuddered through her. Hendra swallowed back a mute, panicked sob, and struggled to block it out.

This stranger had been beaten bloody, too. She had to keep her wits about her.

Zindedis ran by outside, and then the boots stopped. Muttering reached her ears. Loud bangs punctuated the air.

"Over here," she whispered, and scrunched into a corner near the door, below the window. If the soldiers looked in, they'd see no one.

The sweaty, bleeding man squeezed in beside her and Hendra closed her eyes. Nauseating fear threatened to over-whelm her. Foolishly, this man scared her more than the pack of invaders outside.

Fists hammered on the door. The wood panel jerked and bounced with each blow. She drew deep breaths, trying to calm herself. Trying to battle the fear that threatened to overwhelm her good sense.

The invaders pounded louder and harder, rattling the door, but the bolt held. The window above them scraped open, and a black shadow blocked the sunlight streaming into the room. Hendra couldn't breathe, and beside her, the bald man sat as still as a stone.

Finally the soldiers clumped on. Hendra drew a fortify-ing breath, but didn't feel any steadier. Quickly, she scrambled away from the man, until she stood on the far side of the room.

He also stood up. "Who are you?" His voice sounded rough. And he was shorter than she was. It didn't make her feel any safer.

"Who are *you?*"

A mirthless chuckle gurgled in his throat. "I'll ask again." Menace edged his tone. "Who are you?"

The truth seemed prudent. "I'm Hendra. From Dehre."

"Hendra? Dehre?" He moved closer, but the threat in his voice had lowered a notch. "Who is your chief?"

"Mentàll Solboshn. He's my cousin."

"You have the same blond hair." He came nearer, but she raised a trembling hand.

"Stop."

"You don't trust me."

Hendra trusted no man. "Why were the Zindedis chasing you?"

"I know secrets."

"Secrets? What kind of secrets?"

"Take me to Mentàll, and I'll tell him."

Hendra couldn't take him to kaavl camp, even if the man *was* a friend, like he claimed. For the protection of the team, the camp location must remain a secret. Besides that, Mentàll had a bounty on his head. What if this man intended to betray her cousin in order to buy peace with the invaders?

"I can't do that. But I can send him a message."

"I'm supposed to trust secrets to a scared girl like you?"

"Yes. You can trust me."

"I don't." The man strode for the door.

"Wait!"

"You changed your mind?"

"I can set up a meeting, if that's what you want." Carefully, she did not say with whom.

"That's more like it."

Then why did she feel more uneasy now than ever before? Panic rippled through her. She had to get out of this house and away from this man, and she had to do it now.

△ △ △ △ △

Erl and his war party had finally departed late that morning on a new mission. With a gleeful grin, Aali sped to the eating area. Time to put her plan into motion.

She spotted the fair-haired, heavy-set Pogul eating alone at a table. Since no one liked him, she wasn't surprised he was sitting by himself.

Pogul frowned when Aali slid onto the bench across from him. "What d'you want?" He stuffed an apte leg in his mouth and slurped on the bone.

Nasty! She shuddered, but managed a bright smile. "Hey, Pogul. You're a scout, aren't you?"

"What's it to you?" He licked his thick lips. His eyes looked like black pebbles which masked something malevolent inside of him.

Aali's skin prickled, but she continued to smile in a winning way. "I want to try scouting."

"You want to come with me?" An evil smile curled his lips.

"No! Goodness, no," Aali choked in horror. She tried to cover it with a nervous giggle. "I'll do your job for one afternoon. You can take a break."

"What's the catch?"

"No catch. I just want to try it. Uncle Erl won't let me." Dismay flared. She shouldn't have said that.

"So I'd be doing you a favor," he said craftily.

"Take it or leave it. Work, or take a nap."

His laugh made her skin crawl. "You can scout. But I want something from you."

"Forget it!" she flared indignantly.

"Skinny little girls don't turn me on. ...Though you might be fun to play with."

Outraged, Aali leaped to her feet. "You are *disgusting!*" She stalked off.

"Wait a minute," he called after her. "I'm just joking. Can't you take a joke?"

She spun back. "I'm not doing anything for you, you revolting slug."

"Come talk some more."

Aali curled her lip and waited, tapping her foot.

"All right," he said. "You can scout for me. When? Today?"

"No. I'll let you know."

"You'll owe me."

Aali rolled her eyes in dismissal and left the foul Pogul. Maybe she shouldn't have made a deal with him. But too late now. And if he thought he could force her to do an unsavory favor for him, he would be sorry. Painfully sorry. Time to practice with her kaavl stick.

△ △ △ △ △

Methusal sped after Kitran, zigzagging through the dirty streets. Brown cloaked Quasrians stared at them in surprise. Women clutched small children and woven grocery bags close to their sides, but the men looked on with interest.

Zindedi soldiers pounded after them. Methusal spotted more black clad soldiers to the south when they dashed across a street. With a shout, their pursuers alerted those invaders, and the chase intensified.

Methusal used her kaavl to follow the movement of the Zindedis. The cluster behind them was easy to track until they split up. Then she struggled to trace each of their paths. Combined with following Kitran and projecting her hearing ahead, looking for more sources of danger, her brain felt overloaded.

At a maximum, Methusal could only track and follow four systems of movement at once. With eight Zindedis in hot pursuit, she had to forgo that option and flick from one to the next to the next, in rapid succession. Unfortunately, by the time she got to the last pursuer, the first was difficult to locate. She struggled to follow three at the same time.

"They're gaining on us!" she panted to Kitran. "Two are circling north, and two south."

Kitran didn't answer, but dashed on, as if he knew where he was going. Since he'd grown up in Quasr, he probably did. He cut north, and then down an alley between two shacks.

"Two Zindedis are close," she gasped. The northern men were now heading south.

"Tell me where they are," Kitran panted, and darted south, west through another alley, and then south again. "I lost track of the closest pair a block ago."

"The closest two are north. One of the southern men stopped. He's talking to more soldiers. The others are questioning Quasrians."

Kitran ran purely west now, past dozens of blackened homes. Methusal wondered where all the people had gone.

"Are they giving up?" Kitran wheezed.

"No."

"Where's the nearest one?"

"North, and back a street. The other one is close behind."

"Come on." Kitran put on a burst of speed and ducked behind a wild tagma bush beside a dilapidated shack. Panting lightly, Methusal crouched beside him.

"Now what?"

"We'll have to kill them."

"Kitran!" Horror stabbed her.

"We can't outrun them. They won't give up."

Methusal tried to think of reasons why they shouldn't kill the Zindedis. And then she wondered what she was thinking. Wasn't this war? Zindedis had killed Quasrians and members of the Koblani war team. Zindedis had to die if they were going to win this war.

Swallowing hard, she pressed back against the wall and pulled out her mother's bone handled knife. The blade still scared her. It reminded her of the invader's attack on the cliff. She'd flung it at the Zindedi's neck because she couldn't bear the thought of actually feeling it plunge into another living being's flesh. As a result, she'd almost lost her life. If it hadn't been for Mentàll...

The clomp of the invaders' boots were almost upon them. "Two lengths," she whispered, and pulled out her short kaavl stick. It felt more comfortable in her hand than the knife.

Kitran nodded. Methusal noted that he held two knives—one in each fist. To her surprise, he tossed a pebble sideways, so it pinged off the next shack and bounced into the large bush growing beside it. The Zindedis evidently heard it, because they swerved closer.

Kitran noticed her wide, worried eyes. "The closer they are, the better chance we have," he muttered. It was true.

Against guns, they had no hope. Hand-to-hand combat was their only chance to win.

She listened for the other invaders, but the last of those pursuers had faded to the north, following a false path. These two were their biggest threats.

The Zindedis roared and charged the bush. Swords flashed. Kitran leaped up and flung his knife through the first man's throat. The second one bellowed, and his sword arced toward Kitran's head. Without a thought, Methusal swung up her kaavl stick and blocked it. It gave Kitran enough time to plunge his other knife through the Zindedi's heart.

Both warriors crumpled to the ground. Blood seeped from them, and Methusal felt like she was going to be sick. Kitran didn't give her a chance. "Grab his feet," he ordered. He grabbed the shoulders of the first man and dragged him backward, behind the bush. Methusal helped drag the other one, too. Now neither would be seen from the road. At least not soon, and not easily.

"Come on." He grabbed her arm and headed south.

"Where are we going?" She felt shaky and upset by what they had just done. With her help, a man was dead. A fact she'd have to live with forever. What did The One think? Would he view it as murder, or self-defense?

"Kaavl camp," Kitran answered.

Methusal stopped and twisted free from his grasp. "We can't! What about Deccia? We've come all this way. We can't give up now."

"Zindedis are searching for us. We can't risk staying here."

"What about your friend? What if he comes?"

"He won't. Something happened to him."

"You mean..."

"We're not getting that information today. Come on."

"No." Methusal refused to budge. "I will not give up. This is my sister we're talking about. If your friend can't give us the information, then we'll find it out for ourselves!"

Humor sparked in Kitran's dark eyes. "I know how you are when you're in this mood. No one can change your mind."

"Are you with me, or not?"

"The Dehrien won't like it."

"Who cares what he thinks? He wants information, right? We'll get it."

Kitran smiled. "I like how you think. But I'm in charge. If I say it's time to go, we'll go."

"Deal."

The two slipped back toward the middle of town, heading for the General's compound. Hope bubbled in Methusal's heart. *We're coming, Deccia.*

△ △ △ △ △

Hendra wished the bald man would move away from the door. Her churning panic urged her to forget all good sense and dash outside.

She took a deep breath and tried to calm herself. This man had important information. Information the kaavl team needed. She must convince him to give it to her now.

"I can set up a meeting," she said again. "But it won't be until tomorrow."

His eyes narrowed. "Why should I believe you?"

Hendra never lied. It came as a consequence of living in a home where her father told lies every time he opened his mouth. Even thinking about telling a lie made her feel like throwing up. Her cousin felt the same way. Inspiration struck. What would Mentàll do if he was here right now?

He'd trick the man. He'd give enough truth to convince the man to do what he wanted.

Hendra thought quickly, because the suspicion in the man's eyes continued to sharpen. She smiled in an attempt to disarm him. "I don't know your name."

"You don't need to know."

Prickly man. Coolly, she said, "Our war teams are working to free Quasr."

"I know that." He sounded impatient.

"We need to attack the Zindedi's weak points. To find them, we need accurate information. The sooner we get those details, the sooner we can free Quasr." Hendra was a little surprised by the hard edge in her voice. Mentàll would be proud of her delivery.

He advanced closer, invading her space, but Hendra didn't move. Through his teeth, he said, "You expect me to trust you with that information?"

"I am Mentàll's cousin." Time to capitalize on that fact. "Give me the information. It's the same as giving it to him."

"Is it, now?" He seemed to find inexplicable humor in that.

"Will you give it to me?"

"No." He grinned. "You *should* have said, 'Mentàll demands that you give it to me.'"

Was he playing games with her? Giving threats was unfamiliar territory to her, but this man seemed to need them. "I'll tell him that you withheld information," she said in a hard voice. "I'll describe you, so he knows who you are."

The man's stony gaze proved she was getting nowhere. She closed her eyes in exasperation. "Please! We need your help. If we could just combine your information with what Kitran's getting today..."

"Kitran!" He snapped his fingers. "Congratulations. You just said the magic word." The short man jammed his hand down the back of his breeches and pulled out a much folded parchment. He extended it to her.

Hendra regarded it with repulsed trepidation. "What is that?"

"The information for Kitran."

Overcoming her aversion, she plucked it from his fingertips. "*You're* the one Kitran was meeting today? What happened?"

"What happened is I got caught. So did my friend, who spilled the berries about meeting Kitran."

She gasped.

"That's right. He's in trouble. Maybe even dead. But I delivered the goods." He tilted his head. "Tell Kitran I'll be in touch." And then he was gone.

Hendra stared down at the paper in her hand. She had succeeded. Now she had Kitran's information.

Kitran. Methusal! Had the Zindedis found them? Were they in trouble? Hendra slipped out the door. She needed to run to camp and tell Mentàll what had happened. If necessary, a rescue team could be organized immediately.

Δ Δ Δ Δ Δ

Methusal and Kitran crouched in a burned out shack across the street and down a block from the western facing, front gates of the General's compound. Six soldiers patrolled the compound's iron gates, and more strolled through the lush grounds inside. All kinds of trees and flowering bushes grew in the interior of the complex, and beautifully bordered the meandering stone pathways. Methusal had a better view now than she'd had the other night, because the gates were open now, which surprised her. Evidently the General felt confident that his soldiers could protect him during the day. He had certainly deployed enough.

Earlier, they'd circled the compound and had discovered two other entrances. One was on the northern side, and guarded by four Zindedis, and one was on the southern side, and guarded by the same number of men.

Nothing else, however, had been discovered. Methusal stretched her cramping legs.

"Look." Kitran nodded.

Six guards joined the ones already on duty. As Methusal watched, they chatted for a minute, and then changed places. The old guards disappeared inside the compound.

"Could be a weakness," Kitran whispered. "Someone quick could slip in while they're distracted."

"But first we'd need a map of the compound."

"I was in there once, a long time ago."

"You were?" This came as a pleasant surprise.

"I can sketch the compound grounds." With a stick, Kitran sketched a rough outline, including entrances in and out of the Chief's mansion. "I know the Chief's office is down this first hall to the right. I don't know much else."

"What about prisons? Did you ever visit them?"

"No. But I heard they're in the back of the building, and downstairs."

So the dream was true! Deccia was locked in an underground prison.

"Is that Quasr's only prison?"

"Yes."

Methusal and Kitran snacked on dried rations and watched the compound until the sun sank toward the horizon. The guards changed once more, just before Methusal and Kitran scooted west and south, flitting like shadows from house to house until they were free of Quasr, and hurrying through the empty farmlands. A successful mission. Even

Mentàll should be happy with the information they had discovered.

Δ Δ Δ Δ Δ

"You did *what?*" Mentàll did not look at all pleased.
Hendra had arrived back at kaavl camp with Behran, Taltn,
and their bulging cloaks only moments before. The setting
sun already touched the western mountains. On the way
back, she'd told Behran about everything she had done. He'd
been supportive, although not entirely approving. He did,
however, appreciate the warning that Methusal and Kitran
might be in danger. Even now, he gathered up supplies for a
possible raid on Quasr.

Hendra handed the folded parchment to Mentàll. "This
is from Kitran's spy."

"Where are Kitran and Methusal?" An edge underscored
his words.

"I don't know. But the spy thinks they're in trouble.
Zindedis forced his partner to reveal their meeting place."

Her cousin cursed savagely, and swept a hand down the
back of his neck. He gritted, "I am not finished with you,
Hendra," and stalked for the center of camp.

Within minutes, Mentàll had snapped out orders to
Behran, Jascr, and a few other top level kaavl players.
"Search the town. Report what you find and we'll plan a rescue,
if possible."

The men sprinted for Quasr.

"As for you, Hendra." She'd never seen her relative look
so ferocious. "You will stay at base camp tomorrow."

"But Mentàll! I got information. Vital information. I
want to scout. Can't you see that you can trust me with a
mission now?"

"I see I can't trust you to follow orders."

His icy anger shook her. Trembling a little, she said,
"Then what's the point of being here, if I can't scout?"

"You are my cousin. I will not allow you to put yourself in
dan..." He cut the word short.

He wouldn't put her in danger. Just as she'd thought.
Although why he hadn't finished the sentence puzzled her.
Did he think that admitting he cared for her displayed
weakness?

She said, "Then why did you let me come?"

"I understand that you want to prove yourself to me."

Hendra flushed. "It isn't just that. I know I failed you two years ago. Like it or not, I still think I did the right thing. But yes, I do want to prove myself to you...to everyone." She fluttered a hand. "But most of all to myself. I want to make a difference. I want my life to be worth something!"

His pale eyes watched her. "You mean that."

"*Yes!*" She let him hear her passion in that single word. "I won't be the victim anymore, Mentàll. You have to let me go. I can take care of myself."

"That is why you went into Quasr with no cloak." Not much got by him. Her cloak still held the pods.

"I made a mistake."

"You made two. You disobeyed orders."

"Let me go. I can do it," she pleaded.

"Not tomorrow. You disobeyed orders. You will be an example to the team."

"All right." She could accept that. "But the next day?"

"I will promise nothing. You are my only family, Hendra. I will not let you die." He turned his back and left her.

△ △ △ △ △

When Kitran and Methusal neared kaavl camp, Methusal was surprised to spot four men running toward them. One was Behran.

"Thusa!" He slowed to a jog. Relief eased the tension in his features. "Where have you been?" He pulled her into a tight hug and kissed her temple. "We thought you were captured!"

"Why?" Methusal smiled up at him, pleased by his welcome.

"Hendra met your informant, Kitran," Behran said. "He was afraid you'd been captured."

"We almost were." They slowly made their way back to camp, and exchanged the information they'd learned that day.

The Dehrien Chief spotted them the instant they rounded the tall rocks into kaavl camp. Disbelief glimmered, and then his face turned to stone. He strode toward them. "What happened?"

Kitran explained that they'd almost been captured. "Afterward, Methusal and I scouted the General's compound. That's why we're late."

"We wanted to find their weaknesses. It will help us when we rescue Deccia," Methusal added.

The Dehrien gave her a hard glance. "Tell me what you learned," he told Kitran, and led the way to the blackened fire pit. Nearby the Tarst runner, Dastn, talked with Taltn. Since Mentàll clearly didn't want to speak to her, Methusal joined the other two.

"What's going on with the war teams?" she asked. "Is my father all right?"

Dastn smiled. "He's fine. I'm about to head back. Mentàll said these sacks are medical supplies?" He indicated the bulging bags at his feet.

"Yes. They ought to help Doc for a while. How many are injured?"

"A dozen during yesterday's raid. Five seriously."

The kaavl team had been lucky so far.

Dastn tucked a folded parchment into his pocket.

"What's that?" Methusal asked. Then, "Sorry. I don't mean to be nosy."

"Just like Aali." Dastn grinned. "She can't seem to help herself."

With a laugh, Methusal glanced at the Tarst runner with more appreciation. She'd seen him talking to her cousin a few times. He seemed to have taken a protective, big brotherly sort of interest in her. Heaven knew, the more people watching out for her, the better.

"What is it, then?"

"A letter from Mentàll to Erl and Pan. It summarizes all of the intelligence the kaavl team has found so far. And it includes Hendra's information from the spy, too. It's a sketch of the General's compound."

Methusal's heart beat faster. Maybe this sketch had more details than Kitran's map. "Can I see that? Did Mentàll make a copy?"

"I don't know." Dastn handed it to her, but squinted at the sun dipping below the mountain. He'd need to leave soon in order to make it far enough into the hills to escape the wild beasts before dark.

The map closely resembled the one Kitran had sketched in the dirt in Quasr. Only this one included a diagram of the dungeon inside the mansion, and the stairs and halls leading to it. Xs seemed to mark guard locations. More rooms were sketched, but not labeled. Methusal grabbed a stick and swiftly marked the most important details in the dirt. Then she handed the parchment back. "Thanks, Dastn."

"You're welcome." He pocketed the note and hefted the bags over his sturdy shoulders. "See you later."

"See you." Methusal stared at the ground. She hoped she'd marked all of the important information. It looked messy, but it would have to do. Now she needed to memorize it.

"What are you doing?" Behran appeared at her side.

Quickly she explained, and urged him to memorize the layout of the compound, too. While he squatted, scanning the details, Kitran spoke from behind her. "Is that Doltn's map?"

"Yes."

Kitran cursed, which was unlike him. "That Dehrien whip!" He strode for Mentàll, who spoke with a cluster of kaavl players. Kitran looked almost ready to explode.

The Kaavl Commander had barely finished speaking to a Dehrien when Kitran elbowed his way into the group. "Where's Dolton's information?"

Mentàll did not look pleased. "I sent it to Erl."

"But you kept a copy for yourself."

A beat elapsed. "I memorized it."

"Planning on sharing that information with the rest of us?"

The Dehrien's gaze cooled to ice. "I will decide how to use that information, Kitran. Not you."

"And we're supposed to trust you? You live by tricks, Dehrien, and you lust for power. Your Alliance was proof of that! Share the information with everyone."

"You will receive the facts you need for your mission. Nothing more. I cannot have kaavl teams running amok, pursuing whatever plan seems best to them. I have a plan in place, and each team..." he eyed each person in the group, "will follow it. Failure to follow orders will jeopardize our entire mission. And your lives. You must trust me."

"So. This is how you'll keep power over us. By hoarding the information."

"I am the Kaavl Commander. Do not second guess my decisions."

"You arrogant whip!" Kitran said through his teeth. "*You* don't have all the answers. *You* can't think of every strategy. You..."

"If I have questions, I will be sure to ask." The words sounded mocking. "Prove your loyalty to me, and I will give you more responsibility."

Kitran scowled.

"Are you ready for your next assignment?"

"That's another thing," Kitran growled. "No one knows what the other teams are doing. You keep the spying missions a secret. Why? We need to know where the other teams are. If we get in trouble, we need to know where to find each other." Mentàll opened his mouth, but Kitran barreled on, "And why do you send teams to different locations each time? Each team should stay in one area and become familiar with it."

For one split second, the Dehrien's lips curled back in a snarl. Clearly, he didn't like being challenged repeatedly, and especially in front of the whole team. Tone glacial, he said, "I agree with the first. As for the second; new eyes see new things." His gaze flicked away from Kitran, dismissing him. "Here are your assignments."

Methusal would team up with Behran tomorrow. Excitement jumped inside her—until she learned their mission. They were to scout the southern side of Quasr and count soldiers. Deadly dull, and it could be completed in a few minutes. They had Doltn's information. Now they could immediately invade the General's compound and rescue her twin.

She listened as the Dehrien Chief assigned the other missions, but no team was told to rescue Deccia. No team was sent to scout the compound, either! Disbelief choked her.

Before she could address the issue of Deccia's rescue, Mentàll turned away from the group. She followed him, determined to speak her piece, but slowed down when she saw that he'd followed Kitran. The Dehrien reached her kaavl instructor's side. She sharpened her hearing to eavesdrop.

In a harsh voice, Mentàll said, "Show respect, Kitran. If you want to challenge my strategy, speak to me first in private."

"If you can be humble enough to listen, I have plenty to say."

"I know you hate me..."

"You think, Dehrien? Fool that I was, I thought we were friends. That you respected me. But you manipulated me and I will *never* trust you again. Never. You are not fit to lead this team, and I intend to prove it." Face like a thundercloud, Kitran strode away. In that moment, he reminded Methusal more of his volatile brother, Barak, than the reserved instructor she knew so well.

Kitran's anger made her feel uneasy. Emotions drove him now. Not his head.

When the Dehrien Chief headed toward the fire, Methusal fell into step beside him. It probably wasn't the best time to speak to him. Clearly, he was angry. But when *was* a good time to talk to him?

She said, "We have the compound map. When will we rescue Deccia?"

"It is not time."

"When will it *be* time?"

He ignored her, and turned aside to talk to Jascr.

Methusal balled her hands into fists. Why wouldn't he organize a team to rescue Deccia? Was it because she was Methusal's sister? Did he want Deccia to suffer still more?

Someone elbowed her hard, and kept walking. Goric.

"Watch it!" she snapped.

When he turned back, malice gleamed in his murky eyes, confirming her suspicion that he'd done it on purpose. "Didn't your kaavl sense me coming?"

"My kaavl doesn't let me bump into people by *accident*."

"You've underestimated me. I'll prove it soon."

"Ooh, I'm scared." She fluttered her fingers in mock terror. "I'll sleep with one ear open. Or maybe I won't. Your snapping bushes and rattling rocks could wake the dead."

He spit at her. The nasty slime blob landed a handbreadth from her moccasin. "You think you're better than everyone. But you'll fall hard."

"Not better than everyone," she corrected. "Just your kaavl."

With a scowl, Goric strode away.

Once again she'd treated Goric with the same nastiness he'd dished out to her. She'd sunk to his level again. Wonderful.

Goric had upset her, but Mentàll was her real problem. Why wouldn't he rescue Deccia The General could kill her anytime soon. Each delay jeopardized her life even more.

△ △ △ △ △

Methusal's opportunity to speak to Mentàll came much sooner than expected. She'd just sat down with Behran, Taltn, and Hendra to a dinner of dried wild beast and pods when the Dehrien leader arrived.

He paid no attention to the fact she was eating dinner. "Methusal."

"I'll be back," she promised her friends, and took along a few pods to chew on. She took her sweet time strolling to the secluded bend in the stream, however. When she arrived, Mentàll already sat on the large boulder with his tunic over his knee.

Methusal tended Mentàll's wound as best she could. She bit her tongue about Deccia's rescue until she'd begun to adhere the tacky leaves. She didn't want to start an argument while cleaning his wound and accidentally hurt him.

Working quietly for those few minutes gave her time to fully plan a strategy. She'd approach the subject logically. Hopefully, he would respond in kind.

"Do you think we need more information to rescue Deccia?" Methusal was pleased with her opener. Humble, and asking his opinion before swooping in for the kill. She carefully adhered the last, protective leaf.

"Trust me to know the right time."

She counted to twenty. Still, she couldn't resist saying, "Trust you. Because you've proven yourself so trustworthy in the past?"

The Dehrien twisted to look at her. "Are you finished?"

"No! Well, yes, with the leaves."

He stood and faced her. Methusal refused to let his physical size intimidate her. That's what he wanted—she read it in his cold gaze.

She tried again. Unfortunately, her next words sounded even more antagonistic. "Tell me why you haven't planned Deccia's rescue mission."

"I do not answer to you, Maahr." He pulled on his tunic.

"I know." She took a deep breath and struggled to find calm, reasonable words. "But I'm really worried about my sister. The General could kill her at any time. With Doltn's map, it would be easy to break into the General's compound now."

"No." That flat answer dashed every one of her hopes.

She clenched her fists. "Why not? Send me, if you're afraid to go."

The pale eyes turned to ice. "Speak to me with respect."

He wouldn't listen to reason. This had become abundantly clear. He didn't care if Deccia lived or died. Power and control were his gods. And she had had enough.

The glowing fury in her belly exploded.

"How can I respect you? You are a *liar*," she snapped, knowing full well how violently he hated that word. What did she have to lose? He didn't plan to rescue Deccia. Not anytime soon, at least. And she didn't care if he threw her off the team or ordered her to stay in camp. She would not obey. It was past time she took matters into her own hands.

First, however, she'd extract a sliver of revenge. She was finished surrendering to his arrogant decrees. Time to give back a little of what he dished up. And she'd serve it with pleasure.

Tension stiffened the Dehrien Chief's shoulders. "I do not lie. *Ever*."

He'd responded defensively. A first.

Pleased that her words had pricked his cold hide, Methusal pressed on. "How fast you forget your false Alliance." Time to remind him of his past failures. Kitran's attack had made it fresh in both of their minds.

"The Alliance contained no lies."

Technically, that was true. "But you trick to achieve your goals. Playing games with words is deception. That's why Kitran hates you. Petr, too. And many others."

"Fools choose folly, instead of searching out the truth." His eyes glittered with arrogance. "Petr was fooled because he is a fool."

"Pan, too? And Kitran?"

He bared his teeth. "I did not trick your father, did I, Methusal? And Pan is a good man, but his heart is too soft."

"Pan trusted you. So did Petr and Kitran. You betrayed that trust."

His gaze cut away, too quickly for her to tell if she'd scored a jab. "Petr wanted to win the election. His lust for power blinded him."

"And your lust for power ended in defeat."

His features tightened. "Enjoy your fading glories, Methusal. You will never defeat me again."

Part of her believed him. By all accounts, he should have lost power in Dehre two and a half years ago. But he hadn't. Today he was stronger, and more ruthless and determined than ever before. And certainly his kaavl had improved, just as hers had. Unease slid through her.

The Dehrien Chief gave a humorless smile as he watched her expression. "Good. Fear is the beginning of respect. See that you remember it. You do not want to cross me."

"Disgust is not respect." For once, she would win an argument. "Only whips manipulate to achieve their goals. Doesn't it bother you that people hate you?"

"Some are destined to be servants, and others, rulers."

Her lips curled. "And of course you think you're the ruler."

"Aren't I?" He allowed this parry to sink in. "You, however, are spoiled and arrogant without cause."

Arrogant without cause? Spoiled? "*You* are the epitome of arrogance. But obviously you're blind to the truth about yourself. You certainly know nothing about me."

"I know that you want to earn my respect."

She gasped. "I do not! I couldn't want anything *less*."

"Deceive yourself, then." He smiled, clearly enjoying their war of words now. "But know one thing—to gain my respect, you'll have to earn it. No special privileges will be given because you are the Chief's daughter. Prove yourself, if you can. And when it is time, I will put you on the team to rescue Deccia." He turned on his heel and left.

The condescending man! Anger shuddered through her. He thought he held all the cards. But he did not.

CHAPTER TWELVE

METHUSAL DID NOT SLEEP VERY WELL that night. Fragmented, incoherent dreams tormented her. In most of them, her sister begged for help. Over and over again, Methusal struggled to reach her before the General appeared. But snarling wild beasts, attacking whips, and every disaster imaginable stopped her. The last dream had been the worst. She'd finally reached her sister's prison door. She fumbled with the key, searching for the lock, when a hand suddenly grabbed her tunic neck and yanked her backward. Mentàll. He laughed at her tears and dragged her toward kaavl camp.

Methusal awoke, gasping and choking. Her twisted coverlet pressed hard against her neck. After loosening it, she lay still, trying to calm her racing heart.

Pale pink rays of sunshine heralded the dawn. A crisp chill lingered in the air, reminding her of the cold night. A new day.

Today she would rescue her sister, or die trying.

She sat up and surveyed camp. Behran still slept, and so did her other friends. The Kaavl Commander was gone.

Where could he be at this hour of the morning? Meeting with his cohorts? Plotting how to seize their unknown prize? Planning more twisted Alliances?

Her gaze returned to Behran. Sleep relaxed his face, reminding her of the seventeen-year-old boy she'd met eight years ago. Today she'd scout with him. Gratitude surged. Finally, they'd spend a whole day together. Silly as it was, she still felt a little uncomfortable that he and Hendra had spent so much time together lately. She trusted Behran completely. Hendra, too, for that matter. But maybe neither realized how deep their connection went.

Methusal's gaze traced Behran's beloved features. Wasn't she being ridiculous? He loved her. He'd said so. Behran knew his own heart, surely. And he was a man of his word. She trusted him with her life, without question.

"Thusa." Those deep blue eyes watched her. "What's wrong?"

Methusal went for a partial truth. "I'm worried about Deccia."

"We all are."

She glanced at the Kaavl Commander's empty pallet. "Not everyone," she whispered. She moved closer and went down on one elbow. "I talked to him last night. He refuses to rescue Deccia. I don't think he's even formulating a plan."

Behran didn't answer; probably because he knew it was true.

Methusal wriggled a little closer. "It's up to us, Behran. *We* have to rescue Deccia. Today."

"Thusa!" He glanced toward camp, but no one stirred. "We have orders to scout."

"Fine. Afterward we'll rescue Deccia. Are you with me, or not?"

"You think we can rescue Deccia? Alone?"

"Think about it. The whole kaavl team can't attack the compound, because we don't have enough warriors. So we need to sneak in. That means one person, or maybe two at the most."

He watched her steadily. But no fear lived in his gaze, as she'd known it would not. "It's dangerous. We could die."

"You're right." She pulled back. "I don't want to ask you to risk your life just because I want to rescue Deccia now."

His strong fingers gripped hers. "I want to rescue Deccia. We all do. But why today?"

"Because!" Tears filled her eyes. "That General is doing awful things to her I *know* it. I can't let her suffer anymore. I can't. And I'm afraid he'll kill her. I don't know how much more time she has left."

Behran's knuckles gently brushed away her tears. "Okay, Thusa," he murmured. "I'll help. We'll rescue Deccia today."

She crumpled into his arms. Tears of relief and hope slipped down her cheeks.

△ △ △ △ △

Counting soldiers and troop rotations only took two hours. Afterward Methusal and Behran crouched in the burnt out building across from the General's compound. They'd already circled the entire complex three times.

"We'll have to go in the front gate," Behran whispered.

It was the only open entrance.

"Let's wait for the next guard change."

Hours dragged by, and Methusal and Behran rehashed their plan. Behran would distract the guards while Methusal slipped inside. Once inside, Methusal would cause a distraction and Behran would dart in.

Scouting around the compound had given Methusal glimpses inside the gate. She'd memorized the locations of trees, bushes, and doors. Early in the morning she had seen guards in the courtyard. After lunch, they disappeared. Of course she knew they could reappear at any moment.

Six Zindedi soldiers protected the entrance, but two of them currently peered inside the compound.

"The shift change is coming up," Methusal whispered. "Come on."

Behran caught her hand. "Be careful, Thusa." His gaze looked serious, and he tugged her close for a kiss.

"You too. We can do this. Are you ready?"

They slipped out of the blackened ruins and headed west, away from the compound, and toward the next street. There Behran headed north, toward the sea, and Methusal south.

Two blocks south she cut east again, toward the compound's street. She crossed the road and then strolled north, toward the fortified complex. She tugged her cloak tighter around her and clutched a small leather sack meant to look like a grocery bag. It was part of her disguise, and it contained her lunch. A meal she'd likely forfeit today.

One of the guards stared at her as she approached. She forced herself to walk on, but lowered her gaze and told herself there was nothing to worry about. As far as he knew, she was another Quasrian.

"Ohhh! The old racmun..." Behran warbled, approaching from the north end of the street. He staggered into a wall, righted himself, and stumbled on. "OOoh..." The words faltered, and then, "OOoh...the old racmun! Good for the spirits and full of good cheer..."

Methusal smiled. He sounded thoroughly drunk. And he'd caught the soldiers' attention, too. Four watched him approach. The other two greeted their replacements for guard duty.

"OOHH!" High and piercing, this blast caught everyone's attention.

Methusal darted inside the compound. She hid behind a thick bush near the wall and watched the farce outside the gates. Twelve Zindedis watched Behran stumble across the entrance. A few laughed. One shoved him. "Koblani filth," he sneered.

Behran took advantage of the shove, and artfully spun on one foot and collapsed at the gate's edge.

"Get up!" The same guard kicked him.

Men guffawed and others kicked him, too. Methusal cringed, hating the Zindedis more with every blow. Poor Behran! She was supposed to create a distraction, but not until the original guards retreated inside the complex. Having twelve soldiers hunt them down was the last thing they needed.

So she watched Behran silently suffer. He looked limp, as if he had passed out. Methusal couldn't help but worry.

After a while the Zindedis gave up. Apparently the game wasn't nearly as much fun if their victim didn't respond.

The six guards finally retreated inside the compound, leaving their fresh replacements at the gate. Methusal heard doors open to the north, and then slam shut. She peeked around her bush at Behran.

Behran opened one eye. She waggled her fingers, but he faintly shook his head. He closed his eye again.

Methusal changed her crouching position. Her legs ached. Behran must have thought of a new plan. Hopefully one that was less dangerous.

While she waited, she slipped more deeply into kaavl and fanned out her hearing to listen for all sounds within the courtyard. A flying beast chirped, and tree leaves rustled high overhead. Yellow flowers bloomed beside the white compound walls, and their heavy, sweet fragrance smelled divine. A slurping sound tickled her ears.

Methusal crept to the other edge of her bush and peered out. Nothing obstructed her view of the courtyard now. Pebbled pathways meandered through the rectangular compound. Lush foliage with bright pink, yellow, and purple flowers edged the paths of the courtyard, and were interspersed with thick trunked trees with wide, flowing fronds. Long, one story buildings with doors and windows were built into each of the southern and northern sides of the courtyard. Perhaps sleeping quarters for the soldiers, or meeting rooms?

About twenty lengths east was the mansion. The front face of the building took up the western side of the complex. It had multiple windows, and a huge, arched wooden doorway in the middle. There Methusal spotted the slurping soldier. The guard leaned against the wall, gnawing on an unknown fruit. His gun rested against the wall a few paces away. He didn't look worried about a Koblani attack.

She and Behran could easily take him down.

Another glance completed her inspection. On the northern end of the compound a broad, stone flagged path intersected the northern chambers and the mansion. Obviously, it was where the northern gate was located. The southern half of the complex was constructed the same way, except the southern wall of the mansion ended in a large flower garden.

Now, if only Behran...

A touch on her shoulder made her jump.

Behran grinned.

"Behran!" she gasped. "How did you get in?"

"They stopped watching me. We'd better move fast."

Methusal quickly whispered her observations.

"We'll take out the guard first," Behran said, and pulled out two leather kaavl strips.

"You could put on his uniform," Methusal whispered. "Then the soldiers inside will think you're one of them."

"Good idea."

Now to get across the complex without being seen.

"The guards went in the northern doors," Methusal murmured. "Let's cut across on the south side."

The first bush on their planned path was over two lengths away. Methusal's heart pounded, anticipating the sprint. She fanned out her hearing, trying to listen for sounds inside the southern rooms, but heard nothing. Were they empty? Or were people reading or sleeping?

"Ready?" Behran asked. She nodded, and dashed after him to the first bush.

She crouched beside him, heard pounding, and listened.

"Anything?"

"No."

In a series of sprints, they circled the courtyard unaccosted. Methusal couldn't believe it was so easy. Clearly the Zindedi's security inside the compound was weak.

When they were three lengths away from the guard at the huge door, Behran squatted behind a prickly bush. "How's your aim?"

"Pretty good. Why?"

He handed her a palm-sized stone. "We'll need to knock him out. Throw on two. Ready?"

Methusal hefted the heavy rock. Its impact would hurt.

"One...two!"

Behran's rock walloped into the guard's forehead and Methusal's into his adam's apple. Both landed with sickening thuds, and her stomach lurched. The soldier's eyes widened in surprise and he crumpled to the ground.

They waited for any unseen Zindedis to give a cry of alarm.

Nothing. Only the rustle of leaves. Methusal couldn't believe it was this easy.

"Come on." Behran darted out, and she helped him drag the guard back to their bush. Behran stripped off the guard's jacket and breeches, and put them on over top of his own. Methusal tied a kaavl strip around the man's ankles. Behran took care of his wrists and a gag, and then he rolled the man into the base of the prickly bush. The branches and stickers would hurt a lot when he woke up. Behran wadded his cloak and hers into a ball and stuffed them near the man's feet, ready to be grabbed on their retreat later.

"Ready?" His steady gaze held her own. Methusal's heart pounded. Deccia was in that building. Soon they'd rescue her.

"Let's do it."

When they slipped inside the mansion, an involuntary gasp left Methusal's lips. Never had she seen anything so grand before. The entrance hall was enormous—probably ten lengths wide by twenty long, and five lengths high. Three hallways branched to the left and also to the right, and ahead, two more shot straight east.

Sunshine spilled through tall, high windows, and glowed off the polished wooden floor. Ornate rugs lay scattered over it. Sparkles glinted from gold torch holders. Objects of art wrought in precious green and blue stones and interlaced with even more precious gold and silver metal, rested upon tables. Painted pictures of the sea and the Quasr Mountains hung on the white walls.

Methusal had never seen such opulence in her life, and for a moment couldn't stop staring. She'd rarely seen gold or silver before—and that was only in her mother's marriage necklace. That was an heirloom passed down to the sons in the Maahr family for untold generations, and worth a fortune.

Soldiers wandered the hall, but few glanced their way.

Behran whispered into her hair, "Pretend you're my prisoner." He pulled her wrists behind her back and loosely lashed them with a kaavl strip.

Only one hall led to the below ground prison, and it lay straight ahead. They strode for it.

"Where are you going, soldier?" a gruff voice demanded. A burly man approached. Thick gray whiskers peppered his chin, and his wavy gray hair was cropped short. Like all of the soldiers, he wore a black uniform with a sideways red sash fastened across his right shoulder. Metal emblems of various shapes were sewn to the upper left shoulder of his uniform. Obviously an enemy of high rank.

Behran's posture stiffened. "Escorting a prisoner to jail, sir."

The man eyed Methusal. "What did she do?"

"She wasn't wearing a cloak. And I found her stealing food—" he pulled the lunch from her hand, "—from a soldier."

The man's thick lips curled back, revealing yellow teeth. Rough fingers gripped Methusal's chin, and he tilted her face left, then right. The small movement released an acrid scent of body odor. He reminded Methusal of a woolly, unwashed animal. He smiled, and she looked at the floor in order to hide her revulsion and fear. Instinct told her he was a dangerous man. Maybe unpredictable, too.

"Put her in prison, soldier."

"Yes, sir!" Gripping her wrists harder, Behran pushed her forward. Methusal pretended to stumble, so Behran's treatment of her would look harsh.

Swiftly, Behran hustled her down the hall. A few soldiers walking by made lewd comments, which Methusal struggled to ignore.

A panicky fear rose higher with each step that brought her closer to the prison. Methusal wasn't sure why, but she felt suffocated. She wanted to bolt from the General's compound, and run without stopping to kaavl camp. Maybe it was because of the many nightmares she'd had about this place.

A twist at the end of the hall revealed stairs. Behran urged her down, and quickly slipped the kaavl strip off her wrists, but she kept her wrists behind her, still pretending to be tied up. Flickering torches lit the way. A closed door and a guard at the bottom stopped their progress. Just like Doltn's map had said.

Methusal knew what came next, and mentally cringed.

The young guard eyed them with little interest, and pulled out a chain of keys. He slid one into the lock. "New prisoner?"

"Yeah."

The guard pushed the door open. "There you go."

Swift as lightning, Behran punched the guard's throat, and then his nose. Methusal whipped out her kaavl strips and a gag, and within seconds they'd bound the coughing guard. He glared through watery eyes, and Behran quickly dragged him into the prison hall. That's when Methusal stopped. Dizziness hit her. It was the hall from her dreams. Long. Lit by flickering torches. The wooden cell doors had barred windows. Deccia's was the fourth from the end. She stumbled forward.

"Thusa. Here are the keys." Behran tossed them to her, and shoved the guard into a corner. "I'll stand watch outside."

Keys feeling cold in her hand, Methusal walked, as if in a dream, down the empty hall...toward her sister.

All of sudden, she launched into a sprint. This wasn't a dream. Finally, she could rescue her sister. "Deccia? Deccia!"

She stopped at the fourth door and clutched the bars. It was pitch dark in the cell. "Deccia?"

Nothing for an empty, frightening moment...and then a soft shuffle. "Thusa?"

Methusal burst into tears. "Decc!"

Her sister appeared, and her face looked as wan and dirty as in Methusal's nightmares. Her wide eyes looked empty, except for a tiny glimmer of hope. She gripped Methusal's fingers over the bars. "How did you get in here?"

"It doesn't matter. We're going to get you out. I have keys." Methusal wiggled the first key into the lock.

"I prayed," Deccia whispered. "I didn't think it would happen so soon."

Methusal's hands shook, just like in her dream. None of the keys fit. Frustrated, she tried them again. "I dreamed about this place." Tears filled her eyes and slipped down her cheeks. On the other hand, Deccia looked remarkably calm. Was it because she felt patient? Or defeated? Was she willing to accept her fate, whatever it might be? This last thought made Methusal feel sick.

"None of them fit," she cried out.

"Try again. Slower. It's okay."

Methusal started again. "It's not okay." She bit her lip. "I've had dreams about you and this place, and that awful General. I know what he's doing to you, Deccia. I'm so sorry!"

"I've been praying to The One for strength and protection."

"How can you stand it?"

"I don't know," her sister said quietly. "But he hasn't come for me in a few days."

Methusal's last nightmare flashed to mind. "The last time he came, did he threaten to bring you to the garden?" Deccia's face blanched. "Did you try to escape?"

"Yes," she said softly. "But a minute later, a guard reported the attack on the beach. The General left, and he hasn't been back."

More tears blurred Methusal's vision. The dream had been real. She couldn't see the keys or the lock. Taking a deep breath, she swiped at her eyes and blinked. "How many times, Deccia?" For some reason, she had to know. She needed to share every bit of her twin's pain. If possible, she wished that Deccia could transfer all of that horror onto her.

"Three times," Deccia whispered. "Don't tell Timaeus. Please."

"I would *never*."

"If I don't make it out, tell him I love him. I'll love him forever." For the first time, Methusal heard a catch of desperation in Deccia's voice, and an aching emptiness, too.

"Don't talk like that! I'm getting you out. Behran's right outside that door. If these keys don't work, he'll knock it down."

None of the keys fit. After the fourth try, that became clear.

"I'm sorry, Deccia."

Desolation glimmered in her sister's eyes. "It's okay. Just come back. Save me, please...somehow."

"I'll get Behran. He'll knock down the door..."

Deccia's gaze slid to Methusal's right. "Thusa!"

Unfortunately, Methusal had forgotten about kaavl for the last few minutes. A faint whisper of movement tickled her ears and a bag swooped over her head, blacking out the light. She struggled wildly. Where had the man come from? Not from Behran's direction, she felt sure. Probably from the other end of the hall.

Behran.

"*Run, Behran!*" she screamed.

She fought her unseen assailant with all of her strength and kaavl training. Unfortunately, more than one man fought back. They wrestled her into submission on the floor. One tied her hands together, and the other, her feet. Then they dragged her down the hall. The cloth bag felt hot and cloying, and the rough cloth prickled her nose. It smelled like mold and damp. Where was Behran? Where were they taking her?

Methusal wanted to fight, but she was trussed up like an apte.

The men paused. "There's Miln."

Boot steps pounded down the stairs.

"The other one escaped," panted a voice. "I got him good with my sword, though."

"A death blow?"

Methusal listened, horrified.

"No." The word sounded chagrinned. "On the arm."

"Catch him!"

"Men are on it."

Deccia had been praying. Maybe she should start, too. Methusal shot a prayer heavenward as the soldiers dragged her up the stairs. The steps painfully bumped into her back and legs.

"Where are we taking her?" muttered one.

"The General. Commander's orders."

Fear cut into her like a knife. The General. The fiendish rapist. And he was insane, too, according to Timaeus. The General would see that she and Deccia were twins. He would know that she had tried to rescue her sister.

What would he do to her?

CHAPTER THIRTEEN

QUASR

THE MEN DIDN'T PULL THE BAG off of Methusal's head until they had shoved her into a chair. She blinked at the sudden light. Late afternoon sunlight streamed through large windows, illuminating a big room with a polished desk, chairs, a couch, and shelves of books. Behind the desk sat the General. Methusal recognized him from her dream.

"That is all. Leave us." His slightly vacant amber eyes focused on her when the door clicked closed.

He blinked, and a small smile lifted the corners of his thick black moustache and wrinkled into his jowly face. "Well, well, well," he said softly. "My Commander promised a delectable surprise, and here you are."

She said nothing.

"You are Methusal Maahr, the Chief of Rolban's daughter." He watched her, his eyes glittering, like a whip playing with an apte.

Methusal remained silent. How did he know? Had Deccia been hurt and humiliated until she was forced to tell him everything?

She wanted to spit hatred at the horrible man across from her, but that would be stupid. She recognized that he was like Jascr. He liked to inflict pain, and enjoyed seeing people suffer. She would not cry or beg for her life. Pretending that she did not care about anything would be her primary weapon. And her powers of observation. She would learn everything possible about this sickening invader. Every scrap of information would help hasten his downfall.

If she escaped.

The middle-aged Zindedi leaned forward and laced his hands together on the desk. Unable to help herself, Methusal glanced at them. Revulsion lurched when she saw the bloody stump where his right thumb should have been. Just like in her dream. She struggled not to react to the horrifying sight.

With effort, she schooled her features into slack sullenness.

He smiled. "You don't speak much. Of course, I have ways to make you talk."

Methusal slowly glanced around the room, as if bored. She noted the gun mounted on the wall above the window and the sword beneath it.

The General continued to smile. "You pretend to be dull and meek. It will be most enjoyable to find out if that is true."

Methusal silently stared at him.

The General barked, "Where are the Koblani troops?" His nostrils flared, and his amber eyes widened. For a moment, he looked insane.

Methusal struggled not to blink.

"So. You will not tell me. Yet." He sucked in a breath. "That is to be expected." Long, silent moments passed. Methusal wondered what bizarre thoughts might be flitting through his mind. He leaned back in his chair and a conspiratorial smile pulled at his lips. "You may not realize it, but we share a mortal enemy."

Methusal's expression remained impassive.

The General slammed his fists on the desk, and she jumped. He smiled. "Better. You unresponsiveness is not acceptable. Speak when I speak to you."

She sighed, as if bored beyond reason. Dully, she intoned, "Who?"

"So you can speak. Your features are as lovely as your sister's, but your voice carries no melody."

Hope flared. Her plan was working.

Dashing it, he said, "That doesn't matter to me."

Was that a threat? Better to get his mind back on track. In a monotone, she said, "What enemy?"

"Why, the Dehrien Chief, of course. Mentàll Solboshn." His amber eyes gleamed. "Tell me where to find him, and I will free both you and your sister."

What? Not that she believed him for one second. "My enemy does not report to me."

The General leaned forward again. "He is near, though, is he not?"

"All of your enemies draw near. We want you to leave our continent."

"It is my continent now. The fate of your people lies in my hand." He curled his left hand into a fist. "And the treasures of your land will be mine, also." He curled his right fingers in, but no thumb secured them. He squeezed his fingers hard, until they showed white. In fact, they trembled, he clenched them so hard. He stared at them, eyes wide, as if lost in his own little world.

The man must be insane, as Timaeus had reported.

What was he thinking about now? Certainly, he was easily distracted. That fact might prove useful.

"I like to kill, you know," he commented, relaxing. "I killed thousands on my own continent, and I enjoyed it. The fear. The pleas for mercy. It's power, you know. *Power,*" spittle formed at the corners of his mouth, "to hold someone's life in your hand, and then crush it, like an insect."

Methusal swallowed back her horror.

"So you see." He focused on her again. "I enjoy this war. I relish the right to kill every single Koblani. Soon I will unite both continents beneath my brother." His eyes gleamed. "Perhaps he will make me Presidente of this land."

"Your brother is the Presidente of Zindedi?" she blurted. "The whole continent?"

"Thanks to my brilliant military strategies, yes." He unexpectedly lurched forward and grabbed her tunic. With maniacal strength, he yanked her across the desk. Terror billowed as his nose touched hers.

"*Where* is my enemy?" he hissed.

Methusal drew a shallow breath. It didn't calm her panic. "I...I don't know. He tells no one where he goes."

He shoved her back, hard, so she flew backwards and tipped off the edge of the chair. Her bound hands couldn't stop her from hitting her head hard on the wooden floor. A gasp of pain escaped.

"Guards," shouted the General.

A door opened behind her.

"Cart the Koblani filth to a cell. A different wing from her sister."

"Yes, sir!"

"We will meet again, Methusal." He chuckled softly. "Next time you will tell me what I want to know."

The guards dragged her down the hall, and down more painful stairs. Tears trickled down her cheeks by the time they tossed her into a stone cell. The door clanged shut and finally, she was alone. It was dark, except for the sliver of light under the door.

Methusal felt bruised and battered and terrified. How did the General plan to extract information from her? He didn't believe what she'd said about Mentàll, that was for sure. But why did he want to know so badly?

The guards had left her hands and feet tied. At least her hands were in front. Methusal began to work at the knots at her feet. Her prison cell was not included on Doltn's map. Even if someone came looking for her, no one would find her.

△ △ △ △ △

The next few hours in Methusal's small stone cell passed slowly. Escape was possible only through the door. She'd be ready when the guards returned, though. Using her teeth, she untied her hands and feet, and coiled the rope nearby. It would be a useful weapon when the guard returned.

Whenever that might be.

She rehashed through the meeting with the General and her failed attempt to rescue her sister. Methusal blamed herself. She'd slipped out of kaavl. She'd failed to hear the Zindedis approach. They had bagged her like a sleepy apte lying in the sun!

Tears burned her eyes. And what about Behran? Had he escaped?

What a mess!

If Behran didn't make it back to kaavl camp, no one would know where they were.

Even if Behran *did* make it back to camp, Methusal harbored no illusions— the Dehrien would send no rescue team for her. He had refused to rescue Deccia, even though her release would have earned him bonus points with Erl and

Petr. So why would he risk sending a team for Methusal? He hated her.

No. She was stuck here until she figured her own way out.

Hours dragged by. Depression kicked in. The General had probably doubled the guards around the compound by now. They'd be on full alert. Had she made a mistake, trying to rescue Deccia today?

"Listen, Methusal." Again, the Prophet's words whispered through her mind. "Choose the higher way. It is a test to be repeated many times, until you understand."

She was hotheaded. Even mutinous. Wasn't that why Petr had thrown her in jail two years ago? Because she'd refused to listen? Because she'd despised him, and she had followed her own path. Just like now. She hated Mentàll, and had believed that had justified disobeying his orders.

Hadn't she grown? Hadn't she matured?

But this was her sister's life! The Dehrien wouldn't rescue her. Wasn't it up to her to do something about it?

And yet here she was, a prisoner. Behran was injured, and maybe captured. And Deccia was no better off.

Mentàll had called her arrogant without cause. Could he possibly be right?

The thought did not settle well.

Methusal wrapped her arms around her knees and buried her face in them. More tears streamed down her face. What was she going to do?

A scrape came at the door.

Quick as a flash, she leaped up and coiled the rope loosely around her fists. Then she leaned against the wall, pretending to look lethargic and depressed.

The door creaked and opened into the hall, spilling in a thin sliver of light. A hand shoved a cup inside. The guard didn't intend to enter.

Methusal hurtled her body against the door. It hit something solid, and she heard a grunt. She wiggled through the opening and ran straight into a hooded figure. He wasn't much taller than she was, but the arms that grabbed her felt like they were made of ore. She kicked and punched, struggling to free herself, but another hooded guard appeared in her side vision. Pain cracked across her skull, and everything went black.

△ △ △ △ △

Dusk descended on kaavl camp, and then complete darkness enfolded it. Worry twisted tighter in Hendra the darker it grew. Behran and Methusal should have returned hours ago.

Mentàll had shown no signs of worry all evening. He ate his meal and talked with his closest Dehrien comrades, Efron and Tabor. They weren't his friends. Hendra didn't think her cousin had any actual friends. But allies? Yes.

Kitran brooded by himself a short distance away. The shadows made his face look dark and forbidding.

Now the meal was finished and her cousin paced near the fire. Hendra couldn't stay silent any longer, so she approached him. His tense features conveyed displeasure. Irritation, too.

Softly, she said, "Should we send out a search team? I'll go, if you'll let me."

"I will send a team. But you will not go. Kitran!" he barked.

The Rolbani kaavl instructor immediately came. A scowl contorted his features.

Mentàll said, "Search for your Rolbani comrades. Take two men with you."

"About time, Dehrien!" Kitran snapped. "You should have let me go hours ago. They could be dead because of your incompetence!" With a vicious twist of his shoulders, Kitran stalked away. He recruited Goric and Wortn, and sped out of camp.

"Why didn't you send someone earlier?" Hendra dared to ask.

"It is safer to search in the dark." To her surprise, her cousin did not appear to be offended by the question.

Hendra dared to ask a more pointed question. "Did you want to search for them?"

"I did not want to believe they were captured!" Teeth gritted, he said, "Methusal disobeyed my orders."

"How can you be sure?"

"They are not here. That is proof enough." He left her.

Hendra crossed her arms and stared at the cluster of rocks Kitran had just disappeared behind. *The One, please let Behran and Methusal be all right.*

△ △ △ △ △

When she awoke again, Methusal felt disoriented and cold. Metal bit into her wrists, which were now shackled behind her. And her head throbbed.

She felt more afraid than ever. She had tried to escape. Would that stoke the fires of wrath in the General's hellish soul? He had already planned to extract information from her. Now would he intensify his planned tortures?

When would he call for her again?

She was parched. Methusal shuffled on her knees to the door, searching for the water cup. Maybe she could grab it with her teeth and drink. But the cup was gone. Despair choked her.

It must be the middle of the night by now. She curled up on the stone floor. Cold seeped into her bones. How she wished for her cloak, lying snug beneath that prickly bush out front.

She shivered, and curled up tighter. She felt like a helpless animal locked up like this. The General wanted her to feel this fear. He wanted her to feel vulnerable and remember how he had manhandled her in his office, and how he had ordered her dragged out. He wanted her to cower down here and remember his threats. Maybe even to remember his insanity?

Methusal closed her eyes and tried to sleep. If only she could escape! If only Kitran or someone from the kaavl team would rescue her.

It would not happen.

Despair ached in her spirit. Mentàll would send no rescue team. Finally, she would meet the horrible fate he'd always wanted for her.

△ △ △ △ △

Hendra could barely keep her eyes open. She sat by the flickering fire, waiting for Kitran's return. Her cousin silently crouched nearby, poking the burning logs. The rest of camp lay quiet.

Suddenly, Hendra saw Kitran come around the rock. He and Wortn carried a body between them. "Behran?" she cried out. She leaped to her feet.

"What do you see?"

Hendra glanced at Mentàll. Then back at the rocks.

No one was there. "I saw…" For a moment she stared at the stones. Had she fallen asleep? Had she dreamed it? She blinked, and then she saw Kitran again.

Mentàll strode fast for the Rolbani kaavl instructor.

Hendra felt disoriented. What had just happened? Had she actually *seen* Kitran around that corner before he had appeared? Her mind flashed back to Doltn running down the Quasrian street.

But all of those thoughts fled as she ran over to Behran. His face was deathly white, and blood smeared his tunic.

Gently, they lowered him near the fire. "Get his pallet, Hendra," Kitran said, and she hurried to obey. She also grabbed coltac leaves and other healing items from Methusal's stash.

"What happened?" Mentàll knelt by Behran's side.

Kitran pulled out a knife and cut away Behran's tunic. Blood oozed from his chest, and a deep laceration scored his arm.

Hendra gasped. "Behran!"

"He passed out," Kitran said. "We found him halfway from Quasr, collapsed behind a rock."

"Did he speak?" Mentàll demanded curtly.

"He said Methusal is captured. She's in the General's compound."

Mentàll swore once, viciously, and surged to his feet.

Hendra was horrified.

But Behran had escaped. And he needed immediate help. She quickly wet lynnte weeds in the stream and returned. "Let me clean his wounds."

The men moved back, and she carefully wiped away the blood on his chest. That's when she saw the two stab wounds. The one near his side appeared to be a flesh wound. But dark blood oozed from the one in his chest, and she wondered how deep it went.

Behran could die. She could stop the bleeding on the outside, but not on the inside. "He needs Doc!" she whispered.

"Stop the bleeding," Mentàll ordered. "Doc cannot come. Timaeus reported a dozen casualties today."

"But Behran could die!"

"Do the best you can," Kitran said gently. "I'll help you."

She drew a shuddering breath. "I'll need to sew up the wounds. Methusal has a needle."

Wortn spoke above them. "I have racmun spirits."

In swift order, everything was assembled, and the wound and implements sanitized. Hendra had never stitched anyone up in her life, but she'd seen Doc do it multiple times when the invaders had attacked. She hated the thought of poking into Behran's skin and hurting him still more.

"Hurry, while he's still passed out," Kitran urged.

Hands trembling, she began. But she feared that sewing up the wound wouldn't be enough. Only The One could save Behran if he was wounded internally. Hendra prayed with every stitch she made.

Chapter Fourteen

METHUSAL'S EYES FELT GRITTY when she woke up, and she felt frozen from lying curled up on the ice cold floor. Had Behran made it safely back to camp? Was he even alive?

If he was dead, it was all her fault.

Pain ached through her bruised back and legs as she struggled to sit up. It was difficult with her arms shackled behind her.

No guards had come yet. But they would.

Why did they wear hooded cloaks? Were they Quasrians, pressed into service for the General? Methusal thought about enlisting their help, as fellow Koblanis. Then she remembered the vicious blow she had received last night. Even if they were Koblanis, they wouldn't help her.

Soon they'd return and drag her to her fate.

If only she could escape from these shackles! The hard metal bit painfully into her wrists, but that wasn't what hurt most. She'd miserably failed her sister, and Behran, too. Tears slid down her cheeks.

She was so thirsty.

And scared.

How long would she be able to endure the General's torture? Would she break, and reveal kaavl camp's location? And then would he kill her? Or find some other, horrifying use for her, like he'd done with Deccia?

Her eyes burned, and her mouth felt like a fire. She was parched, and her tongue felt thick and sticky.

Her sister had seemed so calm yesterday. She had a strength Methusal longed to possess. Deccia had said she prayed every day. And she'd been delivered from the General's foul attentions at least once already.

Deccia's last words whispered through her mind, "Come back. Save me, please...somehow."

"Save me..." The words murmured over and over through her heart, and burning tears scorched her cheeks. If only she could. If only she could save them both!

The door lock rattled, and Methusal hurriedly brushed her wet cheeks against her shoulders. It wouldn't be smart to reveal how upset she was. She glanced up at the large, hooded guard entering the cell. This was it. Now he'd drag her to the General.

As she faced her imminent fate, horror grew, but so did a sudden, rebellious resolve.

Never! She'd *die* first.

She looked down at the floor as the guard unlocked her hands. The better to drag her, no doubt. Maybe he meant to relock them in front. A plan glimmered.

He was alone—she heard no one else in the hall. Maybe she could attack him, grab the keys, and save Deccia.

Determination grew. The guard gripped her arm and pulled her upright, to face him. He was much taller than the others, and stood almost three handbreadths above her. It didn't matter. *Now!* Like lightning, she swiped her foot behind his and shoved his shoulder back hard, with the heels of her hands.

She heard his indrawn hiss of surprise. Just as she prepared to stomp on his foot and knee him in a most painful place, he seized her shoulder, spun her, and slammed her back hard against him. One hand gripped her left arm, and his other arm immobilized her right shoulder, in a "V" across her chest. She couldn't move. He was much too strong for her, but panic made her fight anyway.

"Stop." The word grated in her ear.

"Die, whip beast," she panted, but his foot unexpectedly snaked between her legs and hooked her right foot, forcing it back. She teetered as he pushed her off balance, and she twisted and suddenly she found herself flat on her back, breath knocked out of her, on the stone floor.

Methusal cringed, waiting for the blow, as the guard crouched beside her.

"You expect me to hit you?"

Methusal recognized that low, harsh voice, and her eyes flew open.

Cold blue eyes stared at her from beneath the shadowed hood.

"Mentàll!" She was speechless with shock. "What are you doing here?"

"Rescuing a mutinous kaavl player." Fury sliced through that whisper.

Relief battled unease. "I had to rescue Deccia."

"Did your plan succeed?" he snarled.

She sat up, feeling vulnerable. "Not like I'd hoped."

"Behran is injured," he whipped back. "You are captured. And where is your sister?"

"In jail." Tears filled her eyes, but she blinked them back and scrambled to her feet. Now wasn't the time to fall apart. "I have to save her now, before it's too late. Give me the keys."

"I will not. You'll come with me to camp." He thrust a damp cloak at her. It was hers.

"No! I'm going to rescue her. Either help me, or get out of my way."

"If the General captures you a second time, what will he do? Kill you. And Deccia."

Methusal didn't reply. She pulled on her cloak. At least it was dry inside.

"You cannot succeed. Guards are tripled now."

"Then how did you get in here?"

He did not answer.

"I have to try! *Move.*" She tried to dart around him, but he gripped her arm, stopping her. She drew a shuddering breath, determined not to crumple before this man. She was so close, and now the Dehrien would stand in her way? Despair tightened her throat. "You don't know what he's doing to her! I can't leave her here. She's my sister!"

Mentàll only watched, his gaze cold and impassive.

Against her will, tears escaped. "You're just like the General! You have no heart!"

"Come. Now." He yanked her hood down over her face, and marched her to the door. Overhead, an army of footsteps clattered. Guards?

"I won't leave without Deccia. I *won't!*"

"You will. Or we will die." He propelled her through the door, down the short hall, and then past an unconscious guard and up the stairs. They entered a wider hallway.

"He'll kill Deccia!"

Footsteps approached, and he pulled her into a shadowed enclave. "No. He has other uses for her."

Methusal gasped in horror. How dare he speak of the General's atrocities so calmly? She kicked him with all of her strength.

He bit back a guttural word as the guard strode by. Luckily the invader didn't hear it. The Dehrien Chief gripped her upper arm and shoved her ahead of him, down the hall. A pause to ensure the side door was unguarded for a moment, and they ran through, dashed across the garden, and then out the southern compound gate and into a rocky alley. Where were the four guards? Had he killed them?

Rain speared her exposed flesh as Mentàll forced her to walk fast beside him. They ducked onto the main street. Dark clouds roiled overhead. Parched, she stuck out her tongue to catch the cool rain.

Methusal still wanted to insist on going back for her twin, but knew it was too late now. Soon, if not already, the guards would discover her escape. If she went back, they'd quickly find and probably kill her.

"Why didn't you help me? We could have rescued her!"

He said nothing until a good fifty lengths separated them from the General's compound, and then he yanked her around the corner of a building. His grip on her arm smarted.

"You're hurting..." She broke off when she saw the contempt in his eyes. A chill crept through her.

"You fool," he hissed. "You could have cost us our lives."

Methusal swallowed.

"Mutiny. Disobedience. Kicking. Struggling against your commanding officer!"

"I didn't want to leave my sister."

"You are a soldier, Maahr! When you disobey me, you disobey your father. You mutiny against Rolban and Koblan."

"No."

"Yes." He shook her arm. "I cannot have a kaavl player I cannot trust. You belong at base camp."

"No!" Horrified, she lowered her voice. "Please. I'm sorry. But I couldn't wait any longer. You weren't doing anything..."

"Rescuing your sister is not my goal. Winning this war is."

Tears of despair tightened in her throat, but she swallowed back the unwelcome, aching lump. "Will you ever send a team to rescue Deccia?"

"Only if the time and circumstances are right."

"Aren't you even a little human? Don't you care how he's using her?"

Mentàll stared at her for a moment. "She is a hostage. He tries to bend us to his will by making threats against her."

"They are more than threats. He is violating her. Repeatedly."

Surprise flashed across his features, and the grip on her arm loosened. "Behran said nothing."

"He didn't speak to her. I did. She told me...she told me the despicable things he's doing to her." Methusal couldn't stop her tears now. Fiercely, she said, "I'd give my life to save her from that."

"You might give your life, but you would not have saved hers."

"You don't care, do you? You don't *care* what he's doing to her. That's because you're just like him! A beast. You would have violated me two years ago, but I escaped. Now you want to kill me!" Rage and more tears stung her eyes, and she wrenched her arm free. She couldn't stand to have him touch her for another moment.

"Do I?"

"Yes!"

"No." His lips curled, and cruel amusement glittered. "You are wrong, as usual, Methusal."

"I don't believe you. But I do believe that you'll wait until you've had your full use of my kaavl before you take revenge on me. You need me to help win this war. Then your promise to my father will end. You're no better than the General!"

A few people who were walking by glanced over at them—probably because of her raised voice. The Dehrien Chief gripped her by the wrist and pulled her to walk on, fast, through the crumbling, half burnt town. "You speak what you do not know, Methusal."

"I know! I know you have no intention of rescuing Deccia, ever."

"You are drawing attention to us."

To her mortification, tears streamed down her cheeks. It hurt, like tearing herself in two, to leave her twin behind to suffer. And she felt thirstier than ever. The rain wasn't enough. Although it killed her to ask, she said, "I'm thirsty. Do you have water?"

The Dehrien unhooked his water skin and shoved it at her. Parched, she gulped it dry. She felt she could never drink enough again.

Mentàll muttered a Dehrien epithet under his breath and dragged her between two buildings.

"Now what are you doing?"

"Soldiers. They've seen us."

If the soldiers recognized Mentàll, they'd kill them both. The bounty on Mentàll's head guaranteed it. For the first time, she wondered why Mentàll had gone to the trouble of rescuing her. Why would he infiltrate the General's compound—the den of the very man who'd put a bounty on his head?

And now soldiers were almost upon them, and she hadn't even noticed because she'd been so wrapped up in her own misery. Would Mentàll really send her to back base camp? She deserved it.

Mentàll pulled his hood lower, to shield his face from the rain and recognition, and in one quick movement he unsheathed his sword and pulled her hard against him. She gasped as her face smashed into the rough fabric of his cloak. She struggled to free herself.

"Stop," he snarled. "Put your arms around me. We are lovers."

"No!" Methusal recoiled.

"Will you fail your mission, yet again?"

She drew a quick breath. Everything in her screamed to bolt from this man, but wasn't it time for her to act to save their lives, instead of behaving like a child throwing a fit because she couldn't get her own way? Wasn't it better to pretend the reprehensible, rather than suffer a real death? Fear of death proved greater than her loathing to touch him, so she slid her arms around his waist.

She'd touched him before, of course, nursing his wounds. But never up close like this. Never before had she realized how shockingly powerful the man was. Hard muscles flexed beneath her palms, and the arms holding her felt as unyielding as ore.

Methusal couldn't decide if she felt scared or secure. The last of her tears stopped, mingling with the increasing rain.

The invaders' boots clomped closer. Her kaavl discerned two men, coming from the south. Thankfully not from the direction of the General's compound. These men wouldn't know about her escape.

She and the Dehrien Chief could take care of them, if necessary.

Mentàll kept his sword in hand, tight against her side, out of view of the street. His other hand slowly slid up her back. Alarmed, she glanced up. But he wasn't looking at her. Those cold, alert eyes watched the street.

The invaders were two steps away now. Methusal tensed, scared, but ready for action. The Dehrien Chief's hand slowly drifted down her back again. Distracted, she jerked her chin up again. As the invaders stepped into view the Dehrien unexpectedly exerted pressure on the small of her back, forcing her closer to him, and his hooded face swept close to hers. His hard mouth crushed her own.

Methusal froze, horrified by this intimate contact with her mortal enemy. She wanted to scream and run away, but couldn't. She shuddered. This contact with Mentàll, and the terror of the guards shorted out her thinking process. She quickly realized the feel of his lips on hers disturbed her the most. And she couldn't push him away. The invaders saw them now.

One hooted, "Rent a room."

In response, Mentàll's grip on his sword tightened against her, and he slid his mouth over hers, changing the angle of his head so he could see better. His bristly chin softly scratched her face, and her skin prickled up all over her body, vibrating with a desire to flee from him.

This cold man's lips felt warm. This disjointed thought disturbed her even further. She stood very still, waiting.

Finally, the soldiers moved on.

The Dehrien broke contact with her and stared over her head, down the street. Methusal gulped in a breath of relief.

He said, "It is safe. Time to go." For the first time, she smelled a whiff of his bad breath that she had last smelled over two years ago.

Methusal quickly staggered back. She followed him between the houses and onto the next street. She gulped, trying to regain her breath, because she felt like she had stopped breathing for a minute back there.

Stop it, she told herself. It was nothing. Just a way to escape from the soldiers. At least he hadn't turned it into anything sexual. In fact, for all the notice he'd taken of her, she could have been a tree, or a rock. Her breath came easier then. Thankfully, it had only been an act, and would not happen again.

Methusal felt better. Things were impossible enough between them now. If he tried to attack her in that way, what would she do? Abandon the kaavl team? But she couldn't, because of Deccia.

At least she didn't have to make that decision right now.

△ △ △ △ △

BASE CAMP

"Today's the day," Aali hissed at Pogul while they stood in the lunch line at noon. She paused behind him, pretending to adjust the food on her plate.

He grunted, and sent her an evil smile. "See you later, pudding pie."

"Blech!" Her mouth curled in horror. "Step off, slug!"

"You owe me."

"You'll get an afternoon off. Nothing else. If you come within a length of me, you'll regret it." She drilled a disgusted stare into him. He didn't scare her. Not really. A slug that revolting was laughable.

He emitted a high giggle.

With an eye roll and shudder, she left him.

As Aali ate her lunch, she reviewed her strategy. She'd tell Doc she was helping Aenill this afternoon, and she'd tell Aenill that she was helping Doc. She smiled to herself, imagining the adventure ahead.

A large shadow blocked the sun. "Little Aali," Dastn said. "Still plotting trouble?" He sat down across from her.

She frowned, but quickly applied a smile to her lips. "Please," she said airily.

That troublesome runner! Ever since Erl had left, he kept popping up like a rocher. Was he keeping an eye on her?

"How sweet of you to sit with me." Her hand fluttered to her chest—still dismayingly flattish. Embarrassed, she quickly directed it to her throat.

The corner of his mouth curled up, telling her that she amused him. "It seemed polite. You were sitting alone."

"I have to go to work now." She gathered up her utensils. "Why aren't you out runnering? Isn't that what runners do? Run?"

"I help Doc move the injured, too. I go where I'm needed. Now it's here."

"I see." She smiled. "Well, sorry to leave you, but I need to work. See ya!" She fluttered a hand and dumped off her utensils.

Quick. She had to set her plan motion before Dastn finished eating.

She hustled to speak to Aenill, and then Doc. Neither suspected her devious plan. Gleefully, she glanced over her shoulder and sped out of camp.

Moving as quiet as a shadow, Aali maneuvered behind boulders and through crevices, until base camp disappeared from view. Then she climbed quickly in the direction of the weapons stash.

Finally she reached the last hill. At the top, she scanned the surrounding peaks and valleys for invaders. Couldn't forget her temporary scouting job, after all.

No invaders in sight. Satisfied, she climbed down into the weapons valley. Barrels, bags, and guns littered the small area. Thrilled, she inspected a small bag first.

The bags contained round bullets, she discovered. Aali put one in her pocket. The barrels contained a fine gray powder. It felt gritty and smelled bad. She also found bags of knives and a few loose swords. One knife looked particularly evil. The blade formed a flat spike, and the hilt consisted of two sharp prongs welded to the primary blade. A weapon from both ends. She cut her finger while handling it, and dropped it with a grimace.

Now for the guns! She counted thirty.

She hefted one in her hands. It was heavy. One end was made of wood, and the other of metal. Holding it carefully, she moved to the edge of the valley and sat on a large boulder so she could inspect the gruesome weapon more closely. She peered in the metal end. It was hollow. Maybe the bullet came out this end. It looked the right size. She pressed her eye to the round hole, trying to see inside. But it was too dark.

Next, she inspected the wooden end. It consisted of a flat piece and a little lever.

Where did the bullet go? Down the metal barrel? She pulled the bullet from her pocket and dropped it down the hollow tube.

But when she lifted the gun, the bullet rolled right back out.

That couldn't be right. How did the bullet stay in the gun?

Aali tested the connection between the wood and metal pieces, and to her surprise it folded open. Gray powder and another bullet lay nestled inside. She carefully tipped it forward so they wouldn't fall out, and snapped it shut again.

The gun was loaded. Her heart pounded. If an invader came now, she could shoot him. Adrenaline surged as her imagination took flight. What if an invader suddenly appeared and crept down that steep slope across the valley?

"What are you doing?" Dastn spoke from above her.

Startled, Aali yelped and dropped the gun. A blast thundered. In shock, she stumbled backward, tripped and fell. She hit her head hard on a rock behind a big boulder.

Kabooom!

A mighty explosion shook the ground. Barrels of gray powder exploded, shooting flames sky high. Pieces of rock and bits of guns and bullets hurtled through the air. Aali cowered behind a boulder, covering her head with her arms, praying not to be hit.

Another explosion thundered, and another...

△ △ △ △ △

Booming explosions shook the ground as Methusal and Mentàll slipped toward kaavl camp. Both stopped and stared at the plume of white smoke streaming skyward from the eastern mountains.

"What was *that?*"

"Looks like base camp."

Her father! And Aali.

"Come," Mentàll ordered. "A runner will tell us what happened."

Methusal hoped everything was all right at base camp.

When they reached the rocky outskirts of kaavl camp, the Dehrien Chief stopped again. The rain had drizzled to a stop.

"It is time to discuss your future on my team." His voice sounded deceptively calm, for she saw the undiminished fury in the pale blue eyes.

"I'm not sorry I tried to rescue Deccia. At least now we know the situation."

"Yes. Let us discuss the situation," he said between his teeth. "Guards are tripled. Zindedis are on high alert. And your boyfriend, Behran, is seriously injured. I'll have to send him to base camp. So I'm down one soldier."

"What happened to Behran?" Fear surged. Methusal took a step toward camp.

He gripped her arm, stopping her. "Do you want to return to base camp with him?"

"Tell me what happened!"

"Behran is critically injured."

Critically. Horror twisted inside her. And it was all *her* fault!

Mentàll hissed, "Now do you feel guilty for your mutiny?" A puff of rank air swirled up her nose.

She felt on the verge of hysteria. Pain and guilt battled within her. And now his rank breath brought her to the brink of physical illness. "Chew some tagma leaves. Your breath stinks!"

His nostrils flared and he reared back, obviously shocked.

Methusal snapped, "I know I'm not perfect. But neither are you. You tried to conquer Rolban. You threatened to rape me and kill me, and now you lecture *me?* What can your mother possibly think of the man you've become?"

Mentàll's face turned ashen, and then red burned his cheekbones. "My mother died when I was five. Do not speak of her again!"

"I'm sorry." And she was. "But that doesn't change the fact that you're just like the General. You think it's all right to hurt people, just as long as it serves your purposes."

"I saved your life! I am the leader of this kaavl team, and you will respect and obey me."

"Maybe I have to obey you, but I don't have to respect you. And all the kaavl and power and violence in the world won't make you a real leader. You only care about yourself. You know that's true. You're just like that maniac who's rap-ing Deccia."

He was silent for a long moment, muscle working in his jaw. Then he said, silkily, "Well, when I take you, Methusal, you will want me."

She felt like vomiting. "You *horrible* man!" She tried to dart by him, but he grabbed her shoulder, spinning her back.

He spoke slowly, voice freezing. "You will not speak to me that way again. Do you understand?"

"You get no respect when you threaten to rape me!"

"You misunderstand. I will never violate you. I promise you that."

Methusal glared.

"*Answer* me."

"I'm sorry," she forced out.

"One more word or act of insubordination, and I'll send you to your father. And you will have no more opportunities to rescue your sister."

Methusal swallowed. He'd do it. He'd send her to base camp with Behran. Finally, she believed it.

"You will follow my orders, Methusal. Do you under-stand?"

Rebellion flared, and the reply caught in her throat.

"Say it!"

"I won't disobey your orders again," she said at last, quietly.

He released her and stalked off, fury evident by the rigid line of his shoulders. Methusal stayed where she was. She didn't understand the man. At all. Because although he hadn't rescued Deccia, the Dehrien Chief had rescued *her* from jail. At his own peril. And she had been a hindrance the whole way.

She slowly headed into camp. Her hotheaded plan had gotten Behran injured, too.

She didn't like herself very much.

Methusal found Behran lying near the fire pit. His face was white, and his eyes were closed. Under his tunic, which had been slit down the front, a bloody cloth was wrapped around his chest. Tacky leaves marked a line down his forearm.

"Behran!" She went down on her knees beside him. Slowly, his lids opened. His deep blue eyes looked dull. Tears sprang into hers, and she gently kissed his cheek. "Behran, I'm so sorry!" She wept.

"'s okay, Thusa," he slurred, and his eyes closed again.

"I shouldn't have asked you to come with me."

"Methusal?" Hendra appeared.

"What's wrong with him? How badly is he hurt?"

Worry darkened her eyes. "He has a slash on his arm, and a few on his chest. But the worst are the stab wounds."

"He was stabbed?"

"Twice. One is in his side, and I think that one will heal just fine. The other is in his chest. I don't know how deep it goes."

More tears burned her eyes. Behran could die. *Die*. And it was all her fault.

"Kitran found him halfway here," Hendra said softly. "He was lucky to make it that far. Taltn has run for help. Pan's team is just south. He should be back soon. Men will carry him to Doc."

Methusal stroked Behran's hair. "I'm so sorry, Behran!" Tears streamed down her cheeks.

"I see Taltn now!" Hendra jumped to her feet and hurried away.

Methusal bit her lip. "Behran, you have to get better. You just have to!"

She felt pressure on her arm, and realized that Behran was gripping it. A faint whisper slurred, "You're...all right?"

"Yes. Mentàll rescued me."

"Good."

The men arrived with the pallet stretcher. "This is the guy?" asked a burly Tarst man.

"I packed up his things," Hendra said.

While the men carefully lifted Behran onto the stretcher, Methusal hovered nearby, anxious with worry. She wanted to go with him. She wanted to make sure he would be all right.

"Hendra." Mentàll appeared in her side vision. "Pack up. You are going with him."

"What?" The shocked expression on the Dehrien girl's face looked tragic. "Why?"

"Doc needs a nurse at base camp."

"But..."

Mentàll gave her a quelling look. "Go. I do not want to worry about you anymore."

After a small hesitation, Hendra left to gather up her belongings.

"Ready?" The leader of the burly Tarst looked impatient. "The sun will go down in a few hours. We need to leave now."

Methusal clutched Behran's hand and kissed his forehead. "Get better soon," she whispered.

He turned his head, and his kiss caught her cheek. He whispered, "I wanted to rescue Deccia, too. Don't blame yourself."

"I love you, Behran." She swallowed a sob. "I'm so sorry."

He squeezed her hand and the Tarst headed for the hills. Methusal followed for a little while, and Hendra soon sprinted to catch up.

"Take good care of him," Methusal begged.

"I will. Don't worry."

And then Methusal's two closest friends disappeared into the mountains. She'd never felt so alone, or so awful, in her entire life.

"Now do you see the importance of following orders, Methusal?" The Dehrien's voice cut like a knife.

She whirled. *"Thank you!* You know just what to say, don't you?"

The Dehrien said nothing.

Guilt and anger consumed her, and she turned it on him. "You like to see people suffer, don't you? Tell me, *why* did you rescue me?" Her voice rose. "Why didn't you leave me to die a horrible death? Wouldn't that please you?" Now she was screaming. She couldn't seem to help herself.

"Control yourself."

"No!" she gasped. She wanted to punch him, but didn't dare.

"You are angry at yourself, not me."

That was true. She burst into tears, and tried to shove past him. But he grabbed her arm, stopping her.

"The truth hurts, doesn't it? You are arrogant and prideful, and now you have learned the cost of your mutiny."

"Let me *go!*" She hated crying in front of her enemy. Hated him for screwing the hurtful truth further into her soul. But what hurt most was that he was right. All of this was her fault. She was at fault for everything.

He released her.

Methusal ran for the hills. She couldn't bear to be in camp for one more minute. Her only remaining friends were Kitran and Taltn. She'd be the only woman among twelve men. A lonely, uncomfortable prospect. Especially since most were Dehriens, including the cruel Mentàll.

△ △ △ △ △

Shaking, Aali huddled against the boulder, waiting for the noise to stop. Rocks rained down around her. Finally, all was quiet. When she gathered the courage to peek around the boulder, the weapons dump was a blackened mess. Cuts scored her arms. And her head hurt.

She felt shocked and numb. Her body still vibrated from the explosions. And what about Dastn, she suddenly remembered.

Aali looked up the slope. She didn't see him. "Dastn? Dastn, where are you?"

On trembling legs, she stood and groped her way up the hill. "Dastn?" Her voice wavered. "Are you all right?"

The runner appeared over the rise. He looked dusty, as if he'd rolled down the hill, but otherwise all right. She gasped with relief. "You're okay! Thank goodness."

His face looked white beneath his tan, and he gripped her arms and helped her to the top of the hill. He pulled her within two handbreadths of his solid body, and worried brown eyes quickly scanned her. "Are you okay?"

She blinked, trying not to cry. "Yes. I...I think so."

His fingers ran down her forearms. "You're cut." His gaze, now darkening with another emotion—likely anger—

focused on her face again. "And you're going to have a bruise on your forehead."

"It doesn't matter. At least we're both okay!" Aali flung her arms around him. She couldn't bear for him to start shouting at her now. She trembled with fright.

He stiffened at the contact. But all the same his arms closed around her, holding her close. Tears streamed down her face and soaked into his leather tunic, darkening it with wet splotches. He felt good and solid and comforting to hold. If only she could stay there forever. If only she didn't have to face the catastrophe she had caused.

As if sensing that she had regained control of herself, Dastn put her from him. His hands curled around her shoulders—whether to prevent her from unexpectedly collapsing, or to keep her from fleeing, she wasn't sure. Maybe both.

"What happened?" His tone was stern.

Aali wiped her cheeks and lifted her chin. She strove for her customary spunk. "What happened is you startled me. I didn't mean to fire the gun!"

"You could have been killed," he said grimly. "And look what happened."

"Those barrels of powder exploded."

He stared down into the valley and Aali followed his gaze. Black marks stained the sides of the valley, and dark scorch marks licked upward like flames. Debris lay scattered everywhere. It was a miracle she hadn't been badly hurt. That boulder had saved her life. She lifted a hand to her hair. It felt gritty, and tiny pebbles rolled beneath her fingertips.

"We need to tell Erl about this." Dastn sounded thoughtful.

"What do you mean?"

"The invaders must have more powder barrels stockpiled in Quasr."

Aali easily followed his line of thought. "Are you thinking we could blow them up?" Excited, she said, "Then we could win the war!"

"Maybe not win it. But it could be a major victory. We'd need to find their storehouse."

Aali stared down at the decimated valley. *She* had made this discovery. By accident, true. But still. Hadn't she said all along that she'd help the war effort?

Dastn gave her a hard look, which squelched her rising emotions. "You're a lucky girl. You could be dead. Will you tell Erl what happened, or shall I?"

△ △ △ △ △

The sun gilded the western mountains pink and gold when Hendra and the Tarst men trotted down into base camp. Behran worried her. The three hour, bumpy trip had taken its toll. His face looked like chalk, and fresh blood seeped through the cloth bandaging, which she'd changed once during the trip.

To make matters worse, frustration simmered in her because Mentàll had banished her from kaavl camp. Yes, she understood that he didn't want to worry about her. But she had managed to get Doltn's map. It would help the war effort. Why couldn't Mentàll see that she was a help, and not a hindrance?

She desperately wanted to stay on the front lines. She burned to do *something* worthwhile to help win this war! And she wanted to stay in kaavl camp for another, entirely personal reason, too—working in the middle of the action forced her to face her fears of violence and men. She wanted to win both victories. How could she accomplish either goal if she was stuck at base camp?

Her foot touched the valley floor. A number of men milled about in camp with packs on their shoulders. Most streamed toward tents. She guessed a war team had just returned.

Blond hair flashed, and Aali rushed up. "Behran!" she gasped, touching his arm. He didn't respond. The Rolbani girl turned a horrified expression to Hendra. "What happened?"

She told the story as they headed for the medical tent.

"He has to be all right. Behran, you have to be all right!" Aali exclaimed. "At least you tried to rescue Deccia. You're a hero, Behran," she told the pale, barely conscious man. Tears wobbled over her eyelids. "Both you and Thusa are. We'll rescue Deccia, don't you worry. And I'm going to help."

"What happened here?" Hendra asked gently. "We heard the explosions."

"I accidentally blew up the invader's powder barrels. Uncle Erl looks mad." The girl shot an uncertain glance toward Rolban's Chief. Right now, he spoke to Dastn, Doc's cousin. She frowned.

"Did you tell Erl what you did?"

"No. He just got here. But it looks like Dastn's telling him the awful news. I'd better make sure Uncle Erl hears the *best* news."

Hendra wondered what that could mean.

"Aali!" Erl's brusque voice didn't sound pleased.

"Uh oh," she muttered. "See you later." The Rolbani girl strolled toward the two frowning men. She didn't look concerned, but Hendra sensed that might be an act.

The Tarst carriers reached the medical tent, and Hendra hurried ahead to lift the flap. From her peripheral vision, she saw Doc stride toward them.

The doctor checked Behran's neck for his pulse. "What happened? Over here." He directed the men to lower the pallet to an empty rectangle of space. Hendra was shocked to see that the back half of the tent was crowded with men lying in rows on pallets. There were so many; maybe twenty or thirty. All were bloody and bandaged. Some were sleeping, and others groaned softly.

Doc's frowning, slightly impatient gaze indicated that he was still waiting for her answer. Quickly, she said, "Zindedis stabbed him. One is a flesh wound. I'm not sure about the other."

"He has a fever. Thanks," he told the men. "You can go."

After the Tarst men left, Hendra squatted opposite from Doc, with Behran's body between them. With careful, efficient fingers, Doc stripped the tacky leaves from Behran's arm and his chest.

"You did a fine job with these stitches." His smoky blue gaze held hers a moment, and an unexpected jolt kicked through her. She'd forgotten how flustered he made her feel. Her heart beat faster.

She looked down. "Thank you."

"Why are you here?" He was direct, as always.

"Mentàll sent me." Lingering frustration bubbled up. Shame, too. "He doesn't want to worry about me going on anymore kaavl missions."

"You don't sound too happy about it."

"I want to make a difference," she murmured. She didn't want Doc to think she was resentful of her cousin. She would never betray him like that.

"You can make a difference here."

"How?"

"I need a nurse. Will you work for me?"

Mentàll had suggested the same. But now, face to face with the idea of working with Doc every day, apprehension tangled inside her. This man disturbed her. But clearly, with all of these injured men—her gaze swept the room again—he needed help.

Doc gathered supplies while she hesitated. He said, "Aali helps a little, and so does Oona. But I need a full-time nurse." He squatted back down. Racmun spirits and various instruments and powders lined a tray. "What do you say? Will you help me?"

How could she say 'no'? Wasn't she afraid of men? And Doc disturbed her more than most. Maybe she could face one of her fears right here with him every day. She licked her lips. "Of course."

A faint smile tugged at his lips. "Good."

"Will Behran be all right?"

Doc inspected his patient. "You're right about the side wound. It should be fine. The other..." he fingered Behran's chest. "It looks bad, but I don't think it cut too far through his ribs. If it did, he'd be dead already."

Hendra felt relieved. "So that's good news."

"He's breathing fine and his pulse is weak, but steady. No swelling of the abdomen. This happened when?"

"Yesterday afternoon."

Doc nodded. "We'll watch him. His fever worries me the most. He has an infection."

Hendra had heard of blood poisoning. It killed men. Her fear returned. "What can we do?"

"Keep his wounds clean. Give him as much water as he'll drink. I'm going to give him pain powder. It'll reduce any swelling and help his body fight the infection."

"Show me how. I want to learn everything."

He smiled. "Good."

Doc showed her how to mix the powder with water and drop bits of it between Behran's dry lips. Hendra helped clean the wounds and apply fresh coltac juice and tacky leaves, and then she set up Behran's pallet. The Tarst were summoned again to move him to his new spot in the hospital ward.

"He'll need several spoonfuls of water every half hour. So will most of these men. Are you ready?"

"Will I need to change their bandages?"

"Yes. And feed them. It's hard work. But I have two men to deal with the nastier jobs."

Hendra was relieved to hear that. "All right."

"You'll do a great job. I'll show you how to measure the blood builder. Then I'll show you the notes I keep on each patient."

Hendra found that Doc ran a well ordered, efficient hospital. It didn't surprise her. Neither did his detailed notes on each person's injury, and his prescribed course of treatment. The approximate time of day for bandage changes and medications were listed on each parchment, which he filed in a box on a table that served as his desk.

"You look overwhelmed," he told her, filing the parchments.

"I'm sure I'll catch on soon. Who watches them at night? Or do you stay here?"

"No. A few men work at night. They start at dinner time."

"That's good."

"I need a break, and so will you. You have a soft heart, don't you?"

"Sometimes." When it didn't freeze into ice.

"Take a break whenever you feel overwhelmed." He glanced toward the open tent flap. "It's about time for dinner. Want to join me?"

Raw, unexpected panic stabbed her.

"Um." She edged backward, toward the door. Working with him was one thing. Eating together was another. It seemed too personal. A step she could not, and would not, take with any man.

Best to draw those lines now. "Uh...I need to unpack. And I'd like to stay with Behran for a while longer."

Uncertainty flickered in his eyes, and then disappointment. "All right."

Hendra ducked quickly out of the tent. She picked up her pack, which she'd left outside, and hurried toward the women's tent. Would Doc think she was a scared apte?

Well, wasn't she? He had to learn the truth sooner or later. She wasn't a whole woman—not where men were concerned. A piece of her was broken, and by now Hendra knew it would never heal. Yes, she would face her fears, and work with Doc during the day. A hard task, if he continued to look at her the way he had today. But soon his feelings would turn to pity and contempt, as had happened with every other man she'd turned away over the years. His pity and contempt might make it easier, and safer, to work with him.

Hendra found she didn't like that thought. Not at all.

△ △ △ △

Methusal sobbed until her eyes felt swollen and her head ached. Behran's injuries were *her* fault. Guards were tripled around Deccia. Now it would be harder than ever—if not impossible—to rescue her. Despair ate at her. She couldn't do anything to make any of this better. She'd have to live with her mistakes forever.

Please The One, let Behran be all right. Protect Deccia. I'm so sorry!

She wept in utter misery until finally she felt dried up from the inside out. Her mouth felt sticky with thirst, so she crept down to the stream and scooped up mouthfuls of cold water. It splashed down her chin and wet her tunic. She didn't care.

And Mentàll. That man had enjoyed grinding in the hurt even deeper. More hot tears slid down her cheeks. She hated him. *Hated* him. And the Prophet had said she should be kind to her enemies? Ha. What good had that done?

"Prophet, why did you have to speak to me? I don't understand *anything!* None of it. Nothing makes *sense!*" Tears ached in her raw throat.

A pebble rolled behind her, and she whirled.

A wizened brown leg appeared around a boulder, then a long, patchwork tunic, and then the familiar brown face and white hair.

The Prophet! Shocked, she blurted, "Why are you here?"

"The One knows our thoughts before we utter a word with our tongue." He looked to the sky. "We will not meet again for many months. He has a word for you, Methusal."

"More words? Ones I can't understand? Much less *do?*"
Maybe she shouldn't talk to the Prophet like this, but she felt
frustrated beyond words.

"You're sad." He sat on a boulder. "Tell me what happened."

Methusal drew a breath. Where to begin? "I wanted to
rescue my sister from that horrible General. It turned out so
wrong. Behran's hurt... Will he be all right?" she asked,
hoping he would know.

"Only The One has those answers."

"I feel like a failure. I can't do anything right."

"It's not wrong to want to rescue your sister," the old
man said gently. "But you must respect the authority of your
enemy. He is in charge of the kaavl team for a reason."

"I *hate* him! He's cruel and he hurts me on purpose, in
every way he can."

"Hurting people hurt others, Methusal."

"I don't think he feels *anything*. He's like an icy, cruel
glacier!"

"Your efforts are not in vain. Do not give up on doing
good. In due time, you will receive your reward."

"I'll receive a reward for treating his wounds?" Her disbelief
rang clear.

"Listen, Methusal. Do not repay evil for evil, or insult
with insult, but with blessing. Love your enemies, like The
One loves you. I fear, however, that you are forgetting
Mentàll is not your only enemy. Be careful."

"I can't *do* it," she cried out. "Not anymore. Why are you
asking me to do the impossible?"

"In our own strength we can do nothing. Pray for The
One's wisdom and strength. Persevere." The Prophet stood.

Evidently he had delivered his word to her. But she
couldn't let him go without asking one more question. "Will
we win this war?"

"Speak to The One who knows." He walked carefully over
the pebble strewn ground, heading west.

"No word for Mentàll this time?"

She felt ashamed when the Prophet sent her a calm,
compassionate look. "He is not ready to listen. But you are,
Methusal."

"Yes." She looked down, feeling gently rebuffed. "I'm
sorry."

"Do not give up." He kept walking.

"Goodbye." Belatedly, she added, "Thank you."

The Prophet lifted his hand and vanished around the corner.

Methusal drew a breath. Strangely, she felt calmer. The Prophet had encouraged her to persevere. That must mean there was hope for the future. And he'd advised her to pray for strength and wisdom. And to love all of her enemies—that most impossible of tasks.

Hurting people hurt others.

Was it possible that Mentàll was hurting? With extreme reluctance, she thought about it. She knew a little about his childhood. His mother had died when he was five. His uncle had beaten him. But that was all in the past.

None of it excused his behavior now.

The Prophet told her again to love her enemies. And *all* of them. Not just Mentàll.

I can't do it, The One. Not when they're so mean to me. If you want me to be kind, please help me. I can't do it on my own.

△ △ △ △ △

After supper that night, Methusal unrolled her pallet. No runner had arrived from base camp today. Questions about the explosion would have to wait until tomorrow. She was worried that the Zindedis might know where base camp was located now.

She felt exhausted from the long day. After crying in the hills and then speaking to the Prophet, she had returned to camp and silently fetched wood and helped cook the aptes the Dehriens had killed. Now she just longed for the peace of sleep. ...If peace could ever soothe her again.

A shadow fell across her legs. The shiver in her soul told her who it was. "One more duty, Methusal."

Weary beyond words, she silently looked up. Would he never leave her alone?

"Change my bandage."

She reached for her healer bag and pulled out the necessary items.

At the stream, he sat on the usual rock and pulled his tunic over his head, revealing his broad shoulders and back.

This morning flashed through her mind, when she had felt the strength of those hard, rippling muscles when he had held her in Quasr. That seemed so long ago. His harsh words, not so much.

He still wore that chain around his neck. It must hold some deep significance for him. Then she noticed the leaf bandages were falling off.

"Didn't Hendra change your bandages last night?"

"I had no time for that. I was missing two kaavl players."

Methusal worked in silence and cleaned the wound, and then dribbled on the coltac juice. She quickly stroked it on, touching him as little as possible.

"Afraid, Methusal?"

"No. I am not afraid." She smoothed down the last bit, and slapped on a clean leaf bandage.

He laughed, and it wasn't a pleasant sound. "You haven't worked the juice into the wound like Doc instructed."

"It's good enough." She stuck on another tacky leaf.

He ripped the bandages off. "No. It is not."

She stared at the back of his blond head, trembling with a surge of anger.

"Do it again," he ordered.

She squirted on more thick gel. Part of her wanted to take her thumb and push it harder than necessary into his wound, but the healer, and better part of her nature, recoiled at the thought. At the very least she could treat him like she would a wounded animal—even though he wasn't helpless, like they were.

Keeping this imagery in mind, she smoothed gel into the puckered line, and then squirted more on her finger and gently massaged it into the split skin, still held together by the rough thread. Besides its healing qualities, the juice would also help smooth out the eventual scar.

He remained very still as she completed her task.

"Does that meet your specifications?" she inquired, before sealing on the first leaf.

"Take satisfaction in a job well done."

His oblique comment reminded her of her behavior when they'd escaped from jail. It had been completely unacceptable in a kaavl player. Again, she wondered why he had gone to the trouble of rescuing her.

She smoothed on the tacky leaves. That question could wait for another time, because other words caught in her throat now. She didn't want to say them, but honesty, and a refusal to retreat from doing the right thing—at least one time today—made them burn on her tongue.

"I owe you an apology."

"Do you." He pulled on his tunic as she gathered up the extra supplies.

"Yes." She met his cold gaze. "My behavior toward you was terrible when we escaped from jail."

"Is that all?" he sounded impatient.

"No." She took a steadying breath. "You make everything so *difficult*. Why can't you be a nice man?"

He dismissed this with a derisive flick of his eyes.

"Thank you...okay? Thank you for rescuing me from jail."

"Do not make me regret it." He stalked off.

She drew another calming breath. At least she'd done one thing that she could be proud of today. Unfortunately simple words could not erase her debt to him. He'd saved her life twice now. Why?

CHAPTER FIFTEEN

METHUSAL FELT BETTER after a good night's sleep. When she first woke up she prayed for Behran, and hoped Timaeus would bring word about him soon. She also prayed for the safety of base camp.

She wondered how in the world they would rescue Deccia now, with the guards tripled. And again she wondered how Mentàll had rescued her. Today she would ask. And she'd find out why, too.

She thought about the Prophet's words as she readied for the day. He had encouraged her to persevere. To try to continue to do good. Did that mean she was already doing a few things right? Maybe she wasn't a complete failure, after all. She felt better, and hoped that might be true. She did want to do the right thing, even if it was difficult.

Kitran squatted beside her as she finished breakfast. "You're banished to camp today."

"I figured as much." Methusal stuffed rations into her pack and set it on top of her leather pallet.

"Nothing else to say?"

"I feel horrible. Are you going to lecture me, too?"

"No. I think you did the right thing."

She glanced at him in disbelief. "You do?"

"Unfortunately it turned out bad. But with the proper planning…"

"What are you saying?"

Kitran's hard brown eyes held hers. "The Dehrien can't be trusted. A point may come when we need to take matters into our own hands."

"Kitran," she whispered, and glanced toward the fire. Mentàll was talking to Efron. "Are you..."

"I'm going to speak to Erl and Pan when we go to base camp. I'll convince them to throw him out of leadership."

"On what grounds?"

"Incompetence. Mentàll is dragging his feet. We should be moving faster. Taking more action."

"Like rescuing Deccia?"

"Among other things."

"Do you think they'll listen?"

"I hope so. That Dehrien can't be trusted. I intend to make sure we win this war."

Kitran left her.

Methusal watched him head out for Quasr with a Tarst team member named Riln. She felt unsettled. Was he right?

She thought again about how Mentàll had rescued her. How had he entered and exited from the compound so easily? How had he known where she was?

Had he received help from the Zindedis?

And yet that couldn't be true. The General wanted him dead.

But she'd heard Mentàll plotting with Efron and Tabor. He was seeking a prize of some sort. The Prophet confirmed it. But did seeking an unknown prize mean Mentàll was disloyal to Koblan?

Methusal felt more confused than ever. Yes, she trusted Kitran. And yes, she hated the Dehrien. But the Prophet had said Mentàll was in charge of the kaavl team for a reason. And her own mutinous mission had ended in disaster.

For now, she'd obey her father; which meant following Mentàll's leadership. If Kitran became Kaavl Commander, or if she learned her enemy was a traitor to Koblan, then she would follow Kitran.

△ △ △ △ △

Methusal hated being confined to kaavl camp. All she could do was worry. At least she'd get to see Behran soon. Day after tomorrow, they'd return to base camp to restock supplies, and Mentàll would meet with Erl and Pan regarding new strategies for the war.

She wished she could do something now to help her sister. Anxiety for her twin made her feel sick. When they returned to base camp, Methusal would talk to her father and beg that a war party immediately rescue her sister.

Late in the morning, after the men left kaavl camp to scout in Quasr, Methusal quickly washed in the stream. She didn't dare undress completely, although she longed for a bath. Then she collected wood for that night's fire, and dragged the wild beast skeleton out of camp. Then she noticed the apte bones everywhere. Black shelled rocher bugs currently chewed on them. Camp was a mess.

She tied twigs to a long branch and swept camp as well as she could. Rochers scuttled as she wielded her broom. One nipped her as it ran over her ankle. It stung like fire. Methusal quickly applied coltac juice to the red, inverted "v" bite, but it didn't help the pain.

In the late afternoon, when she was bored to the point of imagining pictures in the clouds, the kaavl teams finally returned. Each set of men reported their information to the Dehrien Chief, who had just returned, as well. Methusal wondered where he had been this entire time.

She eavesdropped on each conversation. Her rationalization for the dishonorable behavior was that she needed to keep tabs on her enemy. Kitran might find the information interesting, too.

Mentàll apparently wanted to know the exact number of soldiers at different strategic points in town during all hours of the day. A wealth of information, but boring. How did he keep it all straight without writing it down?

Soon afterward, Timaeus appeared and climbed down the mountain. She ran to meet him.

"How is Behran?"

He sent her a compassionate glance. "He has a bad fever. Doc's worried." Tormented hope entered his eyes. "How was Deccia when you saw her?"

Methusal couldn't tell him what the General was doing to her. Deccia had begged her not to. Softly, she said, "She's strong. She'll be all right...for now."

Anguish darkened his gaze, and his jaw clenched. "Tell me the truth."

"She said to tell you that she loves you."

Tears glimmered in his eyes.

Mentàll appeared in her side vision, and so did Kitran. The Dehrien said, "Report on the explosion."

Timaeus straightened his shoulders. "Aali blew up powder barrels in the weapons valley."

"Blew them...*up?*" the Dehrien said, in obvious surprise.

"It was an accident. But a gun fired, and we think a hot spark hit the powder. Once one barrel blew up, the others blew up, too."

The Dehrien fell silent, clearly thinking about that.

Kitran said, "Did the explosion destroy all of the powder? All the bullets and guns?"

"Yes. And the Zindedis tried to cross into the mountains today to find base camp. Pan's war team held them off. But they'll keep trying."

"Great!" Kitran clenched his fists. "And no troops from Eerpor or Wyen have come to help us. How bad can things get?" A scowl blackened his features. "We needed to crush the Zindedis in the beginning! Before the invaders knew what hit them. Instead our war teams are playing games with them. Little skirmishes accomplish nothing, except our men die!" His gaze lit upon Methusal, and then his glare turned on their Dehrien leader. "It's the same with Deccia. We could have rescued her that first night. You didn't. And you've refused to put together a rescue team ever since then. Instead, Methusal had to act on her own. This whole mess is your fault!"

Red darkened Mentàll's cheekbones. "I did not rescue Deccia because I didn't want to tip our hand to the General. I wanted to gather intelligence, and be able to slip in and out of Quasr without detection. A rescue attempt would have warned the Zindedis about our stealth team. I planned to rescue Deccia when troops arrived from Eerpor and Wyen."

Methusal was a bit surprised that the Kaavl Commander had formulated a plan to rescue Deccia. And that he'd answered Kitran's accusations.

Kitran's lip curled. "You say you want to make one massive assault on Quasr? Wake up. Your plan won't work. We need help. It's not coming fast enough, and we can't skirmish forever. Time to change tactics."

"What do you suggest?"

"So *now* you're ready to listen?"

"Speak, if you have a plan," Mentàll said through clenched teeth. "Or remain silent."

"Fine. Here's my plan. Report all of your useless information to Erl and Pan if you want. But plan a massive assault. We need to attack Quasr now."

"We do not have enough troops. It would be suicide."

"Attack their weaknesses. Haven't you found them yet, Dehrien?" Kitran raised an eyebrow. "I didn't think so. You're a failure. I intend to make sure Erl and Pan realize that." With a twist of his thick shoulders, he stalked away.

Methusal stared after Kitran, surprised by how he'd attacked the Dehrien Chief. She glanced at Mentàll. She half expected him to hunt down Kitran and return the favor.

The Dehrien did neither. Face expressionless, he pushed a parchment into Timaeus' hand. "Give this to Erl and return tomorrow for a final report. We will return to base camp the day after tomorrow, as planned."

"Yes, sir." Timaeus tucked the parchment into his pack and sprinted from camp.

The Dehrien Chief's eyes, icy with fury, lit upon Methusal. "Tend my wound, Maahr." He stalked out of camp.

He may not have attacked Kitran, but he *would* attack her. Methusal took a good long time gathering supplies. Tacky leaves were running low. If necessary, she could use other clean leaves and sap.

She found the Dehrien sitting in solitude on his lone boulder with his back to her. His bleached white tunic lay crumpled at his feet.

"I know you're mad at Kitran," she told him. "Don't take it out on me."

He twisted around a little. A snarl bared his teeth. "You think so little of me, Methusal?"

She peeled the tacky leaves off his back. The wound, although red, was beginning to heal. "I'm surprised you let him speak to you that way. If I'd done it, you'd have taken my head off."

"I respect Kitran. I wronged him in the past. I will not make things worse."

Methusal blinked. "Did you just admit you made a mistake?"

"I have made no mistakes with *you*," he spat. "Tend my wound."

Angry words burned, but she said nothing.

"You are humble now? Meek in my presence?"

Methusal bit her tongue. She would not respond. She would follow the higher path, just like she'd vowed to do this morning.

An unpleasant chuckle rasped. "So it is true. You are afraid of me."

Methusal couldn't help but respond to that. "What is true, Mentàll, is that I will treat you like the injured whip you are. Now hold still, so I don't re-injure you." She squirted on the coltac juice and firmly massaged it into the wound. She used a softer touch on the edges of the gash. As a result, there the thick gel slid over his skin like a caress, and he jerked forward, away from her touch.

A snarl contorted his features. "Take care, Methusal, or I will assume you take liberties with me."

Heat, and then ice washed through her. "You're delusional," she snapped. Then she glared, realizing that he'd succeeded in needling her. "I'm being gentle. Or maybe you're not familiar with that concept."

"Don't be gentle," he said harshly. "Do your job."

"I'll do it right, and you'll have to suffer through it."

The One, please help me to want to do it right.

Maybe if she pretended he was Behran... That proved impossible. Maybe an apte. Strangely enough, by the end of her ministrations, Methusal treated him gently because she *did* want to. Because it was the right thing to do. The anger he'd stirred up quieted into an odd feeling of serenity.

She affixed the last tacky leaf. "There," she said mildly. "You're done."

Mentàll faced her with a frown, but when she calmly gazed back, confusion registered.

She said, "I assume I'm to tend your wound once a day now?"

"Yes. Once," he said shortly, and left her.

Methusal watched him go. The man didn't understand gentleness or kindness. Or maybe he just didn't trust her.

She also felt confused about why she felt so calm and peaceful. And toward the end, she'd actually wanted to treat him kindly. How had that happened?

Then she remembered her short prayer. Maybe The One had helped her to do the impossible.

In any case, at last she'd won one battle of their wills. She had treated him kindly, even when he'd done his best to make her fail. Victory tasted sweet.

△ △ △ △ △

Methusal stayed by the stream for a while, instead of heading directly back to camp. The quiet, soothing rush of water over the dark stones comforted her soul.

She stayed until twilight deepened the shadows of the tall rocks into dark purple smudges. Reluctantly, she left the quiet spot and headed back into camp.

Her sense of well-being lasted until after dinner, when she passed by the fire pit on the way to her pallet.

Goric stuck out his foot and she tripped.

She caught her balance just in time.

Those murky eyes narrowed. "Sweet dreams."

Beside him, Jascr chuckled. "Call me if you get cold. I'll come warm you up."

She bit back repulsed, angry words. Neither Goric nor Jascr would make her tumble off of the higher path tonight, though. Ignoring them both, she silently turned on her heel and left them smirking by the fire.

After washing her face, she slipped into her pallet. Rocks bit into her hip, and she wiggled inside the coverlet, trying to get more comfortable.

Something ran across her hand.

What was *that?*

Another something skittered across her wrist and nipped her sharply.

"Ow!" she cried out, and scrambled out of bed. Ryon's light illuminated the rocher that was attached by its sharp teeth to her pant leg. "Uggh!" She grabbed a stick and flipped it off, and then squished it beneath her moccasin.

Methusal grabbed the edges of her coverlet and shook it out, hard. A handful of rochers dropped out and scuttled for the rocks. Trembling, she shook out her pallet again. No more bugs.

She dragged her coverlet pallet over to Behran's old spot and remade her bed. After lying down, she tucked the edges tightly around her, so no more rochers could creep inside. It wasn't likely, as they usually avoided humans. Clearly, they'd crawled into her pallet while it was cold and empty. All the same, hours crept by before she fell asleep. She kept imagining the insects scuttling through her hair. Or creeping over her face and biting her nose.

Chapter Sixteen

Yawning, Methusal rolled up her pallet tight the next morning and stuffed it behind a rock. No rochers would crawl inside it today. Although she heard nothing, she sensed movement behind her. Spinning, she discovered the Dehrien Chief was watching her. A hooded cloak hung from his shoulders.

"You will come with me today."

This was not the news she wanted to hear first thing in the morning. "Why? And where?"

"Quasr. Get your cloak."

After grabbing the cloak and a few meat strips, she discovered that the Dehrien was already striding for Quasr. Was she supposed to follow him like a meek apte? She felt annoyed.

With a sprint, she caught up. "Why?" she repeated. "Kitran and I usually scout together."

"Your last mission made me doubt your kaavl abilities."

She said nothing. He was right to doubt her.

Mentàll glanced at her. "How did the Zindedis capture you?"

She didn't answer for a moment, because she didn't want to expose her failure to her enemy. But she wouldn't lie, either. "I lost concentration when I talked to my sister."

"Can you prove yourself now, Maahr?"

"Yes. It won't happen again."

"We will see."

Since he demanded such frankness, she'd insist upon some answers, too. "How did you find me in the compound?"

He didn't answer.

Frustrated, she said, "Why did you rescue me, when you wouldn't rescue Deccia?

"You want to know?" He stopped again and gave her a thin, unpleasant smile.

Now Methusal wasn't so sure, but said, "Yes."

The smile vanished. Harshly, he said, "I saved you because you are *mine* to deal with as I see fit. I will give that pleasure to no other."

Revulsion was her automatic response. He had meant the words, but she also saw that he had said them to provoke her, too. That hard gleam in his eyes testified to that fact.

She drew a deep breath and looked away long enough to calm her impulsive retort. Then she silently returned his stare.

Surprise glimmered, and then a tiny flicker of...what? Respect?

Victory flared. She returned to the original topic. "Today is a test?"

"Yes. Prove your kaavl skill to me, or you will join Behran at base camp."

"Fine." She would put forth her best effort, and prove herself to both Mentàll and herself. "What is the mission?"

Did disappointment flickered across his face? Had he wanted her to argue the point? Curtly, he said, "A building near the docks is heavily guarded. We will discover what is inside."

After this the Dehrien said no more, which suited Methusal just fine. She ate her breakfast and slipped completely into kaavl. She focused on each nuance of her environment, particularly the texture of the dirt beneath her moccasins, the strength and direction of the breeze, and the cry of a flying beast a half day's journey south. And more.

She felt keenly aware of the Dehrien Chief's presence a length to her left, too. He moved silently.

They slipped into town and headed toward the docks. Two blocks short of the ocean, Mentàll slipped into a burnt, blackened building, and she followed. They crouched in the shadows and peered through a crack in the wall.

Six soldiers patrolled the street in front of the building next door. It was the same, heavily guarded building that she and Kitran had spotted during their first night in Quasr. The soldiers carried guns at a forty-five degree angle across their chests, and strode with clipped precision.

Mentàll murmured, "We will scout the back. Come." He turned into the alley between the two houses.

"Wait! How do you know it's safe?"

"It is. Come now."

Questioning her sanity, Methusal followed him. She hadn't had time to scan the back of the house with her hearing, and here they were, turning the corner.

Empty. No one was there.

"How did you know?" she whispered.

"Are you at the Primary level?"

The note of derision made Methusal clench her teeth, but she said nothing.

The Dehrien Chief looked up the sheer wall of the building. One small window was located almost two lengths overhead.

"Come here."

With reluctance, and still fanning out her hearing to ensure their safety, Methusal approached the Dehrien. She looked up, too. The window looked dirty, and impossibly narrow. "I can't fit through it."

"You can look inside."

"Okay. But how will I get up there?"

"I will lift you." He sounded impatient.

Methusal's mouth opened, but she found nothing to say. His plan would work. She let out a strangled breath. "Fine."

"Face the wall."

With reluctance, she obeyed. His large hands gripped her hips, and then she flew upward, as if she was as light as a feather. She gasped as her stomach dropped, and she instinctively grabbed for the windowsill, which was now at shoulder level. Mentàll's hard hands bit into her flesh, and she knew she'd have bruises later.

Quickly, she tugged on the bottom edge of the window. It didn't budge. Maybe it needed a push. She pressed hard and it screeched open. Methusal held her breath. Sure enough, soldiers approached.

"Soldiers!" she hissed down. The next instant her feet thankfully touched the earth.

"How many?"

Without thinking, Methusal slipped into a visual carry and mentally turned the corner with her vision. She saw three invaders, weapons at the ready. She held up three fingers, and then mimicked holding a gun. The Dehrien nodded and melted to the left, into the ruins of the abandoned building next door. She followed, and then realized what he had asked, and what she had done. Great. Her spirits dropped.

They waited in silence while the invaders scanned the area. Thankfully the Zindedis didn't bother to search their burnt building. The soldiers lingered at the back wall for a long time afterward, joking coarsely with one another.

Methusal's legs ached from crouching, but she didn't dare move. Finally two of the soldiers moved on—presumably to the front of the building. The remaining one patrolled the back. He whistled as he slouched to and fro. Evidently he wasn't too worried about keeping up military appearances in the back.

"Stay here," Mentàll said. Moving as silent as the night, he approached the invader from behind. He punched him in the ear, and then grabbed the rifle and cracked it across his skull. The man collapsed.

Methusal didn't need to be called. She sped out and the Dehrien swung her up high again, to the window. Quickly, she poked her head inside. The interior of the building was dark, and it took a minute for her eyes to adjust. It was full of stacked barrels and bulky bags. No people were inside.

"Down," she whispered.

Once her feet touched the earth, the Dehrien dragged the fallen soldier and propped him up against the wall. Now it looked like he had fallen asleep. His head lolled to one side, and Methusal felt a flash of pity for him. How would the other soldiers react when they found him "asleep" on the job?

"Come." Mentàll's hard hand jerked at her shoulder. "It is no longer safe."

Methusal realized that she had slipped out of kaavl again. Chagrinned, she followed the Dehrien Chief south.

When they'd safely left town and headed toward kaavl camp again, Mentàll said, "What did you see?"

"Barrels. Hundreds of them. Bags, too. It was dark inside, but I didn't see anything else."

"Powder barrels." The Dehrien fell silent.

"And bags. What do you think is in them?"

"Bullets. Maybe other weapons."

An entire house full of ammunition? "That arsenal will keep the invaders armed for months!"

"Exactly."

They walked in silence, which was just fine with Methusal. Soon they'd arrive in kaavl camp, and this mission would finally end.

"We need to discuss one more thing," the Dehrien Chief said when they reached the tall boulders surrounding camp.

"What?"

"Remember when I was injured, in the cave?"

"Yes." Uneasily, Methusal wondered where he was going with this.

"You counted the soldiers around the corner. You tried to convince me that I was imagining things. But I was not. It happened again today. How did you do it?'

She felt a sinking sensation in the pit of her stomach. He had noticed. She tried to stall. "Do what?"

A self-satisfied smile curled his lips. "How did you count the number of men around that corner?"

Methusal hoped for inspiration to rescue her. "I heard them, of course," was the best she could do.

"Do not lie to me, Methusal." The Dehrien turned in front of her, which forced her to stop. She took a step backward. "You also told me they carried guns. Hearing had nothing to do with it."

She frowned.

"Answer my question."

Methusal refused to speak.

Silkily, he said, "As Kaavl Commander, I need to know. Then I can know how to best deploy the resources of the team."

"Right. You just want to know for yourself."

"Also true."

Her enemy could not discover her secret skill. She needed to keep all of her skills—all of her potential weapons against him—a secret. "A little mystery is healthy, don't you think?"

"Not when lives are at stake."

"Don't be so dramatic."

"You do not think I am serious?" A cool edge bit through his voice.

"Oh, you're super serious, all the time. But I won't tell you what you want to know."

The pale eyes chilled to ice. "Let's say you and another member of the team—Behran, for example—are in the General's compound, and about to rescue your sister. Imagine you must turn one last corner. Not knowing your ability, Behran turns the corner and is attacked by a hidden invader. Now, if he had known about your ability to carry with vision, do you think he would have endangered his life? No. He would have asked you to carry first, to see if it was safe."

Her heart dropped, but she remained silent.

The Dehrien Chief closed the distance between them. "You are foolish, Methusal. I have already guessed your secret."

"You know nothing." She crossed her arms and refused to back up. He would not intimidate her.

"Can you carry with hearing, as well?" he asked softly.

Methusal blanched.

"So you can. Both qualities your ancestor, Mahre, possessed."

She didn't like the speculative gleam in his eyes. She tried to look bored. "Is the inquisition over? Or would you like to share *your* secret kaavl abilities with me?"

He smiled. "You will not guess them, Methusal."

"Because you don't have any."

"Never underestimate your competition. I did. But no longer."

She gaped. "Was that a compliment, for *me*?"

"Why else would I allow you to stay on my team?"

"And why else would you rescue me two times?" she agreed. "Except to fulfill your plans to exploit me in every way imaginable."

Mentàll expelled a sharp laugh. "How have I exploited you?"

"You will soon. You're good at manipulating people."

"Even you, Methusal?"

"You may try, but you will not succeed."

"No? Do not be so confident. I am still your commander, and you will follow my instructions."

"Of course. But only regarding the missions."

He inclined his head in agreement, and said, "You will tell the kaavl team about your ability to carry."

It sounded suspiciously like an order.

She tested it. "I won't."

"Will you break your word?"

It was an order, and a deliberate assertion of his power over her. Her eyes narrowed. "I will not give my enemies a weapon against me."

"Everyone on the kaavl team is on the same side."

"Jascr is a threat to me. I don't want him to know. Or Goric."

A frown flashed. "Very well. You will tell the kaavl members you are teamed with."

Methusal bit her lip, surprised that he'd bent a little. She still wanted to shout "*No.*" But she didn't want to be thrown off the team.

"Fine," she clipped out.

"I am glad you see things my way."

"I see *nothing* your way. I will never understand you, as long as I live." Irate, Methusal brushed by him and headed for kaavl camp. Mentàll had forced her to bend to his will, but at least she had managed to salvage some of her privacy. Only Kitran, and possibly one other person would know. Jascr and none of the Dehriens would know. Except for Mentàll, of course.

△ △ △ △ △

Behran thrashed about on his pallet, mumbling unintelligibly. Hendra pressed a cool, wet cloth to his feverish forehead. Day two of his fever. He seemed hotter today, and one of the stab wounds looked purple and ugly.

Hendra knew from Doc's frowning glances that he was worried.

She dribbled cool water between Behran's lips and wished she could do more.

"Hendra. I need your help."

Men had carried in an injured Tarst man minutes earlier. Hendra put aside the bowl of cool water and hurried to Doc's side. Their latest patient was unconscious, and blood seeped from a bullet wound in his arm and from a slash in his head. She guessed a bullet had skimmed his temple.

"We'll need to work fast, before he wakes up," Doc said.

Hendra quickly gathered the supplies and knelt across from the doctor, ready to hand him whatever he needed.

"Knife. Is it sterile?"

"I just soaked it in racmun spirits. Did you know we're getting low?"

"Yes," he said shortly. "Eerporians are sending more with a runner."

"Are they sending troops, too?"

"I don't know. Needle."

Hendra flinched when Doc's fingers brushed hers. "Sorry." She hated her reaction. And it wasn't the first time it had happened.

Doc stitched the patient. After a moment, he said, "Why do you do that?" He didn't look up, so all Hendra saw was the top of his red head, and the edge of his bearded jaw. Did he think she'd feel less intimidated if he wasn't looking at her?

It was a good strategy, because her nerves stopped jumping. However, she didn't know what to say. She wouldn't lie, but she didn't want to tell the truth, either.

He looked up then, and his gaze held hers. "Do you know?"

"Yes, of course I know," she said defensively.

"But you don't want to tell me." He tied off a stitch.

Hendra swallowed. Doc was a good man. She could trust him. But old habits—and fears—died hard. "No," she agreed.

He held out the needle and the curled remainder of the string, but made no move to drop them into her hand, like usual. They rested delicately on his fingers, waiting. Hendra snatched them like a flying beast pecking at an insect. She barely felt the rough texture of his fingers before escaping the contact.

Quietly, Doc said, "Someone hurt you."

Agitated, Hendra slipped the needle into the sterilizer solution. She choked out, "Yes."

"If you want to talk, I'm here. I'm a doctor. I've seen and heard just about everything."

"Thanks. But I'm all right." Her shaking hands dropped the small tumbler and precious, sterile racmun spirits puddled in the dirt. "Oh, no!" Her hands flew to her face. "I'm so sorry! I'll get a new glass."

"Leave it." Doc pulled the dirty cup from her trembling fingers. "Sit down. Take a break."

She obeyed, and told herself to calm down. Doc would never hurt her. He must think she was being ridiculous!

He worked in silence for a moment, and then said with a faint smile, "So that's why you won't have dinner with me. And I thought my scruffy beard had scared you off."

"No. Of course not."

"Good. I won't ask again, if you'd prefer that."

"Maybe...maybe that would be for the best."

"Done. But I'd like to help you, if you'll let me."

"You can't help me," Hendra said bleakly. "No one can."

Doc glanced at her. The set of his mouth looked grim. But he said no more, to her relief.

Δ Δ Δ Δ Δ

Kitran sat with Methusal at the campfire that night, after they'd eaten a sparse meal of rations. No fresh meat had been killed that day.

"What did you learn today?" he asked.

"Remember that big building we scouted on our first night in Quasr?"

"Yes."

"It's filled with barrels and bags."

Kitran frowned. His black brows looked heavier and thicker in the firelight, and his face swarthier. "Powder barrels?"

"We think so."

"We? You and Mentàll?"

Methusal wondered why that distinction should be important. "Yes."

"Where does your loyalty lie, Methusal?"

Taken aback, she said, "You know I'm loyal to my father."

"And then who?" The black gaze held hers. "Me, or Mentàll?"

"That's not a fair question. Of course I trust you more than Mentàll. But my father put him in charge."

"Not for long. I have a plan. It could end this war tomorrow."

"Really?" she said in disbelief. "How? Have you told Mentàll?"

"I'll speak to him now." He stood. "But I guarantee he won't listen."

Kitran strode away, but not toward the Kaavl Commander—rather, toward three of his Tarst friends. From the bits and pieces she'd overheard in the past, Methusal guessed they had become friends when Kitran had been a runner to Tarst years ago. It explained the close friendship she sensed among them now.

The fire felt warm, and although it was dark, she didn't want to retreat to her cold pallet just yet. An icy edge bit through the breeze. The first frost might come tonight. With Kitran gone, though, she felt uncomfortable sitting alone, since she was the only woman in camp. A few men glanced at her. Jascr sent her an evil smile. A contemptuous smirk twisted Goric's lips.

To her relief, Taltn appeared out of the dark and headed for the fire. The boy sat beside her and yawned mightily. He said little. All the same, she was glad for his presence.

Someone threw logs on the fire and it flamed up, burnishing light and heat against her cold skin.

An angry voice caught her attention. Kitran. He and the Dehrien Chief stood near the stream, a good distance away. Kitran's voice rose in volume. Unable to help herself, Methusal focused in to hear the Dehrien Chief's low, harsh voice.

"Now is not the time."

"When will be the time, Dehrien? When the Zindedis have conquered Aestoff, too? That's right. Timaeus told me the Zindedis are battling to take Aestoff right now. But I know Aestoff's leader. He'll fight with every weapon he's got. He won't sit on his hands and *spy*," he spit the word, "for weeks. He's using his kaavl to battle the invaders *now*. Why aren't we doing the same? Where does your loyalty lie, Dehrien?"

"You are insubordinate, Kitran," he snarled. "Listen well. I have dealt leniently with you, because I wronged you. No more. Any further insubordination, and you are gone."

A moment of silence elapsed. Then fury thundered in Kitran's voice. "Erl will hear my full report. Then he'll remove *you* from the team."

"Erl will support me. Defy me at your peril."

"What do you plan to do? Kill me?"

"I do not need to kill you." A curl of humor made the words sound threatening.

"What, then?"

"If you continue your insubordination, I will convince Erl and Pan to banish you to base camp. I am sure Aenill needs help cooking."

Methusal gasped at the insult.

Kitran gritted, "We will finish this at base camp." He strode away, his thick shoulders rigid with fury.

The men at the fire had fallen silent, probably because Kitran's voice carried. Tension simmered in the air as Kitran sat on one side of the fire, and the Dehrien Chief on the other. Methusal decided that now might be a good time to retire.

"'Night," she whispered to Taltn, and slipped over to her pallet and unrolled it. She pulled extra tunics from her pack and pulled them on for warmth. She shivered in the cold. The air near her pallet felt icy after the fire's heat. Then she slipped down into her coverlet and pulled the edge up over her head. She shuddered uncontrollably. Hopefully she'd warm up soon.

Her fingers prickled. Tiny feet scuttled across her neck.

With a cry, she jumped out of her bed. Rochers! A horde of them.

They scurried over her feet, and a half a dozen clung to her clothes with their sharp jaws. Shuddering, Methusal swiped frantically at her clothes and her hair, batting them off her body. One tangled in her hair. A whimper caught in her throat and she grabbed the bug and ripped it from her hair. She pulled out a few strands at the same time it bit her hand.

Tears slid down her cheeks as she carefully patted herself down, but she couldn't find any more of the horrible bugs. Had any crawled up inside her pant legs or sleeves? Methusal struggled to control her hysteria, and methodically checked for more bugs.

None. Then she flung open her pallet and shook it out viciously. How had the insects crawled inside her rolled up pallet?

She glanced toward the fire. Goric and Jascr watched her. Identical grins twisted their lips.

The *wild beasts!* Rage inflamed her. *They* had planted the rochers in her pallet. Probably last night and tonight.

Shaking with fury, all thoughts of a higher path fled from her mind. She stormed to the fire pit. "Think that's funny?"

"Your dance was pretty funny," Goric said.

Jascr said to him, "Maybe she was trying to warm up." To Methusal, "I told you I'd warm you up. All you have to do is ask."

Taltn appeared beside her. "What happened?"

Jascr snorted. "Look. Your brave defender." His smile turned nasty. Threatening.

Methusal didn't want Taltn involved. The boy didn't need enemies like Jascr or Goric. "It's nothing," she told her young friend.

Jascr's lips curled.

After an uncertain moment, Taltn retreated to his pallet.

In a low voice, Methusal told the two men. "You will pay."

Jascr's black gaze flickered down her body. He licked his lips. "I look forward to it."

Goric's glare added his affirmation.

Trembling a little, Methusal spun on her heel. Fine. She'd check her pallet every night. But now she felt more exposed and vulnerable than ever before. Thankfully Taltn was her friend, and Kitran was, too, but he hadn't paid any attention just now. He was probably mired in dark thoughts of his own. Methusal had no doubt, however, that he would defend her if the two wild beasts tried to attack her. Until then, she would handle them on her own.

△ △ △ △ △

Whispers woke Methusal in the middle of the night.

"When?"

A low voice said, "The time is not right."

Mentàll! Adrenaline quickly cleared her sleepy brain.

She tried to relax into kaavl so she could hear better. The two men stood ten lengths away behind a huge boulder. Another secret meeting, apparently.

"Send me," whispered the first voice.

"No. The war is our first priority."

"Do you think your loyalty will earn Erl and Pan as friends?"

"If they become friends, it will strengthen my plans. The Zindedi invasion will benefit me, too. We only need to defeat them, and everything will fall into place."

"What if someone guesses your plan?"

"Let them guess. No one else has the vision or determination to carry out my goal."

"And the prize? That Rolbani girl is sharp. What if she guesses..."

"Rolbanis do not pursue what is most important. Even if they wanted to do so, they would not know what steps to take."

Methusal again wondered what prize he wanted. Maybe ore? Zindedis coveted ore. They had two years ago, and they did now, too. Rich ore deposits lay deep in the Rolban Mountains. Was that the main reason why the Zindedis had come to the Koblan continent? To get Rolban's ore? It seemed logical. And the Zindedi soldiers had mentioned ore on the beach, too, that first night she and Kitran had spied in Quasr.

Did Mentàll want the ore, too? Did he plan to attack Rolban again after the Zindedis were defeated? Did he plan to make Erl his friend, and then stab him in the back? A part of her found this difficult to believe, although she wasn't quite sure why. Maybe it was because she believed he craved power—not ore.

"Fine," whispered the first man. "But remember, no one will notice if I disappear for a day or two."

"Send a message to Calbn tomorrow. Then meet us at base camp."

"Yes, sir."

Calbn. The name sounded familiar.

"And Efron," Mentàll said harshly. "No more questions. You and Tabor must follow me."

"Yes, sir." His reply sounded subdued.

Footsteps scuffed across the pebbled ground. One man had returned to camp. Methusal listened harder. Feet whispered softly over the earth. Mentàll.

Opening her eyes, she peeked over the edge of her coverlet. Sure enough. Mentàll knelt on his pallet now. His Dehrien cohort, a tall, skinny man with thinning dark hair, slid into his own pallet across camp. Efron must be Mentàll's first-in-command. And Tabor, his second-in-command. She hadn't paid much attention to Tabor before, but now recalled to mind everything she'd noticed about him. He was a solidly built man with mud colored eyes and hair. He said little.

She needed to find out what Mentàll was planning. It appeared to be nothing good, however, since it sounded like it would benefit the Dehrien Chief's selfish interests. She'd carefully watch all three men. And when she discovered the truth, she'd stand with Kitran against Mentàll. With two testimonies against the Dehrien leader, surely Erl and Pan would throw him off of the team.

Feeling unsettled, Methusal closed her eyes. Tomorrow at base camp she'd talk to her father about what she had just overheard. And she'd convince him to send a war team immediately to rescue her sister. She prayed that Behran would survive his infection. *Please, The One*. She missed Behran terribly.

CHAPTER SEVENTEEN

JUST AFTER DAWN the next morning, Mentàll sent a scout team into Quasr. One of the men was Efron. The other was Tabor. Today the two would secretly speak to Calbn, whoever he was.

On the hike to base camp later that morning, Methusal fell into step beside Kitran. "Who's Calbn?"

"He's the dead Chief of Quasr's son. Why?"

She wasn't sure if she should tell Kitran about the conversation she'd overheard last night. It would only inflame his hatred for Mentàll. His volatile outbursts unnerved her. She didn't want to upset him further.

"Is he the true Chief of Quasr now? Or do they elect their Chiefs?"

"The M'ntoyans have ruled Quasr for over a century. Calbn is Chief. And if he is killed, his little son will become the next Chief. The line ends with the boy. That's why the Quasrians are determined to hide them and keep them safe. No one knows where they are."

Except for Mentàll.

How did he know? And why was he sending messages to Quasr's Chief?

△ △ △ △ △

After the noon meal Methusal scanned the nearby rock formations, looking for a landmark indicating that base camp was near. She was anxious to arrive and see how Behran was doing, However, as she surveyed the landscape, nothing looked familiar. An uncomfortable thought struck. If she ever had to find camp by herself, could she do it?

Methusal paid more attention to her surroundings from then on. A cliff here, a broken tree there...and a flash of scraggly gray fur. The animal quickly slunk behind a boulder.

She smiled.

"Camp," Wortn shouted from the top of the next rise.

Taltn whooped and ran up the hill. Everyone else quickened their pace. Methusal couldn't wait to see her father, Behran, Aali, and Hendra, too. It would be wonderful to see friendly faces.

Halfway downhill to base camp, she remembered the wolmite. She sat down on a boulder.

"Thusa?" Taltn called. "Are you coming?"

"In a minute."

She waited for the wolmite. He didn't show himself until all of the men had reached the valley floor. Then he slunk out, his fur brushing against a boulder. Sideways, he warily looked at her.

"Come here, boy," she whispered. "How's your paw?"

The animal didn't move. A leather kaavl strip trailed from his leg.

"Let me see," she urged.

Slowly, the beast moved forward.

"Here." She extended her hand.

He sniffed cautiously.

"You're a funny one," she murmured. "You followed me, but you're cautious. I won't hurt you."

After staring at her for a moment longer, the wolmite sat on his haunches and lifted his paw. Gently, he rested it on her knee.

"Let's see." Uncorking her water skin, Methusal lifted the paw and poured water over it. Dirt rinsed away from the wound. "A hard crust." She smiled. "No infection. That's good. I'll give you one more bandage, and that should do it."

The creature sat very still as she gently tended his wound. The wild yellow eyes watched her. On a rare occasion, wolmites had been known to snap at a man's throat. Methusal didn't allow fear to enter her mind. Beasts sensed it. Calm confidence ensured peace. It probably made the animal feel at ease, too.

"There." She smiled. "All done." The wolmite pulled back his paw. "Will you come see me again?"

The beast stared at her, unblinking.

With a faint smile, she whispered, "That's right. Don't give away your plan."

The beast loped off, and then looked over his shoulder, yellow eyes gleaming. Untamed. Bold. Fearless. And she felt an odd affection for him. Then the wolmite was gone.

Methusal picked her way down the hill into camp. She spotted Doc talking to Kitran. As she passed, Doc fell into step beside her. "You have a touch with the wild beasts."

They passed the Dehrien leader's tent now, and Methusal glanced at her enemy, who was talking to his cohorts. "It comes in handy sometimes."

"How is our patient?"

"Mentàll? Fine. The wound stopped bleeding."

"Good. Tell him to come by the medical tent later. In fact, you come with him. I want to show you how to pull out the stitches. They'll need to come out in three or four days."

Horrified, Methusal said, "Take out his *stitches?*" The very thought made her feel queasy. "Won't that hurt?"

"Not much. You'll cut the threads and pull them out, one by one."

"Still..."

"You can do it." Doc grinned with sympathy. "I have every confidence in you."

She followed him into the medical tent, where she spotted Hendra kneeling beside Behran in the back of the tent. Anxiety ratcheted higher. "Can I see him?" she asked Doc.

"Of course."

She hurried over. Hendra looked up and smiled. "Methusal! I think his fever is a little better. We should know for sure in another hour or two."

Methusal touched Behran's flushed cheek. It felt warm, but not blazing hot. Perspiration beaded his brow, and he lay very still. It scared her.

As if reading her thoughts, Hendra said, "He's thrashed around for the last three days. Now he's resting peacefully."

"That's good, then." But Methusal said this to reassure herself. She hated to see him lying there so still. She took his

hand. "I'm here, Behran. Get better, please. I miss you."
Tears filled her eyes.

"You could drop off your pack," Hendra suggested. "I'll
come get you if anything changes."

Methusal didn't really want to leave Behran. But she did
need to speak to her father. And she wouldn't mind washing
some clothes, either. The idea of taking a bath sounded utterly
blissful, too. But that could wait until tomorrow morning,
when it would hopefully be warmer than it was now, in the
cool, late afternoon.

"All right. I'll be back in a little while. But if he wakes up
sooner, please come get me. I'll be with my father."

Methusal dropped off her pack. As she headed for her
father's tent, she saw the slim, slightly built Aali arguing up
at the larger, broad-shouldered Dastn. She smiled to herself.
Her cousin appeared to be giving him an earful, but Dastn
looked down at her with an amused, patient expression.

A bit of their conversation drifted to her sharp ears.
"*Now* are you happy?" Aali demanded. "I'm working from
sunup to sundown, and it's all your fault!"

"Is it my fault you blew up the weapons?"

"It was an accident!"

Their voices faded when Methusal tapped on her father's
tent door. "Papa? It's Thusa."

"Come in." Erl greeted her with a hug and a smile.
"You're looking well." He sat back in his desk chair. "How is
kaavl camp?"

"Hard." Methusal sat down, too. Only then did she realize
how tired she was from the long trek. "Where do I start?"

"Tell me everything."

So she did. About Deccia's mistreatment, and how she
didn't want anyone, especially Timaeus, to know about it.
And she confessed her own disastrous attempt to rescue her
twin, and how Mentàll had rescued her. She finished up with
Kitran's anger toward the Dehrien, and the plotting between
Mentàll and Efron last night.

"I don't know what he's planning, but I don't trust him.
He's after some prize. I don't know what it is. Maybe ore."

Erl frowned. "Do you think he's for us, or against us, in
this war?"

She admitted, "Last night he did say he wants to win the
war. Then he'll set his plan in motion."

"He wants to win the war." Erl rubbed his bristly chin. "You're sure."

"It's his first priority."

"Then that's all that matters. For now."

"Papa. Do you trust him?"

"I have to trust him, in order to win this war."

"And afterward?"

"Afterward, I will proceed with caution."

"What about Deccia? We can't let her stay in that General's prison. He might kill her soon. When will we send in a war party to rescue her?"

"As soon as we can. But we'll need a lot of troops to storm the compound. We don't have enough yet. Especially now. The Zindedis are still trying to break into the mountains to find base camp. A special war team has held them off—for now."

"What about a quick surprise attack on the compound? What if the kaavl team helped?"

"I don't want to put the kaavl team in danger. You're too valuable. The intelligence you've gathered has helped us successfully attack the Zindedis four times already."

"But we have to do *something*."

"I understand how you feel." Grim lines etched into the sides of his mouth. "I feel the same way. We'll rescue her as soon as we can, I promise. In the meantime, we'll keep whittling away at their defenses. At some point, even if the other troops don't arrive, we should be able to attack the compound and rescue Deccia."

"But how long will that take?" Methusal felt sick inside. "I don't want her to suffer anymore, Papa!"

"The General won't kill her," Erl said softly. "She's too valuable for his purpose. But I cannot send men to their certain deaths just because one person is suffering."

Frustrated tears escaped. "It's not *fair*. It's not!"

"I know it's not. But promise me you won't do anything foolish again."

Methusal couldn't speak. She didn't want to concede that her sister had to suffer still more.

"Promise," her father repeated sternly.

Throat aching, she swiped at her tears. "I won't try to break in again."

"I know it's hard, Methusal." Her father gripped her hand. "It's hard on all of us. But I'm afraid it's only going to get worse."

Δ Δ Δ Δ Δ

As the sun gilded the western hills that evening, Methusal washed her dirty clothes in the stream and rinsed her tear streaked face, too. Already a chill bit through the air. She was filthy. Tomorrow she'd wash off a week's worth of grime. Maybe at midday, when it was the warmest. She couldn't wait. And she couldn't wait to check on Behran again. She hoped Hendra was right, and that his fever was getting better.

After hanging up her dripping clothes to dry on a laundry pole outside her tent, she returned to the medical tent to check on him.

She discovered the Kaavl Commander was in there, too. Doc was inspecting his wound, and the doctor smiled when he saw Methusal. "Good job nursing, Methusal. Ever think about taking it up as a career?" The question was unexpected.

Mentàll's cold, unfriendly gaze impaled her.

"I'd never thought about it. I've always taken care of animals."

"People aren't so different." He affixed new leaves with dabs of sap from a small pot.

Methusal glanced at her enemy. "You may be right. By the way, I'm out of tacky leaves. Do you have any sap to spare?"

"On the table." Doc nodded. "Wrap a little in a skin and take it with you."

"Thanks." She headed for Behran. Hendra hovered over him with her palm placed on his forehead.

"Wait, Methusal," Doc said. "I want to show you how to cut the stitches."

Reluctantly, she returned.

"Take a stitch like this. Lift it with the point of the knife." He demonstrated. The tip poked between the tender new flesh and the thread. Methusal cringed, unable to help herself. "Then cut it. Cut each stitch and pull them out, one by one."

"Okay." She felt a little queasy. How could taking out stitches bother her more than tending an open wound? Was she afraid of accidentally hurting a patient? But this was Mentàll.

She found that didn't matter. Hurting him—or anyone—made her feel sick.

Doc eyed her. "You look a little green."

She swallowed. "I'm fine."

"Finished?" the Dehrien demanded.

"Yes."

Mentàll pulled on his tunic and faced them. "Do I see weakness, Methusal?"

She held her tongue. He was baiting her. The hard light in his eyes said so. "I'm not afraid of taking out your stitches," she finally returned. "And if it causes you a little pain along the way, so be it." That wasn't how she truly felt, but this man, as usual, brought out the worst in her.

A nasty smile curled his lips. "So, you wish to prolong your duties."

Methusal abruptly headed for Behran. She wouldn't waste one more breath on that man.

"Thusa," Hendra exclaimed, looking up. "Behran's fever just broke! He's going to be all right."

She rushed to his side. "Behran? *Behran!* Can you hear me?"

His lashes fluttered, and a slit of deep blue peered out. He looked dazed. "Thusa?" he whispered.

"You're all right!" She stroked his cheek and tears of relief escaped. "You're going to be all right."

He smiled faintly. "How could I not...with two angels watching over me?"

Hendra smiled, and Methusal grinned. Behran would live.

Δ Δ Δ Δ Δ

Methusal spent a good hour with Behran, just holding his hand. He slept most of the time, but she was happy just to be with him. By the time she left the medical tent, he had fallen into a deep sleep. Her stomach rumbled, and she followed the smell of food to the tarp covered eating area.

"Thusa," Aali called. She was sitting across from Hendra, and she patted the seat beside her. "We've saved a seat for you."

"Thank you." She smiled and quickly headed for the buffet line.

Matronly Aenill, Pan's wife, spooned up a bread-like pudding, sprinkled with dark berries, onto her plate. It smelled spicy and delicious. "Smells wonderful," she told the cook. "What is it?" Two years ago, while visiting Tarst for the kaavl games, she had learned that Aenill possessed the rare ability to make every dish into an extraordinary, tasty masterpiece.

A smile dimpled into Aenill's ample cheeks. "Just softened grain discs and tagma berries. And a few special spices."

"I can't wait to try it." Her mouth watered, and she piled tender meat onto her plate, and logne leaves, too. She hurried for her table, but a familiar figure in bleached leather intercepted her path.

Now what? Hadn't she suffered her full daily quota of torture yet? "What?"

"You will practice knives with Kitran tomorrow."

Instant irritation simmered. Maybe it was because she wanted a reprieve from dealing with him. Base camp was supposed to be neutral territory. At least, in her mind, it should be. "We're at base camp. I'm under my father's authority here. Remember? Not yours."

He smiled. Obviously, he had anticipated just such a response, and it pleased him. The realization irked Methusal even more. How neatly she'd fallen in his trap!

"I have no authority over you, Methusal?"

"None. Excuse me."

His smile edged up, and looked nastier. "You do not believe your own words. Practice with Kitran, or you will practice with me."

She clenched her jaw.

"Obey me," he said softly.

Methusal counted to ten. It didn't help. Why was doing the right thing so *difficult*? He aggravated her on purpose, but she also let him get under her skin. What would the Prophet do in this situation?

"Fine," she gritted, trying her level best to sound calm. Unable to help herself, she finished with a sarcastic, "Your wish is my command."

His eyebrows flew up, obviously startled. His smile took on a hard edge. "I am pleased to hear you say that."

"Step off," she muttered, and brushed by him. Frowning, she sat beside Aali.

Hendra's lips twitched. It looked like she was trying hard not to laugh.

"What?" Methusal said.

Hendra's smile widened. "You're the only one who dares to stand up to him, you know."

"Someone has to," she said darkly, forking up a bite of the bread pudding. In contrast with her mood, it tasted sweet, spicy, and delicious. "His ego is out of control."

"You're the only one he goads on purpose, too. Did you know that?"

Methusal found this hard to believe, but if Hendra said so, it must be true. "He hates me."

"Yes," Hendra admitted. "But I'm not entirely sure why."

Methusal took a bite of the flavorful meat. It nearly melted in her mouth, and that lifted her mood a bit. "I humiliated him. I defeated him when he tried to take over Rolban. It was a kick to his pride."

"Yes. But I don't think that's the whole story."

"What do you mean?"

Hesitantly, Hendra said, "He said something interesting at kaavl camp, when I asked him why he hates you so much. I think, to him, you personify everything he's ever hated about Rolban. And he's hated Rolban for his entire life."

"Why?"

"I don't know."

"*He's* a slug," Aali interjected. "We should hate him, not the other way around."

Methusal mulled over Hendra's words. Every crumb of information about her enemy could serve as ammunition to defeat him later, when his true plan came to light. Maybe this insight into his complex, obviously twisted psyche would help later, although she didn't see how, at the moment.

Conversation moved on to other topics. Aali wanted to hear about Deccia. Methusal told her everything, except for how the General was abusing her.

"We have to rescue her, and soon!"

"Papa wants to wait until more troops arrive."

Hendra offered, "Timaeus is traveling to Eerpor tomorrow to find out if they're sending troops."

"What about Wyen?"

"I don't know. They're a five day run from here. It'll probably be a few more days before we hear."

"And their troops will take even longer to arrive."

"I won't sit here doing nothing forever," her cousin muttered.

"Don't leap off a cliff, Aali."

"I am *not* a child. Even though everyone keeps treating me like one."

"Do you mean Dastn?"

She scowled mightily. "Don't mention his name. Because of him, I'm banished to camp, working till I'm too exhausted to see straight."

"You look exhausted," Methusal said with an eye roll.

"Don't sniff at my problems. They're serious."

"And they'll get more serious if you run off and do something stupid."

Aali glared.

"Behran is better, Aali," Hendra said, diplomatically changing the subject.

The younger girl's face brightened. "Good." She gathered up her empty dishes. "I'll visit him. Maybe *he'll* appreciate my company." She flounced away.

Methusal tried to hide a smile.

After a moment, Hendra said, "You're lucky to have Behran. He's a wonderful man."

Methusal glanced at her.

Concern darkened Hendra's eyes. "Please don't think...I'm not interested in Behran. Not like that." A few moments passed. "Will you two marry?"

Much as Hendra said she wasn't interested in Behran, Methusal couldn't quite read her expression right now.

Feeling vulnerable to admit it, Methusal said, "He hasn't asked me yet. What about you? Has anyone asked you?"

"Wortn." Hendra's shoulders slumped, and she seemed to close in upon herself. "Jascr wants me to marry him to settle his debts."

"Yuck."

She gave a sickly smile. "I know. If you want to know the truth, I don't think I'll ever marry."

"Aren't there other men in Dehre? Nice ones?"

"Probably. It's not that." Her gaze shadowed.

"Then what is it?"

"I just...I don't...I have a hard time trusting people. Especially men," Hendra looked down. She reminded Methusal of a hurt animal.

Gently, she said, "Because of your awful father and brothers?"

"Yes."

"You need to find a good man. Forget the Dehriens. I haven't seen a nice one yet."

"Except for Behran," Hendra said, with a faint smile.

"Except for Behran," she agreed. "But what about men from Tarst? All of them seem nice... What about Doc? He's gentle and kind. A good guy."

"He is," Hendra agreed. She glanced over at the red-haired doctor, who sat at a nearby table. "He is a good man," she said softly.

Δ Δ Δ Δ Δ

Aali tiptoed through the dark for Erl's tent. Her arms ached from scrubbing pots after dinner, and she was sleepy. But her mission tonight remained clear. And vital. Methusal and Behran had tried to rescue Deccia. Now it was her turn.

Exactly three days had passed since the explosion. Although she felt bad the explosion had notified the Zindedis that the war teams lived in the mountains, enough good had come from the discovery that she chaffed under her unending punishment. She worked under Doc's close supervision all morning, and under Aenill's until dark. Then she was exhausted, and only wanted to tumble into bed—which had been Uncle Erl's strategy all along, of course.

Pogul had been disciplined, too. Now he had to scout at night. Unease slipped through her. Pogul hated her now. She felt it in his hard, evil stares. He hadn't done anything yet, but she knew he was planning something. She wasn't too worried, though. Pogul wasn't the brightest star in the sky. And if she, a kaavl Quatr-leveler, couldn't outmaneuver him, then she should be demoted.

No, what worried and hurt most were Uncle Erl's words on the day of the explosion. On the good side, it turned out Dastn hadn't told him what had happened. On the other hand, he'd put her in a position where she didn't have any choice but to spill the berries herself. She'd confessed what she had done and why she was in the weapons valley in the first place.

"You can't be trusted, Aali," Erl had said. "I told you not to scout. And what did you do, the moment I left?" He shook his head. "I'm disappointed in you."

She'd felt bad. She still did. And she didn't want Uncle Erl to think she was untrustworthy. Dastn, either.

Now she had almost reached Uncle Erl's tent. Pan appeared and Aali quickly huddled against a tree until he entered Erl's tent. She glanced over her shoulder. No one else was nearby. At least Dastn was gone, messengering. His sharp eyes followed her much too often. Uncle Erl must have asked him to keep an eye on her while he was out warring. But tonight Dastn was gone, and Thusa was asleep in the tent. No one was watching her right now.

Silent as a whip, Aali slipped to the back of Erl's tent and sat in the shadows.

Anyway, it was so unfair. Hadn't the explosion given everyone valuable information? Shouldn't they be thanking her? No one seemed to realize how helpful she had been. All the same, she wanted to redeem herself. She wanted to do something vital to rescue her sister, and to help win the war.

But Erl wouldn't let her leave camp, and no one told her anything.

That's why she was sitting in the dark now, ear pressed to Erl's tent wall. Erl, Pan, and Mentàll were holding a top secret meeting right now. She'd heard Pan and Erl muttering about it after dinner. They hadn't noticed her scraping pots nearby, standing half-hidden among the rocks.

She was determined to find out their plans, and to figure out how she could rescue Deccia. She was sick of peeling tubers, and itched for action. Maybe then people would see how valuable she truly was. Maybe then they'd stop treating her like a child.

The icy wind bit through her tunic. She should have put on another. Aali huddled against the back corner of the tent, hugging her arms around her knees, and listened.

Erl had just finished describing the burn marks in the weapons valley. He concluded, "The powder is powerful, but unstable."

Mentàll said, "We have found a building filled with powder barrels in Quasr."

"Where?" Pan asked.

"Near the water, on the east side of town. It's heavily guarded."

"How many entrances into the building?"

"One door, and one small window in the back. The door has four guards."

"And the window?"

"Only one patrolling guard. But it's too small for a man to climb through. And it's high."

"How small?" Erl wanted to know.

Silence. Probably the Dehrien measured with his hands.

Pan spoke. "We'll have to choose the right moment to blow up the building. Maybe we could combine it with multiple prongs of attack. We'd need to wait for the extra troops."

"A final battle plan." Erl sounded thoughtful. "Good idea. But how could we time the explosion?"

"A slow burning candle," the Dehrien Chief said.

"Yes. But it would have to be inside the building. The guards would notice if it was outside."

Silence. "We'll work on that," Erl said at last. "Come to me with any ideas."

The meeting drew to a close. Aali rose from her shadowed corner and crept to the women's tent. An idea glimmered in her mind, and she grinned. She only needed to get one more piece of information. Then, when the time was right, she'd help save all of Koblan, and Deccia, too.

Chapter Eighteen

METHUSAL AWOKE EARLY THE NEXT morning. Dawn lightened the dark sky to pale blue, and then to a soft pink as the sun rose. Camp lay quiet and still. Maybe she'd refresh herself and wash her face in the stream before heading over for breakfast. A quick check of her clean clothes proved they were still wet. Hopefully the sun would bake them dry later.

Grabbing up her leather wrapped bar of soap, Methusal hurried for the private place reserved for the women, and then on to the stream.

She washed her hands in the icy water. It was cold, but not unbearable. How she longed for a bath! She couldn't stand how filthy she felt. The sun edged higher, and a warm beam touched her face. Everything was quiet, except for the rush of the small waterfall and the burbling stream. Overhead a flying beast chirped. Not a soul was nearby.

Methusal glanced toward camp. A few men now thronged outside the food tent, waiting for Aenill to put out the hot water. She glanced up the hill, to the cascading waterfall. No hot water would be found up there. She had planned to take a bath later, when it was warmer, and maybe with Aali along to warn off intruders.

But why not now? She could brave the cold. And no one else was here. In truth, who would be crazy enough to bathe now, in the freezing early morning?

Methusal made up her mind. A bath now would feel heavenly. She didn't care if she turned blue. It would be worth it, just to be clean.

She climbed the hill, slipped between the two protective boulders, and found the little pool just as she had left it—quiet, secluded, and best of all, unoccupied. Hopefully no one would come while she bathed. She'd hurry, just to be safe.

Quickly, she stripped off her clothes and plunged into the deep, icy pool. She gasped with shock from the cold. The water came to her armpits. She swiftly washed her hair and body. She felt surprisingly vulnerable now, and cast a few nervous glances at the path from the camp.

But no one came. It felt delicious to be clean again, although now she shuddered with cold. She wrung out her long hair and tiptoed from the water. Then she realized she had brought no drying cloth. Great. She was freezing, soaking wet, and if she got dressed, her leather clothing would get wet and stick to her skin. And leather took forever to dry. Even worse, these were her only dry clothes. The ones she'd washed last night were still wet.

Although the sun shone low on the horizon, the early morning air was frosty. Teeth chattering, Methusal swiped as much water as she could off of her puckered, bumpy skin. Now what? Get dressed? Stand in the arctic sun for a while longer and hope to dry off? But what if someone came?

Methusal slipped into kaavl and decided to let the sun dry her as much as possible—at least for as long as she could bear the cold morning air. She hugged her arms around herself and shivered. Was she drying? It didn't feel like it.

Just when she'd decided to pull on her leather clothes, she heard the barest sound. A tiny pebble rolled down the slope.

An apte? An adult human would surely make more noise than that. She grabbed her tunic at the same time her gaze swung for the opening to the pathway. The breath stuttered in her throat when she glimpsed short, white-blond hair. A second later the Dehrien Chief appeared, pulling his tunic over his head.

Methusal stared, her own tunic snatched protectively in front of her, while the Chief tossed his to the ground and glanced up. She'd surprised him; she could tell by the quick bunching of his sleek, powerful shoulders.

"Step *off*," she breathed. She could only hope her tunic covered all of her important areas. "Now."

The pale eyes took in her shaking body in one swift, comprehensive glance. She read nothing in them—no lust, no desire—just the usual, cool blue ice. She could not tell what he was thinking, and that made her nervous. He advanced two steps closer. "You did not turn the rock."

"What rock?" She struggled to still her clacking teeth, and also her trembling desire to bolt down the path, away from him. Only the realization that he'd see her naked backside stopped her.

"At the base of the path. Brown means clear, the white side means occupied."

"I...I didn't know." Her body shook from the cold, and from the threat of his presence.

He loosed the knot of his breeches. "Now you do."

Methusal stared in horror. "Stop it!" She averted her eyes.

She heard a soft sound, and glanced back. He'd stopped untying the leather strips, and a small, cruel smile curved his lips. She glared. "Whip," she hissed.

"Go then, Methusal."

"Turn your back," she ordered, but he made no move to comply.

He enjoyed this, Methusal realized with a flash of anger. If only she didn't feel like she was about to turn into an icicle. "Do it," she spat.

"Or?"

Methusal bit her lip hard. To her horror, a quick tear slid down her cheek. What was wrong with her? She couldn't show weakness to this man! "I *hate* you."

"You need a longer tunic."

Methusal gasped with horror. She couldn't lower hers much more, or she'd expose her top half.

"You monstrous man!" She burst into ridiculous tears of embarrassment. At first she didn't see him come closer.

She backed up. "*Don't.*" She hated the high, fearful tremor in her voice. She blinked fast, so she could see her mortal enemy, who was now only a few handbreadths away from her. "If you touch me, I'll hurt you." It was all bravado, and he surely knew it.

"You need to be prepared at all times, Methusal. Haven't you learned that yet?" And then, to her gasp of surprise, he pulled his own tunic over her head, to her shoulders, and then she felt his large hands skim down her waist and hips, tugging it into place. The leather felt warm from his body, and fell halfway down her thighs. Inside it, Methusal still clutched her own tunic, and she stared at him, confused.

"Why?" she choked out.

"I cannot have a kaavl player catch ill. What good would that do me?" He turned his back. "Next time, bring a drying cloth."

Methusal dropped her tunic and pushed her arms through the sleeves of the Dehrien Chief's tunic. The garment felt huge on her, and the sleeves fell a handbreadth below her fingertips. She shoved them up her arms. "I'll return it right away," she informed his back.

"I expect nothing else."

"Well then. Happy bathing." Methusal hastily gathered up all her garments and soap, and sped down the path, heart beating very fast, and still shaking, but not feeling quite as cold.

The first thing she did was change in her tent—thankfully, she was mostly dry by then—and then she tossed the Dehrien's tunic in his large tent. There. That was the end of that disturbing encounter. Next time she would find that rock and turn it. Certainly she'd never let that happen again!

△ △ △ △ △

After a quick breakfast, Methusal visited Behran. His face was pale, and he lay quietly, eyes closed, when she arrived.

"He just ate one of Aenill's dumplings," Hendra said with a smile, and left them alone together.

"You're feeling better?" Methusal couldn't keep the worry from her voice.

Behran smiled a little. "I'll live. But I feel as weak as a baby. I hope you don't mind if I lie here."

"Of course not."

He reached for her hand. His felt warm and solid, which encouraged her. "Tell me. What's been going on at camp?"

Methusal decided to tell him only the positive things. He didn't need to worry. When she glossed over the problems of Goric and Jascr, Kitran's altercations with Mentàll, and her own confrontations with the Dehrien Kaavl Commander, her description of camp life sounded surprisingly sunny.

Behran shot her a narrowed look. "Sounds like paradise."

"I was banished to camp for a whole day. And I worried about you the whole time. I'm glad you're better."

"Tell me what's really going on."

"Later, okay? When you're feeling better."

"Aren't you leaving for kaavl camp tomorrow?"

"Yes, but..."

"Tell me this afternoon, then. And what about the troops? Will the Eerporians fight?"

"We haven't heard yet."

Behran closed his eyes for a moment. "They didn't help during the Great War. Why would they help now?"

"The Great War mostly involved Dehre, Tarst, and Rolban. Our whole continent is in danger now, including Eerpor."

Behran's eyes closed again. Quietly, he said, "I hope they come. We need to win this war, and fast. Before more Zindedis arrive."

"I know." Softly, she said, "You're tired. Rest. I'll sit with you for a while."

Behran tightened his grip on her hand. "Just stay for a few minutes. Don't waste your whole day with me, Thusa. I'll probably sleep for most of it."

She bent to kiss his cheek, but he turned his head to kiss her on the lips.

"Behran." Her cheeks flushed. "Now sleep."

△ △ △ △ △

Later that morning, Methusal entered her father's tent. She wanted to ask about their progress—if any—in the war effort. Last night, he'd said the Koblani forces had won a few victories. But what did that mean, really? How long before they won the war? And how long before they could rescue Deccia, if no troops arrived to help?

More importantly, could they win this war? Methusal was afraid to hear that answer, but she had to find out all she could while she was here. Mentàll would tell her nothing at kaavl camp.

"Come in, Methusal." Erl looked up from his desk. He lay his writing stick on a parchment.

"Papa, tell me the truth. How is the war going? Can we possibly win?"

Pan's voice came from outside, "Exactly what we were going to discuss. May I come in, Erl?"

"Of course, old friend." Erl stood to greet the Tarst Chief.

"Am I interrupting a meeting?" Methusal asked.

"An informal one. We're waiting for Kitran."

A few moments later, when Kitran joined the men in the tent, she said, "Do you want me to leave?" Not that she wanted to, of course.

Kitran said, "This concerns you, too, Methusal. Stay." It wasn't hard to guess the purpose of the meeting.

"Thank you for meeting with me," Kitran said. "I have serious concerns about Mentàll's ability to lead the kaavl team."

"How so?" Erl said.

"We've gathered a lot of information. Useful as that may be, Zindedis still have control of Quasr. More Zindedis are coming. We need to attack them and defeat them now."

"We can't win this war without intelligence," Pan said. "Otherwise, we'll send our soldiers to their deaths. The kaavl team's job is vital."

"True. But it's time for action. Mentàll refuses to act, and he won't share information. Furthermore, he's a liability to the entire team."

Erl's eyes narrowed. "Why?"

"He has a bounty on his head. Invaders are ordered to shoot him on sight."

"I know."

"But he insists on scouting in Quasr anyway. He endangers anyone who scouts with him. Including Methusal, who scouted with him a few days ago."

Erl glanced at Methusal.

Pan said, "It's my understanding that he wears a hooded cloak."

A muscle flexed in Kitran's jaw. "He is unwilling to take action, and he is a liability. More importantly, I don't trust him. Look at the past. He's proven that he's a selfish, underhanded whip. I've seen him meeting with other Dehriens in the middle of the night. He's up to something. I know it, and I don't trust him."

"Did you hear what they said?"

"No."

"I did," Methusal said.

Kitran looked at her in surprise.

"He *is* plotting something. I don't know what, exactly...."

"Plotting the opportunity to sell us out," Kitran interjected.

"We don't know that," Erl said.

"We know he's interested in power," Kitran argued. "We also know he met the invaders before anyone else did. Who's to say he's not working with them? Maybe after they've taken over Koblan they've promised to give him power here."

An uneasy silence fell. Much as Methusal disliked the Dehrien Chief, she didn't believe Kitran's theory. It didn't match up with what Mentàll had told his first-in-command, either. And why would he lie to him? "Kitran," she said softly, "I don't trust him, either. But I don't think he's working with the invaders."

"Prove it," he snapped.

"He rescued me from the General. My death would have helped the invaders. Also, when he spoke to Efron the other night he said he wants to defeat the invaders. He'll pursue his plan afterward."

Kitran scowled. "Plan. So he is scheming against us."

Erl spoke now. "None of us like him or trust him, Kitran. We are in full agreement there. Watch him. It'll protect us from surprises. But for now, he wants to win this war. And the Zindedis clearly hate him, if they want him dead."

"I don't trust him!" Kitran growled.

"I don't, either," Erl agreed. "But so far, he's kept his word to us." He turned to his daughter. "And you, Methusal? Has he kept his word?"

How could she say that Mentàll aggravated her at every opportunity? But had he ever touched her? No. And that was the crux of the agreement. "Yes. He's kept his word."

Pan spoke. "Mentàll has two strengths that we need. That's why we want him to remain Kaavl Commander."

"What strengths?"

"He's fearless. And he's cool in hot situations."

"Cold, you mean," Methusal muttered.

"Yes," Pan agreed. "Nothing—and no one—gets to him."

Kitran bit out, "Unless someone gets in his way."

"Be careful," Erl advised.

"So you intend to keep him as Kaavl Commander?" Visible fury knotted Kitran's black brow into a single line.

"Do you think you'd make a better candidate?"

"I do. My kaavl is at the Primary level, the same as his. I would take action. Needed action."

"For now, I agree with Mentàll's leadership decisions," Erl said. "I think the kaavl team should bide its time until an opportunity for offensive action presents itself. We're planning for a massive attack, Kitran. But the time for that has not arrived yet. Neither have the troops. For now, we'll skirmish, gain information, and prepare for the great battle."

"When the opportunity presents itself," Kitran stated. His gaze hardened. "I couldn't agree more. And when it does, I'll make sure the kaavl team takes the proper action."

"I expect you to follow Mentàll's leadership."

"I will do what is necessary to win this war." Kitran stood. "Thank you for your time. Methusal, we will practice with weapons after lunch."

"Okay." Not high on her list of desirable activities, to be sure.

After Kitran left, Erl and Pan looked at each other. "I hope the troops get here soon. Kitran is a great kaavl player. I'd hate to sideline him for insubordinate behavior."

Methusal couldn't agree more. Unease knotted in her stomach. Kitran had trusted Mentàll, and as a result had been humiliated during the Rolban war. That hurt and humiliation had clearly turned into hatred. If he and Mentàll couldn't work out their differences, the flame of hatred within kaavl camp may explode into something far worse.

△ △ △ △ △

After lunch the men set up impromptu areas to practice sword and knife wielding skills with each other. The very sight made Methusal shudder, even though she knew her knife skills were poor. She didn't want to hurt anyone. Not ever.

Kitran appeared at her side. "Practice time."

She sighed, but didn't argue.

Kitran worked her hard, and she narrowly missed the slash of his knife several times. Once, his blade caught on her sleeve. Another time, his blade pierced the skin of her fore-arm.

"Are you trying to hurt me?" she demanded, swiping at the blood. She sensed the anger still simmering in her instructor. "You're mad at Mentàll. Don't take it out on me."

Kitran lowered his blade. "I'm sorry, Methusal. You've improved. Enough for today."

"Thank goodness!"

"Walk with me. I want to talk to you." Kitran headed for the hills, clearly expecting her to follow. Feeling apprehensive, Methusal did as he bid. Kitran stopped on a high rock with a clear view of the harsh surrounding mountains.

"Why couldn't you talk to me in camp?"

Her instructor's dark eyes bored into her. "I need to know if you're on my side."

"What do you mean? I'm always on your side."

"Against the Dehrien. When it comes down to it, who will you follow?"

"My father ordered us both to follow Mentàll."

"The time will come when the choice will not be so clear. And the time may be sooner than you think."

"What do you mean?" She felt uneasy.

"The less you know, the better. Do I have your allegiance?"

"Kitran..." she felt torn inside. Of course her first loyalty remained with Kitran. But deep inside, she suspected Kitran's heart ruled his head right now. And that heart hated the Dehrien. It was so unlike the Kitran she'd known for years. Of course she disliked and distrusted Mentàll, too...but mutiny?

She tried to make him see reason. "Kitran, you know I'm loyal to you. I respect you. You've been my teacher for years, and I couldn't have asked for a better one. But I'm also loyal to my father. He's the Chief of Rolban. He expects me to obey him, and he expects you to, also. Can't you?" she pleaded. "In a few days we'll start the battle, and then you can attack all the invaders you want."

"We need to take action *now,* or more people will die," Kitran gritted. "Mentàll is a fool! I *know* how to stop the bloodshed. I know how to end this war."

"How?"

"I can't tell you. Not yet."

"Then tell Mentàll," she urged. "Tell Papa. You can work together."

"I've told Mentàll. He says it's not time. He wants to wait, and he's warped Erl's mind with his smooth talk so he thinks the same way. But while we wait, more die! We can't wait any longer. Erl and Pan are *fools* to back Mentàll."

Kitran's harsh words against her father took her aback. "Are you sure? Maybe they're right."

"No. Mentàll is a coward. He doesn't have the guts to take action now, when it will do the most good. And he's convinced Erl and Pan to continue to pursue those small, useless skirmishes."

Methusal didn't know what to think. Who was right? Kitran—or Mentàll and her father?

"Are you with me, or not?"

"I don't know," she said softly. "If you told me the plan, it might help me to decide."

"I can't. If others learn about it, we will all die. You must trust me. Just as you blindly trust Mentàll."

"I *don't* trust him," she said, aghast.

"You act like you do. You come to his bidding whenever he calls." Something dark flashed in his eyes. Contempt?

"I'm trying hard to do the right thing! I want to stay on the kaavl team. I want to help rescue Deccia. To do that, I have to make certain choices."

"To prostitute yourself to the Dehrien?"

With a gasp, Methusal slapped Kitran. "How dare you? I would *never* give myself to that man!"

"No?" His black eyes condemned her. "I saw you return from your bath this morning. You wore his tunic."

Her face flamed.

Kitran twisted the knife further. "Don't deny it. Only that Dehrien wears bleached leather."

"It wasn't...it's not what you think!" she sputtered in horror. "He surprised me. I didn't know about the rock! And I forgot my dry cloth."

"So he stripped off his clothes and you put on his tunic."

"Kitran!" Her face burned hotter. "No! I didn't ask for his tunic. He...he gave it to me." She didn't think it would help her case to say the Dehrien Chief had put his tunic on her. No, indeed.

Kitran stared at her. "Really?"

"Yes, really!" She trembled in humiliation. "And don't you dare think anything else." Now she wondered how many other people had seen her wear Mentàll's tunic. And what they might be thinking. Further mortification burned through her.

"Then watch your appearances. Or others will guess your true allegiance."

Her mouth opened in disbelief. She could not believe Kitran was attacking her like this. She glared. "Humiliating me will not win me to your side."

"I'm just giving you friendly advice. Choose your side with care."

"I have not chosen to follow Mentàll!"

Kitran's discerning black gaze slashed through her. "Maybe not. But he does hold power over you. Admit it."

"He scares me," she admitted. "But I won't let him control me."

"See that you don't. And if you decide to choose my side, my offer is open."

He climbed down the hillside. Methusal stared after him, arms crossed. Kitran hated Mentàll, and so he felt contempt for her, too, for following the Dehrien Chief. Her unfortunate encounter with Mentàll this morning had only added fuel to his fire.

She didn't like how Kitran had just treated her, but she didn't like Mentàll any better. What was the right course of action? Whom should she follow?

△ △ △ △ △

Methusal checked on Behran again, feeling eager to spend more time with him, but he was asleep. He slept through the entire afternoon. When she next checked, late in the day, she found Hendra with her arm around his shoulders, helping him to sit up. She stopped for a second and watched them.

Behran said something, and the Dehrien girl smiled. The scene looked intimate, and entirely natural. Methusal did her best to ignore a ridiculous stab of discomfort.

Then she noticed a steaming bowl of Aenill's savory soup beside Behran, and her spirits lifted with hope. She hurried over. "Behran, are you feeling better?"

Hendra instantly pulled away from him, and she flushed a little. "He said he's hungry. Maybe you could help him, Thusa, while I check on the other patients?"

"Of course." Methusal exchanged places with the other girl, and Hendra hurried off.

Behran grinned at her. "If you'll help me stay sitting up, I'll try to eat."

It turned out that Methusal held him up and held the soup bowl, too. Halfway through, Behran needed to lie down.

"I'll eat more in a little while," he said. At least he didn't look as sleepy now. His discerning, intent gaze watched her. "Tell me everything you left out earlier."

Reluctantly, Methusal did so. But she left out Goric and Jascr leaving rochers in her pallet. It seemed like such a petty thing, and she didn't want him to worry over nothing. Behran seemed most interested in Kitran's mutterings of mutiny. "Will you follow him if he decides to mutiny?"

"I don't know. Shouldn't I obey my father? I mean, I don't want to follow Mentàll..." Frustrated, she said, "It's such a mess. I don't know what to do."

"Do you really think Kitran can end this war?"

"How could he? No. Not really."

"I think you're choosing the right path. Unless Kitran tells you every bit of his plan and it sounds possible, I wouldn't follow him."

"That's what I'm thinking. But I hate how he makes it seem like I'm choosing Mentàll over him. As if I'd ever choose that Dehrien over anyone!"

"Is he still bothering you?"

That was another issue she'd glossed over. "Yes. He likes to get under my skin. He's sick and twisted, and I can't stand him."

Behran nodded. "But he's saved your life twice now. I don't understand that."

He didn't know that Mentàll had only done it so he could have the satisfaction of antagonizing her still more.

"Can we please talk about something else? Has Doc said when you'll be able to leave the medical tent?"

"Another two or three days."

"At least you're safe here. I won't need to worry about you."

"I'd rather be out fighting for Koblan." Behran closed his eyes.

"I know. And soon you will be. But first, you need to eat. Come on. Sit up again. Then you can sleep all you want."

He smiled faintly. "You're a tough woman, Methusal Maahr."

"I never give up on an injured beast."

Behran chuckled, and slowly sat up. "You want to know the truth? I feel sorry for Mentàll. He wants to defeat you, but he doesn't know who he's tangling with. You're one war he'll never win."

△ △ △ △ △

As the sun dipped low on the horizon that evening, the savory smell of meat crisping over the kitchen fire wafted throughout camp. Methusal sat in the dining area with Aali, who'd taken a brief break from her kitchen duties.

"Are you going back to kaavl camp tomorrow?" Aali asked.

"Yes."

"Isn't it awful, being the only girl?"

"It's difficult, especially with Behran gone. But Kitran won't let anyone hurt me."

"You mean like that nasty Mentàll?"

Methusal thought back over her many encounters with the Dehrien Chief, including the uncomfortable one this morning. If he had wanted to take advantage of her, that would have been his perfect opportunity to do so. But he hadn't. "He hasn't touched me. Jascr and Goric are the ones that worry me the most."

"Goric's nasty," Aali agreed. "Almost as nasty as Pogul." She cast a quick glance over her shoulder.

Suspicion flared. "What did you do?"

Guilt flickered across her cousin's face. "You know that explosion? I was in the valley because Pogul let me take his scout duty. Now he's in trouble, too. I think he might hate me."

"Be careful. Pogul's not smart, but he's mean."

"That's what Dastn said."

"Mmhm," With a small smile, Methusal watched Aali's gaze search out and find the Tarst runner. "What else does Dastn say to you?"

She rolled her eyes. "He thinks I'm childish and irresponsible. Pooh on him."

Methusal smiled. She had missed her cousin's irrepressible, spunky spirits.

Aali frowned now. "What are they doing?"

Methusal followed her gaze. All of the men had gathered in a clump in the center of camp. The raised voices of Kitran and a few others drifted to her. Dastn wandered over next, along with Barak. Someone called for Mentàll.

The Dehrien Chief emerged from his tent and joined the throng. Tabor spoke to him. He shook his head, but then Kitran's ugly voice rose. "You were *given* leadership. Prove yourself. I'll bet you can't meet my challenge."

The Dehrien stood very still, and then said words that Methusal didn't catch. Evidently he had agreed, because the men fanned out to different locations.

Kitran glanced toward the dining area. "Methusal! Aali. Come and judge."

"Judge what?" Methusal followed her scampering cousin across the field of mashed flat weeds.

"Two competitions. Push-ups and pull-ups. You count out loud, and we'll follow your lead. Those who don't keep up are out."

It seemed silly to Methusal, but Kitran looked serious. His black, knotted brow scowled at the Dehrien Chief. Maybe this challenge was a good idea. A way for Kitran to contest Mentàll without spilling blood.

"Fine," she said, and noticed that Hendra and Doc had emerged from the medical tent. She waved them over and asked for help judging. A small, amused smile curved Doc's lips, but he stood next to Hendra, ready to judge.

"Come on, Doc," Barak bellowed. "Prove your manhood."

Doc gave a small shake of his red head, but Barak hooted in a friendly fashion. Doc ducked his head, but joined the line.

"Men," Hendra sighed, but her eyes strayed to Doc, who was in push-up position.

"Get ready... Go!" Aali cried.

"One," Methusal said. "Two..."

By the time she reached "fifty," most of the men were out, or straining to continue. Barak dropped out at sixty-five, and Doc at seventy. Dastn made it to one hundred. Soon the only ones left were Kitran and the Dehrien Chief. At one hundred twenty-five, sweat ran down Kitran's face, and the muscles in his arms bunched and strained. On the other hand, the Dehrien looked like an emotionless machine. *This isn't a good idea,* Methusal thought. *What about his injury?*

Kitran collapsed at one hundred and fifty. Mentàll would have stopped too, but his Dehrien teammates chanted him on. "Go, Chief." He continued on to two hundred, and then stopped and sat down, swiping a hand across his sweating brow. He shucked off his tunic, and Methusal saw blood trickling down his back.

"You won't win the next challenge," Kitran snarled.

"Kitran," Methusal said. "Maybe you should stop. It's getting dark."

"There's enough daylight for this last challenge," he bit back, and Methusal flinched at the violence thrumming through his voice.

He wouldn't back down. And she knew Mentàll wouldn't thank her to mention his bleeding injury. "Fine. Where will you do pull-ups?"

Trees were sparse in camp, but they found one with two branches that were the right height. Two men could do pull ups at the same time. Since dusk shadowed the camp, Kitran decided that only the men who'd done the most push-ups would compete.

Doc and Barak competed, and Doc won, probably because his lighter, wiry frame required less wrestling up and down than Barak's large, solid mass. Dastn won his challenge, too, at fifty pull ups—same as Doc. Then it was Kitran and Mentàll. At fifty, Kitran was straining. Methusal urged him on, and so did the other Rolbanis. But at sixty-five, he dropped to the ground.

This time, Mentàll needed no encouragement. He continued on easily to one hundred, and then dropped down in a lithe, leisurely fashion, as if he could have gone on for much longer. As he might have, Methusal reluctantly suspected. She also believed the Dehrien had continued doing the pull-ups in order to screw in Kitran's humiliation still deeper.

Mentàll faced Kitran. Blood ran in a steady stream down his back now. "Another challenge?"

Kitran gritted his teeth and stalked away.

"Come to the medical tent," Doc told Mentàll. "I need to take a look at those stitches."

The Dehrien stooped to pick up his tunic, and approached Methusal on his way to follow Doc. On purpose, she realized with sudden unease, when he stopped in front of her.

That pale gaze froze into her with the force of a blizzard. Intuition, combined with a shot of adrenaline, told her that his show of superior strength had been directed at her, too. To assert his dominance, and his determination to wield authority over her. To remain her Kaavl Commander.

He leaned close, and his breath fanned her temple. She flinched. In a low voice, he murmured, "Choose well whom you will follow."

Her eyes narrowed. Had he heard Kitran's mutterings of mutiny?

His intimidating gaze released her, and he stalked toward the medical tent.

Her heart beat harder. Another threat. She had hoped the challenge would calm the struggle for dominance between the two men. But had it?

△ △ △ △ △

Hendra slipped into the dinner line behind her cousin, who forked a healthy portion of meat onto his plate.

"Are your stitches all right?" she asked, scooping up more of Aenill's delicious bread pudding.

"They are fine." Mentàll reached the end of the line. Hendra expected him to join his comrades at the Dehrien table. Instead, he waited for her. Surprised, she moved out of the way of other people and looked up at him.

He said, "Doc is treating you well?"

"Of course."

Those chilly, light blue eyes seemed to read her soul. "I know you are not happy I sent you here."

Hendra looked down, trying to disguise the pang of bitterness she still felt. "I want to help win the war. At least I'm doing some good here by helping Doc."

"I do not like making you unhappy, little cousin," he said softly.

She glanced up, surprised, and for a second felt hopeful. That hope died a swift death when she saw the uncompromising look on his face. He would not change his mind. She sighed, accepting it—at least for now. "I understand that you want what's best for me."

"I do. And I will warn you to be careful of your friends."

Hendra glanced at the table where the Rolbani cousins waited for her. "You're wrong about Methusal. Just as she is wrong about you."

He smiled humorlessly. "You are sure about that?"

Irritation sparked. "Sometimes I'd like to smack your heads together."

Coldly, he said, "Nothing will settle our differences. Not until I have extracted my last ounce of revenge."

"Mentàll!" Hendra moved further away from the line, so no one would overhear their conversation. "How can you say that? She's a human being..."

"An arrogant, selfish one. She has much to learn, before the price I extract from her is paid in full."

"What are you talking about?"

"Do not look so horrified, little cousin. Methusal deserves every consequence I will give her."

"*What* do you plan to do?" she said, aghast.

"I have promised not to harm her. Let that promise calm your fears. For now, all other means of gaining my goal are fair play."

Hendra didn't like the sound of that. "If the two of you would just sit down and talk like rational people..."

"I am always logical, Hendra. Goodnight."

Hendra watched him go. What had come over the cousin she'd loved and hero-worshiped as a child? Troubled, she made her way to the table.

Aali said, "So, how big is that window in that powder building?"

Methusal measured a space with her hands. Aali nodded, looking thoughtful. "Not too small," she muttered to herself.

Methusal said to Hendra, "Your cousin glared at me while you were talking to him. What was he saying?"

Hendra thought it best not to repeat Mentàll's threats. The animosity between the two was hot enough already. If only they would speak rationally to each other!

An idea, half-formed when talking to her cousin, emerged. If they wouldn't speak to each other, then maybe she could intervene. If she could make each see the other as a real human being, then maybe this war between them would end before Mentàll did something he'd regret forever. True, he was the one who needed to see reason the most, but it wouldn't hurt to lay the groundwork with her friend, first.

"He asked how I'm doing."

Methusal's eyebrows rose, as if surprised.

Hendra thought quickly about how to set her new plan in motion. She forked up bread pudding. "Mentàll watched out for me during my childhood. As much as he could, anyway."

Methusal's brow wrinkled in clear disbelief. Politely, though, she said, "Your mother and his were sisters?"

"Yes. They were twins."

"Twins," Methusal said, obviously surprised. Being a twin herself, maybe she would empathize more with the story. Good.

"Yes. My mother helped my aunt care for Mentàll when he was a baby. I never knew my aunt, because she died before I was born. But if she was anything like my own mother, she was the sweetest, gentlest person in the world."

"Mentàll seems very sensitive about the subject when anyone mentions her."

Hendra was surprised Methusal knew that. "He doesn't talk about her much. Then again, he doesn't talk much about anything. He's a very private man."

Methusal drew a quick breath, as if she wanted to add a comment, but did not. "Does he have any friends?"

"Allies. I wouldn't exactly call them friends. He is close to no one. Not even the women he takes from time to time." Her face warmed in embarrassment.

Methusal chewed meat, and then slowly—possibly reluctantly—said, "And he grew up in your home. I know your father beat him. I've seen the scars on his back."

Tears prickled Hendra's eyes. "Yes." She bit her lip. "My father looked for excuses to beat him. Mentàll never cried. Ever."

Methusal looked disturbed. Sympathy for the innocent and injured clearly battled with her obvious dislike for Mentàll. "That's awful. How long did it go on?"

"Years." The breath caught in her throat. Hendra thought she'd be able to discuss Mentàll's past, but it was her past, too. And it cut like the whip that had flayed into Mentàll's skin. And her own. She bit her wobbling lip and drew a shaky breath. No matter how hard it was to admit, she had to say it all. Methusal had to see the full truth. "My father beat me, too."

Methusal gasped.

"Mentàll..." Hendra licked her lips. "So many times he saved me from a beating."

"What do you mean?"

"He'd turn up out of nowhere, just when my father was about to hit me. Father hated Mentàll so much that he always turned his rage onto him, instead." Tears trickled from her eyes. "Mentàll always took it, and I...I ran." Tears of guilt flowed faster now. "I always left him alone!"

Compassion and other, unknown emotions darkened Methusal's eyes. At last, she said, "I think he wanted that. Don't you?"

Hendra wiped away the tears. "Yes. But I always felt so guilty. The beatings went on until..." She found she couldn't form the next words.

"Until when?" Softly, Methusal said, "What happened?"

Hendra swallowed, and pushed out the rest of the story. It hurt, like peeling a scab off of a fresh wound. "It went on until Mentàll turned sixteen, and I was eight." She drew another breath. "That day I carried water to the house like I always did. Father kicked the bucket over and screamed at me for failing my duty. I was terrified. I said I'd get more, right away. But he was too fast. He pulled out his big whip and hit me."

Hendra involuntarily twitched, remembering the shock and the pain of that lash. "I...I tried to escape, but he wouldn't let me." She shuddered, and couldn't stop her hot tears. "He hauled back to hit me again, but Mentàll appeared out of nowhere and roared, 'Stop it!' Father shoved me aside and flicked the whip at him." Hendra looked down for a moment at her clenched hands. "That's when it happened."

Methusal waited, frowning now. A good sign. Wasn't that the whole point of this story? For her friend to feel empathy for the Mentàll that Hendra knew?

Hendra felt that she needed to put in a clarifying point. "Mentàll had already achieved the Bi-level in kaavl by then."

"Wow," the Rolbani girl muttered.

Hendra hurried on, determined now to get it all out at once. "My father swore at Mentàll, and ordered him to strip off his tunic. He refused. Father snapped the whip again, and it hit Mentàll's shoulder. I couldn't believe what happened next. Faster than lightning, Mentàll grabbed the whip and wrenched it out of Father's hands. He threw it behind him, so Father would have to pass by him to get it. And then..." Remembered horror made Hendra blanch. Maybe this wasn't the best story to tell, after all. But Methusal waited, obviously enthralled.

"And then..." Hendra blinked hard, and looked down. "And then my cousin beat him up. A cold rage seemed to possess him. Every punch seemed...calculated. Precise." Softly, she added, "My father was a strong man, but Mentàll beat him until he was face down, bleeding in the dirt. I couldn't believe what I was seeing. I couldn't believe that *anyone* could defeat the man I'd hated and feared my whole life. But Mentàll did.

"When my father stopped trying to get up, Mentàll snarled, 'You will *never* hit Hendra again. If you do, I will come back and finish the job.' Then he left. He never came home again."

"Where did he go?"

"He lived with his kaavl instructor for a few years. The wife was ill and they needed help around the house."

"And what happened to your father?"

"He recovered. He and my brothers planned an ambush on my cousin. Mentàll must have heard about it. It never happened, because he threatened each of my brothers, separately. I heard them whispering about it later. They left him alone after that. And Father never beat me again, either. I also learned a little kaavl, which helped me stay out of his way. Mentàll saw to that."

"And that is how he became the man he is today."

Hendra wondered if she'd hurt her friend's view of her cousin even more with that story of violence. "I know you hate him, Methusal. And for good reason. But he's not all bad."

"I understand that there's more to him than meets the eye. Maybe he was good back then—and I can see that he still cares about you. To me, that is his only redeeming quality. But he's never been nice to me. It's hard to see any goodness in him now."

It was a start, Hendra supposed.

"What about Mentàll's father?" Methusal asked, surprising her. "What happened to him?"

"I don't know. He was a traveler who passed through Dehre. He never married my aunt. He left her alone and pregnant."

"How awful!"

"My aunt was in love, my mother said. She never saw him for the predatory wild beast he was."

Methusal looked like she wanted to say something, but didn't.

Hendra didn't know if her words had helped or not. Would the feud ever end between Mentàll and Methusal? Or would they need to fight it out and come to their own terms of truce? Next time she would try to reason with Mentàll. She loved him too much to let vengeance destroy his life.

CHAPTER NINETEEN

DAY 16

THE NEXT MORNING, before leaving for kaavl camp, Methusal slipped into the medical tent to say goodbye to Behran. Hendra knelt beside his pallet, smiling. She looked flushed again. Was Behran teasing her?

Discomfort prickled, and Methusal hated it. *Why* did she feel so insecure? She trusted the Dehrien girl completely, and Behran, too.

Unexpectedly, the truth flashed into her heart. Deep down, she was afraid that gentle, kind Hendra would be a far better match for Behran. Hendra was a hundred times nicer than she could ever be. Why wouldn't Behran want someone like Hendra instead of herself—a girl who made enemies left and right, and who still, even now, had trouble controlling her mouth and her actions?

"Hi," she said, moving closer.

Hendra glanced up and quickly scrambled to her feet. She scooped up the breakfast plate. "I'll leave you two alone. You're heading off soon, aren't you, Methusal?"

"Yes."

With an affectionate grin, Behran watched Hendra go.

"I see you're feeling better today." She smiled. "You're sitting up by yourself."

"Doc said I'll be able to leave the medical tent tomorrow or the next day. He said the pain of the stab wound will keep me from exerting myself."

"It still hurts that bad?" she said with dismay.

"Every time I breathe."

"I'm so sorry, Behran." Guilt again overwhelmed her for the part she'd played in his injury. If only she hadn't...

"Stop it, Thusa." Behran gripped her hand. "I'll be fine."

"I know. And I'm glad. I just wish we could spend more time together."

The medical tent flap opened. Kitran. "Methusal, we're leaving."

"Coming." With reluctance, she gave Behran a final hug and he kissed her. "I'll miss you," she whispered.

"Stay safe. I'm sure I'll see you soon."

An uneasy feeling, like a shadow over the sun, slipped over her spirit. Why did she have the inexplicable feeling that everything would change before they saw each other again?

She wanted to cling to him. "I love you, Behran," she whispered.

He smiled. "I love you, too."

She entered the bright sunshine, but her heart ached, as if a piece had been left behind in the tent with Behran.

△ △ △ △ △

On the trek back to kaavl camp, Methusal stayed in the back of the line. She had no desire to speak to anyone on the kaavl team, except for Taltn. The teenage boy hiked beside her. She was glad for his friendly, uncomplicated company.

Kitran and several Tarst men led the way, and next came Mentàll, who was talking to Efron. A quick listen proved they weren't speaking about their secret plan; instead, just the necessities of camp life. After them came Goric, Jascr, and Wortn. Lovely whips, the lot of them. Following them were Tabor and three other Dehriens.

When Methusal looked at the blond giant's back, she couldn't help but remember Hendra's tale of their childhood. She felt another unwelcome stab of sympathy for the boy Mentàll had been. But *not,* of course, for the man he had become. Nothing could ever excuse his attempt to take over Rolban, or his cruel treatment of her ever since.

Clearly Hendra still loved her cousin, regardless of the horrific things he had done. Methusal supposed if a person could ever love someone like Mentàll, it would have to be his family. Probably only those who had grown up with him, and who had seen a few of his good traits, could imagine the good in him now. Hendra did not want to think those qualities were lost forever. But Methusal knew Mentàll's other, dark side, and it was not a pretty picture.

At least at base camp she'd been spared the nightly ritual of tending his wound. Doc had checked it the first night, and again last night, after that silly physical challenge. So tonight that fun ritual would continue. Then tomorrow or the next day she'd get to remove his stitches. After that, Doc wanted her to check the wound for another five or six days, and use coltac juice to further stimulate deep muscle healing.

So much to look forward to.

Beside her, Taltn exclaimed, "Look at that huge rock! It's all white."

Sparkly, too. Taltn jogged up a steep, pebble strewn hill to the boulder. Sun shimmered off of its sheer facets. It looked like a jewel. Methusal had never seen anything more beautiful in her life. It also seemed like they must be returning to kaavl camp by a different route, because she didn't remember seeing this hill before.

She scrambled up the slippery slope after her young friend, and touched the boulder. The rock felt cool and smooth to the touch.

"Look!" Taltn ran to the right. A smaller boulder rested beside a small, scraggly plant. In fact, Methusal now saw that white rocks dominated this small hill. A strange phenomenon. Half of the pebbles rolling beneath her moccasins were white. Methusal picked up a smooth, round stone and slipped it into her pack. Here, at last, was a landmark she would remember.

The kaavl party had disappeared.

"Come on, Taltn. We'd better catch up."

Slipping and sliding, she scooted downhill, but ended up on her hands and knees at the bottom. "Careful. It's slippery," she warned, but Taltn, in his youthful energy, bolted down the hill. A length from the bottom, he tripped on a root and tumbled downhill. He landed hard on his side on the rocky path.

"Ow!" Taltn grabbed his ankle.

Quickly, Methusal knelt beside him. "Are you okay?"

"My ankle. It hurts." Tears glimmered in the boy's eyes, but he grimly pressed his lips together, as if determined not to cry.

"Sit up. Is your side all right?"

Taltn looked. "Yes." A cry choked his voice. "It's just a bruise. But my ankle…" His voice wavered.

"Let me see." Carefully, Methusal touched it. The ankle was already swelling. Gently, she pressed on the bones, and wished Doc was there. She felt no broken bones, but what did she know? "It's probably sprained."

"What am I going to do?"

"When we get back to camp you'll soak your foot in the stream. It'll make the swelling go down."

"But how will I get there?" His lip trembled. "Will I be able to scout anymore?" His voice rose now, sounding fearful and horrified. "Why did I have to run down that hill? I'm so stupid!" A tear ran down his cheek, and he angrily rubbed it away.

Methusal hugged an arm around his shoulders. "Taltn, you are not stupid. Accidents happen."

"I'm useless! I was lucky to get on this team. I'm just a kid. Now Mentàll will send me back to base camp!" His face crumpled.

Methusal tightened her grip. "No, he won't. We don't know how bad this is. Maybe it'll feel better in a few days." She improvised, "Kitran can make you crutches."

More tears wet the boy's cheeks. He didn't look consoled, and in that moment he looked younger than his thirteen years. Dully, he repeated, "Mentàll will kick me off the team."

"He will not," Methusal said sharply. "I'll speak to him. You'll be fine."

"Speak to me about what?" The Dehrien Kaavl Commander had silently arrived. A faint frown creased his brow, and disbelief lurked in his eyes. It was almost as if he couldn't believe that she was treating Taltn kindly.

Methusal stood, so she wouldn't feel so intimidated. "Taltn twisted his ankle. We'll need to carry him to kaavl camp."

"We are nearer to base camp. I will send men to carry him back."

Anguish contorted the boy's features, and Methusal frowned at the Dehrien Chief. "We're halfway to kaavl camp. It would be just as easy to carry him there."

"He will be a liability," the Dehrien returned coolly.

Methusal clenched her fists. "He's just a boy. Have compassion. Being on the kaavl team means everything to him."

"You are not his mother. Let the boy speak for himself."

That young man, to his credit, firmed his chin and wiped away his tears. "I'd like to come to kaavl camp, sir. If I can't scout, I'll work around camp."

Mentàll gave the boy a hard, assessing glance. "Very well. I will send men to help you. Methusal, walk with me."

She didn't feel right about leaving Taltn alone, and didn't move. "I won't..."

"Walk with me," the Dehrien snarled, and walked fast down the path.

"I'll be fine, Thusa," Taltn said. He tried to look brave, but a juicy sniff ruined it.

"I'll see you in a few minutes," she promised, and jogged after the long-legged Dehrien. She caught up with him at the same time the kaavl team straggled back to meet them. After Mentàll issued orders, the majority headed for kaavl camp again.

Tabor and Riln backtracked to meet Taltn, and only then did she turn to Mentàll. A glacial stare impaled her.

"What?" she demanded.

Through his teeth, he said, "Do *not* challenge me again."

Methusal refused to flinch before his intimidating glare. "Someone had to stand up for Taltn. And by the way, listening to reason does not make you weak."

"I let Taltn come for his own sake. Not because of your insubordinate arguments."

"So this is about power. You don't want anyone to think you'd ever back down to me."

"I did *not* back down to you," he snarled, and unexpectedly seized her arm. "Listen well, Methusal." His grip hurt, but she remained silent while the men carrying Taltn walked by. "I have had enough of your backtalk. At base camp. Here." He shook her arm. "It stops. Now."

Methusal didn't want to feel frightened, but she did. All the same, she slowly enunciated, "You are hurting me."

He did not let go. "Do you understand?" He spoke just as clearly, just as slowly.

"I hate you. You're the coldest whip in the universe!"

He laughed softly. "In the universe. What an exalted position you give me."

She glared.

"Do you understand?"

"Or what? What will you *do* to me?"

His chilly gaze held hers. Softly, he said, "I will tell you, if you wish."

All of a sudden, she didn't want to know. He was goading her now, true, but he also hated her. It scared her to think about the vile fate he was planning for her when the war ended. She scowled. "Hendra says you have redeeming qualities. I have yet to see one."

"I saved your life. Twice, if you remember."

"I'm a game piece you need. That is all. When the war is over, you'll show your true colors again."

He released her arm. "You know nothing about me, Methusal. Nothing at all."

She immediately stepped back, but unfortunately spoke before thinking. "I know one thing. If your mother was alive, you would be a disappointment to her."

His shoulders stiffened. "Do not *dare* speak for my mother," he hissed. "You know nothing about her!"

Her temper foolishly compelled her to continue.

"I know my own mother," she snapped. "She wanted me to grow up to be a good person. I'm sure your mother wanted the same. And I'm guessing something else." Something inside would not let her take the prudent path. "I'll bet that besides Hendra, she's the only one who's ever shown you affection in your whole life. Now you're a cruel, lonely man. Is that because of your uncle, or because that's what's in your heart?"

"You have been speaking to Hendra." Rage burned dark smudges across his cheekbones. "Do not speak about my mother again!"

"I'm not good enough to speak about her?" she guessed. "She's so perfect in your mind that my words defile her memory?"

"You know nothing about her! That is why you are unworthy to speak of her."

"Tell me, then," she goaded, unable to help herself.

"My mother was the kindest, gentlest person in the world," he snarled.

"Why didn't you inherit some of her good qualities, then? Or maybe you're more like your father." Methusal winced, and regretted the cruel comment the instant it left her lips.

Shock and pain flashed. Then a mighty shudder surged through her enemy, and a fury like none she'd witnessed before blazed from his black, dilated eyes. "Do not *ever* compare me to that worthless..." he spat a foul, Dehrien epithet, "excuse for a human!"

She felt shocked and frightened to see his control slip. Usually she skirted the safe limits when provoking him. Their verbal battles were like swordplay—seeing who could draw first blood. But her mean-spirited comment had plunged deep. Apparently straight into his heart. His hatred for his father simmered, deep and hot in her enemy—and little wonder. From the little Hendra had told her, the man had been a cruel wild beast, leaving Mentàll's mother alone and pregnant. An unforgivable sin.

Without thinking, she reached out and touched his wrist. It felt wide and powerful, and more fear prickled across her skin. Her involuntary movement shocked her, as did the compassion and deep regret she felt. "I'm sorry," she said softly.

Surprise flashed. After a delayed second, a bit of the stiffness left his shoulders. He stared down at her hand—an unspoken demand to remove it.

She did so. And then turned and left him alone. Nerves trembled through her as she walked away. The wild beast had leaped, snarling, from his lair. What would happen if his control ever snapped? She walked faster, feeling as if a herd of wild beasts was breathing down her neck.

△ △ △ △ △

After they reached kaavl camp, Methusal helped Taltn soak his ankle in the frigid stream, and then Mentàll sent her to pick more pods for supper that night. He sent everyone else to scout Quasr, which made her assignment seem like more of an insult. However, she did as she was told without complaint. Wasn't it time for her to follow the higher path again? She'd certainly jumped off earlier today.

When she returned from picking pods, she reminded Taltn to soak his ankle again. It had swollen to almost twice its normal size. She hoped it wasn't a bad sprain, or worse, broken.

Men straggled back from Quasr, and she eavesdropped on their reports to Mentàll. She especially paid attention to the report of his first-in-command.

"I gave your message to Calbn. He has agreed to wait for the arrival of Wyen's troops." Efron's voice sounded thin and reedy.

"Were you followed?"

"Never," he said smugly.

"Well done, Efron."

Other men, including Kitran, reported invader troop movements and newly fortified positions. It appeared the Zindedis had finally realized that both base camp and the kaavl team were infiltrating Quasr from the east. As a consequence, they'd now assigned a minimal number of troops to the western, farmland side.

"Foolish," Mentàll murmured after this report. "We will exploit their weakness tomorrow."

"They're watching for us now," Kitran interjected. "They know we spy in pairs. We'll need to infiltrate the town one by one."

Mentàll nodded. "You will enter and exit the town alone. But you will remain within sight of one another in Quasr."

A black scowl contorted Kitran's face. "About time you listen to me," he muttered.

No reports were given on the General's compound. Worry for Deccia felt like a constant, sick ache inside Methusal. It felt intolerable to be so near her sister, and yet unable to help her. Praying did not seem like enough. She wanted to *do* something.

Methusal eyed her scowling kaavl instructor. She wondered if his plot to mutiny included a plan to rescue Deccia. She'd need to speak to him about that alone, and preferably away from camp. Maybe she would be able to scout with him tomorrow.

And what if Kitran did agree to rescue Deccia? Would it be worth it to disobey her father and mutiny with Kitran?

Mentàll's voice interrupted her thoughts. He addressed the group. "At base camp I met with Erl and Pan. We discussed strategies and agreed the war teams will continue to attack the invaders at different points each night. First, we will report information to a runner in the afternoon. Using that information, the war teams will move at night and attack before dawn."

"What's the point?" Kitran demanded, his scowl blacker than ever. "We'll sting them, but not kill them. They'll get angrier and more prepared for our attacks. I say we deal the death blow now, and then swarm them on all sides. If we use the element of surprise, we won't need the troops from Wyen to help."

An uneasy murmur swept through the kaavl team.

"What death blow do you mean?" Tabor asked.

Kitran's jaw bunched. "Mentàll knows. I would not dare speak against our leader."

Mentàll watched Kitran with a glacial expression. "Your plan has merit, Kitran. But now is not the time."

"Of course not." Brows lowered, Kitran did not say another word.

Methusal felt uneasy after that interchange.

After dinner, Methusal dealt with Mentàll's injury. It felt strange and intimidating to touch him again, especially after the argument on the trail.

She saw a little dried blood, but it was probably a result of the the physical challenge. The wound was still healing nicely. She matter-of-factly cleansed the firm flesh, and told herself to stop feeling so nervous. He wouldn't turn and attack her like a wild beast. Or would he?

"The wound is almost healed," she felt obliged to report. "Doc said the stitches can come out soon. Maybe in two days," she murmured to herself, inspecting the dried blood.

The Dehrien nodded, but remained silent. He'd said nothing throughout the ordeal. Methusal finished her task in record time. The man unnerved her, even when he sat silently.

Mentàll pulled on his tunic and faced her. "You will scout with me tomorrow."

There went her plans with Kitran. All the same, she said quietly, "Fine."

He gave her a hard look and walked away. He was probably surprised she hadn't argued. She was, too.

Honestly, she was tired of it all. The worry, the constant friction with her enemy, and the confusion about following Kitran.

CHAPTER TWENTY

ALTHOUGH NO ROCHERS had infested her bed last night, Methusal had not slept well. She'd dreamed of those she loved—her sister, Behran, and her parents. In her dream they lived far away, in a place she couldn't reach, no matter how fast she ran. Every time she turned around, kaavl camp was only a step behind her. She could never escape it, nor the leers and whispers of Jascr and Goric.

Dawn pinkened the horizon when she awoke. Her coverlet had twisted around her, and she found it difficult to move her arms. As she wriggled to free herself, she heard whispers behind the rock where she lay.

"The perfect plan!" Goric snickered. "We'll have her running scared by the end."

"We'll have her exactly where we want her," Jascr boasted.

She lay still. Obviously they were plotting something against her.

Pebbles scuffled as the two slunk off.

Methusal freed herself from her coverlet. Shivering, she sat up in the icy air. Though she knew Goric hated her, she felt certain Jascr was the mastermind of this foul plan. In her opinion, Goric didn't have the guts to do anything on his own. She shivered again, feeling very alone. Now she would need to stay on guard every single minute. Great. One more problem to deal with.

Resentment simmered as she readied for the day. She didn't *want* to deal with those whips. She didn't want to be afraid, or watch her back every single second. Why did it seem like things kept getting worse and worse?

Taltn's ankle looked a little better this morning. Kitran had also fashioned crude crutches for him. At least that was one positive thing for today.

After breakfast, she waited for Mentàll with a frown.

"Where is your cloak?" he greeted her.

With a deepening frown, she collected it.

On the way to Quasr she walked a good three lengths to Mentàll's left, and she walked fast. Unfortunately, her bad mood deepened with every stride.

"We will scout the harbor," the Dehrien said.

"Fine," she said shortly.

Silence stretched as they drew nearer to Quasr's west side. They darted from bush to bush in order to remain unseen by the Zindedi soldiers.

Next, they crawled through the fields and spied on the shacks on the outskirts of Quasr. Methusal counted six soldiers; three of whom chatted together.

The Dehrien's shoulder bumped hers. "Do not do anything foolish."

With a grimace of irritation, she twitched away. "I'll do my job. Don't worry. It's clear!" She rose up on her knees. "I'll go first..."

Mentàll jerked her back down by the wrist. Methusal toppled into the tall, soft grass. "Stop it!" She glared. "What are you doing?"

"You are not focused."

"I am!"

"You are upset. Set aside your hatred for me. Do your job."

"This isn't about you!"

Stony impatience stared back. "Tell me what is wrong."

"As if you'd care."

"We will stay here—together—until you tell me what is compromising your kaavl."

Methusal clenched her teeth. Alarmingly, she wanted to snap at him for the way he tormented her, and for every whip who made her life miserable. Tears burned in her eyes. She would not cry. She wouldn't! How mortifying and humiliating that would be, to fall apart in front of her enemy. He'd pounce like a wild beast and devour all of the vulnerable parts she'd expose.

She gritted her teeth. "I am ready. Are you?"

Hard blue ice assessed her. "No tricks. Meet me on the second street, near the beach."

She nodded stiffly.

"Go!" He gave her a push, and Methusal found herself running through the grass before she'd had time to refocus into kaavl. Thankfully it was safe. The guards had drifted further north and south. Navigating through the streets to the rendezvous point was easy.

Mentàll appeared at her side. He wore no hood, but he'd rubbed dirt into his hair to disguise his distinctive white-blond hair.

"What are we doing?" she whispered.

"Walk with me." Mentàll hunched in order to make himself look shorter. His hand gripped hers. "We'll scout the beach, and then the merchant district."

"Let *go* of me!" His hand felt big and warm around hers. And hard, like a vise, when she tried to extricate herself.

"It is our cover." He strode ahead, forcing her to hurry along by his side. "The war team and kaavl teams are made up of men. The invaders won't suspect lovers."

Methusal's face burned. "What is it with you and that term? Pretending to be *friends* is a leap off the bluff of reason."

"They do not know that. Smile at me." His own smile looked stiff and unnatural.

Methusal spluttered into laughter. She couldn't help herself. "You look like you just swallowed a whip bone."

The Dehrien stared blankly at her, as if he'd forgotten how to laugh.

Her black mood evaporated.

The soldiers on the beach paid little attention to them, as Mentàll had predicted.

They slowly walked through the market district. She disengaged her hand from the Dehrien's on every occasion possible, under the guise of inspecting fruits and vegetables. A red, juicy fruit looked especially delicious. Even though they only pretended an interest in buying food while they listened to the gossip around them, Methusal's mouth watered with longing. With reluctance, she replaced it.

"You are hungry?" Mentàll murmured. He handed the woman a coin, and presented the fruit to Methusal. She stared in shock, until she realized he was pretending to be solicitous only for their cover.

She smiled sweetly at him and took a big bite. "*Yum.* Thank you."

Cynical humor flashed in his smile, and then vanished.

Luckily, eating the juicy fruit required two hands. She listened intently as they walked through the open air market.

An old woman's voice said, "Soldiers threw me and my man out of our home today."

"Why?" Horror emanated from the hushed response.

"They're taking over houses on the edge of town. They want to catch those kaavl spies. Particularly that big one, who's the ringleader."

"If I ever see one, I'll get down on my knees and thank them. They deserve a medal for walking these streets." The other woman lowered her voice. "In the daylight, no less! I know with them here, the war teams are still trying. It gives me hope. Maybe they can defeat these horrible invaders."

"I'd be happy to do my part. Give me a broom, and I'll sweep'm out to sea, I will."

Methusal smiled to herself and quietly repeated the conversation to the Dehrien Chief.

"What about those soldiers over there?" He nodded toward two Zindedis who wore multiple medals on their black and red uniforms. They stood two blocks away, and spoke urgently to one another. "What are they saying?"

She licked her sticky fingers and focused, blocking out the man to her right, who suddenly shouted obscenities at a stall keeper.

"We killed one. Tall, skinny. We know he contacted Calbn, because he carried a note. He wouldn't talk. Calbn has to be around here somewhere. Order your soldiers to sweep the northern streets. We'll take the south."

Methusal quickly glanced down at a box of pods and sifted through them with trembling fingers. "I think they killed Efron," she whispered. "They know Calbn is close by. They're searching."

She glanced at the Dehrien, whose face had blanched white. He gripped her hand again and led her fast through an alley, and across the next street.

"Where are we going?"

He didn't answer, but continued to walk rapidly.

"Let go. You're dragging me like a child."

He did not respond, and she jogged to keep pace. "Where are we going?" When he still didn't respond, she insisted, "I need to know, if you want me to help."

"You only need to know what I tell you," he snarled.

Anger overrode her common sense, which included the need to be cautious in a dangerous situation. She wrenched her hand free. "You will treat me like an equal!"

"But we are not equals."

She felt the strong urge to smack him. Unbidden, the Prophet's words returned. "Love your enemies. Treat them with kindness."

Gritting her teeth, she matched his long strides. She would not ask him another question. She would not speak another word to him, period. It might be the only way they could get along.

"Look around that next corner," he ordered, when they drew near the end of the alley.

Without thinking, she automatically carried with vision to the next street corner. She looked both ways, searching for soldiers, and saw two to the south. "Wait."

But he had already slowed down.

The soldiers disappeared. Mentàll moved forward and then cut left, just before she said, "Turn left."

"Look ahead. There," he ordered, stopping between two houses. "Which way is safe?"

She carried with vision. "Soldiers both ways."

"What if we go back, and then south?"

Hardly able to believe she could do it, she looked around one corner, and then another. "It's clear if we head to the..." But he was already moving west. "...west," she finished with a frown. "Then we'll need to head south, but fast. More troops are coming."

Mentàll continued to swiftly lead her west and south. Half of the time he listened to her reports, and the other half he unerringly seemed to know the safe direction moments before she spoke.

"How do you *do* that?" she finally demanded. Luckily, he no longer insisted upon the farce of holding her hand. He led the way now through crumbling, burnt buildings.

He said, "If you know everything, and if we are also true equals, like you wish to believe, then you could tell me."

They slipped down another narrow alley.

Methusal suddenly stopped. "Soldiers are ahead! Twenty or more, both to the north and south. They're heading for a small, partially collapsed building."

Mentàll bit back an oath and slammed back against the wall just before the soldiers marched by, ten steps to their left.

She dared not speak until the clomping boots receded. "Now what?" she whispered.

"We need to warn Calbn."

"Is he in that building?" she said, horrified.

"Of course not. It is a decoy. Efron never met with Calbn, either."

"So we need to get a message to someone."

The Dehrien did not answer. Unknown thoughts flickered across his features. "You will need to go," he said finally. "A small woman can sneak through better than I could. Go to the fifth shack north of the collapsed one. Give the person there a message. Say, 'Doltn has run.'"

"That's it?"

He didn't bother to respond. "Go now!"

Sharpening her kaavl senses, Methusal slipped across the street. She took in multiple input simultaneously, including the receding clomp of soldiers' feet and the bark of the commander's orders. Then she fanned out her hearing and listened for more approaching soldiers. Her neck itched. At any moment she expected to hear a shout, or a gun explode. She swiftly counted shacks.

At the fifth one, she stopped and knocked. Silence. She knocked again. "Please open," she pleaded softly. "I have a mess..."

Someone yanked open the door. A hard hand gripped her arm and dragged her inside. Methusal stumbled, but did not fall. A grim scene met her eyes. Two bloody men lay on the floor. The invaders had been stripped of their uniforms, and were obviously dead. The man who still painfully gripped her arm wore a Zindedi uniform, but it looked too big on his short, balding frame.

"What do you want, and who are you?" A knife flashed and settled against her throat.

She gulped. "I have a message from Mentàll. Doltn has run."

The man chuckled. After a moment, he removed the blade from her neck. "I have, have I?"

"Do you know what that means?"

"I do. Now get out."

"Efron's dead."

"I know. He will receive a proper burial." He shoved her out.

A rude, strange little man.

More soldiers swarmed the streets now around the collapsed house. Angry shouts peppered the air. The soldiers moved south and invaded the next house. Methusal decided to cut west in order to avoid them. She did not know where Mentàll was. Maybe he was waiting for her, but it was too dangerous to retrace her steps. Better to head for kaavl camp on her own.

A sudden roar caught her attention and she paused to listen. "We've got him!"

Methusal darted to the next street, which was parallel to the action, and peered east down the alley. A multitude of soldiers struggled with a large man in a cloak. Mentàll! She could hardly believe her eyes.

Without thinking, she pulled out her red, bone-handled knife and kaavl stick. She had to save him. That wasn't even a question. Maybe she could throw her knife. Her heart pounded hard, and she felt sick.

She crept closer. A Zindedi knife flashed silver in the sun, and a red slash appeared on Mentàll's cheekbone. Horrified, she lost concentration and stumbled over a rock in her path. *A rock.* A big one, too. And others lay scattered about. She resheathed her weapons and hefted the rock in her hands. Two years ago, she and Behran had created a diversion in Rolban when the Dehriens had tried to take over. Maybe that tactic would help her enemy now.

She gave the stone a mighty heave. It cracked into the head of the soldier nearest her. He fell into his comrade, who immediately shouted a warning. He pointed at her and suddenly she heard a gun blast.

It came from the south. One of the men holding Mentàll crumpled. The big Dehrien wrenched free and sprinted south. The man who had seen Methusal froze when the gun blasted, and she took that opportunity to flee toward the western farmlands.

She ran like the wind, and she used kaavl to avoid soldiers in her path. She plunged into the farmlands. Bent double so the soft, waving grasses hid her, she raced for the far tagma bushes. Soldiers panted in her path. Following the smashed grass would be easy. That was one reason why she was running for the thick tagma bushes, and the rocky ground beyond. She'd lose them there.

Methusal had gained a little more ground by the time she left the tall grass and reached the bushes, but she kept going. She threw rocks in one direction, making it look like she took a northern path, when really she headed south. Stepping lightly, she made sure her moccasins left no trail in the dirt.

The soldiers huddled now, north of her, at the first tagma plant. Anger riddled their voices. "She went north."

"No, west!"

"Maybe she went back into the field."

"Who cares about her? The General wants the Dehrien. We'll get a reward if we kill him."

After more mutterings, a few men headed north and the others headed back to Quasr. Methusal, however, waited where she was for a good while, just to make sure no one had remained behind.

Finally certain that it was clear, and no one was following her, she sprinted for kaavl camp.

When the tall boulders of camp were only a three minute run away, Methusal decided to rest for a minute on a rock. Thirst made her mouth sticky. She gulped water and wondered where the Kaavl Commander could be.

She recorked her water skin and waited until her thudding heart quieted. She had been lucky to escape. Her mind flashed to the gun shot.

If Mentàll was in trouble, she'd better hurry back to camp and warn everyone. The thought of the Dehrien being captured or killed worried her. She didn't want anyone to die in this war—not even her enemy.

Sharpening her eyesight into kaavl, she scanned the horizon.

And then she saw him, loping from the west, as she had done. He was alive. For the first time in hours, she relaxed. Much as she disliked him, the thought of him being dead horrified her. The kaavl team needed him. His death would have served a huge blow to the war effort.

He grew larger, as his long legs rapidly covered the distance.

She should head for camp.

As she stood, a faint scratching sound tickled her ears. A whine whimpered from the direction of a scrubby plant.

Methusal rounded the bush and discovered a grizzled old apte, caught in an old rusted trap. Its leg was caught up in a tangled cord. Her heart immediately melted for the sad, pitiful looking creature.

"I'll help you, guy," she whispered. They weren't far from camp, and she knew if the men saw the apte, they'd kill it for supper tonight. She couldn't let that happen. The stripe on his ear reminded her of Chup Chup, her pet at home.

She worked quickly. Mentàll would be here any minute. But the cord was too thick to break, and it was so twisted around the poor apte's foot...

The small, round beast cried when the cord rubbed against its raw leg. He'd been caught for a long time, poor thing. He would have died if she hadn't found him. She let go of the cord for a moment in order to study the tangle.

Her skin prickled up, and she knew the Dehrien was standing right behind her.

"Methusal." A silence elapsed. "Well. Have you found our dinner?" He unsheathed his sword. It flashed silver in the sun as it sliced toward the apte.

"No!" She cringed, waiting for the death squeal. The apte scampered free. Cut cords lay on the ground. She stared up at him.

"Use your knife, Methusal." The Dehrien sheathed his sword.

"I was afraid I'd hurt him. ...Why did you do that?"

"You thought I would kill an animal you were trying to free?"

"For dinner, you said." She still stared at him, finding it hard to believe what she had just witnessed. Now she saw the slash, high on his cheekbone. Blood dripped down his face.

"I am not always cruel. Just most of the time. Remember that." He stalked for camp.

Methusal followed, still trying to make sense of the Dehrien's behavior. It did not match anything she knew about him. Except that she did remember Hendra had told her once that Mentàll had had a pet flying beast years ago. His uncle had killed it right in front of him. Maybe he had a soft spot for animals. Sometimes. She'd seen him kill many for food.

"Tonight you will train more with the knife," he threw over his shoulder. "Kitran will teach you."

She hurried to catch up. "What happened in Quasr? How did they catch you?"

"A soldier saw us. He collected a group and ambushed me."

"I think Doltn shot a soldier to free you."

"And you threw a rock."

Methusal was surprised that he'd noticed.

"You must learn to use the knife, Methusal," he said harshly. "This is war. Men will die. *You* will die if you refuse to use it. Kill, or you will be killed."

She couldn't argue with that. The Dehrien's first-in-command lay dead in Quasr.

She quietly offered, "Doltn said they'd give Efron a proper burial."

"Good." The Dehrien strode into camp. He clearly did not want to speak about it any longer.

△ △ △ △ △

Hendra stopped by Behran's pallet that evening to see how he was faring.

"Are you hungry?" she asked.

Thankfully his color looked better, but he still tired easily. Doc wanted to keep him in the sick tent for at least one more day.

"Aali brought some stew. I wouldn't mind a tart, if you can scare one up."

"Only healthy foods for the patients," she admonished, but smiled. "I'll see what I can do."

"Good." He grinned back. "Don't make me go hungry."

"I won't." She left the sick tent with a light step. Behran always made her feel that way. Doc...

Doc made her feel something entirely different.

Her working relationship with him remained smooth, for the most part. However, every time her fingers accidentally touched his, she had to steel herself not to jerk away like a frightened apte. He made no comment on her progress, although one time, when she'd touched his hand to retrieve a needle, she caught him looking at her with a faint smile. But he'd said nothing, to her relief.

Her stomach rumbled as she entered the eating tent. Tonight she'd sit alone because Aali had to work late. After bringing a tart to Behran, she found an unoccupied table and sat down. She had just forked up a logne leaf when someone blocked the setting sun.

"Mind if I join you?" Doc asked.

Her heart lurched.

"You're taking a long time to answer." He offered a faint smile. "Should I move on?"

"No. Of course not." Hendra tried to ignore the flutters of nerves in the pit of her stomach. "Please sit down. I'd love to have company. Aali is working."

Doc's smile widened, and he sat down across from her. "Aenill is working her pretty hard tonight."

"Poor Aali."

"Aali has a knack for creating her own problems."

Although Hendra had not been at base camp during the explosion, she had certainly heard it at kaavl camp. "I guess she does." All the same, she wished she possessed half of her young friend's courage and audacity.

"Would you and Aali do me a favor early tomorrow morning? We need more tacky leaves. Would you find some? I already asked Dastn if he'd go with you."

"Of course. I'll ask Aali, too."

"Thanks."

As they ate, they exchanged a few quiet words. Toward the end of the meal Hendra began to feel more at ease, and she wondered why she had balked at having dinner with him when he'd asked the first time. Maybe because it had seemed like he was asking her on a courtship outing. She'd certainly never been on one of those before. That thought scared her to death. But this dinner tonight was casual. It meant nothing. Just two co-workers talking.

With reluctance Hendra drew her utensils together. "I should go. I have a supervisor who's a slave driver. He asked me to start work at the crack of dawn."

He gave a rich, quiet chuckle. Lines crinkled at the corners of his eyes, which were a dark, smoky gray in the twilight. "A joke. I believe that's the first I've heard you make."

She felt vaguely offended. "You think I'm so dull?"

"Not at all. I call it progress."

Hendra frowned a little at the enigmatic statement. "What is that supposed to mean?"

"It means you're starting to relax around me. You're showing me your true self." Gently, he added, "Which I like very much, by the way."

His gaze held hers, and her heart alternately thumped and fluttered.

She clutched her plate and utensils. "I...I think I should go."

"Goodnight, Hendra."

"Goodnight." She fled to the dirty dish bin.

What had just happened? All of a sudden the thought of being near him again both excited and frightened her.

△ △ △ △

Moans greeted Methusal and Mentàll when they entered kaavl camp. The late afternoon sun cast a pale, cool light over the disturbing tableau. Two Dehrien men lay on the ground, bleeding profusely, and an angry looking Kitran cinched a blood soaked cloth tightly around his upper arm. Methusal rushed over.

"What happened?"

"An ambush in Quasr!" he roared. "I'm done playing around, Dehrien. It's time to *destroy* those whips!"

Mentàll ignored him and kept walking.

Methusal fetched her healing pack, and with Kitran's help, quickly took stock of the men's injuries. A bullet had shot clean through one man's shoulder. Another suffered from a bullet embedded in his leg.

Methusal knew the shoulder wound would probably heal fine if she doused it with racmun spirits. But the bullet needed to come out of the leg, or else blood poisoning could set in. The wound oozed blood, and her stomach turned at the thought of trying to gouge out the bullet.

"You can do it," Kitran encouraged her. "I'll hold them down. Do the easiest one first."

She cleansed the shoulder wound first, and the man screamed in agony until Kitran thrust a ball of leather into his mouth so that he could bite on it. Tears of compassion wet Methusal's cheeks while she packed in coltac juice and stitched up the wound.

As she'd feared, the leg wound was much worse. Thankfully the man passed out after the first prod of her finger into the bloody hole. She couldn't find the bullet. And although he was unconscious, the man still softly moaned each time she dug in, trying to find the bit of metal. Her hands shook, and she wanted to weep from the horror of hurting the man still more.

Kitran splashed racmun spirits over his hands and pushed her aside. Compassion softened his black gaze. "I'll do it. Sterilize my knife."

Methusal did as he asked, and then he used the tip to prod loose the bullet. The bloody metal bit looked flat and squished, and it also looked too small to cause so much damage. Methusal took over the man's care and washed the wound with the spirits, and then packed in coltac juice, stitched it, and tightly wrapped binding around his leg.

"Now you," she told Kitran. "What happened?"

"A knife wound," he grunted, and pulled off his tunic to reveal a hairy chest. "Nothing serious. Patch me up."

The wound was a handbreadth long and the front portion looked deep. To his credit, Kitran didn't utter a sound when she stitched him up, although his tan looked pale by the end.

"I think I'll take a sip of that," he said, when she'd finished, and took a healthy swig of the racmun spirits before she corked it up again.

The setting sun seemed to set fire to the clouds above the western mountains when Methusal finally told him about Efron.

"Bloody day." Kitran wiped his black beard with his forearm. "And according to Timaeus, no troops are coming from Wyen or Eerpor yet. It's time to move, Methusal. Are you with me?"

With caution, she said, "What are you going to do?"

"Are you with me?" His black eyes looked hard.

"What is your plan?"

"We're going to blow up the ammunition building."

She gasped. "What?"

"No more powder means no more guns. It'll turn this war into hand to hand combat, and we'll win."

It did sound like a good idea. "Why doesn't Papa agree?"

"According to Mentàll, they want to combine blowing up the ammunition building with one big attack when the Wyen and Eerporians arrive. But it's time we face facts: they're not coming. We need to destroy the invaders now, before they kill more of our men, and before more of them might arrive. The Tarst are with me. Are you?"

"It does sound like a good plan. But I don't like the idea of going against my father's orders." She noticed that Mentàll was lurking near the fire, and while she didn't think he could overhear them, she lowered her voice to a whisper. "I'm worried, though. I mutinied when I tried to rescue Deccia. That seemed like a good idea then, too, but look what happened. Behran was almost killed, and guards are tripled in the compound."

"Are you with me, or not?"

"I need some time to think."

"Tell me by first light. We'll leave then."

She watched him go. Should she mutiny with him, or not? The thought of abandoning him felt like a betrayal. The man had taught her kaavl—he had helped shape her teenage years, and he'd always demanded the highest standards from her on every level. Now he needed her help.

And yet loyalty to her father ran far deeper. And the Prophet...he'd said that Mentàll had been given power for a reason.

Whom should she follow? Kitran or Mentàll? No. Kitran or her father.

What choice was right?

Choices. Before she had left home, both her mother and Old Sims had warned her to be careful to make the right choices. Her life might depend upon it. The Prophet had said the same thing.

"Kitran." She rose to her feet and hurried after him.

He waited for her. A frown blackened his brow.

"I can't do it. And I don't think you should, either. I'm afraid something terrible will happen."

"Will you betray me? Will you tell that Dehrien whip my plan?" Black eyes blazed at her. Contempt burned in them, too.

"Of course not."

"Good. Then we have nothing left to discuss."

Methusal's throat tightened as she watched him go. He despised her, because in his mind she had already betrayed him.

△ △ △ △ △

As the sun set, Methusal gathered up supplies so she could take of the Mentàll's wound. She struggled with feeling guilty for abandoning Kitran. But she had to believe she'd chosen the right path.

She met Mentàll at the stream, where he'd already shucked off his tunic. That wound looked better, but she'd forgotten about the one on his cheek.

Quickly, Methusal tended to his back. The stitches could easily come out tomorrow. The last of the dried blood was gone, and tonight she only needed to massage in coltac juice. Mentàll said nothing during her ministrations; as if his mind was elsewhere.

When he pulled on his tunic again, she said, "You have a cut on your cheek. Do you want me to treat it?"

The Dehrien touched his cheekbone, and seemed surprised to discover the wound. "Tend it," he said shortly.

Methusal soaked lynnte weed in the stream, and approached him again. Her steps slowed. She'd never touched his face before. Bandaging and caring for his back was bad enough, but his face...to get so close to her enemy felt dangerous.

He waited without moving, as if carved in stone. Even though every instinct urged her run in the opposite direction, she did not. Up close, she clearly saw the whiskers roughening his skin and the angular lines of her enemy's harsh features. His straight, hard lips. The memory of their fake kiss flew to mind, but she struggled to dismiss it. As well as the humiliating scene at the cleansing pool at base camp.

With a trembling hand, she lifted the water soaked piece of lynnte weed. She hesitated, despite herself. Every bit of self-preservation shouted at her to flee now, while she had the chance.

"I am waiting." The Dehrien's freezing eyes mocked her fear.

"Then hold still," she snapped unnecessarily.

This was terrible. Her hands were shaking! Mortified, she gulped in a breath. *Pretend he's an injured beast. Focus on the wound. It will be easy.*

When she touched the damp lynnte weed to his cheek, the rough bristle on his lower jaw scratched her skin. She jerked back, breaking the contact. *Stop it,* she told herself.

After drawing a steadying breath, she concentrated only on the wound high on his cheekbone. She tried her best to imagine that he was an injured beast—a wolmite, perhaps. As gently as possible, she cleaned the gash. He didn't flinch, or make a sound. Methusal was grateful for that, because then she could pour herself more fully into her fiction that he was a defenseless, hurt animal.

She focused solely on her task, and only on the injury. Next, the thick coltac juice. She broke open the leaf and dribbled it on the angry slash. Carefully, she stroked it over the wound. She put soothing kindness into her touch, just like she did with the animals she helped.

One last step. Methusal applied sticky sap to the points of a leaf, and then pressed it carefully into place.

"There. Finished." With a faint smile, she met the eyes of her sworn enemy and froze.

Uncertainty flickered in his gaze.

Her heart thudded in alarm. "The leaf needs to stay on for one full day."

"Of course." The iciness returned, and she quickly moved away. Her heart pounded. Illogically, she felt as if she'd just faced a terrible danger and barely escaped with her life.

But why? Was it because she had let down her defenses and treated him with an open heart?

Yes. For a few moments she had exposed her tender, vulnerable side to him. And he had seen it.

It was a weapon he could wield against her.

ΔΔΔΔΔ

Apparently Taltn was now Methusal's only friend on the team. Kitran ate dinner on the opposite side of the fire with his Tarst friends.

"Your ankle looks a lot better," she commented.

"I soaked it in the stream six times today. It doesn't hurt as much, either."

"Keep using your crutches. Give it a few more days to heal."

"Don't worry. I will." He gave her a tolerant grin.

Methusal told him the story of how she'd escaped from the invaders today.

He hung onto every word with clear delight. "That'll be me in a few days."

Methusal didn't like the idea of Taltn skirmishing with the Zindedi soldiers, but said nothing. She wasn't his mother. Naturally, he wanted to be a man, but she couldn't help but feel protective of him. He reminded her too much of Aali.

Finally, with a yawn, she retreated to her rolled up coverlet. Although she'd found no rochers in her pallet at base camp—rochers only lived on the plains—and none had appeared last night, she didn't trust Jascr or Goric. The conversation she'd overheard this morning returned to mind. This evening the two had stared at her often across the fire, but she had managed to ignore them. She didn't know where they were right now.

She shook out her pallet, hard.

A cascade of black shelled rochers spilled out, skimmed down her pants and landed on her moccasins. With a yelp, she hopped from foot to foot, kicking them off before they could work their way up her pant legs.

Anger swelled as she swept the horrible creatures out of her sleeping area. She lay down again and tucked the cover-let tightly around her. Goric and Jascr wanted her to live in fear, but she would not.

She closed her eyes and tried to sleep. She could not. The day's events played over and over through her mind. The confrontation with Kitran. Efron's death. The wounded kaavl players.

A Dehrien would head for base camp in the morning and bring back strong men to carry the injured players to safety. Even so, the injured men probably wouldn't leave camp until the day after tomorrow. Until they left, they remained her responsibility.

As her eyes drifted closed, she slipped into a dream. In it Mentàll whispered plots to an unknown teammate. Kitran's face swam before her.

"Trust no one."

"Don't betray me to that Dehrien!"

She dreamed of rochers creeping into her pallet. She woke up repeatedly, imagining that tiny feet were tickling across her skin.

CHAPTER TWENTY-ONE

AT DAWN, METHUSAL AWOKE for the final time. Her lids felt heavy, and her head groggy after the horrible night's sleep. She rubbed the sleep from her eyes and yawned. Then she remembered. Kitran! And his mutiny.

She pushed herself up on one elbow. Kitran and his three Tarst friends were gone.

The frosty morning turned her breaths into white puffs. No one else stirred—except for Mentàll. His gaze locked with hers, and he stalked for her. Foreboding clenched in her gut. She stifled another yawn.

Now he stood at the end of her pallet. He looked enormous and a little other-worldly, standing over her like that, with the golden dawn washing his hair a shimmering white gold.

"Where is Kitran? And the Tarst?"

She returned cryptically, "In Quasr."

"Where?"

Don't betray me to that Dehrien! Kitran's words echoed in her head. "I can't say."

"So, you are choosing to mutiny with him?" Fury sliced through his words.

Her temper flared. "I'm not with Kitran. So how can I be mutinying? Leave me alone!"

He stared at her, his face as hard as ice. "You will scout with Wortn today."

"Fine." She'd lose Wortn, and check on Kitran at her first opportunity.

With a final hard look, her enemy left her.

Δ Δ Δ Δ Δ

Methusal did not speak to Wortn on the way to Quasr. They would enter from the west, as she had done yesterday with Mentàll, and go into town separately. She'd leave him then.

Stocky Wortn crawled beside her in the tall farm grass. Huffs panted from his lips, and perspiration gleamed on his bald crown, which domed above his circular thatch of tawny hair.

"Go in when I say," he puffed, crouched in the grass.

But Methusal heard men muttering inside a shack on the perimeter. She told Wortn so.

A perplexed expression crossed his thick features. "How can you hear that?"

She didn't answer, and instead crept further north. Wortn followed. Three shacks appeared to be abandoned. With caution, she listened to make sure.

"I'm going in now." She met Wortn's black eyes, and felt that she should warn him. "Don't look for me in Quasr, because you won't find me. I'll see you back at kaavl camp."

"But..." he spluttered.

Crouching low, Methusal sprinted through the waving grasses for the outer edge of Quasr. She slipped silently through the crumbling town. More soldiers patrolled the streets today than yesterday, but she managed to avoid them by hiding in alleys or walking beside Quasrian townswomen in the market area, and pretending to be one of them. Slowly she made her way to the east side of town, where the ammunition building was located. So far, she had heard no massive explosion, like the one Aali had set off at base camp, so she guessed Kitran hadn't blown up the munitions building yet.

Had something happened to him? Urgency and worry grew with each step.

As she neared the munitions building, shouts and the clash of swords peppered the air. She ran faster, across a street and down one final alley, and then stopped. To the north, soldiers swarmed around the ammunition building. A crowd of Zindedis surrounded a still form lying in the middle of the street.

A big, crumpled man with black hair.

"No," she whimpered, horrified.

A soldier stepped back, sword held high, and arced it toward Kitran's body. "*Nooo!*" she screamed out.

A hand clamped over her mouth and an arm yanked her backwards, into the shadows. She struggled viciously. But strong arms jerked her tight against a tall, hard body.

"Shhh!" The harsh whisper scorched her ear. *Mentàll.* The soldier raised his sword again.

Methusal moaned in her throat, and struggled to free herself from the Dehrien's large, stifling hand, but he wouldn't release her. Tears streamed down her cheeks as she helplessly watched the soldier plunge his sword into Kitran's still body. Another soldier raised his sword.

Methusal couldn't watch any longer, and averted her face. The Dehrien's hand thankfully loosened. But in her side vision the sword flashed in the sun, and she heard the awful, squelching sound of ripping flesh. Anguished, she cringed against the Dehrien as the sword sliced through her friend. She wept quietly. His hand moved to her hair and pressed her head against him. "Quiet," the Dehrien said in her ear. "Come with me."

"We can't leave him. We can't leave him like that!"

Another man's voice spoke. "We'll get him when it's clear."

She blinked to clear her vision, and saw short, balding Doltn beside Mentàll. The Quasrian man wore a Zindedi uniform. Another man, similarly clad, stood behind him.

"You know where to go," Doltn told Mentàll. "We'll meet you there."

The Dehrien Chief gripped her upper arm. "Come."

She stumbled after Mentàll down the alley, and finally through the door of a house. It was empty, except for a few broken crates. They stopped to wait for Doltn.

Methusal stood with her back to the Dehrien and alternately crossed her arms and dashed away the unending tears. She couldn't look at Mentàll. She wanted to be alone. She could not stop thinking about Kitran lying in the middle of the street. He was dead. More hot tears welled, and she wiped her running nose. If she'd mutinied with Kitran, could she have saved him from this fate? Or would she be dead now, too?

Choices. Her mother had said she'd need to make careful choices. She had chosen not to mutiny. Now Kitran lay dead. *Dead.* She could barely believe it, and pressed her fist to her mouth to stop a soundless cry.

Mentàll paced the room behind her, but she kept her back to him, not wanting him to see her weakness and vulnerability.

A second later the door popped open and Doltn and the other man dragged Kitran inside.

"We'll need to carry him," Doltn panted. "Or the blood will leave a trail for the Zindedis."

Without a word, Mentàll stepped forward and heaved Kitran's big body over his shoulder. He staggered a bit. Kitran's blood immediately soaked into the Dehrien's tunic.

"Where will we bring him?" Methusal couldn't look at Kitran's lifeless body hanging over Mentàll's shoulder.

"We have a safe place where we can keep him until tonight," Doltn said. "Then we'll bury him in the Mehl plot. Come. We need to move fast."

The other fake soldier retreated outside, and then Doltn swiftly led the way across the shack to a door on the opposite side. It emptied into another alley, and after a quick look, Doltn sped across and opened a door on the far side. Mentàll and Methusal followed close behind. Another empty building. This one was half burnt.

Doltn continued to march fast through house after house. Methusal counted six. Some were occupied. In one, wide-eyed children eating breakfast watched them go by. The adults in the house said nothing.

In the sixth house, Doltn descended down steep, dank stairs and they walked underground in a low, earthen tunnel for a good four lengths, and then climbed back up into another house. Men occupied this one, and they sent their little party grim looks.

Then they headed west via a system of underground tunnels.

Sweat dampened the Dehrien's brow by the time Methusal guessed they'd crossed town. "We may need to make use of your underground tunnel system," he grunted, climbing another set of stairs.

"Put him down," Doltn ordered, and peered out a window. He rubbed his hands and nodded. "Safe. For now."

Mentàll went down on one knee and lowered Kitran to the floor. The big man flopped over and lay still. Never to move again. Methusal pressed her hand to her mouth, fighting more tears. Through blurry eyes, she watched Mentàll stare at Kitran for a long moment, and then he slowly climbed to his feet. His shoulder and half of his tunic was saturated red with Kitran's blood.

Doltn cleared his throat. "I'm sorry this happened. Kitran was a good man. My brothers and I grew up with him and Barak." He glanced at Methusal. "I'll notify his mother. The burial will be at midnight. Barak will want to come, if he can."

She nodded, not trusting her voice.

"Say goodbye, Methusal," Mentàll said. "We must go."

A tiny sob escaped from her. With slow steps, she approached and knelt beside Kitran. At least he looked peaceful. "Go with The One, Kitran," she whispered, and touched his arm. After a struggle, she found more words. "I'm so sorry," she said, with a soft, keening wail. "I'm sorry I wasn't there to help you when you needed me most."

She wept more, but couldn't put into words the respect, love, and loss she felt for this big man who had been her teacher and her example for so many years.

"I'll miss you, Kitran," she choked out, and scrambled to her feet. Methusal could not see through her tears.

"Go that way," Doltn murmured to Mentàll. "There is a clear passage all the way to the fields today."

Methusal blinked furiously to clear her eyes, and followed the Kaavl Commander to the door. She managed a nod for Doltn, and then they swiftly strode down the remaining streets to the farmland. As they neared the shacks on the southwestern perimeter, she listened for soldiers, but everything was silent, except for chirps from flying beasts. Doltn was right. This area was clear today.

Mentàll set a brutal pace for kaavl camp. Methusal was glad for the inhuman pace. Sometimes she had to run to keep up. The exertion helped release some of the grief and bursts of anger she felt. Thoughts of cold-blooded murder rose in her, for the first time ever in her life. She fantasized about finding each of the soldiers who had stabbed Kitran's helpless body, and she imagined skewering them with her own blade. What relish, what joy she'd feel to see them crumple at her feet, screaming in agony.

More tears followed these raging, vengeful thoughts, and Methusal sobbed the rest of the way to kaavl camp.

The Dehrien entered kaavl camp. He did not look behind him. Not once had he looked to see if she matched his furious pace. Anger simmered in him, too. She wiped her tears and followed him to the fire, where he stopped. His face looked cut from stone as he observed the five men gathered there. They were looking down on the injured men. Only Wortn was from kaavl camp. One of the newcomers was Barak.

Barak glanced at Mentàll, but didn't seem to sense that anything was wrong, even though his tunic was soaked with blood. "Mentàll!" he rumbled. "We met Zindedis on our way from base camp. We killed four. I don't know how many more riddle these hills."

"They are continuing their search for base camp."

"Yes."

The Dehrien nodded to the three men beside Barak. All were burly and strong. "You three head back to base camp with the injured men. Warn them. Wortn," the pale eyes found his Dehrien compatriot, "go with them, and help carry the injured."

Barak looked puzzled, and for the first time his black gaze, so like his brother's, landed on Methusal. More tears surged to her eyes. His black brows met together. "What's wrong?" he thundered.

"Kitran and three Tarst mutinied," Mentàll said emotionlessly. "Kitran is dead."

"Dead?" Barak stared, and his gaze darted in disbelief from Mentàll to Methusal. "*Dead?*"

"I'm so sorry, Barak," Methusal whispered. "Doltn has him safe. The burial will be at midnight."

"Dead?" The big man's face crumpled. "No. *No!*" he roared.

Methusal helplessly stared at him, unable to fight her own welling, endless tears.

The big man clenched his fists, and without another word lumbered for the hills.

△ △ △ △ △

Hendra, Aali, and Dastn left early to hike up to the easternmost, mountainous tree line. After two hours of hiking they found a good supply of tacky leaves. Aali and Dastn teased and bickered with each other as they worked, and their antics made Hendra smile. She was happy just to quietly pick supplies.

She marveled at Aali's fearlessness. The young girl even flirted a little with Dastn, who dismissed it with amused tolerance.

Hendra wondered why she couldn't be more like Aali. Why did everything have to be so serious? Why couldn't she just laugh with Doc and keep everything lighthearted and fun?

She knew why, of course. It was why she steered clear of even Dastn—a nice guy, and wonderful friend to spunky, irascible Aali.

Hendra felt glum as they headed back. Would she never be freed from this fear? It choked her. She hated it. It was suffocating the life right out of her.

They arrived at base camp just before lunch. Hendra dropped off the supplies in the medical tent and checked on Behran. He was sitting up, and smiled when he saw her.

"Back from scavenging in the wilds?"

Hendra grinned. "Yep. When do you get to eat meals with the rest of us?"

"Doc said tonight."

"Good. I'm glad you're feeling so much better."

"Thanks to your expert nursing."

She flushed. Remembering how much she hated living in fear, she said quickly, "Maybe we could eat together. Maybe lunch tomorrow." Lunch seemed less intimidating than dinner. "That way I can keep an eye on you."

"Strictly medical purposes, right?" His teasing, deep blue eyes grinned at her.

With a smile, she relaxed. "Exactly."

"It's a date," he said lightly.

A date. The thought made her heart want to cocoon up and hibernate. But she knew he was only joking, and so she forced out a high laugh. "Right."

After lunch, Hendra unpacked the supplies and went to work. Doc thankfully made no mention of their meal together last night. However, just as she finished the last job of the evening, he said, "I'm heading out. Care to have dinner with me again?"

Her heart slammed against her chest and her mind went abruptly blank. *What was wrong with her?* Didn't she want to fight these fears? Hadn't she just made a lunch date with Behran? "Um...well..."

"With Behran too, of course. I need to make sure he has recovered enough to leave the sick tent."

"Oh. Well then, yes. Of course!"

He blinked, and Hendra realized how her words must have sounded. He probably felt rejected. She felt bad. "I'm sorry. I...I just... It has nothing to do with you. Please don't be offended."

"I'm not. Don't worry." A long moment passed. Softly, he said, "If you won't tell me what's wrong, will you tell someone? It's going to kill you."

"It's not as serious as that." Although that was how she had felt earlier. Like fear was choking her to death.

"It is." His touched her hand, but she flinched, and snatched it free. Compassion warmed his eyes. He drew a quiet breath. "I won't hurt you."

She stared at him through eyes brimming with tears. And then she fled.

△ △ △ △ △

The men left, carrying the injured for base camp. Grief shrouded Methusal, making her feel hollow and empty inside. She felt very alone. Barak still had not returned from his refuge in the hills. Mentàll had disappeared too, and Taltn was gathering firewood in the low hills.

Methusal paced camp. Her stomach gurgled, but she didn't want to eat. How could she give her body food when Kitran would never eat again? It seemed unjust. Unfair.

"Methusal." The Dehrien's voice commanded her attention. He had returned, and now he wore a clean tunic. His expression was unreadable.

"What?" Defensively, she crossed her arms.

"When did you learn of Kitran's mutiny?"

"You can't blame me for his mutiny."

"When did you learn about it?" he snapped.

"He'd been talking about it for a while. But you know that, don't you?"

The Dehrien didn't deny it.

"Last night he told me his plan. I told him I wouldn't go with him."

The Kaavl Commander stared at her for a long moment. "Why not?"

"Because I'm loyal to my father."

"If you are loyal to your father, then you should have told me last night what Kitran was planning."

"You already knew. How else would you know to go to the ammunition building?"

"I followed you."

She blinked. "But you teamed me with Wortn. How..."

"I know you well, Methusal. I knew you would not follow your assignment."

"Why follow me? You knew all along that he planned to blow up that building."

"I did not know that he foolishly planned to attack it today."

"Why would that be foolish?" Her temper flared. "It sounded like a perfectly reasonable plan to me!"

The Dehrien's icy composure cracked. "Kitran ran to his destruction!" he snarled. "And by keeping silent, *you* are responsible for his death, too."

"I am not!" But she did feel guilty. She had abandoned Kitran. She hadn't been there when he had needed her. Tears sprang to her eyes, but she blinked them back. "Did you truly expect me to tell you last night? To betray an old friend?"

"*I* knew the danger of that mission. Yesterday I learned of new traps the Zindedis had laid."

Fury engulfed her. "You *knew* he planned to mutiny, and you knew the danger, but you didn't tell him? You signed his death warrant! You can't keep all of that information to yourself!"

"I did not know he planned to mutiny today! I did not know, because *you* did not tell me."

"Who cares if I told you or not?" Her voice rose an octave. "You can't keep every bit of information to yourself! What if something happens to you? How will we know what to do?"

"Nothing will happen to me."

"Right." She gave a short laugh. "You have a bounty on your head. Shoot to kill, remember? You're not invulnerable, Mentàll."

"I do not lead by committee."

"I know. Because you think you're smarter than everyone else, and better at kaavl, and better at everything. But you're just a man, Mentàll. You have more flaws than the rest of us put together!"

Fury iced the pale eyes.

"You know it's true," she pressed. "And if you're looking to place blame, look at yourself. You knew Kitran planned to mutiny. Why didn't *you* do something to stop it?"

He agreed with her. For a split second, she saw it in his eyes. Then more fury flashed. Mentàll's hands convulsed into fists, and he stalked away.

Trembling, Methusal sat down abruptly on a boulder. Was he right? Should she have said something? If she had betrayed Kitran, would he still be alive right now? She burst into tears, feeling unbearably guilty and grief-stricken for a situation that could never, ever be put right.

△ △ △ △ △

Late afternoon slipped into early evening. Riln, one of the Tarst men who had mutinied with Kitran, returned with minor injuries. He reported that the other two Tarst were captured by the Zindedis. Other kaavl team members returned, and so did Barak. Mentàll had disappeared from camp.

Methusal and Taltn cooked the evening meal and listened to the men murmur among themselves.

Barak said little, except when spoken to. His black brows bristled together, and his nose and eyes looked red. He wore fierceness like an armor, and it warned off any who might want to offer condolences.

"Tell us about the Zindedis you saw in the hills," Jascr said. Insensitive brute that he was, he didn't seem to mind puncturing Barak's grieving solitude.

Barak cleared his throat. "We killed four," he mumbled. "I'm sure more are crawling in the hills. We've fought them off as best we could. But it's only a matter of time before base camp is discovered."

Alarmed, Methusal said, "Do you think base camp is in danger right now?"

"We're all in danger," he growled with dark gloom. "We're lucky kaavl camp hasn't been discovered yet.

Methusal knew they had been extraordinarily lucky so far. Could Behran and Aali be in danger even now—tonight? Unease grew as she ate. Kitran's death made it clear that horrible things not only could happen, but would happen. Methusal had been scared before, but never more so than now.

"Maybe we should move camp," Riln said.

"Wouldn't be a bad idea," Barak grumbled.

Other men spoke about the idea of having two camps, or a spare camp, should kaavl camp be compromised. A little of Barak's fiery spirits seemed to revive as he argued for the idea of moving camp.

"Where's Mentàll?" Barak asked at last.

No one seemed to know.

"I saw him go that way a while ago." Methusal pointed.

"Get him," Barak said. "We need to make decisions now."

Now Methusal wished she had kept her mouth shut. She didn't want to track down an angry man who clearly wanted to be left alone.

Where's your courage? Since when will you let Mentàll intimidate you?

He always intimidated her. She was honest enough to admit that. She just refused to let him see it.

Methusal washed her bowl, gathered up her medical pouch, and followed the stream west, toward the setting sun. He wasn't at his usual rock, so she pressed on. The landscape grew flatter, with nothing to be seen except for a clump of boulders in the distance. Maybe he had gone there.

She arrived at the tall boulders a few minutes later and skirted around them to reach the other side. She saw him then, sitting forward on a boulder, elbows on his knees, with his hands locked behind his head. As she came closer, she saw that his knuckles were white. He looked like a man in pain.

Methusal stopped, feeling both surprised and cautious. She'd never seen him reveal any emotions before, except for anger. She felt reluctant to intrude into his private space. Like any injured wild beast, he'd probably attack her, as he had done so many times in the past.

But dealing with feral animals was her specialty, wasn't it? She had two choices: either she could wait to be attacked, or she could attack first, with kindness. Besides, wasn't that what the Prophet had said to do? To love her enemies and treat them with kindness?

Unfortunately, everything within her still rebelled at the thought.

Help me, The One, please. I can't do this on my own.

Taking courage in hand, she silently stepped closer. *Be kind,* she told herself.

She didn't plan what to say. The words came out, unbidden. "It's not your fault."

His shoulders jerked, and his hands moved to the sides of his face.

Methusal continued, because it was the truth. She couldn't blame herself, either, although she wanted to. "Kitran chose to mutiny."

"He mutinied because he hated me." She barely heard the low words. "Because I broke trust with him during the Alliance."

She was shocked that he would admit to any sort of responsibility. "Yes, partly," she agreed slowly. "But you broke trust with Petr and my father, too. They chose to trust you on this mission. I've chosen to follow you, and we both know how we feel about each other. Kitran made the wrong choice."

Mentàll rubbed his face. "You chose my side?"

"I chose my father's side. I love Kitran, but ultimately he disobeyed my father. And he didn't research the situation. I hate that he died." Tears clogged her throat. "And maybe I should have said something. You're partly responsible, too. But Kitran is the one who made the choice."

After a moment Mentàll said harshly, "You do not know everything, Methusal."

"I am speaking the truth, and you know it."

"Do you have all the facts?"

Quietly, she said, "Do you?"

"*Go!*"

She would like nothing better. "Barak needs you back at camp. And I need to check your wound, especially after you carried Kitran all that way today."

His fists clenched. "Hurry up, then."

Methusal moved closer. Her boldness was fast deserting her. She would be glad when this chore was over. Maybe now wasn't the best time to do this, after all. The tension between them felt like a palpable, living force.

Mentàll hissed, "Be quick about it!"

"Calm yourself," Methusal snapped back. She lifted his clean tunic. The long, ugly scar looked red. Was that blood? She ran her finger over it. Yes. A little dried blood.

"You've been bleeding."

"Then fix it," he snarled. He ripped the tunic over his head with one fist.

The wild beast had leaped from his lair again. Methusal took a steadying breath. More coltac juice and three adhesive leaves should do it. She broke open four coltac leaves and squirted on the thick, healing sap. Then she gently stroked it down the line of the ugly gash, working it around the rough thread.

Most of the new, dried blood drops were in the upper-most portion of the wound, near his shoulder. It was clear the tiny breaks in the skin were not severe. The new, pink skin firmly held together the wound.

She'd need to take the stitches out tomorrow, for sure. She kept her touch gentle and soothing, treating him like the unpredictable wild beast he was.

She smoothed on the last adhesive leaf. "There. Done."

She was about to step away, but his large hand closed around her wrist, stopping her. Startled, she went very still, and her heart beat faster with alarm. His pale blue eyes pinned her. He said in a low voice, "Your words and your touch always tell me two different stories."

Methusal fought for calm. Surely he didn't think she'd made an advance on him, just because she had tried to be gentle! "I take care of your wounds exactly how I do for any wild animal. Gentleness usually works best."

"You see me as a wild animal?"

"Yes. You're dangerous."

"So you take great care."

"Yes." She didn't flinch from his unwavering gaze. "And The One says to show kindness to our enemies."

He released her wrist. "Go back to camp, Methusal."

She drew a quick, relieved breath. "Barak needs to speak to you. And others want to know if we're going to break camp."

"I will return."

Methusal left him, feeling once again that she had barely escaped from a dangerous situation. So far, he had kept his word to her father and hadn't harmed her. But under the wrong circumstances, she didn't know how far she could trust him.

△ △ △ △ △

Aali heard the news about Kitran when she was helping Aenill serve dinner. Word spread like wildfire about his death, and about the Zindedis who had been killed a good hour into the foothills. Scouts would be doubled tonight around base camp.

Aali quickly ate her own food with trembling hands. All she could think about was Kitran. He'd died while trying to blow up the powder building. If she had been there, maybe she could have saved him. She could have gone through the window like the Chiefs had been planning—but Kitran didn't know that plan. And no one had asked for her help, either. And they never would.

Angry tears blurred her eyes. Those Zindedi wild beasts! They had killed Kitran. She gulped on a sob. Kitran had been her champion when she'd wanted to learn kaavl—even when her father had forbidden it. He was a good man. One of the best in the world! Tears streamed down her cheeks. It wasn't fair. It wasn't fair at all!

Other people sat down at her table, but Aali wanted to be alone. She grabbed her plate and utensils, dropped them off in the dish bins, and hurried into the night. Darkness enveloped her. Overhead, stars twinkled in the soft black sky. It was so quiet. And it even felt peaceful. But how could she feel any peace when Kitran was dead, and she'd never, *ever* see him again?

Men moved past her, heading for the dining tent. Pan's war team had just arrived. Too many people. She wanted to be alone.

She cast a quick glance around her. Dastn always seemed to be nearby these days. While Aali did like Dastn a little—when he wasn't being superior or irritating—she didn't want to be spied upon all day long, either. Especially when her opportunity came in the future to help the war team. She didn't need his interference. Look what had happened when she hadn't been there to help Kitran. No, Dastn was a hindrance she needed to escape. At least he wasn't following her right now.

She touched the short kaavl stick she always kept in a loop in her tunic, and climbed the hill behind the medical tent. She climbed high to a small plateau and sat on the edge. Ryon peeped over the eastern mountain, and shone its pale green glow over the camp below. Again, the peace of the cold night surprised her. How could peace exist when people had just died?

Aali thought about The One. Ancient scriptures said the just would live by faith, and that all who love him would go live with The One when they died. That they never really died at all. Could that be true? She fervently hoped so, and choked on another sob. "Please take care of Kitran, The One," she whispered. "We love him."

"*Who* do you love?"

The ugly snarl electrified her skin.

Aali leaped to her feet in a flash. Pogul stood only two steps away. The shadows made his thick features look menacing in the dim light.

"Why are you here?"

"Time for payback, Aali." The flash of the kaavl stick came out of nowhere. The wooden rod hit the side of her head. Pain exploded. She staggered, and grappled for her kaavl stick.

"Want more?" He lunged forward.

She blocked his next blow with her own kaavl stick.

His thick lips curled back and he swung again, putting all of his weight behind the blow. Aali blocked it, but staggered backward from the impact. Her heel dug into the crumbling edge of the cliff.

Fear made her thoughts crystallize. She'd die if she couldn't figure out how to turn this around.

Pogul swung again, but this time she ducked and pranced sideways, onto a more secure section of plateau.

He spit out an ugly name and tried to skewer her. She whipped sideways and arched her back, avoiding the stick.

She smiled. A little of her confidence returned. "Ready to play, Pogul?"

Aali whipped her stick like lighting, deliberately trying to confuse him. She jabbed and swung here, there, and everywhere.

A blow caught Pogul on the knee, another on the ear, and another in the corner of his mouth. His defensive moves looked sluggish compared to her dancing, speedy attacks. His arms flailed, and Aali connected a hard, satisfying jab to his midsection. He howled and bent double.

She felt too charged with adrenaline to feel afraid now. "Do you want more?" she scorned. "Or will you run away?"

"I'll get you, brat!" Blood dribbled down his chin.

"Bring it," she sneered. "I'll happily give you more."

But Pogul retreated, swearing and limping, down the hill.

Aali realized that she was shaking. She tried to tuck the kaavl stick through the loop in her tunic, but her hands wouldn't cooperate. Suddenly, something grabbed the stick and twisted it out of her grasp. With a choking gasp, she whirled.

Dastn stood there. The green light of Ryon illuminated his eyes and the dark slash of his brows. "Think I was Pogul?" He looked grim.

Aali snatched back her stick. With two hands, she shoved it through the tunic loop. She backed up a step, too. Dastn looked dangerous tonight. Or maybe she was more rattled than she'd realized, and wanted to jump at shadows. "Why are you here?"

"Were you out for a stroll?"

Something inside of her snapped. It was all too much—the explosion, Kitran's death, being chastised by Erl, working like a slave at camp, being watched continually, it seemed, by Dastn...and now the attack by Pogul. She felt frustrated, stifled, and scared.

"Have you been *spying* on me?"

"I notice that you are watching *me* all the time. Should I feel flattered?" He stepped toward her. That one step held the faintest hint of a swagger, as if he was deliberately trying to be obnoxious. It irritated her even further.

"Watch *you*? Please. I'm trying to avoid you, so you'll quit following me everywhere. Like a pet apte!"

"A pet apte?" He looked amused now, and his right brow lifted to match the equally wicked tilt of his spiky hair.

Aali's heart beat a little faster, but she continued to frown. "Don't you have anything better to do?"

Dastn lifted his hands, as if weighing each of them. "Mind my own business...or keep a prankster out of trouble. Now, what would be more interesting?"

"So you *are* spying on me!"

"Sorry to deflate your ego, kid. I'm just following orders."

Kid! Aali narrowed her eyes. "I don't need help. And I don't need a bodyguard—great and hulking though you are!"

He laughed out loud.

"Uncle Erl put you up to this, didn't he?"

"Pretty much."

"I knew it!" she scowled. "I don't appreciate being spied on, or followed around all the time."

"You want me to disobey orders?"

"Stop it! Or this is war."

"War? Sounds like a challenge." Dastn's brow lifted higher.

"One you will *lose.*"

"Confident, are you? You don't think you need a bodyguard?"

She snorted. "I certainly do not!"

"Looks to me like you do."

"Pogul? Please. He caught me off guard. He's no threat."

"I wouldn't be so sure. Refresh my memory. What did you do to him?"

Aali rolled her eyes. "I took his scout shift. You know, so I could find out that vital, potentially war winning discovery. He got switched to nights." She shrugged. "He's not keen on it."

"Apparently not." His dark, unsmiling eyes narrowed.

"Step off, Dastn," she warned. "I don't care what Uncle Erl says. Stop following me, okay? Leave me alone!"

All traces of humor vanished from his features. His face looked hard, and a little frightening. "You are a foolish little girl, Aali." He raised his hand to stop her indignant comeback. "No. You may think you're smarter than Pogul. But he's *mean.* And he wants revenge. And he's patient. Look how he surprised you when you were shocked about Kitran. You ran into the hills. You weren't thinking clearly."

"I handled him. I didn't see you rescuing me, anyway."

"It took me a minute to figure out where you had gone. Don't change the subject. Now Pogul's embarrassed that you beat him. He's mad, so he's meaner. He'll plot and plan for the next time you're alone and defenseless. And then what will you do?"

"He talks empty air," she scoffed. "His kaavl skills stink. What could he do to me?"

Dastn's jaw dropped. "Are you that naïve? Should I describe it to you?"

Her cheeks burned. "No! He wouldn't do that. You're just trying to scare me."

"Aali..."

"No! I don't need you around. I have kaavl. I'm always armed. So step off, Dastn, for the last time!"

The moonlight made the cut of his jaw look hard. "I'll step off, Aali," he said in a quiet, harsh tone. "I'll wait until you call for me."

"That will be never!"

He turned and strode away.

Aali wrapped her arms around herself. She'd succeeded in warning him off—and in infuriating the normally easygoing Dastn.

So why didn't she feel more victorious? Truthfully, she felt scared and alone right now. What if he was right about Pogul?

After several long moments, she straightened her shoulders. She wasn't a child. Wasn't that the whole point? She had to prove herself—not only to Dastn, Erl, and Pogul, but to everyone. She could take care of herself. And she would help win this war.

Koblan needed her now, more than ever. She could prevent another bloodbath, but she'd never escape to accomplish it with Dastn watching her every single minute. She'd done the right thing to make him angry, so he'd back off and quit spying on her. When the war team attacked the munitions building, Aali would be free to go with them, invited or not. She would help win this war, and no one—not Dastn or Pogul—would stop her.

∆ ∆ ∆ ∆ ∆

Barak left for his brother's funeral in Quasr, alone, in the pitch black night. Methusal curled up in her pallet and silently wept. *Oh, Kitran, why did you do it?*

Sleep eluded her. She was wide awake, and aware of each snap and crackle of the fire, and the shuffling sounds of the kaavl team settling in for the night.

Mentàll had told them of an alternate camp site he'd found in the hills. It was located an hour's climb to the southeast. They'd flee there if necessary. Until then, they would remain at kaavl camp.

Methusal shivered, and hitched her extra coverlet higher over her ears and nose, hoping her breath would warm the chilly air inside her doubled coverlet.

And what about base camp? Had the Zindedis found it yet? Were her father, Behran, Aali, and Hendra in danger? Methusal didn't like how helpless she felt, knowing that she could do nothing to help them.

And what about Deccia? Was the General still abusing her?

More tears choked out.

Kitran was dead. Those she loved were in danger. And she could do nothing about it. Nothing. She *hated* it. She gritted her teeth and sniffed.

A thought crossed her mind, and she quickly counted days. Yes. Tomorrow would be the nineteenth day since she had learned of the invasion. It also meant her birthday was in two days. For the first time in their lives, she and her twin would not share their birthday together.

Her twenty-first birthday was supposed to be joyful—the official start of her adult life. Many people got married and started their own families in Rolban when they turned twenty-one. But she already felt like an adult. She felt old, weary, and hopeless. How long would the war drag on? Could they win?

First Efron, then Kitran were killed. Two Tarst and Deccia were captured, and unknown numbers of the war team had been killed or injured. *Why* did this war have to happen?

Why, The One? Please protect us. Please help us.

The One seemed far away. Was he even listening?

Methusal wished Behran was in kaavl camp. She wanted to run into his arms and be held tight. She wanted to feel safe. She wanted to believe that everything would be all right again.

"Please protect Behran," she whispered.

She lay awake for hours, unable to sleep. When the night was more than half gone, sleep finally softened the edges of her mind.

Kitran marched toward Quasr, eager to destroy the ammunition building. He laughed when he spoke to his Tarst friends.

Methusal ran after them. "Kitran! Don't do it. Kitran, no!"

He only laughed still more. The munitions building loomed ahead, looking large and ominous. She didn't see any soldiers, but... "Kitran, it's a trap," she screamed. "Don't!"

But he charged forward. Soldiers suddenly streamed from the building wielding swords, knives, and guns. A Zindedi plunged a sword into Kitran, and he fell. Weeping, Methusal turned away.

Now she stood at base camp in the dark.

Behran and Hendra sat by a fire, and his arm was around her. All of a sudden, howls punctuated the quiet night. Packs of wild beasts galloped down the hills and into camp. Behind them, invaders shot guns, driving the beasts on. Horror blanched Behran's face, and suddenly Deccia floated through the air like a ghost. Was it too late to save her?

Invaders captured base camp. Behran ran to save Hendra, but he didn't see the invader with the sword. Methusal whispered his name, but she couldn't move. The invader slunk forward to attack Behran, who wasn't looking.

Suddenly, Methusal could move. She ran, sobbing out a warning, "Behran, watch out! He's going to kill you." Behran turned, and in a quick stroke, he slew the invader. Methusal ran into the solid comfort of his arms. Her foot suddenly hurt. He lifted her up, and she put her arms around his neck and pressed her face into the side of his bristly cheek. She had never felt so happy to be anywhere in her entire life.

Behran carried her to kaavl camp. It was safe now. A fire flickered in the darkness. He lowered her onto her pallet.

Methusal whispered, "I thought I'd lost you, Behran. Forever."

He hesitated, and then urged her to lie back. "Sleep, Methusal."

"You aren't in love with her, are you?"

"Who?" He sounded confused.

"Hendra." Methusal waited, her heart in her throat.

Another odd pause, then, "No."

Methusal felt relieved, but still unsure. "Hold me—just for a little while," she whispered. She needed the comfort of him being close. She'd felt alone for so long. She didn't want him to leave her again.

He hesitated again, his face in shadows, and looked over his shoulder.

"Just for a minute," she begged. Didn't he want to be close to her anymore? After another long hesitation, he did as she bid. The fire burned low now, and all she could see was the big shape of his body. He lay beside her and lowered one arm around her waist. She felt safe and protected for the first time in a very long time. Joy welled within her.

"Kiss me. Just one time." She reached for his shoulder, trying to make out his face in the darkness. His shoulders felt wider than she remembered. His arm tensed. The muscles felt like polished ore beneath her fingertips. That was new, too. What had Behran done at base camp to gain this sleek, hard bulk? It didn't matter. She was with Behran, and that was all that mattered.

She tilted her head up and pressed her lips to his. Methusal felt his quick, indrawn breath. "I love you," she whispered.

With an inarticulate groan, he abruptly consumed her caress like a parched man drinking water. Heat exploded, and shot to the core of her being. Surprise caught her. This was new, too.

He kissed her long and slow, with a barely leashed passion that made her tremble. He pulled away. "I must go," he said, voice hoarse. He left her alone. Methusal smiled, and fell into a deep sleep. She felt at peace for the first time in a very long time.

CHAPTER TWENTY-TWO

IN THE FROSTY DAWN, Methusal awoke feeling calm and happy, and looked around for Behran. But the ground beside her lay empty except for tiny, frost encrusted plants. Behran wasn't there.

She sat up abruptly.

Only a dream. Methusal drew a deep breath to try to reorient herself. But it had seemed so real!

Barak lumbered by, headed for the stream. His un-shaven, dark stubbled face looked haggard, and Methusal wondered if he had slept at all last night. He spotted her and offered a faint, kind smile. "Morning, Thusa." His voice sounded subdued.

Methusal shivered in the cold, and all of her worries flooded back, and so did Kitran's horrible death. A knot formed in her stomach. She wished she could hang onto the feeling of peace from her dream, but it was a fantasy. She might as well get up. Her body urged a trip to the private place among the rocks.

When Methusal stood up, a sharp pain stabbed into her bare foot. "Ow!"

She sat back down and examined her heel, wondering if a rocher had bitten her last night. No. It was a straight, slashing cut. Dirt infested it.

When had that happened? She stared at it, perplexed. She was sure she hadn't cut her heel last night, before she went to bed. To be sure, she examined her nearby moccasins. No cuts ripped the leather. She stared at her foot again. It was as if she'd gone walking without her moccasins As if she'd gotten out of bed last night...

Her dream flashed back.

She had hurt her foot in the dream. And Behran had carried her back to camp.

Had she slept-walked through kaavl camp last night? Horror spiraled in her. If that was true, what else could be real? Had some man carried her to bed...and kissed her?

Horror gripped her, and she anxiously glanced at her fellow kaavl teammates. Only six men were left now. Plus Barak and Taltn. And Wortn, who was temporarily at base camp. She observed them moving around camp, and watched to see if anyone stared at her, or shared a secret laugh with a friend. Nothing.

She limped to the stream, washed the cut, and then applied coltac juice and a bandage to her foot. Surreptitiously, she continued to survey her teammates. If some man had carried her and kissed her, that man was keeping it to himself. On a team full of mostly boastful men, that seemed unlikely. It must not have happened. She felt a sliver of relief.

Maybe she *had* slept-walked—it often happened when she was upset. Perhaps she had found her own way back to the pallet.

But it had all seemed so *real*. Methusal could not dismiss that feeling. Being carried by a large man...and being kissed. Heart jumping with anxiety, she scanned the team again.

Barak lumbered by with another smile for her. Loathsome Jascr returned her stare and offered a leer. A usual occurrence. Methusal rolled her eyes and dismissed him. Her gaze landed on Mentàll, who dunked his whole head in the stream and shook it once as he came back up.

Taltn hurried her way with his usual, eager grin. His foot must be better, because he was only using one crutch this morning. "Want some pods, Thusa? Barak brought vegetables from Quasr last night."

"Sure." She smiled. "Thanks. I'll join you in a minute."

"Okay." He hobbled back to the fire, where Goric and Jascr now foraged through two leather sacks.

Methusal scanned the men in camp again. Tabor. Riln. Both were large men.

Nothing. She could pinpoint nothing out of place. It must have been a dream. She finally relaxed. The only man who had kissed her was Behran...in her dream.

△ △ △ △ △

Hendra reflected on last night's dinner with Behran and Doc. It had ended up being pretty quiet. Kitran's death had hit everyone hard. Hendra had barely known him, but he'd seemed like a good man, and she knew his kaavl had been excellent.

Doc was especially quiet during the meal, and the few glances he'd given her had looked troubled. Hendra felt bad about the way she'd yanked her hand away from him yesterday.

She remained very quiet during the meal. At the end of dinner the two men started talking about strategic military moves, so Hendra excused herself and went to bed early.

Now, at work this morning, Doc was kind to her, but completely professional. Hendra was sick of being afraid. It had to end. Now. Although she fantasized about going to war, maybe her biggest battle was right here, with Doc.

He said, "Let's check on our worst patient."

She knew exactly whom he meant. The young man had been shot in the knee yesterday. So far, they'd only lost two patients—both from bullet wounds. One in the stomach, and one in the lung. But Viln's knee was a crushed mess. Though it wasn't yet life threatening, the chance of infection was high. And the possibility of his knee working normally again was nonexistent.

Hendra helped Doc by gently speaking to the pale man, and by making him as comfortable as she could. The poor man relaxed a little and swallowed the medicine she offered.

She wished she knew how to fix the broken pieces inside of herself as easily. What was wrong with her? Here she was, safe at base camp with a nice man like Doc, but her fears seemed more out of control now, than when she'd defied Mentàll and scouted in Quasr.

Maybe... If the chance arose to escape base camp and help the war team, she would take it. Maybe that bold move would finally help conquer all of her fears. Maybe then she could finally live again.

△ △ △ △ △

A little later that morning Mentàll ordered Methusal to scout with Riln, the burly Tarst man who had mutinied with Kitran yesterday. She noticed that the Dehrien Chief was rubbing his shoulder—thankfully not the injured one. Carrying Kitran yesterday could not have been good for his injury, and it certainly explained the new blood she'd seen on his back last night.

As they set off for Quasr, Methusal asked Riln a few questions, hoping he would tell her more about how Kitran had died. But Riln only answered her questions with monosyllabic words. He scowled most of the time, and his demeanor bristled angry aggression. Not a friendly man.

Disappointed, she fell silent. They met with Doltn in a shack on the north side of town, and he reported the latest intelligence gleaned from Quasrians who were stationed inside the General's compound. No word on Deccia, but it appeared that the Tarst prisoners were still alive. Guards were quadrupled around the ammunition building. Afterward she and Riln scouted the southern side of town, but discovered nothing of importance. In the afternoon, they headed back to kaavl camp.

Methusal missed scouting with Kitran. She missed his occasional sarcastic comments, and his energy and zest for life. When she reentered camp, everything looked the same. The Zindedis hadn't discovered it yet. One positive note for the day.

Most of the kaavl teams had already returned. She spotted Dastn talking to Mentàll across camp. The Dehrien stood with his back to them as they approached, and she instantly intensified her kaavl to listen. Eavesdropping, she reflected, was becoming a bad habit.

"Eerpor says they'll send fifty soldiers," Dastn said. "They'll arrive at base camp in a few days. No word from Wyen yet."

Instant hope kindled. Would fifty men be enough to finally plan Deccia's rescue?

"Good. Methusal and Riln are here." The Dehrien glanced over his shoulder, and that pale gaze froze into them both. "Listen to their report, and then return to base camp."

"Yes, sir."

Riln quickly reported the sparse facts they had discovered, and the Dehrien listened silently nearby. Dastn chatted with his Tarst compatriot for a minute, and then sprinted for the hills. Late afternoon sunlight gilded the hills pink. Dastn would have to run fast to get home before dark.

Methusal helped Taltn carry firewood for the evening fire, and helped prepare the aptes that Wortn had killed on his way back to kaavl camp this afternoon. The men talked among themselves as she and Taltn prepared the meal, but she noticed that the Dehrien Chief was keeping to himself.

"Looks delicious, Methusal." Jascr appeared at her elbow. His lips stretched into an unpleasant smile. His teeth resembled wild beast fangs.

"Then get in line, just like everyone else."

He licked his lips. "I'm happy to wait. Good things come to those who wait *patiently*."

"Step off."

His smiled broadened. "I'll be back. Promise." He swaggered over to Goric, whose murky eyes glared at her.

A shudder threatened, but Methusal froze her muscles, stilling it. She'd never let those wild beasts know they frightened her. She surreptitiously felt for her knife and kaavl stick. Both at the ready.

Dusk fell, and Taltn started the fire while she strung up the aptes to roast.

"Methusal," the Kaavl Commander said, the instant she had completed her task. He strode toward the stream. Of course, she was supposed to follow like an obedient apte.

Methusal drew a calming breath. After a long delay, during which she gathered up her medical pouch, she followed the Dehrien to the boulder by the stream. Tonight, she knew, would be especially unpleasant, because a new duty awaited. As usual, he waited with his tunic off.

"Take out the stitches," he ordered.

"I was going to," she returned testily.

The wound looked clean, but new dried blood adhered to the upper portion of the wound. It wasn't much, though. For the most part, it looked healed, and the new skin was tender and pink. Definitely time to pull out the stitches—the task she'd been dreading for days.

Reluctantly, she pulled out her bone-handled knife. The tip flashed sharp and silver in the setting sun. She remembered the night, two and a half years ago in Tarst, when Mentàll had held a blade to her throat. Now she held the knife, and he silently waited, trusting that she would not hurt him.

"How far we've come," she muttered. Tentatively, she prodded at the top stitch in his upper shoulder with her fingertip, looking for a place where she could poke the knife under the rough thread.

A long, silent moment passed. Then he said, "What do you mean?"

She found a small opening and snipped the blade up. The thread cut neatly in two. Not so bad. Feeling a bit relieved, she inspected the next stitch. "Remember Tarst, when you held a sword to my neck? Now I hold the blade."

"Are you planning to hurt me?" Faint, arrogant humor twisted through the words.

"If I was a wild beast, maybe I would."

"You believe you are better than me."

Silence slipped by while Methusal thought about that, and she snipped more stitches. Finally, she said, "No. I don't think I'm better than you. But I do try to choose the right path. You don't."

"You are arrogant, as usual, Methusal," he said softly. "You know nothing."

She gave a faint snort. "*You* win the prize for arrogance," she returned. "There. Done cutting." She carefully pulled out the tiny threads. He didn't wince, so she didn't know if it hurt or not.

She soothed on coltac juice, and then dared to put a splash on his cheekbone, too, which still looked angry and red. His pale eyes watched her as she did so, and she moved quickly, not wanting to prolong the contact.

"Done." She pushed the extra coltac leaves into her pouch.

He stood, so he towered over her again. His piercing blue gaze held hers. "Will my wound require more tending?"

Why did his words sound like a test?

She steadily stared back. She could lie, and say "no," and be done dealing with him in private forever. It might end these small goading attacks. He seemed to enjoy provoking her whenever they were alone, and when there was no one else around to witness their exchanges.

"Yes," she said. "Doc says it will need coltac juice for a few more days. It'll help finish the deep healing, and help reduce scarring, too. Plus, you tend to exert yourself and strain the wound. He wants me to keep an eye on it."

Cold blue ice regarded her. "So. You told the truth."

"Have I ever lied to you?"

He pulled on his tunic. "We will see." His smile edged up, and it suddenly looked nasty. "We will see." He stalked for camp.

△ △ △ △ △

Methusal discovered that Goric and Jascr had again infested her pallet with rochers. After sweeping them away, she snuggled down, feeling bone-weary from the lack of sleep she'd suffered the last two nights.

After what seemed like only minutes of sleep, voices intruded into her dreams.

"Nothing has changed."

Mentàll! Methusal drew in a sharp breath and blinked.

"Do you think we will win this war?" That was Tabor's smooth, deep-toned voice.

"We will win." Mentàll sounded grimly matter-of-fact.

She smothered a yawn and listened more intently. Clearly the Dehriens were having another secret meeting.

"So when the war ends, and when your talks with the Chiefs are done... Then you will seize power?"

"No. Then they will cede power to me."

Methusal gasped softly. Mentàll intended to make a power grab—that was no surprise. But he seemed to believe the other Chiefs would *give* the power to him. Had he lost his mind?

No. He was too coldly logical to believe in a fantasy. So he must have some scheme in place so he could achieve the power he'd always lusted after.

Peeking over her coverlet, she watched Tabor and Mentàll return to camp. When she discovered exactly what he was plotting, she would tell her father and Pan. No Chief in Koblan would be tricked into trusting that Dehrien again— not so long as she had breath in her body, and a voice to be heard.

Her thoughts tangled, trying to imagine what the Dehrien might be planning. After a long time she fell into a fitful sleep.

Strands of her hair twitched against her temple. Tiny needles prickled into her scalp, and something smooth slid by the tip of her ear. A tickling sensation crept down her back.

A rocher dropped onto her nose.

Methusal stifled a scream and tore out of bed. She swiped violently at her hair, ripped off her warm tunics, and flicked the rocher off her back. The horrible insect bit her before it fell. The bite stung, and then it burned. Trying to swallow back frightened, gasping breaths, she carefully checked her hair and clothing to make sure she'd eliminated every last rocher. Shivering in the icy night, she pulled back on the tunics. And then she glared across the campfire.

Jascr and Goric slept peacefully. In fact, a snort gurgled in Jascr's throat. An intense, trembling fury overtook her. Those *whips!* Clearly they had dumped a bucketful of rochers near her while she slept. Rochers did not seek out human contact. In fact, they usually fled in fear, biting all the way to safety.

Repay no one evil for evil. The Prophet's words whispered through her mind, but she ignored them. Grabbing up her coverlet, which still crawled with dozens of the shelled insects, she marched across camp and dumped the lot on Jascr and Goric's heads. Jascr snorted, but didn't move. Goric snored faintly with his mouth wide open. Maybe a rocher would crawl inside, Methusal thought meanly.

Still trembling, she returned to her spot and swept it clean of rochers, and then bundled back inside her coverlet. She shivered with cold and with fury. Those whips! Ignoring them wasn't working. Tomorrow she would put an end to this mess, once and for all.

CHAPTER TWENTY-THREE

EYELIDS HEAVY WITH FATIGUE, Methusal reluctantly awoke at dawn. Exhaustion felt like a physical weight, and her head hurt. She wished she could sleep for twenty-four hours.

Her eyes zeroed in on her three enemies, who sat on boulders near the black, cold fire. Goric and Jascr muttered together. Mentàll rubbed his shoulder and the base of his neck.

Mentàll and Tabor's nocturnal conversation returned to mind. She wished she could replay the conversation to her father. Unfortunately, the little she'd heard would not condemn him—by his own words, he did not intend to seize power. Rather, he plotted to make others give it to him. But what he planned to *do* with the power afterward... It couldn't bode well for Koblan.

Goric glanced up and nudged Jascr, who shot her a chilling glare. Rocher bites reddened the bridge of Jascr's nose. Methusal felt both satisfied and uneasy at the sight. Her own rocher bite stung this morning.

She broke open a coltac leaf and smeared it on her back, but knew it wouldn't help much. Nothing healed rocher bites except for time. At least Jascr would suffer, too.

She pulled on her moccasins, slipped her weapons into their tunic loops, and headed for the private place among the rocks. She wanted to be alone for longer than it took to relieve her body's needs, however. Except for Taltn, she felt alone at kaavl camp. She fit in nowhere in this camp of men—and three of those men hated her.

She climbed a faint, winding path among the rocks to a high, solitary place, and sat on a boulder overlooking the valley floor. A cold, bitter wind blew, whipping her hair and sliding into her tunic. She shivered. But it was a bright blue morning; crisp, clear, and beautiful. She looked out over the valley to the right, toward Quasr and the shining, rippling sea. High up like this, and removed from the people and the conflicts below, the day felt peaceful. The soft brown of the plain, which ran west as far as she could see, ended in the dark, soaring outline of the western coastal range. The cold air tasted crisp and metallic.

A faint scrabble of rocks on the path below drew her attention. Unease slid through her. That one path was the only way up or down.

Since Taltn was her only friend in camp, and his ankle was still healing, it probably wasn't him climbing that steep, rocky path. It wasn't Mentàll, either, because he walked in virtual silence. This man was scuffing over the rocks.

Methusal's heart beat faster, and she pulled out her kaavl stick and moved to a safer, more defensive position. Fighting an assailant at the edge of a steep cliff was not the best idea. She chose her position and focused completely into kaavl.

A dark head rounded the corner. Jascr. He'd followed her. His black brows beetled together in a menacing "V," and a knife glinted in his hand.

Gathering her courage like armor, Methusal stepped into his path, which prevented him from climbing any further. "Step off."

His lips curled back to reveal sharp teeth. "We need to settle a score."

Now she saw that rochers had bit red "v's" into his neck and his left ear lobe, too.

"Yes, we do," she agreed. "You and Goric will stop infesting my pallet with rochers."

"You don't like our gifts?"

"Did you appreciate my gift to you last night?"

His lips curled back in a bestial snarl. "You will learn your place!" The knife slashed toward her throat.

With a quick wrist flick, she deflected it with the kaavl stick. Feeling strangely detached, she said, "Do you want to kill me?"

Jascr swung again. This time, not only did she deflect the blade, but a quick double wrist flick disarmed him. The knife fell to the earth.

He lunged for it, but Methusal cracked the kaavl stick under his chin, and then jabbed it into his throat. Lips twisted in fury, Jascr grabbed at the stick, but she kicked him, and then neatly flicked his knife out of reach with her toe.

Jascr crouched, and glared at her.

"Enough?" Methusal wanted to know.

He suddenly straightened and stepped back with a grin. "You will regret that, Methusal."

"Who will make me pay? You?"

He smiled. "You'll never know when I'll come for you. When you're awake. Or asleep. You'll never know."

A black soul lived in him. If the Prophet was here, she'd ask if there could ever be hope for a soul so steeped in evil.

Jascr reminded her of the General. He had no conscience, and he certainly did not care about the higher way. Only threats would persuade him to keep his place.

"Leave me alone, Jascr. Next time I won't be so kind to you. Consider this a warning."

"*Next* time?" He laughed. The sound made her blood curdle, because he sounded so completely indifferent. "Next time *you* will be the one humiliated. Count on that, Methusal Maahr." He licked his lips. "And believe me, I'm looking forward to it. I can't wait to find you defenseless—maybe deep in happy dreams about Behran. I'll come to you then."

Surely it hadn't been *Jascr...* Horror clutched her. But it couldn't be. He wasn't big enough to be the man in her dream. Besides, a wild beast would never stop until he had devoured his victim whole. Coldly, she said, "If you attack me, I will kill you."

"When you're stripped of your weapons, you will fear me," he sneered. "You will regret humiliating me. Be sure of it." Jascr moved to the side of the path and gestured for her to leave. No doubt he meant to search for his weapon after she'd gone.

She couldn't allow that. The point of his knife glinted a half-length away. She pulled out her own blade. "You go first. I don't trust you behind my back."

Red fury mottled his face, but he had no weapons, and she had two in hand. With a vicious shoulder twist, he headed back down the path. She took that opportunity to kick his weapon down the rocky hillside. It clattered, hitting stones all the way down. Jascr whipped around, and when he realized what she had done his black eyes bulged out in rage. For a second she thought he might attack her with his bare fists. She raised her kaavl stick in warning. "I guess we both know how you'll spend your morning."

At a lower point on the path, Jascr cut left to search for his knife. Methusal hoped he wouldn't find it. And she realized for the first time the full consequences of what she'd have to face for not heeding the Prophet's words last night. She'd dumped the rochers on Jascr's head, and now the fight between them had escalated into a war.

Much as she'd pretended to brave, she was scared. She could never be alone again. Never. If he caught her defenseless, not only would he humiliate her in every way his black soul could imagine, but he would also, without a doubt, kill her.

△ △ △ △ △

Doc sat at his desk, head bent, scratching notes on patient sheets when Hendra entered the medical tent that morning. She wondered exactly how early he'd started work, and paused in front of the table. "Good morning." When he looked up, she smiled and held out a plate of Aenill's berry cobbler. "Aenill said you left before it finished baking."

Doc's gaze remained upon her, not the sweet treat. A smile tugged at his lips. "Thank you."

She wanted to lower her gaze, but managed to conquer that fearful instinct. Fantasies of going to war and fighting her fears on an unknown battlefield may help her one day, but today this was her battlefield. "You're welcome. What can I do first?"

"Change bandages. Later I'll need help with Viln, the knee patient."

She nodded, and as she gathered supplies, felt pleased with herself. She had met Doc's steady gaze, and had spoken to him in a calm, professional manner. A small step, of course, but still something.

"Hendra." Behran approached with a pack over his shoulder.

"You're moving out?" she said with pleased smile.

"You don't have to look so happy," he teased. "Won't you miss me? Even a little?"

"Of course." She blushed. "But you're well. That's the most important thing."

With a grin, Behran moved toward the tent opening. "See you later. And Doc—I'll try not to take up too much space in your tent."

Doc lifted a hand in farewell, and Hendra set about her duties. Changing bandages wasn't fun work. The new, pulpy wounds turned her stomach, but the older, healing wounds gave her a sense of satisfaction. Her work did make a difference. People were healing, partly due to her efforts.

"I'm ready, Hendra," Doc said a little later. He knelt beside a worried looking Viln. "Bring the pain powder."

Hendra mixed the powder and helped the young man drink it. Doc took his time unwrapping the knee, and by the time he had finished, Viln had fallen asleep. "This will look ugly," he warned, and pulled back the last bandage.

Hendra's stomach lurched at the blood, mixed with pus, that filled the gaping hole that had been Viln's knee. She swallowed fast and looked away, trying not to be sick. Now she could use a dose of that ice that used to protect her heart. A few days ago she'd realized it had deserted her when she'd started working with Doc at base camp. Now it seemed like she felt everything more intensely than she'd ever before felt anything in her life. Fear. Joy. Horror.

She forced her gaze back to the wound and swallowed again. "What do you need me to do?"

"Hold back the skin like this." Doc used a metal instrument to demonstrate what he meant. Blood and ripped flesh squished together, and Hendra glanced away, trying to find a focal point so her stomach would settle. The bottle of racmun spirits beside the patient's other knee caught her attention. She gazed at it, and took deep breaths.

"You can do it." Doc's voice seemed to come from far away. And then she heard new words, which made no sense at all. "...We're all done, except for one more deep patch here. Oh. This is bad..."

The patient's good knee jerked and hit the racmun spirit bottle. The bottle toppled before she could grab it. To Hendra's horror, the precious liquid pooled all over the floor.

"Oh no!" she gasped.

"What? Hendra, what's wrong?" Doc's sharp voice cut through her thoughts. Hendra stared at him, bewildered. She felt as if she'd been plucked from a filmy dream.

Dazed, she said, "The racmun spirits! It fell..." Distressed, she glanced back, but the bottle still stood upright. She blinked, feeling disoriented. "But..." The truth set in. It hadn't happened. Not yet. She'd seen the future again.

Doc frowned. "What did you see?"

She wasn't sure what to say. After a pause, she said, "I think...sometimes I get glimpses of the future." Did she sound crazy? Weakly, she added, "I think we'd better move that bottle."

Doc immediately moved the bottle to a safer location. His surprised gaze held hers. "You see the future?"

He believed her. No doubt lived in his steady gaze.

"Sometimes. It comes in flashes. I think it happens when I focus on something."

"What did you see?"

"You said we were almost done, except for one more deep patch. Bad, you said. Then Viln's good knee jerked and hit the bottle."

"Amazing."

"I guess we'll see if it really happens."

Doc attended the ugly wound, and to Hendra's amazement the scene replayed exactly as she'd seen it. Doc was so engrossed in cleaning the wound that he didn't realize he'd repeated the words she'd heard in her flash. But when Viln's knee convulsed, Doc glanced up and smiled. "You're amazing, Hendra."

She smiled, feeling inordinately pleased. "It's a kaavl gift, I think."

"I'm sure it is. You'd be an asset to the kaavl team."

"If only Mentàll wasn't so determined to protect me."

"You'd rather be there, wouldn't you?"

"I'm glad I can help you. But...yes."

"You don't need to paint it sweet. I'm a big boy." He finished wrapping the wound. He glanced at her. "I'd like to ask something again."

"What?" Anxiety threaded through her heart.

"Will you have dinner with me tonight? Just the two of us." Hope lived in his quiet voice. "No pressure. Just friends."

A blush warmed her cheeks. He wanted more. She could see that, and couldn't in good conscience lead him on. "I like spending time with you, Doc." A huge understatement. He also unnerved her more than any man she'd ever met. "But you have to realize..." She fumbled for more words. "I...can't. Not right now."

"Is that no forever? Or can I ask you again?"

Her heart pounded harder, and she licked her lips. "You can ask," she said softly. "But I won't guarantee I'll say yes."

"Fair enough." He smiled.

Hendra ducked her head and quickly gathered up the dirty supplies. She'd left an opening for him to ask again. Did she want him to?

Yes. At last, she admitted this frightening truth.

△ △ △ △ △

Methusal scouted with Riln again. His kaavl was adequate, but his company left much to be desired. He'd spotted an apte on the way into Quasr, and had seemed to take great delight in killing it. It made her feel sick. However, he'd also managed to trade the apte for fruit, which he shared with her.

On the way back to kaavl camp, under lowering gray skies, Methusal felt sleepy, and worked hard to keep pace with her Tarst partner. She yawned repeatedly, and wished it would get dark soon, so she could curl up and go to sleep. Three nights of poor sleep were taking their toll. What if Jascr tried to attack her in the middle of the night? Her pallet was on the far edge of camp. Maybe she should move it nearer to the fire, just to be safe.

Back at kaavl camp, she reported her information and then moved her rolled up pallet closer to the fire. Once it was moved, she just wanted to rest for a while; maybe even close her eyes and sleep. But Taltn was hobbling about, gathering firewood for the fire, and she didn't want him to do all of the work. So she helped him.

Jascr and Goric had killed a whip on the way back from Quasr. Appropriate. Jascr elbowed Methusal as he dropped the whip near the fire pit, and uneasiness knifed through her again.

Although she sent him a cold glare, pretending she wasn't afraid, it was a lie. She should have taken the Prophet's advice. She shouldn't have dropped the rochers on Jascr last night. If she hadn't, he would not have followed her this morning, or been humiliated, either. The war between them wouldn't have escalated to this dangerous level.

"Are you okay, Methusal?" Taltn wanted to know a little while later. "You're quiet today."

Dusk had crept in, and she'd set the whip to roasting over the fire. Maybe in two hours she could go to sleep. She stifled another yawn. "I'm tired. I haven't been sleeping well."

"Why not?"

She didn't want to tell her young friend about Jascr and Goric's threats. He'd be no match against either of them if he foolishly tried to defend her. So she settled for a partial truth. "I'm worried about my sister."

"Timaeus said the Eerporians should get to base camp soon. Maybe they'll help rescue her."

"I hope so." She hoped this with of all of her heart.

Clouds had begun to gather overhead in the deepening dusk. Hopefully it wouldn't rain tonight. A soft, chilly wind tugged at her hair, and she thought about pulling on another warm tunic. But she was too weary to move.

"Methusal." The Dehrien's voice startled her. "You are derelict in your duty, yet again."

Every tired molecule in her body rebelled at the thought of getting up and going anywhere, let alone facing another session with the Dehrien.

With a grumble, she climbed to her feet.

"Faster, Methusal. Your procrastination has already wasted enough daylight."

She bit back a snappy reply. After gathering up coltac leaves, she slowly followed him to the stream. The wound required little maintenance now. Hopefully she could speedily apply the coltac juice and zip back to the fire again.

Mentàll waited for her, as always, with his tunic off. But his hand kneaded at his shoulder again—the bad one this time. She'd noticed that he'd been massaging both shoulders a lot lately. Why would his wound hurt more now, than before?

Despite herself, she found that she wanted to know what was going on. Blood trickled from the upper portion of the wound, and she frowned. Not good. In fact, it looked worse than it had yesterday.

"Your wound is bleeding. What did you do today?"

"Nothing," he said curtly, and continued to knead the thick ridge of muscle.

"Put your hand down. I can't see." Not entirely true, but she was afraid that his pulling at the skin might aggravate the wound.

After a hesitation, he complied. She tested the skin around the wound. It didn't appear overly tight, but beneath...she frowned again. Beneath the skin, the muscles felt like hard knots. The wound went deep, she knew that—at least through the top layer of muscle. Could knotted muscles pull the wound apart again?

She remembered that he'd begun to rub his shoulders about the time he'd carried Kitran across town. Carrying the big man for so long had clearly strained his healing muscle tissue.

She wanted to ignore the problem, but the wound was worse. In fact, the skin had pulled apart in one small place. It was a quarter of a fingerbreadth wide. Would he need more stitches, or was the problem only the tense muscles?

Wondering about it, she gently pressed the ball of her thumb into the bunched muscles to the left of the wound, near his spine.

He drew in a sharp breath.

"Does that hurt?" The muscles felt as hard as a rock.

In a low, harsh voice, he said, "A little."

"The muscles are knotted. I think it's aggravating your injury, because it's bleeding again. The tight muscles may be pulling it apart."

"What do you suggest?" His voice now sounded cool.

She didn't answer for a moment, because the very thought of what she was contemplating made her want to bolt. She couldn't be *that* kind to the power hungry Dehrien. Could she? What if he got the wrong idea? Behran was the only man she'd ever touched in such a manner. *Help me, The One.*

Slowly, she said, "I could try to work out the knots. But don't get any ideas," she warned.

"Try it."

Methusal began to knead the area with her thumbs. *Why* had she offered to do this? She hated touching him. But she also couldn't deny that the healing, more tender part of her nature did want all of her patients, wild beast or otherwise, to heal and make a full recovery. Besides, wasn't she choosing kindness, like The One asked? She was doing the right thing.

Still, she felt uneasy as she concentrated on her task. His skin felt warm and firm, and the muscles beneath like smooth stone. And very tense. The knot nearest the wound slowly loosened, but the area around it felt so tight that it would probably seize up again if she stopped with that one knot. She worked the entire shoulder, carefully skirting the long gash, until the knots relaxed. There, almost finished. She smoothed on coltac juice.

Now, however, she noted that his left shoulder muscles looked extremely knotted, compared to the right. And she'd seen him massaging that side more. Stop, or go on? What would be the right thing to do? She wanted to ignore the question, but her conscience would not let her. And she didn't want the wound to worsen—could that happen, if the other shoulder was knotted up?

Methusal hesitantly offered, "I can work the other side, too. Or I can stop."

"Continue." She barely heard his quiet voice. It didn't sound like the Dehrien she knew. It disturbed her, and she felt the sudden urge to escape.

"Okay, then." Ordering gentleness into her fingers, she continued. "Don't expect this again."

After a moment, he shook his head.

It felt strange, to be deliberately touching him like this. It seemed wrong, somehow. This shoulder may not be medically necessary to massage—although, she supposed, tension on one side of his back could affect tension on the other, and therefore the injury. She tried to focus only on the movements, and to forget about whom she was touching.

His muscles slowly relaxed, and she moved to the tops of his shoulders. Her slim hands looked small curled over them. She worked back toward his spine. The muscles at the base of his neck felt like knotted rocks, just like the others had. Patiently she worked those out, too. She'd almost forgotten where she was, and who he was, because she was just focusing on the task at hand. Twilight deepened into a soft darkness, lit only by the faint glow of Ryon through the clouds.

There. Much better. She stroked the pads of her thumbs up his neck to test the tension there. To her shock, his large hand closed over hers.

"Stop." His voice sounded husky.

She froze. "What?"

His fingers remained closed over hers, and he took a deep breath. "That is enough."

Methusal tugged free. "All right," she agreed quickly.

"You have healing hands, Methusal." The Dehrien Chief stood abruptly, and pulled on his tunic. When he glanced at her, his pale gaze looked perplexed and disturbed.

Her heart beat more rapidly. Surely he didn't... "Don't think I was making an advance on you." Twice in as many days she had said that, she realized uneasily.

"I don't," he said harshly. "Goodnight."

He strode toward camp. Methusal stared after him. She had disturbed him, somehow. She hadn't imagined that flash of vulnerability just now.

Feeling unsettled, she splashed stream water on her face and headed back to camp. He wouldn't expect that treatment again, she comforted herself. It would be all right. *Just don't do it again.*

△ △ △ △ △

No rochers infested Methusal's pallet when she went to bed. She edged her coverlet as close to the fire as she dared and closed her eyes. The flames flickered orange images through her closed lids, and the warmth made her sleepier than she had felt all day. In only a moment, she fell asleep.

The prison door clanged open, letting in a stream of light. Deccia cringed against the back wall of her cell. She felt cold. So cold. Frost seemed to seep into her very marrow, and she couldn't remember when she'd last felt warm. The guard had taken her cloak a few days ago, with no explanation of why, and she had dared not protest.

Now he thrust his balding, grizzled head inside and cackled, "It is time. Come, my beauty."

Deccia wanted to scream. She'd rather stay down here and freeze to death than climb to that toasty hell in the General's quarters. He hadn't summoned her in days. She'd dared to hope that he had tired of her. Apparently not.

"Come!" the guard snapped. He reached beneath his cloak...her cloak...for the chains he carried.

Moving on slow, half-numbed legs, Deccia moved into the splash of light. When she reached the door, the short man chained her wrists, grabbed her arm, and hustled her down the hall. She stumbled, because her numbed muscles could not seem to coordinate together.

The little man paid no attention to her stumbling steps and ran down the corridor.

What in the world?

Deccia tripped and fell. The guard barely paused. He painfully yanked her arm until she staggered to her feet again. Then Deccia followed his mad dash up the stairs and down the familiar hallways to the General's office.

"General," the guard panted, thrusting her inside. "As you decreed."

The General turned on his heel with his finger in the air. "Ninety-nine." He wore his full uniform, including the decorated black cap.

The guard mumbled something obsequious. Bowing, he backed out of the door and closed it.

"Well." The invader's amber eyes ran down her body. For good or bad, they looked more focused than usual. He flicked a finger. "Sit."

Deccia sat in a chair. General Greisn perched on the edge of the desk. "You must be wondering why I haven't called for your delightful company."

Deccia said nothing. Agreeing or disagreeing could both set him off. She couldn't figure out how his insane, unpredictable mind worked.

"Of course you do." He pulled out a nasty smoke stick and parked it between his mutilated thumb and first finger. A blazing match lit it. He sucked up a lungful of smoke and stared at her without blinking. Long minutes—perhaps ten—crept by, and he continued to stare.

Deccia knew that he wanted to make her feel uncomfortable, and struggled not to cower.

Finally, he ground out his disgusting smoke stick. "Tell me." He crossed his arms and his amber eyes glittered. "Why shouldn't I kill you now?"

Her mouth went dry. He intended to kill her now? What could she say? The man was totally insane. He listened to no one's logic besides his own.

Had he already made up his mind to kill her? Did he want her to beg for her life, and then gleefully kill her anyway?

The General tapped his polished boot on the floor. "I am waiting."

Prodded by fear, Deccia spoke. "If you kill me, your leverage over the Koblani team will end."

With a sharp wrist flick, he unsheathed a long, deadly sword. He fingered the blade. Fear made Deccia feel sick. "Your Koblani team doesn't value your life. They submit to none of my demands." Blood appeared on the General's thumb. He stared at it, unblinking, as if looking at someone else's appendage. Then he licked it and turned his unfocused eyes upon her. "Tell me why I should keep you alive. Prove your worth to me."

Deccia forced out bold words. "When they defeat you, they will show mercy if you show mercy to me."

"Ha!" Mirth convulsed the man's flaccid features. He slapped his leg so hard the snap ricocheted through the room. Deccia flinched.

His gales of laughter at last quieted, and he stared at her again. He smiled. "I will keep you alive for one more day."

She felt even more uneasy.

His smile stretched wider. "I will keep you alive so that you and your sister can share the same cell. When I kill her, you will witness it."

Horrified, she said, "What do you mean? Have you captured Methusal?"

"I am about to devour your fabled kaavl team whole. I have two Tarst kaavl prisoners. They told me all I wished to know."

"No."

"Yes. So I will keep you alive for one more day, so you can witness her humiliation and defeat."

"You won't..."

"I will crush them beneath my boot!" Spittle foamed at the corners of his mouth. "All who defy me must die!"

Her heart pounded harder.

His unfocused eyes landed upon her again. "Tell me you are grateful." He fingered his sword again.

"For what?"

"Allowing you to live one more day!" he screamed.

Deccia licked her dry lips. In this unpredictable rage, he might do anything. Even go back on his word not to kill her right now. She whispered, "I am grateful."

The General thrust the sword behind him, onto the desk, and advanced toward her. "Prove it."

A sinking sensation emptied Deccia's stomach. She stumbled backward, out of the chair. "No."

He plodded toward her with a twisted, maniacal grin. "Yes."

"*No!*" Methusal screamed, and bolted upright. "*No,*" she whimpered. "Please The One, *no!*" Camp lay quiet and still around her. No one stirred. Dull embers glowed in the fire.

She scooted back under her covers and curled up into a tight ball. Tears streamed down her cheeks, and she prayed as hard as she knew how for her twin. For The One to deliver and protect her tonight.

And she longed for Behran to come and comfort her—even if it was only in her dreams.

He did not.

CHAPTER TWENTY-FOUR

DAY 21

METHUSAL SLEPT ONLY IN SHORT fragments after the nightmare about Deccia. A cold, drizzly dawn awakened her for the final time. She felt so tired that she could barely think straight.

Worry for Deccia twisted like a physical pain inside of her. Again, she prayed for her twin's protection.

Details of the dream returned, too. The General had boasted that he'd forced the Tarst to talk. Did he really know the location of kaavl camp?

Methusal pulled on her cloak and moccasins, rolled up her pallet, and walked over the muddy ground to the stream. She should warn Mentàll. Of course she hoped her dream was only a nightmare, but what if it was more? Deccia had confirmed that at least one of her nightmares had come true.

She splashed cold water on her face and filled her water skin. Then she went in search of the Kaavl Commander.

She found him near the fire, securing his pack. Memories from last night swept back in a flood, and her steps involuntarily slowed. She felt uneasy, remembering how she had massaged his shoulders. How many people had been kind to him in his life? His mother, of course. And what about the women he took on occasion? Or did they use him, as he surely used them?

What if he'd taken everything the wrong way, after all?

"Methusal." His short, cool look dismissed her.

She relaxed. Nothing had changed. "I had a dream last night." Cold rain pattered onto her face.

"I have no time to discuss your nighttime fantasies."

Relief disintegrated into annoyance. "Some of my dreams are real. They come true."

A faint, nasty smile tugged at his lips. "Which ones?"

"I'm trying to warn you! Why do you have to be such a wild beast?"

"Tell me, then, and hurry up. I have no time to waste."

"In my dream the General said he'd extracted information from the Tarst prisoners. He knows where kaavl camp is."

Mentàll knotted his pack. "You want me to believe your dreams are prophetic."

"Not all of them are. But yes, I think this one is." The dripping rain fell faster.

"You have warned me. Your duty is done." He turned away, clearly dismissing her.

The arrogant man. "What are you going to do about it?" she challenged, following him.

He suddenly turned, and she backed up at the snarl on his face. "I will *not* confide my plans in you, Methusal. Go about your duties. When I require your services, I will call on you."

"Require...my services?" She trembled with anger. "How dare you talk to me like that?"

"I speak the truth. As always." His lips curled. "It is hard to hear, though, isn't it? For one as prideful and arrogant as you."

"I am not prideful *or* arrogant!"

"You have proven nothing different to me."

"What about last night?" she cried out, and then clamped her mouth shut.

His looked away. That appeared to have hit a nerve, but as she watched, his face hardened. If she didn't know better, she'd think he was purposefully reminding himself, yet again, why he hated her so much.

"You did what was required. No more."

"You whip..."

"Choose insubordination." He smiled nastily. "I would be happy to chain you to kaavl camp." He stepped closer, clearly attempting to intimidate her. "Is that your wish?"

"Step off," she snapped. "Every kind act is wasted on you, isn't it? *You're* the arrogant one. Do you think you deserve *any* kindness? No!" She clenched her fists in the increasing downpour and left him.

As she stormed for her pallet, Goric stuck out his foot, tripping her. Methusal fell hard, and her hands squished into the mud.

"You slug!" Coming back up, she grabbed him by the tunic.

"Thusa!" Taltn said, stopping her. "Don't do it."

Methusal shoved Goric, and sent him flying backwards on his boulder. Shaking with rage, she scrambled to her feet and ran to the stream. She wanted to be alone. Why did every whip in the world have to attack her? And it was raining! She hated the cold and the wet.

She burst into tears and huddled on a stone near the creek. Her head ached with fatigue, and the tears made her brain throb with even thicker misery. A thought crossed her mind, and she choked out a laugh. "And it's my birthday!"

"Your birthday!" Taltn exclaimed.

Methusal swiped the tears from her eyes. "Shh!" She shot an uneasy glance toward camp. She didn't want Goric, Jascr, or anyone else to know anything so personal about her.

"Why?" With a perplexed frown, Taltn squatted beside her. He wasn't holding his crutches today. His ankle must be feeling better.

"Because no one cares."

"I care," he said gallantly.

"Thanks, Taltn." She sniffed, and tried to stop crying. But the tears continued to leak down her cheeks.

"I heard what you said," he offered. "About your dream. Do you really think the invaders know where camp is?"

"They might."

"I'll scout now, and report back to you. In the meantime," he thrust a dried piece of wild beast at her. "Happy birthday, from me."

Methusal smiled through her tears. "Thank you, Taltn." He grinned back, and darted off. A sweet boy. And she felt grateful beyond measure for his friendship.

$$\Delta \; \Delta \; \Delta \; \Delta \; \Delta$$

Taltn reported an "all clear," but he hobbled a little when he returned to camp.

"Use your crutches," she fussed. "And soak your foot in the stream."

Even though Taltn had seen no invaders, Methusal still felt apprehensive. She folded her extra bedding and clothes into her pack and filled her water skin, just in case they had to flee.

Mentàll gave Methusal no scouting orders, so she was forced to uneasily wander around camp all day. The Kaavl Commander wanted to punish her, of course. But just for that small bit of insubordination this morning? Or was it a general principle sort of thing?

His few glances after their earlier altercation had continually speared dislike, like an ice pick, through her soul. Again, it almost seemed like he was trying to remind himself, over and over again, why he should despise her. It unnerved her, and made her feel more on edge than ever. She was glad when he finally took off for some unknown—likely nefarious—mission at midmorning. Jascr and Goric left, too, so she felt safe alone at camp with Taltn.

Cold rain drizzled all day long. Methusal huddled under a small, protected ledge up in the hills with Taltn and ate dried rations for lunch. A wet, miserable twenty-first birthday, to be sure.

They watched the kaavl team members straggle back into camp at mid-afternoon, looking drenched and miserable. There would be no fire tonight, and she and Taltn shared the only dry spot around. The Dehrien Chief entered camp. His bleached leather pants and white-blond hair made him distinctive, although he wore a dark brown cloak. He wore no hood, though, unlike the other team members. It just proved that he, like a wild beast, was at home in the elements.

"Should we go down?" Taltn wondered.

"No. Why be miserable and wet when we can be miserable and dry?"

"Good point." Taltn rested his chin on his drawn up knees. His crutches lay beside him, and so did their packs. No sense letting them get soaked, Methusal had reasoned earlier.

Goric, Jascr, Riln, and Tabor had arrived. She scanned the plain, searching for the last team. Wortn was on it, and so was another Dehrien. The rain fell from low, dark gray clouds that seemed to touch the plains to the far west. Nothing. She saw no one.

Maybe they had decided to circle in from the east and hug the northern mountains. A stone outcropping obscured her vision, so Methusal mentally carried by placing herself at the edge of the outcropping, and peered around it. Sure enough. Stealthy movements caught her eye. Two men in dark clothing were approaching. She almost relaxed out of kaavl, but one of the tiny men raised his arm.

The man wasn't wearing a cloak. And neither was his partner. Her heart beat faster. They wore all black.

Invaders! Quickly, she scanned for more men, and then fear pumped more adrenaline into her heart. Two more Zindedis trailed the pair she'd just seen. But far worse, six crept up on kaavl camp from the northwest. They were only a minute away, running time.

"Invaders!" she whispered.

"What?"

"Invaders! Taltn, run. Don't look back. You know where to meet up, don't you?"

"Yes." Fear, and then determination blazed in the boy's eyes. He grabbed up his pack just as Methusal vaulted down from the ledge, dragging her pack with her. A last quick glance backward spotted Taltn hobbling up the hill, heading east. Injured as he was, Methusal was thankful he'd get a head start on the invaders.

She slithered down the slippery slope because it was the shortest, most direct path into camp. She could yell a warning, but she didn't want to alert the invaders.

She sprinted into camp and almost barreled into Jascr and Goric. "Invaders," she panted.

Jascr sent her a hard, disbelieving glare, but she didn't care.

The Kaavl Commander looked up at her fast approach, and frowned when he saw her expression. "What?"

"Invaders. Less than a minute away, running time."

"Break camp!" Mentàll's low voice carried to all. "Now."

Methusal sprinted for the hills.

△ △ △ △ △

Methusal never did find Taltn. It was like he had dropped off the face of the earth. Maybe that was a good thing, because two invaders dogged her footsteps for over three hours through the pouring rain. She finally lost them. But by then her lungs burned and her legs ached. Finally, she could head directly for the new camp. She was more tired than she'd ever felt before in her life. Dusk turned into twilight when she reached the small, rocky gorge that would serve as temporary kaavl camp.

She felt lucky to have found it, but she'd smelled smoke drifting on the air, and had guessed it led to the camp. It had. Although how a fire could burn in this damp, she had no idea; not until she climbed down into the gorge and discovered that the fire was burning in the entrance of a deep cave. All of the kaavl team huddled around it, including Taltn.

"Thank goodness!" Methusal sat next to the boy. Taltn had pulled off his moccasin, and his ankle looked swollen in the dim, flickering light. He'd angled his leg out of the cave, so the cold rain spattered down on the injury. It dripped onto her pack, too, since there was no room to place it inside. "Did invaders chase you?"

"No. If you hadn't told me to run when you did, though, I could be dead."

"I'm glad you're all right." The fire felt warm after hours of running through the freezing rain. She held out her cold hands.

"A free cave is ten lengths that way," Taltn pointed. "You could put your pack inside so it doesn't get wetter."

"Good idea." Maybe her pallet could dry out a little before she went to bed, too. Unlikely, but worth a try.

Using the last, faint rays of daylight, Methusal found the tiny, narrow cave. She wondered if any animals were living inside it. She tossed in a few rocks, but nothing ran out. Satisfied, she unrolled her pallet, grabbed up grain discs and a dried meat strip, and returned to the warm fire.

Everyone but Taltn ignored her, which was fine with her. The men boasted about six invaders they'd killed on the way here. They'd done it by playing a vicious game of apte and whip through the rocky mountains. That idea hadn't even occurred to Methusal. The thought of killing anyone—even the invaders—still made her feel sick.

Physical exhaustion, coupled with too many nights of too little sleep soon caught up to her, and she fell silent. Her eyelids felt unbearably heavy. Maybe she should go to bed.

As if in another dimension, she heard Jascr and Goric say goodnight. Taltn whispered goodnight to her and went with them. A little while later, the remaining men made leaving noises to Mentàll.

With a sharp, indrawn breath, she opened her eyes. The men were leaving. This was Mentàll's cave.

She did not want to be the last one here and left alone with him. So she staggered to her feet and stumbled after Riln down the slope and into the rain.

A cold, icy wind swirled through the dark gorge, chasing her into her quiet, empty cave. Shivering, she quickly crawled beneath the ledge outcropping, and then slipped inside her coverlet and wriggled into the narrow cave behind it. The cave wasn't too deep, but at least it covered her to her shoulders. And the ledge sheltered her head from the rain.

But she was so cold! Putting on an extra tunic for the night would be a good idea. She reached for her pack. The drawstring felt loose in her hand. Hadn't she tied it again after pulling out her rations? Maybe not. She pulled it open and felt inside for the garments.

Tiny feet skittered across her wrist, and then a sharp nip bit the back of her hand. "*Ow!*"

More tiny jaws bit her hand; a multitude of them, all at the same time. She tried to brush them off, but the creatures seemed to be in a mad frenzy. They viciously bit her hands multiple times. Then Methusal felt something creep across her stomach, and another up her back. They were in her coverlet, too.

With a sob, she lunged out of the cave and swept her arms over her body. At least a dozen of the horrible creatures clung to her clothes by their strong jaws. They bit her as she knocked them free. Then she yanked her coverlet out and whipped it violently into the drizzling rain. A faint light— Ryon, behind a cloud—illuminated dozens of the nasty creatures scuttling down the rocky hillside.

Now for her pack. That was harder, and took more time. Every item had to be removed, and she had to keep sweeping the rochers out of the cave, because they did not like the rain.

By the end, Methusal wept in misery. The stupid rochers kept coming in. They would not leave! *Goric and Jascr!* She wept harder, fists clenched in fury. Vengeful scenarios swam through her head.

Finally, feeling delirious and utterly exhausted, she sniffled into silence. Rain dripped down outside, making tiny splashes on the rocks. The bitter wind swirled in, too, making her shiver. She sat under the outcropping, but didn't dare slide back into the cave, because a number of the rochers had scuttled back there to safety. So she'd sleep out here, in the freezing cold.

She closed her eyes, too exhausted to move anymore. Too exhausted to cry...to do anything. As she drifted toward sleep, voices tickled her ears.

"I heard a scream." Goric's voice.

"She'll do more than that when we're done with her," Jascr snickered. "Happy birthday, Methusal!"

"But..."

"Are you an apte?" Jascr sneered.

"No. I hate her, too. But maybe this is taking things too far."

"Either you're with me, or you're not."

Silence elapsed. And then a mumbled, "Okay."

"We'll wait a few more hours, until everyone's asleep. I get first crack at her. Time to *pay*, Methusal," Jascr said with a vicious chortle. "Time to pay."

Methusal struggled to pry her eyes open. Had she actually heard their voices? Or had it been a dream? Her eyes slid shut again, too tired to care. Surely Jascr and Goric wouldn't attack her in the night, in a rain storm...

She drifted toward a comforting tendril of sleep.

Rocks clattered down the hill, and she gasped in a cold breath of air.

What was that? The conversation flashed back.

Could it be true?

Her brain felt fogged. She couldn't think clearly.

By sheer force of will, she crawled forward and stuck her head out into the rain. Her thoughts finally crystallized, and she shivered, feeling cold, wet, and miserable.

She intensified into kaavl to listen. No one moved on the hillside. Maybe a small animal had dislodged the rocks. She shifted her hearing to Jascr's cave.

"Taltn's got the right idea," Goric mumbled. "I'm going to sleep for a while. Wake me up when it's time."

Jascr chuckled.

The tiny hairs on Methusal's arms stood up. She hadn't imagined it. They would attack her tonight. In an hour. Maybe two. But she was too tired to keep watch.

Helpless tears slipped down her cheeks. Her brain was completely foggy with fatigue.

Stay awake. She had to stay awake. That meant she had to get out of her cave and away from her beckoning pallet.

If she wandered aimlessly in the drizzling rain, Jascr and Goric would never find her.

The cold permeated her bones. Shuddering, she ducked back under the outcropping. Her face and scalp felt like ice. Did she want to get sick?

She laughed a little. It sounded slightly hysterical to her own ears. Who would care for her?

No one. It seemed both inordinately funny and sad at the same time. Mentàll would have to deal with his wound alone tonight. That would serve him right.

Mentàll. It seemed strange that he hadn't ordered her to tend his wound tonight.

An idea glimmered. Maybe she should go offer. Taking care of the Dehrien's wound would kill time, take her out of this cave, and keep her awake, too. Methusal shivered. And he had a fire. Maybe while she was there, she could come up with her next plan of action.

Mind made up, she grabbed coltac leaves and stepped into the icy, drizzling rain.

△ △ △ △ △

Aali sat alone at the table that night. She didn't know where Behran or Hendra were. Dastn, on the other hand, had taken great pains to give her a wide berth today, although he was still watching her. His glances felt much different than Pogul's, though. Dastn's were protective and alert. He would not neglect his duty to her uncle. It didn't matter what he felt for her personally.

She didn't like the idea of Dastn being mad at her, but she had rudely ordered him to step off. Even though he continued to watch her, he was never close. He didn't ask to eat with her. He never spoke to her. And he let enough space exist between them that when the opportunity arose to save Deccia and all of Koblan, she knew she could easily escape.

Aali fingered her kaavl stick and eyed Pogul across the dining tent. He watched her. A mean expression curled back his thick lips. He was waiting, just as Dastn had predicted, biding his time to assault her again.

She spooned up another bite of Aenill's delicious pudding, but it was difficult to enjoy it.

Dastn had told Erl about Pogul's attack, which had made everything so much worse. Pogul lost his easy scout job, and now he had to serve on Erl's war team. At least that meant he'd be gone from camp often. But she felt the hatred smoldering in him now, like a living, breathing beast. It was worse than before. He wanted to hurt her.

After clearing her place, Aali continued to sit in the eating area. It was either do that or retreat to the safety of her tent for the rest of the night. Neither sounded like much fun.

"Aali." Behran said.

"Hi!" With a grin, she looked up. At least Behran was still her friend.

Behran looked better now, but he still winced when he moved too quickly. "What's up?" He sat across the table from her.

"Not much," she said brightly. She spotted Timaeus across the tent. Rain gleamed in his dark hair, and he carried a plate heaped with food.

He sat next to Aali. "The Eerporians should arrive in two or three days."

"And then we'll be able to rescue Deccia?" she deduced eagerly.

"I don't know. I hope so." Worry lines wrinkled Timaeus' brow all the time now, and his dark eyes looked bleak. Aali wanted to comfort him, even though she worried terribly about her sister, too. She patted his arm.

"She'll be okay, Timaeus. Deccia is strong."

He nodded, but said nothing. He ate quickly, and slashed into his meat with short, vicious knife strokes. Aali wondered if he imagined he was flaying into the General with that knife.

A cold breeze lifted the awning, and she shivered. Clouds obscured the moon, and rain pattered outside. The damp seemed to seep into her bones. She could never get completely warm on nights like this.

Hendra joined them a little later, and so did Dastn. He sat near Timaeus, and spoke to him in low tones.

Aali cleared away plates as people finished their meal. Popping up and down from the table gave her something to do. Everyone was so quiet!

After she'd cleared the last plate she sat quietly, too, but only for a few deadly boring minutes. It all seemed so awful, suddenly. And unmanageably depressing.

"We're a bunch of slugs," she said. "Just sitting here, like we're dead, or something. Let's sing."

"Not much to be happy about," Timaeus said, and abruptly stood.

"Timaeus! I'm sorry," Aali leaped up too, but he raised a hand. He wanted to be alone. "She's my sister, too," she said, with wobbling lips.

"Maybe singing's not the ticket, Aali," Dastn said grimly. With Timaeus gone, only a short length of bench separated them. She missed his easygoing grin. And the way he used to tease her. It was her own fault, of course. She'd told him to step off and never return. Unfortunately, that didn't make her feel any better.

"Obviously," she said.

"How about we play Truth or Lies," Behran suggested.

"Good idea," Aali agreed. "I'll go first. Behran, when did you reach the Bi-Level? And when did Thusa?"

He grinned. "On the same day."

Aali looked at Hendra and Dastn. "Truth, or lie?"

Both agreed it was the truth, as it was.

"Okay, Hendra, here's one for you," Behran said. "Why won't you eat a meal with Doc? I've heard him ask you twice now."

Hendra flushed. "I...I just don't want to," she stammered.

"Because he has red hair?" Aali supplied helpfully. "Or maybe he has wild beast breath?"

Hendra glanced sideways, into the night, as if she wanted to flee. "Something like that," she said softly.

Behran said, "I think that is a lie."

Hendra's eyes filled with tears. She leaped to her feet and rushed into the dark, drizzling rain.

"Hendra." Behran said a soft word against himself and quickly followed her.

"Guess it's just you and me," Dastn observed. "Who will leave first?"

"You, of course," she said with narrowed eyes.

"I'll ask the question."

"Fine."

"What are you plotting?"

"Plotting!" she said indignantly. "I haven't done anything for days. How dare you accuse me?"

"Answer the question."

After a moment, she gave him a small smile. "You'll know when the time is right."

"I knew it."

She ignored this. "Now it's my turn to ask a question."

"Shoot. Or maybe I shouldn't say something so explosive."

Aali smiled, despite herself. "Maybe so. Here goes." She drew a deep breath, "Will you please stop being mad at me?"

He stared at her, clearly taken aback. In fact, she felt a little shocked by her own words.

She went on, "Even though I don't want you to spy on me for Uncle Erl, I want us to be friends again."

"So it's that easy."

"Yes. If you want it to be. Do you?"

He ran a hand down his face. After a moment he said, "You drive me crazy."

"So?" she said impertinently. "I drive lots of people crazy. Can we be friends again?"

"Is this an apology?"

"It's a peace agreement. You agree to give me space. Then we can be friends."

"No deal." He stood.

She frowned in hurt and surprise. "You don't want to be friends?"

"Friends apologize, Aali. They're not rude."

"Step off," she muttered.

"I think this is how our last conversation ended. Guess you're the last one standing." He strode into the night.

What had she just done?

Aali hated that he was angry with her. It hurt badly. And she missed his friendship more than she ever could have imagined.

Scuffling pebbles beneath her moccasins, she made her way to her tent. She was the first one in. She crawled inside and curled up into a small ball and pressed her hands to her face.

"I'm sorry, Dastn." she whispered. Her throat ached with tears. "I don't want you to be mad at me. But I have to help save all of Koblan."

△ △ △ △ △

"If you still require my services, I'm here."

Methusal stopped at the entrance of the Kaavl Commander's spacious cave. It was so different from her own tiny nest, which was barely sheltered from the rain. Here, the warm, welcoming fire still burned at the entrance, and she noticed for the first time that the cave extended several lengths back into the hillside.

Mentàll sat on a rock near the fire, writing on a parchment. He raised a hand, indicating that she should wait until he deigned to speak to her.

The warmth of the fire beckoned, and she eagerly held out her cold, rocher-bitten fingers to it. The heat made the bites burn.

At least now she could think more clearly.

She could not stay awake all night. And no one would hear her struggle when Jascr and Goric attacked her, either, because they'd probably creep up on her while she was sleeping and gag her. And what would happen next, she couldn't bear to think about. She needed to hide somewhere they wouldn't find her.

"I am ready, Methusal." Mentàll shucked off his tunic. He was still sitting, because the cave wasn't tall enough for either of them to stand. Ducking a little, she made her way over to him, coltac leaves in hand.

She said, "I see it's finally stopped bleeding." So the massage had done some good, after all. She squirted on the thick gel and ordered gentleness into her touch.

He said nothing, which she found rude. After all, she had come here of her own volition. And performed her duty like a good kaavl soldier. She wanted to make short work of the task, but at the same time she didn't want to return too quickly to her cave, either.

"There." She threw the leaves outside and rubbed the remaining juice over her still smarting hands, hoping for a little relief from the pain. She moved nearer to the fire, longing for the heat to warm her chilled bones and anxious heart. She still didn't know what to do about Jascr and Goric.

Mentàll pulled his tunic back over his powerful shoulders. His cool look dismissed her. "You may go."

"Thank you," she returned sarcastically. "But I'm freezing. Can't I stay here for a minute?"

That glacial gaze did not look welcoming. "By all means. I will enjoy your company." Mockery edged his words.

She turned away. This day kept getting worse and worse! She wouldn't beg, but he hadn't ordered her to go, so she'd stay for another minute. Unfortunately, she felt like a beggar soaking up scraps of warmth.

"No reply? No fiery comeback, Methusal?" The Dehrien Chief moved by her and tucked the parchment in his pack. He dropped onto a boulder near the cave entrance, directly in front of her.

Great. Now *he* wanted to torture her, too. Why had she come here?

Fiercely, she whispered, "Leave me alone." It really was too much. Her hands stung, she was freezing and in danger of being attacked by two men, she was worried about Deccia, and Kitran was dead. When would this war end? And it was her birthday! And that awful Dehrien chose right now to torment her still further.

Helpless tears welled in her eyes, and she averted her face, not wanting to let him see her misery. What satisfaction he'd feel if he saw them!

So, she'd go now and endure the cold. She'd be cold all night, anyway.

Tears teetered on her eyelids. She couldn't stop them! Throat aching, she quickly turned away from him.

"Warmed so quickly, Methusal?"

Not answering, she stepped out of the cave. Her vision blurred, so she couldn't see the dark, rocky hillside very well. Still, she stumbled on, anxious to flee. A stone that looked substantial rolled suddenly underfoot, and she slipped and fell hard on her hip. Pain smarted, and she couldn't swallow back her choking sobs any longer.

She struggled to her feet, but a hard hand gripped her upper arm. "Come up here." Mentàll hauled her back to the fire. "Sit down."

Methusal obeyed, but looked at the floor. She would not let him see her tears.

"Speak, Methusal." He sat on a nearby rock.

"No." Why wouldn't he leave her alone?

"Look at me."

After an unwilling moment, she wiped her cheeks and met his narrowed blue gaze. Wary hostility lurked there, but she sensed an odd reluctance, too, evidenced by his next words. "You are injured?"

"I'm okay," she denied.

"Your hands are bleeding."

She looked at them. Now dirt smeared into the welts left by the bug bites. She bit her lip, and several more silent, miserable tears ran down her cheeks.

He disappeared for a moment, and then reappeared with a shallow bowl filled with water. "Clean your hands before they become infected."

She washed off the dirt and a few imbedded pebbles. Her hands stung still more afterward. She pulled two coltac leaves from her pocket and broke the gel over her left hand, and then rubbed the two together, and the backs, too. They hurt, as if dozens of bugs were still biting her.

"Why are your hands bleeding?"

Methusal felt reluctant to reply. "Bug bites," she said at last.

"Only rochers leave bites like that. Where did you find them? In your cave?"

"Yes. Sort of." She didn't want to say anymore. The Dehrien Chief couldn't care less about her problems with Goric and Jascr.

"Your cave is infested with rochers?"

Methusal pressed her lips together.

Hard fingers lifted her chin, forcing her to meet his gaze. "Answer me when I speak to you, Methusal. The truth only." He removed his hand, to her relief.

She admitted quietly, "Bugs were in my pallet. I shook them off outside."

"Rochers live on the desert floor. Not here."

She bit her lip, but remained silent.

"Tell me how they got in your pallet," he ordered. "No more games, Methusal!"

"Jascr and Goric have been putting them in my pallet for the last week or more. Never so many. And now..." she paused, reluctant to tell him the rest.

"Now?"

"Now..." She blinked back more threatening tears. *Stop crying!* She couldn't believe she was about to tell him the rest, but the words tumbled out in a rush. "Goric hates me, and Jascr, well... I think...I heard them..."

He waited silently.

"I overheard them talking about me. They plan to attack me tonight. Jascr said it would be my b-b-birthday present!" She burst into a torrent of tears, feeling pathetic and embarrassed, but at her wit's end. "But I *can't* stay awake all night! I'm so tired..."

Mentàll uttered a series of harsh Dehrien curses and stood abruptly. She cringed, not sure if he was directing them at her. He stepped into the dripping rain—the only place where he could stand upright.

"Why didn't you tell me sooner?" He sounded furious.

"I hoped if I ignored it, they'd stop. And why would I tell you? You hate me. Why would you care?"

"I am in charge of order and discipline on this team. Insubordination... rape... how could I not care about that? It hurts our entire team!"

"I have no proof. And they'll just deny it."

Rain dripped through the Dehrien's blond hair, making it spike up. His hands clenched into fists. "I will deal with Jascr and Goric. Get your pallet. You will sleep with me tonight."

She gasped. "I won't!"

That pale gaze froze to ice. "Take your chances, Methusal. Jascr and Goric—or me."

"Can't you warn them off?"

"Of course. I will throw them off the team. And then what? They will hate you more, and now have nothing to lose. They will attack you in the night and not only violate you, but kill you."

True. Methusal could think of no response.

"Get your pallet."

To her complete surprise, the Dehrien accompanied her to her cave and waited while she gathered up her things. She shook out everything to get rid of the last of the rochers.

"Now go to my cave." He disappeared into the night.

Carrying her pack, Methusal navigated over the slippery rocks back to Mentàll's cave.

The firelight looked warm and welcoming. At least she wouldn't be cold tonight.

She crept inside, took note of where the Dehrien had spread his own pallet, and then found a corner as far away as possible, in the back of the cave. All the same, unease slid through her when she thought about spending the night alone with him.

A little of the warmth from the fire drifted back to her corner as she unrolled her coverlet. She lay down and curled up, pulling the damp leather blanket over her. Maybe she would be asleep by the time he returned.

She yawned. Exhaustion numbed her brain, but rightly or wrongly, she felt safe here.

Methusal drifted on the edge of slumber when Mentàll returned. His silent footsteps stopped at the end of her pallet, and she tensed. Silently, he watched her. Long moments passed, but she kept her breaths even, pretending to be sleep. He muttered something that sounded suspiciously like, "Happy birthday, Methusal," and moved to his own pallet.

After a moment, she heard the soft sounds of him pulling off his tunic, and then she closed her ears, not wanting to hear more. Silence fell. Warmth from the fire drifted in waves over her, and in the safe silence she fell into a deep, dreamless sleep.

Chapter Twenty-Five

METHUSAL AWOKE TO THE SOUND of a crackling fire. Pale, shadowed sunlight barely reached her corner of the cave. She felt relaxed and safe, and for the first time in many days, rested, too. She hadn't dreamed about Deccia. She wasn't sure if that was a good thing or a bad one. In her last dream, the General had threatened to kill her in one day. That day could be today. Surely if Deccia was in danger she would feel *something*. That knowledge, however, gave her little comfort.

Methusal heard a silent movement. Someone had stopped at the end of her pallet.

Last night's events rushed through her mind. She was in Mentàll's cave. And he stood over her now. Tensing, she kept her eyes closed.

"Get up, Methusal. Do not pretend to sleep, as you did last night."

Reluctantly, she opened her eyes. This part of the cave was high enough for him to stand with only a faint stoop. She wondered suddenly if he had watched her sleep this morning, while she lay defenseless and unaware.

Probably. Unease slid through her.

He watched her like a wild beast with an apte. "You are afraid. Do you believe I intend to take Jascr's place?"

"No."

Surprise flashed. "You trust me?"

Methusal sat up, but still held the coverlet close to her neck as a means of protection against both the cold morning air and Mentàll. "You will keep your promise to my father."

She hoped so, but didn't know. Not really.

"Yes." At last, he turned his back. "We are heading to base camp. Pack up."

Methusal quickly did so, and at the same time chewed on meat strips from her ration pack to satisfy the demanding rumbles in her stomach. As she exited from the cave, she realized how it would look if others saw her leave Mentàll's cave.

Heat burned her cheeks, and she glanced quickly around. After the cleansing pool incident, this would appear to be the ultimate moral failure on her part. To her relief, she saw no one. She heard them, though, around the next bend, near a large fire. Quickly, she made her way there. Early morning sunlight gilded the tops of the mountains pink, but the gorge lay in shadows. A clear, cold day. At least the rain had passed.

Mentàll said, "We will head now to base camp. Each team will take a different path, in case invaders try to follow. Be alert." His gaze rested upon her. "I see we are all here. We will leave shortly."

Methusal looked for Goric and Jascr, wondering if they were still in camp. Goric slouched on a nearby boulder, frowning. To her surprise, Jascr stood only a length away, and she caught his eye quite by accident. He scowled and moved away, but not before she saw the huge purple bruises darkening his jaw.

"Morning, Thusa." Taltn hobbled up, carrying his pack.

She nodded after the retreating Dehrien, remembering that Taltn had shared a cave with Jascr and Goric last night. "What happened?"

"Mentàll came looking for them last night." Taltn grinned. "Want the whole story?"

"Sure."

"I didn't hear the first part, because I was asleep. Scuffling woke me up, and when I opened my eyes, Mentàll had Jascr by the throat against the wall." Taltn lowered his voice, clearly immersing himself into the tale. "Quiet-like, but vicious, he said, 'What is your plan for Methusal?'

"'Nothing she doesn't deserve,' Jascr said. 'Since you won't keep her in her place, I will.'

"Mentàll must have tightened his hold, because Jascr turned purple, and his eyes bugged out. Then Mentàll hissed,

'Methusal is *mine* to deal with. I will do it in a way that pleases *me* most.' He shook Jascr hard.

"'You are an apte,' Jascr whispered. 'She scorns you. She mocks you. *I* scorn you.' He spit at him.

"Mentàll punched him hard, twice, and after a minute, let him go.

"Jascr said, 'When you're finished with Methusal, give her to me. I'll make that Rolbani—he said a bad word—pay.'

"Then Mentàll punched him so hard that Jascr's head snapped back. He said, 'You will *never* touch her! *Never.*' He slammed Jascr against the wall again and shook him by the throat. Deadly-like, he said, 'If you do, I will kill you. Do you understand?'

"Jascr looked scared for the first time. He gurgled, 'Yes.'

"Then Mentàll let him go, and Jascr collapsed on the ground."

Taltn grinned. "Goric hid in the back of the cave the whole time. And you can bet I stayed quiet, too. Then Mentàll snarled that Goric had better keep his place, too. When Goric whimpered that he would, Mentàll left."

Methusal smiled at the picture of Goric whimpering in the back of the cave. And she felt vindicated by the thought of Jascr lying crumpled and defeated on the floor. Not that Mentàll had done it solely for her, of course. Instead, according to Taltn's story, he alone wanted the full rights to torment her, and refused to allow anyone else that pleasure.

"Mentàll said they're both off the team," Taltn informed her. "When they get back to base camp, they'll transfer to Pan's warrior force."

"Good."

Taltn's smile faded. "What did Mentàll mean? When he said you're...his?"

That hadn't settled well with her, either. "He thinks because he saved my life once—twice, if you count rescuing me from prison—that the rest of my life belongs to him. You know, like the ancient legends say."

"Oh."

"The truth is, he wants revenge, and he won't let anyone else extract it from me except for him. That pleasure belongs only to him." Methusal hated the familiar, sick feeling of dread she felt when she thought about it.

"He hates you that much?" Taltn sounded both horrified and disbelieving.

"Yes. You heard how I defeated him in Rolban two and a half years ago?"

The boy nodded.

"He promised my father that he wouldn't harm me during the war. But when the war ends, so does his promise. I don't know what he'll do to me then." Methusal often wondered when and how he planned to attack her... And yet sometimes, she wondered if even Mentàll fully knew. Was his plan evolving over time, so he could slice closest and deepest to her heart?

"Are you sure?" Disbelief still lurked in Taltn's voice. Surely he didn't suffer from the same misguided hero-worship as Hendra!

"I'm sure he hates me. But I'll be ready to defeat him, no matter what he tries to do." Taltn's raised brow indicated he doubted the bravado in her words.

The warning blare of the slug monster shell made her jump.

"Invaders!" Taltn spun around.

Mentàll barked, "Split up by caves. Kill all invaders who follow. Do not let them find base camp. Go!"

Methusal slipped into kaavl. She heard the invaders now. About twenty of them, by the sound of it, and she scrambled up through the rocks to find a hiding place from which to attack. Taltn did the same, and hobbled away as fast as he could. Again, worry for her friend plagued her, and she prayed for his safe passage to base camp.

A group of invaders dropped into the rocky gorge, and Jascr and a few other bloodthirsty Dehriens rushed them. Guns blasted, but no kaavl player fell. Instead, the invaders fell to their quick kaavl knives. More invaders appeared, and streamed in from the north and south.

It was time for the kaavl team to lure the invaders further into the hills, and to separate them from their teammates. Little did the invaders know they were in for a deadly game of whip beast and apte through these rocky foothills. Even with the guns, the invaders had no hope of matching even a Quatr-level kaavl player in these mountains.

"Methusal." The Dehrien Chief stood on the hill just above her. An invader shouted, and he dropped down on the other side. A gun blasted.

Quickly, she followed.

"This way," he ordered.

Mentàll had commanded them to split up by caves. So she was paired with him for this frightening game. It reminded her of the first invader attack, when they had traveled to Quasr over two weeks ago. Invaders had almost killed them both then. But now they were more experienced.

Methusal tried to swallow her fears as she followed the Dehrien Chief deeper south into the hills, heading away from base camp. A pack of invaders followed them. No doubt they'd seen Mentàll and wanted to earn the bounty on his head.

She sharpened her hearing, listening as she ran, while at the same time looking for likely hiding places from which they could attack the enemy. Grunts punctuated the Zindedis' progress, and one said, "The blond one. Take his head to the General."

"The girl's, too. Match it with her sister's when the General kills her." A wheezing laugh.

A chill rippled through her. Never. The invaders would *never* take Koblan. And they would never kill her, Deccia, or anyone else she loved, as long as she could do anything to stop them.

She noticed twin peaks rising ahead. They were the midpoint of the Quasr Mountains. She'd never been this far east before. She hurried on, wondering when Mentàll would decide to stop. He ducked around a corner, and she stopped just short of bumping into him, although her sleeve brushed his.

It was the perfect place. They could escape uphill, or fight in any direction.

"How many?" the Dehrien muttered.

Methusal easily completed the visual carry. "Six. They're splitting up so they can surround us."

"Where?"

"Two south, two north, and two straight for us, on either side of this rock."

"I hope Kitran taught you well."

Methusal tensed, hearing footsteps, but saw the invader before he rounded the corner. She saw his black, narrowed eyes, the gun held at the ready, and his crouched, mincing steps. His neck was vulnerable. Moving with fast precision, she rounded the corner and hurled her knife straight into the invader's exposed flesh.

He gurgled, dropped to one knee, and then collapsed. The life blood ran out of his body. Methusal's hand shook as she freed her blade, grabbed the gun, and slung it over her pack. *Don't think about it,* she told herself. *Not until it's over.*

Mentàll had killed his attacker as well, and they moved together to higher ground and waited for the remaining Zindedis. Methusal whispered locations, and after a series of quick turns and swift knife thrusts, the other four fell as silently as the first two had. Mentàll killed three with cold, brutal efficiency. Methusal killed one more.

By now, she felt on the verge of throwing up. She had never killed anyone before. And now *two.* She followed Mentàll to still higher ground, to a rocky hillside located just below the snow covered twin peaks. The wind blew in harsh, freezing gusts up here. Why had he chosen to climb this high? And why had he stopped?

The Dehrien grabbed her elbow and pulled her toward a dark, narrow sliver. It was an opening to a cave.

"One more," he breathed, staring at her. The strange, triumphant light in his eyes frightened her. One more? Who did he mean? *Her?*

And then she heard a scrabble of rocks above them. She'd missed a soldier. This one must have arrived from a different direction. She focused harder into kaavl, and listened.

Only one system of movement reached her ears. He was the last Zindedi on this high, lonely mountain.

The Dehrien Chief pulled her further back into the cave and positioned himself at the cave's entrance, sword at the ready. The invader threw a rock, obviously trying to trick them into exposing their position, but Mentàll did not move. He flicked a glance at her, and she pointed up and to the right, and lifted two fingers, for two lengths. He nodded, and then turned out, sword flashing, into the early morning sun.

A gun fired. And then nothing.

Was Mentàll dead? Horror filled her.

Focusing again, she forced her mind into another visual carry, but it ended up being unnecessary. The Dehrien Chief reentered the cave, wiping his sword on his breeches. Blood also smeared his tunic sleeve. Methusal looked down. Blood stained her clothing, too.

She turned, and was abruptly sick. She shuddered uncontrollably, and clutched at a rock imbedded in the cave wall. The scenes of death and gore she made happen made her heart clench, and she vomited again, gasping. Tears dripped down her cheeks.

The Dehrien watched her. "You did well."

"I'm a good murderer?" Methusal's nose and mouth dripped.

He said nothing for a moment, and then, "I hear water."

Methusal stumbled after him, further into the cave. Pockets of light shone down where breaks in the cave ceiling let in the sun, much like their caves in Rolban did. She saw the tiny stream of clear, fast running water, and knelt to wash her face and hands. She drank deeply of the cold water, too, trying to cool the scorch in her soul.

She held her head in her hands. *I'm so sorry, The One! I'm so sorry. Please forgive me.*

"Self-defense is not murder, Methusal."

She squeezed her eyes shut. "I know."

"You did what you had to do to survive."

She said nothing, but her throat ached.

"The war is not over." His voice was hard. "You will kill again to save Koblan."

"I don't want to kill anyone!" she cried. "I'm not cruel and heartless like you!"

"Get up, Methusal. It is time to move on." The cold words felt like a slap in the face.

She stood with a glare.

He said, "And I am not a murderer, either."

"Right," she retorted. "You started the war in Rolban. Five people died. And let's not forget Renn and Liem!"

"I killed none of them." He frowned, clearly not pleased to be confronted with his past failures. "And as you know, Verdnt, the invader, started the war."

She could not believe his audacity. How dare he try to escape blame for the two hour war on Rolban? "You intended to take over Rolban! Your Alliance was only a cover, remember? You used it to send your best warriors, disguised as *merchants* to my home. Did you think we'd let you take over without a fight? If so, you're just as crazy as the General!"

"The General wants ore and power. My people were dying!"

"No, they weren't." The words flipped out before she remembered the truth.

The icy condemnation in his eyes hardened into disgust.

She remembered the horrible conditions she'd witnessed in Dehre during the Inter-Community Kaavl games several years ago. She remembered the filth and hatred, too. And Hendra had said they had suffered through several droughts.

"I'm very sorry they were suffering so terribly. But you never asked for help, did you? Because you hate Rolban."

"Did you have enough food to help?"

"No," she admitted, remembering how low the inventory had been in the supply room. "Verdnt must have told you that."

He didn't deny it.

"And," she continued, "we didn't have much food to eat the next year, either, because you tricked Petr into giving you our seed grain. The uncured grain only gave us half a crop."

"And that same seed grain saved the lives of my people."

She was glad the Dehriens had not starved. But still...

"So you see," Mentàll said harshly, "Rolban would never have helped us."

She threw up her hands. "If we'd had our seed grain, maybe it could have yielded a huge crop for both of us. If we'd known about Dehre's problems, we could have tried to share more. We did sign the Alliance, you know. We wanted to take steps to build trust and trade agreements between our communities."

His expression remained icy and impassive, as if he did not believe one word she said. In exasperation, she said, "Mentàll, the hatred from the Great War had ended. I mean, it had until you rekindled it. But the hatred never died with you, did it? You hate Rolban. Why?"

"You are wasting time by dredging up the past," he snapped. "It is done. Rolban won. Let it go."

"Like you have? You hate me, and why? Because a girl kicked a death blow to your pride."

He advanced on her. "I despise you for more reasons than I can *count*."

Methusal held her ground. "Will you break your word to my father?"

His fists clenched, and his gaze froze fear into her veins.

"One day that promise will no longer protect you," he said softly.

Methusal met him eye for eye, but shivered inside. She was relieved when he turned away. However, their war of words had accomplished one positive thing. It had helped her to forget, for a while, the carnage they had left behind.

She followed him back to the mouth of the cave. There the Dehrien stopped and looked up the hill, to the twin peaks towering high above them.

The unholy gleam in his eyes returned. He murmured, "This is it."

What did he mean? Methusal looked at the two peaks more closely. Two peaks, just like on his medallion—and like something else, too. She glanced at his neck, where the silver chain was barely visible, hidden beneath his tunic.

"The Quasr twin peaks are on that medallion you wear," she said.

"What?" He blinked, as if she had broken his concentration.

"Your medallion. It's from Quasr, isn't it?"

He did not pull it out, but his thumb touched the lump under his tunic. "Quasr? No. It is from Rolban."

"Rolban's symbol is three peaks. Not two."

His eyes dilated, and for a second he looked totally disoriented. "Quasr?"

"Who gave it to you?" Methusal dared to ask.

"My mother." His grating voice sounded perplexed.

"But wasn't she from Dehre?"

Mentàll dropped his hand, and a cold mask descended over his features. "We will take a break here."

He was surprised to learn that his medallion had come from Quasr. Methusal stared at the Quasr mountains again. The peaks had reminded her of one other thing, too...

In a flash, she remembered her tablet necklace, which Mentàll had taken from her over two years ago. And she also remembered the Dehrien legend that her ancestor, Jotham, had scratched the location of the *Second Book of Kaavl* on the back of it. Two mountain peaks were etched into it, as well as additional unreadable scratches, ending with the letter "r." Quasr.

Were Quasr's twin peaks where Jotham—or his Dehrien captors—had hidden the book? Mentàll and Verdnt had originally thought the clue had pointed to Rolban. But had Jotham or the Dehriens hidden the book in *this* cave, of all places?

Had Mentàll come here on purpose?

Methusal's heart suddenly pounded harder, and she slowly moved back into the cave. The ancient book was what Mentàll was searching for. His prize. And it must be part of his unknown, treacherous plot, too. It must be part of the reason why he'd been in Quasr in the first place, trying to meet with its chief.

She could find the book. Excitement pumped through her. She could find it first, and hide it in her pack before he ever knew she'd found it.

Methusal scanned the cave walls as she slipped further inside. The book had probably been hidden on a ledge, or in a protective crack in the rock. It would be in a location high enough from the ground to be protected from a flood, but not near a ceiling crack, which would let in rain.

Mentàll had reentered the cave and now scanned the walls, too.

Methusal followed the stream deeper into the cave. Light still filtered in through cracks here and there, dimly lighting her path.

Nothing... Nothing.

The cave ended just ahead, and she spotted a rough shelf outcropping. *A bundle rested upon it.* In a step, she pulled down the package. A rectangular object, two handbreadths wide and three high, was wrapped in a protective layer of leather.

Holding her breath, she reverently pushed back the dusty wrapper. It was an old book, covered in dark leather. Words tooled in silver ore read...

Second Book of Kaavl

Methusal pulled it to her chest, heart racing. She'd found it. The book the Dehriens had stolen from Rolban and from her ancestors. Here it was, at last.

The hair on the back of her neck prickled up. She'd been so excited about finding the book that she'd momentarily forgotten about Mentàll's presence. Her mortal enemy. Rolban's mortal enemy. And another Dehrien.

If only she had easy access to her pack, she could slip the book inside without him noticing.

He still may not realize that she had found it. Maybe he wasn't even looking at her. He was probably still scanning the walls, as she had done.

Quietly, she shrugged down her shoulder and lowered the gun and her pack with one hand to the floor. The other protectively held the book tightly pressed against her. With a casual foot, she kicked the pack open

She didn't hear Mentàll. So she stood very still, listening. And then she heard his silent breaths, handbreadths behind her. She froze.

"Find something, Methusal?" he said silkily.

A hard hand gripped her shoulder, forcing her to turn.

Everything within her screamed out a silent, *No!* She had found it. It rightfully belonged to the Maahrs and Rolban. A Dehrien would never steal it from a Rolbani again.

She glared. "Take your hand off of me."

Although he complied, Mentàll's gaze riveted upon the bundle in her arms.

"You found it." That icy gaze impaled her. "How did you know?"

"It was my necklace you stole. I'm not stupid, like you want to think."

His gaze returned to the book, as if drawn by a magnet. "I do not think you are stupid, Methusal. Quite the opposite."

He wanted the book. She saw it in the determined gleam in his eyes. She began to feel uncomfortable, and said, "It's time to go, don't you think?"

She reached for her pack, but his hand bit into her arm, stopping her. "Give it to me," he said softly.

Methusal froze. "I will not. I found it, and it belongs to Rolban. All your plotting and planning doesn't change that fact."

"Plotting? Planning?" His eyes narrowed. "Have you been *spying* on me, Methusal?" The last came out in a hiss.

Methusal sealed her lips.

He stepped closer, intimidating her by his sheer physical size. "What have you heard, Methusal?"

Through gritted teeth, she said, "Enough."

"Enough what?"

"Enough to know you've been looking for something here all along, before the war started. And that you've been trying to form alliances all over Koblan. That's why you met with Quasr's Chief, isn't it?"

He said nothing, but his pale eyes were slits.

"What's your plan, Mentàll? To seize power all over Koblan?" She laughed at the absurdity of it. "You have enough ego to think you could, though, don't you?" She stepped backwards, away from him, but her heel hit the wall of the cave. She was trapped. The only way out was past Mentàll. "If you want the book, you'll have to steal it, just like you've stolen everything else."

"I have stolen nothing."

"My necklace. And you tried to steal Rolban from us, too. That's your only way, isn't it, to get what you want? Force and manipulation!" Anger spurted through her words.

"Give it to me."

"I don't think so," she said through clenched teeth. Although she sounded confident, she didn't feel that way. How could she prevent him from taking it? He was a lot bigger than she was. And a lot stronger, too. Right now he towered over her. He was too close. But she wouldn't let him intimidate her.

"No?" His voice was soft.

"No."

He could kill her. He could easily kill her and take the book. Mentàll still possessed that thin, once illegal sword. Not to mention his knife. Both were razor sharp. He'd threatened her with the sword once. She didn't trust him. She knew he was capable of anything. And she stood in the way of his goal.

"Give me the book." Impatient anger bit through the words.

"Or what? You'll kill me? Doesn't your word mean anything?"

The bands of his neck tightened. She'd hit home. But still, he didn't come any closer. He didn't make a move to threaten her more than he threatened her now, with his close physical presence.

His pale eyes gleamed. "You will learn, Methusal, that I am a man of my word."

The book's rough leather ripped through her fingers. Still not stepping back, he moved it into her line of vision. "And you will learn one more thing. You are no match for me. Remember that." A twist of his shoulders, and he stalked away.

"You dirty *thief!*"

He turned back. "I found the cave, and I am the thief?"

"*I* found the book! It belongs to Mahre's family. *My* family. And Rolban. Not to you."

"It belongs to the Kaavl Master."

"Didn't you forfeit that title when you declared war on Rolban?"

"Verdnt declared the war."

"But it was your plan all along. You are a selfish, lying whip!" The inflammatory words erupted before she could stop them. Did she want the wild beast in him to attack her? No. She was just so angry that she couldn't seem to control her tongue. "But you're a coward," she told him. "Stealing is the whip beast's way. You have no honor."

His cheekbones seared red, and he slowly retraced his steps and stopped three handbreadths from her. He tossed the book to the side. "Then fight me for it," he said in a quiet, deadly voice.

"I can't fight you."

"You possess only one weapon, Methusal. Use it, and if you win, I will give you the book."

What weapon? She was confused. Kaavl? No. Her knife? Certainly not.

"You are a despicable man," she told him. "You have no intention of giving me that book."

"Why?"

"Because you want it. And you hate me."

"And you hate me."

"Then we're evenly matched on that score." She glared.

"You do not intend to fight for the book you profess to want so desperately?"

"I would if I could."

"If only you knew, Methusal."

What did he mean by that? Then it came to her. Words! All of their battles during the war had been with words. Why not this last, most important one? She hesitated, trying to think of the best way to attack. She knew she had the power to get under his skin. "How do I win?"

"Make me lose control, and I will give it to you."

"Lose your temper?" she probed.

"I will give you one minute." He smiled, and it wasn't a nice one.

Methusal found that she suddenly wanted to meet that challenge. She wanted to get under his skin. To irritate him. To upset him, because she knew she had that power. That was clear enough.

Deliberately, she said the most inflammatory words she could think of. "You are a whip beast. And a liar." She enunciated the last word slowly, knowing he hated nothing worse than being called a liar.

His eyes remained cold. "Waste your time on childish games if you wish, Methusal."

She spoke without thinking, "So, I'm a child now. Two years ago, you asked me to be your wife. Was I a child then, too?"

His pale eyes flashed. Danger...and success. "You were nothing to me then. Or now. Continue at your own peril, Methusal."

"I'm not afraid of you." She was, but her voice remained steady and even, thanks to years of kaavl practice. And something perverse inside drove her on to continue this dangerous line of questioning. She felt like she was playing with fire, but found she enjoyed the heat. Was she cruel to want to reflect back the cruelty he'd shown to her? Was that what made her *want* to disturb him? Or was it because since the beginning of the war, all she'd seen was danger. Had she acquired a taste for it?

"I'm not a child, Mentàll. Then. Or now. And you know it. So don't try to dismiss me as one."

"It is not wise to provoke me."

"Isn't that the point?" Methusal tried to ignore the warning frisson of danger in the pit of her stomach, and pushed on. "You're afraid of me, aren't you? Why?"

His eyes slitted, and a bit of fear lurched through her heart. Had she already pushed him too far? But surely he wouldn't hurt her. He'd given that promise to her father. All of a sudden, though, she suspected she'd been a fool to trust his word so far.

She stiffened when his palm cupped her chin, tilting it up. His breath drifted down. It smelled clean, like freshly chewed tagma leaves. "I fear no one. Especially not you, Methusal."

She didn't like him standing so close, nor the fact that he towered over her by almost three handbreadths. Her head barely topped his shoulder. She felt a breathless, reckless sort of fear. "Then why do you hate me so much?" She answered her own question. "Because you know I can hurt you."

"You do not know what you are saying."

Methusal suddenly guessed, "I remind you a little of your mother, don't I? She was kind to you. I've tried my hardest to be kind to you too, even though you've treated me like a whip. Is that it? Do you see qualities in me that remind you of her? And you hate anyone tarnishing that precious memory of her. Especially me. Right?"

"You know nothing," he snarled, releasing her. "You are nothing like her!"

Methusal pressed on. "Then how would she like it if she could see you now? Is this how she'd like to see her son behave?"

Mentàll spat a Dehrien epithet, and his lip curled. "You do like danger, don't you?"

"So I win?" she challenged in a whisper.

"I have one more response to make. And then we will see."

"Let me go." She struggled, suddenly terrified, but felt his hard fingers grip her arm, stopping her. The little imp inside of her had driven her too far. She'd wanted to push the boundaries. Wanted to challenge him, for she sensed there was something inside of him that only she could provoke out of him. Something that he didn't want out. As much as she hated him, that thought intrigued her. Besides, she'd wanted to win the challenge. To win back the book, if she possibly could.

He didn't loosen his grip. "You need to learn something, Methusal. If you choose to play with fire, you will be burned."

She swallowed and stared up at him, chin trembling slightly. She willed it to stop. "Leave me alone." He wouldn't make her cower to him. She wasn't afraid of him. "Let me go!" she repeated more forcefully.

"Are you giving up?" He didn't move.

Attack! Methusal's defenses screamed. "I'm right, aren't I? You *are* afraid of me." Her chin was steady now.

His lips stretched into a humorless smile, but his eyes still watched her carefully. "I am not afraid of you. It is the other way around."

"You're wrong."

"Am I?" Methusal didn't like the way he kept looking at her. He had promised her father that he wouldn't accost her, but what did that mean? Wasn't he accosting her now?

All of sudden, she backed up a step. Her heel hit the wall of the cave, and her back slammed against it. She twisted, trying to escape, but Mentàll's arm suddenly barred her escape route. She stared up at him with her back pressed to the wall, and swallowed again, trying not to look frightened, even though her stomach turned cartwheels, and she wanted nothing more than to flee from this man as fast as she could.

"I think only one thing will decide this challenge, Methusal." His words were soft.

Visions of his razor sharp knife shot through her mind. She gulped, and jerked her neck back.

He laughed softly. "Nothing so drastic."

"Let me go." Her whisper trembled, and she hated it.

"I will. In a moment." His hand that gripped her left arm relaxed and moved to cup her shoulder, while his other palm reached up to brush across her temple. His fingers slid through her hair. Firm. Sure. Sensual.

She knew what he intended even before he did it. "No," she breathed out in a panic.

"Or Behran will be jealous?" His words mocked her before his mouth swooped down to capture hers. It felt hard.

She struggled violently to free herself, but his steely hand on her shoulder kept her from moving. She jerked her head back against the wall. Still, she couldn't escape the hard lips, or the rough bristle of his chin scratching her face.

A quick sob welled up, and to her dismay, a tear trickled down her cheek, toward her ear. She hated it. She hated him, for being able to make her cry. The tear slipped toward her hairline, where his hand was still tangled in her hair.

The pressure against her mouth abruptly eased. Before she could wonder why, the punishing assault lightened. She felt his lips, warm, and now bewilderingly softer, moving against hers.

To her shock, the sensation burned.

All of a sudden, she realized she wasn't struggling any longer, and her tears had stopped. Her heart pounded in her ears.

He lifted his head, and then, as she stared, unblinking, he bent toward her again. His mouth skimmed across her own. It felt like a flaming feather whispering across her sensitive skin. She stared up at him, eyes wide, unable to move, as his head raised again. Mentàll's pale eyes had dilated almost black, and he stared at her for long, inexplicable seconds, his breaths harsh.

That wasn't what she had expected. Not at all. She had expected complete violence from him. He stepped back abruptly, and his lips curved into the familiar, cold smile. "Perhaps that is what you wanted all along."

"No!" The words tore from her lips, and she jerked free. She wanted to flee from the room, but couldn't. Her legs felt odd. Tingly and rubbery. Like she'd come face to face with her worst nightmare, and still lived to tell about it.

"Or did you want it to be Behran...again?" Mentàll watched her closely.

It took a second for his deliberate words to register, and then shock rocked through her. Appalled, she said, "It was you."

Like an explosion, the dream flashed through her mind. The feel of the man holding her. The hard, sleek muscles, and wide shoulders. Bigger than Behran. Different than Behran. She had tried to ignore it and forget it. But not now. She had kissed him! And he had thoroughly kissed her back. And she had felt...

"No." She shook her head. "No!"

"Yes, Methusal."

She shook her head violently. "I don't believe it!"

"Have you asked him yet?"

"Asked him what?"

"If he's in love with Hendra."

"No!" Horrified, Methusal shuddered. *No*. It couldn't be. It couldn't be! No no, no, *no, no!* She had betrayed Behran. She had betrayed herself...with that horrible, horrible man!

"I think you have lost the challenge, Methusal."

She hated his self-confident, mocking laugh, and balled her hands into fists. Things were going from bad to worse. Then she saw the book at her feet, and in a heartbeat, scooped it up and ran.

Δ Δ Δ Δ Δ

Methusal knew she didn't have a chance to escape Mentàll permanently. She darted out of the cave, moving as fast and silently as she knew how. She heard him, equally silent, and faster, behind her. Even if she could escape now, he'd accost her at base camp and take the book from her then. No. Right now, all she wanted was a chance to look at the book alone for a few minutes.

She remembered a break in the rock just outside the entrance. It created a thin passage to the other side of this rocky peak. She slipped through it just before her enemy reached her. He was too big to get through. He'd have to climb around. It bought her a few minutes, and she sprinted up the next hill, and then backtracked carefully to a cave she'd seen when she'd followed Mentàll earlier.

Methusal ducked silently inside and sat, pulling the dusty old book onto her lap. She knew he'd find her. The question was, how long did she have to examine the book?

Carefully, she opened the cover. Cracked leather strips tied the book together, and the parchment looked brittle. The first page read, "'Second Book of Kaavl,' by Mahre."

Gently, she turned the page and read, "To my family and all of my kaavl descendants." Signatures were scrawled below the inscription. Mahre. And a list of Maahrs. Her heart pounded, recognizing the names. Apparently her family name had been changed directly after Mahre. She read seven names. The last was Jotham Maahr, her direct ancestor, and the man who had been taken captive by the Dehriens during the Great War. Now, coincidently, the book had been found by herself—Mahre's descendent—and a power hungry Dehrien, too.

Methusal heard footsteps at the cave entrance. Reluctantly, she closed the book and rose to her feet. "I wanted a chance to look at it."

He held out his hand.

Silently, she relinquished the precious book to her enemy. "Take good care of it," she warned. "My ancestors wrote their names in that book. By rights, it belongs to Deccia and to me."

He did not reply, and strode in the direction of camp. Fuming, Methusal followed, but made a quick side trip to the cave to collect her pack and the gun. The book belonged to *her*. She was the one with the right to read it. Her powerlessness in the situation, and the injustice of it all stoked her fury higher with each step.

Someday, somehow, she would get that book back. For all of Rolban.

And he would give it to her.

She didn't know where that thought had come from, but she liked it. Someday, she'd make him give it to her. Forever.

△ △ △ △ △

The first person Methusal saw in base camp was Behran.

Relief and joy overwhelmed her, and she flew into his arms. At the last second she remembered not to slam into his injured ribs.

"Behran!" She hugged him as tight as she dared, and buried her face in his neck. It felt good to be with someone who loved her. To feel like she wasn't alone anymore. He hugged her back, and kissed her hair.

At last she released her grip, afraid she might be hurting him. She touched his face. "You're all right. You're out of the hospital!"

Deep blue eyes gleamed down at her. "Doc says I'm going to live."

"Oh, Behran! I'm so happy." Tears slid down her cheeks, but she didn't care. Especially not when Behran brushed them away and kissed her tenderly.

His kiss was nothing like that Dehrien's. Stiffening, Methusal tried to push that thought out of her mind. Following on the heels of that thought was guilt for betraying Behran when she'd slept-walked and kissed Mentàll. Of course, in her dream, she had thought he was Behran. Unfortunately, that knowledge didn't salve her conscience.

Behran frowned. "Are you all right?"

"Of course!" She managed to smile, and gently hugged him again. "Are you completely healed?"

"Not yet. But I'm well enough to scout again."

"You are?" Joy bloomed, and then worry dampened it. "Are you sure?"

"Come on, Thusa." With a grin, he slung an arm around her shoulders and urged her toward the eating tent. "Aali's dying to talk to you. I'm sure Hendra is, too."

"How are they?"

"Fine. We spend hours together every evening talking. Or playing games or singing, if Aali has her way."

She smiled at the thought of seeing the others. And she wouldn't feel guilty about Mentàll, either. He'd love to know that he could torment her, even when he wasn't present.

△ △ △ △ △

Methusal felt much better after spending a good amount of time with Behran and Aali. Her father wasn't in camp, but he would arrive back soon, according to Dastn. Methusal noticed that the Tarst messenger and Aali didn't seem to be on speaking terms at the moment. During lunch they sat at opposite ends of the table, and afterward Dastn disappeared.

Hendra said a quick "hi" before grabbing two plates and returning to the medical tent. Behran's smile for Hendra seemed warm, but the Dehrien girl paid little attention to him. Methusal got the feeling that she had run off to the medical tent on purpose.

Taltn hadn't arrived yet, and that worried her. Then again, neither had Jascr nor Goric.

After lunch Methusal washed her clothes and took a bath—after turning the rock, of course. Then her father and Timaeus arrived at camp at the same time, coming from opposite directions.

"Papa!" Methusal ran to hug him. She was relieved that he looked well, and appeared to be uninjured.

After hugging her back, he looked at her hard. "Are you all right?"

She smiled. "I'm fine."

"I heard about kaavl camp. Did everyone make it here safely?"

"Everyone but Taltn, Jascr, and Goric." Her worry intensified as she glanced at the angle of the late afternoon sun. Surely Taltn was all right. Surely he would show up soon.

Timaeus spoke up. "Chief. I spoke to the Eerporian war team. They'll arrive sometime tomorrow."

"Good. I'll meet with Pan and Mentàll now and discuss strategy."

"When will we rescue Deccia?" Methusal asked anxiously. She still was sensing nothing from her sister. It worried her.

"Soon, I hope." Her father frowned.

The three Chiefs spent several hours in Erl's tent, discussing the war and strategies. Methusal couldn't help but eavesdrop from time to time as she helped Aenill, Aali, and Oona prepare the evening meal. Then she felt guilty, and stopped. Had she lost all sense of ethics? She'd gotten into a bad habit by spying on Mentàll all the time.

Pan and Mentàll exited from Erl's tent just before sundown, and spoke for a few more moments outside. As Methusal carried pots to the buffet table, she wondered what plan the three Chiefs had decided upon. And what that would mean for Deccia.

Her skin prickled up.

"Methusal." That harsh grate came from behind her. She lowered the last pot onto the table.

Wariness tightened in her stomach as she faced him. "What do you want?"

"Do you feel threatened?"

"After what you pulled in the cave, I don't trust you at all."

"Perhaps you feel guilty, instead." His eyes glinted.

How did he know? Or had that been his goal all along—to upset her by interfering with her relationship with Behran?

"You're the one who should feel guilty. After all, you stole the book from me."

"And yet you handed it to me without a fight."

She was tired of talking to him. "What do you want?"

"My scar requires your attention."

"Why? You can do it yourself now."

He smiled. "But I know how much you enjoy it."

"You mean you know how much I *hate* touching you."

"Always?"

"Of course, al..." Methusal broke off, remembering the sizzling kiss she'd shared with him in the dream. When she'd thought he was *Behran*. When his smile curled up, she exploded, "You're cruel! Why would you pretend to be Behran? Are you that desperate?" She wouldn't even think about the kiss in the cave. He had forced that one upon her.

"Desperate for what?"

"For love and affection—even if it's stolen!"

"I can have any woman I want."

"Not me," she contradicted. "And unfortunately for you, there's no other woman at camp who will meet your base needs."

He said nothing.

Methusal waved toward the western mountains. "Go to Quasr. Hundreds of women live there. But leave me alone!"

"I make my choices, Methusal. Not you."

"And persuade one of them to massage you, too." She flung a coltac leaf at him.

The Dehrien caught it. "I want *you* to do it."

"Why?" She spoke between her teeth. "Unless you *like* me to touch you."

His face gave no hint of his thoughts, although the hard gleam in his eyes intensified. He smiled, then. "I enjoy it."

Her heart pounded. "You sick bastard!" She swiftly strode out of the dining area.

Mentàll caught her arm, but she wrenched free and glared at him. "Why did I ever try to be kind to you?"

"You tried to be nice to me?" Disbelief registered. And a hard watchfulness.

"I did. Like The One wants me to be. I tried to treat you like an injured whip."

"You mean when you take care of my scars."

"Yes."

"Perhaps that is why I want only you to touch me." He baited her.

Her eyes narrowed. Seeing this, he continued smoothly, "You have the healing touch, Methusal. I will not allow my scar to be treated by anyone less skilled."

Furiously, she hissed, "You like to torture me!"

He neither confirmed nor denied it.

All of a sudden, she desperately wanted to lash back. How dare he constantly manipulate and upset her? Instinctively, she knew which words would slice straight through his icy soul. "You're just like your uncle!"

Mentàll drew a quick breath. Instant red burned his cheekbones. "You are a *fool*."

She took an involuntary step backward, but continued to glare.

"I am *nothing* like him! I do not drink racmun spirits, I do not lie, and I do not beat women or children. A fact you should be grateful for right now."

"But you *are* cruel. Like just now. You deliberately try to hurt and scare me."

"You are not easily frightened, Methusal."

"Good thing, or I'd be a wreck by now. But that's just the way you are. You'll hurt anyone to get what you want."

"I choose only actions that will help me accomplish my goal."

"Your goal of what? Revenge on me? When will it end, Mentàll? What is your final plan to destroy me?" Lately, this question had begun to torment her. Although he'd repeatedly said he didn't want to kill her, that fact didn't make her feel any better. Look at how he tormented her now, and the war wasn't even over!

His pale gaze narrowed, but he said nothing.

"You say you aren't like your uncle, but you *are*. You inflict cruelty on me, just to see me hurt. Isn't that what your uncle did to you?"

"You provoke me at every opportunity, and I cannot retaliate?"

"When the war is over, what will you do?"

"You do not *want* to know, Methusal," he bit back. "But it will be a fitting punishment."

"So you *are* like him, then." She turned and stalked away. She would not deal with his scar. She would not.

Instead, she headed for the protection of her father's tent. However, even though she was irritated, she felt just a little bit pleased. She had left Mentàll angry. A rare victory for her.

△ △ △ △ △

"Methusal, come in." Her father motioned her through the open tent flap. "We've made a plan to rescue Deccia."

"Really?" Finally, some good news.

A grim smile crossed Erl's lips. "We'll take out the munitions building, attack the ships, and raid the General's compound all at once. We'll attack at dawn, the day after tomorrow."

"Thank goodness! I hope it works." And she hoped the attack wouldn't come too late to save Deccia's life.

"You sound tired, Thusa." He sent her a sharp look. "Kitran's death has taken its toll on you."

"What about Aestoff? And the troops from Wyen? Have you heard from them?"

"Still no word from Wyen. I'll send a runner south to check on them soon. But we can't wait any longer. With the Eerporians' help, we'll hopefully turn the tide of this war. As for Aestoff—they're holding their own, with Var's help. For now."

"Good. As long as no more ships arrive, maybe we can win."

"Spies have seen more ships, but they're heading south. Southern Koblan is fighting for their lives."

That was terrible news. "Papa, how can we fight so many invaders? They keep coming."

"They'll run out of ships, sooner or later," Erl said grimly. "But that brings up another problem. We know nothing about the land across the sea. When this war is over, we'll need to learn all we can. I hope we can capture a ship so we can take a look at their charts and books, which would tell us more."

Methusal nodded, and sighed quietly. A tough fight lay ahead.

Erl eyed her. "What is it? What else is bothering you?"

She didn't want to burden her father. The whole weight of the war campaign rested upon his shoulders. He didn't need to worry about her petty problems with the Dehrien Chief. She was an adult, after all. "I'm fine, Papa."

"You are not. I can see that."

"I'm tired. I'll see you tomorrow?"

"Methusal. Are you having a problem with Mentàll?"

A tiny sound indicated that someone had arrived and now stood in the doorway behind her. She knew who it was before Erl spoke. She should have known he would never leave her alone. Never.

Erl said, "Mentàll. How are you?"

"I am well. I hope I am not interrupting?"

Erl glanced at Methusal. "Is he?"

Methusal felt suddenly weary. "Mentàll needs my help. I'll see you tomorrow, Papa."

He frowned. "Treat her right, Mentàll."

The Dehrien Chief inclined his head.

Methusal pulled two coltac leaves from her pocket. "Let's get this over with," she muttered. Mentàll led her to the stone outside of his tent, and sat down and pulled his tunic off. Silently, she massaged in the juice.

"Done. Are you satisfied?"

He caught her wrist before she could turn away. "I am sorry, Methusal."

More than a little shocked, she met his pale eyes. "You're what?"

"You heard me." That hard gaze held hers. It said she could accept it or not.

What kind of an apology was that? Methusal stared back, not sure how to respond. As an afterthought, she tugged her wrist free.

Did he mean it? As always with him, multiple layers obscured his true motivations.

"Thank you," she said shortly, and left him alone.

Only time—and his future behavior—would tell if he was truly sorry for getting under her skin tonight. She felt too tired to think about it any further.

△ △ △ △ △

Hendra entered the dining area late, still feeling worried about Viln. Doc had remained behind in the medical tent to keep watch over the young man who had been shot in the knee two days ago. The Tarst man was burning up with fever. Even worse, now angry red marks were streaking out from the wound. A bad sign. A few minutes ago Doc had said he may have to amputate the leg. "I'll reassess tomorrow morning," he'd said. That admission had pained him, she knew.

Hendra hoped they wouldn't have to amputate. Just thinking about the horror of the procedure made her feel sick. Would the protective ice finally return and insulate her heart then? It hadn't frozen her emotions since that first Zindedi ambush in the hills. It was also the day when she had first met Doc. These days she continued to feel each emotion more painfully than the last.

Doc had stopped asking her to dinner. Truthfully, she felt both relieved and disappointed. Despite her rejections, he continued to treat her with warm, persistent friendship. Sometimes, when he looked at her, the understanding patience in his eyes made her heart skip. He liked her very much. But she also sensed that he had decided to let her set the pace. He'd take his cues from her. At that rate, their relationship would go exactly nowhere. Frustration and relief battled in her soul.

Now she spotted her cousin sitting alone at a table in the corner, and carried her plate over to join him. With Methusal back, she didn't want to sit with Behran, as she normally did. The two needed time alone to reconnect.

"Hendra," her cousin greeted her with a faint smile.

She grinned back, pleased to receive one of his rare smiles. "You are well?"

Harsh lines sculpted his face again. "As well as possible. Jascr, Goric, and Taltn are missing."

Hendra was sorry to hear about Taltn, the sweet Tarst boy, but she wouldn't mind if Jascr disappeared forever. "I heard how the invaders found kaavl camp. Do you think base camp is next?"

"Not if we destroy them first. The day after tomorrow we'll attack Quasr."

Excitement sparked. "How?"

Mentàll outlined a few sparse details, but she learned that the Koblani team also planned to rescue Deccia and the two captured Tarst men, too. Her feelings of excitement increased, but she carefully stifled it, so her perceptive cousin wouldn't suspect what she was thinking. "I hope you succeed. Methusal is anxious to rescue her sister."

Mentàll glanced at Methusal's table. It wasn't the first time his gaze had lingered in that direction, Hendra noted. Although the upcoming battle plans simmered in her brain, she took a moment to observe her cousin.

Mentàll's intent glance, which was focused on Methusal, possessed an air of watchfulness. Almost as if he was looking for something in the Rolbani girl.

Hope kindled. "What do you see?" she said softly.

Mentàll's hard gaze slid back to Hendra, and for a second she didn't think he would answer. She also suspected that she'd misinterpreted his motivation. But she pressed on anyway. "Now do you see that Methusal isn't a horrible person?"

A silent moment elapsed. "I see I do not have all of the facts about her," he returned. "But I will *get* all of the facts."

Unease replaced Hendra's fading hope. "What do you plan to do?"

"I will find the truth. And then..." For the first time, uncertainty crossed his features. After a long moment, he frowned. "Then I will decide what to do with Methusal Maahr. Whatever pleases me most, you may be certain of that."

He picked up his plate. "Goodnight, Hendra." After dropping off his utensils, Mentàll disappeared into the night. Hendra frowned after him, but then her mind returned to the plan to attack Quasr and rescue Deccia. She'd been thinking for a while that she could help infiltrate the General's compound. Thankfully, she had finally figured out how to control her flashes of the future. The key was to focus on one particular location, and relax. She'd duplicated it a number of times during the last few days.

Now, after learning about Deccia's upcoming rescue attempt, excitement lurched within her. The compound would be the perfect place to use her kaavl ability. In close quarters, and with guards around every corner, the team could really use her short flashes of the future. If she could see which people would be in certain halls a few minutes in the future, surely that would help the war team.

So far, she'd told no one but Doc about her unusual kaavl ability, and she didn't plan to broadcast it now, either. If Mentàll learned of it, he might suspect her plan and order her to stay at base camp. No. When the war teams left, she'd secretly follow. Then, when it was too late to send her back, she'd approach Mentàll, confess her skill, and ask to join the rescue team. Surely he would agree. Or maybe he would be angry. She cringed a little, thinking about his displeasure.

But it would be worth it. Saving Koblani lives was worth it. More excitement surged. To think that maybe she could help defeat the Zindedis—it would be wonderful. Better yet, by going, she'd be able to confront both of her fears—her fear of men, and of war. She couldn't wait for the challenge.

Her one regret would be leaving Doc in the lurch. Hopefully he would understand. Maybe she'd leave him a note, explaining where she had gone. Yes. That idea salved her conscience a little.

She would miss him.

This realization drifted up from her subconscious, and she gingerly touched it, testing the inexplicable emotions wrapped up with it. Probing it too deeply, however, made her feel uncomfortable, so as she finished her meal, she turned her mind back to working out the logistics of her war plan.

Soon she'd prove to herself, Mentàll, and even Doc that she wasn't a scared, useless apte of a girl. Even if she died helping others it wouldn't matter, for finally, her life would count for something.

△ △ △ △ △

After dinner Methusal and Behran took a walk beneath Ryon's soft, greenish white light. His arm around her shoulders felt warm, and she leaned into his side. She felt peaceful walking beside him. And she was grateful to Hendra, too. The Dehrien girl had made more efforts than necessary to make sure that Methusal and Behran had plenty of time alone.

Again, it wasn't Hendra who worried her. It was herself. Every day for weeks now, Methusal had faced one truth: the only two things she inspired from men were hatred and revenge. Just look at Mentàll, Jascr, Goric, and even Pogul. What was wrong with her?

She was grateful beyond measure that Behran loved her, but she wondered if some day he'd finally wake up to the truth about her, too. Then would he search for someone more gentle, tactful, and kind? Someone like Hendra?

She hugged Behran tighter and blinked back tears. Maybe exhaustion could explain her unusual depression.

Behran spoke into her hair. "Are you all right, Thusa?"

His warm breath and the gentle way he said her name inspired more tears. She sniffled, but didn't tell him of her self-doubts.

"I'm worried about Deccia."

"We're all praying for her."

Methusal had sensed nothing from her sister for almost two days. Did that mean Deccia was all right? Or did it mean she was dead?

No. Everything within her recoiled from that thought. No. It couldn't be too late. Surely she would feel something if Deccia was gone.

Worry for her twin made her remember about Taltn, too. Had the Zindedis captured him? Killed him? Looking up at the clear, dark green sky, she silently prayed for Deccia and Taltn's safety.

Long moments passed, and Behran rubbed her arm. "I haven't asked you, but what's been going on with Mentàll? Has he bothered you since I left kaavl camp?"

She wasn't sure what to say. Should she tell him about the kisses that Mentàll had stolen from her? They would upset Behran. And what purpose would that serve? Especially since they'd need to work together to attack Quasr.

Telling Behran would create more problems than it would solve. Besides, neither incident meant anything. Hopefully, soon she could erase them from her mind.

"You've been quiet for a long time."

Methusal forced out a small laugh. "Yes. He's bothered me. It's what he does best. But I can handle him. Don't worry."

"Are you sure?"

"Of course." She redirected the subject in an effort to reassure him. "In fact, he even apologized today."

"Good." More time passed, and then Behran said again, "You're sure you're all right?"

Methusal hugged him. "Of course." But she wasn't. Why couldn't she tell him so?

Behran stiffened. "What's that?"

Ryon's pale green light bathed three figures descending into base camp. One limped noticeably.

"Taltn!" Methusal cried, and took off at a run.

She passed Jascr and Goric on the way. Jascr's arm was crudely bound up. She pulled Taltn into a hug. "We've been so worried about you! What happened?"

Taltn grinned when she released him. "Hey, Behran." He hobbled on, using makeshift crutches. "Invaders chased us. We split up a couple of times. A bullet grazed Jascr, and one exploded into a rock near my head. Then Jascr killed two Zindedis."

"You're lucky to be alive." Methusal was a bit surprised that Jascr and Goric hadn't abandoned the Tarst boy. It would have been far easier for them to escape if they'd sacrificed Taltn.

"I ran," Taltn said grimly, heading for the medical tent. "I didn't care how much it hurt. Still, I could barely keep up with Jascr and Goric. Goric did help me make some crutches, though."

Behran said, "We're glad you made it, buddy. Methusal's been worried sick."

Taltn grinned. "I couldn't let down my team. And I didn't want to die, either."

Methusal and Behran followed the three kaavl players into the medical tent. Several lanterns lit the interior. Doc peeled back the bandage on Jascr's arm.

With a lifted eyebrow, Behran eyed the bruises on Jascr's jaw. "What happened? Did the invaders beat you?"

"No. Mentàll did." Taltn snorted. "After he found out Jascr planned to jump Methusal."

"What?" Behran exploded. His blazing gaze swung first to Methusal, then to Jascr, who scowled, and then back to Methusal again. "Why didn't you tell me?"

"I didn't want to think about it." That was true. Remembering it now made her feel sick. A yawn worked at the corner of her mouth. "I'll tell you everything tomorrow, if you want. I'm exhausted. I haven't slept well in a week, I think." Except for last night. She dismissed that thought.

"Night, Thusa," Taltn said.

"Keep off your foot," she fussed, and offered a smile which turned into a yawn. "I'm glad you're okay."

"I'll walk you to your tent," Behran said.

Outside, camp lay quiet in the dark. A lamp flickered in the Dehrien Chief's tent, and in Pan's tent, too. It seemed strange to see everyone parceled off here and there, separate from each other. So unlike kaavl camp, where everyone slept out in the open together.

But this was better. And safer, too.

She stopped outside the women's tent. At least here she didn't have to worry about rochers, or Jascr attacking her in the middle of the night. She wasn't alone anymore.

Behran kissed her, and held her tight for a moment. "I love you, Thusa. You know you can tell me anything."

"I know. Goodnight." She slipped into the tent. The moment the leather blanket covered her, she fell into a deep, dreamless sleep.

CHAPTER TWENTY-SIX

A COLD, PINK DAWN woke Methusal. She felt rested, and her head felt clear this morning.

People were already filling the dining tables when she arrived for breakfast. Frying apte meat tantalized her nose, as did the sweet, steaming scent of steeped tagma leaves. She filled a plate and looked around for her friends. Aali madly waved a hand to grab her attention. Behran and Hendra sat with her, and they appeared to be deep in conversation.

The table looked full, and Methusal's steps slowed.

"Good morning, Thusa." Behran's warm grin lifted her spirits.

Hendra jumped up and grabbed her half empty plate. "Sit here. I need to go to work."

"But you're not done."

"I'm full," the other girl insisted.

"Well, sit with us at lunch. I haven't had a chance to talk to you yet."

Hendra's face lit up. "All right. See you guys later." She hurried off.

"That was nice, Thusa," Behran said. As she sat opposite him, he said slowly, "Hendra seems to have the odd idea that you think she and I..."

"I know," Methusal cut him off. "And I know it's not true. I wish she'd stop leaving."

Behran grinned. "I think maybe she might, now."

"Good."

Behran curled his hand over hers. In a low voice, he said, "I want to spend more time with you today. It's been almost a week, and I feel like I've lost you somewhere."

"I'd like that, too."

After breakfast, Methusal and Behran hiked into the low hills and found a rocky perch to sit on. They spent the morning talking. She told him about Jascr and Goric, about Kitran's awful death, and about her sleepless nights, and nightmares about Deccia.

"I never knew you had so many prophetic dreams."

"They're all about Deccia. I think it's because we're twins."

"Have you had other prophetic dreams? I mean, not about Deccia?"

"Once. Two years ago I dreamed about men fighting. I think it predicted this war." She fell silent, remembering the other part—that Mentàll had chased her. She'd run for her life, but in the end had slammed up against a locked prison door. She'd had no way to escape. The One had told her to *listen*.

And she realized that she had been listening during this war. The Prophet had told her to be kind to her enemies. While she'd failed with Goric and Jascr, she had done a fair job with Mentàll.

Would her obedience make any difference to the end of her dream—when Mentàll had closed in on her, determined to destroy her?

Or would her choices make no difference after all?

Methusal became aware that Behran was watching her with a quizzical expression. She tried to smile. "That's it. I don't want to have more prophetic dreams."

"Sounds like you've had a tough time at camp. But you still haven't told me about Mentàll." Deep blue eyes searched hers.

"He's been a wild beast. What more can I say?"

"Has he hurt you? Physically, I mean?"

"Never." Methusal wasn't sure if kisses counted as an assault. And she still didn't want to tell Behran about those, anyway. She was afraid it might drive a wedge between herself and Behran, and for no reason. He had nothing to be jealous about. She hated Mentàll. Both he and his kisses could go to the devil!

Behran still watched her.

She forced a smile. "Mentàll's a nuisance. But nothing he does matters. Not really."

Finally, he nodded. "All right."

Methusal hugged him, but she still felt guilty. Maybe she should have told him everything.

△ △ △ △ △

After the walk with Behran, Methusal helped Aenill and Aali prepare and serve lunch. She stood at the end of the serving table, ladling gravy over wild beast meat. Behran, Hendra, Taltn, and her father greeted her with smiles. Goric ignored her. Hatred burned in Jascr's eyes. He'd let his black beard grow. The stubble helped mask the mottled bruises left by Mentàll's fists.

She poured a dollop of gravy on his plate and averted her eyes, waiting for him to move on. He didn't. Instead, he leaned in close and whispered, "I am going to kill you."

Before she could respond, he was gone.

A cold sensation washed through her. Her false sense of security, based on the belief that Jascr was afraid of Mentàll, and would therefore leave her alone, evaporated like the morning mist. Her hands trembled as she ladled out gravy for the next person. She forced them to be steadier

When she finally filled her own plate, she hurried for the far table, eager to join her friends.

"Hi," she greeted them. "How's the gravy? I made it myself."

"Yum!" Aali proclaimed, and Taltn nodded, too.

"It's delicious," Hendra agreed. "By the way, Doc wanted to tell you that your bullet wound patients are doing well."

"Oh!" she said, pleased.

"Medicine could be a whole new career for you, Thusa," Behran suggested.

Methusal became aware of a prickling sensation in the back of her neck. Someone was staring at her. "Doc mentioned that, but Sims may not like the idea. He'd have to find a new apprentice."

"Sims loves you," Behran said. "He'd walk through fire for you."

The malevolent stare burned into her flesh. She hunched a little.

"In his mind, you're his granddaughter. He'd approve of any decision you make."

"If we defeat the Zindedis, I'll think about it." The idea of helping people heal did appeal to her. But the inevitable sickness, pain, and death...she wasn't sure if she could handle that very well.

"What's wrong?" Hendra said quietly.

Methusal glanced over her shoulder. "Jascr. He threatened to kill me a few minutes ago."

Taltn snorted. "Didn't Mentàll warn him off?"

"Maybe he's not scared."

Hendra shrank down a little in her seat. "He's a whip," she whispered. "And evil. Take his threats seriously, Thusa."

Behran gritted, "I'll warn him off."

"No." Methusal touched his hand. "Just leave it. I don't want to make things worse."

"What could be worse?"

"Him coming after you. Or maybe Aali or Hendra."

"I can tell by the look on his face that he won't back off. I'm going to talk to him."

Behran strode over and spoke in a low tone to Jascr, but the Dehrien only smiled. Methusal focused in time to hear Jascr tell Behran that he could go to a descriptively unpleasant place.

Behran flushed. "Touch her, and you'll answer to me."

Jascr continued to smile like a wild beast.

When Behran sat at their table again, anger darkened his features. "Don't go anywhere alone, Thusa. Promise me."

"I've beaten Jascr before."

"Promise me."

"I won't go into the hills alone. I promise."

"I'm going to report this to Erl and Pan."

Methusal doubted that would do any good. But she wouldn't live in fear, either. Jascr's Chief hadn't succeeded in making her cower. And neither would Jascr.

Δ Δ Δ Δ Δ

Hendra quietly went about her duties in the medical tent after lunch. Her thoughts were anything but quiet, however.

Jascr scared her. And Methusal worried her. Jascr's threats hadn't seemed to faze her. That was a mistake. Hendra knew, more than anyone else, exactly how horrible...

Long suppressed images and sensations exploded in her mind.

She shuddered and gasped, and grabbed a tent pole for support. Cold prickles washed through her. She felt unbearably dizzy and closed her eyes.

"Hendra?" Doc's voice seemed to come from far away. "Hendra." She felt a steadying hand on her arm, and Doc directed her to a chair. Her chest felt unbearably tight, and each breath wheezed in with labored effort. She felt like she was going to die.

"Hendra. Look at me." Doc sounded worried. Gentle fingers touched her chin, urging her to look at him. He crouched before her.

With effort, she opened her eyes. His smoky blue gaze became her anchor in the storm. Tears slipped down her cheeks as she labored to breathe. Something touched her lips. Black spots danced before her eyes.

"Breathe into this." A leather bag. Hendra tried to concentrate on breathing.

"You're all right." She became aware that Doc was rubbing her shoulder. Finally, after excruciatingly long moments, the tightness left her chest and her breaths became more normal. Doc removed the leather bag, and she swiped at the tears wetting her face.

"I don't know what happened." Her voice trembled.

"This has never happened to you before?"

"No!" More tears escaped. "I'm so scared."

Doc's hand convulsed on her shoulder, and he looked like he wanted to pull her into his arms. He did not. Instead, his hand covered hers. "You had a panic attack. What were you thinking about before it happened?"

It took a moment to remember, and then she shuddered. She slammed shut the door on the painful images and memories tumbling into her brain. Hendra realized she was squeezing Doc's hand. The pressure had turned both of their hands white. "I'm sorry!" she gasped, freeing him. "I'm so sorry."

Doc recaptured her hand, and his firm touch felt gentle. "It's fine, Hendra. Can you tell me what you were thinking? It upset you."

"No! No, I *can't*."

"Maybe you should lie down for a while."

"I'm fine." Hendra stood up, but her head swirled. She reached for support, and Doc was there. She clung to his shoulder to steady herself. Hard, sinewy muscles rippled beneath her fingers as he pulled her closer, and wrapped a strong arm around her waist.

"You're going to lie down for a few minutes."

"But what about the patients?"

"Come back when you're feeling better." He steered her out of the tent.

"But..."

"I am your supervisor, and you will listen to me." The faint smile in his voice gentled the words.

Hendra stumbled several times during the short walk. Luckily her tent was only a few lengths from the medical tent. She pulled free of Doc's supporting arm at the door. His embrace didn't frighten her—perhaps because her overloaded brain couldn't process more fear. "I think you're right." She smiled weakly. "I do need to lie down."

"Take all the time you need."

Hendra slipped into her tent, and her last backward glance caught Doc's troubled frown. "Thank you," she whispered, and closed the flap.

She crawled into her coverlet and pulled it to her chin. Still, she trembled from the panic attack, and from the awful images that had triggered it. Those images had remained buried for so long. Her mind remembered the facts, of course, but the sensations, the emotions—the fear, the panic—it felt like it had just happened now.

Why?

Hendra began to cry. She didn't want to remember. She didn't *want* to remember. Why wouldn't the ice protect her anymore?

△ △ △ △ △

Brightly clad Eerporians descended into base camp late that afternoon. Barak roared, and pumped his fist in the air. Camp reverberated with cheers.

Methusal's spirits soared as she counted the soldiers. Fifty Eerporians would be added to their own weary hundred and twenty. With their help, they could rescue Deccia. With their help, maybe they could finally turn the tide of this war. The Zindedis still outnumbered the Koblani warriors by more than four to one.

The Eerporian warriors wore colorful flaming red, purple or blue tunics. The purple clad ones carried bows and arrows, and the red team carried a long sword at each hip. The Eerporian war leader, dressed in a yellow tunic, met her father, Pan, and Mentàll in the center of base camp.

"Welcome, Nazu!" Erl said, and shook the Eerporian leader's hand.

After lengthy greetings and introductions, Erl spoke quietly to Nazu, and then her father ordered everyone in camp to split up according to their war party. The blue clad Eerporians joined the kaavl team, and the reds and purples mixed into Pan and Erl's war teams. Nazu joined her father's team, as well.

Methusal noticed that Barak had joined the kaavl team, and so had a number of other strong warriors. She sat on the hard, pebbled ground next to Behran and Taltn.

Erl raised his voice in order to be heard. "Each team leader will discuss strategy now. Listen well. Tomorrow each team must complete a vital task during the attack. In short, we'll arrive in the dark. Mentàll's team will attack the General's compound. Pan's team will engage the soldiers on the east side of town. They will draw attention away from the munitions building, which my team will blow up. After that, our warrior teams will circle south and fight as seems prudent.

"Just to be clear, we do not plan to finish the battle tomorrow. We cannot win—not yet. We will attack, inflict as much damage as possible, and then retreat. When Wyen reinforcements arrive in two days, we will have enough warriors to press on to the finish. I've just learned they're sending one hundred men."

One hundred men! Relief made Methusal cheer right along with everyone else. Finally, some good news.

Erl said, "Now, I'll let your leader explain your specific strategies."

Mentàll surveyed the kaavl team. Supplemented by the warriors, it was forty-five members strong now. His harsh voice spoke, drawing all attention to him. "We are entrusted with the most vital mission of all. Tomorrow we will ambush the General's compound. Our goals are to kill the General and free Koblani prisoners. The mission will be difficult, but I am confident we will succeed.

"The plan is as follows. Our new kaavl team warriors will first kill all guards in the outer courtyard. Then the kaavl players will join the warriors and storm the mansion."

Mentàll outlined a detailed, room by room attack upon the General's mansion. It was a well thought out plan. The plan paired Methusal with Behran. Both would attempt to free the prisoners. Mentàll and a few others would hunt down the General.

"I wish I could go, too," Taltn muttered. "Instead I have to help Aali and Aenill cook."

Out of the corner of her eye, Methusal spotted Aali skulking near Erl's team.

Her father's mission sounded dangerous. Aali's accidental explosion had proven how volatile the powder must be. One spark could blow up the entire building.

How did her father plan to plant the flame in the munitions shed and escape before the explosion blew them all to smithereens? Blowing up that building might be the most dangerous job of all. And that didn't even take into account the problem of the guards. Trying to blow up that building had already cost Kitran his life. How many more men would die tomorrow?

Dusk darkened the sky when Mentàll concluded with, "Rest early. We leave at midnight for Quasr."

So they would march tonight!

Warriors sped toward the delicious smells wafting from the dining tent. Methusal decided to wait until the main crush subsided, and then she'd eat by the fire. Likely the tables would be filled for quite a while.

"Coming, Thusa?" Behran asked.

"Soon." She'd spotted Mentàll striding for his tent. "Do you want to eat by the fire tonight?"

"Sure." Behran followed her gaze. A faint frown touched his brow. "Isn't he healed yet?"

"Almost." She squeezed his hand. "Be back in a minute."

She pulled a coltac leaf from her pack and followed the Dehrien Chief toward his tent. For the first time, she realized that he hadn't provoked her all day. In fact, he had said nothing to her at all.

The Dehrien turned abruptly, just short of his tent. "Methusal." That cool gaze pinned hers.

She lifted the coltac leaf. "Are my services still required?"

He watched her for an uncomfortable moment. "How eager you are to do your duty."

"I'm not *eager*," she retorted, recoiling a step. "If you've had enough, just say so."

"No." He shucked off his tunic. Those icy, unreadable eyes held hers. "I have not had enough."

A flush warmed her cheeks, but she bit her tongue so she would not respond.

He turned his back to her, but did not bother to sit down, like he normally did. She felt very aware that he towered over her as she slicked the gel over the warm, scarred skin. Only a small scab remained at the top.

"It is better?" he asked.

"Almost completely healed. There. Done." She rubbed the remaining juice over the backs of her hands. They still smarted, but not as badly today.

He faced her and pulled on his tunic. "Thank you, Methusal."

"You're welcome." She could not figure him out today. Nor that watchful, probing look he kept giving her. She'd noticed it earlier, too. During breakfast, she'd caught him studying her with a faint frown.

She became aware that she was staring at him, and he continued to watch her right back.

"Well." She took a step backward. "I guess I'm finished here."

Mentàll smiled faintly. It was one of his remote, calculating ones. "Are you?"

Gritting her teeth, she spun on her heel and left him. She wished he didn't possess the power to needle her so skillfully.

△ △ △ △ △

"I'm back." Hendra entered the medical tent late that afternoon. Doc sat at his desk, making quick notations on a parchment.

The Eerporians' arrival had finally prompted Hendra to get out of bed. She felt disgusted with herself for pathetically lying there for so long. Hadn't she decided that she'd beat her fears into submission? The Eerporians had again reminded her of that vow. As did thinking about tomorrow's rescue mission. She was sick to death of living in fear. She wanted to make a difference—she wanted to truly live. And that meant facing all danger head on. Now.

She offered, "The Eerporians are here."

He smiled. "I saw. Are you feeling better?"

"Yes. I'm sorry." Hendra helplessly waved her hand. "I've never gone to pieces like that before."

He frowned. "I'm sure you haven't."

"Should I give the men sips of water?"

"Aali did that." He gave her a measuring look. "I need to amputate. Can you help me? Or should I call one of the men?"

Hendra's heart lurched. She tried to swallow back the sick sensation suddenly churning inside her. Here was an opportunity to conquer her fear. She could do it. She must. "Will...will the powder keep him asleep?" *Was that her squeaky voice?*

Doc's steady gaze held hers. "Yes. Can you handle it?"

She swallowed. "Yes. Of course. Just tell me what to do."

"Sterilize the instruments and your hands. I've already moved him to the surgery tent."

Hendra hurried to do as he asked. In the surgery tent, the young man looked peaceful as he slept. Doc had given him enough powder to numb the pain, as well.

"Are you ready?" His steady gaze watched her over his mask.

"Yes."

"Hand me the knife."

Hendra followed his instructions to the letter. But the enormity of what they were doing to the young man sickened her. She knew they were saving his life, but at such a cost. And the blood... The horror of it all overwhelmed her, but still, the ice did not come. She couldn't hide from the gore, and the awful knowledge that Viln would lose his leg forever. But she was determined not to fall apart. Doc needed her to be strong. So she concentrated on carefully following each of his instructions. She focused only on her task.

And then it was done. Hendra felt relieved, but her fingers trembled from reaction. Doc had been remarkably swift, which she knew would bode well for the patient's recovery.

As she cleaned the instruments, a tiny bit of confidence settled into her spirit. She had faced an extremely difficult task, and had completed her job well.

Doc said, "He'll need blood builder when he wakes up. And he'll need to be watched all night."

But she'd leave with the war party at midnight. Not only that, but she'd need to get some sleep beforehand. "I can help after dinner for a little while. But maybe we should ask some of our old patients—the ones not going on the war party—to help during the night. I know most of them are itching to do something—anything." Maybe a few of them could help Doc tomorrow, too. He'd certainly need it, since she planned to abandon him. She tried to ignore her feelings of guilt.

"Good idea. Will you ask them?"

"Yes." The trembles had quieted now, and she gathered up soiled cloths to bring to the stream for washing.

"And Hendra..."

She glanced back at him. His mask hung down his chest, and weary lines etched into the sides of his mouth. "Great job. I couldn't have done it without you."

"Thank you. But you're the one who deserves the praise," she said softly. "You're a wonderful doctor."

His lips lifted with pleasure, but it was the smile in his eyes that made her heart warm, and then race. Flustered, she gathered up the last of the cloths and left the tent.

The old patients agreed to help out in the medical tent. They'd start an hour after dinner, when her shift ended. One man even agreed to come back in the morning, if Doc needed help. This had been accomplished by Hendra's subtle suggestion. She couldn't tell Doc where she meant to go tonight, because he might try to stop her. But she wouldn't leave him in the lurch, either. As it was, she felt bad enough, leaving him without warning, although she had left him a note in the patient box; a place where he wouldn't look until morning.

Two hours past dark, Hendra left the amputee, satisfied he was doing as well as could be expected, and he was sleeping comfortably. She told the new helpers what to watch for, and to get Doc if anything changed.

She met Doc just outside the tent door.

"How's our patient?"

"I think he's going to make it."

"Good." The light of Ryon accentuated the tired lines at the sides of his mouth.

"You look exhausted." For one crazy moment, she wanted to smooth away his lines of worry. What would his skin feel like? His beard? She suddenly realized that she was staring at him. He watched her just as intently.

"I...I guess I should go," Hendra said, but her feet didn't move.

His warm hands lightly cupped her upper arms. She didn't flinch, although deep in her mind, a tiny voice warned her to flee.

"Thanks for staying, Hendra. Above and beyond the call of duty, as usual."

"I'm happy to help." Unable to stop herself, her gaze ran over his lips, neatly outlined by his beard, and then looked up into his eyes. She felt breathless. "Good night, then."

"Good night...sweet Hendra." He leaned closer, and then hesitated, his warm breath touching her lips. They tingled. She swayed the barest fraction closer to him.

He seemed to understand that her small movement meant acceptance, and so he closed the remaining distance and gently kissed her. It lasted only a wonderful moment, but in that second, something shifted between them.

And then the panic began.

Her heart beat wildly. He still lightly held her by the arms, but all of a sudden his hands felt constricting. Again, the thunderbolt of old memories splintered through her mind, and the moment of pleasure shattered. Doc's face disappeared, replaced by the man from her past. How he'd held her, forcing her to submit...

Hendra jerked backward. "Let go!" she choked out. "Don't touch me. Ever again!" Tears blurred her vision, and she fled to her tent.

She collapsed on her pallet, weeping with misery, and hating herself for surrendering to the mind bending fear. That fear had turned Doc into a monster, and had killed the special moment they had just shared.

She had just punished him for something he'd never done. Could he ever forgive her?

Could she ever forgive herself?

Finally, in that moment, she realized that her fear would never end—not unless she did something huge to fight it. She was right to go on this mission tonight. She had to conquer her fear, finally and forever. She must!

△ △ △ △ △

The plan was set. Tomorrow morning Koblani forces would make multiple pronged attacks upon Quasr. Deccia would be rescued, and the munitions building blown to bits. The only thing the leaders didn't know was the part Aali intended to play.

She carefully filled her pack with the candle she'd experimented with, as well as other supplies she'd need. Soon, she would help to save all of Koblan. She couldn't wait.

△ △ △ △ △

Methusal pulled her coverlet up to her chin and thought about the mission ahead. In only four hours they would march.

So much adrenaline licked through her that it took a long time before sleep pulled her into its gentle, seductive current, pulling her down...down, down into a well of blackness and complete silence.

Methusal was completely alone. She stretched out her arms and touched dirt on either side. In a sudden panic, she whirled around in a circle, tracing the walls of the room. It was a tiny, earthen room with no door and no windows. Fear stabbed her.

"Methusal." Behran's voice.

Methusal flew upward, but part of her still remained behind. Bereft and terrified, she cried out, "Wait." She fought to go back, but couldn't.

A voice followed her flight skyward. "Help me...help me." The cries grew fainter, until finally black silence swallowed them up.

"Methusal!"

Methusal sat straight up, gasping with fear. Behran stood in the tent doorway. "Behran." Tears burned her eyes. "It's Deccia," she cried out. "She's in a pit! How will we ever find her?"

Chapter Twenty-Seven

THE ENTIRE KOBLANI WAR PARTY, over a hundred and seventy-five strong, marched for Quasr at midnight. Ryon lit their path, and the kaavl team led the pack.

Methusal felt jumpy and tired, and worry for her twin ate away at her. An hour wore by, and then two. What had that horrible General done to Deccia? Where was she?

The path widened, and Behran walked up beside her. "Tell him," he urged.

"He won't listen. The last time I warned him about a dream, he sneered."

"He needs all of the facts."

Methusal mumbled another thing Mentàll needed. Fortunately, Behran didn't seem to hear. "Okay!" she said. "I'll go. Wish me luck."

She strode faster to catch up with the Dehrien Chief, who of course led the whole procession. She shouldered past Barak to gain the Dehrien's side.

"Methusal." The Kaavl Commander didn't look at her. "What do you want?"

"I had a dream about Deccia tonight."

He made no reply.

"I don't think she's in prison anymore. I think she's at the bottom of some deep, dark pit."

"A pit."

"Yes, a pit."

More silence elapsed, and then he unexpectedly said, "I know where she might be."

"Where?"

He turned his head suddenly, as if listening.

A voice whispered behind Methusal, "Excuse me."

Methusal let the person pass by. Long, white-blond hair glimmered in the moonlight.

"Hendra!" Displeasure darkened Mentàll's tone. "What are you doing here?"

"I'm here to help. And don't order me to go back, because I won't go." Hendra's face looked resolute.

Methusal fell back in line in order to give them privacy, but she wasn't finished speaking to Mentàll yet. Curiosity inspired more unfortunate eavesdropping.

"I ordered you to stay at base camp."

"Please listen. I have a secret kaavl ability. I think it will help your mission succeed."

"How?"

"If I concentrate, I can see a few seconds into the future."

A short silence elapsed. Mentàll must feel as taken aback as Methusal did. The Dehrien finally said again, "How?"

"First, I concentrate on an object. Then I see a flash of what happens near that object in the future. It can be a few seconds in the future, or up to a few minutes."

"You cannot tell how far into the future."

"No, but it's usually within a minute."

Mentàll remained silent for a long time. "I do not want you on the team, Hendra."

"But..."

"You are here now," he said grimly. "I cannot send you back, so you will stay with me. Cover up your hair. I do not want the Zindedis to suspect that you're related to me."

"Don't treat me like a child, Mentàll!" Uncharacteristic anger hardened Hendra's voice. "I want an assignment. I want to help win this war!"

Mentàll walked in silence for so long that Methusal thought he wouldn't answer. At last, he said, "I will pair you with Behran. You will help rescue the Tarst prisoners. Tabor, Wortn, and Riln will go with you."

"I thought Methusal was with Behran."

"Methusal requires my help to rescue Deccia. She will pair with me."

Methusal wasn't sure what to think about this change in plans. She knew Mentàll planned to kill the General first. She wanted to rescue Deccia first, just in case the prison guards were under orders to execute prisoners if the compound was attacked.

"Thank you, Mentàll."

"Go tell Behran your assignment."

Hendra retreated back down the line.

Methusal strode up beside Mentàll. "I heard that we're teamed up now. Where is the pit?"

"You do not need to know."

She counted to ten, and then spoke as reasonably as she knew how. "I understand why you want to kill the General first. But I need to rescue Deccia first. What if the prison guards are ordered to kill the prisoners right away? I can't let her die."

"It is too dangerous, Methusal. You need a partner to watch your back."

He was right, in a perfect world. But war was anything but that. She tried a new tack. "What if you're killed? I need to know where the pit is."

"Speak the truth. You plan to desert me and rescue Deccia on your own."

"I want to look for Deccia while you kill the General."

"Do not *test* me, Methusal!" Frustration lashed.

Clearly, he was already upset about Hendra. However, she didn't appreciate him taking his wrath out on her. She snapped, "Isn't your plan going how you want it to?"

"Methusal…"

Her own frustration exploded. "Your cousin just told you she has an extraordinary gift. And what did you do? Lecture her! Try to see someone else's perspective for once. Deccia's life is at stake. I need to find her. Immediately. Now, will you help me, or not?"

Unexpectedly, Mentàll grabbed Methusal's wrist and dragged her to the side of the path. Others marched by, and a few threw them curious looks. His fingers bit painfully into her skin. "*I* am the leader of this team, Methusal. Insubordination is unacceptable! From you. From Hendra, who *disobeyed* my order to stay at base camp. I choose the strategies. They are designed to make our mission succeed, and to protect lives. You will obey me, or you will go back to camp."

The moon cast his harsh features into dark planes, and he towered over her, gripping her wrist hard against his tunic. His muscle beneath felt like stone. Her heart beat uncomfortably fast as she stared up at him.

At last he released her. "Do you understand?"

She stepped back. "Tell me where the pit is," she insisted, but in a quieter voice.

"You will do what I *tell* you to do," he snarled, and strode to regain the lead of his kaavl team.

Methusal rubbed her smarting wrist. Maybe she should have tried to be more tactful. She didn't think that would have helped, though. The Dehrien was as hardheaded as a rock.

△ △ △ △ △

Aali skulked silently at the end of the kaavl team line, hoping no one would notice her. She couldn't take the risk of being ordered back to camp. She wore her hood up, so no one would recognize her.

She'd sensed someone following her for the first hour or more, but was relieved when she saw Hendra brush by a little later. At least it wasn't Dastn.

Aali yawned, and wished she'd slept before marching. But she had been too afraid of accidentally sleeping through the whole night. That idea had horrified her so much that she'd stayed awake. Now she would have to stay awake for two days in a row.

No problem, she told herself.

She stumbled over a rock, and made herself concentrate harder into kaavl. They were hiking downhill now. Good.

When the team reached the plains floor, Aali's nerves spiked. Finally, it was time to face Uncle Erl. He couldn't send her back now. She ran to catch up.

△ △ △ △ △

Mentàll stopped the kaavl team on the plains floor. A few lights shone in the distance. Quasr was still a twenty minute run away.

"From now on, we will move silently. Each kaavl player will team up with a group of warriors. They will help the warriors sneak past Zindedi defenses on the outskirts of Quasr. This is key, team. We must arrive at the compound unseen. We cannot risk the General finding out and fleeing to safety. Understood?"

The warriors nodded and fingered their sword handles, as if impatient to begin the battle.

"Each of you will perform a vital task. Can I trust you to do as required?"

"Yes!" Barak rumbled, and the others echoed agreement.

Methusal's heart ached, thinking about her sister, but the Kaavl Commander's gaze seared into her, demanding compliance. Rebellion surged, but she squashed it.

She had to do the right thing. Not just for Deccia, but for the entire team. Although it was difficult, she lowered her eyes, silently agreeing to his wishes.

"Good." Satisfaction grated. "We will achieve our goal if we are swift and deadly. Do not forget—we will not battle to the finish today. Inflict as much damage you can, and retreat when prudent. Let's go."

△ △ △ △ △

"Please, Uncle Erl!" Aali cried out. The kaavl team was already heading toward Quasr. She had to convince her uncle of her plan, and quickly. She showed him the candle. "Look. I've experimented. I know exactly..."

"Aalicaa!" Erl thundered. His face looked dark in the moonlight. She uneasily suspected it might be purple. "I won't let you risk your life. Go..."

"How will you get into the building, then?" She interrupted. "Methusal said the only way in, besides the front door, is a high, small window. She showed me how big it is. I can sneak inside!"

"We plan to kill the soldiers, and then shoot a gun inside. The spark will trigger the explosion. We don't need you..."

"Then you'll die!" she cried dramatically. "I know how fast that powder blows up. Instantly! And if that building is *full* of powder...it might blow up a whole block of Quasr!" Maybe she was exaggerating a little here. But then again, maybe not. That explosion had gutted the weapons valley. And it had probably contained only twenty bags of powder.

Erl frowned, but said nothing, giving Aali the opportunity to rush on. "I think we should sneak up on the back of the weapons building. Kill whoever is in our way, and then let me sneak inside. The candle will burn down in two minutes, giving us lots of time to run. Then the whole building will blow up, and it'll kill all their soldiers. Wouldn't that be better than fighting them first, and losing our warriors during that battle, and then during the explosion, too?"

Erl still scowled, but his fingers rubbed his chin. A thoughtful gesture. He was considering her plan. Her spirits soared, but she remained silent, giving him time to think.

"Show me your candle again," he said abruptly.

Aali eagerly showed him the candle and the wooden holder, and the bit of parchment she'd brought. "Aenill had a bunch of burned down candles. I experimented until I found out how thick the candle should be. I've done it lots of times. It's safe."

He snorted. "It's not safe. And I don't like the idea of putting you in danger."

But Aali sensed he was weakening. "I *want* to do it. And think of all the Koblani lives we'll save."

Erl scowled harder. Finally, he muttered, "All right! Gather round, men. We have a new plan."

Aali's heart soared with excitement as Uncle Erl gave new orders to the men. Soon she would help to save all of Koblan.

Or die trying.

△ △ △ △ △

After eliminating several pairs of Zindedi soldiers who were patrolling Quasr's northeastern border, the Koblani forces slipped into the sleeping town.

After entering Quasr, Erl's warriors headed for the munitions building, leaving the kaavl team and its warriors to slip silently to the General's compound.

There, the Zindedi guards at the gates gave a brief, violent struggle, and then the new kaavl team warriors streamed into the complex. Long moments later, Methusal heard a great shout of alarm, and lights flared on all over the mansion.

Methusal crouched in the shadows of the burnt out building near the compound. Behran, Hendra, Tabor, Wortn, and Riln waited with her. Once the courtyard was cleared, it would be the kaavl players' turn to help navigate the difficult, possibly booby trapped hallways of the mansion. And rescue the prisoners.

Barak ran out. "Now!" he thundered, and dashed back into the fray.

Methusal wondered where Mentàll had gone. She was supposed to meet up with him. As they slipped through the open gate, she saw him sword fighting a Zindedi. A vicious thrust, and the invader crumpled to his knees.

Pandemonium still reigned in the courtyard. Half-dressed soldiers lunged at Koblani warriors, but Methusal spotted a mostly cleared path to the front door. She dashed for it, but a hand gripped her arm. Her heart beat with panic, and she yanked out her knife.

"No!" cried a man, his eyes wide with fright. He wore only a night robe. "It's too late! He's gone!"

"Who's gone?" Methusal struggled to free herself from his clutching fingers.

"The General! He escaped out the passage. You're too late!"

"What about the prisoners?" she said urgently.

He waved a fluttering hand in the air. "Dead!"

"No!"

"Methusal!" Mentàll's voice drew her attention. "Come. Now."

"But the General. The prisoners!" Her voice rose. "He said..."

"We will discover the truth for ourselves."

△ △ △ △ △

Methusal followed Mentàll's broad back into the mansion, and then hesitated, overwhelmed with the urgent need to rescue her sister.

A rough hand shoved her. Barak. "Hurry up!"

Although it hurt, like ripping herself in two, to abandon Deccia for the moment, Methusal stepped away from the prisoner hall and quickly followed the Dehrien Chief down a hallway to the right. Barak dogged her footsteps. His heavy, panting breaths reminded her of a wild beast hunting its prey.

Zindedis ran down the hall in both directions, but Mentàll killed the ones in front, and Barak killed the ones behind. The violence and the blood and the screams all over the mansion scared her.

Heart pumping wildly, she held her knife and kaavl stick at the ready, but neither were required. The Dehrien Chief strode swiftly down the hall and stopped beside a large door. He opened it a crack.

"What do you see?"

He was speaking to her. Methusal slipped by and peeked through the slit into the room. One direction looked clear, but the other was impossible to see from her vantage point. She concentrated upon a bookcase, and carried with vision. Now she had a clear view of the room from the position of the bookcase. It proved to be an opulent study. In fact, it was same room where the General had interrogated her when she had been captured. The gun and sword still hung over the window.

Her gaze swept the room. "Empty," she whispered.

Mentàll pushed open the door and directed her inside. Barak closed the door behind them.

She glanced around, and this time she noticed a little more than she had the first time she'd visited this office. To the right was a small sitting area, with a couch and two chairs. A large painting hung on the wall nearby. Bookcases lined the walls to her left. A closed door bisected the bookshelves. Barak opened it.

"A closet," he said.

Straight ahead were the wide, curtained windows, and beneath them squatted the huge, polished desk. A mug sat on it, and the Dehrien Chief crossed to touch it.

"Warm," he muttered.

"The General was just here, then."

Mentàll stood at the bookcase now, and ran his fingers over the joints.

"What are you doing?"

"Quasr is riddled with tunnels, and so is this mansion."

"Do you think the General escaped through a tunnel?"

"It is possible."

Mentàll must think one of these bookcases hid the entrance to a tunnel. Methusal moved to the opposite end of the same bookcase and pressed on the seams in the wood, just like the Dehrien Chief was doing. How might a bookcase move? A button? A lever?

Outside, to the east, guns thundered. Methusal's heart beat faster. Pan's forces had just attacked the Zindedi barracks. Soon Erl's team would blow up the munitions building.

The sounds of battle abruptly intensified in the hall, and the office door burst open. Seven Zindedi soldiers poured inside. Terrified, Methusal's hand convulsed on a book. She shoved it hard, propelling her into a quick spin to face the enemy.

A groan shuddered behind her. Cold, dank air crept up her spine. She didn't have to look to know she'd accidentally found the passage.

A Zindedi soldier curled back his lips and screamed, "Attack!" He lifted his gun and sighted it at Methusal.

Δ Δ Δ Δ Δ

Aali's heart felt like it was thundering as hard as a herd of urchets. Right now she stood at the back wall of the munitions building. So far, so good. Only one soldier had noticed them. He was dead now.

Luckily, she, Erl, and two of the warriors had made it back here before Pan's fight began. The soldiers at the front of the building had been dozing. Not any longer, however. Two Koblani warriors watched to make sure the Zindedis didn't creep around the corner and surprise them while Aali planted the candle.

"Here's the rope. Pull twice when you're ready to come up," Erl directed.

Her hand shook a little as she accepted it.

"Are you all right?" he asked sharply.

"Just nerves," she scorned with a shaky laugh, and looped the rope over her shoulder. A burly soldier held the other end secure. A small bag in her teeth held the necessary items for her espionage mission.

"Up you go." A great Tarst warrior gripped her by the waist and Aali flew up toward the window, which was high above. She swallowed back a cry of fright, and grappled for the window ledge. The window swung up, just like Methusal had said it would. She heaved herself forward, on her tummy. The window bumped and scraped across her scalp, and then her back, as she slithered headfirst into the pitch dark interior.

Horizontal wooden beams supported the walls inside, and Aali grabbed one. Carefully, she scooted sideways, supporting her body weight with the heels of her hands on the support beam. Finally, one ankle slid through, and when she allowed that foot to drop, it unexpectedly jerked her other foot through the opening, too. Her full body weight yanked down on her hands, which were gripping the beam, and they slipped. A terrified, scrabbling slide followed, and she crashed into a wooden box with one foot, and a powder bag with the other.

Ow! She stumbled backward, landed on her rear, and awkwardly sprawled back with both feet in the air. A hard corner of a box dug into her thigh. Her supply bag fell out of her mouth. Heart racing, Aali gingerly tested herself for injuries. Nothing appeared to be broken.

Ignoring twinges of pain, she felt for her supply bag. Anxious seconds ticked by until she found it. She pulled the rope once, to signal that she was okay.

Now she was glad that she'd practiced in the dark. With annoyingly shaky fingers, she set the candle on a nearby barrel. Then she pried open the top of another barrel with a knife. Gritty powder touched her fingertips. Good.

She lay a leather cloth over it, and then set up the candle base on top of this. She fiddled with the rolled parchment, edging the flat end under the candle and directing the other end into the powder. Then, for safety purposes, she found a level piece of dirt and stood up before she lit a tiny flare. The flickering orange taper pushed the shadows away, illuminating at least fifty barrels, and hundreds of bags of bullets. The Zindedis had come expecting a huge resistance. Either that, or they planned to stay for a while.

Aali took a steadying breath, and lit the candle. She blew out the taper and yanked hard on the rope, twice. Strong arms pulled her swiftly up, and she grabbed the window and hauled herself out. Waiting hands caught her as she fell headfirst toward the ground.

Dawn glimmered in the east, now.

"Good job, Aali. Now go back to base camp," Erl ordered.

"But..."

"Go!" He shoved her, and the Koblani warriors scattered.

She cast one more glance over her shoulder, and then ran for the mountains as the shadows fled from the land. As always, the light would chase the wild beasts to their caves. Soon a brilliant, dazzling explosion would chase the Zindedis home, too.

She'd done it. She didn't even care that Uncle Erl had banished her to base camp. Once the munitions building blew up, all of Koblan would finally be free.

△ △ △ △ △

Hendra followed Behran at a dead run down the hallway. She didn't have time to concentrate, or to see into the future. Tabor, Riln, Wortn, and Koblani warriors flanked them, and made short work of two guards at a door and one at the bottom of the stairs. Behran clearly knew where he was going. The last door clanged open, and cool air touched her cheeks. A long, torch lit hallway met her eyes. Wooden doors with grilled windows lined it.

It seemed eerily quiet. No Zindedi guards were in there.

"Hello?" Behran shouted. "We're here to rescue you. Tell us where you are!"

Silence.

Behran frowned. "Split up. Look in all the rooms."

Hendra and the warriors peered into each of the rooms. All locked. All empty.

Behran's frown deepened. "Thusa said they'd moved Deccia. Maybe the Tarst prisoners are with her."

"Is there another prison? Didn't Mentàll rescue Thusa from a different prison hall?"

"Yes. But we need to keep something else in mind, too. Thusa said there are dozens of passages under Quasr. I'll bet there are a lot are under this compound, too. The prisoners could be anywhere."

Hendra realized that now was her chance to focus and see how secure their position might be. She concentrated first on one end of the hall. Clear. Then the other. A guard peeked around the corner. Glee curled his lips, and he motioned, obviously to someone behind him.

"It's not safe!" she gasped. "We need to go. Now! That way!" She pushed Behran back the way they had come, and they all dashed back up the stairs to the main hall.

"Maybe one of the servants knows where the prisoners are," Hendra said. The hall they were in now was deserted, but she felt on edge. She focused on the next corner, but saw nothing. She heard fighting, though, in the distance.

"We don't need a servant," said Riln, one of the Tarst men who had mutinied with Kitran. His comrades were the prisoners. "Give me a Zindedi and I'll flay the truth out of him."

"Keep going," Behran said. "Maybe we'll find another passage to the prison."

Hendra concentrated on the hall ahead and watched for Zindedis. A blond-haired one popped out of an upcoming doorway. "Watch out, Behran! That door."

Riln shoved by and flattened himself against the wall beside the door. The Zindedi crept out, followed by two more. Riln grabbed the one first by the throat, and other warriors killed the next two. Blood squirted down the walls and Hendra turned, wanting to be sick. All of these weeks helping Doc heal people. And now, to see life taken so swiftly and ruthlessly.

Riln shoved his Zindedi prisoner against the wall and pressed the knife tip into the young man's throat. The invader wasn't old. Maybe nineteen, Hendra guessed. He looked terrified.

"Bring us to the other prison," Riln ordered.

"I...I..."

"Now!" Riln pressed the blade up, and a drop of blood slid down the edge and settled on the hilt.

Hendra looked away.

The soldier must have agreed, because Riln shoved him down the hall. The young man stumbled.

Concentrating into kaavl, Hendra saw more Zindedis, a pack of them, erupt from an adjacent hallway. Quickly, she relayed the news to the others.

"Bring us somewhere safe. Quick!" Riln growled to the Zindedi.

The young man's eyes rolled up into his head. He looked ready to faint from terror.

"Where is the prison?" Riln roared.

"Th...there. Two doors down..." His knees buckled.

Riln dragged the man by the hair and they both ran down the hall. Terrified, Hendra followed. Now she heard the Zindedis coming in real time. They didn't have time to make it in the next door. And who knew what waited for them there, anyway? What were they going to do?

And then, just as the Zindedis rounded the corner, a mighty explosion shook the mansion. Hendra staggered into the wall. The Zindedis stumbled and fell. Bullets ricocheted, and Riln's prisoner screamed.

△ △ △ △ △

The ground shook, and Methusal grabbed at the bookcase, trying not to fall. Half of the Zindedis fell to their knees. Unfortunately, not the one who was pointing the gun at her. His shot fired wild, thank goodness.

Quickly regaining his balance, Barak let out a mighty roar and threw his knife straight into the Zindedi's throat. The man crumpled, but the six others struggled to bring their guns back to their shoulders. Mentàll's knife felled another. Just as swiftly, his flying sword skewered another. With a shaking hand, Methusal threw her own knife. It missed her intended target by a mile, but it sank into a Zindedi's stomach. With a gurgle, he doubled over.

A gun fired as Methusal threw her kaavl stick end over end through the air. Her stick exploded in midair. Barak's glinting knife distracted another soldier, and the bullet flew wild and imbedded in the wall. Barak's weapon found its mark, however, and the Zindedi fell.

The remaining Zindedis looked at their fallen comrades. Still, the ground trembled beneath their feet. One struggled to reload his gun. The other, obviously the officer, shouted, "Get reinforcements!" The two ran out.

Methusal, Barak, and Mentàll quickly retrieved their weapons. Mentàll grabbed a flickering lantern and slipped into the dark secret passage. Barak closed it behind them. Hopefully it wasn't a dead end, or a trap of some kind. And hopefully part of the passage hadn't collapsed during the explosion. Methusal didn't like the thought of having to return to the General's study if the tunnel ahead had collapsed. Soldiers would surely be waiting for them to return, with guns drawn.

The cold, dank passage led steadily downward. The flickering light illuminated boot prints.

"Those tracks look fresh," she commented. "The General must have come this way."

Mentàll did not answer.

She tried again. "Where is that pit you were talking about?"

He did not answer that, either. Frustration grew.

"Shh!" He stopped. "Listen."

She heard a faint sigh. "Is that the wind?"

"No." The Dehrien handed the lantern back to Barak, and moved forward again, into the dark. They came to a fork in the passage. The fresh boot prints went right.

"I will follow the General," Mentàll said. "Barak, you and Methusal go down the other path. It leads to the pit."

Methusal wondered how he could possibly know that.

The lantern Barak held lit their path, and Methusal briefly wondered how the Dehrien was managing without one as he stalked down the General in the other passage. How could he see? Or perhaps, like a wild beast, he could see better in the dark than in the light.

The sigh she'd heard before grew louder. Now it sounded like rushing water.

Barak stopped a little later, and gestured with the lantern. "Look."

The tunnel ended where a rushing stream crossed their path. It appeared from the right, and disappeared downhill into an oval opening to the left. Methusal took the lantern from Barak and crouched down in order to see better. The cool scent of damp earth reached her nostrils. Wet rocks gleamed in the light. A dirt path bordered the right side of the stream. Were those boot prints?

"Look at the path," she whispered. "Someone walked on it recently. Let's see where it goes." Bent double, she waded into the cold stream and into the waist high tunnel to the left. Rushing water surged around her ankles. It was freezing cold, as if it had just melted from the high Quasr Mountains.

Barak followed silently. Methusal tried to walk on the dirt path, but it proved to be muddy and slick, so she returned to the stream. Her feet grew numb as she walked steadily downhill. How much further underground did this stream go? And where did all of the water empty out? It couldn't possibly empty into the ocean. They were well below sea level by now.

Methusal followed the stream around a long, slow corner. Then she stopped with a gasp. A huge, underground lake pooled inside of a massive cavern. A few steps later she was able to straighten up, and Barak stopped beside her. Awe registered on his swarthy face.

Glittering crystal stalactites dripped from the domed ceiling, which she estimated must be three lengths high. But she saw no outlet for the lake. The cavern seemed completely enclosed. She didn't see a pit, either.

"Deccia!" she cried out. Her voice echoed.

Barak thundered, "Deccia!"

Her ears strained. Was that a faint cry? She focused into kaavl and listened intently.

"Deccia!" Barak roared.

The blast hit Methusal's kaavl sensitive eardrums like a punch to the head. She reeled, covering her ears. "Stop, Barak!"

After the ringing subsided, she listened again, as hard as she could. She'd thought she heard a faint sound ahead, and to the right. She hurried that way. "Deccia!" she called again. Now she spotted another faint path. It led to a small hole in the wall, and it was barely big enough for a man to get through.

Methusal crawled inside and lifted the lantern. It was another cave, and as dark as pitch. Water dripped somewhere. She crept further inside. The dirt was soft here. And the wall to the right...she touched it. The soft earth dented beneath her fingers. It wasn't a wall at all, but rather a mound of freshly dug dirt, piled as high as the ceiling. It must be at least one length high.

Someone had dug a pit in here. Horror engulfed her.

"Methusal," Barak rumbled. "What do you see?" He knelt at the opening and peered inside.

"Deccia's close. I know it. I feel it."

Barak scrambled through, and Methusal carefully walked forward, holding the lantern high. The light illuminated only blackness—black dirt, black walls, and black floor. Each step felt like it carried her deeper into nothingness. To her right, the wall fell away and sloped downward. "Deccia?" she called.

"I'm here!" cried a faint voice.

"Deccia!" Methusal ran forward, but Barak grabbed her arm. He stopped her just in time. A pit yawned open at her feet.

Barak took the lantern and lifted it higher, illuminating the deep, narrow pit. The light shone onto Deccia's upturned, grimy face. She was at least three lengths down.

"Deccia, are you all right?" Methusal cried out. She went down on her knees at the edge.

"Hold on, Deccia. We'll get you out." Barak unstrapped his pack and pulled out a coil of rope. He tied one end into a loop. "Put the rope around your hips and I'll pull you up."

Methusal grabbed the lantern and held it high so they could all clearly see the loop rope descend into the pit. When Deccia grabbed it, her heart soared. Quickly, Barak pulled her sister out. Deccia tried to sit up, but collapsed sideways into a fetal position.

"How long have you been down there?" Methusal whispered in horror.

"A few...days. I'm so...thirsty."

Barak already held his water skin to Deccia's lips. Cradling her head, he urged her to drink. She gulped, but more water washed onto her face and neck than went into her mouth

"We have to get her out of here," Barak said grimly. He gently lifted Deccia in his arms and retraced their steps to the small opening. After he set her down, he crawled through first, and then Methusal helped her sister crawl out. Then Barak lifted Deccia in his arms again and they headed back the way they had come.

Going uphill, bent double, through the icy stream was hard work, and Methusal didn't know how Barak managed it.

Once out of the stream and in the main tunnel again, Methusal offered more water to her sister. Deccia drank weakly, and then her head lolled back on Barak's arm. She looked like death warmed over.

If they hadn't come today to rescue her...

Fear made Methusal feel sick. Why would someone dig a pit like that? It was insane. But look who they were dealing with. The General. The man was cruel and insane. She wanted to rip his *eyes* out. The violence of her emotions scared her.

She wondered how they would ever escape from this labyrinth of tunnels. One path led to the General's quarters. This one led to the pit. That left only one other path—the one Mentàll had taken to follow the General.

Methusal longed for sunshine. It seemed as if they'd been walking underground for hours.

Mentàll met them just before the fork in the path. "You found her."

"How did you know about the pit?" Methusal wanted to know. "It was freshly dug."

He sent her a cold look. "I have sources, Methusal."

Barak spoke. "Did you kill the General?"

"No. But the path leads east. It is our only way to escape."

Mentàll led the way. Deccia now appeared to be unconscious in Barak's arms.

The path climbed steadily uphill now, and it ended at a ladder. The Dehrien Chief crawled up first into the empty shack, and then reached down to help Barak with Deccia. Her sister looked like a lifeless doll, and tears filled Methusal's eyes as she knelt beside her in the hut. "You'll be all right, Deccia," she whispered. "You will."

"Barak. Carry Deccia to base camp. Methusal and I will return to the compound."

"Yes, sir." The big man scooped up Deccia again.

When Barak slipped out the door, Methusal recognized their position. They were in the southeastern area of town. Shots rang out to the north, and swords clanged two buildings west.

"Be safe!" she urged. Heart in her throat, she watched Barak lumber down the nearest alley. She prayed for their safe passage to the foothills.

"Come, Methusal." The Dehrien silently slipped west, heading toward the General's compound again. With a final glance after her sister, Methusal followed.

△ △ △ △ △

The floor still quaked beneath Hendra's feet, and it took a moment for her to realize what had happened. Bullets pinged into the wall around her. Then Tabor grabbed her arm and dragged her through a doorway. But not before she saw that Riln's prisoner had been shot. In addition, a Koblani soldier lay face down on the floor.

Tabor shoved her after Behran and three other warriors into a short, dark passage, and slammed the door behind them. He turned the lock for good measure.

Two smoking torches on the wall lit their path, and led to a door at the far end.

Zindedis pounded on the first door. A gun blasted, and a hinge gave way.

"Quick!" Hendra gasped. Behran barged through the next door and ran down the stairs. Rank, cold air assailed her nostrils. It smelled horrible, like a garbage heap, or a sewer.

A man retched behind her. Riln. Hendra pressed the hem of her tunic to her nose and followed Behran through the damp, drippy room to another door. And then they were in a well-lit hall. It had clean, shiny wooden floors.

What in the world? What kind of a place was this?

"Split up. Check the rooms," Behran said.

Hendra ran to obey. At the same time, she focused kaavl glances at each end of the hall. So far, no Zindedis would come. And the room she peeked into looked like sleeping quarters. Perhaps for servants, or lower ranked officers.

At the end of the hall, Riln waved a hand. "Come on," he urged. "Stairs."

More stairs led downward. How deep did this mansion go, Hendra wondered. It looked huge on the outside, but with these underground corridors, who knew how many blocks the complex covered.

At the bottom of the stairs, the hallway split.

"I'll go left," Riln said. "Who's with me?"

Several Koblani warriors ran down the hall with him. Hendra, Behran, Tabor, and the others went right. At the end, they faced two doors. One led to a dark hall, and the other led to a short hall with barred doors. The prison!

"Lelm!" Tabor growled. "Cratn!"

"Here!" cried a man's voice. "We're at the end of the hall."

Several warriors sprinted down the hall and attacked the door with their bare hands. Behran found a key. Within moments, the Tarst prisoners exploded from the cell and hugged their comrades.

Finally, a happy sight. Hendra smiled, and cast a focused glance toward each end of the hall. Nothing. She swept a gaze down the hall again, and froze. A door in the middle might have moved. She watched intently. Suddenly hordes of Zindedis charged out. On a hunch, she glanced further down the hall, to the door they'd first come through. A pack of Zindedis flooded through that door, too.

"Behran!" Hendra turned panicked eyes to him. At first she didn't think he'd heard her.

"What is it?"

"Zindedis! Coming there...and there!" Hendra flew down the passage, trying all of the other doors. They only opened into cells. There were no more passages. Now the men caught wind of her panic. Tabor and the other warriors pulled out their swords.

Behran backtracked to the Tarst prisoners' cell door at the far, safe end of the hall. "Hendra. Come here."

Tears pooled in her eyes, and she stumbled toward him. "We can't escape. Behran, we can't..."

Behran pulled up her hood and shoved her behind him. "Don't let them see your hair. We can't let them know you're a woman."

A blood curdling cry rent the air, and Zindedi soldiers poured out of the two doors, just as she had foreseen. Terror overcame her. They were trapped.

△ △ △ △ △

As Methusal and the Dehrien Chief backtracked to the General's compound, the clash of weapons and the roar of guns grew louder. To her surprise, Goric darted across the street, toward them. She recalled that he'd been assigned to Pan's war team. He looked panicked and lost.

She caught his arm before he could sprint south. "What's going on?"

"Zindedis swarmed the compound." A brief flash of bewilderment hardened those murky eyes. "Everyone's escaping."

"Everyone?"

"Some of the team split up and headed north. Warriors are still fighting, but..." Did shame flit across his features? "I'm not good enough with the knife. Let go! I need to run."

"But what about Behran? Did you see him?"

"No!" Goric twisted free, and ran south as if the devil pursued him.

During this small drama, Mentàll had continued to advance toward the compound. She ran to catch up. "Goric said Zindedis have overrun the compound. Some of the kaavl team escaped. But not..."

"Shh!" Mentàll ducked behind a broken fence. From there they had the perfect view through the southern gate into the compound. It looked quiet. Flowers in the garden swayed in the gentle breeze. No soldiers were posted at the gate.

"Kaavl players might be captured," she whispered. "We need to find out, and save them."

"It is not safe."

Methusal carried with vision. "The garden is empty. We could sneak in that door. Where does it lead?"

"Downstairs, to the servants' quarters. And to the prison where they held you."

"See? If they've captured more prisoners, that's where they'll be. We should rescue them."

"Are you finished?" He sounded sarcastic.

"Come on!" She leaped to her feet.

"It is not *safe!*"

But she saw and heard that all was clear. It was safe for now.

She darted inside the compound. Mentàll followed, fury clear in every stiff line of his body. She flattened herself against the wall and projected her hearing inside the door that led to the prison. Chaos. Shouts. Swords clashing. A scream. A clang of metal; perhaps a door closing.

A gruff voice said, "We killed one, Commander. The other six are in the cell. Including the blond one you stabbed a few weeks ago. I punched him in the ribs, and he threw up. He was trying to protect some skinny, blond-haired boy. I threw them both in prison."

Horror gripped her. Behran! And maybe the other person was Hendra.

"That Dehrien Chief has to be close," someone stated in deep, clipped tones. "Scour the grounds. Kill him on sight. Good thing we had this plan in place. None of them will escape alive."

She heard a rush of movement from the compound courtyard to her far right, but it barely registered. She could barely think. Behran was captured.

It was just like Deccia, all over again.

"Follow me, Methusal," Mentàll ordered.

"No! Behran's captured! So is..."

"Now!" His hard grip hurt her arm as he yanked her behind a nearby bush.

She struggled to free herself. "We have to save them! No one is inside the door. It's safe. Hurry!"

"Come! *Now*."

A pack of invaders spilled around the corner. They let out a great shout. "Get them!"

They had been seen. Methusal fled after Mentàll for the southern gate.

Evidently she wasn't moving fast enough to please him. His painful grip on her wrist forced her to fly behind him. They ducked through the gate just as a gun exploded. The compound wall shattered above her head.

At a dead sprint, they reached the main street. Pandemonium reigned. People ran screaming in every direction. Soldiers fired guns in the air.

The Dehrien sprinted down a narrow alley and cut right, to another street. He was fast. She couldn't keep up. "Mentàll!" she gasped. "Wait. I can't..."

"Stop, and you die," he snarled. "Run!"

A pack of soldiers charged after them. More guns fired, and a bullet pinged off the wall beside her. Another creased her sleeve. Terror lent wings to her feet. They ran down one alley, through a burnt house, and then zigzagged through multiple streets and alleys. Most of their pursuers fell far behind.

They reached the bush studded plains, but still the Dehrien Chief did not slow. A few shots followed their darting path as they took cover behind bushes. The gun fire gradually slowed down to intermittent blasts. The few remaining soldiers seemed to be giving up. Odd. She wondered why.

Her breaths came in harsh gasps when they finally reached the foothills and ducked behind a large rock. She put her head down on her knees, trying to regain her breath. The instant she did, she turned on the Dehrien. "We left them behind!"

"Yes. We are no good to them dead."

Methusal clenched her fists. "Don't you care about anything except saving your own hide? We could have saved them! That doorway was clear!"

"The prison passageway was not."

She glared at him. He had left them behind, just as he had left Deccia behind weeks ago. Anguish made her feel sick. "We left them to die!"

"The General will use the prisoners as bait. He will not kill them. Yet."

She wanted to scream at him, but did not. "*Behran's* there! And Hendra." Shock dilated the icy eyes. "That's right. Hendra. Your cousin. *Now* do you care? If you'd known, would you still have run, you coward?" She tried to spring to her feet, but he gripped her hard by the shoulders and forced her back down again, to safety.

"Silence!" he hissed, shaking her a little. "You do not know what you are saying."

"I *do!*" she shouted, and abruptly burst into tears. "And I hate you. *I hate you!*" She grabbed his tunic and tried to shake him, but could not. He was immovable. "I *hate* you!" she said in a low scream. "You left them!" Gulping sobs erupted, and she could not stop them.

"Stop it." He still gripped her shoulders.

"No! I *won't.*" She struggled to free herself, but couldn't. That didn't surprise her, either. Gulping on a sob of grief, she fell forward. To her consternation, her head hit his chest. She jerked away, but couldn't go far.

"Methusal."

She closed her ears, weeping harder. "They're going to die," she choked out in a keening wail. "And it's *our* fault. We should have saved them!"

"Methusal." Against her will, he pulled her closer to him. His arms coiled around her, so she couldn't wriggle free, and she found her face against his shoulder. She wept harder, in complete humiliation. She struggled, but it was no use, and finally, after a long time, she quit trying, and crumpled against him. Only then did the arms that felt like bands of ore around her relax a little.

He felt warm and solid, but not comforting. How could she find comfort in the arms of this hard man, her worst enemy?

The Dehrien said nothing until she snuffled into silence. She wiped her running eyes and nose on her sleeve. Only then did he let go. She sat back and averted her face.

"Now we will have the truth, Methusal." The quiet words sounded cold.

"Your truth, of course."

"You want to be dead?"

"I'd rather be dead than a coward!"

He drew in a hissing breath. "We are free. How could we help them if we were dead?"

"We could have done *something* to rescue them. There had to be a way."

"Did you count the soldiers, Methusal? Eighteen chased us."

She had not realized that. She'd been too overcome with worry about Behran to pay attention. "We could have broken into the servants' quarters before they saw us. Then..."

"No. It was not safe. I told you that. And they saw me."

"They saw *you*. Not me. I could have..."

"Methusal," he gritted. "Think logically. They saw us too quickly. Your plan could not work. I would be dead! And so would you, because you are with me. How would that help Behran? Or Hendra?"

Methusal said nothing.

"We lost that battle. See? Warriors are retreating, as planned."

She looked. Koblani warriors dotted the plain and took shelter behind thick bushes. A line of their fiercest warriors formed a barrier, battling Zindedis who tried to follow the retreating troops. That's why the soldiers had stopped following them.

Harshly, Mentàll stated, "We will return and finish the fight when the Wyen come. You are a soldier, Maahr! Use your brain instead of your heart."

She glared. "Lucky for you, you don't have one. Must make your life so simple."

Red etched his cheekbones. "I saved your life."

She forced herself to meet the icy eyes. "Thank you," she enunciated clearly.

Now he looked disgusted, and stood abruptly. He climbed the hills toward base camp. Methusal followed, but at a good distance. She didn't want to see him. She didn't want to speak to him.

Unfortunately, Mentàll was right. It was hard to admit it. They couldn't have saved Behran or Hendra. Logically, she knew this. But her heart could not stand the thought of Behran being imprisoned by that insane, sadistic man. She wiped away the tears that kept falling.

She had been wrong to run into the compound against orders, too. It had almost cost them their lives.

Mentàll had saved her life. *Again.*

The familiar hills near base camp appeared. The Dehrien Chief drew further ahead of her, and Methusal ran to catch up. As they descended into camp, she gripped his arm. He shook her off like an annoying insect.

"Mentàll. I'm sorry."

Those pale eyes remained cold. It disturbed her more than she liked. Whether it was true or not, Methusal felt like she'd gained a scrap of his respect over the last few weeks, and didn't want to lose it now. "I'm sorry I disobeyed your orders and ran into the compound. Thank you for saving my life. And I'm sorry I called you a coward."

"Is that all?"

"I was angry. And I took it out on you. Will you please forgive me?"

The rigid set of his shoulders relaxed. "*You* are begging for *my* forgiveness, Methusal?"

"Don't press your luck."

"Apology accepted. Report to Erl when he arrives."

"I will."

A mask settled over his features, and he strode off, leaving her alone. Methusal watched him go. Something was wrong. Something more than her insubordination. It was easy to guess what it was. Hendra was a prisoner. So was Behran, and probably other kaavl players, too.

She wondered if the invasion had done any good at all. Or had they only lost more people to the ruthless Zindedis?

Behran. What would the Zindedis do to him?

△ △ △ △ △

To her relief, Methusal found Deccia lying on a pallet in the medical tent. Barak had managed to carry her home safely. Aali was spooning broth into her mouth, and she glanced up when Methusal approached. "Thusa! Deccia's going to be all right. Doc says she's just dehydrated."

"Good." She felt even more relieved when Deccia offered her a weak smile.

"Can you take over?" her cousin asked. "Doc's mad at me for skipping off today. He has lots of work for me to do."

Methusal accepted the bowl and spoon. Dryly, she said, "I'd think you'd want a nap, after staying up all night."

"I had a little one in the hills. At least I did until Barak came with Deccia."

Doc appeared. "You made it back fast, Methusal." He glanced toward the tent opening. "Is the whole kaavl team back?"

"No." She bit her lip. Tears stung her eyes, but she blinked them away. "I...I have bad news."

Doc's face drained completely of color. "Hendra."

"And Behran. They're both captured."

Aali gasped. "No!"

Doc's hand curled around a nearby tent pole, and he stood very still. His knuckles showed white, as if he were in great pain—or fighting for calm. After a long moment, he let go. "Thank you, Methusal. Aali. I need you in the back."

Aali's skin tone looked sickly. Uncharacteristically silent, she followed Doc's instructions.

"Thusa, that's enough." Deccia refused the spoon, and struggled to sit upright.

"You should lie still," she fussed.

Stubbornly, though, Deccia sat up and leaned against the tent wall, which was supported by a pole in that section. She whispered, "I feel a hundred times better. I'm so relieved I'm out of that black pit."

"I dreamed you were in a pit. I just *knew*..." For a moment, Methusal couldn't say more. The unspeakable horror she'd felt in her sister's place, and the fear... "I dreamt I was you, Deccia, so many times. And every time the dreams came true. Before the pit, I dreamed..." She broke off, remembering how the nightmare in the General's office had ended. Deccia wouldn't want to be reminded of that horrible episode.

"Tell me." Her sister's eyes looked calm; too calm. Almost dead. "It can't be worse than what I've already lived through."

Methusal bit her lip. "I dreamed you were in the General's office. He said he knew where kaavl camp was. He said he'd spare your life one more day, but he'd kill you as soon as he found me. He...he asked if you were grateful." Her voice broke. "And...and then..." She found she could not finish. "My dream ended, so I didn't see, but... I *prayed*, Deccia. I prayed he'd leave you alone."

Deccia's sigh sounded exhausted. "The One answered your prayers, and mine, too. A guard interrupted before..." With visible effort, she said, "He told him the kaavl team had escaped. He ordered me thrown into the pit, instead."

"They *threw* you?"

"It was narrow. I hit the walls going down." She looked at her hands. "I dug in with my fingernails. It slowed my fall. Maybe that's why I didn't break any bones." Her voice turned soft and bleak. "After a while, I wondered why I had bothered. Time passed so slowly. It seemed like an eternity. And then...and then I knew," her voice broke. She drew a shaky breath. "They had left me down there to die."

"Oh, Deccia!" Methusal hugged her sister tightly. Deccia didn't cry, and that worried her. In fact, she didn't respond at all. "Are you tired?" she said anxiously, gently releasing her grip.

"Sleep won't make me feel better, Thusa." Deccia closed her eyes. Her skin looked translucent, and tightly drawn over her gaunt face. She had been malnourished and mistreated, but she looked clean. Someone must have helped her bathe.

"Deccia, I'm here. Whenever you want to talk..."

"I know." Her twin's lips quivered, and she reached for Methusal's hand, which she quickly clasped. "I feel so dirty, Thusa." She drew a quick, choking breath. "I feel awful, like I'll never, ever be clean again."

"I love you. All of us love you. And especially Timaeus. We'll help you get through this. You'll never be alone again."

"I want to sleep now." She curled up on her side.

Methusal pulled the coverlet over her shoulders. "I'll send in Timaeus when he gets back. He's checking on the Wyen war team."

"No. Please. But you come back. Promise?"

Deccia didn't want to see Timaeus? Methusal's worry doubled. "Of course. Rest for a while. I'll be back soon."

Deccia lay quietly, and Methusal went to find Doc, who frowned at a parchment on his desk. When he glanced up, his gaze looked blank, as if he was lost in thought.

"Will Deccia be all right?"

The Tarst doctor immediately focused and glanced back at Deccia. "Physically, she'll be fine in a day or two. But emotionally... Do you know what happened to her?"

"Yes." But she said no more. It wasn't her story to tell.

He nodded. "Be there for her, Methusal. Listen to her. She's going to need it."

"I will. I'll be back soon." She pushed through the tent flap and into the early afternoon sunlight. The brightness blinded her. It seemed strange to enter the well-lit, cheery sunshine, while inside her sister lived in a black pit of misery; in a nightmare that would likely haunt her for the rest of her life.

Tears blurred her eyes. She wanted to scream to the heavens, *Why? Why did this happen to her?* What harm had Deccia ever done to anyone?

Yes, she was glad that her prayers had been answered, and that Deccia was safe now. But it didn't seem like enough. Not nearly enough. Her mind turned to Behran, and worry nearly choked her. *What's happening to Behran, The One? Please protect him, and Hendra, too!*

Δ Δ Δ Δ Δ

Hendra sat huddled with her arms around her knees, in the back corner of the dark cell. Behran sat beside her, and Tabor and Wortn beyond him. Four other warriors, as well as Lelm and Cratn, paced the tiny cell. Two lay dead in the hall, both shot through the head. Hendra wanted to close her mind to those images, but could not. She pressed her wet cheeks against her drawn up knees. She hoped Riln and the Koblani warriors had escaped.

Guards shouted in the hall. It seemed to be their favorite pastime.

"Now?" demanded one.

"The blond one," roared another.

A head darkened the window, and the door lock rattled.

The blond one? Did they mean her? Had they figured out she was Mentàll's cousin?

Hendra hugged her knees tighter, and tried to quiet her panicked breaths. Would she die a coward, and bring disgrace to Dehre? No. Never. But that feeble bit of determination didn't quiet her fears.

The cell door swung open, and the guard lifted a torch high. The bright light made Hendra squint like a burrowing apte. She scrunched against the wall, tugging her hood down to make herself look smaller.

"You!" The burly guard pointed at Behran. "Come now."

"Behran!" Hendra whispered, clutching his sleeve. "No."

Behran pulled free and stood. "Why do you want me?" He sounded fearless.

"General wants to question the prisoners." The guard grinned. A black gap appeared where his front teeth should be. "Guess you're first." When Behran didn't move, the guard forced him out.

Behran glanced back as he staggered out. His blond hair drooped across his forehead. "I'll be back."

"You hope," sniggered the guard, and slammed the door shut.

Behran! Hendra pressed her fingers to her mouth to silence a scream of protest. No! *Please, The One. Protect Behran. Protect us all!*

△ △ △ △ △

Worry for Behran intensified as Methusal left the medical tent. *Please protect him, The One!* Again, she wondered if her prayers did any good. Yes, Deccia had been protected and rescued. Maybe The One did listen. But so many bad things had happened, too.

And what about all of the other things The One required of her? Being kind to her enemies, for example. What good had that done? Did it make any difference? She had tried to be kind to Mentàll. He still hated her. She'd failed to be nice to Jascr, and he hated her, too.

Sometimes she wished The One was right here, so she could ask questions and *understand*. Walking by faith was a hard road to travel.

Her stomach rumbled, so she swerved by the dining area to grab a meat strip. Aenill was nowhere in sight, but meat roasted on the spit out back. It smelled delicious, and her stomach gurgled.

When she turned to leave, Jascr blocked her path. Her gasp of surprise turned into a choke, because he stabbed a knife into her tunic. Right at her heart.

She went very still. Her kaavl stick had been blown to bits, but her knife...

"Don't move," Jascr smiled.

"What do you want?"

"You. Dead."

"Do you plan to kill me now?"

His knife stroked her tunic, slitting a hole in the leather. "Soon."

She forced herself to remain still while she weighed her options. A sudden move and Jascr might stab her through the heart. "Why not an honorable battle to the death?"

He continued to smile, which gave her the creeps. "Your death will not be swift, Methusal. I promise you that."

Her hand crept toward her blade. "Your hatred is wasted energy, Jascr. I've done nothing to you. Why do you keep harassing me?"

A kaavl stick hit her hand, knocking it away from her knife. She winced, despite herself.

"You are easy to hate. You are arrogant, prideful, and you *humiliated* me. I will humiliate you."

"You sound just like your cousin."

Jascr showed his teeth. "As I said. You are easy to hate."

Goric appeared in her side vision.

"So, two whips will attack one defenseless woman. Your honor astounds me. And your *bravery*...well, it's the stuff of legends."

Goric cast Jascr an uneasy glance.

Jascr pressed the knife harder, so it bit into her flesh, but she willed herself not to flinch. "You will pay, Methusal. You, *Mentàll,* and everyone else who has ever humiliated me." He held the knife still another long moment, and stared into her eyes. With seeming reluctance, he retracted it. He leaned closer. "Watch your back. Because it will be *me*. I will get you when you least expect it."

Jascr walked away. With a quick, skittish glance at her, Goric disappeared, as well.

Methusal trembled where she stood. Jascr's sudden attack had surprised her. He could have killed her. She had to find another kaavl stick, and right away. And she had to remain on guard at all times from now on.

△ △ △ △ △

After eating the meat strip and finding and shaping a new kaavl stick, Methusal found Pan's wife and helped her chop tubers for dinner. She still felt shaky from the encounter with Jascr, and didn't want to be alone. And she kept worrying about Behran.

When she'd finished, Aali appeared, carrying a soup bowl and plate. Her cousin's skin tone looked healthier than it had in the medical tent when she'd received the news of Behran's imprisonment. In fact, right now Aali looked remarkably energetic for someone who had only had a few minutes of sleep in two days. Exhaustion had begun to erode at the edges of Methusal's mind, even with her four hours of sleep.

"Guess what, Thusa?" Her cousin pushed the dirty dishes into a tub of water and joined her at a table.

"What?" Methusal covered a yawn.

"Deccia ate all of the soup, and some bread, too! Doc is really happy. He says she'll be herself in no time." Apparently this good news was the source of Aali's revived spirits.

Methusal didn't want to put a damper on Aali's hopes. But it would be a long time—if ever—before Deccia was herself again.

"*And,*" Aali finished with flourish, "Deccia's actually sitting up, and she even smiled once."

A shadow blocked the sun. Voice husky, Timaeus asked, "Deccia's *here?*"

"She's asking for Thusa," Aali informed him.

"I need to see her. You don't mind if I go first, do you?" Timaeus' urgent tone and longing gaze beseeched Methusal.

Methusal remembered that Deccia had said she didn't want to see Timaeus. Hopefully she would change her mind, now that she felt a little better, but still... Gently, she said, "Why don't I go first? I'll make sure she's ready."

Aali added helpfully, "She'll want to brush her hair."

"Okay," he agreed with clear reluctance. "But tell her I can't wait to see her. I don't care what her hair looks like."

"I will," Methusal promised. As she stood, she remembered Timaeus' mission. Insight flashed, too, as to why he'd been assigned to do it. Maybe it had been designed to keep him safely away from the battle in Quasr, and Deccia's rescue, too? Maybe it had been meant to keep him from acting on impulsive emotion. "When will the Wyen arrive?"

"Tomorrow morning. Is Dastn back yet?"

"No," Aali said. "He's still messengering for the war team in Quasr."

Outside, the sun hovered above the western ridge. Dusk would soon arrive. Hopefully Dastn, her father, and the rest of the war teams would arrive soon, and safely.

"The mission was a success, wasn't it?" Aali asked. Then she frowned. "Except for Behran and Hendra, of course."

"I hope so," Methusal agreed. "When Papa gets back, hopefully he'll have an idea of how many Zindedis are left."

"The tide has turned," Aali predicted. "Now that the munitions building is blown up, their guns are useless. Soon we'll be able to rescue Behran and Hendra."

"Erl blew up the munitions shack?" Relief rang in Timaeus' voice.

"*I* blew it up," Aali corrected.

"*You* blew it up?" Methusal exclaimed. Timaeus stared at Aali with his mouth agape.

"Yes." she grinned, clearly pleased by their reactions. "I had it all figured out. When I told Uncle Erl my plan, he agreed to it. So I crawled inside, lit a candle, and the warriors dragged me out. Then we ran and...KABOOM!"

"That's wonderful, Aali!"

"Awesome," Timaeus agreed.

She looked pleased. "Maybe now people will treat me seriously. I'm not a kid anymore."

"Does that mean you'll give me your dessert tonight?" Timaeus teased. "You've probably outgrown that, too."

Aali rolled her eyes, but smiled.

"I'll check on Deccia. See you soon," Methusal promised, and headed for the medical tent. Hopefully, her sister was doing better, as Aali seemed to think.

△ △ △ △ △

An hour passed before the prison door banged open, and the guards thrust a bleeding Behran back inside the tiny cell. He staggered toward Hendra, and the guards grabbed Tabor and hustled him out.

Behran leaned against the wall, holding his ribs. He slid to the floor, his eyes half closed.

"Behran. Behran! What did they do to you?" Hendra whispered. A bruise darkened his cheek, and blood dripped from his split lip. But the way he clutched his chest made her worry. "Are you bleeding? Did they open the wound again?"

He drew in a slow breath. "The Commander...the one who stabbed me...took great...joy...in punching me."

"That's awful! Are you bleeding?" she asked again, urgently. "Should we check the stitches?"

He moved his hand, but no blood darkened his tunic. "I guess...I'll live." His faint smile resembled a grimace.

One of the warriors said, "What did they want?"

"Location...of base camp."

"Did you tell them?"

"I gave...directions...to Aestoff."

The warriors guffawed. One slapped his knee. "Good one."

Silence ensued. Talking seemed to hurt Behran's ribs, so Hendra said nothing else. Instead, she observed him as a patient. He took slow, shallow breaths, as if trying to ease the pain. Maybe it helped, because after a while he seemed to relax a little.

Hendra dreaded each clomp of the guards' feet in the hall, because each time she wondered who they'd haul away next.

After untold, interminable minutes crept by, a commotion erupted in the corridor.

"Straight ahead. March!" shouted a guard.

A number of feet shuffled in the hallway. Keys clanked in the lock.

"Get in there!" A guard shoved a man inside. It wasn't Tabor. Rather, a Tarst warrior whom Hendra had seen around base camp. And then another man—a Koblani warrior—followed. And more. At least eight additional men crammed into the tiny cell. Men backed up against Hendra and pressed against her folded legs, and another pushed in on her right. She breathed faster. Panic unfurled inside of her.

Last of all Tabor staggered in, sporting a black eye and a bleeding nose. All told, eighteen people were jammed into the prison cell.

"Nighty night," chortled the guard, and slammed the door.

The men standing above Hendra rumbled in low voices to one another. She huddled harder against the wall, wishing they would go away.

"Are they going to leave us here all night?" asked one warrior. "There's not even enough room to sit!"

"The whips. Stuffing us in here like rochers."

Men finally began to sit down. One sat directly ahead of her and pressed against her knees. A whimper started in the back of her throat, but she cut it off. Another shouldered into her right side. His hip touched hers, and she cringed away in horror. She leaned into Behran, unconsciously seeking his protection. His shoulder touched hers, but that didn't scare her as much as the creeping revulsion of the strange men touching her did.

Unfortunately, when she moved, the man to her right moved, too, and filled up the empty space. His arm pressed into hers. Fear billowed, and she helplessly shuddered.

"Are you all right?" Behran whispered.

She didn't answer.

"Come here." Behran slid an arm around her, giving her room to scoot closer. With reluctance, she did so. When the man beside her tried to move again, Behran's hand stopped him.

"Hey," growled the man. Then, "Behran?"

"Wortn."

Wortn? Hendra cringed further into Behran's side. Jascr's friend. He'd offered to marry her for a price—to pay off Jascr's steep debts. She shuddered again, unable to help herself.

She closed her eyes, trying to ignore the sights and sounds and feel of so many men pressing in around her. Tears filled her eyes. She couldn't block it out. *She couldn't.* Terror blanketed her mind and she gasped on a sob. If only the ice would come!

"What's wrong?" Behran's voice seemed to come from a great distance. She couldn't answer. The presence of the men pressed in on her. She couldn't escape. She *couldn't* escape! Her breaths came in gasps, and her chest felt tight. She moaned, and began to cry.

"Hendra?"

Her chest hurt. She couldn't breathe. As she choked for air, black dots danced before her eyes. Doc had held a bag to her lips.

She didn't have a bag. But maybe she could breathe inside her tunic? She pressed the leather to her nose, hoping it would help. And silently despairing that it wouldn't.

"Hendra." Behran rubbed her back. She shuddered harder, and concentrated on breathing. In, out. In, out. She was grateful when he stopped touching her.

Slowly, as excruciatingly long minutes crept by, her breathing slowed. Her senses gradually came into focus again. Hendra kept breathing in a slow, soothing rhythm, and kept her eyes closed. Now it wasn't so bad. If she didn't look. If she didn't *see.*

"Are you all right?" Behran sound worried.

She took a shallow breath. "Not... Not really." If she'd wanted to face her fear of men, now was her opportunity. And already she was drowning in failure.

"Don't worry," Behran said in a low voice. "I'll protect you. I won't let anyone hurt you."

Hendra wanted to cry. Faintly, she whispered, "Thank you, Behran."

She knew he would keep her safe—as well as he was able, anyway. But this demon—the fear of the men pressing in around her—was one that she must face on her own. Either she could learn how to control it now, or sometime during the night she would lose her mind.

Hendra closed her eyes. One painful breath at a time.

△ △ △ △

Methusal found Deccia sitting up in the medical tent, and hurried to sit beside her. "Aali said you're feeling better?"

"Physically." Her sister smiled, but it didn't reach her eyes.

"Timaeus is here," Methusal said softly. "He wants to see you. He's been worried sick."

At last, tears welled in Deccia's eyes. "I want to see him, too. But Thusa..." She looked quickly away for a moment, and then whispered, "I don't feel *right* to see him."

"You mean because of what the General did to you?"

"Of course!" She bit her trembling lip. "I'm ruined for him. I'm not pure or innocent anymore. I'm spoiled."

"He *loves* you. He won't care."

"You don't know that." Deccia drew a shuddering breath and wiped at the tears slipping down her face. "I'm afraid to tell him. I'm afraid I'm too *weak* to tell him."

"You don't need to say anything yet."

"But I *should*," she said in an anguished whisper. "I don't want to lead him on. He thinks he's getting something...something that doesn't exist anymore. I'm ruined for him, Thusa, don't you see? I have to tell him."

Anger at the General overtook Methusal, but she tried to erase the trembles from her voice. "I agree that you should tell him. But not until you're ready. Certainly not today, if this is how you're feeling."

"But I don't want him to waste any more time on me. I'll feel like I'm lying..."

"Stop it!" Methusal could barely suppress the fury she felt toward the General for hurting her sister in this way. "You are not ruined! You're still Deccia—the sister I love. And you're the woman Timaeus loves, too." More gently, she said, "You've been hurt. The wound is in your heart, and only love will heal it. You have to let Timaeus love you. Give him that chance."

Deccia pleated the blanket between her fingers. "I will tell him. But not today. Not yet."

"Take all the time you need. And if you want someone with you when you say it, I'll be there. All of us love you, Deccia. We'd do anything for you." Tears blurred her eyes, and she pulled her twin into a tight hug. "I love you. You're still just as wonderful as always. Don't let the General steal your self-worth."

Deccia wrapped her arms around Methusal and finally collapsed into deep, gut wrenching sobs. Afterward, Methusal helped repair the damage with a cool wash cloth and a hair brush.

Timaeus paced outside, waiting, when Methusal exited from the medical tent. Anxious, dark pain lived in his eyes. He knew. He'd probably known all along. And he loved her. Deccia was lucky that such a wonderful man loved her. "Is she ready?"

She managed a smile. "Yes."

"I'll be careful," he promised softly, and ducked into the tent.

Methusal knew that Timaeus would not pressure her sister. He'd let Deccia tell him in her own time, in her own way.

Tears blurred Methusal's vision. Hugging her arms around herself, she stumbled for the stream. She needed a splash of cool water to soothe her hot, aching eyes. But nothing could soothe her heart, except to see Deccia well and whole again.

△ △ △ △ △

After washing her face in the stream, Methusal went looking for the Dehrien Chief. Shadows darkened base camp. As usual, she needed to deal with his wound. Better to get it over with now, rather than be ordered to do so later. She was in an odd mood, because she actually wanted to face unpleasantness right now. Hopefully, in a few days the last scab would fall off. Then she could be done with him forever.

He wasn't in his tent. And she hadn't seen him at the stream a few minutes ago, either. Methusal checked the dining tent. He wasn't in there, either.

"You have the look of searching for someone," Aenill called, carrying a large pot to the buffet table. Heat flushed her perspiring face.

"Mentàll. Have you seen him?"

Aenill sent her a sharp glance. "It's an unusual day when you'd be looking for him, miss."

Methusal felt uncomfortable. "I just..."

"Or have you mended differences? I noticed you don't seem to mind his company so much anymore. Ever since returning from kaavl camp, I mean."

A flush scored Methusal's cheeks. My goodness, what could Aenill possibly be thinking? Did she think something had happened between them—could she sense that Mentàll had kissed her? Certainly not! Hastily, she lifted a coltac leaf. "I've been tending his wound. It's nearly healed, but..."

"But you need to find him." Aenill's perceptive glance scanned Methusal's face.

"Or he'll hunt me down later. The lesser of two evils."

"I see." Pan's wife gathered up her potholders. "I saw him head east, into the hills. "But I got the feeling he wanted to be left alone."

Nothing so small would stop her. "Thank you."

Still feeling disturbed, she climbed up into the rocky hills. Why in the world would Aenill think...? But Kitran had thought the same, she remembered, after she'd worn Mentàll's tunic after bathing. Circumstances could paint entirely the wrong picture of reality.

Maybe she'd better heed Kitran's advice about watching appearances. After all, Mentàll was still plotting some grand, unsavory scheme for Koblan. So her actions had better not give the false impression that she trusted him now.

Where was he, anyway?

Large boulders sent long, dark gray shadows over the hillside. The sun felt warm, but it was chilly in the shadows. Night would arrive soon. She shivered.

Maybe he was lurking at the very top of the hill. Knowing Mentàll, he'd probably want to feel like he was king of all he surveyed. She climbed to the pinnacle, but still didn't see him.

Maybe she should go back to camp.

A bit of warmth still touched the air up here, although the small breeze felt chilly. Pink and gold rays from the sunset toasted the pebbled earth a faint bronze color.

What a perfect view. The Tarst Peaks, to the south, were outlined in white snow, and the back of them were cast in shadow. Below, the men of base camp looked like insects. Ryon was already rising on the eastern horizon. It was full, so it would be bright tonight.

Methusal relaxed into kaavl and listened to the sounds around her. She didn't want Jascr to catch her unaware again. A faint noise tickled her ears. It came from her left, and it was down a bit on the back side of the hill. She intensified into kaavl and listened harder.

A man's breaths. Adrenaline made her pulse spike. Jascr? Or Mentàll?

Her hearing pinpointed that the man sat halfway down the hill, behind a huge boulder. A scratch of sound indicated foot movement.

Methusal unsheathed her knife and crept toward the sound, her senses on high alert.

She pressed her back against the boulder and crept left, downhill. Another step and she would see...

Just when she realized that she should carry with vision, silent footsteps whispered from her right. With a gasp, she whirled, knife arching up in self-defense. The Kaavl Commander caught her wrist, stopping the knife a handbreadth from his throat. Hard fingers pressed into her nerves, and all feeling left her hand.

"Methusal," he gritted.

Her fingers helplessly dropped the knife.

"You did not come to kill me, did you?" Predatory watchfulness lurked in those blue eyes. They looked threatening—an expression she had not seen in a while. Fear slid through her.

"No. Of course not. I...I came to tend your wound." His calculating suspicion did not abate. "I heard you," she explained. "And I didn't know if you were Jascr."

He released her wrist. Painful tingling returned to her hand, and she scooped up her knife with her other hand and resheathed it.

She didn't like him looking at her like that, so she turned her back on him and edged around the boulder, like she'd meant to do all along. Smaller boulders sank into the hillside here. The spot provided a beautiful view of the eastern mountains, which were now cast in shadows.

"What are you doing here?" She didn't have to look to see if he followed her. She sensed his presence, like a prickle down her spine.

"I was thinking."

When she glanced back, she saw that he still watched her with that same assessing, unreadable gaze. With one slow, deliberate movement, he pulled his tunic off, baring his shoulders. He turned his back to her; a silent order to tend his wound. Standing there, towering over her like this, he felt like a threat. He intended it—she sensed that to her very bones.

Methusal's fingers trembled a little, but she blamed that on her still tingling hand. With quick precision, she broke open the coltac leaf and rubbed it into the scar. She didn't want to touch him. She didn't want to notice anything about him, either, but couldn't seem to help herself. The heat from his skin warmed her fingers, and the muscle beneath felt supple and firm. She could not finish quickly enough.

"The last scab is gone," she said, rubbing the remainder on the backs of her scabbed hands. "It's healed."

Mentàll pulled on his tunic, and she felt relieved by that; even more, when he moved away to stare out at the horizon.

"What were you thinking about?" she dared to ask.

A short silence slipped by. "You enjoy danger, don't you, Methusal?"

"I must."

Long, silent moments elapsed. She thought he wouldn't answer at all.

At last, he said, "You would not understand."

"You're upset about Hendra."

The faint tightening of his shoulders indicated that she'd scored a direct hit.

She said, "I'm worried about Behran, too."

"Hendra was *my* responsibility!" The angry, harsh words shocked her into momentary silence.

"But she wanted to go..."

"She was *not ready to go*." He clenched his fists. "I should have sent her back."

Now she understood. He blamed himself for her capture. "She wanted to help win the war."

"She could be dead. Or with the General." His fingers dug into his short hair. "If he knows she is related to me..."

"We'll find her," she said softly. "Behran, too."

He abruptly sat on a boulder and leaned forward, locking his hands over the back of his head. The Dehrien reminded

Methusal of a wild beast. Unpredictable. Dangerous. But in pain.

She understood his pain. She'd felt it for Deccia, and now for Behran. Her heart ached with him for Hendra, too, and for all who were missing, or whose lives were lost. Impulsively, she touched his shoulder. "We'll rescue her. She'll be all right."

His shoulders tightened. They felt like hard, impenetrable ore, and she quickly removed her hand. Did that coldness permeate his heart? Or was that what he wanted everyone to believe?

With surprise, she said, "You love her."

"Of course," he snapped. "She's like my sister. She is the only family I have."

"I didn't think you cared about anyone but yourself. I see I was wrong."

"You know little about me, Methusal."

That was true. She could admit to one thing now. "I was wrong. You're not like your uncle, are you?"

Narrowed eyes looked up at her. Voice harsh with disbelief, he said, "You do not think I am cruel to you?"

"Yes. You are. And you're ambitious, ruthless, and you'll do whatever it takes to accomplish your goals. I'll certainly never trust you. But tell me. Am I the only one you're deliberately cruel to?"

Affirmation flashed, but he did not reply.

"Why?" For once, she wanted to know the truth. "Because I hurt your pride when I defeated you in Rolban?"

Anger flared. He would not admit it. That same pride refused to allow it.

He gritted, "Your kaavl does not equal my own."

"Maybe not," she admitted. "But is that why you're so cruel to me?"

The Dehrien rose to his feet, his emotions clearly in check again. "No. *Your* pride and your arrogance, Methusal, explain my feelings for you. It has given me great pleasure to keep you in your place."

"You whip." Fresh anger trembled through her.

"You wanted the truth, Methusal."

"Your *truth* cuts like knives."

"Then hear this. You cut under my skin." Tone freezing, he finished, "I do not want you there."

"I understand that feeling perfectly." How could this man be such a paradox? In pain one minute, and cruel and hurtful the next?

Without another word, she headed back to camp. Dusk had deepened, but Ryon's green light shone bright enough that it was easy to see the path.

The Dehrien Chief followed, but at a distance.

When she reached base camp, Dastn greeted her with a friendly grin, and swerved over to walk beside her. His friendliness salved her spirits. "You okay?"

"Yes." She forced a smile. "Did my father make it back safely?"

He nodded. "What about Aali? I heard she blew up the munitions building."

"She's fine." Methusal glanced into the dining tent. "Funny. She should be helping Aenill right now. Maybe Doc needs her. I'm sure she'll want to tell you all about her adventure."

His smile dimmed. "Probably not. See you at dinner, maybe." He headed for the medical tent—perhaps to look for her irrepressible cousin. Methusal hoped the lingering rift between Aali and the runner would heal soon.

While talking to Dastn, Mentàll had entered the packed dining tent ahead of her. No tables were available, but she did see her father. He sat across from Riln, who had apparently escaped from the General's compound, too. They spoke earnestly, obviously exchanging information. She didn't want to interrupt their conversation. Maybe she'd grab a plate and eat with Deccia in the medical tent.

She followed the Dehrien into line. He told Oona, "The food smells delicious."

Oona dimpled a smile up at him, and rewarded him with an extra helping of wild beast meat. Appropriate. Methusal averted her eyes from the admiring glance Oona slid over the Dehrien, and scooped up her own food. At the end of the line, Oona scraped together the last of the tagma berry dessert.

"Lucky you," she bubbled up to the Kaavl Commander. "You get the last piece."

Great. The Dehrien would get two portions of dessert, and she would receive none. Methusal plucked up a roll and sidestepped Mentàll in order to get out of line, but he backed up. She almost walked right into him.

Unable to help herself, she glared. "Do you mind?"

The Dehrien directed a thin smile at Oona. "Give the dessert to Methusal."

Methusal frowned harder. "Take your own dessert. I don't want it."

Oona glanced from one to the other, dessert dripping from the spoon. She looked confused.

With one arrogant wrist flick, Mentàll stole Methusal's plate and held it out to Oona, who plopped the dessert onto it. Then he shoved it back into her hands. His unreadable gaze held hers for a long moment.

She frowned more. Why had he done that?

"You are holding up traffic." The Dehrien headed outside, and since she had unfortunately planned to do the same, Methusal followed. He did not stop, however. Evidently he was finished speaking to her. Good. He headed for his tent.

"You're still a wild beast," she mumbled.

"Perhaps," he murmured. But he kept walking, as if he had not spoken at all.

What game was he playing now? Confused and unsettled, she headed for the medical tent. She would never understand him. Never.

△ △ △ △

Good spirits bubbled inside Aali as she hurried out the back flap of the medical tent and into the night. Uncle Erl had just congratulated her in front of Deccia and Doc about how well she had done. Without her, probably the whole mission would have been a disaster.

Well, he hadn't actually said *that*. But close enough.

Aali wondered if Dastn had heard of her success. She hadn't spotted him in camp yet. Soldiers were still straggling in. Ryon's light showed more men trudging down the far hill and into camp. She skulked behind the dining tent. When she peeked inside, she felt doubly glad that Aenill had let her eat early. The dining tent was full.

Ryon shone extra bright tonight. It was almost as light as the daytime. Perfect. She hiked up into the low hills behind the dining tent.

She felt about ready to crawl out of her skin from the excitement of the day. By rights, she should feel exhausted, since she'd had no sleep last night, but elation pumped up her spirits as she again remembered Erl's high praise. With the munitions building blown up, the whole tide of the war surely had changed. And she'd played an instrumental part in that.

And Deccia had been rescued, too. Except for poor Behran and Hendra's capture, the day couldn't have gone any better. Surely they would be rescued soon, too.

Aali climbed higher. Maybe she shouldn't be out here alone, but she hadn't seen Pogul in ages. Maybe he'd died in the battle. In any event, she didn't want to think about a slug like him right now. She wanted to climb the highest peak. She wanted to be on top of the world, because that is how she felt. *Finally,* she had proven herself. Now others would treat her with respect. Like an adult.

Rocks tumbled down the hill behind her. Had she dislodged them? Maybe she'd better practice kaavl.

She reached the top of the hill. Impulsively, she spun in a circle, arms outstretched. So what if she looked immature? No one could see her. She wanted to crow in triumph, too, but didn't dare. Base camp would hear her.

She stopped and crossed her arms, hugging them to herself, and looked up at the star spangled sky. A cold, crisp breeze ruffled her long hair. It was so beautiful tonight. It looked otherworldly, with Ryon bathing the world in that cool green light.

Half of the battle had been won today, she just knew it. And soon the Wyen would arrive and help defeat the Zindedis. Behran and Hendra would be rescued soon, too. No dream seemed too impossible on this wondrous night.

"Enjoying yourself?" The hiss came from behind her. She spun. Something snagged her hair. A hard yank nearly pulled her hair out by its roots.

She cried out, and a meaty fist connected with her jaw. Pain exploded.

Pogul.

With a flare of fear, she fumbled for her kaavl stick. Pogul punched her multiple times, hard and fast.

The painful assault disoriented her. She could barely think straight. But she finally freed her kaavl stick and swung at him. He seemed to have been waiting for it, because his own stick connected with hers, and sent a vibration up her arm from the impact. The stick trembled in her tingling hand, and like lightning, Pogul struck her forearm. She dropped it. When had he gotten so fast?

Panic screamed in her mind. *Pick it up!* But Pogul didn't give her the chance. He hit her with his stick again and again, connecting with her shoulder, her stomach, her head. She staggered backward and tripped over a stone. She fell hard on her backside, and lifted her arms in self-defense.

Pogul came closer, his grin leering in the moonlight, holding the stick raised high above his head. Aali kicked him hard in the kneecap. His thick lips curled back in a snarl, and he swung.

Pain shattered through her brain, and the night sky went black.

When Aali came to, she was lying on her stomach, and ropes bit into her wrists. Pogul gave these a hard tug, as if he was tightening a knot. Her brain felt fuzzy with pain, but she struggled to regain her senses. She struggled to slip into kaavl.

Pogul knelt beside her. What did he intend to do? He chuckled, and fear filled her. He didn't know she was awake. That was an advantage. If only she could stand up, maybe she wouldn't feel so vulnerable.

Tensing, she gathered her strength. She rolled quickly away from Pogul, up onto her knees, and then onto her feet. He sprang up too, glowering at her in the moonlight.

"You will pay, Aali. I'm not finished with you."

How could she defend herself with her hands tied behind her back? Awful, choking fear set in. She couldn't. She darted for the path downhill.

"No, you don't!" With a lunge, Pogul grabbed her shoulder. She staggered, but kept her feet.

"Let go!" she ordered through her teeth. "Uncle Erl will make you pay. Dastn will be here any minute. He'll beat you up!" A pathetic, idle threat. Dastn wasn't back yet. If only he was! If only he was following her and spying on her. But she'd chased him off, and now she had to face Pogul alone.

"No one will save you." He smiled. "Everyone knows you stupidly ordered off your faithful guard. You and Methusal are the same. Both arrogant. Both of you deserve to pay for what you did to me. I'm just happy I get to hurt one of you."

"Uncle Erl will find out."

"I don't think so. No one will ever find out."

What did he mean by that? Did he plan to *kill* her? Horrified, Aali elbowed him and twisted free, but Pogul swiftly grabbed her by the throat. He threw her to the ground. "Now you'll know what humiliation feels like."

Terror coursed through her. "Dastn!" she screamed.

But Dastn would never come. She had made sure of that. She was alone.

"*Dastn,*" she sobbed out, and kicked Pogul as hard as she could. She kicked in a frenzy. Some blows landed. Others met the air. Then Pogul landed on top of her, and all hope left her. Aali screamed again, long and piercingly. Someone had to hear. She didn't want to die! She choked on a sob.

Pogul grabbed her hair. "No," she cried out. "*Stop it. You're hurting me!*" Then Pogul's hand smothered her cries.

A large figure bolted like black lightning into her peripheral vision, and Pogul's weight lifted. Gasping, Aali scooted back and rolled into a sitting position. She could not see Pogul anymore. Only the broad back of her rescuer. Bones crunched as the man hit the scout with vicious ferocity.

Pogul dropped to the ground within moments, with dark blood smearing his face. He didn't move.

Her rescuer finally turned, and the light of the moon illuminated his familiar features.

"*Dastn?* Dastn! I didn't think you were back."

"I'm here." Dastn knelt beside her, and his large, blood smeared hand felt gentle on her cheek. "Are you hurt?"

"He punched me a lot. My hands are tied," she whispered.

He quickly freed her hands, and helped her to stand. Aali hurt all over. Her ribs, her stomach. And her arms and legs; everywhere Pogul had kicked her. It was only then that she realized the enormity of what he had planned to do to her.

"Dastn," she choked out, and wobbled toward him. He caught her in his arms and held her tight against him. She burst into tears. "I was stupid. So stupid!"

"Shhh," he whispered. "It's all right. He'll never bother you again."

"How do you know? He lives in Rolban! I'll never be free from him."

"What's going on?" Uncle Erl's voice surprised her. And then she heard other footsteps, too. "I heard you scream, Aali. Are you all right?"

"Yes," she sniffed, but didn't let go of Dastn.

The runner quickly explained what had happened, and at last she pulled free and wiped her eyes.

Pogul sat up with a groan. Barak grabbed him under the armpits and hauled him to his feet. Erl said in a deadly voice—one Aali had never heard before, "If you survive the next attack on the invaders, you'll spend the next three years in jail."

Pogul spit out something. Maybe a tooth. "I'm not scared."

"You should be," Erl sounded grim. "I hope your fighting skills are up to par."

"He's ready to fight a girl," Dastn said in a low, vicious voice.

"I can see that. Tie him to a tree for the night, Barak."

Aali followed the men back to camp, but slowed down before she reached her tent. She grabbed Dastn's hand before he could melt away into the night. Solemnly, she looked into his dark eyes. "I'm sorry, Dastn. I've been totally rotten to you. Please forgive me."

His hands closed gently around her forearms. His thumbs stroked them once. "I've already forgiven you, Aali." He smiled—the familiar one that curled up at just one corner. Sunshine slid into her soul. "But thanks."

Impulsively, she went up on tiptoe and kissed his scratchy cheek. "Good night." With a smile, she slipped inside her tent. A long moment later, she heard his footsteps recede into the night.

CHAPTER TWENTY-EIGHT

HENDRA FELL ASLEEP sometime during the night, and when she awoke, she was grateful that she'd had that short reprieve from fear. Big, burly men still surrounded her and touched her legs and arms, but no one had harmed her. Of course, few probably knew she was a woman.

At dawn, the guards ordered them all out of the cell. Her muscles protested when she stood, and fear again filled her. Where were they taking them? Zindedi guards poked the Koblanis with guns, forcing them into a single line down the hall. They shoved the men into a dark room. At the back of the line, Hendra crossed her arms and shivered, wondering what was going on. When men filed back out another door, she felt relieved.

The instant she set foot in the room, its smell told her the room's function. Horror crawled through her. She would have to relieve her body in front of all of these men? Boards lay over three holes in the ground. Some men squatted over them, and she hastily averted her eyes. Tears of panic and absolute horror burned in her eyes.

"I'll shield you," Behran whispered. "I won't let the guards know you're a woman."

Tears slid down her cheeks, but she nodded.

When it came her turn, she did her business as quickly as possible, and did not look at anyone. But she felt some Koblani men looking at her. They knew she was a woman. Her skin crawled with fear and mortification. Afterward, she hurried out of the rank smelling room. Her body felt better, but she felt as degraded and filthy as the dirt hall she walked down.

"In there!" A soldier shoved her shoulder and she stumbled back into the cell. She found a new corner to sit in. Behran appeared, and she felt better when he joined her. The room filled up with men again, and she closed her eyes and cringed against the wall.

The door clanged shut again.

"Where's Wortn?" A man asked.

Men shuffled about. But a quick survey proved that Wortn was gone.

Although Hendra felt no love for the man, fear crept through her. Why had the guards taken him? What was happening to him? And most terrifying—who would be taken next?

△ △ △ △ △

All of camp buzzed about Pogul's attack on Aali last night. When Methusal went to breakfast, the stocky young man sat tied to a tree in the middle of camp. Paradoxically, it was the same tree where the men had competed to test their strength last week.

If she hadn't already seen her cousin's purple bruises, she might feel sorry for the way people stared at Pogul and whispered about him. But he deserved it. Even now, Goric walked by and cast him furtive glances. Maybe he was contemplating his own fate if he decided to help Jascr attack Methusal. She could only hope.

While in the buffet line she saw Aali sitting across from Dastn at the table. Her long hair straggled across her cheeks, probably trying to hide her multicolored bruises. But she giggled at the runner, clearly in high spirits. Judging by his tolerant grin, Methusal deduced that they had made up.

She held her full plate and hesitated, not sure if she should interrupt and sit with them.

"Morning, Thusa." Timaeus spoke behind her, and when she turned, she saw that Deccia was with him.

She greeted her sister with a glad, one-armed hug. "Doc let you out?"

"Just for meals. He wants to keep an eye on me for a while longer."

"That's wonderful."

"Thanks for the clothes, Thusa." Deccia smoothed her hand down the tunic Methusal had leant her. "Timaeus buried my old ones this morning." The shadow in her eyes said she wished she could bury the memories associated with them, too.

"Of course." Methusal only wished she could do more for her sister.

After breakfast, Methusal quickly washed a few dirty clothes in the stream, and when she headed back into camp at midmorning, she saw waves of warriors in brown tunics descending into camp. The leader carried a fluttering, royal blue flag imprinted with a gold cross.

The Wyen. She stopped in her tracks, holding her dripping laundry, and watched the warriors stream into base camp. A hundred big, burly men were a fearsome, wonderful sight. And the Wyen were known for their fierce temperaments and courage. Her spirits soared. With these men, surely they could beat the Zindedis, even if they were outnumbered four to one.

She sprinted for the medical tent to tell Deccia the good news.

Lunch ended up being a big party. The Wyen roared with laughter, and more than a few fondled their sword handles. They itched for battle. A good sign.

After lunch, Erl called a giant meeting.

"The Wyen report that Aestoff has defeated the enemy. They are free!"

Methusal cheered. She glanced at the faces near her—all were jubilant—except for Goric, whose face bore no expression at all.

"What is more, the Zindedi ships that were sailing for southern Koblan have turned around. They seem to be heading home. The first set of ships are also fleeing. Quasr is the Zindedi's last stronghold. Tomorrow morning we will attack, and we will fight until every last Zindedi is gone."

Another cheer swelled.

"We will attack Quasr from the east and from the south. The kaavl team will attempt to slip into the General's compound. They will kill the General and free the captives. Whatever it takes, we will fight to the end. Are we ready?"

A roar of affirmation answered him. The Wyen's energy seemed to have infected base camp's weary troops. Methusal's hopes surged, too.

Wyen's leader strode up beside Erl, and he shouted encouraging words, punctuated by energetic fist pumps, to the troops. Methusal couldn't help but grin with excitement. Surely everything would be all right now.

A short, balding figure caught her eye. He stopped by Erl's elbow. Doltn! When Foreboding tempered her jubilant spirits when Mentàll joined the two men. Methusal concentrated intently in order to hear Doltn's words. It was difficult to filter out the Wyen's cheers.

"Mentàll." Doltn shook the Dehrien's hand. "I bring bad news. One of the prisoners is dead."

Mentàll's face blanched. "Who?"

"Wortn. My men found him on the plain this morning. We buried him. A note was on his body."

Erl said, "What did it say?"

"The General sends a message to you, Mentàll. Meet him alone, at dawn in the compound, or he will kill Hendra. After that, one prisoner every hour will die."

No emotion registered on the Dehrien's face.

Erl spoke. "The Wyen have arrived. We will attack Quasr at dawn."

Doltn kept his gaze on Mentàll. "You may want to come earlier."

The Dehrien inclined his head. It looked stiff. "Warn the Quasrians that we are coming. We will require their help to defeat the enemy."

Doltn nodded. "Done. And Mentàll, I know passageways the General knows nothing about. I can get you and a few others inside the compound without being seen. But be warned—don't let the Zindedis see anyone with you. The General has ordered death for anyone who is seen with you."

"Understood."

"I want to go with Mentàll." A new voice spoke. Timaeus. Methusal had been concentrating so hard to block out the roars of the Wyen commander that she hadn't seen Timaeus approach the trio. Pan joined them now, too.

"That's not a good idea," Erl said.

"I *have* to go," Timaeus said with quiet force. "And I *am* going. I know I don't know kaavl, but please don't try to stop me."

Erl sent Timaeus a measured glance, but nodded. "All right."

"Thank you."

Deccia wouldn't be happy to hear about this.

"Who else do you want with you, Mentàll?" Pan asked.

"Methusal and Goric. After them, send in Riln and Barak and a few warriors. But I will face the General alone."

Methusal was surprised that he'd asked for Goric, but then she realized their kaavl team had dwindled to only four, including Goric. Taltn's ankle prevented him from helping out, which frustrated him, but also relieved her. She didn't want him to die in the war.

"A good plan," Erl said quietly. "We wish you every success in saving Hendra."

Methusal was glad that Mentàll would give her the chance to help save Behran and the others; especially after her poor performance on the last mission. But the Dehrien's other plan disturbed her. Facing the General alone would be a suicide mission.

Troubled, she listened to the last of the Wyen commander's speech. Afterward, Mentàll stepped up and suggested that everyone practice sword fighting in order to sharpen up their skills for tomorrow. The Wyen greeted this with shouts of zeal. Methusal did not feel the same enthusiasm.

The men dispersed and unsheathed their swords. Mentàll strode toward her. "Practice with Goric, Methusal."

Although she didn't like the idea, she went in search of Goric. He looked equally unhappy with the arrangement, and the instant she pulled out her knife, he attacked her with swift, vicious slashes.

She barely held her own, and felt relieved when the Eerporian leader, Nazu, ordered everyone to switch partners. A medium height, stocky Wyen approached, but when she looked at him, he abruptly turned around and headed in the opposite direction. Their brief eye contact, however, hit her like a punch to the solar plexus. Those dark, dead eyes were familiar. But she couldn't place him.

She watched the man thread his way through the crowd. He approached another Wyen soldier. It almost seemed like he wanted to avoid the Rolbani, Tarst, and Dehrien warriors. Why?

He shot a glance over his shoulder, and then she knew. Kilum! The old Tarst runner. Kilum had disappeared after Verdnt's death at the end of the short war in Rolban. Everyone suspected that Verdnt had had an accomplice. Kilum had disappeared directly afterward. He had never been questioned.

Unsettled, Methusal ran for her father and reported what she had seen.

A frown settled between Erl's brows. "You could be right. I'll ask the Wyen leader what he knows about him. We'll keep an eye on him."

Methusal hoped that would be enough. If Kilum was a Zindedi, like Verdnt, he could be a spy in their midst. Or he could sabotage the attack. At least her father knew the facts. She would have to trust him to do the right thing.

△ △ △ △ △

Methusal felt relieved when Nazu finally called an end to weapons practice. The sun hovered just above the western mountains now. She felt sticky after knife fighting with four warriors. And since they'd go to war tomorrow, she'd like to get a bath. But she'd better hurry.

Unfortunately, after gathering up all of the necessary items, she found the rock turned at the bathing place. Someone else must have had the same idea. Disappointed, she wondered what to do now. Soon the sun would set, and her hair took a long time to dry.

Perhaps she could wash her hair in the stream while she waited. It didn't require privacy. Just a deep enough place to do it.

She picked her way through the rocks, past the little waterfall, and then followed the shallow stream west, through the little valley which wound through the low, rocky slopes. It was quiet there. Not a sound could be heard, except for the rushing gurgle of the stream. She felt for the reassuring handle of her knife. Although she heard no one, she wanted to be ready, just in case Jascr tried to attack her.

The stream did look deeper here, but stonier, too. The fast flowing water frothed white in places as it churned over the rocks. Maybe she could find a quiet pool a little bit further on.

Methusal climbed over a rock, and then turned the corner and spotted a thick, green bush growing into the stream. It blocked her path. The bordering, rocky hill was steep right there. Cautiously, she stepped on a few stones in the creek and peeked around the bush. She caught a glimpse of a deep pool on the other side, and a small, sandy bit of shore. It looked like the perfect spot to wash her hair, if only she could get past the bush without falling in.

Balancing carefully on the wet stones, she edged by the prickly bush. Twigs scratched her cheek when she made her last, safe hop to the other side.

Relief transformed into consternation.

Mentàll knelt at the pool's edge, naked from the waist up. Sleek muscles rippled as he splashed water over his torso.

He spotted her and swiftly stood. At least he wore breeches, thank goodness. But water streamed down his powerful, wide shoulders to his chest muscles, and dripped down the flat planes of his stomach. Her gaze screeched to a halt, and jerked back up to his face.

The pale eyes narrowed, and looked calculating. Did she see a trace of amusement? Couldn't be.

"I...I'm sorry," she said quickly, hating her stammer. "I didn't know you were here."

"Then why did you come?"

"I wanted to wash my hair, and someone's at the pool."

With predatory grace, he grabbed his tunic and swiped it across his face, and then lowered it, still gripped in his fist. He seemed larger and more intimidating than ever before. Yes, she'd seen him with his tunic off before, many times. But never so unexpectedly, like this.

Her heart beat uncomfortably hard. She licked her lips. "I'll leave you, then."

He smiled then, a small one. "Do I frighten you?"

Her eyes narrowed. "Of course not." She searched for another topic to prolong her stay, so it wouldn't look like she was running away from him. For good measure, she stepped over the last stones, and up onto the dry beach. A good length still separated her from the Dehrien. "I heard what Doltn said. Do you really plan to meet the General alone?"

"I will confront the General on my own terms. Not his."

Foreboding settled like a dull, dead weight in her chest. "You know he plans to kill you."

"Does that worry you?" He sent her an inscrutable look.

She drew a short, exasperated breath. He was trying to get under her skin again. "Much as I dislike you, your death won't help us win the war."

"And when the war is over? Then will my death be acceptable to you?"

She rolled her eyes, but managed to suppress a flip retort. "I want peace for Koblan. But when the war is done, tell me. What will you do? Will you plot to destroy the peace we've fought for?"

"How little you trust me."

"Is it any wonder? Only two years ago you tried to take over Rolban."

The sun gilded the western mountain tops and turned his shoulders a warm bronze color, which distracted her for a moment. She remembered the warm, firm feel of his skin last night, when she'd rubbed in the coltac juice.

The Dehrien watched her, his ice blue eyes sharp and calculating.

She was staring. Methusal flushed. Searching for an excuse for her inappropriate behavior, her gaze landed on the silver medallion he wore in a chain around his neck. His mother had given him that medallion, and he never took it off.

The medallion came from Quasr.

In a rush, facts finally clicked together. "That medallion belonged to your father, didn't it?"

At last he pulled on his tunic. "Yes."

More insight flashed, and her jaw dropped. "Quasr's symbol is two peaks, just like on your medallion. Rolban's is three, but you didn't know that, did you? Few people do. Rolban's third peak is lower than the others, and it can only be seen if someone is high in the mountains. But you knew Rolban's symbol was mountain peaks, so you believed your father was from Rolban."

"Yes."

"That's why you hate Rolban so much."

The Dehrien Chief did not answer.

"I'm right," she pressed, amazed to finally understand the root truth that drove him. "Your father abandoned your mother in Dehre, and she died in shame. And you hate him for that. So you grew up hating Rolban, too."

"I was wrong."

"What?" she exclaimed in disbelief. "The great Mentàll Solboshn was wrong to invade Rolban?"

His eyes flashed. "Rolban would not have helped us two years ago."

"But you didn't give us that chance, did you?"

Red suddenly burned his cheekbones. "For *years* Rolban watched Dehriens die in misery and poverty."

"Was that how your mother died?" Despite herself, she felt a flare of compassion.

"We lived in filth!" he spat. "And disease took her. No one helped her."

"Does that mean your fellow Dehriens didn't help her, either?"

"Rolban has everything!" Hatred shook through that harsh voice. "Plenty of fresh water, protected croplands, and a secure community. Dehre has nothing, but still Rolban has never lifted a finger to help us."

"That is because of the Great War, which Dehre and Tarst started. And you started the war with Rolban!"

Mentàll clenched his fists.

Everything made a warped kind of sense now. Fiercely, she said, "Even if your father had been from Rolban, you had no right to invade us. It was wrong!"

"I had to save my people. We had run out of food. They were dying!"

"If you had truly wanted help, you would have asked for it. And we would have done *something*. No. You wanted power. That's what you care about, isn't it? Being Chief of Dehre and Kaavl Master weren't enough. You wanted to take over Rolban. You'd take over *Koblan* if you could, wouldn't you?"

"You know nothing, Methusal," he snarled. "Nothing at all."

"I *do*. It's the truth, isn't it?"

He did not respond.

"Listen to me, Mentàll. Great leaders see beyond their own desires. They try to understand situations from every perspective. You've been so close-minded and filled with hatred that you can't *see* the truth. You've hurt innocent people. And still my father trusted you with this mission. He's a bigger man than you'll ever be."

Mentàll scowled and looked away. But his fingers dug into his scalp. Methusal recognized the gesture. Self-condemnation. Her words had struck into his heart.

She wanted to turn and stalk away, but the prickly bush blocked a dignified exit. Instead she crossed her arms and, at a sensible pace, headed for the stepping stones.

Harsh, agitated breaths made her glance back. His knuckles were white, and his jaw clenched, as if he was struggling to reject the pain of the truth that she had revealed. It unexpectedly stabbed at her heart.

Why? How could she possibly feel sorry for him? Did he finally see that he was wrong to invade Rolban? Did he feel guilty about it? Did he see how hatred had warped his mind, and destroyed lives?

Surely not. Surely he was not humble enough to realize all of those things. No. Instead, he would probably attack her again, as he had last night.

Unease crept down her spine, and she walked faster for the first stone.

Mentàll's voice chased her, "I do not answer to *you,* Methusal. I answer to no one but myself."

"Your ego has led you down a pretty path so far, hasn't it?"

The Dehrien Chief said nothing. It surprised her.

Methusal found the pool unoccupied when she returned, and took a record fast bath. And she wondered why she didn't feel more triumphant about her verbal victories.

When she toweled off, she realized the truth.

She did feel sorry for him.

But why? Because he'd watched his mother die in poverty and shame? Because he'd suffered years of cruelty at the hands of his uncle? Because he'd labored under false beliefs all of these years? Yes.

All of it, combined, had ruined him. It had made him into the cold, self-serving, power hungry...lonely man he was today. One determined to take control of every situation he could. Power had become his only desire, and his only security.

And so he'd driven himself to become Dehre's best kaavl player, and had won the title of Chief of Dehre by the age of twenty-four. Then he'd become Kaavl Master.

In anyone else, those feats would be considered remarkable. But hatred had frozen his soul. He had made cruel decisions, and people had died. He had attacked Rolban out of a warped sense of justice for his dead mother, and to punish his father, and therefore Rolban, too. And maybe also in there somewhere was part of the reason why he had chosen to hate her, too.

Did he now truly regret having invaded Rolban?

She didn't know. Mentàll craved power. Look at the alliances he was trying to build all over Koblan. Why would he do that? It could only be to obtain power for himself. And yet how could he possibly gain power over all of Koblan?

Ultimately, she feared that the man only cared about himself and pursuing his own selfish purposes. Woe to anyone who stood in his way.

Didn't he hate her because she'd kicked a terrible blow to his pride, and defeated his bid for power in Rolban? Yes.

But that wasn't the whole story. Insight flashed. She also reminded him of what he hated most about Rolban—his father. He'd labeled her as selfish, prideful, and arrogant from the start.

At last, understanding glimmered. She reminded him a little of both of his parents—one he loved, and one he hated. Combined with the blow she'd delivered to his pride, and the way their personalities clashed, it was no wonder he possessed such violent emotions toward her.

What was his ultimate goal? What final victory did he seek, and who else would he hurt in order to gain his goal?

She could not feel sorry for him. He was no longer that hurt, innocent child who had suffered so long ago. He had grown into a dangerous man. A wild beast could only remain a wild beast.

△ △ △ △ △

Late in the day, when Hendra's stomach hurt from hunger and her mouth felt as dry as dust, the cell door swung open. Guards threw in loaves of bread. The first hard loaf hit her in the head. Behran snatched it before someone else could. A guard laughed and hurled in the last loaves. More men shoved in a big jug of water. The door swung shut again.

Tabor sprang to his feet. "Where's Wortn?" he shouted. He was foolish to draw attention to himself, Hendra thought. Or brave.

The guard secured the lock, but grinned through the barred window. "Dead."

Dead?

Horror made Hendra curl in on herself. She hugged her knees tightly with her arms.

"*Why?*" roared her fellow Dehrien.

"A warning. Your leaders must meet the General's demands."

"What demands?"

"You will see. But that one," he pointed at Hendra, "will be the next to go."

Terror flashed. *They knew who she was.*

The guard gave an evil laugh. "Yes, pretty one. The General can't wait to meet you. And if your cousin refuses to sacrifice himself for you, you will die."

Δ Δ Δ Δ Δ

Methusal visited her sister after dinner. Deccia lay on her pallet with her eyes closed. Her face looked pale.

"Are you all right?" Methusal dropped down to her knees.

Her sister blinked, and slowly sat up. "I'm just tired."

"Rest. You don't need to get up."

"I want to. Even though I'm tired, I get bored lying here all day."

"Has Timaeus visited you?"

She nodded, but the closed look in her eyes said she hadn't told him yet.

"We'll leave for Quasr at midnight."

"You need your rest, then."

"Soon."

"What's wrong?" Deccia eyed her. "You have that look. You're upset about something."

"I'm worried about Behran. The General will start killing prisoners soon."

"Yes. But that's not it."

"How do you know?"

"I *know* you, Thusa. Spit it out."

Methusal stared at the tent rafters. Should she share what was really bothering her? But saying it out loud would make it seem so...real. She didn't want it to be real. She wanted the confused feelings to go away.

"What, Thusa?" her sister insisted gently.

"Okay. You'll think I'm insane, but..." She bit her lip. "It's Mentàll. He's driving me crazy."

"You hate each other."

"It isn't that." Methusal threaded her fingers together, and then apart. She wanted to drop the entire subject.

"Then what is it?"

"He confuses me," she blurted.

"Confuses you how?"

"He's hard, and antagonistic and hateful. And other times, like when he opens up about his past...he was horribly abused, Deccia. He's vulnerable then."

"Hmm." She waited.

Reluctantly, Methusal continued. "I've tried to be kind to him, like the Prophet said, but it's only made things worse. Now, instead of hating him all the time, sometimes I feel..." What did she feel? She offered the safest words she could find. "Sorry for him. Like tonight, when I found out why he hates Rolban so much. It's because of his mother, who died when she was sick and living in poverty. He blames his father, who abandoned her. He thought his father was from Rolban. Oh Deccia, I'm so mixed up!"

"You feel sorry for him because of his past? Or because of the hurt he still feels now?"

That question cut closer to the root of what disturbed her the most. Slowly, she said, "It's what I see now. Sometimes I get the feeling there are deeper things going on inside of him. Things he doesn't want anyone to know."

Concern lurked in Deccia's eyes. Her sister was an empath. She did care about people. "Like what?"

"Pain. Sometimes vulnerability. Loneliness. I don't know why I see those things, or why I care." There, she'd said it. She cared—at least a little—about how Mentàll felt. How warped was she?

Deccia remained silent for a few moments. "Here's what I think. You've been caring for his wound, right?"

"Yes."

"I think you see him as one of your hurt, wounded animals. You care about those animals. I know you do."

"Of course I do."

"I think that when you've cared for his wound, your heart opened up to him a little. With animals, that's okay. But Thusa, he's not an animal. He's a man."

"I know."

"Do you?"

"*Yes*. I know he can't be trusted. I know he's dangerous. That's why I don't understand why I care when I see he's hurting. I should hate him, but I don't—at least, sometimes I don't. It confuses me, and it's driving me crazy."

Deccia nodded. "It's not wrong to feel compassion for someone. Maybe that's why the Prophet told you to be kind to him. So *you* would grow."

Methusal hadn't thought about that possibility. Then she thought about Behran again. More guilt surged.

"What, Thusa?"

"You don't want to hear my problems. You have enough..."

"I *want* to hear. It gets my mind off of myself, and frankly, that feels good."

Methusal threaded her fingers together again. "I feel guilty about something. I haven't told Behran yet, and I wonder if I should."

"What?" Concern drew her sister's brows together.

Methusal drew a breath and looked at the rafters again.

"*Tell me.*"

Voice barely audible, she confessed, "I kissed Mentàll."

"What?"

"I thought he was Behran."

"How? What in the *world*..." Deccia's mouth was wide open.

"I slept-walked after Kitran died, and dreamed I hurt my foot. Behran carried me back to camp." In a small voice, she said, "I asked him to hold me, and he did. Then I kissed him...and he...he kissed me back."

"Behran?"

"No."

"*Mentàll* did?" Deccia's eyes looked wider by the minute. "Wait a second. How did you find out the dream was real? And that it was him?"

Now Methusal felt the overwhelming desire to confess everything. It felt as if she wanted to purge herself of a great sin. "He kissed me again, Deccia. On a different day."

Her sister only blinked in shock.

"Remember when I told you that he stole the *Second Book of Kaavl* from me? It happened then. I told him to give the book back. He said he would—if I made him lose control."

"Lose control?" Incredulity sharpened Deccia's voice.

"Yes. You know. Make him lose his temper. We fight all the time, so I thought it would be easy. I guess I succeeded too well. He wanted to get back at me, so he kissed me. Then he asked if I wished it was Behran again. Like that night when I'd slept-walked."

"Oh, Thusa!" Deccia sounded distressed.

"And now I've kissed him twice. I feel like I've been un-faithful to Behran."

"It's not your fault when you have no control over it!" Deccia burst into tears. She put her hands to her face.

"Oh, Deccia." Methusal hugged her tight. "You haven't told Timaeus?"

She gulped. "No. I'm afraid to. I can't even deal with it myself."

"He loves you. He wants to be there for you."

"But what if he...he doesn't want me anymore?" She pressed both hands to her mouth, and cried harder.

"Of course he will. He will never abandon you. He loves you! You know that."

Her sister gasped on more sobs. "I want to believe that. But what...what if I'm pregnant?"

Methusal had not thought about that horrible possibility, and hugged her sister closer. Softly, she said, "Even so. You have to tell him as soon as you can. He'll help you get through this. He *loves* you, Deccia."

Deccia wept for a long time. Finally, she wiped her eyes with her sleeves. It hurt Methusal to see her sister in so much pain. "I wish I could do something to help you."

"Just accept me. And listen."

"Of course!" She gave her sister a final, fierce hug. "Somehow this will turn around. You will be all right."

"I hope so." Deccia sniffed, and rubbed her eyes. "Now, back to you. It's not your fault, either. You didn't have a real choice either time. Think about it. Mentàll took advantage of both situations. First, you were dreaming and sleepwalking. How is that your fault? Mentàll shouldn't have pretended to be Behran. He's a whip beast, Thusa. He got a nice girl to kiss him—that probably never happens. He's pitiful. You should feel sorry for him.

"And the second time, he played you just right. He managed to hurt you three ways—he got the book, he repulsed you by kissing you, and then he rubbed it in that you'd mistakenly kissed him back at kaavl camp. I think he's trying to get under your skin."

That made sense. "Yes. He likes to torture me. And I know he has some kind of revenge planned for me after the war is over."

Deccia eyed her. "You've formed quite an enemy." After a pause, she said, "You don't provoke him, do you?"

Methusal flushed. "Maybe. Sometimes. But I won't let him intimidate me. I won't be afraid of him."

"Aren't you?"

"I don't want to be. And I don't like feeling confused about him, either. Sometimes I *hate* him and sometimes I...I *don't*." She drew a frustrated breath. "What is wrong with me?"

Her sister sat silently for a moment. "I think you've been spending too much time with him. In a forced way, of course," she added thoughtfully. "Taking care of his wound. Running from the invaders together—twice. You were teamed on kaavl missions, too. I think you need space away from him."

Methusal's conscience wouldn't be quiet. "I hate thinking that I've been unfaithful to Behran. I haven't told him what happened. I keep telling myself it meant nothing, but..."

"Do you think Mentàll could be playing mind games with you?"

"Well, of course. He hates me."

"Because you defeated him in Rolban."

"Yes."

"So he wants to punish you."

"Yes. He's admitted that."

"Well, maybe this is his way. Your relationship with Behran means the world to you, right? Mentàll knows that. He's a brilliant strategist. Maybe he's figured out the best way to hurt you is to sabotage your relationship with Behran.

Your kissing him by accident might have given him the idea in the first place. So he kissed you again. Maybe he hoped you'd feel guilty. He'd probably love it even more if he could drive a wedge between you and Behran."

"Maybe." That did make perfect sense. Didn't Mentàll want to wreak the ultimate revenge upon her? How best to do that than to cut straight to her heart?

"Remember all of the facts, Thusa. He stole the book from you. He tried to take over Rolban. And now you say he's been meeting with Chiefs all over Koblan. He's a power hungry wild beast. You can't trust him."

"I don't!"

Deccia sent her a shrewd look. "Are you sure? I'll bet he wants you to trust him, even a little. It lets him get under your skin, which allows him to plant doubt and confusion in your mind. You've been forced into close contact with him for too long. You need to step back, and see him for who he really is."

"I know who he is." But maybe Deccia was right. Maybe she had begun to trust him a little. On the kaavl field, at least. Deccia's logic made a warped kind of sense, which exactly matched Mentàll's mindset.

"Thank you, Deccia. You've helped me see things a lot more clearly."

"Don't blame yourself for those kisses," her twin admonished. "Try to forget them, if you can."

"I'll try." Methusal didn't want to talk about Mentàll any longer. "When will Doc let you leave the medical tent?"

"Tomorrow."

"Good."

"Thusa?" Aali's voice came from behind them. She tapped Deccia's shoulder.

With a faint smile, Deccia looked back. "*I'm* your sister, Aali."

"Decc! You're wearing Methusal's clothes. I couldn't tell you apart."

Methusal smiled, too. Aali's confusion reminded her of long ago, when she and Deccia had deliberately tried to trick people. "What do you need?"

"Your presence is requested by the great Dehrien Chief."

"What does he want now?"

Aali shrugged. "I don't know. But you'd better not keep his Mightiness waiting." With a grin, she scampered off.

△ △ △ △ △

Methusal headed for Mentàll's tent. Anger simmered in her. It grew hotter the closer she came to his door. Deccia was right. Mentàll continually manipulated her, just like he always manipulated *everything* to get what he wanted. How could she possibly have felt confused about him for one second? He wanted to hurt her. She *knew* that. He chose every word, every action, to hurt her. *Every* one. She clenched her fists. And being nice to him had played directly into his hands.

Of course he'd love to tamper with her relationship with Behran. He relished every opportunity to torment her. Just as she didn't doubt that he'd hurt all of Koblan, if necessary, just to serve his own selfish, power hungry purposes.

Rage trembled inside her by the time she reached his tent, and she snatched open the flap without knocking.

A single lantern cast a warm glow over the spartan interior. Its single occupant sat at the table, but he put down his writing stick at her approach.

"I'm here," she stated. "What do you want?"

"Respect, Methusal." He stood. "I am still your commanding officer."

"Whatever."

"You are angry with me."

"And why shouldn't I be?" she snapped. "You plot and manipulate to get what you want. The *book*. Rolban." She trembled, but stopped short of accusing him of trying to sabotage her relationship with Behran. "You only look out for yourself. You don't care who you hurt. Or maybe that's your plan—to hurt as many people as possible. And during this whole time you're plotting to gain your...your selfish, *wicked* goals!"

He stared at her for a long moment, as if surprised by her outburst. Then, moving with predatory grace, he closed the distance between them by half. "And what do I want now, Methusal?" he asked silkily.

He absolutely would *not* intimidate her.

"Power. Control." She stood her ground. "Your games won't trick me anymore."

"Games?" Those cool blue eyes watched her carefully.

"You don't fool me, Mentàll. You've been after that kaavl book for years. You stole it from me. You've been setting up alliances all over the continent. Why? Do you plan to take over Koblan, community by community?" She would get all of her answers right now. "And why does the General want you dead?"

Mentàll turned his back and crossed to the table, where the lantern glowed and a book lay. "Those are a lot of questions, Methusal," he said mildly. "I will answer the last one. I went to visit Quasr's chief a few weeks ago. To sign an alliance, as you said. Only I met the General, instead. The Chief was dead."

In a harder voice, he said, "The General tried to kill me. I killed two of his men, and I would have killed him, too, if a pack of invaders hadn't charged into the room. I slashed his chest, and cut off his thumb. He did not appreciate it."

So, that explained the mystery of the General's missing thumb. "Why are you setting up alliances all over Koblan?"

Mentàll smiled, but it didn't reach his eyes. "I have a vision, Methusal." He did not elaborate.

"You *are* up to no good," she breathed. "I told my father we couldn't trust you. I'll tell him again, when this war ends."

His smile curled up. "Is that a warning?"

Apparently her words didn't concern him.

She was ready to leave. "Why did you call me here? To tend your wound?"

Mentàll hesitated for the barest fraction of a second, and then said, "My wound is healed." He lifted the book from the desk. "Tomorrow the war will end for many of us."

The quick, involuntary vision of her own mortality, and even that of this man, her enemy, flashed before her eyes. Much as she distrusted him, she could not imagine him dead. The thought made her feel slightly sick. She drew an unsteady breath. "I know." After a hesitation, she added, "Good luck."

"Good kaavl," he said, and extended the old book to her. Her mouth dropped open. With suddenly trembling hands, she accepted it. "I expect it back in my tent before we leave for Quasr."

Methusal just stared at him. The hated confusion roiled in her again. "Why?"

"I will say...I do not want to see good kaavl go to waste." He turned his back on her. A clear dismissal.

"Thank you." Feeling even disturbed, she left, hugging the book tightly to her chest. Why would he be so generous? To win her trust? To manipulate her still more?

It didn't matter. She'd learn all she could from the *Second Book of Kaavl* tonight. Hopefully it would be enough to win the battle, and to last for the rest of her life. For she knew she'd never touch the book again after she returned it to Mentàll.

Chapter Twenty-Nine

Day 26

GUARDS SLAMMED OPEN the prison door, waking up Hendra and the others. The lanterns the guards held blinded her. One strode in, grabbed her by the arm, and dragged her to her feet.

"No!" Behran tried to shove himself between Hendra and the guard.

An invader punched him in the ribs, and Behran doubled over with a sharp gasp. Tabor, her cousin's first-in-command, landed several hard punches on one guard, but that earned him a brutal crack on the head with the butt of a gun.

The Zindedis dragged Hendra from the cell.

Terror screamed in her mind. What would that insane General do to her? And Mentàll. Would he come?

He couldn't! They'd kill him. Tears slipped down her cheeks.

All too soon the Zindedis thrust her into an opulent office. A polished wooden desk, positioned beneath curtained windows, appeared to be the centerpiece. No light shone through the dark windows.

The guards left her alone in the office. Before she could get her bearings, however, footsteps sounded behind her, coming from the direction of the bookcases at the far end of the room. A door clicked shut.

She spun.

The General stopped less than a handbreadth away from Hendra. The top of his head barely reached her eye level.

Terror churned in her heart, but she didn't dare move. Something told her that any sign of fear would only encourage the man to behave abominably.

"So, you are the Dehrien's cousin." The General's voice sounded smooth and slick, like oil before it burst into flame. "Your fellow Dehrien was most forthcoming. Until I killed him, of course."

Horror sickened her. Wortn. So that's how the Zindedis had known she was in the cell. She didn't blame Wortn. Who knew what horrible things the Zindedis had done to him.

The General pulled back her hood. Her long, white-blond hair slid through his stubby fingers. "You and your *cousin*," hatred seethed through that word, "could be brother and sister." He stared into her eyes. "Do you think he will rescue you?"

"Yes." Faced with the most awful threat imaginable, Hendra's nerves settled into quiet stillness. Fear still gripped her, but a tiny sliver of ice finally encrusted her emotions. Without blinking, she observed the General as though he were an insect.

The General smiled, showing his yellow teeth. "You are arrogant, just like he is. I will relish making him pay the ultimate penalty for what he did to me."

"What will you do to him?"

"You should ask what I will do to *you*."

Hendra did not respond.

The General chuckled, and moved to his desk. She drew a shallow breath of relief.

A smoke cloud curled above the General's head when he turned to face her. "If he does not show up, I will kill you and throw your body onto the plains, like I did Wortn's. If he does come... Well, then." He smiled, and fiddled with his cigar. "I will humiliate you in front of him. When he is apoplectic with impotent rage, I will kill you. And then I will kill him. Slowly, of course." He smiled. "Do you think my plan has merit? Or should I refine it still more?"

Hendra felt cold, to her very marrow. "When will he come?"

He tapped his cigar, and it dropped ash onto the floor. "By dawn. Only an hour left, my dear. Do you have a last request?"

"I'm hungry. And thirsty." Hendra couldn't believe the words left her lips. What was she thinking, to say such things?

The General chuckled. "Good. A healthy appetite is one I am happy to indulge. Guard!" When a guard appeared in the door, he said, "Bring this delightful young woman fresh meat and bread. And tea, as well."

"Yes, sir." Within moments, the guard returned with a steaming tray. The General indicated that she should sit and eat. So she did. With the General observing every bite, and every chew, she slowly ate the food before her.

And she prayed for Mentàll's protection, and for wisdom for him, too. Because she knew he would come. He would never allow her to suffer and die at the General's hands.

△ △ △ △ △

Methusal hurried after the kaavl team onto the plains floor. She was exhausted. She'd managed to read three pages of the *Second Book of Kaavl* before falling asleep. Those few pages had opened up her mind to so many new possibilities with kaavl—such as the idea that kaavl concentration could be intensified with quick flashes from one sound or sight to another. The mind was a tool, Mahre had written. It only needed exercise, like a person's body, to strengthen and unleash one's true potential in kaavl.

Now, during this last bit of the trek to Quasr, Methusal tried to rapidly assimilate kaavl input. She wished she didn't feel so dull and sleepy. Hopefully, when she reached town adrenaline would burn off her lethargy.

With foreboding, she noted again that Jascr was hiking with the kaavl team. Obviously, Mentàll had asked him to come along. But why? Surely Mentàll didn't trust him.

Tension knotted tighter inside her as they neared Quasr. Was Behran all right? Did the prison guards have orders to kill the prisoners as soon as Koblanis were discovered in the compound?

To be on the safe side, Methusal and the others would move swiftly. She wondered if Mentàll still planned to face the General alone.

A man appeared from behind a bush, and her heart jumped in alarm.

Doltn. He fell into step beside Mentàll. "The General wants you to meet him in his office. Alone."

Mentàll grunted.

Doltn continued. "Be warned. An alarm will sound if Koblanis are seen on the compound. Prisoners will be executed immediately. Are you ready?"

"Yes." Mentàll sounded impatient. "Do you know of another passage that ends in the General's office? Not the one behind the bookcase."

"Yes. It is ready."

"Good. Lead me to that passage first, and then direct Methusal's team to the prison passageway. Direct the remainder of the team to a passageway that comes out near the office."

"Done."

Lights blazed in Quasr, and the dark figures of soldiers paced the perimeter. It looked like the number of guards had tripled since their last attack.

Doltn did not appear concerned. He indicated that the kaavl war team should stop behind the closest bushes to Quasr. Then he put three fingers in his mouth and emitted a series of lonely chirps.

Soldiers in the nearest section parted. They headed north and south, leaving a clear path for the kaavl team to enter Quasr.

"My men," Doltn said, with evident pride. "We killed the Zindedis, one by one, and took their places. All Quasrians in the compound will help you in any way they can, too. They have been instructed to wear brown cloaks, so you will know who they are."

Methusal, Mentàll, Barak, Timaeus, and the remainder of the kaavl war team sped into Quasr. Both Timaeus and Riln carried bows and arrows strapped to their backs. There was no need to hide their weapons tonight.

Although Methusal's heart pounded with nerves, they filed, unmolested, into an abandoned house. Doltn lifted a trap door. "This passageway branches off into smaller tunnels that lead into the mansion. I have men stationed below. They'll kill any invaders who show up."

Doltn seemed to have the mission well organized.

Mentàll descended into the dark pit. "And Calbn? Are he and his family still safe?"

"Yes. They are in a new location underground. He's itching to fight. He hates that I get to have all the fun."

Below ground in the musty passage, hooded Quasrians handed the kaavl team lanterns. Doltn led them west.

Methusal was amazed by the extent of the labyrinths. The passages appeared to be old, and only a few seemed naturally formed. Why had ancient Quasrians dug so many passages?

They passed many branching passageways before reaching a major fork in the underground tunnel system. Five Quasrian men waited there. Two wore Zindedi uniforms, and all five followed the kaavl war team down the left passage.

Doltn spoke as they walked. "As you requested, Mentàll, one of these men will accompany you. The other will go with Methusal to the prison."

So, Mentàll wouldn't face the General completely alone. But one ally to help him face off against the General and the soldiers he'd have in the office didn't seem like nearly enough. Mentàll's plot seemed risky. Even foolish. She could not explain why that bothered her so much.

"Here." Doltn stopped where the passage branched in three directions. "The prison team will go down the right passage. The left one, Mentàll, leads to the General's office. The middle one ends in a supply room in the center of the mansion."

Mentàll faced the kaavl team. "Most of you have your assignments already. Methusal will lead the prisoner rescue team. Kill all Zindedis. We will not leave the compound until it is ours. Good kaavl!"

"Good kaavl!" Methusal echoed back, somewhat surprised that he had placed her in charge of the prisoner rescue mission; especially considering her many past failures in kaavl.

The Dehrien Chief and the uniformed Quasrian disappeared down the dark passage.

Methusal said, "Goric, Timaeus, Barak, and Riln, you're with me. I guess the rest of you need to go down that middle passage..."

"We know our assignment," Jascr sneered. His hard eyes bored into Methusal. "And believe me, when I'm done, *all* of my enemies will lie dead at my feet."

Methusal turned her back on him and headed down her passage. "Come on." She could not worry about Jascr now. Behran and the other prisoners were waiting.

△ △ △ △ △

Faint rays of the sunrise glinted through the General's window. Hendra had finished the food, and servants had whisked the dishes away long minutes ago. The General had disappeared, too. She sat alone in the huge office, feeling terrified.

What would happen next? And most worrying—where was Mentàll? She didn't want him to risk his life to rescue her. And yet she knew he would.

A soft sound whispered from her left. Heart pounding, she quickly looked up. A huge painting above the sofa slid to the right, and a dark passageway appeared behind it. To her shock, Mentàll and a Zindedi soldier crawled out.

Mentàll quickly glanced around the room. The Zindedi— or likely uniformed Quasrian—did the same.

He was here. Sudden relief filled her. Mentàll was *here*. She ran and flung her arms around him. After a brief hesitation, his arms closed tightly around her, too.

Everything would be all right now. Mentàll would keep her safe.

He said in a husky voice, "You are all right?"

"Yes." Tears slipped out, and she pressed her cheek into his warm tunic. "Now that you're here."

"Quick," he said harshly. "Get in the passageway."

A latch clicked across the room. One horrified glance took in the bookcase sliding sideways. The General and a horde of Zindedis burst into the room.

"Now!" Mentàll shoved her hard, toward the sofa.

A score of metallic snaps ricocheted. All guns pointed at Hendra, Mentàll, and the fake Zindedi. She didn't dare move.

The General strolled toward Mentàll. Hatred burned in his eyes, making them smolder like amber fire. "So, we meet again."

"Let her go," Mentàll said flatly. "I have come, as you requested."

The General snapped his left fingers. "Get the girl."

A Zindedi surged forward, eager to do the task.

Mentàll and the Quasrian blocked the way.

"Shoot the fake soldier," the General ordered.

"No!" Hendra cried out, but a gun exploded. The Quasrian crumpled to the floor. She gasped with horror.

The Zindedi reached for Hendra.

"No!" Mentàll snarled. His quick twist of the soldier's wrist sent the Zindedi to his knees.

"Shoot him!"

"No!" Hendra threw herself in front of her cousin. "I'm here! Don't shoot."

The General smiled. "A woman with spirit. I will enjoy my revenge. Seize them!"

Soldiers rushed forward. Despair gripped her. If they captured Mentàll, he would die, and it would be all her fault.

"No," she sobbed out, and made a wild grab for one of the guns. To her surprise, she yanked the weapon out of the soldier's hand. With all of her strength, she swung it. It smacked into a Zindedi's head.

Unexpected pain slashed through her arm, and a gun rammed into her stomach. With a gasp, she bent double.

In a flood, the Zindedis swarmed around them both, like a horde of black rochers.

△ △ △ △

The uniformed Quasrian who led the prisoner rescue team through the passageway seemed to be moving at a slug's pace. Fear coiled tighter in Methusal with every minute that passed. Time was running out. She felt it, deep in her gut. Patience suddenly gone, she grabbed the lantern from the Quasrian and sprinted down the dark passage.

"What are you doing?" he snapped.

She didn't bother to answer.

The passage ended in a dirt wall and a ladder. Methusal held the lantern high and spotted the wooden trap door overhead. "Where does this lead?"

"A supply room in the prison ward."

"I'll see if it's safe." She handed the lantern to the Quasrian and climbed the ladder. With care, she lifted the trapdoor a finger-width and peeked out. Dark. She carried with vision, struggling to see something in the dark room.

Light seeped from under the door leading into the hall. Quickly, she focused her vision on that point, and then under the door and out into the hall. Four soldiers patrolled the passage. Sounds came from the cell directly across from the supply room.

She listened intently. Breaths from sixteen men. It appeared that the Zindedis put them all in one cell. She fanned out her hearing, focusing on each room in the hall. No more signs of life could be heard, except for the faint scratch of rochers.

It wasn't until Methusal lowered the trap door that she realized what she had done. She had carried instantly, from place to place, as quickly as her thoughts. Although she had practiced with vision on the other missions, this was unfathomable. Had Mahre's new precepts sunk in so quickly?

Perhaps they had seeped into her subconscious while she had slept a few hours ago. The book did belong to her. She felt this more clearly than ever before. It was almost as if the blood she shared with her ancient ancestor sang to her, enabling her to understand his words on a deep level that she did not understand.

The others waited expectantly for her report.

"The supply room is empty. Four soldiers are patrolling the hall. All of the prisoners are locked in one cell. It's directly across from the supply room."

Barak blinked. "You could tell all of that by looking into the dark?"

"Kaavl, Barak," Riln said, with a loud hand clap on the shoulder. "That's why Mentàll put her in charge."

Respect flashed, and then disappeared in Goric's murky gray eyes.

The praise felt good, but Methusal didn't dwell on it. "Maybe kaavl is my strength, but fighting isn't. Barak, how should we attack the guards? We don't want them warning the Zindedis that we're here."

"We may not be able to stop them. We'll attack the guard holding the keys first. And we'll take down the others as soon as possible. Then you can release the prisoners, Methusal. When the men are freed, we'll leave the prison and fight more Zindedis."

Except the prisoners wouldn't have any weapons. An obvious detail she didn't need to state.

"Let's go." She quickly climbed up the ladder, and the others followed.

In the supply room, Methusal carried with vision again under the door and scanned the hall. "Five guards...now seven!" Frustration sharpened her words. "The guard with the key is at the far end of the hall."

"Maybe we should wait a minute," Timaeus suggested. "Maybe they're having a meeting, and the new guards will leave soon."

Methusal watched. Currently, two guards were strolling toward the supply room. The other Zindedi guards remained where they were, including the key holding guard. The two closest Zindedis flanked the prisoner's cell door. In a whisper, she relayed this news to the others.

"We need to act now," Barak rumbled.

"I agree," Riln said. "Barak, we'll kill the two across the hall first. Then Timaeus and I will shoot the others with arrows."

It seemed like a good plan. Methusal nodded.

Riln's hand twitched at his side, and he pulled out his knife. "Ready, Barak?"

"Now," agreed the big man, and they simultaneously turned into the hall. Methusal heard a shout of surprise, and then a gurgle. Barak and Riln dove back into the supply room.

Guns exploded in the hallway.

Timaeus knelt at the door's edge and threaded an arrow into his bow. Riln stood above him and did the same.

"One, two," Riln muttered. "Now!"

Both men popped their bows into the hall and sighted. Arrows flew at the same time three guns discharged.

Both men jerked back, thankfully unharmed.

Methusal carried with vision. "Two men down," she reported. But one of the Zindedis who had guarded the cell was stirring. He glanced into the supply room, and his eyes widened. "G...g...Gg..."

A crouching Goric must have seen, for his knife flashed to hand, and he flung it across the hall. It stuck in the man's throat. Methusal averted her eyes, feeling sick.

Even so, she forced out, "Good job, Goric."

His opaque eyes looked hard, and for a moment he stared at Methusal as if he didn't comprehend her words.

Then disbelief flashed. After a second, he muttered, "Thanks."

Timaeus and Riln let fly another duo of arrows. More guns blasted. A chunk of wall exploded where Riln's head had been a second earlier. One arrow found its mark, and the other one winged an invader. The remaining invaders swiftly reloaded their guns.

"Two Zindedis left," she reported. "The guard with the keys is dead, but he's still at the other end of the hall."

"Ready, Timaeus?" Riln grunted. "Stick out your bow. Draw their fire first."

The plan drew one man's fire, but the other Zindedi cunningly waited.

"First me, then you," Riln ordered, and sighted down the hall. A blast exploded before the Tarst man had a chance to take his shot. He jerked back, just as a clump of his hair went flying.

"Riln!" Methusal gasped. The big man toppled backward and fell hard onto her. She crashed to the floor.

Timaeus took his shot and Barak barged out, armed with a knife and a sword. Timaeus and Goric ran after him.

A quick glance told her that two invaders still stood in the hall, frantically reloading their guns. The Koblani men were easy targets, charging down the hall like that. And Riln...

Blood seeped from the side of his head. Fingers shaking, she touched the wound, searching for a bullet hole. But she found only a long, burrowed wound. The bullet had grazed the side of his head. He would live. With relief, she quickly split a coltac leaf, applied the gel, and stuck the leaf on for a bandage.

She heard the dreaded sound of a gun snapping, ready to fire.

An explosion thundered. Barak let out a mighty roar, and kept charging. Goric stumbled to one knee, but Timaeus took his place and threw his knife with swift, deadly accuracy. A Zindedi grabbed his throat and collapsed, gurgling blood. Barak skewered the last man with his sword.

Timaeus helped Goric up. Blood seeped down Goric's leg. It appeared to be a flesh wound.

Riln groaned.

"You're going to be all right," Methusal said, and pushed him off of her lap. Only one thought rang in her mind. *Behran.* More Zindedis could arrive at any minute.

"The keys, Methusal!" Timaeus hurled them down the hall. They slid on the floor, and stopped at her feet.

She fit the key in the lock and shoved open the door. *Behran.*

Men surged out of the tiny cell.

"Thusa!"

Relief shuddered through her when she saw him. "Behran!"

And then Behran pulled her into his arms and buried his face in her hair. "Thusa."

"*Behran.* I was so afraid! Did they hurt you?"

He kissed her. "A few punches in the ribs. I'll survive."

"Zindedis!" Barak roared. "Fight, men!"

Methusal turned. A few of the prisoners had already stripped the guards of their weapons. But with bloodcurdling screams, more Zindedis flooded into the hall.

△ △ △ △ △

Hendra watched the Zindedis shove the painting back into place, closing off the secret passage. Men stood guard on either side of it.

She strained against the bonds tying her wrists together behind her back. What hurt more was seeing her proud cousin standing there tied up, and suffering multiple, brutal punches from the Zindedis. He could do nothing to defend himself.

"Stop," she cried out. *Oh The One, help us! Please!*

"Halt." The General raised his hand and strolled toward his prisoner.

The punching stopped. Now the guards on either side struggled to keep Mentàll under control. He jerked his shoulders and flexed his arms, wrestling for freedom. The Zindedis who gripped his arms grimaced, staggering under the force of Mentàll's movements.

"Cease!" the General barked. "Listen. Now I will decide your fate." Rage and something else swirled through his strange amber eyes.

Hendra stared. What would he do now? A scene flashed before her eyes...

The General grabbed Mentàll by the throat and screamed, "Shut your filthy mouth!"

Mentàll's face turned red, and he struggled violently. A Zindedi stuck his gun into Mentàll's back.

"Shall I shoot him, General?"

Hendra gasped, and blinked.

Now the General stood a full length away from Mentàll. *The future.* "Mentàll, don't!" she cried out. "Whatever he says, don't answer!"

The General pivoted and struck her hard. Her face snapped right. Tears stung her eyes, and she tasted blood. Stepping closer, he gripped her hair and pressed his florid, awful face close. Softly, he said, "Shut *up*. You will have my attention soon enough, pretty."

Hendra shuddered.

"Good." He smiled, and released her.

Rage seared Mentàll's cheekbones a dark red. Hendra sought his gaze and shook her head, urging him not to speak.

The General approached Mentàll again. "Do you want to know what I will do to your cousin before I kill you?"

Mentàll's contemptuous gaze looked as cold as ice. But Hendra sensed his volcanic rage underneath, burning to lunge free.

The General smiled. "But no. That might spoil the fun. Perhaps I should show you, instead." He strolled back to Hendra.

Fear boiled up in her like a coiled black monster. It attacked before the General could. Her lungs closed, bound by black terror. She could not breathe. She could not escape.

She gasped for air and let out thin, choking, animal moans.

"Fight *me!*" Mentàll's roar seemed to come from far away.

A high-pitched whine rang through her ears.

"Fight me, you dirt eating whip!" Her cousin let loose a string of violent curses.

Still, her lungs refused to cooperate. Terror swelled. She couldn't breathe! Hendra struggled to connect with reality;

to focus on a tangible object that might pull her from this whirlpool sucking her down into hell.

The General launched himself at Mentàll and gripped his throat with short, stubby fingers. He screamed, "Shut your filthy mouth!"

A gun snapped. "Shall I kill him, General?"

In the space of one second, Hendra saw another flash of the future. Horror choked her. *Disaster.* Unless...

She let loose a bloodcurdling scream.

△ △ △ △ △

Barak and the freed prisoners fought the Zindedis who flooded the prison hallway. Riln staggered out of the supply room, but Methusal pulled him back. "You're injured, and I need your help."

"What's your plan?" Behran asked.

"Goric, Timaeus, Tabor!" She cast Behran a pleading glance. "Will you come, too?"

Behran followed her down into the tunnel. The injured men, Tabor, and Timaeus did, too. The others stayed behind to help Barak.

A sharp, unexplainable anxiety filled her, and she ran down the passage with the lantern in hand. Its light seemed dimmer, but she didn't stop to figure out why. She said over her shoulder, "Mentàll and Hendra are in trouble! They need our help."

"How many weapons have we got?"

"I have an extra knife." Timaeus passed it to Behran. "What's the plan, Thusa?"

"We'll take the passageway to the General's office and see what's happening. We'll attack, if we need to."

Timaeus told Behran and Tabor, "Mentàll's alone, except for one Quasrian. He's meeting with the General to try to save Hendra. Hopefully, the rest of the team has rallied to help him, but if not...chances aren't good for their survival."

They reached the fork in the passage, turned, and ran on. Methusal carried with vision, but saw nothing but darkness ahead. The lantern's light sputtered, threatening to go out. Faint sounds touched her ears, but she couldn't tell what they were.

A few seconds later the passage narrowed, and she heard the sound of quiet breaths. Yes. From one man. And he was close! Two lengths ahead. She slowed down and held up a hand. "Someone's here," she whispered.

"Get behind me, Thusa." Behran took the lantern.

Before she could turn sideways to let him pass by, a black-haired man stepped from the shadows. *Jascr!*

"What are you doing here?" Jascr wasn't helping anyone, that much was for certain. Warning twisted through her gut. "Tell me why you're here."

A snarl contorted Jascr's face, and he whipped out a knife. He clearly intended to block the path to the General's office.

"What are you *doing?*" She stared from the knife to Jascr's hate filled eyes. "Move! We need to help Mentàll and Hendra."

"They can die, and so can you!" He lunged forward and his knife sliced upward. Pain seared her abdomen. *Jascr intended to kill her.* And the passage wasn't wide enough for someone to come alongside and help her.

She whipped her kaavl stick to hand and struck his arm. He growled and tried to slash her again. She blocked. He dodged back and forth, slashing, jabbing. The thin light from the lantern glinted on his deadly blade. Behind him, faint lines of light caught her eye. It was the entrance to the General's office. Methusal focused her hearing. A choking gurgle came from the room. Someone was in trouble!

She spun her stick, flashing it faster and faster, trying to confuse him. Jascr's eyes widened, and then narrowed. His facial muscles contorted into a snarl, and she knew he planned to put all of his strength into one final thrust. His hand went back, and the knife arched. Swiftly side-stepping, she hit his wrist, and then swung her stick hard at his head. It connected with his ear. With a silent, open-mouthed cry, he crumpled to the floor.

Riln shoved by and kicked Jascr out of the way. He nodded toward the sliver of light gleaming into the passage. "What's going on in there?"

Her stomach burned, but a touch told her the wound wasn't deep. All the same, it needed tending. Moans came from the other side of the painting. She carried with vision by looking through the crack.

"A guard is on each side of the painting," she whispered. "Two guards are holding Mentàll. He's on the left side of the room, about two lengths forward. Hendra is to the right, sitting on the General's desk. The General is facing Mentàll, and maybe fifteen Zindedis are behind him."

Goric whispered an oath.

"Yeah," Riln muttered. "Okay, here's the plan. I'll jump through the painting and kill the guard on the left."

"I'll take the one on the right," Behran offered.

"Good," Tabor agreed. "Methusal and Goric, kill the guards with Mentàll. I'll start in on the others." He gripped a Zindedi knife in each of his fists.

"I'll take down the General," Timaeus stated grimly.

Tabor hesitated. "All right. After that, kill as many Zindedis as you can."

From the General's office, Mentàll suddenly snarled, "Fight *me!* Fight me, you dirt eating whip!" His violent expletives made Methusal's hair raise.

A gun snapped. "Shall I kill him, General?"

Methusal gasped.

Riln muttered, "Now!"

But she grabbed his arm. "Wait! If you startle the guard, he might pull the trigger."

"Mentàll could die either way," he said impatiently.

"We need something inside the room to distract them." Methusal winged a desperate prayer heavenward.

"I'm not waiting!" Just as Riln charged forward, Hendra let loose a bloodcurdling scream.

When Riln burst through the painting, Zindedis stared at Hendra, and then their gazes flew to Riln. Their mouths opened in shock. Before they could raise their guns, however, the two passageway guards were dead and Riln had already hurled a knife through the throat of one of Mentàll's guards. Timaeus killed the other. Goric stumbled as he came out, and fell hard on his injured knee. He moaned in agony as Methusal rushed forward to cut Mentàll's hands free. Tabor's knives swiftly felled two Zindedis.

Guns exploded before the General could open his mouth to issue orders. A bullet whistled by Methusal's cheek and Riln grunted in pain. Suddenly, Timaeus' blade flew through the air, deadly and true. The General's eyes widened, completely focused for once in his life. Timaeus' knife sliced straight through his jugular vein. With a choking gasp, the General grabbed for his neck and toppled backward, spurting blood.

A commotion erupted from the hall, and Barak and the freed prisoners surged into the office.

Zindedis fired into the melee, and two prisoners fell. Methusal freed Hendra so she could duck and find cover. Zindedis pulled out swords and fought with deadly fury. The fight seemed to last an eternity, although it was likely only a few minutes. In the end, the Koblanis overpowered the Zindedis, who were less skilled with their swords than they were with their guns.

Methusal felt dizzy, looking at the carnage around her. Over twenty men lay dead on the floor. Five were Koblanis. She quickly looked for Behran, and relaxed when she saw that he was all right. He was helping a wounded Koblani sit up.

Timaeus approached. He looked a little stunned, and leaned up against the desk beside Methusal and Hendra. In a low voice, he said, "I can't believe I killed him."

"Come on, men!" Barak roared. "Collect their weapons!"

Methusal's stomach burned with pain, but she struggled to ignore it. The men needed weapons, and fast. Then they could hunt down the remaining Zindedis in the compound.

She pulled knives and swords from the dead Zindedi guards who lay near the painting. It gave her the creeps to touch their warm, unmoving bodies. She wanted to be sick.

"Here." She thrust the weapons at Barak. A second later he led the charge into the hall. Most of the men followed him.

Methusal felt a sharp twist of nausea, and sat down on the sofa beneath the tattered painting. Maybe she should tend to her wound.

"Methusal!" Goric shouted.

What...

"Behind you!"

Methusal felt the air displacement which warned of Jascr's approach before she saw him. She ducked and rolled onto the floor. A new, sharp pain pricked into her side. She rolled again, struggling to escape from him.

Where was her knife? A foot in her midsection stopped her. It pressed down hard on her wound, and she moaned in agony. Jascr stood over her. A triumphant smile curled his lips. She struggled to free her knife or kaavl stick, but before she could, Jascr raised his sword high, and drove it down.

"*Thusa!*" Behran shouted.

As if in slow motion, she watched Jascr's blade plunge toward her. *She was going to die.* In a futile attempt to save herself, she raised her arms to block the blade. Out of the corner of her eye she saw a knife fly through the air. Straight and true, it hit Jascr's sword hand. His hand jerked, and the sword deflected sideways. It pierced the edge of her tunic and pinned her to the floor.

Before Methusal could move, Jascr whipped a knife into his other hand. Lips curled back in a snarl, he lifted his arm to strike. A sword flashed forward in her peripheral vision, and so did bleached leather. Jascr's gaze flickered, and his eyes opened wide. Mentàll plunged his blade straight through Jascr's heart.

"I warned you, traitorous cousin," he hissed. A vicious wrist twist, and he pulled his sword free. Jascr collapsed onto the floor, his black eyes lifeless.

Methusal pulled Jascr's sword free and struggled to her feet. She glanced from Mentàll to Jascr. Her hand cupped her stomach, which hurt like a fire. "You killed him," she whispered.

Behind her, Hendra quietly wept.

"He is a traitor," Mentàll grated. "And Timaeus' knife saved you." As had the Dehrien Chief's sword, but that remained unsaid. He had saved her life, yet again.

"Thank you." Methusal sent a grateful glance toward Timaeus, and even Goric. His warning had saved her life, too. Those murky eyes flashed in acknowledgement, and an almost smile tugged at his lips before he looked away. Had she been wrong about him? Maybe he wasn't irredeemable, after all.

Her gaze sought Behran's. He strode toward her, his face pale. The next moment, she was in his arms.

Mentàll turned away to clean his sword.

"I'm all right," she whispered.

"Thank The One." He held her tight, and then looked into her eyes. "Are you sure?"

Methusal didn't want Behran to worry about her stomach wound. Other Koblanis, injured far worse than she, groaned on the floor. Tabor was one. He was holding his shoulder. Blood seeped through his fingers. She slipped coltac leaves into Behran's hand. "Will you help me care for the wounded?"

After a hesitation, he nodded and headed back to the Koblani he'd been helping before Jascr's murder attempt. Timaeus was tending a wound on Hendra's arm. Runners carried coltac leaves, too. That was a good thing, because she hadn't brought enough for everyone.

Now she only needed to take care of her own wound, and then she could help the injured, too. Methusal turned away and lifted her tunic a little so she could see the injury. Blood seeped down, darkening the waistband of her breeches.

"You are injured." Mentàll's voice startled her.

A flush scored her cheeks when she saw him looking at her bare stomach. Hastily, she lowered her tunic. "It's just a scrape."

"Now you will lie to me?"

Methusal couldn't read the expression in those ice blue eyes, but his frown indicated displeasure. "I'll live," she told him. "Is there something you want to speak to me about?"

His gaze returned to her stomach, where her injury was now covered by her tunic. That was why he had spoken to her. The truth was in that one look. Instead, he said mildly, "You disobeyed orders."

How like him, to try to assert his authority over her one second after a victory. Happy inspiration flashed. "I helped save your life. Won't you thank me?"

"You do not listen well, Methusal."

She smiled. "And aren't you grateful?"

He inclined his head. "You did well. But in the future, you will follow my instructions."

The audacity of the man! "I will follow you *nowhere* in the future, Mentàll. This war is over, and now I can be rid of you forever."

"You remain under my authority until we return to base camp."

She gasped with complete exasperation. "Your absolute lust for power amazes me." She sketched a hand toward the room. "People need help. We're fighting to win the compound, and all you can do is stand here and lecture me?"

"So, you admit the war is not yet over. You will follow my instructions."

He was baiting her. And he was enjoying it, too. She could tell by the quick, calculating gleam in his eyes.

"Step off," she advised. "I have a wound to tend."

"I am still your commanding officer, Methusal."

"Leave me alone. Please. Sir. *Now*."

△ △ △ △ △

Hendra wiped the tears from her cheeks. Jascr was dead. The years of hatred and fear—the relief to know he would never harm her again—had all exploded into a violent torrent of emotion. She sat very still, so Timaeus could finish tending her wound. Thank goodness Jascr hadn't killed Methusal.

Right now Methusal stood toe-to-toe with Mentàll, and they clearly were arguing about something. Her friend was a sight to behold, with her dark hair flowing and eyes blazing.

A smile tugged at Hendra's lips when she observed the inscrutable expression on her cousin's face. In Dehre, no one dared to stand up to Mentàll. Even kaavl challengers, hoping to win the title of Dehrien Chief, came with respect and fear to make their challenge. Not Methusal. Hendra's admiration for her friend grew. Thusa wasn't afraid of Mentàll, even though she knew he hated her. Hendra eyed her cousin more closely. Or did he?

As Methusal threw another barb at him, Hendra knew her cousin well enough to see a flash of respect—and amusement? Couldn't be. She had not seen Mentàll amused by anything in years.

"Finished." Timaeus had smeared on coltac juice and wrapped a cloth around her arm. "Doc will need to take a look at it."

"I'll show him. Thank you," she said softly, and glanced back at her cousin, who now strode toward the door.

Mentàll's attitude toward the Rolbani girl had changed. She didn't know if that boded bad or good for her friend.

But at least one threat had been eliminated. She glanced back at Jascr. No more tears fell.

△ △ △ △ △

By the time Methusal and the others exited from the General's compound that afternoon, all of the Zindedis inside were dead. The carnage that she'd seen made her feel sick.

Barak had suggested that they cart the corpses to Zindedi ships and burn them. It all seemed so awful.

Erl and Pan joined Mentàll in the General's compound, and they circled into a group to talk. Methusal sat with Behran nearby and listened. Already, the war was over. The Quasrians had taken back their town. The Wyen, combined with the unified Quasrians, had made all the difference. An unknown number of Zindedis were captured. All of them would either be imprisoned or executed.

Erl agreed with Barak's proposed plan. First the ships would be searched for important items, and then they would burn several of the large boats. The Zindedi ships which were fleeing from Koblan's southern coast would see the burning wrecks, and bring word to their evil Presidente that their mission had failed.

"It's likely that some Zindedis will escape and make it back to their homeland," Erl said. "Doltn and his men are combing the tunnels, but that could take all night."

"The Wyen have agreed to stay here, and so have the Eerporians and a few of my men," Pan said. "Barak wants to stay, too. We'll help the Quasrians clean up their town, and we'll tend to the wounded."

Erl nodded. The deep lines in his features made him look older and wearier than he had a few weeks ago. "Success. It feels bitter. We've lost many good men, including Nazu."

Movement caught Methusal's eye. A dark-haired man of medium height exited from the General's mansion. A stranger. He wore all black, although his black clothes looked well-tailored. Alarmed, she stood up.

Mentàll stood too, but his smile made her relax. He greeted the man with a handshake. "Calbn. I am glad to see that you are well."

Quasr's leader!

Calbn shook Pan and Erl's hands, too. "Thank you for coming to Quasr's aid. We are forever indebted to you."

"We are Koblanis," Erl said.

Calbn smiled. "And we are friends for life. Will you return in the future for a feast? After we've cleaned up Quasr, I would like to show you my town as it should be. And I would like to formally express our thanks, as well."

"I would be honored," Erl said, and Pan and Mentàll agreed. The men talked quietly about security issues, and Methusal squeezed Behran's hand.

"I can't believe the war ended so fast."

"Thanks to the Wyen."

The warm sun soaking into her skin felt nice, and the scent of flowers blooming in the beautiful, lushly foliaged courtyard smelled divine. Methusal wondered if this might be what heaven felt like. Peace. Warmth. And the joy of knowing that the people she loved most were alive and safe.

$$\Delta \; \Delta \; \Delta \; \Delta \; \Delta$$

Later that afternoon Methusal, the kaavl team, and most of the Rolbanis straggled back to base camp. A few Tarst came, too. Methusal wondered about Kilum. Was he still with the Wyen, or was he a Zindedi? She shivered, and Behran slid an arm around her shoulders. Glad of his comfort, she leaned into him.

"Are you all right?"

"I hope the Zindedis never come back."

His arm tightened. "We'll be watching. They won't take us by surprise again. Remember, knowing our enemy gives us power."

"Knowledge won't bring peace."

Behran remained silent for a moment. "True. Only a peace agreement will do that."

But would a power hungry enemy ever accept such a thin reward? Methusal watched her own enemy climb up the hill ahead of them. She felt certain no reward so small would ever salve his lust for power and domination.

She didn't believe that peace with the Zindedi would come any easier.

An unwelcome thought entered her mind. The war was over. Mentàll's promise to her father had now just ended. What did he plan to do to her?

△ △ △ △ △

At base camp Hendra slipped into the medical tent, holding her arm close to her side. Timaeus had done a good job patching it up, but it throbbed painfully.

Doc crouched beside an injured soldier in the back of the tent, speaking to him in low tones. Patiently, she waited.

As if sensing he was being watched, Doc glanced up, and then he went very still. A small eternity seemed to tick by. His gaze seemed drink in everything about her. With a final word to the warrior, he stood. "Hendra."

"Doc," she said softly.

He joined her and gently touched her arm. "You're injured."

"Just a cut."

He led her to the supply table and gently dealt with the wound. Finally, his fingers left her skin. Hendra did not feel relieved by that. Rather, a small sadness, which surprised her.

With the supplies put away, Doc looked at his hands, as if not sure what to do with them next. They fell, restlessly, to his sides. "I was worried about you."

"I'm sorry. I left you here with no help."

"You wanted to help win the war. I understand that."

She nodded.

"Good. Just so long as..." He stopped.

"As long as what?"

His gaze looked troubled. "As long as our kiss didn't make you run away."

"Of course not." Her face warmed. "I'm sorry for shouting at you. I feel horrible. I didn't mean to make you feel bad." Tears wet her eyes, and she looked quickly away. Licking her lips, she swallowed. "Being captured turned out to be a good thing. I needed to face my fears. They're not gone. But they are better."

"What happened in prison?"

Hendra told him everything.

"You were trapped in a cell full of men?"

"I had a few panic attacks. They got better as time went by. Behran helped me."

"He makes you feel safe."

"Yes."

He nodded, but she couldn't read his expression. "Hendra..." He hesitated, and then motioned to two adjacent boxes. They both sat down. Holding her gaze, he said, "I know it's hard, but will you please tell me what happened to you?"

Confused, she said, "I just did."

"No. A long time ago. What *happened* to you? Why were you terrified when I kissed you? Why have you been having panic attacks?"

Hendra closed her eyes. More tears threatened. She forced them back, because she was sick to death of feeling weak and afraid.

"Tell me. Please."

She had never told anyone before. She'd almost confessed it to Behran in prison, when he had kept giving her those worried looks. But he had never asked her. And Doc wanted to know. He truly did. And he was long overdue an explanation for her behavior.

"It's a long story."

"Luckily, I'm in charge. I have all the time in the world."

Hendra smiled faintly. But worry darkened her thoughts as she thought back to that awful time in her life. Would she have another panic attack telling Doc about it? She laced her trembling fingers together and told herself to face this fear, too.

She began, "My father was an evil man. He beat everyone in the house, and called us names, and worse. My brothers grew up to be just like him. He hated Mentàll the most, but when Mentàll beat up my father and left home when he was sixteen, my father turned his hatred on me and my mother. I was eight. He drank lots of racmun spirits, and in his rages he swore I wasn't his daughter. I didn't have his dark hair and eyes, like my brothers do. I look more like my mother. Still, I didn't understand why he hated me so much."

Doc looked grim.

"One day, when I was thirteen, my mother introduced me to a tall man with a long face and sad eyes. She said he was my real father. But they warned me never to tell my other father. I could tell they loved each other, and I was glad they had told me the truth. I was relieved I didn't share any blood with that awful man who had raised me.

"It turned out I wasn't the only one who learned the secret. My brother Jascr followed us that day, and overheard.

Actually, Jascr is not my true brother. His mother died when he was born, and after that, his father married my mother. Anyway, soon after I learned about my real father, Jascr came to me. He said, 'I know your secret. We don't share blood, do we, little sister?

"He scared me, so I stayed quiet. Then he said, 'I think I'll tell my father the truth. I'm tired of hearing your mother scream in the night. Maybe he'll finally kill her.'

"I cried, 'No! Please. Don't.'

"Jascr seemed to consider it. 'I won't, then. But you'll have to do me a few favors.'

"I quickly agreed, and said, 'What kind of favors?'

"'You'll see.'"

"I didn't trust him. He was as mean as his father, and just as big, even though he was only eighteen. So I used kaavl to escape him from then on. If I was alone in the house, I left until someone came home. When I was out, I tried to stay with friends. That went on until I was fourteen."

She fell silent, and tears silently slipped down her face.

"What happened next?" Doc said gently.

Hendra slipped back into the awful memories, and her tears overflowed. "He found me hiding in an outbuilding one day. He knows kaavl too, and he used it to find me.

"He said it was time for me to start paying back the favors. I tried to escape him! I tried...but I couldn't. He had a knife...and...and he pinned me against the wall. He said since we weren't related, he got to touch me."

Hendra's tears came faster now. "He said to...to stay still, or he would hurt me really bad. He scraped the knife across my throat to show he meant it. Then...then he touched me..."

She couldn't go on. Sobs choked her, and she struggled to breathe. "I felt so filthy!"

"Did he violate you?"

She shook her head. "He attacked me so many times...before my mother died. Maybe twenty or thirty." In a whisper, she said, "I couldn't tell anyone.

"He grew more violent. As long as he could make me cry, he was happy. He always got this *awful* look on his face then. Triumphant. And evil. When he cornered me when I was fifteen, he finally realized he wasn't hurting me anymore. I felt cold inside, like I was dead. I still feel that way sometimes."

Hendra bit her lip, and blinked. "I knew then that he planned to do more than scare me that time. I saw it in his eyes.

"I prayed to The One to help me. To send someone—anyone—to help me. But Jascr threw me on the floor and started ripping off my clothes. I screamed. I didn't think anyone would come." She fell silent, reliving the horror she'd felt.

"And then?" Doc pressed gently.

"And then...I don't know how, or why, but Mentàll was passing by. He never came to our part of town anymore. I still don't know why he was there. But he heard me scream, and slammed the door open. He looked like a fire-breathing giant. He grabbed Jascr by the hair and threw him off me. Then he beat Jascr until he couldn't get up, and then some more. Mentàll said he'd kill him if he touched me again. And he *would* have." Hendra shivered, and wiped her cheeks.

Doc handed her a cloth to blow her nose, which she did, in an undignified manner. He didn't seem to notice. "Was that the end of it?"

"Jascr never touched me again. But soon afterward, someone murdered my true father. And my father—Jascr's father—beat my mother to death."

"Jascr told him the secret."

"I'm sure he did." Grief threatened to engulf her. "I stayed with friends after that. And then I turned sixteen, and my other father died in a fight. He was drunk, as usual. None of my brothers wanted me in their homes. And I wouldn't have gone, anyway. Mentàll had just become Chief. He said I could live in one of his tents. And so I did. It's the only place I've found peace in my entire life. So I've lived there for the last seven years."

"Mentàll has never harmed you? Or requested special...favors?"

"No! Never. He's never touched me. He's more of a brother to me than either of my half-brothers."

"Good."

"So now do you understand why I behave the way I do?"

"I have always understood, Hendra. But I thought it might help for you to tell me."

She heaved an anxious breath. "You don't think any less of me? You don't think I should have escaped, when he...he did those things?"

"How could you?" Though his voice was tender, anger darkened his eyes. "Jascr had a knife. He threatened your life, and your mother's, too. If Jascr was here, I'd want to kill him myself."

"Jascr is dead," she said quietly, and again felt overwhelming relief. Surely it must be wrong to feel so happy about his death. "Mentàll killed him when Jascr attacked Methusal in Quasr today."

Doc stared at her for a second. "Good."

"I agree. But isn't it wrong to feel that way?"

He shook his head. "I'm a doctor, and I've pledged to save lives. But so help me, some men deserve to die." For a second, the taut lines of his face looked a little frightening.

"I'm tired. Maybe I should go."

Doc's gaze held hers. "Thank you for trusting me, Hendra."

She gave a small nod.

He reached out, and then hesitated, hand hovering beside her face. Then he stroked a gentle thumb across her cheek. "I want to check your wound tomorrow."

His touch comforted her. With reluctance she stood, and he rose with her.

"Rest, Hendra," he said huskily, and headed back to his patients. He understood why she'd run away when he had kissed her. She was grateful for that. She wasn't ready to let anything like that happen again, though. Not yet. Even though the panic attacks had subsided in jail, the fear and even the memory of all those hordes of men still crawled through her.

Clearly something was still wrong with her. Pieces were still broken, deep inside. Going on the war mission had helped. But she still wasn't completely healed, as much as she'd tried to make it sound that way to Doc. As much as she wanted it to be true.

A few minutes later, on her pallet, Hendra closed her eyes. To her surprise, she discovered that a little peace had slipped into her soul. Doc was right. The telling had helped...a little.

Δ Δ Δ Δ Δ

That night, after dinner, Methusal sat high on the rocks with Deccia, overlooking the dark valleys and peaks behind base camp. It was a little lower than the spot where she'd tended Mentàll's wound for the last time. The newly risen moon and stars shone down on the barren landscape. The solitude soothed and comforting her after the violence she had experienced that day.

"Do you think The One answers our prayers?"

"Yes. He answered mine in prison."

"And I prayed that you and Behran would be rescued, and for the war to end. All of those things happened. Finally. But so many people died."

"People die in wars, Thusa. I think we should be grateful that this war has ended."

"Yes." Methusal realized that she'd never thanked The One for any of it. But he had listened to her. He had answered her prayers. So she thanked him now, and knew he was listening. Even though horrible things had happened, some good had come from it. Would everything turn out right now, at the end? Carefully, she said, "Have you talked to Timaeus yet?"

"No." Deccia said in a small, quiet voice.

Methusal gave her a quick hug. "Tell him. He loves you. It won't change his feelings for you."

"I hope you're right."

A pebble rolled behind them, and a frisson of danger shot down her spine. *No.* She didn't want to deal with him now. She wanted to enjoy the peace and solitude just a little while longer. She felt his presence behind her.

"Methusal."

She didn't respond. Maybe he would go away. Wishful thinking.

"Methusal." A hand closed around her upper arm. "You have something that belongs to me."

After a long moment, during which she contemplated arguing with him, Methusal reluctantly stood. She didn't want to fight with him anymore. "I forgot to return it when we left so early."

"Where is it?"

"I'm surprised you haven't searched my pack and stolen it. Again."

Deccia stifled a snort.

"Perhaps we need to speak in private." Mentàll's soft words held the hint of a threat.

Deccia stood, too. "Do you need help, Thusa? To keep what is rightfully yours?"

"No. But thank you." Methusal's gaze battled Mentàll's.

"Will you break our deal, Methusal?"

She wanted to say 'yes,' but couldn't. He had given her the book in good faith. She would be worse than a whip if she broke the implicit bargain. Even though she'd found the book. Even though it belonged to her family. No. She would do the honorable thing.

"No," she said at last. "I'll give it to you."

In the moonlit darkness, they all climbed down the mountainside. On the outskirts of camp, but still in the last, tall, rocky jumbles of the foothills, Deccia said, "I need to go talk to Timaeus."

"Oh, Decc." Methusal hugged her. "Tell him. He loves you."

Deccia slipped ahead, toward Timaeus' tent. She hesitated outside, and then pulled aside the tent flap. An orange light glowed within, and then she slipped inside.

"He doesn't know?" Mentàll spoke.

"I never told anyone but my father...and you." Methusal bit her lip. Her heart grieved all over again for her sister. "I didn't want anyone to know. And you. You made me so angry. Because you're just like him. The General."

"Insane?"

"No. A predator."

"And yet you came to my tent so willingly last night. And you walk with me now. Alone in the dark."

"We're not alone. We're at camp."

Mentàll's fingers loosely encircled her forearm, and he stepped back a few paces into the shadows of the rocks, pulling her with him. Base camp disappeared from view. Only stars illuminated his large form.

"Now we are alone. Do you trust me?" His hand encircled her wrist now.

Chills ran down her skin. Her palms felt clammy. "You won't hurt me."

"The war is over. All agreements are ended."

Methusal stood very still. "What do you want from me?"

"Are we still sworn enemies, Methusal?"

"I don't trust you."

"And yet you do. You are standing here, alone with me."

"Help is only a call away."

"And yet you know that would not stop me." Nothing so small would hinder him, if he wanted to carry her off and behave like the General had done with Deccia.

"You won't. You kept your word to my father. You're too self-controlled to behave irrationally."

"So, you establish that I am not like the General at all."

He had twisted her words.

"But you do want complete power and control, like he did. And you'll stop at nothing to get it."

"You know nothing about me, or my motivations or plans, Methusal."

"I know they benefit only you."

"Like winning this war?"

Methusal said nothing for a moment. Then, "You don't want anyone else to take over Koblan. That's your ultimate plan, isn't it? You want that pleasure all for yourself."

"So now you know what brings me pleasure, Methusal?"

"*No.*" The word vomited out. She didn't want to know.

She felt his thumb slide along her jaw. A sharp gasp caught in her throat. "Stop."

"Then step away. Go to Behran."

Infuriated by his behavior, Methusal raised her free hand to smack his face. He caught her wrist. His hand felt wide and powerful. He was much stronger than she was. She could not escape through brute force.

"Let go."

"Only if you promise not to hit me."

"Only if you promise not to touch me again."

His teeth flashed white in the semi-gloom. "I make no promises I cannot keep."

What was *that* supposed to mean?

He released one of her wrists, but still held her immobile with the other. His thumb softly grazed her lower lip. Another quick breath hissed through her teeth.

He spoke. "Remember that night you slept-walked? I carried you back to camp and you kissed me."

"I thought you were Behran." Methusal trembled. She felt like she wanted to jump out of her skin and run away. Why was her heart beating so fast? Why wasn't she struggling to escape? Her breathing accelerated, anticipating his next words, yet ready to deny them.

"You knew it wasn't Behran. You knew it was me."

"No!"

"You saw me."

"No. Your face was in the shadows."

"Not when I carried you into camp."

"*No.*" She struggled violently to free herself. "You're wrong! I hate you, Mentàll. I hate you!"

He let her go suddenly, and she staggered backward. "Then go to your Behran. Enjoy many happy years together." He sounded mocking, like he pitied her.

Methusal caught her breath. She should go to Behran. But she found that she wanted to finish this argument much more. "I know you hate me. You've been waiting to take revenge on me for almost three years."

"You know nothing, Methusal."

"Don't deny it. I saw it in your eyes when you came to Rolban. Not to mention how you've threatened me every minute since then."

He said nothing.

Methusal rushed on, "So you've been waiting. But you couldn't physically hurt me, or you'd lose your precious position of power in the war. And you needed me on your kaavl team. So you decided to destroy me subtly, two ways. First, by trying to torment me at every opportunity. And lately, by trying to kill the only thing that means anything to me. My relationship with Behran.

"You think you're slick and smooth, but I don't feel guilty about those kisses. *You* are the one who kissed me. I've done nothing wrong. Honestly, is that the best you can do? Because you lose. You haven't driven a wedge between Behran and me—we *love* each other. You can't begin to understand what that means!"

With a step, he closed the distance between them and pulled her flush and hard against him. His large body confronted every nerve ending on her skin. His mouth touched hers, burning her, and the shock of it felt like an earthquake shuddering through her.

"No," she gasped, but he did not release her. It wasn't a punishing kiss, like the one in the cave. Rather, the exquisite torture she remembered from her dream. Searing and persuasive, and with a bewildering touch of gentleness, he imprinted the feel and smell and taste of him upon her senses. The virile scent of male...and clean leather...and the faint, sweet taste of tagma leaves he'd begun to chew at her request.

A flame licked through her blood.

Tears etched her cheeks. Her fingers fisted the light colored tunic he wore, and she pushed against his chest, which felt like a warm, immovable rock. His hand pressed the small of her back, urging her even closer. And still he kissed her. Slowly. Branding her mouth and then, in a coaxing, shocking thrust, her tongue, too, with his caresses.

Her mind whirled and her body felt like molten ore. She had never been kissed like this before. She clutched his tunic tighter as her senses swam in a warm, velvet blackness.

He lifted his head, and she stared up at him, heart pounding. With a guttural word, he kissed her again, even more deeply. Shaking, she allowed it.

Behran had never...

Behran.

A spark of coherency entered her thoughts.

What was she doing?

She pushed at him with trembling, weak arms. "Stop," she whispered against his mouth. "Please stop."

He raised his head.

"Now that," he said in a low voice, "gives me pleasure."

Trembling, Methusal spun and fled. She stumbled over rocks and roots until she reached camp. She saw Behran and Hendra sitting together at the fire. She had to get rid of that book now. She couldn't face Mentàll again, after tonight. She yanked it from her pack and turned to discover that her tormentor had followed her. He looked cool, and in complete control. As if nothing had happened.

Methusal thrust the book at him. Was it all a game? Was he really trying to destroy her relationship with Behran, like she had accused him earlier? She couldn't dismiss the thought. Otherwise, how could he be so calm now? Was it all an act? Was he so experienced that he could make her feel like she didn't know herself anymore, and yet remain unaffected himself? It appeared to be so.

"Take the book and don't come near me. *Ever* again," she ordered.

He gave her a thin smile. "Goodnight, Methusal."

No promises he would not keep.

Methusal fell into bed, exhausted. She couldn't talk to Behran or Hendra right now. She couldn't face anyone.

△ △ △ △ △

Methusal tossed and turned for over an hour, but couldn't fall asleep. Her thoughts tormented her as she relived Mentàll's kiss, over and over again. *Why* had she allowed him to kiss her like that? Despair ate at her, and she felt horribly guilty. What was *wrong* with her? Was she a masochist? Did she like his negative attentions?

And Behran. He said he loved her. Surely he did love her. Then why did she keep wondering, in the back of her mind, if he would end up wanting Hendra? Tears slipped down her cheeks. She felt utterly alone and miserable.

A long time passed, and she stared at the tent ceiling. She wasn't falling asleep.

Why was she lying here, feeling depressed and sorry for herself? And guilty. She hated Mentàll. She *loved* Behran! And he loved her. Who cared if Behran sat with Hendra now? She *knew* they were only friends. She'd go out and sit with him.

Methusal crawled out of the tent and headed toward the fire, where Behran and Hendra still sat together on the log.

"Hi," she greeted them.

"Hi, Thusa." Behran's instant grin was warm. He took her hand and tugged her down beside him. "I was wondering where you were."

"I'm going to turn in." Hendra stood up with a quiet smile for both. "Night."

Behran put his arm around Methusal and pulled her close. "Where were you?"

"Talking with Deccia. And then…" Methusal wouldn't say what had happened with Mentàll. "I thought I was tired, but it turns out I'm not."

Behran rubbed her arm, and she unaccountably shivered. "Are you okay?" She heard the concern in his voice. He held her tighter.

"Of course. Why wouldn't I be?" But she did not feel all right. She did not feel better at all. In fact, being close to Behran like this made her feel even guiltier. She wanted to cry.

Behran quietly held her close for a long time, and then she felt his warm breath in her hair, "You're not all right. What's wrong?"

She shivered. "Nothing. I'm cold." Out of her peripheral vision she saw Mentàll prowl by the fire. She averted her gaze. A yawn worked at her mouth.

"You're tired. Go to sleep, Thusa."

"But I want to spend time with you," she insisted. "I want to talk. We've barely spent any time together during the war, and then you were captured..." A wide yawn caught her by surprise.

Behran's presence did comfort her, a little. He made her feel safe.

"I want to talk to you, too, Thusa." His dark blue gaze found hers. It looked serious. "But we'll have plenty of time tomorrow." He kissed her.

She quickly kissed him back. Her guilty conscience pursued her. And yet why should she feel guilty? She hated Mentàll! He had instigated those kisses, after all. And she *knew* he was deliberately trying to undermine her relationship with Behran. And yet she could find no explanation for why she had allowed him to kiss her—or, even more alarming, her disturbing response to his caresses.

And then, finally, a logical explanation presented itself. Mentàll was an experienced man. Surely, in a purely physical sense, he knew how to make a woman's head swirl with confusion.

Of course. That's all it was. The kiss had meant nothing. *He* meant nothing to her.

At last, she felt a little better.

"Night, Behran." She hugged him, and he held her tight.

He released her with a husky, "Night, Thusa."

Methusal snuggled into her coverlet in the women's tent, hanging onto the thread of peace she had found. Mentàll had skillfully manipulated her. She would not feel guilty for succumbing to his experienced wiles.

Finally, she slipped into the sleep of exhaustion. Her dreams rehashed the battles in the General's compound.

The screams of the wounded. Behran rescued. Relief. Joy.

Now she was safely back at base camp. Everything was okay again.

Everything was all right.
The fire leaped high in the dark sky. Warm. Bright. A man's possessive, protective arm slid around her. Only this time, she knew it was a dream. Her memory supplied all of the details. And when the leaping firelight illuminated the planes of his angular face, it was not Behran she saw.

She abruptly sat up, her heart driving in hard, staccato beats. Icy night air bit into her skin. Images from the dream lingered, making her shiver. She lay back down, and pulled her coverlet over her head. Finally, she drifted toward sleep again...and a variation of the same dream.

For the rest of the night, Methusal tossed and turned, feeling infested with a sickness.

At dawn, exhausted and tearful, she made a vow. Never again would she speak to Mentàll. Never would she allow him within three lengths of her! His lies and manipulations had addled her brain.

Her relationship with *Behran* was real. Nothing had changed. Nothing else mattered.

△ △ △ △ △

When Methusal woke up for the last time, just after dawn, Mentàll's tent was gone. Surprise and relief tangled inside her. The Dehriens had struck camp. Well, a few of them had, anyway. She still saw Hendra and a few Dehrien warriors in camp. What was the Dehrien Chief up to now?

Erl approached. "Good morning, Methusal." He noticed the direction of her gaze. "They're gone. He left you this." He handed her a folded parchment.

Apprehensively, Methusal unfolded it. With surprise, she saw it was the first full page of instructions in the *Second Book of Kaavl*, and it had been copied in bold handwriting. At the bottom the Dehrien Chief had scrawled, "Methusal, here is page one. Mentàll."

She handed it to her father.

He read it silently. "Why did he give this to you?"

"I don't know." Methusal had a feeling she didn't want to know. But she did know that she would remove that man from her mind. She wouldn't allow his lies or manipulations to ruin her life.

△ △ △ △ △

Deccia joined Methusal at breakfast. By her bright eyes and happy smile, Methusal deduced that her talk had gone well with Timaeus last night. Her smile dimmed, though, when she eyed Methusal.

"You're upset. What happened?"

Methusal didn't want to say. She didn't want to admit that she was still troubled about last night. But she was. The memories wouldn't leave her alone.

Maybe she should tell Deccia. After all, her twin knew everything else. Perhaps an objective opinion would help resolve her lingering feelings of guilt.

After checking to make sure no one would overhear, she said in a low voice, "Mentàll kissed me again last night." Her cheeks unfortunately flamed as she remembered it.

How could such a cold man kiss her with such passion?

She hated that fleeting thought. It was so *wrong*. He'd only kissed her to confuse and upset her still more!

Open-mouthed, Deccia stared back. "He did? Why?"

"Because he...wanted to." This appeared to be the truth, even though other reasons had surely motivated him, too. Tormenting her, being number one.

Deccia remained silent for a full minute. Conflicting emotions flitted across her face. "So. How do you feel about that?"

Methusal gasped. Fiercely, she said, "I *hate* him. I love Behran. That man only wants to confuse me."

"But you won't let him."

"Of course not! At least he's gone. Thank goodness. Now I won't ever have to see him again. I *won't* feel guilty. And I won't tell Behran, either. It deserves to be forgotten. *He* deserves to be forgotten."

"You're right. Forget him, Thusa. I think it's perfect that we're going home now. We both need to put this war behind us."

"Time for new beginnings."

Deccia smiled. "Timaeus still wants to marry me."

"I knew he would. But are you ready? After what happened?"

"I love Timaeus. I still want to marry him," Deccia said quietly. "We've decided to go ahead with our wedding next month. But once we're married... Timaeus understands that

I'll need to go slow." Tears brightened her eyes. "He loves me so much. What did I do to deserve him?"

Methusal hugged her tight. "You're wonderful. And you deserve the very best. You and Timaeus are going to be very happy."

"I hope so. I hope everything turns out for the best for both of us."

△ △ △ △ △

Methusal spent the morning by helping to pack up camp, and then ate a quick lunch with Behran. They would leave soon. Erl wanted to hike to the plains by nightfall. Urchets already waited nearby with heavy loads on their backs. Sleeping tents and the dining tent had been taken down, and all of the kitchen utensils had been packed up for transport back to Tarst.

Behran sat beside Methusal on a log by the fire, while Erl oversaw last minute preparations for the trip. Behran's easy grin was absent. He looked serious.

"What's wrong?"

"Nothing." He pulled her hands into his warm ones. "I did a lot of thinking while I was in that jail cell." His gaze searched hers. "You mean the world to me, Thusa. I'm not sure why I've been waiting." A small silence elapsed, as if he was searching for the right words to say. "What I want to ask is... Will you marry me, Methusal?"

"*Behran.*" Surprise shot through her.

A smile lit his deep blue eyes, and he waited.

Why couldn't she speak? Hadn't their relationship been steadily building toward this over the last two and a half years? Isn't this what she'd been hoping and longing for all along? Her spirits lifted.

"Yes." She suddenly smiled. "Yes, Behran, of course I'll marry you!"

He grinned. "You've made me a happy man," he said softly, and kissed her.

Behran's kiss made her feel happy. Like she had come home. She slipped her arms around his neck and kissed him back. This is where she'd always longed to be; right here in his arms.

The long, awful war was done. Now it was time to live again.

△ △ △ △ △

From the moment she woke up the next morning on the plains, Methusal sensed that something was watching her. But every time she scanned the hills, she saw nothing. So she dismissed the feeling.

The seriously injured patients had been transported to Quasr yesterday. The others rode on urchets now.

As they left the Quasr mountains behind, Hendra dropped back to talk to Deccia. Surprise flashed on Deccia's face a few minutes later, and the two fell into a deep, obviously intense conversation. Deccia wiped tears from her eyes every now and again.

Methusal didn't want to interrupt. She walked with Behran and Aali. Her cousin's bruises had lightened to a dull purple. At least Aali never needed to worry about Pogul again. He had died in the last offensive against the Zindedis.

The feeling of being watched once again tickled her senses. It didn't frighten her, but it did puzzle her. She intensified into kaavl, and struggled to identify and separate out the sounds produced by the urchets and seventy trudging men.

She heard the faint scratch of claws on rock.

Quickly, Methusal turned her head and pinpointed the location. The wild, yellow eyes of the wolmite watched her. She had almost forgotten about him.

The wolmite stepped out into the open. He was not limping. He was healed. She smiled.

Methusal walked on, but she still felt his eyes watching her. She glanced back. The animal had stopped moving. He stood high on a lonely hill at the end of the Quasr foothills, watching her go.

She felt an odd sense of loss that she probably would never see him again. "Goodbye," she whispered. "Take care, wild one."

△ △ △ △ △

The three day trek went quickly for Hendra. Before leaving base camp, Doc had suggested that she share her past with Deccia. She was glad she had. Deccia had seemed to feel relieved to discover that someone else knew how it felt to be abused by a man. Hendra hoped their conversations had helped Deccia as much as they had helped her.

The Tarst Mountains loomed very close now. Up ahead, Doc said goodbye to Erl and Methusal. Soon he would say goodbye to her, too. Hendra's heart felt heavy. He headed back toward her, and she moved forward to meet him.

She didn't want to say goodbye. A lump filled her throat. She didn't want to say goodbye at all.

"Hendra." His gaze held hers. "I wish you could come home with me. You're the best nurse I've ever had."

A flush warmed her cheeks. Softly, she said, "Thank you." And then, because neither of them seemed to know what to do next, Hendra reached for Doc. She wanted to hug him. She needed to touch him. And so she did—and by doing so, she felt another barrier inside her crumble.

His muscled arms closed around her, and for a fleeting moment, he held her secure against him. "Until we meet again, fair Hendra."

She swallowed. "Until then."

An empty hole opened in her heart as Hendra watched him go. She'd miss him. She'd miss him terribly. But goodbye was for the best. She wished it could be different; she wished that with her whole heart. But what could she offer Doc, or any other man? Nothing.

Not yet.

△ △ △ △ △

As Methusal watched the Tarst people head home, she thought about Doc's final words to her.

"You have a knack for healing. My advice—think about becoming a nurse or a doctor. We need all the help we can get."

Methusal would think about it. Certainly, in the war she'd seen more suffering than she'd ever seen in her entire life. It had felt good to help people. Her thoughts slipped to Mentàll, but she tried to shut them out, as she'd battled to do over and over again over the last few days. He was gone. He'd never trouble her again. It was time to move on with the rest of her life.

Nursing. Yes, she would like to learn additional skills, so she could help more people. Maybe when she got home she'd talk to Rolban's doctor and see if he would take her on as a part-time apprentice. Of course she'd talk to Sims about it first, but she felt certain he'd approve of anything she wanted to do. She smiled at the thought of returning home and seeing him, and her mother, too.

Her mother's last warning before Methusal left for war unexpectedly whispered through her mind. "Know, Methusal, if you go, your life will never be the same again."

Hanuh was right. She had changed. But she couldn't put her thumb on exactly how. She had learned to obey The One, even when it was hard, and she'd learned to trust that The One heard her prayers, too.

But besides the good ways in which she'd grown, she felt unsettled, too, but wasn't entirely sure why.

Was the war truly over? Or would the Zindedis come back with more men and more arms? And what was Mentàll really up to? What was his plan for the Koblani continent?

Methusal walked faster for Rolban's mountain, eager to arrive home, and to forget the dark uncertainties still lingering in her mind. She longed for familiar sights and smells, and for the comfort of home. She yearned to live within its protective walls once more, and never leave again.

Because in some inexplicable way she knew that if she stepped outside of its borders again to contend with her enemies, her life would never be her own again. She would have to face her deepest fears. Face the truth of who she really was, and what she wanted. Never again would home protect her.

She prayed for the end of war. For no more death or grief. No more broken hearts, or the pain of losing good men like Kitran. Surely the Zindedis had learned their lesson. Surely they would never attack Koblan again.

EPILOGUE

ZINDEDI
THREE WEEKS LATER

"PRESIDENTE." The clerk bowed. "You have a visitor."

The Presidente of Zindedi straightened his jacket. Perhaps it was a report on the invasion of Koblan. He hadn't heard from the General in almost two months. It made him feel uneasy.

Of course, it took two weeks to sail between the two continents. He did the math. A month to take over Koblan? He would never have believed it.

He smoothed his moustache. "Enter."

A young man who wore the black uniform of the Presidente's imperial navy stepped through the door. He snatched the cap from his head. A Commander's hat. But the soldier facing him was little more than a boy.

The Presidente made no effort to stand. How could this pup be a Commander? His brother would never allow it. Eyes narrowed, he motioned the soldier in. "Speak."

The young man licked his lips, and his eyes darted about the room, as if he wanted to be elsewhere. Finally, his gaze met the Presidente's. "I have a report on the battle for Koblan. Sir!"

The Presidente impatiently waved for him to continue.

"Sir, the invasion has failed. The General is dead."

"*Dead?*" The Presidente rose from his chair. "Failed?" He could not believe his ears. "That is impossible!" he roared.

The young Commander jumped. He licked his lips again. "I'm sorry, sir. Forty-one of us in Aestoff escaped, and so did three ships. The southern attack ships escaped, as well."

"But the ships in Quasr? And the men?"

"Captured. And dead. All ships were seized by Koblani forces and most were burned."

The Presidente sat down again. All dead. All captured. And his brother was dead? The greatest military strategist in Zindedi's history? Fury rose in him, suffocating his ability to breathe properly. "How did this *happen?*"

"Koblani forces united. For a while, we thought we would win Aestoff, but when they learned that the northern kaavl soldiers blew up Quasr's munitions, kaavl warriors blew up Aestoff's, too. We didn't see them coming, and couldn't protect ourselves against them. After this victory, the Koblanis became like savage wild beasts. Their kaavl warriors attacked us at night, and led their strongest warriors in to slit our throats. Our guns only helped for a while. Without powder, they're worthless. Some of us escaped, but the rest...perished." The young man twisted his cap in his hands.

"*Kaavl,*" the Presidente hissed. Verdnt and the spy in Wyen had warned of kaavl. What was this kaavl? Only two Zindedi spies had managed to learn it, and Verdnt had died during the Rolbani war. His mind returned to his brother, and a foreign emotion rose in him. Grief. Followed by rage— a more comfortable emotion.

"What happened to my brother?"

"A Rolbani killed him. I don't know who. But reports tell us that their two best kaavl soldiers in Quasr were Methusal Maahr and Mentàll Solboshn, Chief of Dehre. They are allies."

"But they are enemies!" How could this be? The Dehrien had attacked Methusal's home. And she had beat him in kaavl. How could a man accept defeat from a woman, and then ally with her? He must be no man at all.

"They still hate each other," the Commander interjected. "But they fought together to free Quasr."

The Presidente needed something to hit. Something to crumple, or something to throw. But he would display no temper in front of this young pup. No tales to tell to his comrades. His anger turned on the soldier. "And how did you become Commander, soldier?"

The soldier straightened his shoulders, but fear flared in his eyes. "I was the only one who knew how to sail the ship home, sir. Before he died of his wounds, the Commander gave me his title."

"Do you want to *keep* your title?" the Presidente shouted.

The blood drained from the young man's face. "Yes, sir!"

"Then write up your report. I want no detail left out. None! Do you hear?"

"Yes, sir! Right away, sir!"

"Go!"

With obvious relief, the soldier bolted from the room.

The General grabbed a vase of flowers and hurled it across the room. It shattered against the door. Then he threw his inkwell and books, one after another, across the room. Five of them. Ten. Twenty and more. Still, his fury was not satisfied.

His breaths came hard and fast. Years of sitting behind the desk had thickened his body, and pains shot through his chest. Heart thundering, he collapsed into his presidential chair. Fury and rage still boiled in him.

He would have vengeance! He would burn the blood of this Methusal and the Dehrien, as well as the unknown murderer. They had killed his brother! And their kaavl wins in Quasr had turned the tide of the war. Their victories had become his defeat.

Unconscionable. He would not stand for it! He clawed at his head, and beat his forehead with his palms. *Think! Form a plan.* An unaccustomed emotion choked his throat. Not a sob! No. He would not succumb to weakness, even for his brother's sake. Instead, he would avenge his death. And Rolban's ore would become his.

He had invested too many men, ships, and arms to concede defeat.

A map. He needed the crude map of Koblan that the spies had produced. A dig through a drawer produced it.

His thick finger ran over the sketch, looking for a weakness...any weakness he could exploit. And then he saw it. The Iignon region. It was an eastern, rocky shore bordered by sheer mountains. No one lived there. Ships could anchor there unseen. It was near the Tarst and Rolban Ranges. A hard hike, but stealthy soldiers could easily climb through there undetected, and slip down into Rolban.

The Presidente sat back, and his breathing became quieter as a plan developed. He would get Rolban's ore. He had made a mistake, trying to take over the entire continent, when only one village was needed. First, he would build up his weapons store again. And then he would draft more men into the military.

It would take six months. He wanted to be fully prepared. This mission could not fail. In addition, he would prepare missives to his remaining Koblani spies, preparing the way for the attack. Particularly to the man in Wyen. He knew the Tarst terrain best.

This mission would have to be swift and stealthy.

He smiled now, dreaming of Rolban's defeat. He imagined cutting down every man, woman, and child. And he imagined that kaavl whore, Methusal, begging for her life. He chuckled to himself. A tasty treat.

Pictures grew in his mind; his soldiers, harvesting the ore from Rolban's deep, rich mines and transporting the ore to waiting ships to be sent home, to Zindedi. A marvelous idea struck him. He would manufacture arms in Rolban, and use the Rolbanis as slave labor. So be it. Women and children would be allowed to live.

Rolban's fall would be discovered by her neighbors, of course. But Zindedi soldiers would guard her borders, and protect the path from Rolban to the Iignon. Rolban would become his stronghold in Koblan. More weapons would be made, and then Zindedi forces could capture other villages, too. That idea wasn't necessary. Only a pleasurable possibility.

Soon, he would have Rolban's ore. And then he would rule the world.

The Presidente poured a drink of racmun spirits. Nasty stuff the Dehriens made, but it seemed fitting right now. "To you, brother." He lived the glass high. "I swear to you that the Dehrien Chief will die, and so will Methusal. Rolban will fall! And we will finally harvest her ore!"

Flying spittle spattered his fine sleeve. He'd hated to see the foam on his brother's lips. He licked his mouth and flung the glass higher. Dark amber liquid sloshed out. "For you, brother. Revenge will be sweet! It is done."

Somewhere in hell, his brother laughed.

"Prepare a place for me," he muttered, swallowing the fiery liquid. The spirits burned his throat, leaving it raw. Best to get used to the fire. He twirled the glass in his hand, and stared at it with a brooding frown. "Yes, brother. Someday I will join you."

△ △ △ △ △

ROLBAN

DECCIA'S WEDDING TOOK three weeks to plan, but it had been worth every minute Methusal thought, as she stood beside her sister at the ceremony. Hanuh stood on Methusal's right. Winter flowers decorated the Great Hall. Delicious smells wafted down from upstairs. Every Rolbani sat in attendance, happy to see two of their own marry for love. Pan and Aenill had arrived too, from Tarst. Mentàll had been invited, but he hadn't shown up. Thank goodness.

Deccia looked radiant as she exchanged vows with Timaeus. She wore a soft, simple leather gown with clear gems sewn on the "V" neckline, at the sleeves, and at the waist and hem. It matched the gold and gem entwined marriage necklace at her throat; an expensive Rolnnt family heirloom. Timaeus looked handsome in a dark brown, fine leather tunic and breeches which matched his eyes. Quiet happiness lit his smile, and the deep love he felt for Deccia glowed in his eyes. He truly loved her. Methusal felt joy for her twin. She deserved such complete happiness.

The man of The One announced them man and wife, and whistles and cheers erupted. Timaeus kissed Deccia, and Methusal clapped enthusiastically.

After the lingering embrace, the newlywed couple moved with the wedding party to the stairs. Following tradition, the women ascended first. Aali, Hanuh, Methusal, and Deccia climbed partway up, and then Timaeus, and all the men who'd stood with Timaeus filed up as well. Each person in the wedding party remained on the stairway, each on a different stair. The guests streamed upward to the dining room, offering congratulations along the way.

Deccia graciously thanked Pan and Aenill for coming. Aenill pressed Methusal's hand as she passed, and whispered, "I brought tagma berry cobbler. I hope everyone will enjoy it."

"Thank you, Aenill!" Methusal smiled. It had been her favorite dish at base camp.

More people filed by, and suddenly white-blond hair and broad shoulders appeared in Methusal's peripheral vision. Her heart unexpectedly skipped, and then it plummeted to her moccasins. *Mentàll.* When had he arrived?

Timaeus shook Mentàll's hand. "Thank you for coming."

"I am sorry I was late," the Dehrien Chief murmured. "I left Aestoff yesterday."

A three day journey.

Mentàll took Deccia's hand and bowed over it. "You are a beautiful bride."

"Thank you." Happiness lit Deccia's smile, making her look radiant.

Mentàll blinked, and he glanced at Methusal. Stonily, she stared back.

He joined her on her step, and Methusal quickly tucked her hands behind her back.

"Methusal." He inclined his head.

Deccia offered brightly, "Methusal and Behran are engaged now. Isn't that wonderful?" She smiled at Methusal. "They'll be next."

"Is that right?" Ice blue eyes held hers.

She felt compelled to say, "Yes, it is."

"Congratulations." A hint of mockery curved his lips.

"Thank you," she said coolly, although she felt quite certain his comment had possessed no sincerity at all.

"I brought a gift for Deccia and Timaeus, but also one for you."

"What is it?" She eyed him with suspicion.

"Page two." With the barest smile, he offered her a folded parchment.

Methusal stared at it, and her heart suddenly pounded harder. It was page two of the *Second Book of Kaavl!*

"Do you want it?" He watched her closely.

Of course she did! Against her better judgment, she accepted the paper filled with the precious words of her ancestor. "Why?"

"Could it not be a peace offering between our communities?"

"If that was true, you'd have given it to my father."

"I finish what I have begun, Methusal."

Her eyes narrowed as she tried to follow his meaning. "Why does that sound like a threat?"

"It is a promise." After letting that comment sink in, he moved up a step to greet her mother.

He dipped his head slightly. "Hanuh Maahr."

"Mentàll." Though respectful, Hanuh's clipped voice sounded more like a warning than a friendly greeting. She searched his features with a troubled, almost severe look.

The Dehrien Chief met that look directly. His respect for her was evident. After a moment, he moved on.

Finally the last guest passed by, and Methusal and the wedding party joined the others in the dining hall. Petr had reserved a table, and already Erl, Pan, Aenill, and Mentàll sat with him. When Methusal entered the hall, Behran appeared by her elbow. She held onto his arm, glad for his presence. They'd sit with Deccia at Petr's table, too. Methusal stood back, letting the others seat themselves first. That gave her and Behran the end spots. Perfect. Now almost an entire table separated her from Mentàll.

After a prayer of thanks, the people at the main table filed first to the buffet line. Methusal scooped up a plateful of delectable morsels, and took an extra-large portion of tagma berry cobbler. Aenill had brought plenty.

Back at the table, talk ebbed and flowed around them as they ate the delicious food. Even though he sat over half a table away from her, the Dehrien Chief's voice repeatedly cut into her thoughts. She couldn't seem to ignore him. She reasoned that her unconscious mind still sought out the threat he was. Even so, it disturbed her, and she wished she knew how to turn it off. He wasn't a threat any longer. She would never see him again after this.

"Did standing up there today make you think about our own wedding?" Behran asked.

"What?" She blinked at him.

Patiently, he repeated the question.

"Oh." Methusal smiled. "Yes. Of course."

"Do you want to set a date?"

Now silence from the other end of the table distracted her. "Um. I don't know. I'm not...not ready yet." The realization disturbed her.

Puzzlement flashed across his face. "Why not?"

"I don't know." She searched her heart for the truth, and fumbled for words. "I think with Deccia's wedding, and the war, I just feel...overwhelmed."

He nodded, but his perplexed look lingered. "Maybe we could decide in a few weeks?"

Methusal looked away, and tried to ignore a peculiar tension she felt, deep in her soul. "Maybe."

With a frown, Behran fell to his food, and Methusal felt bad. What was wrong with her? She pressed her hand over his and whispered, "I'm sorry."

Understanding gentled his smile. "It's okay, Thusa. The war got to all of us. It's all right. We all need time to recover."

She nodded, and felt a little better. She finished dessert, listened to speeches, and finally the long wedding reception ended. Rolbanis drifted into the hall to go home to their compartments. Pan and Aenill and a few other guests from Tarst retreated to their temporary compartments. They'd go home tomorrow.

Behran talked to Timaeus.

Everyone seemed happy. Laughter rang in the air. But Methusal wanted to be alone.

She slipped downstairs to the Great Hall, seeking peace from the questions tangling through her mind.

She watched a few Dehriens and the Rolbani friends they'd made during the war walk by and head for the gate. At least the war had built some strong friendships between their communities.

She leaned against the rough wall and closed her eyes.

"Escaping?" Mentàll said.

Methusal jumped. "I need a break." This was the last man she wanted to see.

"I would think you would want to be with your fiancé now. Perhaps planning your own wedding."

Methusal couldn't help it. She scowled. "What do you know about matters of the heart? You have to have one, first of all."

"Defensive, Methusal? Perhaps I make you feel uncomfortable."

"You make me feel *nothing*. Kindly leave me alone."

"I only want to congratulate you again on your engagement."

He mocked her. Those cold eyes laughed at her.

She glared. "You don't know anything about love. You think it's ridiculous, don't you? Everything is a game to you. It's all about power and stroking your own ego. You're a cold, lonely man whom no one loves. That's why you laugh at me and Behran. You don't understand it. You never will."

Methusal watched with fascination as his cheekbones darkened to a dull red. She had gotten under his skin. She'd seen him cold and angry before, but this was a topper. Regrettably, this pleased her.

"You do not know what you are saying." His voice was soft.

"But I do." Methusal couldn't believe how calm she felt. He would never accost her on her own turf. Not now. Not at home, with scores of people to come to her aid. And she felt furious with him. She wanted to hurt him, just as he had hurt her, over and over again.

He took a step closer, so he seemed to tower over her. She narrowed her eyes, but refused to step back. She snapped, "The only emotions you manipulate in people are fear, loathing, and disgust. But usually nothing. Nothing at all."

He drew a harsh breath, and she saw with a detached, satisfied eye that the muscles in his shoulders flexed, and another clenched in his jaw.

He said, "Those are the emotions you felt when I kissed you at base camp."

Methusal blanched, but tightened her suddenly trembling lips. "Absolutely. Nothing."

"Then let's repeat the experiment."

"No!"

"I think so." He stepped so his broad back hid her from the crowd behind him. A large hand cupped her jaw and he swooped closer.

Methusal could only let out a breathless, squeaking, "No," before his warm lips seared into her own with mind bending intensity. Violent emotions pummeled her.

She shoved him away, hard. "Stop it."

He stared at her, pinning her with that ice blue gaze. "Disgust? Fear? Or nothing at all?"

Tears burned. "I *hate* you."

He gave a sharp laugh, and his lips curved into a cool smile. "Not indifference."

"Get away from me."

He said in a low, harsh voice, "You know nothing about me. Yet." Turning on his heel, he strode toward the gate and his large silhouette was gradually swallowed up in the glare of the sun.

Heart pounding, Methusal turned to see who else might have witnessed that encounter. Behran stared at her from across the hall. Shock froze his features. She swallowed as he crossed the distance between them.

His jaw clenched. "What was that about?"

"Nothing! Just Mentàll being hateful. He said he wanted to congratulate us on our engagement, but..."

Behran took a step toward the gate. "I'll *punch* him..."

"No, Behran." Methusal caught at his sleeve. "He's not worth it. Forget it. I'm going to." She would.

Behran didn't relax. "I don't trust him."

"Neither do I. But don't let him ruin our happiness." She hugged him and felt him gradually relax.

He smiled, and the look in his dark blue eyes filled her heart with a gentle happiness. She smiled, feeling safe in his arms.

Behran said, "And don't worry about setting a date. When the time is right, we'll know. For now, we'll just go on as we have been."

"Are you sure?" Methusal felt both relieved and grateful.

He smiled slowly. "I'm sure." And he sealed his promise with a kiss.

The End

Δ Δ

Author's Note

I SINCERELY HOPE you enjoyed *Kaavl Quest* as much as I enjoyed writing it. There are two more books in the quadrilogy. *Kaavl Calamity* is next, and it will be published in the fall of 2016.

One final note. As a small press author, getting my books before readers is a real challenge. You can help! If you liked this book, please consider writing a short review on Amazon, B & N, or the retailer's website where you purchased the book. Each review encourages Amazon and other online retailers to promote the book to more readers. Each and every review counts, and means so much!

I love to hear from my readers. Please drop me a note at jennettegreen@jennettegreen.com.

Best wishes always,
Jennette

www.ingramcontent.com/pod-product-compliance
Lightning Source LLC
Chambersburg PA
CBHW020239120726
47904CB00001B/23

* 9 7 8 1 6 2 9 6 4 0 1 3 6 *